KEVIN WILKS AND THE POWER STONE

By

Kevin N Shortland

Table of Contents

Dedication

I dedicate this book I have written to my late mother and father for all the support and life lessons they taught me as I grew up.

Also, to my brother Paul for his patience in handling me as we grew together.

Finally, to my Wife Barbara for allowing me to take time to accomplish the wish to write a book.

Lastly, to my three sons, Stuart, Steven, and Matthew, who have been another driver in writing and publishing this book.

Acknowledgement

I would like to that the whole team in Amazon Publishing Pros for all their hard work in getting this to press.

Also, to my friends and colleagues I have and still do work with for their support in completing this accomplishment.

About the Author

My name is Kevin Shortland. At present 59 years old, and I work within the food industry as an auditor. Growing up, I was very sport minded and gained many medals and cups playing football for my hometown, but I decided that it would not make me a living.

Growing up, I guess you could say I was a pain in the backside for my family and teachers at the schools. I always asked lots of questions of all of them and did not believe in what I was told unless they could provide me hard facts and evidence that what they said was true. This is a trait of Kevins Wilks that I put into the character he is.

I was also in the British armed forces, where the characters of the friends I met also added an influence to my writing background for characters.

I get asked who is or was my influence by many people both in writing my book and the job I do. My answer to all is your family. Not just mum, dad, brother, or sister, but uncles, aunts, cousins, and grandparents. Many interesting stories are told by all these people that stay in your mind. In truth, they are the greatest storytellers in the world. As a child, you look up to those people and admire them for what they went through during the years they were growing up in. We all can influence each other in our walk of life.

Did anyone influence me in writing the book – Well, I have to say I am a big fan of KK Rowling and John Grisham. They gave me thoughts of adventure with twists in the plot that need to be thought of before they can be revealed.

I have to say that I have always had a passion for writing, right from a young age. Always used to write short stories in a journal but did nothing with them.

I see many things around many different places and countries I visit doing my job. It is some of these that give me the inspiration to use in the series of books I am writing. Kevin Wilks and the Power Stone is the first in the series.

Chapter 1

New School Issues

It was a bright early morning as Kevin lay sleeping peacefully, dreaming of being a great footballer and earning lots of money, having lots of girlfriends, and having a particularly good life. Suddenly his dreams disappeared when a burst of sound echoed from his alarm clock, telling him once again he must move out of his bed and get ready for a day of new beginnings.

The new beginning was that today. He goes to a new school. No longer was he a massive fish in a shallow pool at his old school. Now, he was an exceedingly small fish in a very big ocean. Kevin had a brother already at this new school, three years older than him, and by the way, he told stories about this school. Kevin was not looking forward to going.

As he moved from his bed and opened his curtains, the bright sunlight blazed into his bedroom, making him shield his eyes. He then turned and walked from his bedroom toward the bathroom. As he passed the stairs, he could smell the aroma of toast coming up the stairs towards him, which made his stomach groan.

As he turned the door handle to enter the bathroom, he found that it was locked. "Oh, come on," he cried, "I need the loo." "Wait your turn," came the reply from his brother Paul already in there. "You should have got up earlier while I was on my paper round." Kevin started to get a little mad and started to knock continuously on the door shouting, "Hurry up, you stupid idiot." Paul, now getting a little mad himself, started shouting through the door at Kevin to pack it in, along with the occasional call to his mum to stop Kevin from bothering him.

At this point, their mum appears at the bottom of the stairs and shouts at Kevin. "Pack it in, Kevin. Wait your turn. Any more of this, and I will tell your father when he gets home, you have always been a little headstrong, especially if you do not get your own way, and you know dad will not put up with it, you will be for it, now just get dressed first then wash when your brother comes out". Kevin sneered down the stairs at his mother without saying a word. "Go on," his mother called back to him, "and don't give me the evil eyes, my boy, or you will find yourself over my knee, no matter how old or big you are." With that last thud on the door and a muffled "Prat" coming from Kevin's mouth directed at his brother, he went back into his bedroom to dress.

Finally, the door opened to the bathroom, with Paul stepped out with a smile on his face, "what's to smile about" Kevin asked, "first day at my school, lots going on, lots of young kids going in the bushes, oh and don't ask me to protect you because I will be one of those chucking you in." Paul laughed loudly as he started his descent up the stairs. "Mum, did you hear that? He is going to throw me in the bushes." "Now stop that," came mum's reply, "Paul, you will do no such thing. Remember when you were dumped in those blasted things and tore your blazer sleeve and trousers? Dad went loopy, straight down the school, complaining to Mr. Easter, the principal. It had better not happen again, or your dad might just hit someone this time. I never saw him so angry before, so that is why you will have nothing to do with it. Paul and Kevin stay far away from those bushes. Do I make myself clear"? "Yes, mum," came the reply in a solemn sound. "I do wish you two would get on with each other rather than fighting and bickering as you do. I also had brothers and sister's when I was young, but we never fought as you do. It is time you to start to love and help each other, do you hear me"? Another reply of a soft "yes, mother" crept from their mouths. "Anyway, eat your breakfast, then off to school with you. I shall not be far behind you, now get a move on." There was a reason for his mum's comment, and that was she was one of the school cooks at school, and all her friends in the kitchen knew to see everything that went on and would certainly tell her if they saw or heard anything suspicious. Knowing that, Kevin felt a bit better. After all, who is going to take on a mad mum, hey??

As Kevin rode his bike to school, he started thinking not about the usual things that a thirteen-and-a-half-year-old boy does, like football, girls, and sleep, but a strange thought came into his head, a thought of fear. Not sure why he felt this feeling, but he peddled on towards the school, waving to his mates Vinnie, Ivan, and Paul as he sped by. Once he had turned onto park drive and carried on towards the school gates, he thought he saw a man standing, staring at him from over the hedgerow. The man was dressed in what looked like a long black coat or something like a coat. Kevin was not sure as the hedgerow hid the full visionary sight. One thing he was sure of was that the man was staring at him.

He looked quite old and had a beard stretching down to his waist. The man was staring straight at Kevin and never took his eyes off him as he rode by. Kevin, feeling a little disturbed now, peddled faster, and dashed to the school gates where he was met by some other friends, Amanda, Susan, and David, as they were dropped off by bus at the school as they lived quite far away.

As the friends all walked together down the long chase of the school to the bike shed, chatting about what they got up to over the summer holidays, the boys were met by Paul and his mates.

"So, new blood," Paul said as his mates chuckled, "back off," Kevin shouted, "you know what mum said." "Ooh, I'm scared," Paul replied, "you know what's going to happen. It's inevitable. Catch you later, bro." Paul and his mates turned and walked away, discussing how, when, and where they would get the friends. As Kevin parked his bike, telling his friends not to worry, his mind drifted back to the old man he saw. "Kevin," came the voice of his friend Vinnie, "you, ok? you are in a world of your own!" As Kevin snapped out of his thought, turning to Vinnie and saying, "What, oh nothing, I just saw an old man in the park staring straight at me, I didn't know him, but it looked as if he knew me the way he stared." Vinnie and the rest of the gang just laughed, "probably just a nutter," Vinnie replied, "my dad said there are still some of them about, just keep in a bunch and do not let yourself get caught on your own. Come on. We had better get to assembly and work out a way to keep away from your brother and his mates." With that, the gang went off to their class registration before assembly.

The school looked massive, with corridors all over the place with classrooms set off in all directions. Well, it was only natural on the first day in a new school. The boys got lost during walking and ended up late on the first day of registration. The teacher Ms. English spoke abruptly to them for being late. "So, you finally decided to join us, did you"? The boys tried to say sorry, but Ms. English just continued calling the morning registration for the rest of the form. After she walked up to the two boys and gave them a map so they would not be late for any lessons or registration again, Ms. English explained to them that if they were late again, they would have to do break time detentions. It was funny, Kevin thought, but that was a perfect way to get out of the bushing, so Kevin mentioned it to his mates, but they were not up for it.

Kevin, well, he was never one for rules and did not believe in anything that he was told unless undisputable evidence could be provided to make him believe what was said was true or have got to do it. His parents had trouble before at his junior school. One parent's night, the head teacher Mr. Davis told his mum and dad, "Kevin is like a horse, you can take him to water, but you cannot make him drink." Both his parents had previous heated discussions with him regarding different subjects, especially religion, but Kevin just disputed their comments which got his parents even madder. Kevin used to say if there was no substantial evidence to back the comment up, then it was just a story or a belief of a person, not fact. Therefore, he got into so much trouble throughout his school life and caused his parents all sorts of grief by doing it.

Kevin would argue with teachers and adults about anything if they did not have the evidence to back it up. His main fights with people were about religion, ghosts, and magic. This would be a very trying time for the teachers and his parents this year, but Kevin always looked forward to a good argument, especially one that he thought people could not win against him.

His mother knowing how Kevin is had looked at his timetable of lessons and saw that Kevin's second period had religious education with Mr. Godwill on the very first day and was overly concerned about the fact that she had to see Mr. Godwill and explain to him about Kevin. As she parked her bicycle in the bicycle shed, she wondered what to say to the teacher about Kevin when her friend Lilly called her. "You alright, June?" "Not really, Lil. I need a few minutes to see Mr. Godwill and explain to him about Kevin. First day at a new school, and already I have a bad feeling that something is going to happen and be bad." "Boys," replied Lilly, "I suppose it is a mother's thing that we want to protect our young. I had the same feeling about Gordon. Well, maybe not what you are feeling, but still, it will be all right. They must learn and learn the hard way. You watch. They will thank us for it overall. I will see you in a few minutes". Lilly turned and walked back into the kitchens, and Kevin's mum followed the paths to the main teacher's study.

As Kevin's mum explained to Mr. Godwill all about Kevin, she could see in his eyes that he was not really interested in what she had to say. As she finished, Mr. Godwill stroked his beard and said, "Yes, yes, do not worry, Mrs. Wilks, I have dealt with more troublesome lads than your Kevin. I remember your Paul was not the easiest lad to teach at first, but now look at him, getting good grades in all he takes. Who knows, this school may be the making of your Kevin also, do not worry". With that, Mrs. Wilks thanked Mr. Godwill and returned to the school kitchens, ready to start work.

So, the first school day began. Kevin and his friends are late for registration and now standing in line for lesson one, Chemistry, when Kevin's brother walks by with his little posse of friends following him. As they passed, Paul gestured to Kevin about going in the bushes, Kevin just gave him a smirk back, and the moment had passed.

In chemistry class, Kevin sat by the window, occasionally looking out a crossed the football and rugby fields towards the park. Although he was not particularly interested in chemistry or thought not, somehow, he was still drawn into the lesson by small pieces of information he could hear from the teacher Mr. Chandler. These small pieces of information were brought to Kevin's attention by the word Fact. As stated before, Kevin would argue with anyone if there was no supporting evidence to back up the statement, so to him, this was a challenge to prove this was indeed true or just another hearsay story.

As Kevin started to ask questions to Mr. Chandler regarding the authenticity of the information that he was teaching to them, it became apparent to Kevin that this item that they were being taught was that of identity. Mr. Chandler produced research from reputable chemists that all analyses were completed and recorded through the atomic values of metals, gases, organics, and liquids; therefore, Kevin relinquished his glazes out of the window to concentrate on the lesson. He had found a lesson that he liked and did not argue with.

The bell went for the class to finish and move on to the next lesson. This was going to be the hardest of the lot as it was religious education, something that Kevin had a big dislike for and argued with anyone till he was blue in his face, or the person he was arguing with just turned away in a discussion.

With the bells heard all over the school, June, Kevin's mum, now looking at the clock and realising it was crunch time, seemed to have a look of dread on her face. "June," called Lil, "you ok? You look like you have seen a ghost?" "If only," replied June, "it's Kevin's second lesson now starting," "so?" replied Lil. "It's RE with Mr. Godwill." "Oh, I see," replied Lil quietly. Lil had been a long-term friend of Junes and knew all about Kevin's likes and dislikes and how he argued with anyone about anything, especially if they could not back up certain statements with particle evidence, even if she had been on the wrong end of a discussion with Kevin, so she knew how strong-willed he was. Lil laughed, trying to take June's mind off the situation, "you see, Mr. Godwill, didn't you?" mum nodded, "well then, if he is not prepared for the encounter, well, more fool him." Lil looked again at June, and they both started laughing and continued their work.

As the pupils moved into the RE class, Kevin made for the back of the class. "Wilks," shouted Mr. Godwill, "up the front" gesturing to a seat, Kevin stopped, turned, and answered, "oh, I will be fine back here," "this is not a request, young Wilks, now move it," cried Mr. Godwill. Kevin's mates gave a chuckle as he passed them by to the seat the teacher had pointed to. "Now, let's get started, shall we?" As the lesson continued, Kevin had no interest in what Godwill was saying and let his mind wander to other things when a loud shrill came at him from Godwill. "So, what do you think happened, Wilks?" Kevin just looked blankly at the teacher and replied, "about what?" Mr. Godwill was not at all amused, "about what? Don't you mean about what, sir? At least if you have no interest in this subject, you could show a bit of respect, boy." Kevin looked Mr. Godwill straight in the eyes and answered, "Respect, Sir, is earned, not given" the class just looked on in total disbelief, "what" replied Godwill, "I said," replied Kevin, but was interrupted by Godwill, "I know what you said boy, and I think you owe me an apology for it," Kevin looked hard at Godwill, "Sir" he said with a smirk, "do you really believe in what you teach? Where is the proven fact that this all took place and that it is not simply the ranting of mad men written down in story form pushed upon people like me to believe in as you do? Where are the proven facts, the physical evidence? Does it not state Jesus fed five hundred or thousand men and women, I forget now, on some loaves of bread and a few fish? So now we must believe he was a magician also. Also, that he rose from the dead is a good trick, I think, since no one else has achieved that in all history! Now, do you not think just through these few trivial things that this is a true account? Or am I right? Is it just stories that have been passed down through time and impressed on people's minds to believe in?"

Mr. Godwill grabbed Kevin by the ear and hauled him towards the door. "Out, get out, boy. Your mum warned me of this. You shall see the headmaster. I will not have you disturb my class with your attitude." As Kevin felt the pain in his ear like it was being torn off and marching towards the door, he worked himself loose, turned at Godwill, and asked, "I only want you to prove or disprove what I have asked you. Is that too much?" Godwill opened the door, "Go, wait outside the headmaster's office, go" he shouted again. As Kevin walked down the main corridor and reached the principal's office, he saw an elderly gentleman stepping out from it. "Can I help you, son?" asked the old gentleman, "I don't know, sir. I was told to stand outside the headmaster's office," replied Kevin. "For what reason?" replied the old man. "Oh, I may have ruffled Mr. Godwill's feathers in class about RE," Kevin replied. The old man looked at Kevin, then spoke again, "Hmm, your Kevin, Kevin Wilks, am I right?" "Yes sir," Kevin replied, "I have heard quite a bit about you, young Wilks, a bit of a hot head you youngsters call it. You believe in nothing unless there is a scientific fact to prove or disprove, and will argue the point no matter what, am I right?" "Yes sir," Kevin replied, "has my mother been talking to you by any chance or my brother?" Kevin noticed that the old gentleman, although knowing his name, seemed calm and controlled. Especially after knowing that he had upset a teacher on his very first day, this man understood the way he thought and acted. Kevin had heard how strict the new principal was, but if this was the head, Kevin did not feel frightened at all. He noticed that the old man's stature was slightly bent towards his left side, with a medium white beard and a happy smile, definitely not someone to be scared of, or maybe as this was Kevin's first brush with the trouble he was taking it easy on him, still Kevin did not worry, he was quite relieved. The old gent smiled, "why do you ask that, son?" he murmured, "well, it is a large school, a lot of students, and you seem to already know me. I mean my name. Therefore, I can only assess that my mother or brother must have informed you that I may get into trouble from time to time and be seeing a lot of you, am I right, sir?" "There you go again, always trying to think logically and work out what is right and what is not. There are things in this world and time that cannot be explained. Not everything is defined through physical evidence. Some things can only be summarised and take complex chemical formulations. Where did they get their origins? Why give them silly letters and numbers, I could go on and on, but my point is, young

Wilks, since time began and man and animals roamed through this green land, not everything can be explained. Not everything can be verified that occurred. Therefore in some ways, you are right to question things, but you must also be big enough not to try and criticise people's beliefs. People need to believe in things they know. It gives them strength. They will go through tough times, just like your strength is your belief which calls you to not believe anything that cannot be produced, to verify certain things, or can have hard physical evidence produced. Although sometimes it can block your sight on what is real and what is not."

"Many years ago, back in the Middle Ages, it is written, magic and mythical beasts were amongst the lands." Kevin smiled, then said, "don't tell me you believe in them, sir?" "Why not?" the old man replied, "you seem to think that just because they are not apparent in our time now, they do not or did not exist." Kevin smiled, "but sir, where is the proof, and if they did exist, why have their descendants not carried on their profession, if you can call it one? No, back then, in the Middle Ages, I believe that there may have been some people called magicians who made potions, potions for ailments, potions that a little like our pharmacists of today put together for our medicines to help us when we are unwell. Do we call them magicians? I think not!" "There you are," replied the old man, "replied Kevin, "you stated your belief, a belief that magicians were potion makers, so that tells me that you do have some thought that they did exist, although not in the way of wand carrying spell book making people, in the curing of people ailments or the enchanting of the persons mind into believing certain things." Kevin looked a little puzzled at the old man, "I suppose if you put it like that, then it could have happened, but wait, no, there is no such thing as magic. You will never make me believe that. Tricks we see from so-called magicians are by using mirrors and quickness of the hand only." The old gentleman just smiled and then said, "I do not have to. The seed of doubt has already been sewn in your mind to even think about it. All I ask is to take this book and read it. You may find it illuminating."

The old man handed Kevin an old brown book. "Just read it. Who knows, it just might have the power within it to convince you, ok?" The old man smiled again with that, turned, and walked back into the office, where the door shut. Kevin looked at the title of the book. It had the title of the book called **the pharynx**: As he stood there about to open the cover, the office door swung open again. This time it was not the old gentleman but a middle-aged, balding man. "What do you want, boy" bellowed the man, Kevin, now a little scared, nervously answered. "Mr. Godwill sent me to stand outside the headmaster's office, sir." "Did he? Well, you must have done something to upset him. I am Mr. Peterson, the headmaster. Stand there until Mr. Godwill comes and lets me know what's going on, ok boy!", "yes, sir," Kevin replied. It seemed strange to Kevin, for as he stood there awaiting Mr. Godwill, he could hear telephones ringing, people talking, and music being played in the teachers' staff room, but he never heard any of that when he was talking to the old gentleman, nothing, just the old man's voice and his own. Did he really meet and speak to this old man, or did he imagine it? Well, the book in his hand verified that something was given to him. Therefore, it must have been real. Then there was when he came out and went back into the headmaster's office. As Kevin still stood outside, he could not be sure that the old man was not still in there, or was he?

As Godwill arrived and knocked on the headmaster's door, Kevin felt a little uneasy. Both the headmaster and Godwill came out and ushered him into the office. As he went through the doorway, Kevin placed the book on a small table next to the office door. There was no sign of the old man in the office. Kevin looked confused but then snapped out of it to listen to the principal now ranting at him about respect and order in his school. The whole thing ended with Kevin being given three detentions after school and going on report. With that, Kevin was ushered out of the head office and away for break time. The rest of the day seemed to go pretty quickly for Kevin, he and his friends had managed to keep well out of the way of his brother Paul's gang and avoid the bushing that they were said to be going to get thrown into or so they thought.

They managed to get through the rest of the day, finding their classrooms and registration class on time with no other problems, but now as everyone was leaving the registrations and moving down the school pathways, there stood Paul and his gang waiting. "Well, look here, thought you avoided us, little brother, I think not," Paul laughed, "Back off, Paul, I am not in the mood," Kevin replied. "Oh, is that so? Well, we will just have to get you in the mood. Get him, lads." With that, four of his help mates grabbed Kevin and lifted him high, stopping him from struggling. "Now, what were you saying, little bro?" "I warn you, Paul, if they push me, you are going to pay big time!" "OH, I'm so scared," Paul laughed. "Ok, boys, ready, swing, one, two, three," Kevin screamed at the top of his voice. "Paul," "Now" shouted Paul as they let go. Kevin went flying and landed at the top of the bushes, which stood a good six feet. As he fell through the thick prickly thorns cutting his hand's face and ripping into his new uniform, he knew although he played no part in this, he was going to get the blame from his mum. There was only one thing for it, revenge when he got out. Kevin's friends had long scarpered, so they were not next. This also did not please Kevin. Eventually, as Kevin came to a halt falling, he carefully eased himself out of the bushes. There stood his brother and pals standing laughing, and Kevin just could not hold it back. He strode up to his brother, still laughing, and head-butted him right in the nose. This soon stopped his laughs, especially when he felt the pain and saw his blood running down his face. Kevin then turned to Paul's mates, who now could see that Kevin was truly angry. They decided that retreat would be the best possible defence, so they just ran away. Kevin now turned to his brother sitting on the floor, holding his nose.

"Why, I asked you not to, why," Kevin asked his brother " Paul looked up with tears and blood trickling from his nose, "it's only supposed to be a bit of fun. We all had it done, so why not you? You are going to be in big trouble when I tell mum of this". Kevin knew this and was not looking forward to going home. Paul had gone to the toilets to see to his nose before going home as Kevin looked at the rip in his blazer and trousers. "Mum is going to kill me," thought Kevin, "Paul will wriggle out of any punishment as usual, and I will end up with all the flack as always" With that, Kevin got his bicycle from the sheds to ride home only to see he had a flat tyre and no pump. "Great," Kevin thought as he wheeled his bike out of the gates and started his journey home.

As Kevin neared the park, he saw the old man there staring at him again, "Who are you? What do you want?" Kevin shouted, "Nothing, now Kevin," came the reply, "you know my name" Kevin replied, "it is true, I do. I can help you master Kevin if you wish?" "Help me how?" asked Kevin. The man pointed a stick at him and uttered the words "Compare-relapsum." There was a bright light and then nothing. Kevin shielded his eyes from the light, and as it died away, he looked back towards where the man was and noticed that there was nobody there, only a smoky appearance of an old man disappearing with a faint voice saying, "you owe me," and then completely disappeared. Kevin, now thinking about what was going on, looked at his blazer and trousers. No rips, no cuts, no scratch marks on his hands or face, and his bike tyre were pumped up again. Kevin really could not believe what had happened or not happened. Was he dreaming all this? Was he asleep, but then reality set in when Paul rode by with his nose still slightly bleeding and blood stains on his shirt? Kevin felt more confused than ever now. He got on his bike and rode off towards home thinking how he could explain this to his mum and dad, let alone his brother, who played some part in the events that took place.

As Kevin rode up the path of his house, he could only imagine that Paul would have laid it on thick and put the blame on him regarding the state of his bloody shirt and his nose. Instead, he had not said a word, only that he got a football kicked into his nose during break time. Kevin thought he was off the hook, but unfortunately not, as Mr. Godwill had a word with his mother about the confrontation in his class, and she was going to make him pay for it. Before he could speak, she had grounded Kevin for a week. He had tea and then sent to bed early. As Kevin climbed the stairs, he was still puzzled as to why his brother had not told on him. Both hated the sight of each other, but still, it could have been worse, Kevin thought.

Paul confesses

As Kevin lay there on his bed with nothing to do, his mind wandered to the events that had happened today. The man in the park, the man outside of Mr Peterson's office, the repairing of his clothes and bike, and the healing of his scratches. How do you explain what had happened? Did they happen? Or was it just his mind playing tricks on him? Either way, he was feeling very confused about the whole thing. As Kevin was thinking with increasing intent about the day's events, he heard the slight knock on his door, then in burst his brother with his finger to his lips.

"What do you want," Kevin asked, "and why did you not dob me into mum?" Paul looked at Kevin, answering, "keep it down." Kevin could see by Paul's look that he was not happy about something, "What's up? You seem a little worried. Is it that if you tell mum about me, then I will split on you bushing me?" "That's just it," Paul replied, "think Kevin, did we really bush you? I mean, when you came out of those bushes, you had scratches, and your uniform was gashed, but there is no evidence that these things took place, no scars, no missing threads on your uniform, and I know I let your tyre down on your bike, but you managed to get the tyre inflated and ride home, how, how". Kevin looked at Paul then answered, "I don't know, I have thought about all the things that had happened during the day, and some do not add up." Paul looked at Kevin and then said, "What do you mean some do not add up? Did something else happen?" As Paul finished, he heard his dad Derek mention that he was just going for a wash which meant coming upstairs to the bathroom, so Paul again put his finger to his lips, opened the door, and left Kevin's room, quietly uttering the words "Talk later".

As Kevin lay on his bed now pondering more on the day's events, he was interrupted again by dad coming through the door. Kevin thought, "that's it, I really am in trouble now," you see his mum was strict, but his dad, well, he was like a regimental sergeant major, thinks that all young people should go in the forces to harden them up and not be the softies that they are. Kevin moved up towards the headboard, making as small a target as possible should his dad lash out at him, but instead of being angry, dad handed Kevin a chocolate bar, and he put his finger to his lips as if to say shush, then smiled. "I hear you had a bit of bother with that RE teacher. What's his name?" Asked dad, "Mr. Godwill," replied Kevin, "that's right, Godwill never liked him, always had it in for your brother. It was him that broke his spirit. Oh yes, he was just like you, hot-headed, always up for trouble and arguments. Godwill was always getting something on him to make him have detention, and eventually, the poor boy just broke. Some say it was a blessing as they couldn't handle him when he was in one of his moods, always breaking things or trying to blame others for his wrongdoings, quite a hand full. When he broke down and stopped being the nasty little urchin he was, people seemed to love him again. Still, I think that we are what we are, and no matter how much hate there is in a person, there is also that little bit of goodness. You just have to dig deep to find it. With you turning out to be the same as your brother was, well, it's like reliving it all over again," Kevin looked at his dad and spoke softly, "I'm sorry, dad", his dad stared him in the eyes, "I know you are son. Well, if Godwill thinks he can run rough shot over my boys, then he had better think again" Dad ruffled Kevin's hair as he smiled, "be good and quiet tonight, and I will see if I can get the grounding lifted, ok," Kevin smiled back and replied, "thanks, dad." "Oh, just one thing Kevin, you might want to rethink how you ask questions to adults. After all, we did have that trouble at your last school also. It's time to start growing up now, mate. Show some respect to your elders," dad paused, "even if they are irritating, ok?" Kevin, now relieved that he was out of trouble, agreed, "ok, dad, I will try." "That's all I can ask you to do, and who knows, you might just become polite like your brother," he said, smiling as he left Kevin's room. Later, as Kevin lay there now reading his schoolbooks, he remembered the book the old man had given him. As he searched through his bag, he finally came a crossed it right at the bottom. He lifted it out and looked at the front cover. It was brown, old, and a little worn around the spin and the edges, with the word 'Pharynx' embedded into the front cover. Before he opened the book, his mind went back to the meeting with the old man, what they had talked about, and disappearing. Then Mr. Peterson and Godwill took Kevin into the office and finally ushered him out to the outside for a break. At no time could Kevin remember picking up the book and placing it in his bag. Kevin opened the book but was surprised that half of the book's pages were blank. Only a few had some writing on, and then it was no more than ten words on the whole page. Kevin, even now more confused flicked through the book again; as he did, he noticed that by doing this, the words on certain pages now formed sentences. He began to flick through again, now more slowly, trying his hardest to make out what the sentences said. As he did this for the third time, Paul raced up the stairs and into Kevin's room.

As Paul opened the door and gazed upon the book Kevin was holding, he cried out, "oh no, he didn't," Kevin looked bemused at Paul, "what, who did not do what?". Paul just looked at Kevin and then said, "where did you get that from? Who gave it to you, Kevin?" Kevin, now looking surprised, answered Paul, "whoa there, boy, calm down. I got it from an old man, I thought he was the headmaster as he came out of his office while I was waiting for Godwill to arrive." Paul asked, "this old man, what did he look likc"? "Well," replied Kevin, "just an old man, quite nice actually. He knew my name, so I thought he was the principal. Why"? Paul turned to face the window with his hand stroking his chin, "was this man about your height, slight white beard, slight bending towards the left"? Kevin looked surprised, "Yes, that's him, do you know him, who is he?" Paul turned towards Kevin, "oh, I have seen him before," Paul replied, "What about the other man, in the park?" Kevin looked puzzled, "the other man, in the park, when did you see him"? Kevin asked. As Kevin looked at Paul, he could see that there was a worried expression on his face, "When," repeated Paul, "ok, this morning, I saw him for the first time this morning, why"? "So, this has all happened today," Paul asked, "yes, of course," replied Kevin, "what is going on, Paul? Why do you sound worried"? Paul looked at Kevin, this time it was with a thoughtful look, which Kevin did not really understand and thought a bit creepy as they both used to hate each other, but now it seemed as though Paul was genially worried about his little brother.

The time was getting on, and the cry from their mother was to tell them it was time to wash and get some sleep. Paul looked at Kevin and then said, "bro, it's the footy trials Friday evening. I want you to come with me to them, try out for the under thirteen's, and who knows, you might just get in the squad", Kevin turned away, "I can't, remember I'm grounded" came Kevin's reply, "No, no" Paul replied, "I heard dad talking to mum, and he's got the grounding lifted, although mum thinks he is going soft in his old age, no, you can come, just make sure you don't do anything stupid for the rest of the week to change her mind, alright!", "I don't know, do you really think I have a chance?" asked Kevin, "well, you'll never know unless you try," replied Paul, "I'm busy for the rest of the week, what with after-school games, then the youth club, so we need to get together Friday, ok," Paul told Kevin. "Listen, don't forget to bring that book with you. We need to talk more, away from anyone who can hear us, and try not to speak to either of the old men you saw. It's important you listen and do as I ask for once," "why" asked Kevin. "What's the book got to do with this?" "Just bring the book," Paul replied," you are not going to believe any of this until I show you something." "Ok, ok, I will bring the book, but why wait till Friday?" Paul looked at Kevin and then spoke, "I'm busy every night up till then, so it will have to be Friday. We need to spend quite a bit of time together so I can explain", Paul stopped in mid flow, "look, keep your head down, nose clean, mouth shut, and don't go telling any of those friends of yours about this, they will think that you have gone bananas", with that Paul walked out of Kevin's room to the bathroom.

As Kevin lay in his bed, flicking through the book, he wondered about what Paul could have meant, not going to believe any of it until he showed him. Was this going to be another trick to get Kevin in trouble, or was there really something that Paul knew? After all, Kevin had not seen the worried look on Paul's face in a good three, three, and a half years. What could it be to make him worry like that, and what's the book and the two old men got to do with it? By now, Kevin's brain hurt trying to work things out, so he decided to put the book back into the school bag and go to sleep.

The morning came quickly; the cool autumn sun bursting through Kevin's curtains to wake him. As he got up, washed, and dressed for another day at school, his mind automatically thought back to his conversation with his brother. Paul had long been up and gone to do his paper round before school started. As Kevin got to the foot of the stairs, his mum was waiting, ready to issue the orders of the day. "Not a particularly good start, young man, yesterday, was it? I certainly hope today is better. Your dad has persuaded me to lift the grounding due to the football trials on Friday. But just you heed my warning Kevin, any more nonsense, and you will be grounded, not for a week, but for a month, is that clear? You need to keep that irritable nature out of sight and no back-chatting with any of the teachers, especially Mr. Godwill. Now go eat your breakfast and then off to school. Go on." Kevin grabbed a slice of toast, and off he rode to school. As he neared park drive, he could see the old man still staring at him. Kevin just turned away and peddled on, remembering what his brother had told him.

The day went very quickly and without any problems during Kevin's classes. Kevin still had to complete the daily detention that Mr. Peterson had given him, but Kevin did not seem to mind it, and he did keep his mouth shut about the previous day's events, not telling anyone at all.

As the week went on, Kevin saw less of his older brother, as he was busy with school football, basketball, and chess matches or youth club table tennis, football, and snooker matches. Kevin was looking forward though to Friday, partly the football trials but also what Paul was up to. He still was a little doubtful about what was going to go on after the trials with his brother. One thought was that he really was going to show him something amazing, or the other thought, something that was going to get Kevin in big trouble, but he had put his mind to it that if it was trouble, he was going to be ready for him, after all, he had hurt his brother only a little while ago, so he may need to do this again.

The days came and went, Kevin finished his detentions and had been relatively good throughout the week, and Friday was now here. As Kevin lay sleeping in his bed dreaming of football stardom, he was woken by Paul, "listen" he said quietly, "keep out of trouble today and don't be late for the trials. Remember to bring the book, see you at the park at half five, ok", Paul winked at his brother before leaving to do his paper round.

Well, the day went without any problems, and Kevin, now at home, got ready for the football trials. Dad was there, "alright, Kevin, now, just be yourself. You don't have to try and be all smart and technical with the ball. Just play as if you were in the school playground, and you'll see, you'll be in that team as quick as a bullet." "I don't think I had better do that, dad. If I played like I do in the playground, they would send me off before I even started," Both of them laughed. Even mum had a little smile on her face. "Well now," mum said, "your meeting Paul down there. Please try and keep out of his way during his trials. I don't want him coming home blaming you that he never made the team, ok," "yes, mum," replied Kevin, "and mind you come straight home together when it's finished, alright." Kevin answered again "yes mum, I hear you", "now, off you go, and be lucky, both of you".

Kevin picked up his bag and was on his way out of the door when he realised he had forgotten the book, "hang on, forgot something", he raced upstairs and fetched the book out of the bag and was carrying it down the stairs when mum saw it, "what you got there then?" she asked, "oh, just a book I said I would lend to Vinnie" Kevin replied. "Oh, well, you had better get going, or you will be late, forget your head if it wasn't screwed on," she laughed, and with that, Kevin cycled to the park. As the football fields were on a different side of the park from the school part, Kevin did not think about the old man he saw standing there, staring at him daily. Kevin pulled up at the entrance, parked his bike next to others that were there, and went and joined all the other children who had come to try out.

Paul had come straight from school as he had been playing basketball there against another local school. He crossed over to his brother, "ok Kevin" he asked. Kevin nodded, "bring the book?" Kevin nodded again, "ok, see you here after the trials. Have a good one, little bro" with that, whistles were being blown, and the people in charge were moving the now crowd into their year categories.

The trials were great. First, they did stretching, then jogging, and finally, they were placed into teams to play against each other. For the first half hour, Kevin was in the centre of defence, tackling, and organising people to stop others, then asked if he would do time in goal which he tried. Kevin did very well in both positions. He saved many shots and even a penalty. After the trials, the adults in charge told everyone that they would decide who would go forward for the team and who will not. They would make their decision over the weekend and get it to the schools to put on their notice boards with the names and the next training sessions. Kevin was incredibly pleased with how he had done. He could not have done any better. Now all he could do was wait and see if he would make the next training session. With all this going on, he had totally forgotten about the meeting with his brother. As he started to go towards his bike to talk to Vinnie, Paul called to him. "Kevin, where are you going," Kevin looked round and remembered the talk. "Listen, Vinnie, I'll catch you later. Big bro wants me." Kevin returned to where Paul was, "what, you forgot our chat", Paul asked, "no, I, ok, I did, just for a minute though, sorry", Paul looked at Kevin, "you could be, believe me, now come on, follow me".

Kevin followed Paul as they made their way over the park towards the rock garden. "What are you doing here? Not thinking of throwing me in there, I hope, because if you are, I'm ready for you. I will head butt you again," Kevin said. "Quiet down, Kevin. I'm not going to throw you in there. Now listen, I want you to sit there, keep your mouth shut, and listen to what I have to say. No matter what I tell you, you do not open that mouth of yours until I am finished. Is that clear?" Paul was now making a stern finger gesture at him. "This is for your benefit, mine also. You cannot tell anyone about what I am going to tell you or show you, agree!", Kevin looked at his brother and once again saw the worried stare in his eyes, "ok, ok, just get on with it. We do not have that much time". Paul got up and started to pace up and down, "Well," Kevin said, "Don't rush me," Paul answered. "Ok, I wanted you to turn your mind back three and a half years ago. What can you remember?" Paul asked. "Well, " Kevin said, "not much, I was only eight, but I do seem to remember you were getting into quite a bit of trouble that year, both at school and home, and you really took a major dislike to me, you were nasty to mum, dad, gran, and granddad, in fact, everyone. Didn't mum also nearly put you in a care home because she couldn't handle you?" Paul lowered his head then spoke, "ok, I remember, go on," "go on, what do you mean to go on? I cannot remember anything else apart from you being a right pain in the backside. Anyway, what has that got to do with what happened this week?" Kevin asked.

Paul walked over to the rocks near the waterfall, moved three stones back, muttered some words that Kevin could not quite hear, then pulled out of a space a canvas bag. He looked around as if he was checking that no one had seen him do this, then walked back and sat down next to his brother, "Three and a half years ago, I was just like you, strong-willed, outspoken, and going to a new school. You see, I, too, saw and met both old men. By the sound of it, the one you met in the school is a man called Jarez, and the other in the park, is his brother, Matrees. Like you, I met Jarez. First, he too handed me a book, but this book was a slightly different, unusual colour, and had a different context in the book". "What do you mean different context" Kevin asked. Paul reached inside his bag and drew out another book. It was red, old, and had a worn appearance too.

On the front, in big, bold letters, read 'The Camphyr.' "Flick through the book and tell me what you see," Paul told Kevin. Kevin flicked the book, "Not much, some squiggles of writing on certain pages, but nothing I can make out. Why?" Paul held his finger up for Kevin to stop. "Now turn the book upside down and flick from the other side," Kevin did as Paul told him to, and the squiggles now turned into words that Kevin could recognise but not understand. "So, is this it, the massive thing that's going to blow my mind away? Your right. I think not," Kevin blurted out sarcastically. "There you go, after all, I said. You have to open that cesspit you call a mouth and shut your brain off before you talk. I don't know why I am bothering you," Paul said, holding his head in his hands. "Neither do I," Kevin replied as he started to get up to go. "Sit down and listen, just for once, after I have told you and shown you things. Will you, I hope, understand." Paul shouted at Kevin. "So, this is not what you planned to show me?" Kevin asked, "No," Paul replied. "ok, I know how stubborn and set in your ways you are, but I need you to let go of all that and be as open-minded as you can be. I do not want to hear that you don't believe in anything I tell you until I have finished. Then and only then you can talk as much as a donkey brays for all I care. All I know is that this is real. If you agree, we will start. If not, then," Paul paused, "then things could end up being very serious, not just for you, but for a lot of people, do you agree?" Kevin did not know whether to laugh or just get up and go until he looked his brother in the face and once again saw the cold stare of worry. "Ok, I'll listen, but" Kevin was interrupted by Paul shouting at him, "no buts, ok?" Kevin nodded in agreement. "Three and a half years ago, I was really just like you, Jack the lad, cocky, head full of sport, girls, and argumental thoughts. I was a new kid on the block at a new school, where some of my friends had come with me from the junior school; some had left me to go to other schools. I would miss them as we had been together for a long while, and we all knew where our place was, but in this new school, I was going to have to make new friends again, and I was not looking forward to it. You are lucky; you had me there," Kevin interrupted, "lucky you and your gang threw me in the damn bushes. What's lucky about that?" Paul stared at Kevin as if to say shut up, "anyway, I did not have the best of starts" Kevin, instead of speaking this time, pointed to himself, "yes, just like you, and just like you I met Jerez first, you described him down to a tee, He is a patient man, but his brother, Matrees, well he has a very hasty nature. They are brothers, just like you and I, and just like us, they argue. The only thing is, when they argue, it causes chaos, and people get hurt, even end up dead" "what, you mean they kill people?", asked Kevin. Paul looked at the floor and answered, "Yes, I have seen it", "so what, they shoot people or stab them with a knife?", Paul shook his head to indicate no, "then how, why are they after you?, what is this all about, and what's with the books?, are they some sort of record on killings?" Paul stood up quickly, "What did I say? Keep your mouth buttoned; your brain is going into overtime yet again. You are in a fantasy world. I am not talking about Al Capone or Bugsy Malone. These men are," Paul went quiet, "what, these men are what?" replied Kevin. Paul bent down and drew what Kevin thought looked like a stick from the bag, "They're Wizards," Paul replied, "Wizards," Kevin replied, and then started laughing, "you really had me going there. I thought you were in trouble and someone was out to get you, Wizards. There are no such things; next, you'll tell me there are witches and mystical creatures". Paul looked at Kevin and then spoke, "glad you find it funny. I knew you would react this way, but here's a real kick to your funny thoughts, I am a magician also, and I believe you also have the gift. That's why they have come back" "Gift, gift, there is no such thing. You don't really believe all that nonsense, really, do you? Look, if they existed hundreds or even thousands of years ago, where are they now?" Kevin, still chuckling to himself, rose from the seated position he was in and turned to Paul. "I suppose that's your wand then," and laughed more. Paul looked hard at Kevin, then spoke, "you don't believe me do you? I can sense it in your laughter. I knew you were not adult enough yet to understand the true existence of magic. Well, let me prove it to you, then we will see who is laughing". Kevin, still laughing, managed to say, "so what are you going to do, turn me into a toad?" "oh, I could easily do that" Paul replied, "but then you wouldn't be remembered what you have seen, no hold out your hand", Paul said, Kevin still very amused asked, "why", "just hold out your hand and point to a small stone on the floor with the other, well go on, just do it," Paul demanded, "all right, but I don't know what you're trying to prove". Kevin held out his left hand looked for a small rock and pointed to it saying "that one, is that ok my mighty magician" still laughing. Paul stared at the rock Kevin had chosen, pointed his wand at it then spoke, "**incantartum leverat**" the rock slowly twitched, then moved, slowly it raised from the ground and travelled towards Kevin's hand, all this time Paul was moving his wand to the momentum of the rock until he lowered it into Kevin's hand. Kevin just stood there, not laughing at all now, "go on," Paul said, "explain that no strings around the rock are there, no wind or a big bird flying overhead to accomplish it, explain."

Kevin felt the rock all round, nothing attached, no breeze, he had no explanation. "good trick" Kevin came out with, "can't explain it at the minute but somewhere there is an explanation for it", Paul turned away in discussed, "what is there to explain, it is magic, it is real, no tricks, believe me", Paul answered now getting really annoyed, "what else do you want me to do to prove it, start a fire" he pointed his wand at a small bush and uttered the words "**firentium sparksum**" a blinding light shot from the wand and hit the bush which started to burn, "put the fire out" Paul then said, again he pointed his wand at the burning bush and uttered "**disquelch firentium**" again a light shot out of the wand and hit the bush, this time water appeared all around it and put the fire out, "what more, I can make it as though nothing had happened, the same spell that fixed your clothes, cuts and scars", again pointing at the bush said "**Compare-relapses**" , one final time a light shot from the wand to the bush, this time the bush turned back into the living greenery it had been before the event. Paul now turned and looked at Kevin. His facial expressions had changed, and he no longer wore a cocky grin but a look of disbelief. He walked over to the bush. He could still see little scorch marks on some branches. Also, the ground it stood on was wet.

"No, no, this did not happen, it's not true, there are no people called witches and wizards, there are just stories, you are not a magician or wizard, it's a dream, and I will wake up in a minute" Kevin tried to convince himself, "well," said his brother Paul, as he walked over to him and pinched Kevin, "ow, that hurt, what did you do that for"? Asked Kevin, "if you were asleep, then that would have woken you up. Also, in the morning, you will have a bruise there to let you know that what you saw here today is very real, not a story, and by the way, remember I told you that you may have the gift to", Paul then went into his bag once again and fetched out a bundle of parchment papers and handed them to Kevin, "Magic is passed down through genes through ages, this is our family tree, have a good look, and you will see those I ringed on the tree, they were said to be magicians, it is up to date, you might just be amazed at what you find out". Paul now a bit more relieved even managed a small smile, "believe in the unbelievable Kevin, I have kept this secret for three and a half years, I so wanted to tell mum, dad even you, but I knew you would all think I was a nutter, that is why I was so bad, no-one would understand me, but now, you need to know what lies ahead and believe me, brother, it will be hard and dangerous. There is information to understand, to learn, what is right and what's wrong, and which path to take. All I can say is that you must not tell anyone, and I mean anybody, not even mum and dad. The more you know the secret, the more you will upset people and be cast out. The book you have, study it, for it contains spells, spells that can help you, but beware, there are also spells in there that can cause you more turmoil than good. You yourself will have to learn which to use, when to use, and believe in why you used it. As you use the spells, you will find that the blank pages will fill with other spells just like mine." Paul picked up his book and flicked through it, showing Kevin. "Well, for now, I think you have enough to take in. Best we get off home, come on grab the book, family tree and let's get off."

Kevin did as his brother asked, and they walked a crossed the park to get their bikes. As they walked, Paul put his arm around his brother's shoulder and said, "well, I said it would blow your mind away, didn't I," Kevin looked briefly at Paul, then spoke, "you sure did." With that, they got on their bikes and rode home. As they arrived, mum was there to greet them, "well" she said, "how did it go", Kevin looked at Paul first, then back to mum, "great" Kevin replied, "just great" Kevin smiled at Paul, "oh I am so pleased, so when will you know if you both made the teams, how many boys were there, you didn't hurt anyone did you?", Paul stopped his mum there, "we will know by the end of school on Monday, not until, so we cannot tell you any more ok". "Anyway", Mum continued, "granddad called and asked if you to want to go fishing in the morning after Pauls paper round. I told him I'm sure you'd love to, didn't do wrong, did I?" mum said, "no", replied both Paul and Kevin, "that will be great", with that both the brothers settled down to an evening of deep thought before they had tea and then bedtime.

Chapter 2

Something Strange Caught

That night, as Kevin lay in bed, his small side lamp pushing out as much light as it could, he could not think of anything else of what his brother had revealed to him. He was trying to make sense of it all, how the rock got to his hand, the bush burning, then put out, the books, the funny language, and last but most of all, the wand. If magic did really exist, why does it need an element to channel its energy through it? , it was only good science that proved this fact. Then he stopped, but this is something that science cannot explain. There is no physical evidence that proves or disproves the facts of the case. As he thought this, he felt a little pain on his arm where his brother had pinched him, mumbling to himself, "I guess you could call this a proven fact," then smiled.

He reached for his bag and took out the family tree and the book. As he opened the family tree, he saw great lines drawn down the page with people's names he had never heard of, dating back to the late fourteen hundreds. Some of the names had circles around them, and some with question marks beside them. But as he followed the lines, he came to the Wilks family outline. There was their great-grandad's name with great-grandma alongside with the tree line showing their children's names, as Paul had said, had circles around them, some just question marks beside their names, then on to granddad and Grandma Wilks, Granddad Wilks was circled, grandma, just a question mark. The lines showed the children's names, Kenneth, Malcolm, John, and Derek, their dad, and Christine. John and Malcolm had circles around their names. Christine had a question mark beside her name, so what did this mean, Kevin thought to himself. The tree lines seemed to disappear from Kenneth, John, and Malcolm, probably because they had no children, but Derek and Christine both had children.

As Kevin looked closer and over the page, he saw their part of the tree, Paul and Kevin. Paul circled Kevin with a question mark and a semi-circle. His brain was now starting to hurt a little. He put the family tree back into the bag and now picked up the book.

Kevin ran his hands over the book's cover. He could feel that the book appeared to have had a lot of use in its time and turned the book like his brother had shown him. As he flicked the heavy pages, he could now make out lesser amounts of the writing that was on the pages. He stopped at a page where it was blank, with no marks, no indents, just the blankness of the page. He whispered softly, "why are you blank? There must be a reason," as soon as Kevin had finished speaking, writing started to appear on the blank page. Kevin watched as the letters appeared in a sentence that he had read. 'There is always a reason for doing something. It is within your mind that the purpose of that reason lies. Choose what the purpose is, and that will define the reason.' Kevin looked at the page, "but I don't understand what purpose, what reason"? The book revealed more, 'when you want something bad, you will stop at nothing to get it. When you want to forget something, you try and block its presence from the mind. You must decide the right path, right or wrong, good or bad. Only you have the power to decide. But beware, there are others amongst you who will try and sway your mind.' Kevin, even now more confused, flicked more pages of the book and stopped on a page that read the repair spell. Kevin looked at the words written under the title. It read, '**Compare-relapsum,**' a spell to fix all breakages, cuts, tears, or anything separated from the main body of the object. "That's the spell both Matrees and Paul had used," Kevin thought to himself. He quickly flicked through more of the book and came a crossed the fire and water spell his brother had used. There were more spells within the book that looked a bit complicated in the wording to say, so Kevin decided to close the book. As he did, the book flew open to the blank page once more, "now what" Kevin asked. As if asked, the page once again started to fill up with writing. Kevin read what it said. 'It is written that an article will appear, and possession will have toiled for it. One good and one bad will pursue the article for themselves. The article will ensure power though all may not be as it seems, for the two art one.' Kevin looked very puzzled at the sentence as it slowly disappeared from the page. He slowly muttered in a quiet voice, "I still do not understand, and not quite sure of what to do about what you are showing me." As he closed the book completely, this time making sure it was not jumping back into life, Kevin decided to see if Paul was still awake.

As he slowly undid his door to stop any squeaking, he heard a voice coming from Paul's room and a light glow from under his door. Kevin crept closer. He pushed his ear up against the door and heard Paul's voice say quietly, **"Iluminum Cantarta"** with that, the light shone brightly from under the door frame, then slowly disappeared to reveal nothing but blackness. Kevin tapped at the door and called to his brother quietly, "Paul, you awake?" Kevin opened the door and saw his brother dive into his bed, "shut the door, stupid," "there's no need for that," Kevin said, "what do you want?" Kevin looked at his brother and then spoke. "Cannot sleep. I cannot get my head around what has happened in just a short space of time. My mind is all over the place. Things I know cannot happen have happened. There is no explanation for any of this. How did you cope? I need help to understand it all." Paul looked at Kevin, then answered. "I did say it would blow your mind away. It will take time for you to adjust to the fact that this is real, not fiction, not dreams, very real. It will be hard, extremely hard. You will have to really believe in the fact that you may be a wizard too, now with that comes great responsibility. Great strength is required from you, inside your mind and body, and you will encounter many different things along your journey, just as I did. Some things will be good, some bad, but you must rise above them, take them in your stride, but most of all, if you doubt yourself just for a second, it could be your downfall." Kevin looked at Paul and nodded as if to say he understood. "So, what was that you were doing before I came in?" Kevin asked. "It is a light charm. It illuminates an area for a brief period but can be extended if the charm is concentrated on for a longer period," Paul replied. Kevin stood up, then turned towards Paul and said, "I looked at the family tree," "neat isn't it" Paul replied. "Hmm," Kevin mumbled, "so what is the thing with the circles and question marks?" Paul eased himself up in his bed and replied.

"All those names circled have dealt in magic. It has been proved through time and records, all with question marks beside their names have not been recorded using magic but have been said to have used it."

"So, that means Uncle John and Uncle Malcolm are also magicians or wizards, and Aunty Christine, then she may be a witch!" Kevin answered. "That's right, how neat is that? It took me ages before I found out all the histories of the people. Wizards, witches, and warlocks have been in our family gene line for hundreds of years, skipping certain generations, but still, the art has been passed down the line through time." "You know I am having great difficulty trying to work all this out, it still does not seem possible, but I know through what I have seen with my own two eyes and the pain I have felt" Kevin stroked the arm he had a bruise on from his brother, "it has to be true".

"At last," Paul said, "you need to be more convinced; a good wizard must be focused on every little detail. Everything he does, sees, smells, and touches can mean a great deal to him. I know this must have hit you like a ton of bricks, Kevin, and scuppered your great logical mind, but now you can move forward and embrace the time. You have a lot to learn in a brief time. Someone once said that the greatness of a person comes with time, whilst sometimes greatness is thrust upon that person. No one knows what your destiny will be, but at the end of the day, this is happening to you for a reason."

Just as Paul finished speaking came their mum's voice, boys, what are you doing?" "Nothing, mum," replied Paul, "just talking about the football trials". "Well, it's getting late now, off to sleep with you or you will be dead tired in the morning, Paul", "ok mum" replied the boys together, then Kevin crept back to his room and got into bed where he fell fast asleep in a very short time.

Kevin was woken quite early by the banging of the front door and the muffled sounds of greeting and leaving. Paul was on his way out to do his paper round, whilst dad was on his way in from working nights at the hospital. Kevin leapt out of bed, got dressed, and ran downstairs. As he turned the corner from the stairs, he nearly went straight into his dad. "Whoa there, Kevin, what's the hurry? house not on fire, is it?" Kevin looked up at his dad and replied. "No, sorry, dad, need to get outside and dig some worms for fishing today, that's all." Dad looked at Kevin and then said, "hmm, never seen you so excited overfishing before like this. Who are you going with?" "Granddad and Paul," replied Kevin, "well, mind you behave. Granddad wilks is not getting any younger, you know, no arguing with your brother, and keep well away from the waters side," dad replied. "Dad, I'm not a baby now. I promise to be good," replied Kevin. Dad bent down to whisper in Kevin's ear, "if you catch any eels, make sure they're dead before you bring them home, you remember how mum went mad last time your brother brought some home, and they started to swim again when put in water", dad smiled at Kevin then continued, "better still, let your granddad take them home for nan and him, ok". Dad gave Kevin a little wink of his eye which made Kevin smile, "ok," replied Kevin. "well, those worms are not going to put themselves into your box on their own. Mind you, only dig at the bottom of the garden where nothing is planted. If you dig any of your mum's plants up, then she will have both our hides. Now go get them son", dad patted Kevin on the back as he grabbed the shed key and went outside to get his worms.

As Kevin began digging, he wondered if there was some sort of magic to get the worms up without digging, but then thought perhaps that would be an idol, so he totally forgot about it and carried on digging until he thought he had got enough for all of them. Time passed quickly as Kevin sat in front of the television, watching all the same programmes he watches every weekend. Paul walked in with a cheery "hello," mum answered him with, "everything ok dear, here grab some toast, Granddad will be round soon." Paul munched on the toast as he walked into the sitting room, "don't forget a plate with that. There will be crumbs everywhere" mum shouted. Paul, quickly getting a plate, came back into the room. "Got enough worms then, Kevin"? Asked Paul. Kevin nodded. "Enough for us all"? Kevin nodded again, "better had, mind you. Granddad is bringing maggots also, so we should be ok"! Paul mumbled as he continued to eat his toast.

In no time at all, granddad had arrived in his car, ready to take the boys fishing. With a tap on the door, he went in to see them. "Hello, you two, ready then? Fish do not wait for anyone", as he started to say, "it's the early bird", the boys jumped in to finish the sentence, "that catches the worm, we know, granddad", the boys said together. Kevin looked at his granddad Short then said, "never really understood fisherman saying that. It's alright for birds catching worms, but what's it got to do with fishermen"? Everyone just laughed, and the boys got their tackle together and put it in the boot of the car. "Now, mind you behave, boys, no playing granddad up, you hear," "yes, mum came the reply from both Paul and Kevin, "and I will not go near the water's edge, ok," Kevin added. "Bit like a record playing. I already had that speech from dad," Kevin mumbled to Paul so his mum could not hear him. "So, boys, where to?" asked granddad, "how about the little Holland" Paul blurted out, "my friends said that they have just restocked it, and it's fishing well just opposite Baxter's Barn." "Then Baxter's barn, here we come," replied granddad, and off he drove there. As they arrived at their destination, granddad pulled up alongside the barn, which stood on the opposite side of the road, it was on a bend, and the river followed the course of the road. The river itself was not that deep or wide, so granddad was happy with the location. The party got out of the car and unloaded the tackle. As they crossed the road, granddad said, "ok, where do we set up then", Paul motioned towards places that were worn down ahead of them, "Kevin and I could go here, and my friends said that there was some big fish being caught just round the bend so if you want to go there", Granddad looked, he could see a patch that was also worn down, "I don't know" he said, "a bit far away if anything happened to you for me to get to you". "Now, grandad, what's going to happen," Paul asked. "I don't know" replied granddad, "one of you could fall in". "We will not do that, and besides, both of us can swim. Why not try that spot for a while and just keep coming back every now and then to check on us? If there is a problem, we will be able to alert you quickly enough" Paul replied back. Granddad looked at the bend place where he could see a bit of activity in the water, "ok, but mind you behave, I'll be listening, I'm only just a short distance away." Both Kevin and Paul nodded and went down the riverbank.

As the two boys got to the edge, Kevin started to move towards a flat place on the riverbank when Paul called to him. "No, not there. I think you ought to fish from this spot", Paul said, "why?" asked Kevin, "I don't rightly know, but I have a feeling that you are going to catch something pretty big from there today." Kevin looked at Paul, shrugged his shoulders then moved to the spot. As he did so, Paul raced up the riverbank and looked at the barn. His eyes followed a path from the barn, over the road, down the bank, and into the river, where he stopped and stared. "what's up" Kevin called to Paul, "nothing, just checking the flow of water so I can see where is best to cast into", "oh" replied Kevin, "so where's my best spot?", "right in front of you, about ten feet out. You don't want to be too shallow with the hook, either. There looks to be a bit of a dip there, so it might have quite a few fish in it", replied Paul. The boys set up the tackle, and Kevin cast out to where his brother had told him to.

The daylight was good, with a slight windy breeze coming down the river. Birds were circulating in the sky around them to see if there were any loose food snatches they could make, but overall, quite a lovely day and location, Kevin thought. As the day went on, the party had caught quite an amount and assortment of different fish. Granddad was as good as his word. He kept coming back to the boys on a regular basis to check on them and how many fish they had caught and also to have their sandwiches together. By now, they had been on the riverbank for a good three hours. It had been so peaceful. Only the bird's song and a wisp of a breeze kept them company as the boys fished. Kevin was having so much fun that he had totally forgotten about the previous day's events until Paul started to talk to him.

"So, now you have slept on it, how do you feel? What are your thoughts"? "About what"? Kevin asked. "About what"? Paul answered sarcastically. "About you having the gift of magic." "But I don't know if I do or don't," Kevin replied, "do or don't what"? Paul asked. "Whether or not I am gifted and can perform magic, when did you know"? Kevin asked Paul. "When I received my wand, I just had the feeling that I could do it," Paul answered, "do it," Kevin said "do it, perform magic," replied Paul. "Oh, so who gave you the wand, a magician"? Kevin asked. "No," replied Paul sternly, "then who"? Repeated Kevin. "It wasn't so much of a who, more of a where," Paul said, "what do you mean where?" Kevin asked again. "What, you a parrot, repeating everything I say?" Paul scolded back. "Sorry for asking" Kevin came back sarcastically and turned to his rod, looking out over the water at his float. "look" Paul said, "the reason I wanted you to fish there and the reason we are here, is not through my mates saying what I told granddad, I was sitting right where you were when my line got tangled up on something on the bottom. As I pulled the line in, it brought to the surface a bundle bound up like a cord tie. It was covered in weeds, so I opened it and found the wand and" Paul stopped speaking dead in his tracks of speech, "and what" Kevin asked, "and a necklace. A necklace with a small emblem inscribed into a stone, the markings, or words I still have not worked out to this day." "So, where is the necklace?" Kevin asked. Paul lowered the top of his tee shirt to show Kevin the necklace. "Always worn it since the day I got it, never took it off. I thought it was a good omen. Even wore it, though. I gave the art up for the past three years until it all started to happen to you. Now we must work out what is going on."

Kevin and Paul continued to talk about what had happened, especially about what had come up in the book last night. " So the book stated that an article would be found, a fight for it would occur, power given from it, perhaps it is this pendant," Paul said. Kevin looked back at Paul, "I don't think so," he said, "I didn't know of your pendant before the writing appeared in the book, and if it brings power, why has nothing been done within the three years you have had it to gain it. No, there is something else." "Oh, mister logical mind once again," Paul scoffed at Kevin. "look, you brought me into this world. I didn't ask for it, you said I have to believe in myself to become a magical person, but you also need a clear, calm mind to think of all these things. That's my specialty, so grow up, and we need to find out more about your pendant, agree?"

Kevin asked. Paul, Not like the way his little brother had spoken to him, but somehow felt it the right thing to agree to.

Granddad appeared round the corner cheerfully, singing a little tune to himself. As he came into the boys' view, he shouted, "we will have one more hour, then call it a day, ok, boys", Paul and Kevin both acknowledged agreement. As granddad turned and went back to his fishing spot, Kevin turned to Paul and said, "you said you pulled your wand and the pendant out of the water here. Is that why you wanted me to fish this spot, in case it repeated itself? The odds are astronomical for this to happen. It's just not going to happen" Kevin said to his brother. Paul looked at his brother, "well, you can't blame a bloke for trying or believing."

Kevin shook his head, but as he did so, he noticed what looked like a large white dove flying towards them upriver. As it reached Kevin's spot, it stopped moving forward and hovered in front of Kevin for a good three seconds, staring him straight in the eye, "Paul" Kevin called quietly, "look at this." Paul turned his head in Kevin's direction and saw the dove hovering, and then the dove turned, swooped down near Kevin's float, and dropped something from its beak. A kind of pellet that landed beside the float and then sunk. The dove then turned and flew off, but as it did so, Kevin's rod twitched and started to move. Kevin caught hold of the rod and started to reel in the line. Paul ran over to Kevin and tried to help, but Kevin just shrugged him off. As Kevin continued reeling in the line, it was clear what was on end was very heavy or caught up on something. Kevin heaved harder and harder, but the line was stuck fast. "Let me try" Paul called, "no, it won't beat me. If it's a fish, then it's a mega big one." Kevin kept pulling and reeling in line, "look" Paul cried, "it's not going to come. You're better cutting the line and leaving it." "It's not going to beat me", Kevin grunted as he fought hard to haul his line in, his face now turning red. "You are not going to beat me", he called out again, then suddenly, the line went slack. "Well," cried Paul, "either, if it was a massive fish, it has gone, or if it was tangled, then it's snapped the line and freed itself". Kevin started to reel in the line, and as he did, he noticed a big air bubble appear where his float was. He continued to reel in, still a little tight but needing no fight now.

As his float rose out of the water, Kevin noticed something had risen to the surface. Kevin pulled his line tight and towards him. As the float got nearer, Paul looked in disbelief. "I told you, I told you, "He repeated. Kevin dragged what looked like a medium-sized package to the bank. He bent down and lifted it from the water. Weeds were all around it. Kevin cut the weeds from around it and laid them down on the floor. "Well," Paul said, "well what" Kevin replied. "Open it", Paul cried. Kevin, a little apprehensive, untied the knot from the cord around the package holding it together. He looked at his brother, Paul's face now aglow with excitement, motioning for him to reveal what was within it. Kevin peeled back a flap of the now completely dry cloth, then another flap to reveal the corner of another book. As Kevin completely opened the cloth, there in front of him sat along with the book, an ivory wand.

By its side, another object, it looked like a half-moon shape made of metal with small rings around it on a silver chain. Paul stared at Kevin, "bloody hell, look at that wand," Kevin picked up the wand and stared in disbelief at it, "what do I do now?" Kevin asked his brother, "well," Paul started to say but was stopped short as he noticed the white dove returning towards them. Nervously he pointed down the river to Kevin, who looked and saw the dove also. Again, the dove stopped and hovered right in front of them, then flew to the ground where the book was. It pecked at the corner of the book, which flew open. Both Paul and Kevin moved closer to see what was written on the first page. It read, 'to be chosen for a task is a great honour, to undertake the task to the end, will bring a hero, although long gone, I, Merlin, will be your guide, mentor friend and advocate, through the time of your peril and joy', Kevin closed the book quickly. "Bloody hell," Paul called out again, "that looks like that's Merlin's wand. It's supposed to be a myth." "Kevin looked at Paul, "but Merlin was a myth, wasn't he? King Arthur, Camelot, and Merlin, they were just stories, weren't they? There is no evidence to say they existed, just stories." Paul replied, "Stories nothing, you must believe in yourself and believe the whole idea of magic and magicians, this is reality, this is happening, you have Merlin's wand and spell book, you could be as great as he was, hundreds of years ago. Even though I only dabbled three and a half years ago before I, well," Paul changed the subject quickly, "the wizards I met and got to know all talked about the possibility that Merlin's wand was real, only no one ever found it, many have tried. It was said that it will only be found by a good, powerful wizard, who will use it to rid the plains of dark, devilish wizards and witches." "Why me then" Kevin asked, "A person who did not believe in magic or its people but entrusted me with this, am I likely to find the sword Excalibur too?" Kevin asked in a sarcastic voice. Paul shrugged his shoulders, "I can't tell you because I don't know, there may be one person who might be able to help, but I can't have a word with him until Monday. For now, I suggest you pack those things away and keep them safe."

All this time, the white dove was standing on the floor, not moving, just cooing. Kevin looked down at the dove and said," well, I must thank you for what you did". The dove cooed at Kevin, "I wish you could understand me, and I could tell what you were saying," Paul looked over to Kevin and said, "what are you doing now? Come on, leave that dove alone and get those things packed up ". Kevin put the wand and the book into his fishing bag and started to turn away from his rod when he heard a voice in his head say, "do not forget the time stone" Kevin looked round but saw no one, "did you say something Paul?" asked Kevin, "no, why?" "Oh, I could have sworn I heard someone say don't forget the time stone." Paul dropped his bag, "you what" Paul asked. Kevin repeated what he had said. "The time stone, that's the time stone." "I guess so," said Kevin, "I swear I heard someone say don't forget the time stone, so I guess it must be." Paul again turned and said, "I don't believe it, you have got Merlin's wand and the time stone, it is said that those two items are the most powerful items within the realm of magic." Kevin now getting a little mad cried out, "well, I didn't ask for them, here you take them."

Kevin tried to hand the items to his brother, but when he let go, they remained within his hands. He shook them violently, but with no movement" Paul looked at Kevin and then said, "Sorry bro, it is you that you have been picked for this task, and these are the tools you need to complete it. Only he who has been chosen can brandish the wand and stone. Only he who has the power and goodness of heart will overcome all his foes with these elements at his disposal. Admit it, bro. You are in it for the long haul". Kevin turned and eased the wand, stone, and book into the bag. As Paul started to take his tackle apart, Kevin tried hurling the bag back into the water. As it left his arm, it looked as though it was on its way back into the river when it did a u-turn and landed back at Kevin's feet. Paul looked at Kevin, "Told you, bro, in it for the long haul" Paul resumed taking his rods apart, smiling to himself. "If I were you, I would put that time stone around your neck for safekeeping," Paul called to Kevin. "Once it's on, it should disappear like mine until you need to see or use it, then it reappears. Well, it should do." "Should do, but we know nothing about this thing," Kevin replied, "what if it is bad for me?" Paul looked at Kevin smiling, "I would hardly think it would hurt you if it were with the most powerful wizard's wand and his spell book. Merlin was a good wizard, remember, trust me."

Kevin looked a little hesitant but looped the chain over his head. As the stone came to rest on his chest, he felt a complete calmness run throughout his body. He felt quite good in himself, very fit, and incredibly happy. Kevin returned to packing the fishing rods and tackle away and also placing the book and wand into the bag. Paul called out, "oh, one more thing, your wand." "What about it" Kevin replied, "place the wand anywhere around your body where you can easily access it and be comfortable with" Paul replied. "What do you mean?" Kevin asked. "Well, like this," Paul said as he drew his wand from the side of his body. "But I didn't even see it there," Kevin gasped in surprise. "No, you won't," Paul answered. "Like the stone, once positioned, it stays there and becomes invisible, only you know its whereabouts, and only you can retrieve it. The best thing is you don't even feel it on you, no matter what you do, and that includes swimming, but it's there." Kevin thought about the best place he could put it in case he did need it, then decided to place it on his left thigh, easily accessible for him as he was right-handed. As soon as the wand was placed where he wanted it in position, it disappeared. "There you go" Paul said, "feel anything?" Kevin shook his head as if to say no. "Now, go for a quick draw. Go on." Kevin snapped his right hand over to his left thigh. As the hand touched the thigh, he felt his fingers wrap around the wand and withdrew from its resting place. With one quick movement, the wand was in his outstretched hand in front of him. "See, told you so", Paul said, "now put it back and let us get this lot packed up before granddad comes."

Kevin replaced his wand in its position and did as his brother asked. It was quite lucky, really, for as the last thing went into the bag, granddad appeared round the corner, walking towards them. "Ok, you two" he asked as he stood in front of them, "absolutely," Paul answered with a big smile on his face. "Well, catch much, let's see" granddad asked the boys. The last thing to be put away were the keep nets of the fishing tackle. Paul pulled him in to show that he had a hefty haul in it. There were all sorts of fish, including a couple of good eels. "Not bad" granddad replied, "And what about you, Kevin?" he said. Kevin pulled in his keep net, not as many fish as Paul, but bigger fish and a good couple of eels also. "Well now, I guess your mum will be pleased with those eels you two caught her" granddad said. "Oh, I don't know" Kevin replied, "she is not a great lover of them. Perhaps you might want to take them for Nan and yourself. I'm sure you two would enjoy them more than mum and dad." "Well, if you think so, young man," granddad replied," that is most kind of you. I must say it has been a real pleasure fishing with you two today, and your mates were right, Paul. A good catch for all of us. We will have to come again, come on time to get moving towards home."

The party walked up the bank and over to granddads car, put the fishing tackle in the boot, and got in. As they drove along heading back to their homes, Kevin kept looking out the back window, "what are you looking at, bro" asked Paul. "Oh, nothing" replied Kevin, but secretly he was looking for the white dove, which had decided to fly a short distance behind the car all the way home to their house. As the boys got out of the car and emptied the boot, Kevin saw the white dove perch itself on the TV aerial of their house. The next thing he heard was his mother's voice. "Everything ok, dad?" she asked granddad. "Everything's fine, June, they have been as good as gold, and we all caught quite a good haul of fish," granddad replied. "Oh, good," she said as if she really didn't want to hear that, "only four eels though, to which the boys have let me have for your mum and me, hope you don't mind" he answered. "No, no, you have them. I know how much you two like them," mum answered now with a bit more happiness in her voice. Kevin looked at his granddad, who winked at him. "Well then, better be going, be good for your mum, boys, we must do this more often, bye." With that, granddad got in his car and drove off as Kevin, Paul, and their mum waved at him. "Thank goodness for that," mum said, "I thought I was going to get lumbered with those blasted eels you lot keep catching. I really do not like them, boys, so please, if you do catch any more, either release them again or take them to your granddads, ok." Kevin and Paul laughed, "Ok mum," the boys said together. They all then went into the house for tea and quiet time.

That evening as Kevin watched TV before getting washed and into bed, his mind kept him thinking about the catch at the river, the dove, and all the week's events as he sat watching TV thinking. He ran his hand gently over his left thigh in slow motion so as not to be seen by anyone who may notice. The wand was still there as his brother had said it would be, also the stone around his neck, but neither was visible. Kevin felt quite tired now and decided to go up to bed. As he lay there, he pulled up from the bag the book he had pulled in at the river with him to have a look at. "Night dear," his mum called, "night mum, night Paul" Kevin replied. As he lay in his bed, he took the book onto his lap, opened it, passed the first page, and on into the book. There were all sorts of different marks and writing on the pages, none of which Kevin could recognise. He flicked through page after page, wondering what the marks and words he did not understand as they were in a foreign language to him, said. "I wish I could understand this" Kevin said quietly, "I'm no good with foreign languages."

A slight glow came from the stone he had around his neck, and the words suddenly went from complete jargon that he could not interpret to words that Kevin could now understand. Kevin, a little startled, stared at the book and slowly read the contents. Not all were spells or magical writing; the book was like a journal also. There was mention of a wizard called Bartholomew, killed by a warlock called crandloss. There was also an entry about the last unicorn, its death, its blood, and the hereafter. Kevin flicked through more and came across more spells for all different things, some to do with good, some bad, like a killing spell. There were also spells for torturing and harming, but also counter spells for healing. A lot of useful information was in this book. It would take Kevin a long time to go through and try to understand it all. He questioned himself if he really wanted to be bothered by it all. He kept asking himself, is this real? He only had to feel his left thigh which he did and drew the wand from it. It was very real. Kevin just did not feel the belief in himself to be who his brother wanted him to be, a great wizard. Kevin closed the book, put it on the side table, turned off his light, and closed his eyes.

Visions

As Kevin slipped into a deep sleep, it was not long before he started to dream. Some things were clear, and some quite misty things he could see were present in his mind as he slept. Although quite misty, the first vision soon cleared. Kevin could see a young boy playing outside the front of a small house, about the same age as himself. The boy's father, known later to Kevin as Cormious, came out of the house and called to him." come, Merlin, we need to go into the woods to collect some special items. You can help me." As the boy Merlin looked up at his father, he gave a broad smile, then got to his feet, and off they went into the woods. The woods were completely covered in bushes, trees, and thick-rooted grass bunches. Small animals like rabbits and deer were seen moving from bush to bush, keeping a watchful eye out for anything the two may do as they passed by. As the two ventured further into the woods, they saw three beautiful unicorns grazing on the grass, "quiet Merlin," the boys' dad told the boy and beckoned him closer towards him. As Merlin got close, his father pointed towards the unicorns. "See those Merlin, one of the most beautiful creatures ever to exist on this world, many, many years ago they were vast in numbers, now they are very few." "Why?" asked Merlin. "Many folks, including wizards, have killed these magical creatures for two things, Replied Cormious. "Their magnificent horn on its head is noted to harness a powerful energy, one that can keep evil away, whilst the silver blood that runs through its veins is also said to carry magical qualities. It is said that anything, man, beast, or plant life, ingests any of the unicorn blood, it will enhance the life existence of many folds of the person or vegetation."

Merlin looked at his dad and then asked, "do you mean they will live forever?" "Oh no," replied Cormious, "not forever. There is nothing that can make you live forever. It just helps you live longer than you would, that is all. But mind, for although these creatures are of good nature, they also carry a curse." Merlin looked at his father with a worried facial expression. "Oh yes," his father continued. "It is also said that anything that kills a unicorn and drinks of its blood will turn evil and be cursed throughout the whole of their life." "Cursed father," Merlin asked. "Cursed," replied Cormious. "The elders have said that one was seen slain by a young wizard, who drank the blood and had his soul torn in two." "How asked Merlin?" "It is said that the wizard just split in two, one part of the wizard still good, repenting for what had taken place, the other doomed to be cursed with evil for the rest of his life."

Merlin's father could see that his son looked a little scared by what he had just told him, so he beckoned him away from the grazing unicorns. Merlin followed his father, still even deeper into the woods. At last, they came to a clearing where a great elm stood towering above the whole of the woods, which was over five hundred years old. "Here we are then," Cormious called to Merlin. "Where father?" asked Merlin. "The special place we need to be. Now, I want you to gently break a small piece of wood, about the length of your two hands, from that tree. Go on. It won't hurt you." Merlin walked towards the tree, and as he did, he felt uneasy, a feeling that someone was watching him, apart from his dad. There was no one else around, so why did he feel like this? Merlin reached the tree and looked at the branch he was going to break. "Sorry, "he whispered towards the tree as he broke the piece needed off a small branch. "That's fine," he heard whispered back. Merlin spun round in a start but could see no one. He ran back to his father and handed the piece he had got to his father. "Now, you look after that until we get home", his father said, then heading back towards their small village. They collected berries and shoots, then continued back home.

It was getting towards dusk when they reached home, and Merlin's father told him to finish off his tasks before tea time, so Merlin did as he was asked. After tea, Cormious asked Merlin for the piece of wood he had collected earlier that day. Merlin handed it to his father, asking, "What are you going to do with it." Merlin was always inquisitive and always wanted to know what was going on. "Patience, young man," replied his father, "come with me, and you will see." Merlin followed his father out of the house. "Right," called his father, "make a small fire, then collect those six stones and place them in a circle around it." Merlin did as his father had asked. "Sit down, be quiet, watch, listen, and observe, his father told him. Merlin sat on the ground, crossed legs in complete silence. Through the back of the woods came an old man who had a lean towards the right side of his body and was dressed in an old set of robes. The old man walked to the fire, stooped down, and warmed his hands. "Is this the young one you wish to initiate?" asked the old man to Cormious. "It is, sir. He is my son, Merlin, now of eleven and a half. It is time for him to take on our ways and help our people in our course," replied Merlin's father. "Then so be it," replied the old man.

Merlin watched and listened as the old man began chanting a rhyme as he moved firstly left of the fire, then right. Merlin felt a breeze forming that engulfed him as he sat watching. After a long time, the old man held out his hand, and Cormious placed the piece of wood into the old man's hand that they had collected from the wood earlier. The old man, with one last chant, threw the wood into the fire. There was a loud bang, then a plume of smoke, then finally, the wood shot from the fire towards Merlin and stopped right in front of Merlin's face. "Take it, boy," called the old man. Merlin looked at his father, who was smiling at him, "go on, don't be afraid," whispered his father. Merlin slowly held out his hand towards the stick, it had changed in appearance, no longer a plain old piece of wood from a tree, but it had a turned handle and a strong centre piece with carvings on it sitting proud. Merlin closed his fingers around it, and as he did, he felt a deep sense of power and peace rip through his entire body, one that nearly made him let go of it. A final spark shot from the fire into the dark sky and slowly faded as it made its way back down to earth. The old man looked at both Merlin and Cormious, then said, "It is done. You, Merlin, have entered the family of the druids. A sect that upholds helping all those that are weaker than you, but only of good nature. You will travel a great distance to complete tasks that are asked of you, and to complete these tasks. You will have to stay true to the cores. You will need to learn many things in your lifetime, things sometimes that you think are of no use or purpose. But they will help in unpredictable ways of which you have not even dreamt. You are now a trainee wizard. What lies in your hand is your wand. Through it, you can muster great power and magic. Use it wisely, for sometimes magic can be a burden as well as a blessing. The old man looked at Cormious, who bowed, "time for me to leave," the old man said, but just before he did, he turned to Merlin and said, "I feel it in my bones that you could do great things, Merlin, be true, and the path will always guide you back home". The old man turned and walked off into the woods.

Merlin turned to his father and asked, "who was that man? what did he mean initiate? and what magic? Merlin's father laughed, "so many questions. I will tell you all you need to know tomorrow. For now, go wash your hands. Tomorrow, we will start your training. Now, let us go and tell your mother the news." With that, Merlin rose from his position, still looking at his father, puzzled but did as he was asked. The night went quickly. The next morning Merlin's father met him with a large rusty coloured book, "here," said his father, "this is for you. You will need it to write down all your spells and potion-making you are going to learn. You could also write things that you need to remember, like places, people you meet, or something else you see. Whatever you write in there, make sure it remains a secret so only you know of it. I will teach you how to complete starting tomorrow. Some of the more powerful magic you will learn through your years will be taught by the senior wizards and warlocks." Merlin butted in on his father's conversation, "so is it like a school," he asked, "yes" replied his father. "A school where you will learn many splendid but often dangerous things if used wrongly. Therefore you must listen well and practice hard, I will help in any capacity I can, but I am only a mere potion maker, but still, we will see".

Merlin was curious but a little scared, but still managed to smile at his father, "you promised to tell me about the old man and initiation father" Merlin asked, "so I did. Well, the initiation is into the druid sect. Our people have long been able to use magic. This spans back many hundreds of years. Some people fear us as they think we are the devils, always causing harm and casting gloom over their lives. That is why we live in small villages all over these lands. The reason is in time, someone comes across us, and we must move on, or there might be trouble". "Trouble father" asked Merlin, "but why? We are good people. I have never seen any person of the village harm another soul, so why must we move on if we are seen?" Merlin's father put a hand on his shoulder and then replied. "Not all druid wizards' are good. Oh, they start out good, but something inside them turns them evil. It could be the lust for power, or it could be that they develop a hate for someone or something, but they do go bad. You must heed the words of warning and follow the correct path. Never stray from it, Merlin, or you, too, might just end up bad. Do you hear me, son?" Merlin smiled at his dad and then replied, "I will always be a good father, just as you are." Cormious smiled and ruffled Merlin's hair, then said, "right, take your wand and book. We will tell your mother the good news, then I want you to go down to master Wilfred's house, he will be waiting, and oh Merlin," called his dad, "you are not the only trainee wizard that will be learning, so mind you be good, make friends and no arguing with Mr. Wilfred, ok," Merlin smiled then replied cheekily, "as if I would father, but what about the old man, you said you would tell me," Cormious looked at Merlin then stammered as he spoke, "one thing at a time, I will tell you later as you grow up, all you need to know of him is that he is an elderly wizard, ok? "Ok," Merlin replied, and off he went. Cormious walked back inside the house to his wife Driomatus to give her the news of Merlin's initiation into the Druids.

The dream seemed to fog up again at this point, but as Kevin tried to make things out in his mind, it slowly came clear once again after a brief time. The next vision Kevin saw was that Merlin had grown now. He must have been in his early twenties and had, by what Kevin could see, learned new spells and magic. As Kevin looked on, he saw Merlin in the woods with another young wizard, practicing casting spells at inanimate objects, setting them on fire, putting them out using water, making objects levitate, and all sorts of things. Both boys were laughing and having what looked like an enjoyable time. This frivolity continued day after day, with both boys meeting in the woods after class to try out their new gifts. They now have with every day that goes by, they learn new spells or potion-making and are always eager to try them out. Then, one day Merlin's friend never showed up after class. Merlin waited and waited, but the boy never turned up. Merlin decided to turn back to the village and go home when he heard cries coming from that direction. Merlin raced towards the village, smoke now appearing in the sky in the direction of the village. Merlin's heart pounded as he ran, not knowing what the commotion or the smoke meant, but as he neared the end of the woods, he stopped and crouched down.

There in the village were men burning houses and taking people away from their homes. Merlin could see his mother and father lying in front of their house, motionless. He wanted to run out and go to his parents but was scared to. As he looked around where the men were, he caught sight of his friend, Crandloss. Merlin could see he was not hurt or tied up but standing, talking to the leader of the men. Kevin heard the man talking was called Jarone, who sat on a black horse. Merlin could see that he was the leader of these bad people in his village and caused the devastation of the community. Merlin thought hard about how he could help in a situation like this. Luckily, he had carried his book with him as he had time before and after class to practice what he had been taught. He quickly flicked through the book and came to a disarming spell that would remove all weapons the men were holding. With a flick of his wand and the chant of "**firentay, Consunium, Derivarm**," there was a flash from the sky which hit all the men holding weapons with a high electric charge making them drop their swords and weapons. Then Merlin chanted, "**Windinium Ferosciate.** "A high-impact wind tore through the village sweeping the men off their feet and pushing them from the village. The men, now looking scared, did not know what was going to happen next or where it would come from. Looking at each other decided enough was enough and decided it would be better for them to high tale it out of there, so they ran.

Now only the leader and Crandloss stood in the village. "It's Merlin," Crandloss said to Jarone, "he is only a trainee, not that strong yet, so he should be easy to get," "easy," called the man, "I do not think scaring my men away, and the easy thing after capturing the old wizards and killing people. If he is such an easy wizard, then you deal with him. I will wait back at the camp for you to tell me the deed is done. Come to me when you either have captured him or killed him, although I would prefer it if he were alive as he would add to my coffers when I sell them over to the king." Crandloss bowed to the man, then replied, "it shall be so my lord." With that, Jarone galloped off out of the village.

"Merlin," called to Crandloss. Come out. They have gone. Merlin wanted to run down to the village, but something was stopping him. He felt a presence with him holding him back, then heard a voice in his head, "beware, Merlin, your friend is no friend at all. It was him that led these men here to do what has been done. You must do what is right, be careful". Merlin now felt as though he could move easily and decided to go to the village. As he stepped from the edge of the woods staring at Crandloss, his wand held tight, he circled round to where his mother and father lay. "What have you done, Crandloss? Why bring them here?" Crandloss shook his head, "they caught me and tortured me into the whereabouts of the village. I could do nothing." "Lies Crandloss," Merlin shouted back. "I thought we were friends." Crandloss again shook his head before answering. "Friends, friends Merlin, we are wizards, wizards with power, in time the power will grow so much that no one will question or stand before us without worthy cause, so what if some have to be cast aside for us to get where we want to be." Merlin lowered his head but did not take his eyes off Crandloss then spoke, "we have been given this gift to use it for good, what good have you done here? You have killed, maimed, and had our people trussed up and marched away, ready to be sold into slavery or, worse, to die for people's amusement. How dare you claim that the power we have is for personal use. You have been taken into the black side with the greed for money and absolute power over weaker people. Your heart, once pure, now has the blackness, you are no longer a person I can call a friend, but you must be stopped before you do any more damage."

As Merlin stared at Crandloss, he noticed a slight movement of his arm. Before Crandloss could raise his wand, Merlin cast the unarming spell at him, "**Transisomb**," but Crandloss just waved the spell away using his wand. Crandloss laughed, "your weak Merlin, I predicted that you would use that, now let me show you what power is," with that Crandloss waved his wand, chanting, "**Firentium Sparksum**" a fire bolt shot from Crandloss's wand. Merlin chanted, "**Disquelch Firentium**" a huge bolt of water shot from Merlin's wand to quelch the fire flow. "Very good, Merlin," called Crandloss, "you have been paying attention in class, but what about this? "**Electro Seethe**," again a surge shot through Crandloss's wand producing a bolt of lightning towards Merlin, "**Eversage Momentum**," Merlin cried. As the lightning got to within four feet of Merlin, it slowed in speed, then stopped and disappeared. "You see, Crandloss, extra lessons paid off, something you were not happy to do, **Crevatious Septimium**" Merlin cast back Crandloss's spell towards him. This time it connected to Crandloss's body which sent him shooting backwards, slamming him hard into one of the walls of a house. Crandloss lay on the ground almost unconscious but gained his senses and rose back to his feet, still stumbling around. As he prepared to raise his wand again, Merlin called out the last spell once again, "**Crevatious Septiium**" another bolt shot from Merlin's wand and carried its force towards Crandloss. This time Crandloss managed to deflect some of the power that the spell had, but still withered in pain as it hit him again. Crandloss, now on his knees, looked up, "seems I underestimated you, Merlin. This is not over. We will meet again" with that, Cranloss clapped his hands over his head, and there was a large bang, then a plume of smoke. As it disappeared, Crandloss was nowhere to be seen. Merlin now turned his attention towards his ill-fated parents. He knelt and cradled his father's head in his lap, stroking his father's hair.

As he did this, tears rolled from his eyes, dropping onto the forehead of his father. Merlin's father gave a small gasp as they hit his forehead, "father you're still alive," Merlin whispered to his father, slightly opening his eyes, "I am but dead, son, but You must go to the end of the land and seek Postromus, he will help you continue your journey. We die to keep you safe, Merlin, but although we are no longer in body, we will always be in your thoughts and your heart." Merlin, now crying floods of tears, answered. "Don't go, father. I'm scared. I need you." Merlin's father smiled at his son, then, with his last breath, said, "Be true, Merlin, and you will remain strong. You must not turn to blackness for revenge. Promise me, promise me, Merlin." Merlin closed his eyes and said in a quiet voice, "I promise, father," as he opened his eyes, he could see that his father had passed on. There the vision turned foggy, and Kevin could see no more. Kevin now sank into a deep sleep. No more visions, just blissful sleep.

Kevin was woken the next morning by his mum bursting through his bedroom door, "come on, sleepy head, it's past ten o'clock. Unusual for you to still be in your bed at this time, even if it is the weekend. Do you not feel well?" Kevin wearily yawned and pulled himself up the bed, "I don't know," he replied, "I still feel tired and feel like I have no energy." "Hmm," his mother replied quickly, "I hope you did not catch anything from that riverbank apart from fish. I cannot have time off work to look after you, so you had better rest up today and take a few medicines to help you revive yourself, ok". Kevin hated medicine. It always left him with a bad taste in his mouth and made him feel worse than before he had taken it, but he just smiled at his mum and replied, "Ok, mum." Kevin got out of bed and drew back his curtains. Unfortunately, it was not a nice-looking day outside. In fact, it was a bit dull and overcast, looking as though it was going to rain.

As Kevin looked out from his window, he noticed the white dove perched on the lamppost opposite his bedroom but decided to take no notice of it. He quickly dressed and went downstairs. As he hit the last step, he heard his brother Paul walk in through the back door. "Alright, Kev, you look a bit peaky today," said Paul as he smiled. "Listen, I'm going down the spinney later. Why don't you come along?" "Oh, I don't know about that," called their mum, "he's only just out of bed, and he's feeling a bit poorly," "mum," called Kevin, "I'm not poorly, I just didn't sleep to well last night that's all, perhaps a bit of clear air later will help pick me up." "Well, if you're going out there, then mind you wrap up well. We don't want you getting any worse, ok?" Kevin looked at his mum and answered sarcastically, "Yes, mum," "fine," said Paul, "We will go after lunch."

The spinney was a small set of woods in the middle of a field that his brother and some friends found a while back. They used to go there to swing on trees and play games like hide and seek, so he told his mum. Although his mother was a little apprehensive at first with the boys going there because she did not know who owned the land these woods were set in, the school used them to run through during cross-country season and had not received any complaints from farmers or people around that area. The woods were dense and set back from the road. To get to them, you had to follow the field's outline until they led into it. As they were only a short distance from the school, their mum had allowed Paul to go there. So, the boys set off on their bikes towards the spinney that afternoon. As they rode, Paul kept asking Kevin if he was alright. Kevin just nodded each time he was asked but never actually replied and continued peddling. As they continued, Kevin caught sight of the white dove flying around the area where they were. Although he thought it odd, he just kept going forward. Finally, they reached the field and could see the spinney. "Come on," Paul said and got off his bike and wheeled it around the field's edge. Kevin did just as his brother did until they reached the edge of the woods, where they laid their bikes down. "You're going to love this place," called Paul. Kevin just smiled.

"What's with you today, Kev? You seem subdued, not yourself," Paul paused, then continued, "never mind, when I show you this, it will bring a smile to your face." He took out his wand and called "**Optimus**

31

Reveal." A doorway appeared in thin air to which Paul undid the door and passed through it. Kevin held back, apprehensive of going through the door. All of a sudden, Paul popped his head out of the doorway, calling for his brother to follow him. Kevin moved through the doorway very slowly, but as he did, he now found he was outside no more, but in a large room that had chairs, tables, lights, and all sorts of bottles containing liquid and different things in them. "it's a safe house," His brother said," I was shown it three years ago. I come here every now and again to get away from things. Now, what is eating you? You hardly said a word coming here, and I certainly thought you would be more excited than what your face showed when you stepped in here." Kevin walked further into the room and sat down, "I don't know," he said, "I had a dream last night, not a particularly good one either", Paul laughed, then replied, "what, you had a nasty nightmare," and continued laughing. Kevin looked at Paul quite seriously." I do not know what it was, but it was very strange, and I could not really understand it. I want to, but I do not know where to start. I do not usually dream, and if I do, then I certainly do not dream of what I did. If I do dream, then it is usually about me becoming a superhero". His brother laughed again, then said, "Perhaps I can help. Tell me what you remember, and we will see if we can figure this out between us." Kevin took his coat off and then started to tell Paul all about what he had seen in his dreams. When Kevin finally finished speaking, Paul stood from his seat, paced a little then replied, "Well, it is evident that you have been shown this for a reason. Merlin, Crandloss, the old man Postromus They all play a part in Merlin's life, some good, and some evil, to what extent, I do not know, mind you" Paul continued, there is someone I can ask who might know, although it will have to wait till tomorrow. Yes, that is what we will do, we will see him and ask for his guidance".

Kevin looked puzzled, "that's twice now you said you would talk to someone on Monday. Who are you going to talk to?" Kevin asked. "Ahh," replied Paul, "it will be another surprise for you, another thing that you will not believe your eyes." "Oh, Whoopee," Kevin replied sarcastically. "Anyway," Paul said, "I brought you here so we can make a start to practice your magic," Kevin looked at his brother, "I don't know, Paul," answered Kevin, "what?" Paul answered quickly and as if he was annoyed. "You do not know, do not know what, that you do not feel like it, or is it that even being here, and what you have seen and been told by me, you still do not believe in magic or who you really are? Look, Kevin. You need to wise up. I know it is hard for a thirteen-year-old to take this all in. Think back to your dream about Merlin. He was the same age as you when he started. He, too, must have been scared witless, but after a while, he accepted it and embraced it. That is what you must do". "Oh, really, Paul," Kevin hissed back at his brother, "why do I have to, just because some crackpot story wizard, who, incidentally, still has not been proven to exist, did. Why do I have to do the same? Answer me that." Paul looked hard at Kevin, then answered crossly back at his brother. "Some crackpot wizard. He is the most powerful wizard ever to walk the earth". Paul paused, "ok, what about me? What about what I can do? What about this place, Mr. logic? If this all is not happening, where are you now, still at home in bed, dreaming it all, are you?" Kevin lowered his head and then spoke, "I don't know, perhaps a freak, and this place only exists in our minds, to which we are both asleep and dreaming the same thing." "What," Paul answered, "now that is codswallop, and you know it, you need to come into the real world, boy" "that's what I was in before you jumbled all this in my head.

Now I don't know what's real and what's not. I've had enough. I don't want to be part of it anymore. I want to go home and just forget it all happened, ok?" Paul could see Kevin getting angry, so he decided to do as he asked. Paul knew from his experience through the years that Kevin packs a mean punch, even for a boy of his age, and knows just exactly where to land it to do the most damage and hurt you.

The boys left the safe house and peddled home in silence. Along the way, Kevin turned for a quick second to see if he could see the white dove, but there was no sign of it. That evening, Kevin just sat watching the television, hardly uttering a word to anyone. If they did speak to him, he answered with as little as he could get away with and with a quite snappy attitude. Paul and their mum went into the kitchen and started to whisper. "What's the matter with Kevin? Did you two fall out again?" asked mum, "no, I do not know what's wrong with him. He seemed ok when we were down the spinney, then he just snapped at me and said he wanted to come home, so we did. He never spoke a word on the way home either." Paul replied. "Well, something's bothering him, that's for sure," replied mum, "unless he doesn't feel too good, he did lay in bed later this morning than what he usually does." Kevin could still hear them and decided to join the conversation, "there is nothing wrong with me" he snapped, "yes, I can hear you in there, I just want to be quiet for a change, is that a crime?" he asked. "No, dear," replied mum, "well, if you say you are alright, then we will respect your peace and quiet, my dear, alright Paul", she asked as she turned to him. Paul nodded and went and sat back down.

As night closed in, Kevin decided he would go to bed and try and get a decent night's sleep, hopefully forgetting all about the events. As he opened his door, there sat Merlin's spell book, sitting on his bedside table, right in front of him. Kevin quickly grabbed the book and put it in the bottom of the wardrobe under a pile of clothes. He also took off the time stone, removed the wand, and put these with the book. "If I can't see them or feel them, then there is a good chance I might forget all about them," he thought to himself. With that, Kevin pulled back his bed covers, got in, and snuggled down, ready to go to sleep. Just as he was dropping off, his door opened, and in stepped Paul, "now what?" Kevin asked in an abrupt way, "Look," Paul started, "I know this has come as a complete shock to you. It did to me also, but it can be good. Look at the things I can do, what I can use them for", Kevin broke Pauls speech by interrupting abruptly, "oh really Paul, what are you going to use them for to do good with ay? can you put out a fire that's burning, or save a cat stuck in a tree, maybe take on a gang of gunmen and save people from getting shot, you'd become a superhero or nutcase in the eyes of normal people. If people saw what you could do, they would have you carted off to the local nut house in the blink of an eye, and then there's my life, one boy a nut, so the other must be, there goes my life as well, well, what do you say to that?". Paul looked at Kevin now getting angry himself, "No" replied Paul "people with our gift have to keep it secret, there are things we can do and can't do, your right in a way if people saw me do the things you just said then yes, I would be classed as a nut, but it doesn't have to be that way. There are other things we can do to help. There might be times when we can help save a person's life if no one is watching or cast a spell to get a cat out of a tree. You just make it look as if it is helping itself. Therefore, no one thinks you helped. It is a matter of training and sleight of hand, it all comes in time, and you just have to believe in yourself and what is happening". "No I don't" replied Kevin, "no one makes my mind up for me, not you or a story book wizard, my mind is my own,

33

only I control it, and that's how it is always going to be, now, I have put all those magic things", Kevin said sarcastically, "into the wardrobe where they will stay until I think of a way to either destroy them or get rid of them", Paul looked at Kevin shaking his head and smiling, "you just don't get it bro" Paul said, "Get what?", Kevin replied, "you can't get rid of any of those things, they have been handed down to you, no matter what you do to them they will always end up back with you, you'll see" Paul answered, then chuckled to himself as he went to open the door. As he passed through, he turned back to Kevin and said, "Like I said, bro, you're in it for the long haul," then off he went to his bed. Kevin just gestured for him to go, but Paul never saw it as he had already started to leave. Kevin snuggled down once again, closed his eyes, and drifted off to sleep.

Chapter 3

Kevin's Torment

The next morning, Kevin was woken by the sun shining brightly through his curtains, so he decided to get up, get washed, and have some breakfast. "You are feeling better today, dear," asked his mum, "I wasn't ill yesterday, mum," Kevin replied," just nervous about I will make the team, that is all." "Of course, they let you all know today don't they, oh I'm sorry dear, I thought you were coming down with something, forgot all about the football trials, it will be alright, you'll see, you'll make the team, I have every confidence both you and your brother getting in" replied mum. "Now, come on, eat your breakfast before you go off to school." His mum ruffled Kevin's hair and smiled as if to indicate she had a happy feeling that this was going to be a good day for all.

Kevin decided to leave earlier than normal and peddled slowly to school. As he got to the parking lane, Vinnie, Ivan, and Paul were on their way also. Kevin stopped by them and walked alongside, now chattering about the football trials and how they think they did. Time flew by as they walked and talked, and before they knew it, they were at the front gate of the school. As they entered the school grounds, Kevin rode down the chase and parked his bike up in the bike sheds, then went to be reunited with his friends. They all had a kick around, joined by other friends until the bell went for them to go to registration. The day was going well at present for him, he felt. Kevin, still a little nervous, waiting to know if he had made the team or not, now walked towards his next class when his brother came running after him. "Wait up, Kevin, Paul called. "I've had a word with that bloke I told you about, and he can see us after school." "What bloke, who is he?" Kevin replied. "Arrr, can't tell you that just yet," replied Paul," you would never believe me even if I did tell you, so it's better to wait and see." "Look, Paul," Kevin said, "I told you yesterday, I don't want to be any part of this. It's not happening, not now, not ever, get it", "oh I think not", Paul said, "like I told you also last night, in it for the long haul, you'll see, just meet me at the edge of the grass in front of the science block after registration this afternoon, ok", "maybe" replied Kevin, "just be there", Paul said and ran off down the hallway.

Kevin continued his day, getting to classes on time and having quite a good day with lessons he liked. However, he never liked languages, especially French, as he thought the teacher had it in for him as he always got picked first to say a phrase, and really, he could not remember any of it, so she just got annoyed and shouted for him to sit back down with a comment "I really don't know why you bother coming to class. You never remember anything we learn, and it is a waste of my time and yours and a disruption to the class you are being here." When his last class had finished, he saw Vinnie running towards the sports gym, "wait up, Vinnie, where's the fire" Kevin asked, "it's up. The list is up," replied Vinnie in a nervous voice. Both boys ran on to see the list, hoping that their names were on it. As they rounded the corner, there in front were many others trying to see if their names were on it or not also. Kevin and Vinnie pushed their way through the crowd, trying to get closer to see if they were on it. As they got to the front, they could see that both their names were on the list. Kevin looked crossed to the other list to find his brother had also made the team. As Kevin read down the list, it stated there would be training every Wednesday evening in the park, and the teams would be picked that night to play at the weekend. Kevin thought to himself, "I must not get in trouble, or I will blow this." Kevin and Vinnie struggled through the waiting people to get some space. As they emerged, Mr. Sidney, the sports teacher, stood with a smile on his face. "Well done, you two," he said, "guess I will have to keep my eye on you to see about getting in the school side." Both boys looked at each other and then back to Mr. Sidney, "thanks, sir," they said together, and then they ran off outside, laughing and chuckling at each other. Kevin thought this day just couldn't get any better.

The day passed with Kevin on a real high. The school had gone well, he had got on the football team, and the sun still shone brightly. As he left registration and headed towards the bike shed, his brother Paul called to him. "Oy, Kevin, I said at the grass area in front of the science block. Where are you going?" Kevin changed direction towards his brother. As he met up with him, he smiled and then said, "isn't it great we both got on the team?" "yer great," replied Paul, "well you could be a bit happier about it" replied Kevin. "Look, I'm happy, alright, but now we have to see someone," answered Paul. "Who," Kevin asked again," you won't say. If I don't know them, then I'm not going. You know what dad said about strange men". "Trust me," Paul replied," You know him, all will be revealed in a minute, now come on." Paul led Kevin into the school and along the corridor to the RE room. "Mr. Godwill," Kevin said, "You have got to be kidding." "No, I'm not, remember, all is not as it seems," Paul replied. As he finished speaking, the door opened, and Mr. Godwill stood in the doorway. He looked up and down the corridor, then ushered the boys in before closing the door. He turned towards the boys and then said, "well, your brother has been telling me a bit about what has happened to you, young Wilks. It seems a bit farfetched, but who am I to question anyone before I hear all the facts." Kevin looked at Paul then said, "so what's my big, mouthed brother been telling you, sir?"

Mr. Godwill pointed to the big desk at the front of the class, where three chairs were. "Sit," said Godwill, "and we can discuss it in more detail." Both boys sat looking straight at Mr. Godwill, "well, where shall we begin" he asked. He looked at Kevin and said, "why don't you start, young Wilks? Tell me what you think has happened. We have time." Kevin looked at Paul and then sighed. "Ok, when I tell you, you are going to think we are both nuts, but we are not, sir. I can assure you of that." "Carry on," said Mr. Godwill.
Kevin started telling Mr. Godwill all about what had happened, leaving nothing out. They were there for an exceptionally long time while Kevin did his talking, but the daylight never got any darker. As Kevin finished, he still emphasised that he did not believe in any of it. Mr. Godwill smiled, "what's such funny, sir" Kevin turned to his brother with a stare of amazement. "See," Kevin said. "I told you people would think we were nuts." "Oh, people would, but I don't. You see, I guess Paul never told you about me helping him. It took some time, though," replied Mr. Godwill. Kevin looked blankly at Mr. Godwill, then said, "you helped him, sir, in what way?" Mr. Godwill explained to Kevin about Pauls journey into magic. Kevin sat listening, trying to make sense of it all. Finally, he said, "so all those times Paul was in detention, you were teaching him stuff?" "That's right." Kevin turned to Paul and spoke. "Dad thought you were being bad at

school, getting detention after detention, that's why he disliked Mr. Godwill, but you couldn't tell him, could you?" Paul nodded in agreement. "Hang on, if you helped Paul learn his magic stuff, then you must be," Mr. Godwill butted in, "a wizard also." Kevin shook his head, "no way, this is not happening. You, Paul, and now me, magic, no, no, it's not real," Kevin said. "Oh, it's very real. I can prove it, young wilks." "How?" Kevin snapped back. Paul looked at Kevin and then said. "You know you took the time stone off and put your wand and book in the wardrobe," Kevin nodded as if to say yes, "feel your neck, feel your thigh, go on." Kevin nervously felt his neck, and there was the time stone hanging around it. He touched his thigh, he gently pulled from it the wand, he looked over at Paul, "check your bag," he told his brother. Kevin undid his bag, and there, sitting at the top, was Merlin's spell book. "But how? I do not understand." "In it for the long haul, told you," Paul laughed. Mr. Godwill held up his hand and then spoke, "that will do, Paul. You see, Kevin, magic is a powerful and beautiful thing, used correctly, but if not can be as harmful as a bomb going off. The reason these things stay with you is that you have been given them to complete a task. One that we still do not know yet, but in time we will. You are an extraordinarily strong-minded individual, and so was Merlin, it was written. Therefore, you have the connection. You have seen some of the visions for his upbringing, he is showing you this for a reason, again, one to still be worked out, but the three of us can do that, and there are others who can help. Also, do not think of it as if you are on your own because you are not. You just must believe in yourself, your talents, and the friends who can enhance it all." "That's the problem," Kevin replied, "I do not believe in any of this. I have no talent as a magician, I do not want to learn magic, and I certainly do not want to end up looking like a nutter. Look, I am sorry, but it is not happening, ok? I told you, Paul, it is not happening." Kevin got up and walked towards the door. As he grasped the handle, Godwill spoke, "remember what you said in class, Kevin. Respect is not given. You have to earn it. This is your time to earn it." Kevin turned and looked at Godwill, then turned back and walked out of the classroom.

As Kevin stepped into the corridor after closing the door to Mr. Godwill's classroom, he suddenly had an uneasy feeling shoot through his whole body. "What's the matter," he heard a voice come from beside him. Kevin turned quickly to see it was Jerez standing there. "Leave me alone," called Kevin as he started to run down the corridor, Jarez just paced after him calling, "wait, it is no good. You will not get out of here, not until you have listened to what I have to say". Kevin kept running, but the corridor seemed to get longer and longer. There was no end to it, no doors to get out. Eventually, Kevin came to a halt. "What do you want of me," cried Kevin; "there's no need to shout," replied Jerez as he stood next to Kevin. "I heard all that went on in that classroom. It must be hard for a young person like you to have so much put upon you in a brief time but listen. It does not have to be. Remember what I told you the last time we met? People all have some sort of belief. It makes them stronger. That is what you need to do, believe. You have been chosen because of your talents, talents you do not know you have yet. There was a reason for this happening."

Kevin tried to speak, but Jerez held his hand up to his lips as if to say quietly." I know you do not believe in what has happened. You keep telling everyone, but who are you really trying to convince, other people or yourself." Kevin looked at Jerez, "I don't know," replied Kevin. "I'm confused, a little scared, and above all else, worried that I can get hurt, just like Merlin's family in the dream." "of course, your confused, and if you weren't scared, I'd call you an idiot, but being scared is not a terrible thing. It can cause you to pull on any strength you have and strength you didn't realise you have also", replied Jerez. "As to danger and being hurt, well, you face that every day, coming to this school on your bike. It is just that you do not think about it. Listen, young wizard, yes, I called you wizard because that is what you are going to be whether you like it or not. It is in your genes passed down through ages. Logic in your mind says that there were never any or never will be any wizards or witches or anything else connected to magic, but, and I have said this before. It is very much real. I am real. You're real. Paul is real, and even old Godwill. You see," continued Jerez, "although you need those physical things of proof to verify that something happened, not all things can be. Magic comes from your soul, your heart, and here." Jerez touched Kevin on the side of his head just above the eye. "This is your power. This is your strength. The better and purer the mind, the more you can do with it. Believe in yourself, Kevin. Believe that you can do remarkable things, and it will, I assure you come easily".

As he finished speaking, Godwill appeared from the classroom. "Jerez, what business do you have here," he commanded, "nothing, sire," replied Jerez. "I was just talking to the young wizard." "Leave him be, he has a lot to contemplate, and he certainly does not need you twittering in his ear," replied Godwill. "Just think about what I have told you, Kevin," Jerez started to fade into the air. As he did, he called, "believe in yourself, believe," and then he was gone. Godwill walked up to Kevin and put his hand on his shoulder, then spoke. "Only you can choose what path you take. No one should force you into anything you are not one hundred percent committed to. Therefore, until you decide what you want to do, no more will be said. Should you wish to embrace the commitment, then I will be here for you just like I was with your brother. Now go home, relax, and enjoy the evening". Mr. Godwill turned and went back into the classroom where Paul still was.

Kevin could now see doors leading off the corridor to get out. He made for the exit and ran to his bike. He peddled fast down the chase and out onto the road toward home. "Should I try speaking to him tonight Godwill?" asked Paul. "No," Godwill replied, "if we keep trying to get him to realise his ability, he may turn against us, he could end up going from good to bad, and if he turned bad and realised his magic ability, it could be dangerous for a lot of people, especially you, as you live with him. No, let him be, let him unravel his mind and come to terms in his own time and by his own means, but" Mr. Godwill continued, "stay alert, keep watch from a distance to make sure no ill fate comes to him. I have a feeling that something big is going to happen along this journey. I do not know what, but there is something in the air, and with Matrees showing up again like that, there is sure to be foul play around. Knowledge is a major attribute of us magical people. Without realising it, your brother is one of us. His strength will be useless. Even when his power surfaces on its own accord, he needs the knowledge to control it, or it could end up controlling him." Paul nodded in agreement and then left the classroom. He headed home once he had retrieved his bike from the bike sheds.

That night as Kevin lay in his bed, he felt for the time stone and his wand. Both were there. He closed his eyes and tried to drift off to sleep, but no matter how hard he tried, he just kept thinking about what Godwill and Jerez had told him. Time after time, he heard their speeches talking repeatedly going through his mind. Kevin grabbed at his pillow and curved it around his head as if trying to shut out the noises, but it was to no effect. Kevin sat upright in his bed, trying to quieten the voices with his hands closed around the sides of his face, trying to make sense of them and all that had happened. Then suddenly, quiet, they all stopped, he thought about them no more, he lay down and closed his eyes, and drifted off into a deep sleep. Kevin got a very restful sleep that night and was woken the next morning when his brother returned from his paper round by the banging of the back door.

Kevin leapt from his bed, got dressed, and ran downstairs. "Easy, Kevin," his dad called as he ran into the kitchen, "where's the fire," he asked, "nowhere," replied Kevin, "just wanted to catch Vinnie at the park before we go into school to practice, that's all." "You boys," dad said, "still, I remember when I got in my first major team, I was." His dad was then interrupted by Kevin, running out of the door shouting, "that's great, dad, see you later," as he shut the door behind him. His dad just stood there shaking his head, thinking to himself, "youngsters, they never have time to talk to you nowadays, always in a hurry," with that he shrugged his shoulders and went and sat in the living room and grabbed the newspaper, and started to read it.

Kevin met Vinnie down the park with a few other friends and started to kick the ball around, all thinking they were premier players when time sped by, and it was time to get to school. All that day, Kevin concentrated on his lessons, and the day went quickly. Not any part of the day did his brother Paul approach him, but Kevin did not really think about that until he got home. When his brother finally walked through the door, all his brother said was, "alright, Kev?" and he walked on. Kevin, now a bit confused, thought he would surely try and talk to him about the magic stuff, but no, not one word. All night the air was silent. They just sat there watching the television. Hardly a word was said, even over tea. After watching the television, Kevin decided it was bedtime for him, so he got up, kissed his mum goodnight, then turned to his brother Paul and said, "night Paul," Paul looked at his brother and just smiled and said, "night Kev." With that, Kevin went upstairs got into bed, and closed his eyes.

As he lay there, he felt sure his brother would be close behind him, wanting to talk, but nothing happened. Paul stayed downstairs watching television. Kevin now struggled with the way his brother was distancing himself from him, but it also made him cross. "What's he up to," he thought to himself, "he has been a nuisance ever since this whole magic thing came on the scene, so why now does he act as if nothing happened?" As he had no answers, he decided that at least he could now forget everything and concentrate on doing what a normal boy does. Or could he? How was he going to face Mr. Godwill, knowing he was a wizard also?

What if he let it out by accident when he was talking to his friends, what if? Kevin stopped himself there. He tried to clear his mind of all the thoughts, so he concentrated on thinking about football. That did the trick, he was soon drifting off to sleep, but he was brought back to normality when he heard a creak from where the wardrobe stood. Kevin turned on his bedside lamp and looked towards it, the door had swung open, and that was all. Kevin got out of bed and closed the wardrobe door before getting back into bed. As he lay down and went to turn off his small light, he noticed that Merlin's book now sat on his bedside table. Kevin stared at the book, wondering how it got there, had his brother been in his room and put it there? "No," he thought to himself, "it definitely was not there when I got into bed, so how did it get there, and why is it there," he asked himself. As he looked, the book opened and flicked through to an empty page, Kevin took the book onto his lap and flicked through more pages, but it always returned to the same blank page. Kevin stared at the page, there was nothing on it, but then writing started to appear. It read, 'Talk to me, Kevin,' Kevin sat back quickly, still holding the book, watching the writing now disappearing. "Talk to you. Who are you?" he asked quietly. Again, the writing appeared in the book, 'Merlin' it said. "Merlin," said Kevin, "do you really think I believe this rubbish? I bet this is Paul doing something. I thought he would. He's been too quiet over this whole thing just lately." As Kevin spoke his last word, more writing appeared in the book, 'It has nothing to do with your brother. I am Merlin.' Kevin watched the writing disappear again, then said, "Alright, prove it," Kevin said sarcastically," you can't because you are nothing but a story thought up by someone." Again, the book began revealing more, 'how shall I prove it to you? Do you not think that you are being able to do magic is not just cause, or were you being able to read what I have written here? You view all existence through the material and physical volume. Your mind is strong on these ideas, which is good, as it acts as an immensely powerful strength to you. I lived hundreds of years before you. I saw many good and many black things within my existence. Time does not stop for anyone or anything. Throughout the years, I have wandered through time, keeping a hold of all bad black magic that could reappear and cause havoc and destruction. The time is here. That is why I chose you to act for me.'

The writing slowly disappeared from the page. "Hang on," Kevin said. "You still have not proved that you are the actual Merlin to which I am talking. So far, you have told me a load of jumble nonsense that makes no sense at all. If you are Merlin, how have you existed for all this time? "The book was blank, and no writing appeared, "Ha, got you, I knew this was a trick, and I bet it was Paul's doing. He has got to get up earlier than that to catch me out". Suddenly. The book began revealing itself again. "To try and understand the whole situation, there is but one way to make sense of all this,' Kevin looked at the book and then spoke, "oh, and how do you plan to do that? Oh great, Merlin," he said sarcastically.

The book again went blank; Kevin had a feeling that something was going to turn up, so he waited in silence for what seemed an age. The book finally revealed its next bit of writing, 'we must meet.' Kevin leaned back and laughed. "And how do you propose we do that," Kevin said again sarcastically, "after all, you're a fictional character, a story, nothing else. Oh, this is good. Paul is really pulling all the stops out." The book revealed more, 'Kevin, Paul has nothing to do with this. I promise you, I am Merlin, and we will meet, but to do that, you must believe in everything that is going on, I keep a watchful eye over you every day, but I cannot materialise in flesh and blood as you are until I have grown very much stronger. That strength will come from you, we will meet one day as two people standing side by side, but for now, there is only one way you will be able to see me, and that is through the astral plain.' "Astral plain" Kevin said, "and where is that when it's at home." 'The astral plain is within your mind and your heart, a place where only you can take yourself through concentration and self-belief. It is one of a dense region. When we sleep, many tread a path through it without realising. As you make your way, I will be waiting for you on the far side of a brook sitting by an old oak tree. I will wait, if necessary, until you get there. The writing began fading as Kevin watched, "well," He said, "I guess you will have an awfully long wait in front of you." The book did not reveal any more writing, so Kevin closed it and put it back on the bedside table. Once he had done this, he shot out of bed and went busting through his door, ready to go into his brother's room. He stopped in his tracks as he heard Paul say goodnight to his mum before coming upstairs. As Paul got to the top of the stairs, he saw Kevin standing there.

"Alright, Kev, thought you were asleep," he said, "very funny," Kevin answered, "I knew you just can't leave things alone. How did you do it", "do what" Paul answered with a bit of a bewildered look on his face. "Put Merlin's book on my bedside table and knew I would look at it." "Whoa," Paul said, "get in here and keep quiet." Paul ushered Kevin into his bedroom and shut the door. "Now then, what did I do?" Kevin started to talk to his brother all about the book, how it got there, what appeared, and the conversation he had or thought he had with the book. "Well, I can assure you, Kevin, I had nothing to do with that. I was downstairs all the time with mum watching the telly. She could prove it." Kevin looked away from Paul and then said, "so, how did it happen? I know I am not asleep. I know the book got there somehow. I know what I said when I read the writing each time it appeared." He turned to his brother and then said, "You must have had a hand in it. Come on, how did you do it?" "Honestly, Kevin, it wasn't me. Perhaps it was Merlin trying to contact you." "Here we go. I knew it would only be time before you threw that rubbish back to me." "No, really, Kevin," Paul said, "I had nothing to do with what you just said, and I am not here to throw things down your throat about it. You are right. If you do not want to believe in any of it, then so be it. It is purely your choice, your mind that you have to know, it's hard, I know, I was like you before I chose the right path, but hey, you do what you think best, the only thing I will say then I will leave it all alone is, you're not alone, there are people to meet who are exactly like you, people you wouldn't even think of that have the magic touch" he said with a smile a wave of his hands. "Now, be off to bed with you. I have got to get up early for my paper round. It's alright for some lying in bed. Now get out of here." Kevin smiled back at Paul, then left his bedroom and returned to his. The bedside light was still on, no book on the bedside table, so Kevin made himself comfortable and closed his eyes.

The next morning, Kevin woke, remembering it was the first training day for the new team that he was picked to play in. He got up, washed, and had his breakfast before racing off to his bike to meet Vinnie down at the park for practice. As he got there, he saw Vinnie looking glum, "what's up, Vinnie?" Kevin asked, "Hurt my leg last night," replied Vinnie, "sure hurts a lot," "how did you do that? I thought you would be more careful than that before training. Can you kick a ball?" asked Kevin. "Don't think so," replied Vinnie, "hurts to even stand on it." "Looks like you're not playing this weekend for sure," Kevin said. Vinnie just looked at the ground in sadness. "Look," Vinnie said, "I am going home. This really hurts. Will you let the teachers know, Kev?" "Sure, buddy. Is your mum or dad home?" Kevin asked. "No," replied Vinnie, "but my big sister is, so I will be ok. I just got to rest it. Oh, and can you let them also know at training tonight?" "Sure will," Kevin replied, "go get that rested up, mate. I'll check on you later" Vinnie waved goodbye as he limped off home.

The day passed quickly, as the previous days had, but Paul still stayed silent again, not bothering him with any of the magic stuff, so Kevin just got on with what he was doing. School finished, and Kevin raced home excitedly to get ready to go back down the park and have a good night's workout, hoping to impress Russ and Brian, the teams' managers. Kevin rushed his tea down him before packing his bag with his boots and shin pads. "Whoa, slow down, Kevin. Anyone would think you have a train to catch," his mum called to him. "There's still plenty of time before the training starts, and after all, it's only a kick about." Kevin looked at his mum quite crossly before answering, "it may only be a kick about, as you put it, but if I show I'm willing and always arrive early, then they might think that I am dependable, and that could help me get in the team, is that not so mum?". Kevin's mum smiled, "that's right, my boy, go on," she said, "mind how you bike there, make sure you keep a good lookout for cars and lorries." "Mum, I'm not ten. You know, I can look after myself now, I don't need you to hold my hand" Kevin answered cheekily. "Go on, get off to your football, play well dear," Mum answered, "I will," Kevin said as he raced off on his bike. When Kevin arrived, there were already quite a few boys already there and kicking about. Kevin parked his bike up and went to join in. Eventually, all were there, including Russ and Brian; they split the boys up into two teams to train before the game at the end of training.

The evening was a little brisk, but none of the boys seemed to mind that, as they were hard shuttle running, dribbling, and controlling the ball over a circuit. At last, the time had come for the end game; this was what Kevin had been waiting for. He was determined that he would put everything into it to try and make the starting team for the Sunday morning match. The game started with Kevin in a defensive role. He tackled hard and put every effort he could turn into it. He was quite good in the air also, heading the ball away from the goal and setting up his forwards to score. After about half an hour, Russ decided to change some of the positions. Kevin's was one of those. He took Kevin out of the defensive roll and put him in goal. Kevin was not too happy with this but did as he was asked. Again, Kevin put all his heart and soul into his playing. He saved many a shot, caught the ball cleanly from the opposing team's corners, and had an incredibly good kick on him to clear the ball. At the end of the training session, all the boys were huddled close together to hear what Russ and Brian had to say. Kevin thought he had done enough to at least make it onto the substitute's bench for the game.

"Right boys," Russ said," that was a very good night's training, the first of many. We have had a very good response from all of you. The key element is commitment. That's what I'm looking for. Now as there are a lot of you, we will be experimenting with the team on a regular basis. Some of you may not play a lot, others will, but do not be disheartened. We are trying to get a second league started, so we can play both an A team and a B team. This will allow us to keep an eye on all of you and see who is progressing well, just like a premier team does. Now then, the team for this Sunday's game, after a long talk between Brian and myself, will be the team selected." Kevin listened inventively as Russ was going through the positions; Kevin's name did not come out in any of the main positions, but he was first out for the substitutes. Although a little bit disappointed not to make the starting team, he was happy to at least be on the bench. As the crowd of boys started to walk away, both Russ and Brian approached Kevin. "Good night training Kevin" Brian said, "you have some particularly good attributes to your footballing skills; you have strength and awareness for the defensive roll and a good pair of safe hands for goalkeeping. It is good when we can have someone like you on the team to put in various positions; it means we can cover a lot of positions with the smallest amount of people. It is going to be a hard game Sunday. We are playing Holbek bank, a side that demoralised us in both games we played against them last year. We need to be a lot better this year, and with your strength and footballing capabilities and hopefully a few more like you, we just might do it. See you Sunday morning, Kevin, do not forget your boots." Kevin, now smiling, answered, "oh, I won't. See you Sunday," and raced off to get his bike, then peddled as fast as he could home.

That night, all he could talk about to his mum and brother was the training session and what Russ and Brian had to say to him at the end of it. Kevin had now gone from being disheartened to extremely excited. His mum tried to quieten him down on several occasions, but it was no good. His enthusiasm just flowed right out of his body and his mouth. "Ok," his brother Paul called, "enough is enough. Sundays are still days away. A lot can happen before then." "What do you mean?" asked their mum, "oh come on, mum, something is bound to happen to get him grounded before the match. We all know what he's like." "Shut up," Kevin snapped back, "I have not been in trouble for a while, have I? I'm not going to blow this. I'll be there. You watch". "Well," their mum said, "he has been good lately, and he seems that he wants to do it, so good of you, boy, you show them and us." Paul murmured under his breath, "pity he didn't put as much effort into his belief about himself for other important things," "what was that Paul," their mum asked, "Speak clearly, I can't hear a word you say when you mumble," "oh nothing mum, just mumbling to myself" he replied, but knew Kevin had heard him, as Kevin looked straight at him and had a big sarcastic grin on his face. "Anyway," mum continued, "it's time for you two to hit your beds. Paul, you got your paper round in the morning, and you," she said, pointing to Kevin, "need to calm down, or it will be midnight before you get to sleep. Like Paul said, you do not want to keep me awake all night, or you just might face a grounding," she said with a laugh. Both boys kissed their mum and then raced upstairs to get washed and into bed. After a while of mad noise with the two boys arguing about who was getting washed first, it all went silent. Peace had come to the Wilks household.

More visions

As Kevin fell into a deep sleep after all the excitement, once again, his mind wandered off into the world of dreams. A fog lay heavy in what he could see, but after a minute, it began to clear. As it cleared, he could see Merlin standing over two graves, his mother's and father's. Merlin had not moved for a long time, just standing there staring down, tears still in his eyes. A rustling from the edge of the woods made him turn quickly with his wand outstretched, "wait," came a voice that he knew. It was Bartholomew. Bartholomew was also a student of Master Wilfred's and studied at the same time as Merlin. He ran down to where Merlin stood, "Bartholomew, why did you not let me know what was going on through thought casting like Master Wilfred taught us? and how did you escape?" Merlin asked. As Bartholomew crouched down to catch his

43

breath he uttered, "Easy really", he said," the guards are quite thick, I told them that Master Wilfred was hurt and needed water and attention, as they opened the cage door that we were in, I jumped out, and ran here as fast as I could, I don't think they followed me, not after what they were talking about, how you conjured up the elements to run them off", Bartholomew paused, " I'm sorry about thought casting, I just forgot in the heat of the moment, I didn't know you could do all that Merlin, who taught you?". "Master Wilfred" replied Merlin, "but, with you escaping, has that not put the other elders and people in more danger?", Merlin asked Bartholomew, "it was Master Wilfred's plan, because I was the fastest runner, he wanted me to come and get you, see if the two of us could help free them and get away". Merlin now moving to what was left of the village houses centre was looking for something, "what are you looking for Merlin?", Bartholomew asked, "A wand" Merlin replied, "but you have it in your hands", came the reply from Bartholomew, "not for me, for you, one wand is nowhere near enough to handle that amount of men holding the others, then, there is Crandloss, we will still have to deal with him, Ahh", Merlin stooped down and moved a wooden flask out from under a broken table, "this will do nicely, think you can use that?", he asked Bartholomew, "just give me the chance" he replied, "Right said Merlin, you know the way to the camp, let's go, we will wait until night fall then give those bandits something to be very scared about, and release the others. With that, Merlin and Bartholomew set off to the camp.

Kevin's vision again clouded over for a minute and then cleared. When it did, it was nightfall. The camp was in sight, and Merlin and Bartholomew were crouching behind a thick set of bracken. Merlin looked closely at the camp layout deciding on a plan of attack, "are you ok, Bartholomew?" Merlin asked, "a little scared," came the reply, "me also, but we must do this. It will be dangerous, so you need to be focused one hundred percent. You need to make sure no one gets behind you. Whatever happens, keep vigilant, and especially keep your eyes peeled for Crandloss. I will circle around to the east side. You come in on the west side. You need to cause as much mayhem as possible, make them think we are of large numbers, and use fire, water, and lightning if you can, but watch the direction you choose to point it in. If you see Crandloss, try to get to me as soon as you can, two are better and more powerful than one." Bartholomew nodded in agreement, "now off you go, wait for my signal, then let the show commence," "but what will your signal be?" asked Bartholomew, "Hoh, you know it when it happens, now go." Bartholomew circled the camp and stayed in a position close to the edge of some woods so he could see the camp. Suddenly there was a clap of thunder, and an electric bolt flew into the main hut where most of the bandits were. "The sign," thought Bartholomew. He leaped from the woods casting fire spell after fire spell, followed by immense wind spells soon after. The bandit guards ran this way and that was trying to avoid the commotion but could not. Some were hit and paralysed by Merlin's lightning, and some were burnt by Bartholomew's fire. As the torrents flew from both the wizards' wands, more of the bandits ran from the camp into the woods, trying to escape, howling in pain. Then the door flew open to the main hut in the centre of the camp. There in the doorway stood Crandloss and Jarone. Crandloss held his wand tight, whereas Jarone had a long thick sword. Both men walked from the hut into the centre of the camp. They now stood between Merlin and Crandloss, "so you came for them," Crandloss shouted to Merlin, "and brought your little friend also, well, well , well, think you can defeat me again, Merlin," called Crandloss, "I don't know about that" Merlin replied, "but I wouldn't be here if I didn't think so, what do you think Crandloss?", Jarone made a quick move towards Bartholomew, but he was too quick for him and cast a fire spell at Jarone's sword which made the metal glow red with heat and Jarone call out in pain as it burnt into his hand. At the same time, Crandloss cast a lightning bolt towards Merlin, which engulfed Merlin and sent him flying, crashing down on the hard earth. Bartholomew cast a disarming spell towards Crandloss, who just cast it aside as if it was a fly. "Weak, both of you, now you will feel my power, now you will obey me until I have no more use for you, then I will do away with you." Whilst Crandloss was talking, pointing his wand at Bartholomew, Merlin cast a thought over to Bartholomew, "cast a water spell, Bartholomew, now." As he finished his thought, Bartholomew called out, "**Disquelch Wateriade**", a water blast shot from Bartholomew's wand. At the same time, Merlin called out, "**Firentay, Consunium, Derivarm,**" A lightning bolt shot from Merlin's wand, which, now had clambered to his knees, Crandloss didn't know which spell to repel first, and because of it was hit by both at the same time which added to the lightning's power. An enormous loud bang was heard, a cry of pain, then a second bang, a plume of smoke, then silence, only the cries of Jarone holding his bleeding, blistered hand. Crandloss had disappeared. "Have we killed him?" asked Bartholomew, "no, it only made him realise that good will always win over bad," Merlin replied as he slowly got to his feet.

Both wizards moved slowly over to where Jarone was huddled in a heap, "please spare me," he cried, "why should we?" replied Merlin, "you have my parents killed, friends maimed, tell me, oh mighty one, why should I spare your miserable life, why not take a life for a life, tell me that." Merlin was terribly angry remembering what fate his parents befell. "Wait, Merlin," came a voice from the cage. It was Master Wilfred's. "If you kill this man, will it bring back your parents? No, nothing can ever do that, but if you kill him, you are no better than the man that led him to us, Crandloss. He is on the black side now. If you kill this man, then you, too, will start on that dark journey. Is that what you want? I know your father would not have wanted it." Merlin looked down at Jarone and then said, "if I spare your life, will you promise to give up this terrible existence you lead? Will you change and help those too weak to fight for a good cause? If you do not change, then you will die. Your fate lies within your own hands now, bandit. What is it to be?" Jarone stared Merlin in his eyes. He could see the end of Merlin's wand just inches from his head, "I promise," came a terrified response from Jarone, "remember," Merlin said, "if you break your promise, the curse I have put on you will kill you. Therefore, you must think before doing things. Are they for the good or not? Do you wish to live or die? The choice is yours". Merlin turned to Bartholomew, "fix his hand, then release the elders and others, take them to a safe place, far away from here, be vigilant, learn well, Bartholomew, you may need the powerful knowledge and power sooner rather than later should you meet with Crandloss again." Bartholomew took hold of Merlin's arm and led him away from Jarone, "Curse," whispered Bartholomew, "I didn't see you perform a curse spell," Merlin grinned then replied, "I didn't, but he did not know that does he?" Bartholomew grinned, then winked at Merlin. "But are you not coming too?" asked Bartholomew, "Unfortunately not. I have a quest to complete given to me by the last breath of my beloved father. This I must do, Farewell friend. I am sure we will meet again." Merlin shook hands with Bartholomew and then left the camp.

Once again, the vision went cloudy and then became clear once more. This time Merlin was travelling through thick forests, climbing mountains, and being helped by a crossed river. Finally, after travelling for many days, Merlin arrived at a mountain pass. The opening to the pass was large and exceptionally long. Merlin could see many bones and pieces of armour, swords, shields, and other weapons, scattered along it. Merlin took out his wand and continued slowly along the path, keeping a lookout for trouble all around him. Suddenly there was a mighty roar, and a large fire-breathing dragon appeared from a siding. Merlin stood still as the dragon flapped its massive wings and soared into the air. Merlin stood still, stuck to the spot with fright. The dragon twisted and turned in the air and then made a flight path toward Merlin. As it closed in on him, all he could do was cast the water spell **"Disquelch Firentium,"** a blast of water shot from Merlin's wand and connected with the dragon's front of its head. The force also took the flight of the dragon away from Merlin, but still, he could not move because of fright. As the dragon passed over Merlin, now without its mighty fire, it turned for yet another pass. Merlin cast a thought spell, "I am Merlin. I mean, you no harm. I am in search of Postromus, my teacher." With that, the dragon veered off to the side and turned once again in the air, as before it looked as though it would be coming straight towards Merlin but flapped its wings to slow its speed down before finally coming to a halt, landing in front of Merlin about ten feet away. Merlin then heard a voice that asked, "why do you seek Postromus?", Merlin looked at the dragon and then spoke, "my parents have been killed by unjust men. On his death bed my father told me to seek out the one they call Postromus, it is he who will help me continue my journey".

Merlin heard the voice again, "to what journey do you refer, young wizard?", "a journey of learning, a journey to help harness my powers to save the weak and help them fight the bad. I am young inexperienced, and need guidance. This is my quest. Can you help the dragon show me the direction I need to take?". The dragon moved closer, "and what is your name, young wizard?" Merlin heard in his mind, "Merlin, I am called Merlin." The dragon backed away on hearing this, "you are the son of Cormious," Merlin heard the voice say once again, "yes, did you know of my father?", "I knew of him," replied the dragon through the thought spell, " what makes you think I will help you?", "I don't know," Merlin replied," it was my father's wish, I have never met this person, so I do not know what he even looks like. That is why I need help, dragon. Will you let me pass and continue my search for this man, or do we need to fight more?". "Whoa, young wizard, firstly, you have met Postromus. It was he who initiated you into your sect. Secondly, I will let you pass, and lastly, Postromus will be waiting for you once you have reached the crossroads further along the path," replied the dragon. "How do you know that dragon?" asked Merlin, "let us just say that I do. There is no need for us to fight anymore. Now go. Postromus is a busy man. He will not thank you for keeping him hanging about". With that, the dragon flapped its large wings and flew high in the air until it had disappeared. Merlin continued his journey until, like the dragon said, there was a crossroads in the path. A large oak tree stood in its path displaying its wide greenery and thick branches. Upon one of the branches sat a white dove but no Postromus.

Merlin sat at the base of the tree, waiting for Postromus to show. He had only just sat down when he heard a voice talking to him in his mind, "hello, young wizard, and what are you waiting for, may I ask?" Merlin got to his feet and looked around but could see no one but the dove in the tree. "I am waiting for

Postromus" Merlin directed his conversation towards the dove, "do you know of him?" he asked, "indeed I do. I know that he is a very busy wizard and does not like to be kept waiting, so you had better choose your path and go on to great him," came to the reply. "But I know not which path to take," Merlin said, "does everything in this part of the land command magical abilities?" "some people and animals do," came the reply once again, "now choose your path, wizard." Merlin walked to the beginning of the left path and looked down it, then did the same to the right path. He ended up back at the base of the tree. "What's the matter, wizard? You can't make your mind up. That's not good. It shows a bit of indecisiveness," Merlin heard the voice say. "No, it's not that at all," Merlin replied," Mr. Dove, as you are high in the tree, and you can clearly see down both paths from there, perhaps you could answer me a question or two?" "Very well, wizard, what are they?" came the reply. "does the left path have woods and thick bracken further along the road?" the dove looked then replied, "it does," then Merlin asked, "the right path, does it have the same?", again the dove looked then replied, "no, it is open all along the path but comes to an end with a rocky mountain range, why do you ask?", Merlin looked at the Dove and said, "to the left, there is woods and thick bracken where I might get attacked from bandits or wild animals to the right clear open space where I could easily see anyone or animal that tried to attack. My father regarded Postromus as a friend and entrusted me into his care to learn the magic to help the weak and needy. I do not think, as a friend, Postromus would put me in that kind of danger; therefore, I will choose the right path to follow, thank you Postromus".The dove flew down from the tree and landed on the road near Merlin, there was a bang and plume of smoke, as it cleared there stood an old man, "Very good Merlin, I was told of your logic to understand and work problems out, you are correct, I am Postromus, and it would be a pleasure to help you continue on your journey, come, you will stay with me, you have a hard time ahead of you, there is much to learn and much to see." Postromus led Merlin down the right path until they reached the mountain area, **"Optimus Reveal"** called Postromus. A large part of the mountain wall moved to the side, revealing his living quarters. "it's not much, but it's safe and warm," Postromus said to Merlin as they both entered the room. The wall moved back, and the mountain face looked as if nothing had happened.

There, Kevin's vision went foggy again but slowly lifted to show Merlin and Postromus talking some years later. Merlin had been learning a vast number of things under the guidance of the wizard. He now knew and could use spells that were so powerful that he would be safer along his long journey. He learned how to cast binding spells that would enhance the powers given to him to fulfil his every need, along with magical potion making, another part of his arsenal. Merlin was a good and quick learning pupil, Postromus liked that, and many a day, they changed their selves into animals and relaxed, occasionally playing a game of hide and seek. Merlin was incredibly happy living with such a great master wizard who devoted time and patience to teaching him what he had been taught or learned for himself. Many of the spells and potions Merlin had been taught he recorded in his book; little did he leave out until one day, his new friend, the new wizard, taught him the way to reverse dark magic spells.

These were alarming for Merlin to cope with, so many things, terrible things, he would have to do should the need arise to reverse the badness of dark black magic. In some instances, he knew that one day he would have to kill. Merlin was not happy with this thought, as killing rips the soul apart and can transform a good-hearted wizard over to the dark side. Postromus could see this in Merlin's face and eyes, "killing," he said," as you know, is bad, bad for the soul, bad for the person or animal you have to kill, but it is necessary for you to survive, there is one way to help lessen the chance of falling into that domain." "What is that?" asked Merlin, "To help prevent the blackness from taking over your heart, you must find a slain unicorn. When you do, you must take some of its silver blood, and drop, just a few drops in your mouth. Unicorn blood has a magical effect, it protects the good and has the magical effect of prolonging life, but beware, drink too much of that blood, and it will still prolong life, but instead of protecting you, it will speed along the dark passage of the person." Merlin was shocked, unicorns were beautiful creatures and were very rare to find, "why would anyone kill a unicorn?, what damage do they do to people, I cannot believe that this is true, surely you jest?", Merlin asked, "jest I do not, I have tasted the blood of the unicorn, look at me, I am five hundred years old, I worked out that I may still have a good two hundred left, but mark my words, Merlin, there will come a time that you will have to heed my warning and do as I did them many hundreds of years ago to help save this green land we live in from powerful foes, I know it's not nice but the deed will have to be done."

Merlin got up and walked outside, disheartened by the thought that one-day Tominsolus may just be right. As Merlin stood looking down at the floor, Postromus walked behind Merlin and said with a comforting voice.

"Come, I have something to take your mind off things." He took Merlin up to the pass where he had first met the dragon, "why are we here?" Merlin asked, Postromus pointed to the mess of bones and swords scattered around the front of the pass, "did you kill all these men?" Merlin asked in a quivering voice, "no" replied Postromus, "they are merely an illusion to keep folk away from my home. Not one person lost their lives here, and that's how it will stay. Look at the patch by that large stone", Merlin moved towards a large boulder and looked, "what am I looking at?, there are only small stones scattered about the base of the boulder", Postromus moved over to where Merlin stood, "look harder Merlin" he said, "don't look with your eyes, look with your soul and heart." Merlin bent down and grabbed a handful of stones. They all looked the same. Apart from one, it had a small glass-looking splinter coming out of its side. Postromus called out, "**Ilustria**," the pass where all the bones and swords were noted was now just a pass with lush green grass. "See Merlin, it is merely an illusion, oh be it a very good one, but no harm has become of anyone or anything, as I said." Merlin rose to his feet, looked crossed at his teacher, and smiled, "that's better," Postromus said, "we will begin learning this tomorrow. For now, you will need to rest and relax. It takes a great lot of strength and will to bind an illusion spell. Come, let us go and eat." As Merlin and Postromus started back to their home, he again called out, "**Ilustria Evapsum**," the pass returned to its sight before with bones, swords, and armour scattered about it. There, Kevin's vision fogged up and then went completely black. Nothing to see, just blackness, Kevin fell into a deep sleep for the rest of the night. Kevin woke the next morning to rain pelting hard against his window, "looks like I'm going to get soaked today," as he looked out of the window. Just as he was about to come away from his rain-soaked window, he caught sight of the white dove once again. It was perched on the lamppost opposite his bedroom. The dove had its head tucked hard under its wings, keeping itself dry, "poor thing," thought Kevin, then closed his curtains. He then washed, dressed, then ran downstairs to get his breakfast. Eventually, his brother returned from his paper round a little soggy. Kevin grinned as he saw his wet brother coming through the door. Paul just grinned back sarcastically to his brother and then ran upstairs to change. It was time to leave for school for Kevin. The rain had slowed to a mere drizzle, so off he peddled. When he got there, he went to see if Vinnie was turning up, but Vinnie did not appear, so off to the registration, Kevin went with his other friends. The school day just flew by. A new day came and went without Kevin getting into any trouble or being pestered by his brother about magic. The weekend had arrived; Kevin was excited, only a brief time to the match now.

Kevin was outside for most of Saturday, practicing heading and kicking the ball. He hoped he would get a chance to take part in the game to show the managers that he was good. Eventually, nighttime came, and after eating his tea, he sat watching television thinking how he could become a great footballer, how it would be great to be recognised around the world, and never have to worry about money because of his wages. Kevin, every now and then, smiled to himself, "what's up with you" his brother said, "got wind," then laughed, "no," replied Kevin sharply, "nothing is wrong with me. Why should there be?". "Leave your brother alone, Paul," mum said, "he's probably just a bit nervous about the game tomorrow," "right" Paul said sarcastically. Kevin had enough of his brother's sarcasm, so he decided to get an early night, "night, mum," he called as he went upstairs, "Night, dear," came her reply.

As the night got blacker and time went on, Kevin drifted off to sleep. It was not long before he started to see a vision appearing. Only the vision he was seeing was not like the others he had seen. These were as if they speeded up, a lot faster than the others. First, he saw Postromus and Merlin practising what looked like making spells. Kevin could not make out everything they were saying, so they could not understand the spells they were making. Next, the vision moved onto Postromus telling Merlin that dark times had started. Many Unicorns, dragons, and griffins had been killed, but for what use neither knew. The vision sped forward again. This time it slowed. Postromus and Merlin sat by a fire, talking. Although slowed, the vision was still moving at a pace. Kevin was sure he heard a name mentioned but did not remember it, along with a thing called the time stone. That is all he got from that part.

As the vision picked up the pace once again, it slowed to show that in the next part, Postromus was in combat with Jarone and his men, Crandloss was nowhere to be seen, but Postromus was fighting in the form of the dragon and got wounded badly, Kevin heard him call for Merlin, but just before he appeared, Jarone thrust his sword into the dragon. The shrill of pain echoed through the past, then silence. With a loud bang, Merlin appeared and cast the lightning spell on the men surrounding the now-dead wizard. All the men were hit by its power which made them fly crashing into the mountain walls that surrounded the pass. As Merlin looked at Postromus, tears slowly rolled down his cheeks as they did that night his parents had been killed. He turned to Jarone, "I thought I had taught you a lesson the last time we met," he snapped at Jarone, "you lied. Crandloss told me that there was no curse on me, for that you shall also meet your maker, just like your parents and this stupid old man." With that, Jarone ran at Merlin, his sword held aloft, ready to strike him down, "**Firentay, Consunium, Derivarm,**" called Merlin. A high-voltage bolt of lightning shot from his wand catching Jarone's sword, and the electricity flew up the sword and into Jarone, sending him flying through the air.

"You shall not kill again, Jarone. You had the chance to leave and get away from Crandloss's clutches, but still, you chose to stay and fight for him. Tell me before I kill you. It has been your men killing the unicorns and other magical animals. What for?" Jarone lay battered, bruised, and bleeding from his collision with the walls, "I will tell you nothing. Go ahead and kill me, for if I talk, then he will only do your bidding instead". Merlin looked at Jarone, "very well" he said standing over Jarone, "I know what will make you talk," Merlin called out, "**Excelious Painclos**," Jarone screamed with pain, "now tell me, why are you killing these beasts?", Jarone screamed "no, I won't say," Merlin concentrated more on the spell, the pain increased in Jarone's body, he screamed once again, "ok, alright, he is killing them for their magical abilities, everyone killed he takes something from them, I know not what but it makes him more powerful." Just as Jarone finished speaking, Merlin heard the dreaded words come from a siding in the past, "**Lithio killentious**," Jarone screamed in desperate pain, then silence, his body lifeless.

Merlin knew it was the killing spell. He turned quickly to see Crandloss standing there brandishing his wand. "Oh come, come, Merlin, our past two meetings have been barbaric, do not you think we need to either talk or at the least duel like what every wizard is shown? I would prefer to talk and reason with you, but I see that you are not happy with the events that have happened." Merlin stared constantly at Crandloss then said, "and why would I be amused, you have had my parents killed, now my friend, why don't you just go for the hat trick and kill me also", "oh, don't think it hasn't crossed my mind, but, I know the old fool that Jarone managed to kill, under my influence I must add, potions make people think there immortal do you not find, I know he was a very accomplished wizard, one that I know would have passed on his knowledge and power, I prefer to offer you an alliance, the two of us ruling this miserable land, and making other parts our own also". "at what cost Crandloss, Killing more innocent people and magical beasts, no I will not be part of that" Merlin answered, "very well, but I feel that a duel will not benefit either of us at this time so until we meet again, and I promise, the next time I will not be so forthcoming", With a loud bang, and a plume of smoke Crandloss disappeared. Merlin stood looking around at both Postromus and Jarone.

The vision moved on. Kevin could see things happening to move through the vision, but for just split seconds, when it stopped, Merlin had aged what looked to Kevin about another ten years. Merlin was at the mountain home, where he had lived with Postromus. Merlin now had a book in his hand, going through it page by page, and what looked like the time stone hanging from his wrist on a silver chain. Merlin was unhappy with a thought cast by a previous wizard. It was Bartholomew; he was in trouble calling for help. Merlin clapped his hands together and materialised back at his childhood village. In the far opening, he could hear spells being cast, he quickly made his way toward the commotion, and as he broke through the bracken, he could see Bartholomew fighting against a dark shape. Merlin turned his wand towards the shape and called out, "**Firentium Sparksum**", fire shot from his wand and hurtled towards the dark shape. As it got within three feet of the foe, it disappeared. Merlin knew that there must be a magic shield repelling certain spells cast at the foe, so she tried a different spell. "**Firentay, Consunium, Derivarm**," lightning bolts shot from his wand, but instead of disappearing, this time, the lightning shot from the foe and directed itself at Bartholomew. With a scream, Bartholomew dropped to the floor; Merlin moved out closer to the foe. He did. He could see it was Crandloss, now clearly with a dark complexion. The two wizards cast the lightning spell at each other at the same time. Sparks flew as the energies of both wizards connected halfway between them, both wizards holding tight to their wands, concentrating on each other, energies flowing, the light from the connection shining brilliantly throughout the area. Eventually, Crandloss cast another spell, " **Crevatious Septimium**," The lightning bolt now intensified and struck at Merlin, sending him backward. As he tumbled, he called out, "**Weathio Corpus Evrader**," High winds shot through the trees with hail and lightning thrown at Crandloss. As both hit Crandloss together, he withered in pain and broke off the attack, fleeing into the woods.

Merlin picked himself up, slowly moving over towards Bartholomew. As he stood over him, Bartholomew was hardly breathing, his body showing intense burning from the lightning that had been directed at him. Merlin now bent down and held Bartholomew's head in his lap, "I'm so sorry, my friend, I should have come sooner. I should have known Crandloss's evil would search out my friends and destroy them to get to me", Bartholomew gasped, "it wasn't your fault, he is led by the dark side, he has heard of the life expectorant from the unicorn's blood," Bartholomew gasped again, "he seeks to live indefinitely, he said that you hold the key to that, I didn't know what he meant, then he turned on me." "Hush, my friend, we need to get you better, save your strength," Bartholomew looked Merlin in his eyes, then said, "too late for me, watch your" there, his voice faded away, his head turned slightly, then went lifeless. Merlin had lost another friend, his anger at this growing. With a big cry heard through the woods, he shouted, "Crandloss." The vision sped up once more and then slowed to see Merlin rushing towards a shape kneeling over a dead unicorn drinking some of its blood, "what have you done" called Merlin to the dark shape. As it turned, Merlin saw it was Crandloss, the silver liquid around his mouth. Crandloss shuddered, then let out a cry as if in pain. Merlin stood looking at Crandloss. His shape was altering. In fact, it was splitting. Merlin took a few paces back, still watching Crandloss's body squirming about and slowly looking as though it was separating. A plume of smoke filled the air, a shrilling cry coming from within it. Merlin held his wand tightly, pointing towards the smoke. Suddenly the smoke cleared, and there instead of Crandloss, were two characters, one standing, one kneeling, looking at the unicorn. Kevin got a good look at both the men; it was Jerez kneeling over the unicorn and Matreese standing. Merlin moved closer towards Matreese, "too late, Merlin, no better left inside me. I have shaken that weakness from me; you had your chance to be my aid. Now when we meet again, I shall finish it. Once again, a large plume of smoke engulfed Matreese and then cleared with no sign of him. Merlin, still holding his wand, pointing now at Jarez, knelt over the body of a slain unicorn.

"Put away your wand Merlin. You need it not here, as My brother said, I am his weak side, Jerez, the good of him, now the bad part has intensified his powers throughout his body. You know that once the blood has been tasted of the unicorn, it will enhance the ability to lengthen the life span of that person; the struggle will be long, arduous, and very dangerous to defeat him. Every day that goes by, he will get stronger and you weaker. You know what you have to do". Merlin knelt, stroking the dead body of this once magnificent creature. Tears again swelled in his eyes, slowly falling from his face upon the head of the Unicorn. Merlin scooped some of the unicorn's silver blood into a small container. As he did, a light shone down from above, a harmonising sound surrounded the woods where the two were, and then the horn of the unicorn fell from its head. Merlin picked the horn up, and with a command and a clap of his hands, Merlin was transported back to the house of his fathers.

As Kevin watched, Merlin set to work in his old father's house, shaping the horn into a handle shape. He put both the handle and his wand together in what Kevin could only see was a homemade vice. Merlin then tipped some of the unicorn's blood over the wand and began chanting some words, again Kevin could not make sense of all the words being spoken by Merlin, but after a second chant, in which Kevin made out Merlin mentioning Postromus, there was a blinding light, a tremendous loud bang, smoke and thunder rumbling above Merlin's father's house. As all the commotion calmed, Merlin stood now with the wand in his hand. He dipped his finger into the container and dropped a few drops of the unicorn's blood into his mouth, "now," he said, "this is where it ends. Kevin's vision ended abruptly. No more sights or sounds, just the blackness he had seen at the end of other visions, so why was he still trying to see something, he waited a while longer, but nothing appeared, so Kevin dropped off into a deep sleep.

Chapter 4

Can It Be?

Kevin woke quite early the next morning. As he wiped his eyes, he remembered the dream he had that night. He looked over towards the wardrobe and wondered if the book was still there or if it had got back into his bag once again. He pulled back his covers and walked a crossed the room to the wardrobe. He slowly undid the door and looked under the pile of clothes he had put it under. There it was. It had not moved. He pulled it out and placed it on his bed. As he looked at it with a nervous expression now on his face, he wondered why he had been shown the life of Merlin. It had not been a good one. After all, he had his mother, father, and best friend turn evil and two close friends also killed, so why show him? Kevin slowly opened the book. Page after page of spells that he recognised in his visions, potions he did not, names of people met, and a list of items, berries, herbs, tree leaves, and some long words all put together that at the end of it read, The Flamel Power Stone.

Kevin remembered hearing this name before in the vision mentioned by Postromus but had no idea what it was all about. Kevin closed the book, put it back in the wardrobe, and shut it up. He had better things to think about today, it was the first game of the season, and he wanted very much to be part of it. Kevin got dressed and went downstairs quietly as it was still early in the morning; he got out his boots, went and got some shoe polish, laid an old newspaper on the ground, then started to clean his boots. Kevin heard a key go in the door lock from outside. It was his dad on his way in from work, "hello Kevin, what's up? can't sleep?" Kevin looked at his dad, smiled, then answered, "Bit nervous, that's all" "what's to be nervous about? I heard you did well in the training session. You'll be fine" "but what if I stink dad, there are better players out there than me," Kevin replied. His dad bent down, ruffled his hair, smiled, then said, "Kevin, it doesn't matter what other people think of how you played. As long as you give your best every time you walk out on that pitch, then that's all you can do. Look, there are loads of youngsters, all going through the nerve thing every day, whether it is because of a football match, or a day at school, every parent will tell them exactly what I told you. It's a kind of pass-me-down phrase that has been said for generations, don't be that scared person. Believe in your own abilities. You need to get your self-confidence flowing from every part of your mind down through your body. Once you have done that, let the others be nervous about how good you really are. I believe in you. I know Russ and Brian will also. Once they get to know you, you go out there and knock their socks off, ok?" "Thanks, dad, it's just what I needed to hear," Kevin replied, "you're welcome, my boy. Now, are you going to put the kettle on for me? All that talking has made me dry," both Kevin and dad laughed as he got up and did what his father had asked.

Time soon passed with the whole household up, and breakfast was eaten. Kevin grabbed his bag and started off towards the door when his brother called to him, "wait up bro, I'm coming to watch you, see how you get on" "do you have to?" replied Kevin, "your match is in the afternoon, don't you want to get ready for it?". "there will be plenty of time for that, besides, I can see if you're good enough for the school house team," Kevin looked at his mum as if to ask her for help in this matter, "oh don't be silly Kevin, it will be nice having your brother there cheering you on, now smile and off you to go, be good dear," Both boys grabbed their coats and went off to the park. As they arrived, Kevin saw Russ and Brian putting up the nets in the goal mouths and their sons putting the corner flags out. "Good look Kev," his brother said," hope you get on. I'll be watching from the stand," Kevin went off into the dressing room to meet up with his teammates. In next to no time, the opposing team was there, changed, and ready to start the game. As the referee blew his whistle for kick-off, Kevin sat alongside the other substitutes. He looked around to see his brother with some of his friends and Mr. Sidney, the sports master at the school. Unfortunately, the game did not start well for Holbek. Within five minutes, they were a goal down. Another went into their net after another five minutes. Kevin and the other substitutes were all calling to the players on the pitch to mark the opposing side and tackle them hard, but to no avail. Kevin heard Russ say to Brian, "looks like we are going to get another drumming just like last season," Brian nodded in agreement. As the ball went down the wing towards Kevin's team's goal, Sandy, one of the centre halves, went in for a tackle and got his foot stood on. The referee blew for a free kick. Sandy gradually started getting up onto his feet again when Kevin whispered, "be too hurt to continue. Let me have a go," with that, Sandy sank back down to the ground. "It's no good, Russ," Brian said. He can't put any weight on his foot. You'd better get a sub ready." Russ got up from his space in the stand, looked at the substitutes he had then said, "ok, Kevin, get warmed up. You are going on" Kevin jumped up and ran down to the pitch, running up and down the touchline to warm up; eventually, Russ called to him, "right, we need a bit of strength in the back there, so help them out, get forward for the corners if we get any, but make sure you get back to defend, ok?" Kevin nodded in agreement and ran onto the pitch. As he got to his place he called out "come on, we are better than this, let's get at them." With the restart, Dedger took the free kick down the wing to Holly, who got a cross into the box but was put out for a corner for Kevin's team. As the corner was taken, Kevin stepped back three paces. The ball was headed away from the goal by the opposing defender right toward Kevin. With a big grunt, he connected with the ball, "get in the goal," he screamed as the ball left his foot and shot through the air and into the top right-hand corner, Goal. With his first touch, Kevin scored a stunning goal. All the team gathered around him, congratulating him, while Russ and Brian, and were thumping the air in approval. The game continued, and Kevin was called upon time after time to make goal-stopping tackles, but occasionally as the opposing player was going to shoot, would whisper, "miss the ball," the player would take a wild swing at the ball and fall over, Kevin's teammates collected the rogue ball each time, this happened regularly. Also, the forward would shoot the ball over the crossbar or wide of the posts. The half-time whistle went, and the teams ran back to get their half-time orange and team talks from their managers.

The second half went much as the first half, apart from the opposing side not scoring any more goals. Still, time after time, their forwards missed easy chances. Paul was beginning to get a little suspicious as he watched the game go on. He kept a good watch on Kevin and the number of times his mouth moved when there was a goal-scoring chance for the opposing side. After fifteen minutes of the second half, Kevin's team got another corner, Kevin went into the penalty area, and as the ball came crossed, he jumped high and headed the ball goalwards, "get in there," he shouted as it left his head. The ball seemed to swerve and ended up sitting in the back of the net. With a loud roar, Kevin's team was level. Once again, his teammates ran to him to congratulate him. Russ and Brian were running up and down the touchline, jumping and hollowing with joy. The game continued and was nearing its end when the opposing forward got through into the eighteen-yard box and clashed with the keeper coming out to stop him. The referee blew his whistle and pointed to the penalty spot. There was a lot of arguing between Kevin's teammates and the referee, but he had none of it and waved them away. As this was all going on, Bob, the keeper, was in great pain. He had hurt his leg and could not stand on it. Again Brian indicated that he would not be able to continue and needed replacing. Russ called Kevin over to him, "you are doing great, Kevin, but I need you in that goal now. Think you can save it?" Kevin smiled at Russ and then replied, "I'll give it a go if you want me to." Russ got out the reserve goal-keeping jersey and handed it to Kevin, "do your best. That's all I can ask you to do" Kevin took off his shirt and put on the goalkeeper's shirt as he ran back onto the field. He ran across to Nutty, Holly, and Wayne to have a quick chat with them. All three looked over to Russ and saw him clap his hands and shout, "come on, you can do this." With that, Kevin's teammates he spoke to went onto the halfway line in the centre circle, and Kevin went into the goal mouth. As the players waited out of the box, the forward placed the ball on the spot and turned to walk away. "Now, where are you going to put this, my man?" Kevin heard a voice in his head say," I will look to the right to make him go the wrong way, then slot it in the left about halfway up." Kevin looked a bit astounded but knew he had to go the right way. The referee blew his whistle, and the forward started his run-up. The game was now in injury time, and this had to be the last kick of the game.

As the forward ran up to take the kick, Nutty, Holly, and Wayne ran to the sides of the pitch. The forward did as he said he would do. He looked right, then kicked towards Kevin's left. Kevin flew through to his left, caught the ball, and, as he landed, rolled over and let a long throw go down the wing. Holly collected it and sprinted down the line. The opposing side's defence started to run towards him. Holly crossed the ball over the defence and right onto Nutty's head. As the ball left Nutty's head, the opposing keeper was coming out to get the ball but missed it. The ball shot into the back of the net, and the opposing side's team all sank to their knees as the referee blew first for the goal and then for full-time. Holbek had won, and fans ran onto the pitch, celebrating, cheering, and holding Kevin aloft on their shoulders. Paul was looking not so happy and waited at the bottom of the stand for his hero brother. As the teams started to come off the pitch, Mr. Sidney congratulated Kevin on a magnificent game. "That was sure one hell of a game you played, young Wilks. If you do that weak in, weak out, you'll definitely be on the school side. Who knows, you might even make the national side." "It was a great game," Russ added, "but you have to prove that it was not just a one-off. If you can do that each week, then we can have a good season, go on get washed up, and get in the warm", Russ ruffled Kevin's hair as he ran off to the dressing room.

After a long time in the dressing room, getting washed and changed and talking about the game, the boys started to leave. Paul was waiting, and he did not look happy. "What's up with you?" Kevin asked his brother; Paul grabbed hold of Kevin's arm, "come with me," he said in a stern voice. Kevin had no choice but to go with him as his grip was firm, and Kevin was being dragged along. As they came to a spot that was covered by trees and bushes, Paul let go of Kevin's arm and checked to see if they were not being followed. "What are you doing?" Kevin asked. Paul turned quickly and stared at Kevin, "well?" he asked, "well, what?" Kevin replied, "tell me," Paul started," you, Mr, who doesn't believe in magic, what the hell do you think you were doing?" "what are you going on about" Kevin snapped back, "oh, so you didn't use thought magic to get on the pitch or make those guys miss kick the ball every time, oh and what about the goals you scored, my you must be good enough for the big time," Paul then turned away then back again, "and that save and set up for the goal, that was genius, what, did you ask him which side he was going to put it, and he obliged by telling you, unsuspectedly."

"What are you talking about" Kevin answered, "those guys were useless. It is not my fault they could not kick the ball properly, and Sandy was injured. I had nothing to do with that using your mumbo-jumbo magic. And for your information, those goals I scored were all me. What, wish you could do the same?" "ok," said Paul, "so, you never uttered the words, miss it, when the guys were about to shoot, or get in there, or get in the net, for the goals." Kevin looked at Paul and said, so what if I did? As I said, the goals were all for me. The bad footballing was all of them." "And what about the penalty? Did you ask the thought where you are going to put it" Kevin looked at Paul and said quietly, "I might have" "and you got a reply, didn't you? You heard his thought about what he was going to do", "no" replied Kevin, "don't lie," cried Paul," I know you do well," Kevin snapped back quickly, "alright I thought I heard something about the way to dive, what's all this about? You really have some sour grapes there, bro." "I'll give you sour grapes. Hold out your hand," Paul commanded, "what?" Kevin replied, "hold out your hand," he said again, "why," asked Kevin, "you are going to accept what's going on even if it kills me," Paul snapped, "right, I want you to concentrate on anything that could help you do something," "what, are you mad?" Kevin said, "Look, if you don't want my fist in your nose, you will do as I say, ok." "Alright, alright, calm down. I'll do your stupid thing, but don't think I will believe in this nonsense. How do I know it's not you making things appear? After all, you are a wizard", he said sarcastically, "just shut up and concentrate," Paul snapped, "ok" said Kevin trying to calm his brother, "so what do you want me to concentrate on, money, booze, fags", Kevin said once again sarcastically. "none of the above" Paul snapped, "you have to want something that will do you some good, like if you were hungry then you could wish for a sandwich or chocolate bar, or if it was dark you could wish for a light, something like that," "so what's wrong with money, that could do me some good" Kevin asked, "like how" Paul asked, Kevin, started to laugh before saying, well, if I wished me some money, I could buy the sandwich or light," "very funny, now let's do this, alright," Paul said back sarcastically.

"Ok," replied Kevin, "so what do you want me to wish for?", "I don't want to know. You think of something you could do with, and remember, it has to be able to help you in some way". "right, ok, I can do this," Kevin said and closed his eyes, "what are you doing?", Paul asked, "shush, I'm concentrating" Kevin replied, "did you have your eyes shut when you whispered the guy to miss, or the ball to get in the net, or the way to dive for that matter?". Paul snapped once more at Kevin, "this is not a game, Kevin, now come on," "all right, you win. I'll do it right, ok here goes". Both Kevin and Paul fell silent, Kevin's face was full of concentration, but after a minute, nothing happened, "no, I got nothing," Kevin said, "you're not trying," Paul snapped, "you have to really want it, just like you did at football, so concentrate on something you really, really, want, or need to help you do something, now try again." Kevin held out his hand and stood concentrating, "look at the item" Paul whispered, "see it in your mind, and project it into your hand, you can do this", Kevin stood absolutely still, his face full of concentration again, suddenly a shape of a pencil started to appear in the palm of his hand, "concentrate Kevin, more concentration, it's nearly here", finally it materialised into a physical shape, "look" Paul said, "feel it, it's real, try using it", you did it, I knew you could, now tell me, you still don't believe in magic". Kevin folded his hand around the pencil and broke it in two, he looked at it closely, it was just as a real pencil is. Kevin looked at Paul with a confused blank stare, "you think I did it, and put it in your hand, don't you, oh come on bro, a pencil, you really think I would know that was what you thought of, a pencil" Paul turned away in disbelief, "ok, he said as he turned, "let's try something else, just one more time, it should be easier this time because you know how to get there, right, just picture it in your mind, and project it to your hand, so, let's do it". Kevin held out his hand again before Paul could say anything. Kevin had a chicken sandwich in his hand, "you see, you see, you can do magic, you can" Paul turned, clapped his hands, and laughed, "you cannot say now that magic is not real and that you used magic on that field probably without knowing it, but you did use magic." Kevin, still with a blank look on his face, took a bite out of the sandwich he was holding, "look" Paul said," try practicing, but you must do it where no one can see or hear you, just in case you shout out in disbelief, also try not to conjure up too much stuff, and don't take it home, mum will think you stole it, are you listening to me bro?", Kevin looked at his brother, still a bit shocked, "Ok Come on let's get home, I've got a game this afternoon, without using magic, perhaps you need to come and see how it's done," Paul laughed then slapped Kevin on the shoulder, "let's go, bro," both boys went and got their bikes and went home.

Kevin was silent all the way home, as they reached the corner of their road, Paul called out to him, "cheer up Kevin, mum will notice some things wrong, you have to separate this from normal life", "but I'm not normal, am I?", Paul stopped his bike in front of Kevin, "look, I was just like you, but I had help to put my two lives into perspective, you also can get help, I can help you, and goodwill, just try and look happy for now about winning the game, I'm not going to say anything, and neither are you, so change your face, put on a smile and we will talk things through after my game, ok". Kevin nodded in agreement. They finished their ride to their house, where mum was waiting for them, "so", she said with her hands held out to the sides, "Kevin looked at his mum then at Paul, "he's in shock" Paul said quickly, "he scored twice, great goals, then had to go in goal at the end, and saved a blinding penalty to help his team win, it was", Paul paused, "magic", Kevin looked over at his brother, "what" he said, "you had a brilliant game" Paul said with a smile on his face. Kevin got off his bike and put it in the shed. "well, he doesn't seem too happy about it," mum said, "oh, I'm just a bit tired," Kevin replied. I'll be full of it when I have had a rest" "well, I hope so," mum replied, come on, let's get some dinner. Your brother has his game this afternoon. You going to watch?" Kevin just shrugged his shoulders and mumbled, "I don't know." "don't mumble, Kevin, you know I can't hear you when you do that," mum replied, "at least you can support your brother as he did you, but if you don't want to, no one is going to force you," "just give me a little time then I'll be ready, I'll go and watch him," Kevin answered, "that's better, it's nice to see you two getting on with each other these days, it certainly better than the constant fighting you used to do," mum gave a little smile then went into the kitchen to get some dinner ready for them. Kevin looked at Paul and beckoned him to him, "we have to talk, Paul," Kevin said quietly, "I know," Paul replied, "how about the spinney after the game?" Kevin nodded as if to say ok. They then sat down and waited for their mum to bring them some sandwiches before going to Pauls's afternoon game.

The afternoon game went quickly, Paul's team ran out of easy winners, but as Kevin watched the game, he reflected on the dreams he had, what he could now do, and what he needed to do next. He was not really focused on the game but managed to watch still bits and pieces. After the game, Kevin waited for his brother to come out of the dressing room. Paul came out, saying his goodbyes to his mates and catching up with Kevin. "You alright, bro?" his brother asked him, "what do you think?" Kevin replied, "come on, let's get to the spinney." Both boys got on their bikes and went to the spinney. As they got to the point where Paul had opened the safe house, he stopped, "feel like doing the honours?" he asked Kevin. Kevin looked at the spot and said," **Optimus Reveal**" the doorway became visible, and Kevin looked at Paul, "see, I told you" both boys went in. After both Kevin and Paul sat at the table, Paul looked at his brother and then asked, "ok, let's hear it. What's bringing you down about all this?". Kevin looked at his brother and started telling him all about his dreams and visions and the night he was contacted by Merlin throughout the book. Paul listened intently as Kevin talked and talked about all that had happened, including Merlin wanting to meet him in the Astral Plain. Paul clapped his hands, smiled, then repeated.

"The Astral Plain" "what is it? Where is it?" Kevin asked, "never been there," Paul replied, "It's a place that is beyond anywhere, a place which it is written, that only great wizards can get to, it is a place that no bad can get either, Supreme wizards watch over it with their immense powers ready to fight back black and dark wizards trying to get there and destroy it, and Merlin wants to meet you there. You know what this means don't you?" "No, what?" Kevin replied, "You are going to be a great wizard also. It makes sense now." "What does?", Kevin asked again, "why you have been given Merlin's wand, his spell book and the time stone", Paul replied, "for what use though?", Again Kevin asked, "I don't know, but I suggest you meet him there when he asks you, I think you will find out why". "so how do I get there", Kevin asked again" is it a special hidden place like this, with a magical door?", Can't tell you, like I said, I have never been there, somehow you will be given the way to get there, until then, don't tell anyone about any of this, I'll have a word with Godwill tomorrow and see what he has to say, ok", Kevin nodded in agreement, "well little bro, it's taken time, but I think your just about there now, I think you have changed your perception on the magic thing, it's going to be an adventure, one that may get a little sticky at times but, you have plenty of friends and people to help you on that journey, welcome to the clan", Paul held out his hand offering it to be shaken, Kevin grasped Pauls hand and shook it. "You had better be there for me when I need you," Kevin said to his brother, "I'll be there. I'll always be there, bro," Both Paul and Kevin smiled at each other, finished their handshake, then decided it was time to go home.

The Astral Plain

When the two boys arrived home, it was getting near teatime. Dad was there also, so he wanted to know all about how the games went. Both boys took turns describing how they helped their sides beat their local rival teams. "Well, that's splendid," he said after listening to them, "I bet you are relieved, Kevin. After all that worry about how the game would go, I told you, you believe in yourself, and magical things can happen." Both boys looked at each other and laughed, "your right there, dad," the boys said at the same time.

After tea, it was time for Kevin to reflect on how the day had gone, and now he was desperate to try other things just to see what he could and could not do. Paul could see on Kevin's face that the excitement was there. No more would he deny that magic did not exist. The only trouble was now he had to keep a closer eye on Kevin just to make sure he did not do something stupid that could not be explained. Paul got to his feet and turned to Kevin, "I've got some Geography homework that I think you might be able to help me with, Kevin, don't suppose you'd give me a hand with it upstairs"? Mum looked at Paul and said, "Geography homework. How is Kevin going to help you with that? He's only just started that school. You would have learned a lot more in the three years you have been there than him in a couple of weeks or so." "you know that I'm not brilliant at Geog. Kevin seems to know where a lot of places are and what goes on in them. It must be all that logic in his brain that helps him", Paul said as he laughed, "I'll see what I can do," replied Kevin, "but don't shout at me if you get any answers wrong, ok," the two boys raced upstairs. When they got into Pauls room, he turned to Kevin and said, "that was lucky, now listen to little bro, I can see in your face that you are bursting to try magic now at the drop of a hat, you can't do that, I told you, you have to keep the two lives separate," "it's easy for you to say" Kevin replied, "no, it isn't, I know exactly what you feel," "so how do I feel if you know so much?", Kevin blurted out.

Paul looked at Kevin, shook his head, then said, "you feel like a boy that has been given the run of a sweet shop, and you don't have to pay for a thing. I know. I was exactly like you. I wanted to whip my wand out and cast spells the first day I got it, but there is a time and a place for everything, and this is not it. If you must practice your thought casting, remember to try and only conjure up things you will eat, and I mean eat all of it, or mum will find crumbs or disregarded pieces of rotten food in your room and then start to get angry, or even suspect that you're stealing them from someone or somewhere. Keep the items small. At least that way, you can smuggle them out of the house into your locker at school or even the school bins. I know it will be hard, but I got through it with the help of Godwill, and you will too. Kevin looked at Paul and said, "it doesn't feel right" "what doesn't feel right? that you're a wizard, someone that can do magic" Kevin nodded. Paul looked at his brother and said, "I know what you mean, but it is going to be great. At least now we can really connect as brothers should do instead of fighting. I'll tell you the truth, bro, sometimes, when we were fighting, after I found out that I could do magic, just sometimes, I really wanted to use it on you, not to hurt you but to shut you up, at least now we have more in common than the usual brother relationship, we can practice our spells together, learn new ones".

Kevin looked at Paul and said, "What, like Merlin and Crandloss, see what happened to them, one good, one bad." "But that won't happen to us. We are brothers. They weren't. We will look out for each other.

You'll see." Kevin looked at Paul and then replied, laughing, "You'd be better, or you're going to be in for one bad fight, bro." "Anyway," Kevin said, I still wonder how I am going to get to this Astral Plain and who I will see and talk to?" Paul sniggered, "well Merlin cloth ears, that's who." "But how will I recognise him? will he be old? Wearing a long robe and a pointed hat, like fiction is written of his appearance, where is this place? Is it far away or close? Will I have to walk, bike, or what? What if someone else is there?" Paul held his hand up for Kevin to stop talking, "I don't know," he said," why don't you open your book and ask it?" Kevin clicked his fingers, "open the book and ask," he said excitingly, "why didn't I think of that?" Kevin went into his room and got the book out of the wardrobe, with it in his hands he ran back to Paul's bedroom and shut the door, "right, let me find the right page" he said to his brother, "Here we are." Kevin had found the blank page that the writing had appeared on just those few short nights ago. "Well?" Paul said as his brother looked blankly at him, "what do I say?" Kevin replied, "ask it how you get to the Astral Plain?". Kevin looked back towards the book and asked the question, the book page stayed empty, "maybe, Merlin's not there, maybe I was asleep and dreaming when I saw the writing appear on this page," Kevin said to Paul, "I don't think so" Paul replied with a nod of his head telling Kevin to look at the book. As Kevin looked at the page, writing appeared, 'to get to the Astral Plain. You must be first invited. Secondly, you must want to go there. Finally, you must open the subconscious part of your mind and let it explore all that there is to be seen and heard. The writing disappeared. Kevin looked at his brother, "do what," he said. Paul smiled, "look, it's quite simple," he said to his brother. "Firstly, you have to be invited. You have by Merlin. Secondly, you have to want to go there. Well, I would say that's something you definitely want to do, isn't it?" Paul looked at Kevin as he nodded in agreement. Finally, open your subconscious, that's easy, you do that when you go to sleep, so the journey takes place when you are in bed asleep, it's a bit like your visions, you know, when you were watching Merlin's life reveal itself, you could almost imagine you were there". Kevin looked at Paul then asked, "But if I'm asleep, won't it be just a dream, a dream that everything happens in it because I want it to?" Writing again started to appear again on the page, 'although you see it as a dream, it will be in fact reality, nothing you want to happen will, only what must be said and done, you will see and remember all that goes on within the confinement of the Plain.' The writing disappeared once again. Kevin looked at the book and asked one last question, "when? when will this take place?" the writing appeared once more with just one word,' Tonight.' Kevin looked at his brother, "tonight," he said, in a slightly hesitant way, "I don't know if I'm ready for that to happen this quickly. I'm only just getting used to what is happening" "calm down, Kevin," Paul said, "if you weren't ready, I'm sure Merlin wouldn't have asked you to meet him. There must be some reason for it. You don't have to be scared; nothing can happen to you there. Anyway, you do have the most awesome powerful wizard with you once you get there, so I would just say enjoy it, see what it's all about, and just remember as much as you can. I know I would be very happy if it was me going there".

Kevin again glanced at his brother and then spoke, "so why don't you go in my place" Paul laughed then answered, "Because you have been chosen by Merlin to meet him, not me. It's not like school, where you can hand a note in as an excuse to miss a day's school. You need to grow up, bro. This is a big honour for you, so grasp it with both hands and enjoy it, ok?". Kevin looked nervously over to his brother, then nodded in agreement. "Ok," his brother said, "time for you to go and get ready for your journey, we will meet at the spinney after school, and you can tell me all about it, alright mate"? Kevin again nodded as if to say ok. With that Kevin closed the book and took it back into his room where he hid it back in his wardrobe. He went to the top of the stairs and shouted down "goodnight" to his parents. "Have you finished already?, his mum called back" it's still quite early yet, Kevin, for bed" "I know, mum," he called back, "feeling quite tired, must have been the game took it out of me earlier today," "alright dear" called mum, "sleep well," she replied, Kevin hoped he would also, as he closed his door and got comfortable in his bed. It was not long before his eyes shut, and he fell into a deep sleep.

It was not long before things started to happen, the wardrobe door opened, and Merlin's book floated from where it was over to the bedside table next to Kevin's bed. The book opened, and the pages turned until it got to the blank page. A quick blinding flash came from the page, and Kevin saw himself now in a meadow. As he looked around, he could see a path with woods on both sides of it, the sky was clear, but no sun could be seen. Kevin started to walk down the path, flowers were out in a blaze of glorious colour, but one thing Kevin could not see or hear were any songs of birds. He thought this strange but continued along the path. As he walked further, now well in the woods, he came to a clearing where he could see an old village, some of the buildings were blackened, as though they had been burnt. Beside one of the houses were two graves with thick wooden crosses embedded into the earth with names on them, but Kevin could not make them out due to the crosses now in bad repair. As he walked through the village, Kevin realised that it looked just like Merlin's home village that he had seen in the first vision, but how could he be there, and what was the significance of it? Kevin continued further down the path, and eventually, he came to a large brook surrounded by tall, large old oak trees. Under one of these trees, Kevin could make out a shape of a person, just sitting there, staring into the blue water of the brook. He moved forward towards the person quite hesitantly.

"Don't be scared young Kevin. It is I whom you seek, Merlin." The figure stood up and turned towards Kevin. The figure was that of a man in his late sixties, Kevin thought, but again, Kevin felt confused. If this were Merlin, then how could he look like this if he were hundreds of years old? "Come, sit with me. You must have a thousand questions you wish to know the answers to. I will try my best to provide answers for most of them, although I cannot promise they will be what you want to hear." Kevin walked over and sat on the ground by Merlin, staring at the man claiming to be one of the oldest, most powerful wizards known. "Staring is un-nerving young wizard," Merlin said to Kevin in a kind sort of way. Kevin turned his head away from looking at Merlin and instead stared into the brook. "Well, now, where shall we begin?" Merlin said. As he did, he held out his hand, "first things first, take my hand Kevin" Kevin looked at Merlin once more, then said, "excuse me," "take my hand, you want to see if I am real and prove to you I am who I say I am, is that not right?", Kevin still looking at Merlin moved his hand towards Merlin's. Just before they connected, Kevin withdrew his hand, "hang on, what will this prove? I am asleep in my bed, so how do I know if I touch you, that the feeling is real?" Merlin smiled, "always the doubter, that's why I chose you," he replied, "everything you see, smell, hear and touch is real here too, just like you and me, although your body is at your home, your soul is here. It is that part of your body that tells you, what is real, and what is not. After you wake, you will remember all that has happened here, and to help you believe it more, I shall give you a parting present to take back with you when it is time, now touch my hand if you would please." Kevin again moved his hand towards Merlin's, this time both hands connected, "tell me, Kevin, what do you feel?" Kevin held Merlin's hand and replied, "skin, bones, a pulse moving through from your wrist, and a few hairs." Merlin held his other hand to his chest then spoke, "thank goodness," he said with a smile, "at least I know I am still alive," Merlin winked at Kevin who smiled back at Merlin. "Now, Kevin, let's answer some more of the questions you are asking yourself on a regular basis. Yes, I am real. We have established that" he said, smiling, "how old am I? Hmm, well, if I told you I was over five hundred years old, you would not believe me. Unfortunately, it is also true. How can that be? Well, I will get to that later, but you have seen some of what has helped me get to this age in your visions. No, there never was a King Arthur or a kingdom called Camelot", Kevin interrupted Merlin's speech with, "yes, I knew it was just a story" Merlin held his hand up to Kevin as if to say stop, "but, there was a man Called Arthur Pendragon, he was a noble man, but as far as ruling a kingdom, well that is untrue, and although there was not a kingdom called Camelot as I said, there was a village, somewhere near what you call York now I believe. So now we come to the main questions, ask away." Kevin looked at Merlin then said, "if magic," Merlin stopped him there, "if magic, remember, this is real. You need to think before asking questions, young man. You are part of this sect now, so please, start again", Merlin said. Kevin thought for a second, then asked once again, "magic began many thousands of years ago. How?" Merlin looked at Kevin and smiled again, then spoke, "men and women many thousands of years ago discovered by chance that they had immense capabilities for being able to learn new languages and new ideas.

With these ideas came improved brain capacity, a capacity that could, if harnessed, do what people thought were unnatural things. There were few at first, but as they mated through time, more people with these gifts emerged. A sect got together and started to improve their abilities using potions and developing gods to follow. Alchemists sprung up with more extensive knowledge and more ways that could harness a person's strength from inside them. Over hundreds of year's progressions, new languages brought new rhymes; these rhymes, as we know them today, are called spells, spells that can produce energy to help people in ways they never knew, or dark spells, spells for doing harm to your friends and family." Merlin got up and moved closer to the brook, staring into it. Kevin looked over at Merlin and said quietly, "I was sad when I saw your parents killed. I don't know what I would do if mine died" Merlin turned towards Kevin but said nothing, "is that why the village is here, so you can pay respect to your parents?" Kevin asked. Merlin gently nodded then said, "you have a wise old head, on those young shoulders, come, I need to walk while we talk if that's ok with you?", Kevin nodded then rose to his feet, "good, my bones get a bit achy if I sit too long," Merlin replied with a smile.

As they walked, Kevin asked all sorts of questions, and Merlin did his best to answer them. Sometimes Kevin got the answer he knew, sometimes not, but they walked and walked but never seemed to be far from the brook. As they rounded a bend, there was an old oak tree standing tall in the middle of the meadow. Kevin pointed to the tree and said, "I remember this tree. This is where your father brought you to get a piece of it for your first wand" Merlin looked at Kevin, smiled, then said, "very good, you remember what

I sent you in your vision. What else can you tell me?" "the old man, at the village with the fire, Postromus, wasn't it" "that's correct," Merlin answered, "and Crandloss," continued Kevin, "your friend, you two used to practice your spells here, but then he went bad, why was that Merlin?" Merlin turned away from Kevin and sat again at the base of the tree, "I don't know, I have pondered that thought for these five hundred years or more, greed takes over some men, some want extreme power, I guess Crandloss wanted both". "so why kill your parents on that night and help that man, Jarone capture your friends", Kevin asked, "to get to me", Merlin answered, "you see Kevin, I was a good wizard, never had a bad thought in my mind, I always did as I was asked by my parents and the elders, I even took extra lessons from Mr Wilfred, Perhaps Crandloss knew I could become a supreme wizard one day, and he wanted it for himself, he wanted it so bad that the only way to get it was to embrace the dark art and do away with me", Merlin stopped there, "so why did he have to kill your parents", Kevin asked, Merlin looked at Kevin, his eyes had tears in ready to roll down his cheeks, "so I was alone, if you are alone then you can't be much of a threat", "but that's not true", Kevin replied, "you got rid of Jarone's men, and beat Crandloss, surely he would have second thoughts on how strong a person you actually were?". "Unfortunately, not," replied Merlin, "as you remember, he took to killing others that I became friends with Bartholomew and Postromus, once again I was alone." Kevin now getting a little mad asked, "and how did he defeat the great dragon?, in your vision he was killed by Jarone's men by sword, how?, Postromus was a great wizard, why did he not do as you had done and summon the wind, hail and lightning, I don't understand", Merlin answered, "one thing you need to know Kevin about magic, to turn oneself into an animal takes great strength, to keep that shape needs immense concentration, but, in the animal form you have no barriers, you cannot spell cast, unfortunately with the amount of men at Jarone's command, if they did not run, then there was nowhere to hide, Postromus died because of this, you must remember this one fateful thing, for if you do not" Merlin again stopped in mid flow, "I could be killed also", Kevin said. Merlin looked away from Kevin still silent, but then said, "Yes", that was all, nothing else added.

Kevin, now a little scared, walked around the tree. As he entered Merlin's sight, he stopped, "Well, I guess I need to learn how not to get killed, ay" Merlin smiled up at Kevin, "I knew I chose well from the first moment I saw you. I just knew," Merlin stood up and offered his hand to Kevin once more. This time there was no hesitancy for Kevin to take it and shake it. "The journey will be long and arduous young Kevin, you up for a challenge"?, Merlin asked, "Well, at first I wasn't, but nobody likes a bully, so I think it's time to kick someone's butt," Merlin let go of Kevin's hand, "what's wrong," Kevin asked, "have I said something I shouldn't have?". Merlin looked into Kevin's eyes and then spoke, "It's not about doing people harm. The magic you possess is for good. The reason I chose you is that I thought with your youth and inner strength, you would be the one that can possibly save me." Kevin stepped back a little bemused, "save you, why? how?" he asked, "I don't understand." Merlin stood looking at Kevin, "the reason I gave you my wand and book is to help you" "help me, do what" Kevin asked, "do you remember in your vision anything about a person called Marcus Dwight?" Merlin answered, "I heard his name mentioned but nothing about him, why?". "Marcus Dwight was a great alchemist and wizard," Merlin began, "he lived in Germany as you know it today. During his life, he came a crossed a way to produce a substance to live forever", Kevin answered, "forever but that's impossible, isn't it?", Merlin shook his head, "you have seen in the vision, that a few drops of the unicorn blood, can enhance the life expectancy of a person," Kevin nodded, "that is what both Crandloss and myself did, all those years ago, to get us through to now, but the effects are wearing off, and without the product, we will die within ten of your years' time. Well, this product, if you keep it with you produces a magic spell around the person to keep him at the age he is, forever". "So where is this Marcus Dwight now?" asked Kevin, "unfortunately, he is no longer with us", Merlin said, "you mean he is dead", Kevin replied. "yes", Merlin replied, "well it didn't do him any good did it?", Kevin said rather sarcastically, "The reason he is dead", Merlin said, "is that after two hundred years his loved one and children passed away and he found himself alone, a bit like myself, but, many wizards heard of this product which he named the Power Stone, wanted it for themselves, this is what I think Crandloss, I mean Matrees, now needs to survive", Kevin butted in, "that means you also", "correct", Merlin said, "here is the thing, because Marcus was tired of being alone, and always having to be on his guard from others who wanted to possess the stone, he tried to destroy the stone but failed, eventually a number of people tried to kill him to gain this stone and unfortunately, succeeded". Merlin gave a little sigh.

"Marcus had put a part of his soul into the rock along with other good and dark items to produce it to enable to sustain ever after life. "And how do you know this?" asked Kevin, "I know this because Marcus was a friend of Postromus. Eventually, a wizard by the name of Cederic gained the stone and had it for many years until, one day, he, too, was found dead. No one knew of the whereabouts of the stone ever again. Searches have been done for it over the ages, but non returned with the prize. It seems that Cederic hid the stone so well that it seemed lost forever. However, my good friend and teacher Postromus came a crossed a small piece of the stone which he passed down to me during my training with him. The piece I refer to is that stone hanging from your neck. It's called the", Kevin again butted into Merlin's conversation, "the time stone" "Correct once again," Merlin said, "Postromus gave me that stone along with the book, The Pharynx, Marcus Dwight's personal book. It is supposed to hold the clue to the next bit of the stone". "Hang on. You said that Marcus tried to destroy the stone but never succeeded, so how is this part of the original stone"? Merlin smiled and then replied, "the wizard Cederic must have succeeded where others failed before hiding the stone. It was written that the stone was supposed to have been hidden intact in one piece, but that piece you have hanging around your neck is a piece from it, so my conclusions are that he succeeded. The only problem is, where are the other pieces, and how many did he break it into." Again, Kevin butted into Merlin's conversation, "but how do you know it is part of this stone? Have you seen the power stone for yourself? Did it really exist, or are these just stories"?

Merlin smiled at Kevin and then said, "patience, young one, the stone you wear omits a power from it. Any good or bad wizard can feel the power it omits. There is a passage in the Pharynx that gives a clue to where something of importance is held with other things mentioned, but I cannot be sure it is the stones' whereabouts. Kevin stared at Merlin, then said in a shocked voice, "I have that book. Jarez gave it to me on our first meeting," Merlin smiled, "I know. I gave it to him to give it to you." "But why him," Kevin asked, "isn't he the split brother of Matrees? Surely, he would make a connection through it?" "not really," Merlin replied. Remember in the vision what Matrees said to me about his new brother, Jarez? he said that Jarez was his weakness, something he did not want to be associated with as it would affect his power. Therefore, the ideal person to give the book to look after, cunning hey", Merlin winked at Kevin, who smiled back. "I looked through the book a million times, but I can't find any clue within its writings. This is why I needed to find someone that has the gift of magic, and a logical mind for solving puzzles, You." "So, what is the clue about?" asked Kevin, "before he died, Postromus mentioned that somewhere in the book, he mentions a name of a place, and a significant point to the whereabouts of the stone, if it's there, I can't find it," Merlin replied. "Well, maybe I can help get these pieces of stone, so it will help you," Merlin nodded his head as if to say yes, "but," Merlin continued, "one thing is for sure, when and if you find the places of the stones, it will not be easy to get to them. Cederic was a wizard and did not want any dark art person getting hold of them, so I guess he would have put a spell or an extremely challenging task surrounding the piece to stop this. It may even be so strong that it may kill. I know I would if I was him." "Great," Kevin said," now you tell me, anything else you want to tell me, like there's going to be monsters and dead armies coming after me"? he said sarcastically. Merlin stared at Kevin, "this is not a telly vision show Kevin, it's very real." "Sorry," Kevin said, "so, what's the story with this time stone? Does it stop time or move me through time"?

"None of that, unfortunately," replied Merlin, "It's a piece of the Power stone that enhances your powers. It also lets you thought cast, so you need not speak, but your thoughts can be heard by the one you are conversing with, provided they know how to thought cast themselves, although it is pretty good for listening in on what others think, but beware, thought casting also can reveal your location to any dark art wizard who also possesses the magic. It also produces a shield to protect you against certain dark magic; it may not stop the full effect of the spell but will lessen its effects on you". Merlin led Kevin further along the path, "so what is the pendant that my brother Paul wears?, and where did he get his wand from"?, Kevin asked, "think," Merlin said, "you tell me, it was in the visions," Kevin thought as he walked, he could see the clearing before him that he saw in his vision, "Bartholomew," Kevin shouted, "it was here where he fought Crandloss trying to protect the unicorn but failed, I remember seeing you come from over there in the bushes casting a spell that seemed to bounce off Crandloss and," Kevin stopped there, Merlin walked over to a place where there was a small cross in the ground, written on it, were the words, 'here lies Bartholomew, a young, good friend of many, you shall be missed.'

Merlin bent down and held his head in his hands, "your right, I killed him," he said with a disheartened voice, "but it was an accident. I saw it. The spell bounced off Crandloss and hit Bartholomew. How?" Merlin stood, looked at Kevin, then turned quickly away, "I should have known he would use the dark shield. It all happened so quickly, I didn't have time to think, that is why Bartholomew died before his time", Merlin paced quickly over to Kevin and grabbed his arm, "no matter what, you must be able to think straight and in an instant, if you don't then one of your dear ones may end up this way, you have to be strong but patient, learn all you can as quickly as you can, do you hear me?", Kevin nodded, Merlin let go of Kevin's arm, "every day for the last five hundred years I have regretted the deaths of all those I called dear to me, wondering if there was something I could have done back then that might have ended this, but there was nothing, nothing at all, nothing at all," Merlin repeated as he walked away from the graveside and back onto the path.

Kevin followed behind him, just walking and looking around. As they walked further, Kevin could see the brook once more and caught up with Merlin, "so the pendant, you were going to tell me" Merlin lifted his finger then spoke, "the pendant is a very old druid healing stone, it will heal all minor and even some major illness, cuts grazes even bones, and I know what you are going to say next, but unfortunately for Bartholomew, I was wearing the time stone which enhanced the power of the spell, which also doubled in strength as it came away from Crandloss's shield, he had no chance of surviving that power, no one could," Merlin reached the oak tree at where Kevin met him earlier, and both sat down again. "I guess I'm going to be very tired tomorrow," "why," asked Merlin with a slight smile on his face, "well, I have been up all day and almost all night here with you. We must have walked miles and talked for ages," Kevin said. "Merlin laughed, "what's so funny"?, he asked, Merlin continued to laugh and slowly spoke, "you really need to use that brain of yours more, I thought you would have noticed a few more things by now", "like what?", Kevin asked with a rash reply, "think", Merlin answered," what happened when you met Jarez"?, Kevin thought back, and then started to speak, as he did so, he got up and walked around, "Well, when I met Jarez it seemed as though we were the only people there, especially the first time, there were no phones ringing, no peoples voices, nothing, just the two of us talking until he disappeared into Mr Peterson's office, the second time, again no noises, the corridor seemed to be never ending with no doors in it, and he caught me up very quickly", "so" Merlin said, "so I don't understand, was there a sort of time delay, or time stop"?, Merlin clapped his hands, "very good, you're getting there", he said, "but if that's so, then how did Godwill be able to move within the time frame"?, Kevin asked. Merlin beckoned Kevin to sit, which he did. "It's not a time frame, but a time envelope. It enables time to continue, but at a very reduced speed. For every hour that passes within it, normal time only passes one minute.

Because of its momentum, the only things that can move within it are those of magic nature, hence why Godwill could enter it". Kevin looked at Merlin and then nodded his head, "so what you're saying" Kevin said to Merlin, "although we have been talking for about eight hours, only eight minutes have actually gone where I am in bed"?, "that's correct," Merlin answered, "great, isn't it, it's brilliant for being able to slow everything down when you need to, and have a good thing, I use it regularly to help broaden my mind, you should try it also, mind you, don't use it when old Godwill is around, I don't think he would be so happy," he said as he winked at Kevin. "So how do I do it"? Kevin asked, "oh, it's a simple spell, it's in the book under time divination, you ought to look it up when you get back, try looking a few of the other spells up and practice them also, but, your brother is right, you need to keep your magic life away from the normal life that's why it's best to use the time divination spell first to slow things down before trying to set fire to something or doing something else that can be seen, ok"?, Kevin nodded in agreement, "Well, I hope I have answered some of your questions", Merlin said, "I guess we have chatted for a long while, I'm getting tired myself, but one last thing before you go, be assured that I am always watching over you and will be of help whenever and however I can, you have help there as well in your brother, Godwill and a few others, that you yet will meet, now it is time to leave", Kevin rose to his feet and helped Merlin get up also, "how do I get out of here"?, he asked, "just follow the path you came in on and it will lead you right back to your time", Kevin turned and thanked Merlin, "oh, one final thing", Merlin said, "make sure you and your brother are at the safe place tomorrow at four o'clock", "why"? Asked Kevin, Merlin scratched his nose, "it's a surprise," he said.

Kevin turned and followed the path he came in on, back through the village to the meadow and beyond. The next thing he knew was that he was waking up in his bed, he looked at the bedside table for the book, but it was not there. He then looked at his clock. Merlin was telling the truth. It had been only ten minutes that had passed from when he got into bed. He didn't know what to do. Does he grab his book out of the wardrobe and start looking through it for spells to learn, or leave things till tomorrow and see what is going to be at the safe place? His thoughts were interrupted by Paul's loud footsteps bounding up the stairs, ready to go to bed, "Paul," Kevin called out to his brother as he heard him get towards the top. With a burst of his door opening and his brother standing in the doorway saying, "what," Kevin beckoned him in and to close the door. "What"? repeated Paul as he shut the door, "what do you want now?" Kevin held his finger to his mouth and let out a quiet "shush" Paul looked at his brother and whispered, "what do you want"?, Kevin smiled at him then spoke, "I've been" "what do you mean you've been," replied Paul, Kevin smiling up at him nodding, "you mean you've been," Paul said again in a whispered voice, "but how?, you have only been up here ten minutes, Crickey, that was a quick visit, or did he get annoyed with your constant babble about not believing and turfed you out"?. "Not at all," Kevin replied, "we talked for ages, we walked, I saw his village, the place where Bartholomew died, the oak tree where he got his first wand." Paul interrupted, "what, all in ten minutes"? Kevin looked at Paul and smiled, "there is something called the time divination that slows time to nearly a standstill. Merlin told me it works on something like an hour within the time envelope is equal to a minute in real-time. That's what the Astral Plain works on. It also was the same when I met Jarez both times. Merlin reckons it's in his spell book". Paul looked at Kevin, then said, "you for real, bro, I hadn't heard of any time divination spell before," "well," Kevin said," only one way to find out."

Kevin got out of bed and undid the wardrobe door, got the book from under his clothes, and opened it. As the two boys flicked through it, looking at many spells written on different pages, they came a crossed it, 'Time divination,' it said at the very top of the page with an outline for its uses. "There it is," Kevin said. Paul looked at what it said. As he read down the page, everything seemed quite simple, especially the casting spell, but at the end, it read, 'only a strong, wilful, and talented wizard, witch or warlock can cast this spell. "ok," said Paul, "let's give it a go and see if you're telling the truth," "hang on" said Kevin, "what do you mean if I'm telling the truth, besides, it does state that the one casting the spell has to be strong, wilful, although I'm not sure what that means really, and also be a talented wizard, witch or warlock, can we say we are any of these things"?, "only one way to find out, and if it doesn't work then we can always ask Godwill about it tomorrow, ok?", Kevin nodded in agreement. "Ok," Paul said once more, "keep your eyes on that clock if what you have been told the second hand should almost come to a standstill" Kevin nodded as if to agree. "**Timearium Discourse Afentium**," Paul said with his arms held outwards. Kevin watched the clock. The second hand continued at the same rate, "well, maybe we are not all those things it says. We'll ask Godwill in the morning," he said as he stood up, ready to leave. "hang on, what about if I try"? Kevin blurted out, "you, how can you be all those things? You have only just come to terms with the fact that magic exists, don't make me laugh", Paul said sarcastically, "won't hurt for me to try it, would it"?

Kevin replied, "ok, go on then, prove that you're better than me," Paul said sarcastically again. Kevin focused his mind as Merlin had told him to when casting a spell, **"Timearium Discosure Afentium,"** he said. Paul watched the clock. The second hand continued to move at its normal rate, "there you are, see, I told you," Paul said this time very sarcastic, Kevin gave a little cough, "what," Paul enquired, Kevin's eyes moved towards the clock, the second hand was hardly moving, "it's probably the battery gone in it, that's all," Kevin looked at Paul then said, "well, only one way to find out, I'll go downstairs for a drink that way if it hasn't worked then mum, will be none the wiser will she"?. This time Paul nodded in agreement. Kevin opened his door to complete silence, no sound coming from the television downstairs, which they could usually hear. Kevin knew it had worked; it was just like when he had met Jarez.

Kevin ran downstairs to see what he could only describe as his mum sitting there like a zombie, unaware of what was taking place. "Paul," Kevin called, "you'd better come down here and look at this for yourself" Paul followed Kevin's lead and ran downstairs and into the sitting room. He walked over to his mum and waved his hand in front of her face, not a single movement with any part of her body or eyes. "Crickey," Paul said, "it's true, but how"? Kevin explained to Paul what Merlin had told him and especially that only magic people could move about the time frame whilst the spell was cast; as they sat there, Kevin told Paul all about what had gone on in the Astral Plain, all about Merlin showing Kevin his life story and about the items both he and his brother had, where they came from and who they came from. Paul already knew what his pendant was and a little about it as Godwill had explained bits of it to him all those years ago but did not know from who it was handed down. As the boys talked, Paul was asking questions of his own that sometimes Kevin could answer and some he could not, but both knew now why this was happening and what the possible outcomes could be. After a good what seemed two to three hours of the boys talking, they decided to call it a night.

"So," Paul said, "did he tell you how to end this time spell"?, Kevin tried to remember if Merlin had said anything about it but couldn't remember him saying so, "Not really," Kevin replied, "not really, then how on earth are we going to undo this spell oh masterful one," Paul said sarcastically, but also a bit scared, "let's check the book, there must be something in there to do it, don't you think," Kevin said hesitantly, both boys raced upstairs and flicked through the book one more. Finally, they came to a page with the heading stating, 'Cancelling spell' "well, go on," said Paul, "you started this, so you must be the one to finish it, I guess." Kevin again concentrated, then said, **"Evreko,"** once Kevin had chanted the cancelling spell, both boys watched the clock slowly. The second hand moved one second, then another, and another. Finally, the clock was working as before they had cast the spell. They could also hear the noise from the television. "Phew," Paul said, "I think you need to practice and remember a lot of those spells in that book, bro. Well, times are back to normal, and I'm up with the birds to do my paper round, so I think I've had all the excitement for one night. I'll see you tomorrow", Paul was just about to leave Kevin's room when Kevin called him back, "oh, one last thing, Paul, We both have to be at the safe place tomorrow at four"c "what for," asked Paul, "don't know," Kevin said," Merlin just told me to tell you, apparently there is going to be a surprise there for us, so don't be late," Paul stuck his thumb up as if to acknowledge that he would be there. Kevin closed the book and put it back in the wardrobe. He then climbed into his bed, turned off his light, and closed his eyes.

Chapter 5

Now to Learn

The very next morning, Kevin awoke feeling particularly good about himself; as he lay in his bed, he now believed not just in himself but that magic was real and that he was a wizard. To prove this to himself, he held out his hand and wished for a bar of chocolate, and in just a murmur of a second, there it was in his hand. He chuckled to himself, took a big bite of it, and sat back with a satisfying look on his face. As he ate the chocolate bar, all sorts of things were running through his head. How he could stop bullying in the playground, get robbers caught in the act and held so police can catch them, and how he could do good for his family. All sorts of things roamed through his head until a thought shot back in there. It was both Merlin and Paul, both talking at the same time. "You must now learn to keep your magic life separate from your normal one," he heard them say. The satisfying look slowly disappeared from his face, "what good are magic powers if you can't use them to help those you care about," he thought to himself. With that thought, the wardrobe door opened, and the book floated out onto his lap; it opened at the blank page that had been his guide to Merlin.

Kevin looked at the page, and writing appeared, 'Morning young Kevin, I feel you have a problem about what you can do and can't do regarding your gift' the writing disappeared, "Yes," Kevin said, "I know that I must keep them secret, but what if there are times that I could use my gift to help someone, even save their lives?, am I to sit back and just watch what goes on, even if they lose their lives"?. Writing appeared once more, 'unfortunately, my answer has to be yes, for if you are caught producing magic within sight of normal people, what do you think will happen'? Kevin thought for a moment, then answered, 'that I was a bit weird"? The writing continued, 'not weird, as you say, but a danger, as people have thought of us down throughout the ages. You would be someone that everyone would fear, and those that were not scared would want to get you to help them with evil doings. To accomplish this, they may hold your family to ransom, threatening to kill them if you do not do as they ask. I have seen all this through my years, so to ask a question of you, would you use your gift in full sight of others now, knowing you could be helping one person but putting your whole family in jeopardy because of it? Kevin understood what Merlin had said; he was just a little deflated by knowing that he had a wonderful gift but could not use it.

Writing appeared on the page once more, 'you need to get your mind into a clear-thinking mood and keep it there. I shall say this once more then you will have to work things out for yourself, as I do not intend to keep informing you of the rights and wrongs of magical use. What is the one thing you have in your hands that can help people by using magic but not getting caught by normal folk'? Kevin started to think, "I don't know, I guess it could be" he stopped in mid-sentence and then blurted out, "the time envelope, of course, time slows down to nearly a standstill; therefore, I could move people out of the way of dangerous things, thus helping them without being seen using magic." The page stayed bear for a second, then writing appeared once more, 'exactly' it said, 'but, remember, magic people can move within the time frame also, so although you were doing some normal folk good, it could also give away where you are, this would not be good in the event of an evil wizard like Matrees, so I caution you not to use it for long times of periods and not on a regular basis, now you must begin your learning, go to Godwill, he will gladly help you on your journey, watch, listen and learn quickly, Kevin, time is not our friend, I will always be here should you need my help,' with that the page went blank, and the book closed.

Kevin heard mums footsteps coming up the stairs, so he hid the book under his bedclothes. The door burst open, with mum was standing there, "did you say something, Kevin? are you alright?" Kevin looked at his mum and smiled, "of course, I'm alright, mum," he replied, "I thought I heard you talking or calling, that's all, dear," Kevin thought quickly, "oh, I was just singing to myself, that's all mum." "you, singing, in the morning, you must be ill," mum laughed, "can't be that you're looking forward to school, so what's the story?" she asked, "oh, I don't know, perhaps I have learned that it's no use hating something that isn't going to change, so, you might as well just go with the flow," he replied, "Crikey, that's a bit deep for you in the morning, still, as long as you stay out of trouble, who am I to question your moods?". Mum gave a hearty laugh and then turned to go out of the door, "come on then, lazy bones, out of that bed and get ready for school; breakfast will be waiting," she closed the door and went back downstairs. Kevin got out of bed, put the book back into the wardrobe, dressed, and then ran downstairs for his breakfast. After peddling to school, he was met by his friend Vinnie, "I heard you had a mental game Sunday," he said, "well it wasn't bad for my first," Kevin replied, "not bad," Vinnie replied, "I heard you scored twice, saved a penalty and set the winner up, that's bloody good in my reckoning," he said with a smile. "Well, let's just say I had a bit of help in the matter," Kevin said, "with the rest of the team, I mean," he said quickly. Vinnie just nodded, "come on, let's get in there for another day of boredom," Kevin said to Vinnie as both boys walked down the chase and into school.

The day seemed to go very quickly until it came to lunch, possibly because Kevin liked the morning subjects he was taking, but as lunch finished and the afternoon bell rang, Kevin was walking down the corridor towards his next lesson when he noticed that he was getting nowhere, and there was no noise. He stopped and turned, he already knew that it was going to be Jarez standing there, "Hello young wizard", he said, Kevin looked at Jarez then answered, "Hello Jarez, what can I do for you"?, "Oh, so you know my name now", he said, "your name, how you come to be, and your brother, the only thing I'm not sure of is what your purpose is being here?", Kevin replied, "oh, it's a simple one", he said, "it's to keep watch over you whilst you are here, as you know Merlin watches over you most of the time, but even wizards need sleep", he said, "so", Kevin said, "apart from watching over me, what else do you do", "Well, I'm also here for you to ask questions and give advice to, whether you follow the answers that I give is your choosing, but Merlin has instructed me to help in any capacity that I can, so wizard, do you have a question for Jarez?". Kevin thought for a second then asked, "when you and your brother were together as Crandloss, why or what made him go into a split personality forming two other beings?" "Good question," Jarez said, "Well, Crandloss was being held back from obtaining ultimate power by his good side" Kevin looked at Jarez and pointed to him; Jarez nodded, then continued, "to be able to gain more power than any other wizard he had to find a way of disposing this side from his soul, there was only one way to complete this thing, he had to

71

kill. Killing rips your soul apart and drives you to the dark side. The other thing was to kill the unicorns and drink their magical silver blood." Kevin butted in, "by drinking the unicorn's blood, it enhances your life span, so he would have longer than normal to complete this" "Yes," said Jarez, " whether you drink a lot of the blood or just a few drops, still, will give you the desired effect and length of time, But, to drink a lot also turns your soul black," "how," asked Kevin, "I saw Merlin taste a few drops, and he is ok, isn't he?", "Merlin's fine, "replied Jarez, "but as Crandloss had already killed the unicorn in question, then drank its blood, it turned good to evil. Crandloss knew this, and that is what he did, and you know the rest." Kevin turned away from Jarez and then said, "if you are his weakness, then what good are you to me?" Kevin asked. "Oh, I am very useful to you, young wizard; I have knowledge of Crandloss that I carry within me, knowledge of weaknesses he still has, although he is not yet aware of, I can be of great assistance to you when the time comes." As Kevin was just going to ask what assistance he needed, time resumed to its usual time frame; Jarez had gone, and the clock continued to tick that was on the wall. Kevin ran off to his next class.

The day continued just as it had in the morning, with classes rushing by; after registration, Kevin was on his way to his bike when he was met by Mr. Robertson, the school's PE teacher. "Great game, young Wilks," he said, "thanks, sir," Kevin replied, "think you can keep that up all season, or was it just a lucky game," he asked. "Well," Kevin replied, "I certainly am going to try and continue with my form, so, no, I don't think it was a lucky game, sir; just watch this space," Kevin said with a smile, "oh I will, and if you do continue to get even better, then there will definitely be a space for you on the school side, that's for sure," Mr. Robertson said as he walked off. Kevin now turned his attention to getting down to the spinney. He wondered if his brother would have remembered. As Kevin got close, he could see his brother's bike already there. Kevin ran over to the safe place and into the room after revealing it. His brother was standing there with a look of bewilderment on his face, "what's up with you," Kevin asked. Paul moved away from where he was standing. There behind him was a bird perch with an egg sitting in the middle of the bottom shelf, "a bird's egg, what on earth do we need a bird's egg for" asked Kevin, "I guess Merlin thinks we need a pet for some reason," Paul explained. "So, we have to come down here every day to feed it when it hatches," Kevin said, "guess so," Paul replied, "what good will that teach us," Kevin asked, a little disheartened. Paul just shrugged his shoulders as if to say he didn't know. The clock on the wall started to chime at four o'clock, and as the last chime was heard, movement from the egg started to happen; eventually, after a struggle, the egg top broke, and out of it, a small head appeared, then the body. Kevin looked at it, then at his brother.

"What an ugly-looking bird," he said, "oh, I don't know," both brothers heard a voice come from behind them. It was Godwill; he had quietly let himself in without the boys noticing. "Give it time to grow up; you'll change your mind then," he said. Kevin turned to Godwill and asked, "but Sir, whatever is it, what type of bird is it, an owl, a hawk, what?" Godwill laughed, "you have much to learn young Wilks", he said, "No, this is no hawk, or owl, it's a phoenix", the boys looked at each other, "a phoenix", both said together, Godwill nodded, "but sir, they were a myth, weren't they?", asked Kevin. "what, like magic was until you knew the truth, no, they were and are very real, they are one magical creature that has survived the ages, not many left in existence, but are a most beautiful and wondrous bird, they have special abilities also", he continued, "just one tear from the phoenix can cure poisons and heal cuts and abrasions, it can carry immense weights even though it is not a very big bird itself, also they are very loyal and would give their lives up to save the one that the bird belongs to, so you see, Merlin has given you this for a reason, not just to prove how to look after something". The boys again looked at each other, "so how do we feed it or what do we do to look after it?" Godwill laughed, "why not look it up in your book from Merlin Kevin, there is bound to be information in there, along with other things you need to look at". "that's right, Merlin told me when we were in the Astral Plain, that I need to start my learning, and that you would help me learn", Godwill looked at Kevin, "you have been to the Astral Plain?", Kevin nodded, Paul also, "you also Paul?", "No," replied Paul, "just Kevin, perhaps you need to tell Godwill what happened there, and maybe he can also help," Kevin agreed, "but first," he said, "Timearium Discosure Afentium" Time was put into very slow existence, "Well, we don't want mum getting on at us for being home late," "very impressive," Godwill said, "now, tell me, the Astral Plain, tell me everything." All three sat down whilst Kevin told Godwill and Paul every detail of what happened. Even though Paul had heard it before, he explained what was said between him and Merlin, occasionally glancing over to the phoenix to ensure it was alright.

When Kevin had finished, Godwill got up, "so, that is why Jarez and Matrees are among us once again. They search for the Power stone to gain immortality". Kevin butted in, "well, Matrees anyway, not Jarez, he is the good of Crandloss, why would he want this? Besides, it was him that Merlin chose to give the book to, so he could give it to me". Godwill stroked his beard, "there is much for both of you to learn; you will need to learn in stages; from each set you learn, more will become clearer. For now, I suggest we meet here at least once a week, if not more, and work on your lessons in the art of magic. Matrees would not be here if he did not know something of the whereabouts of one of the artifacts you have just mentioned, and he, as we all know, is a wizard of dark art. Therefore we must train you in the art of repelling evil spells and protecting each other. We start tomorrow after school," Godwill then walked out of the safe room casting the cancelling spell. All time returned to its present, and then he walked away. "Well, we had better get home and find out what this little fellow needs to survive on," Kevin said to Paul, Paul nodded in agreement and off they went home.

Once home, both boys hardly said a word to their mum but decided to go upstairs into Paul's room and look through the books they had. As they looked, Paul came a crossed the section regarding the life and feeding of a phoenix; both boys read what it said was needed for the phoenix to survive. Also, there were a few tips on how to get the bird to like its owner. "Well, that shouldn't be too hard," Kevin said, "all we got to do now is work a roster out when we will do it" "Oh no," Paul said, "the phoenix is a one-person bird, Merlin told you about it's coming, so you're the one who needs to look after it." Kevin was not best pleased, but he knew his brother was right, and who knows, the two of them may become remarkably close, he thought. "Paul looked at Kevin then asked, "so, you going to knuckle down now bro and get some serious learning and practicing done, I can help you to, we can go to the safe place and you can do your time stopping bit and we can practice till our hearts content until we get really good at this stuff, what you say?". Kevin turned to Paul and replied, "we have to be careful using the time spell, Merlin warned me, although it is a neat thing, it also could give away our location, so we will only use it in short bursts and in a different location each time, is that clear?", Paul scrunched his nose up then replied, "ok, if you say so", Kevin got up to leave his brothers bedroom, but before he could his brother called out, "so what now?", he asked. "now dear brother", Kevin began to say, "I need a little more information regarding a few things from Merlin", "why not ask them here, with me, or is it secret?", Paul asked, "no, not really, but we have to be careful in case mum gets suspicious, after all, it was only a short while ago we were fighting like cat and dog, now look at us, hardly out of each other's pockets, to change that quickly in such a short time, I think I would be suspicious to wouldn't you?".

Paul looked at his brother and then nodded, "I suppose your right, but you will tell me when you find out whatever you're going to ask Merlin, won't you?" Kevin smiled at his brother, "don't I always, bro!". With that, Kevin took his book into his bedroom and sat on his bed. Just as he was about to open it, he heard his mum coming upstairs. Quickly he hid it under his bedclothes, "and what are you two doing up here so early? not had a falling out, I hope?" she said to Kevin, "no mum, I just came up here to read and get a better knowledge of the classes we had today, you know, try and make sense out of them," Kevin replied. His mum put her hands on her face which had a worried look on it, "so who have you challenged and upset now Kevin, that logic mind of yours will get you in deep trouble someday", she asked, "honestly mum", Kevin said," I have upset no-one, and I don't intend to, I just need to understand the things they teach us, you know that, and believe me, I think I am getting to do that without upsetting anybody". "you're not lying to me Kevin are you, because I will soon hear about it if you do, the teachers know me at the school and will make a beeline straight to me if something's going on", she asked with a quizzical tone, "have they been to you lately regarding my attitude or anything else?", Kevin asked, "Well no, guess not", she said looking thoughtful this time, "no, and there not going to", he replied," I've changed mum, I realise now that something's are what they are, perhaps I need to reassess my logic at how I look at things, also I need to think before opening my big mouth and put my foot in", Kevin's mum looked now at him with a loving face, "well", she said, "it's been a long and painful journey to get here, I just hope it lasts that's all", Kevin smiled at his mum, "I don't know if the journeys over yet mum, I still have five years to work on, but I promise, I will try", his mum just smiled back at him, "that's all I can ask of you son", after saying this she closed his door and went downstairs.

Kevin retrieved the book from under the bedclothes, opened it at the blank page, and then asked, "Merlin, tell me about Crandloss." The page was blank for a while, and then the writing appeared; it read, 'why do you want to know about Crandloss? You have seen what he is about in the vision,' the writing disappeared. "I know what you showed me, but I need to know more, where he came from, his family, and how he grew up," Kevin asked, 'of what use will this be to you,' the book spelled out. "Logic states," Kevin began, "to understand someone, is to need to know of their existence, by knowing if he had a happy or sad childhood, then that would determine his mood. If he got on well with other people and had friends and people he talked to, it all goes to give a clear understanding of that person and their mentality. With this knowledge, I could be one step in front of Matrees. You were once a friend of Crandloss, so please, tell me, you did promise to help if you could; here is your chance," Kevin replied. The page stayed blank again for a while longer, then burst into paragraphs. 'Crandloss was the son of a witch and a potions master, much the same as I was. He always had a relevant, content home life, especially with his mother, Teresa. She was a particularly good student and turned into a successful, powerful witch, whilst his father, Tolomas, took to the art of potion making; he also became well known within that field. Although Crandloss was more sided towards his mother, he was still a happy boy in his father's company. Then one day, after Mr. Wilfred had been teaching us, A wizard by the name of Veraticus was passing by and took a shine to Crandloss's mother. Tolomas tried to warn the wizard but to no avail. Well, things got ugly, and a fight began, but Tolomas was killed, and his mother was taken from Crandloss by Veraticus. In a small village, you soon get to know everyone, and everyone becomes friends. We lay Tolomas to rest in a grave near the back of their house, but as the service went on, I heard Crandloss utter a promise that never can be broken, the promise of revenge. I alone heard it, and he knew I heard it; he turned his head quickly towards me and smiled, smiled as though all his problems had just disappeared".

"Over the next few years, he stayed with Master Wilfred, learning different spells and potions just as I did, and I would like to think we became good friends, which seemed the case until that fateful day when he turned his back on his kin, and handed them on a plate to Jarone and his men. The rest, you know.' Kevin pondered at what he had read, then continued, "There is still more to know and understand, like, did he have a first name, I have only known him as Crandloss, and did he go in search for this wizard and his mother, what happened there." The page lit up with writing as soon as Kevin had finished speaking; Kevin read what it said, 'Why do you need to know this, Kevin? I see no point in it. How will this help you understand the person he was and what he intends to do?' Kevin just replied, "you asked me to use my mind. When I do you question it, I am here to try and help you gain these artifacts. Matrees also seeks them; he was once Crandloss, so I need to understand everything about his life, what drives him, and what possibilities are his weaknesses, now will you help me understand this, or do I have to do this on my own?", The page once again bare, started to fill up with writing. His first name was Ardrano, but most people called him Crandloss. As to did he go in search of his mother and this other wizard called Veraticus, well, the answer is yes, but not alone. Bartholomew and I helped search for them; that is why it is so painful to speak of this. Both Crandloss and I were of the same age, but poor Bartholomew was a little younger and less experienced, but he wanted to help his friend, or what we believed to be a friend. Unfortunately, we did not find either of the two in question, and after searching for half a year, Bartholomew and I gave up and returned to the village, but Crandloss continued his search. As to whether he found them, I don't know, I heard stories that he had and fought the wizard, other stories that he never saw his mother again, but one thing was for sure, on his journey, something happened to turn his soul black. There were stories circulating that he had fought other wizards and gained their powers, also that he had been killing unicorns, Griffins, and Dragons to also gain the magical power of each beast. Now answer me, Kevin, what help has this given to you opening my heart to devastation on this person?'. Kevin got up and walked around for a bit, then answered.

"Well, before I tell you what I think, there is one last question I have to ask, do you have any knowledge of this wizard Veraticus?" writing appeared once more, 'only stories that cannot be verified,' "well, you know me by now, and what I needed to be verified Merlin, but that all went out of the window when all this happened, didn't it?", Kevin said, the writing appeared again, ' Stories say he came from the North, a powerful wizard with no goals in his life, only to seek power and glory, what he wanted he took, no matter what the consequence, he had no friends, family, or people who cared for him, that was his way, he was a user, one who gained power through good, evil or by deception, no person that I spoke to throughout the ages can remember this wizard, there is nothing written down of what was said to have happened to Crandloss's family, only hearsay. So, you see, Kevin, this is just another story, a waste of time, but you asked, and I have delivered. Now, tell me of your thoughts.' Kevin sat back on the bed, "Well," he said, "in my mind, Crandloss is definitely in search of the artifacts of the Power stone. Is it to be more powerful than you? Maybe, but I think there is a second thing behind this. I believe that he has a certain amount of knowledge about Veraticus and his mother. I think that somehow, he believes they are still with us even now in this time and age, which is why he needs the artifacts to help sustain the time to find them. Yes, he killed many people and magical beings, if what you said is true, to gain more power and knowledge of certain things, things he believes can help in his search. He promised revenge for his father's death which you heard, and on your search for this wizard, you and Bartholomew turned back after a time to Crandloss. This was a betrayal, one that needed to be addressed. That is why he led Jarone's men to camp, had your parents killed, and then set about revenge on Bartholomew, which he did by having him killed using the dark shield you knew nothing about. The trouble is, he never actually killed Bartholomew. It was the deflection from your spell that did it. Crandloss still had a grievance against you, so he killed unicorns, griffins, and dragons, one more takeaway of power from good to evil. He had not contemplated on you learning as quickly as you did or the things master Wilfred had taught you. Therefore, he was powerless against you in the two fights you showed me in the visions. There is a slight doubt in my mind that now lingers; you say these were only stories of the happenings of Crandloss's family, what happens if they are true, and that this Veraticus managed to do the same as both you and Crandloss and taste the blood of the unicorn. This would mean that they actually still exist, and somehow Crandloss has stumbled upon this, and that's why he needs the artifacts to help find them before it is too late", there Kevin went silent.

The writing in the book reappeared, 'my, for one so young with an old and wise head upon his shoulders, you have given me a lot to think about, for that, I thank you, what you have just said may just be true, but we need to be on our guard, if Matrees makes the connection that you are in possession of the first piece of the Power stone, he will stop at nothing to get his hands on it. You must learn quickly, Kevin, go to Godwill and start your learning. It may just save your life and others associated with you. I will be in contact when I have deliberated what you have said and the page goes bare once more. Kevin spoke again, "wait, one more thing" the page returned writing, 'what is it?', "We also have to think that there may be a second party also with us, looking for those artifacts also, Veraticus. If what I think could be true, then we must take this knowledge into consideration". The writing appeared again, 'you are correct, although our main concentration must be on Matrees, we know he is here, now, Veraticus is at present a story and thought only, I will tend my books and see if I have missed anything regarding this person, thank you, Kevin, I feel for the first time throughout my life, that my quest has gained a true and talented wizard to share my journey with,' the page went bare, and all had been said for that particular time, although Kevin's thoughts now turned to this wizard Veraticus. In one swoop, the danger had intensified from one to two. Merlin was right. Kevin needed help from his brother and Godwill if he was to be ready should any confrontation come. Kevin decided that he had better let Paul know exactly what had gone on and what was said, but he knew it was annoying to be told things twice. Therefore he decided to let Paul know that he needed to talk to both Godwill and him together tomorrow after school, which is what he did.

Chapter 6

Potions and Football

That night was quite peaceful, with no visions and no thoughts. Kevin just had a decent night's sleep which he had not really had since this whole thing started. As morning came, he was woken up by his mum calling him to get ready for school as it was getting late. Kevin leapt out of bed, got dressed, and raced downstairs, "why didn't you wake me earlier, mum?" he asked, "well, it won't do you no harm having the occasional late sleep. Besides, your brain needs a bit of relaxation. I heard you calling out some names in the night; who's Crandloss and Veraticus, people you studying in History?" Kevin looked at his mum then said, "yes, that's right, just two olden time people in the medieval age, why have you heard of them?", mum thought for a while then replied, "nope, can't say I do, but we were taught different things to what they are now, so it's no good asking me my dear," Kevin heaved a sigh of relief, "oh well," he said, "they're not very well known anyway, just learning about woodwork and metalworking in that age," his mum looked at him and said, "nice," then quickly did him some toast before he left for school.

That day at school was just like any other, lessons that he wasn't really interested in, but he had to do and take note of what was being said. All through the day, Kevin concentrated on his classes waiting for the bell to go at the end of the day. Finally, it came, and he met up with his brother in front of Godwills class. Both boys eased through the door after knocking on it. Godwill stood looking out the window, "come in, boys, I have been expecting you," he boomed in his loud voice.

"So, what can I do for you today?" he asked. Kevin walked over to him and then said, "there have been more developments that I need to verify," Godwill turned to look at him, "oh yes," he replied, "please, tell me." Kevin Paul and Godwill sat around the teacher's desk. Just as Kevin started talking, Godwill held his hand up and cast the time spell, "you never know when you may be interrupted. It is best this way. Now continue! he said. Kevin told Godwill what had been discussed with Merlin and about the possibility that there could be that second party also searching for the artifacts. After Kevin finished, he asked Godwill if he knew about Veraticus, "can't say I know anything regarding this person, and if, as Merlin has stated that it may be just a story, then there may be nothing on this subject anyway." Kevin asked, "but you hold books, books throughout the years. Could you not check to see if anything is mentioned? Any information on this wizard will help" "well, I guess I could, but it won't be an easy task. There are hundreds of books I hold regarding different things that have happened or spells made throughout the years, I will look, but we also need to start your learning, young wizards" Paul looked at Godwill, "what do you mean wizards," he asked, " where do I come into this equation, I have already gone through the learning stage," "true," Godwill said, "but there is still much for you to learn, I feel there will be a major part on this journey that you will play a part in, so to teach you both from the beginning and get you to practice together would be the best thing, besides Paul, it will give you a chance to help your brother when I'm not with you both, do you not agree?", Paul agreed but with a certain grudge in his attitude. "Right, I'm free after school every Wednesday and

Friday, so I suggest we meet at the safe house on Wednesday and get down to tricks," Godwill said with a smile, "get it, tricks," he said, both boys looked at each other then back at goodwill and gave a sarcastic smile back towards him. "Right, I suggest you look at the books you got in the potions section. We will start with them on Wednesday," Godwill said, then cast the canceling spell, "now, off you go. I have some research to do," with that, both boys left the class and went home.

That night both boys studied their books regarding potions together in Paul's bedroom, "so what good are potions" Kevin asked his brother, "well, I haven't had much teaching in the preparation or use, but each potion has a use, don't ask me what, as I don't know, but, they're used for something," Paul replied. As they looked through their books, they saw recipes for potions regarding love, hallucinations, poisons, enchanting, and a few others. After a good two hours of studying the ingredients and uses, Kevin closed his book, "enough is enough for now," he said, "perhaps being taught by someone that can explain the uses may help, rather than looking at some words in a book." Paul looked at Kevin, then smiled, "your attention span was always weak; you never take the time to study what you are supposed to, you may have a logic mind, but you need to be able to lengthen that attention span," Kevin replied sarcastically, "really, we'll see when we both get learning how each of us picks things up, and who needs that extra help and who doesn't. Mind you, you have had a start on me already, but I will soon catch you up and overtake you". Paul just laughed, "Really, it's not as easy as you think to learn this stuff correctly. There is a lot of willpower required, and reading, lots of reading, and I look forward to the challenge."

Kevin picked up his book and then went off into his bedroom; as he put his book back that he got from Merlin, he remembered the book first given to him by Jarez. He ran downstairs and got the bag that he had taken to school, there in the bottom sat the book. He took it out and ran back upstairs to his bedroom. As he sat on his bed, he remembered what his brother had told him on the way to read it. He turned it over, moved it upside down, and then started to flick through it. Kevin read everything that was in that book twice; he leaned back, trying to remember what Merlin had said regarding the clue to the next artifact. "a sentence with a place name and a significant point, all within it," repeatedly he went through the book, the only mention of a place was Nottingham, Sherwood Forrest, nowhere else could he see anything mentioned apart from a small phrase later in the book regarding the place of a berry called the lassingro berry. It is supposed to be used for healing certain kinds of poisoning. According to the phrase, it is supposed to be in the North West of the forest under a waterfall, but Kevin didn't really take any notice of this. After all, he had just been looking at berries used in potions, and he was not really paying any attention to it. Kevin put the book away. This time he put this book under his bed where his old toys were, out of sight of his parents.

That night, Kevin's mind passed between thoughts of Crandloss, Matrees, Veraticus, and Sherwood Forest. He tossed and turned but could not get them out of his mind. Eventually, he decided he needed to find some answers, or he would never get to sleep. Kevin focused his mind and cast the time spell. Time slowed; Kevin got out of bed and ran into Paul's bedroom, "wake up, Paul," he called. Paul sleepily rubbed his eyes, "what is it," he said wearily, "can't sleep," Kevin said, "what, are you mad? It's", there Paul stopped speaking, then, "you've controlled time again haven't you," he said staring at his clock, "I thought you said we have to be careful using that," Kevin shrugged his shoulders, "I know," he said, "but something's bothering me," "what, what's bothering you," Paul said and plunged his head under his covers, Kevin pulled the covers back, "I can't get Crandloss, Veraticus, and Matrees out of my mind, and I have gone through Flamels book to see if I could find out about the second artifact," "and," his brother said, "Well, there is a mention of Nottingham and Sherwood Forrest, but that's all," "so," Paul said, "have you informed Merlin of this?", "Well," Kevin said," no, it's rather late to be waking a supreme wizard don't you think?", "oh, but its ok to wake me, look either tell Merlin now, or wait till tomorrow, is anything likely to change overnight?", he asked, "I don't think so", replied Kevin, "then leave it till tomorrow", Paul said, "and regarding Crandloss, Veraticus and Matrees, well you already have Merlin and Godwill looking into Veraticus, perhaps you should also ask Jarez to as well", he smiled, "we both know what happened to Crandloss, so I wouldn't worry about him, and Matrees, have you seen hide or hare of him lately in the Park?", Kevin shook his head, "well then, I shouldn't worry over him either until we know what's he up to, now return time and go to bed and sleep, please", Kevin looked at his brother then said, "suppose your right, I guess my mind is just occupied by so many things, sorry", Paul pulled his covers up to his chest as Kevin left his bedroom, "its ok", he called, "I was just like you, your minds going to go into overdrive and you will get a few nights like this, you just have to learn to shut it off until its needed. It will come in time and with training. Now close the door, put time back to normal, and I will see you tomorrow, ok?" Kevin raised his hand to say ok, then closed the door, went back to his bedroom, got in bed, then canceled the time spell. He closed his eyes and drifted off to sleep.

Kevin woke on Wednesday morning already thinking about the after-school learning with Godwill. He was extremely excited and just couldn't wait. He got up, dressed, and ran down to get his breakfast. Mum stood at the kitchen door, still in her dressing gown. "Well, I don't know," she said, looking puzzled, "one day, I have to get you up as you are sleeping late. The next, you're up with the lark. I just don't understand you." Kevin looked at the clock; it was just a few minutes past six in the morning. Paul had not yet gone on his paper round, "oh well, I must have had enough sleep, or I wouldn't want to get up, would I?" he said. Mum just looked at him and shook her head, "Well, I guess you can get your own breakfast today. I'm going to get a shower", and off she went. As Kevin got his toast, Paul came downstairs, ready to get off on his morning job, "morning bro, you're up early, or have you been to sleep" he asked, "oh, I went to sleep alright, quite a good one in fact, just woke early, why, is there a problem?", Kevin replied, "no, not at all, just not used to seeing you out of your bed this time of the morning." Kevin was just buttering his toast when his brother snatched it out of his hand and ran out the door shouting, "thanks, bro," laughing as he went, Kevin put more toast on for him. That day at school flew by again until just after the lunch bell had gone, Kevin was walking down the corridor towards the Geography class when he noticed once more no exit doors getting closer, no classrooms getting closer. He stopped and then said, "hello, Jarez," He said, "good day, wizard," he replied, "I have reason to believe that you are troubled, is there something I can possibly do for you?" Kevin turned and looked at Jarez, "yes," replied Kevin, "tell about Veraticus," Jarez took a step back, "why do you wish to know about this man" he said with a quiver in his voice, "Merlin mentioned him and what had happened to Crandloss's family, now tell me, is, or was, he real, or just a story?". Jarez looked straight into Kevin's eyes, then replied, "again I ask, why do you need to know, young wizard?" Kevin stepped towards Jarez, "you have answered part of my question with the way you looked at me, so Veraticus was real," Jarez lowered his eyes then spoke softly, "yes, Veraticus was and is a real person, he is part of the problem that caused my existence."

Kevin looked at Jarez and could see he was emotionally distressed, "sorry to ask," he said, "but perhaps you can explain a little further," Jarez sank to the floor, sitting crossed-legged, "so, what do you need to know," he asked. "Well," Kevin said, "you said Veraticus is responsible for your existence. Tell me more" "Crandloss, Bartholomew, and Merlin searched for this man who killed our father and took our mother," Jarez started; Kevin butted in, "I know of this, and I know Merlin and Bartholomew returned after a long search with no findings," "true, but Crandloss continued his search, he was so intent on finding this man and reaping revenge over our father's death that he changed. He changed so much that every man or beast that he came crossed could not help him on his quest; he killed. Magical people, magical beasts, stealing their powers as he went, gaining knowledge and power, until one day, he caught up with Veraticus. Crandloss was seething with grief. Still, his only thought was that of killing this person or being killed in the process; it did not matter either way to him" "so what happened" Kevin asked, "Crandloss challenged him to a duel. Of course, his mother, Caulpolsier, was there, and she pleaded with Crandloss telling him that she had planned to leave his father as she loved him no more; she loved Veraticus. Crandloss would not listen to her. He claimed Veraticus had enchanted her with potions or a spell." "Then what?" Kevin asked, "Then they dueled, spells cast backward and forwards, neither gaining ground on the other until," Jarez stopped there, "until what?".

Kevin asked again; Jarez rose to his feet and gently hugged an iron pillow that was next to him, "until mother joined in on Veraticus's side, the power of both was just too much. They cast the lightning spell together, and it hit Crandloss full on; even though he had cast the evil shield he had learned, the power still got through and caused him serious harm, almost life-threatening. But they nursed him back to health and took him under their wing. There they taught him the dark art of black magic, evil, strong, and exceedingly difficult to repel. He stayed with them for a while, being taught about the life-enhancing unicorn blood and the inner power it gives you in a dark way. They had taken to the dark side and enjoyed that evil sensation; it was Veraticus that turned Crandloss against all good magic beasts and men that possess it. That is why Crandloss killed Bartholomew and had Postromus killed by Jarones' men. He thought that if Merlin were alone, then he would not be so strong." Kevin put a hand on Jarez's shoulder and then spoke again, "but why does he want to kill Merlin? Is it because he uses magic for good?" partly," Jarez said, "but it is also because Merlin and Bartholomew gave up the search for his mother, along with Veraticus turning him even eviler against good, and lastly, he knows that Merlin holds the first piece of the Flamel stone, the power stone that will give either his mother, Veraticus, or him, eternal life." Kevin looked down towards the ground in thought then said, "but Jarez, how, his soul has split into two different beings, you, and Matrees, how is this possible?", Jarez turned and stood toe to toe with Kevin, "enough, I have told you what you need to know, now I must be off," with that Jarez disappeared and time returned to normal.

Kevin continued to his class, and the rest of the afternoon was uneventful. Now he looked forward to the end of the day and starting his learning regarding magic. As the bell went after registration, Kevin made his way to the safe place in the spinney; Paul was already there talking to the phoenix. As Kevin entered the room, Paul turned to him and said, "so what are we going to call this little fellow" Kevin shrugged his shoulders before answering, "what about fireball" the phoenix gave a little twitter, "it seems to like it," came a voice behind Kevin, it was Godwill, "ok, fireball it is then," Paul said with a smile. "Right, let us get down to work, shall we, gentlemen," boomed Godwill. Both boys took up seats around a table that was there, "no, not over there, over here," Godwill said, pointing to a bench with different items on it. There were mortal and pestles, berries, small bottles of different plants in them, and some with what looked like disgusting stuff in them to the boys. "What about the time spell? Are we not using that?" asked Kevin, "why do you want to use that? you can't keep using it to gain momentum all the time", replied Godwill, "but mum will get suspicious if we are late and there is also football training tonight," replied Kevin, "you must get your priorities in order to be able to study this and take it all in," Godwill said, not at all happy.

"Very well, just for today, we will use it, but I suggest we meet on a Friday night instead of Wednesday, and you work out a story to tell your parents that won't cause suspicion, ok?" Godwill concentrated then bellowed, "Timearium Discosure Afentium," time slowed, and the boys got down to work mixing and cooking different potions, easy ones first, like love and enchanting potions. Towards the end of the class, Godwill got them to produce a hallucination potion which was put with the others on the shelf clearly labeled up. Godwill explains what each potion did one by one. "The love potion is as it means. It will make anyone fall in love with another for a brief time. It is not a gift to get with any girl you fancy, so please be responsible and do not use it as so. The enchanting potion is just like the love potion. Although it has a longer-lasting effect, some say it is overrated, but when a person falls under its influence, not only is it used for infatuation, but it can also function as a truth serum. The hallucination potion is a strong part of the arsenal; it can help in very sticky matters. It tricks the person under the influence into imagining inanimate objects come to life and attack them; it may cause the person to injure themselves, giving you time to escape should you need to. Well, a good lesson, boy. You have done well, although it is not wise to evaluate these on yourself due to the harm they could cause, especially regarding females. If you followed the recipes, then there should not be a problem. Well, all there is to do now is to return time and go home." Godwill was about to cast the canceling spell when Kevin interrupted, "excuse me, sir" "what is it, Kevin?", Godwill asked in a harsh voice, "have you had any luck regarding Veraticus?", Kevin asked, "not yet, I do have other things to do also you know," he replied, "only."

Kevin continued, "I have" both Godwill and Paul looked at him. "Where, how, who from?" asked Paul, "let him speak," Godwill said. Kevin beckoned both to the table, sat down, and told them what Jarez had told him earlier this afternoon. "I can't say I trust that individual," Godwill exclaimed, "why not" asked Kevin, "if anyone knew of this, I would put my money on him. After all, he was once part of Crandloss", Godwill stroked his beard in thought, "but how do you know he was telling you the truth and not just telling you what you wanted to hear?", he replied. "Well, if you had seen the torment in his face when he was telling me, you'd understand," Kevin replied in a hasty voice. "remember Kevin," Godwill said, "wizards can do many things, lying and emotions come natural to us, it's the only way we can keep our secret from the natural world," Kevin got up of the seat, "but why should he lie to me, he is, I mean was, the goodness in Crandloss, and if that was a show just for me then it was a very good one. Although I am twelve and a half, I judge myself to understand the true character in people. He was telling the truth, I am sure of it", Kevin answered back. "Very well, Kevin," Godwill replied, "but before you tell anyone else, especially Merlin, let me go through the books to see if there is anything that can verify his story. We will meet here tomorrow after school, and I will let you know what I have or haven't found out." All three looked at one another and agreed, "very well then," Godwill boomed, "tomorrow," With that, he boomed out, "Evreko," the clock on the wall started to move its second hand, "now, we must leave," he said as he turned and walked out the door, the two boys followed him, closing the safe place and hiding it once again. Godwill disappeared into his car and drove off while the boys got their bikes and cycled home.

That evening, the boys went down to the park as planned for football training. Again Kevin put in a particularly good performance, running around, controlling the ball, shooting, and goalkeeping. At the end of the training, Russ walked over to Kevin and spoke to him, "Bob's still injured, so I need a good set of hands this week in goal. You up for it, Kevin?" he asked. Kevin really wanted the center-half position but knew at least this way. He would get to start the game this time. "You bet," he answered with enthusiasm, "ok, you have the slot," Russ replied," be here at nine Sharpe Sunday, as we are away this week, ok? You can get a lift with me. See you Sunday," Kevin thanked Russ and waved as he walked away. "yes," Kevin said as he jumped in the air with his arms aloft, "no need to see that you made the team this week," he heard, it was his brother Paul, "that's right, I'm in goal, although I would have liked to play outfield," Kevin replied, "and are we going to be a good normal kid, or a magical, fantastical one this week," his brother asked. "Well, I don't know, what if I suck doing the normal stuff, I will get dropped again and probably not get a second chance," Paul laughed, "you know somewhere along the line, you won't be able to help yourself, just be careful, make sure no-one sees what you're up to, and don't make it a regular occurrence. Every now and then, if your team is well ahead, make a blunder. It will show people that you are only human, ok?"

Kevin understood his brother this time. He was right. Magic could be used to help him, provided he also showed he was no exception player, just a good one that still makes mistakes. It was perfect. As the boys walked to get their bikes, Mr. Robertson approached them, "Good workout, boys. Listen, the school footy trials are coming up next week, and I want both of you to attend. Paul, the seniors' trials are on Tuesday, and Kevin, the juniors, are on Friday. What do you say". Both boys looked at each other, then smiled and replied, "we'd love to" Paul turned to Kevin then said, but hey, bro, don't you already have something to do on Fridays after school with that other thing?", Paul winked at Kevin who looked a little bemused, "what?", he asked, "you know, that other thing that you think is magic," Paul replied. Kevin then caught on to what he was saying, "I guess, but I'm sure missing one evening isn't going to cause any problems, don't you think? I'll be there, Mr. Robertson," Kevin replied, "Good, see you at school tomorrow," he said before walking away. Paul looked at Kevin with a face like thunder, "what?" Kevin asked in a second, "Godwill has already changed the day from Wednesday to Friday because of the football training for this team. Now you want to blow him off on another, boy, is he going to do his nut? I wouldn't want to be in your shoes, I can tell you. Teacher, he might be, but when it comes to this stuff, he's more than that. He's going to think that you are not taking this seriously, and if he does, he might just forget about teaching us what we need to know. Are you really that dim? Doesn't that worry you in the slightest?" replied Paul, "back off," Kevin shouted, "I'm a kid of twelve. I like football, I didn't ask for this to happen, and now I have the chance to be in two teams and do what I enjoy doing. You want to take that away from me, well, it's not going to happen; if Godwill doesn't accept that I need to miss just one of his silly extra classes, then that's his problem, not mine, I can deal with it, I suggest you do to". Kevin got on his bike and peddled away, leaving his brother standing there shaking his head. When the two boys finally got home, Kevin could see the white dove had reappeared on top of the lamp post, "what's that all about" he said to his brother after he had caught him up, "I don't know," Paul answered sharply, "who cares, you don't that's for sure," and he pushed his bike into the shed, then went indoors.

Kevin followed him in to find that his mum was standing there waiting, tapping her foot, and looking a little cross, "what's gone on, Kevin?" she asked, "what do you mean?" he replied, "well, your brother has come in here with a face like he has been chewing a wasp, something has gone on, and to my knowledge, it's usually got something to do with you, so, let's have it, no lies." Kevin thought for a moment, then answered, "nothing has gone on, mum. Mr. Robertson saw us at training and asked us both to go to the school footy trials next week. Paul's is on Tuesday, and mine is on Friday. I guess he just has a touch of sour grapes because I have gotten into two teams quicker than he did. He is mad because he knows that I'm better at this age than he was, I guess". His mum looked at him, "are you sure that's all? You two haven't been fighting because if you have and I find out, both of you will be grounded, and neither will play for any team. Do I make myself a clear young man?" "clear as day," Kevin replied, "I will find out if something has gone on, you know that," his mum came back with. Kevin just nodded, "right, go get washed and then get some tea," his mum said still not sure whether to believe him or not but gave him the benefit of the doubt, Kevin ran upstairs to the bathroom, as he was going in, he could see Paul sitting on his bed, "thanks a lot," he said, Paul just stuck out his tongue then closed his door.

After a very quiet tea, Kevin watched TV before going to bed, "well"; he said, time for me to go to bed. I'm feeling a little tired, night, mum" his mum had just about forgotten the mood she was in and replied, "night" Kevin didn't even say a thing to his brother. He just ran upstairs to his bedroom. On entering it, he noticed that Merlin's book was on his bedside table, Kevin hoped that his mum had not found it and put it there, but then again, surely, she would have mentioned it. The book opened itself to the blank page, and writing appeared; Kevin read what it had to say. 'You seem troubled, Kevin. Is there something I can help with? It said Kevin sitting on the bed, "I don't know if I can do this," he said, "Paul's in a bad mood just because I want to go to the school football trials on Friday after we had arranged to meet Godwill at the safe place for magic tuition," 'so' the book came back with. "Well, Paul reckons that Godwill will go crazy if I don't show and will probably not teach us what we need to know" the page went blank, then again the writing appeared, 'so what do you think is more important, football, or magic?', "that's not fair," Kevin replied, "I'm twelve going on seventy-six. I feel since this has come to light, all twelve-year-olds want to play football, be normal, like girls and do what a twelve-year-old is supposed to do".

Writing appeared again, 'and you feel you cannot do both?' "No, well, I do not know. I understand the seriousness of the matter and what I have to do, but" Kevin paused as he spoke, 'but what?' the writing said, "But I keep remembering what you, Paul, and Godwill said about keeping a separate life for magic and normality, I'm trying to do this, I'm trying to keep hold of my childhood by doing the natural things like playing football, and growing up to take on this magic stuff. How do I explain that to old Godwill, who will want to tear me a new backside when I tell him I cannot make Friday?". The book came back straight away, and as Kevin was reading it, it looked as though the first part of it was laughing. After the chuckling sloppy writing at the beginning, it continued, 'Godwill will understand if you tell him exactly what you have just said. It is in no one's interest to take away the childhood of a person why, and it is at this age that the most learning in life takes place. Explain to him, and mention that his childhood was not so different from your own. I know. I watched him grow up, and that was not without a couple of blemishes on his character. He may be stern, but if talked to, he can be an exceedingly good listener; now, fret no more, Kevin, talk to him tomorrow. The page went blank. Kevin was just going to close the book when more writing appeared, which said, 'have you found out anymore regarding Veraticus? I can find nothing in my books', Kevin thought and remembered what Godwill said that afternoon, "not yet, but I will keep looking. I have asked Godwill to look also," 'good, the more the people, the more chance we have in finding out if it is true, sleep tight Kevin,' the writing read, then disappeared. Kevin closed the book and put it back in the wardrobe before climbing into bed, but before this, he looked out of his curtains to see the white dove flying away from the lamppost. He thought nothing of it and got into bed, closed his eyes, and drifted off to sleep.

The very next morning, Kevin woke and went down to breakfast as normal; Paul had already gone off on his paper round, and mum and dad sat at the table eating breakfast and chatting away. "Morning, mate," dad said, "Morning" Kevin replied, "I hear things are happening rather quickly for you on the football side," dad said with a smile, "seems that way," Kevin responded, "well, I hope it all goes well for you, just remember, concentrate at school, get your homework in on time, and there shouldn't be any problems," dad replied with a smile. Mum also was looking a lot better, with no worried look on her face from the evening before, so Kevin thought he was out of the bad books once again. "Oh," mum said, "did you see that book I found in your wardrobe? I found I left it on your bedside table" Kevin looked up in a start, "oh, yes, I saw it there," he replied, a bit nervous. "Funny book, lots of foreign writing in it, a few pictures of what look like strawberries or some sort of berry; what's that for Kevin, and where did you get it?" Kevin thought quickly, "Vinnie lent it to me. His sister studied the old methods of medieval medicine long ago, and he thought it would come in handy to try and understand what they used and how it helped people. Mind you, I think a lot of it is just nonsense, just bits and pieces, berries and twigs to help cure someone from the hiccups or a cold, yer right" Kevin's mum and dad looked at each other before mum spoke, "you still have that ruthless streak in your nature don't you?, why does everything have to be black or white with you, if it can't be proved, it didn't happen, I don't know why your friends put up with you sometimes Kevin, I really don't. If you think like that, then perhaps you had better give the book back," she said, "well, I will, but I still like looking at it. It makes me laugh how people actually believed that this nonsense actually helped them all that time ago," Kevin replied. His mum just turned away as if to say, 'yer, whatever.' Kevin knew he had convinced his parents regarding the book and that he did not have to hide it anymore. He just had to be careful when he was using it to contact Merlin. "oh, I forgot," Kevin said, "Susan also leaned me another book. I think it's called the Pharynx, another one on medieval stuff, so you might find that in my bedroom also", mum looked at him, "why lend it to you, don't they take the same classes?", "not all," Kevin replied," some are in different grades, you know that mum, it's just her sister did this class, she's not, so like Vinnie, she thought it would help, that's all." "Well, mind you look after them," mum said," that one I put on your table looks incredibly old, I don't want their parents coming after me if something happens to it" "I will," he replied. "Well, Godwill was right about one thing, wizards can lie well," he thought, then he collected some books, and off he went to school to stand up to Godwill.

Kevin's day at school went without any hitches, meeting up with Vinnie and friends at the break and talking about the football trials for the school and the forthcoming game this weekend. Class after class went by until the final bell went for the day. It was at this point that Kevin remembered that he had to talk to Godwill about Friday. He started to feel uneasy. Although he remembered what Merlin had told him the night before, he still did not feel that Godwill would take the news as easily as Merlin had said. Kevin made his way to Godwills classroom, knocked on the door, and went in. Paul was already there. Kevin guessed that he had told Godwill all about the Friday because the look on Godwills face was not that of a happy person. "so young Wilks," he began in a stern manner, "you think that football is more important to you than learning things that one day may, just save your life," "not so sir," replied Kevin, "then tell me why you will not be at the safe place for a lesson on Friday, or has your brother told me a lie?" Godwill boomed, "one lesson, that's all, I promise, just for the trial," Kevin said nervously, "and why should I take this as so when you have changed one day already for another game of football?" Kevin looked Godwill straight in the eyes, then replied, "I know what is asked of me. I know that I have a lot to learn, and learn I will, but I am twelve, not seventy. You all say about keeping magic and normal lives apart. This is what I am doing. Did you not also have an uneasy growth from childhood to adulthood, sir? There are things that must be done and will be done, but do not take my childhood away from me to do those things, please".

Kevin lowered his head after speaking. Godwill walked over to the window and peered out, stroking his beard, "very well," he said, "I am here to help you; you have been chosen by Merlin to do his bidding. Go to your football trials Friday, but I will expect that any day you miss learning with me, you shall do twice as much the next lesson, and you will take yourself away to a confined place and practice spells your taught if you still want to do this, then you have to be able to fit both in with the time we have got. Think of it as if you miss a lesson after Friday, you will have detention the very next time. Some will be with using the time spell, others not, so you need to use whatever is in front of you to convince your parents you are doing something else on those days. Do I make myself clear?" Kevin nodded in agreement, still a little scared. "Now that is done, I can inform you of my findings on Veraticus," he said a bit lighter heartily. Unfortunately, Godwill had not found out too much regarding this person, only that he did exist, there was a small piece of writing recorded in the fourteenth century about it, but there was not much about him, only that he had been named in this passage and mentioned dark, black magic, along with it. Towards the end of the passage, there was a mention of a woman with him, called Caulpolsier, Crandloss's mother. That was all. "So, what Jarez told me could be true," Kevin asked, "possibly," replied Godwill, "but I still do not trust a being that has been given life through these events; good he is supposed to be but beware, there may be a secondary thing to this that we have not worked out yet," replied Godwill. "Tell him nothing of your findings. Only use him for the information you require. Now it's time to leave, or your mother will suspect something if you are late home. May I suggest we meet Monday after school and start on spells if that is ok with you, Kevin? You don't have anything planned for then, do you?" he said kind of sarcastically, "no, I have nothing planned, sir, Kevin replied, "good, Monday it is, now go, I have some more books. I need to go through." The two boys walked out of the class and over to their bikes; Paul was smiling but shaking his head, "now what?" Kevin asked his brother, "you are the luckiest person I know; if I had done that at your age, old Godwill would have gone to town on me." "Well," Kevin replied smugly, "you did not have Merlin in your corner then, did you?", Both boys laughed and continued their way home, laughing and talking as though nothing had gone on.

Chapter 7

Spells

All that evening, the two boys were once again talking and playing with each other, which caused their mother to think that everything was once again good, "so," she said to the boys, "good day at school" Paul turned then answered his mum, "well I did," he said, "me too," Kevin blurted out, "that's good, no arguing or anything Kevin with anyone?", Kevin looked at his mum then replied, "not that I can recall, why?, has someone said I did?", "no," mum replied with a smile, "just asking, that's all. Tea will be ready in a little while, ok?" the boys nodded then continued to talk, sometimes quietly, so mum couldn't hear them loudly about school stuff, so she could. After tea, Paul wanted to do his homework, so he went up to his bedroom. Kevin stayed downstairs watching TV with his mother. "Funny," she said after a while, "what is mum?" Kevin asked, "oh, how you two go to your bedrooms to do your homework" she replied, "nothing funny in that" Kevin answered, "wasn't it you that told us if we did our homework downstairs while the telly was on we would concentrate on it, we would spend a lot of the time watching or listening to it instead of doing the work?", mum smiled over at Kevin, "your right, of course, Kevin," she said, "you must have a recorder up there in your brain, keeping tabs on what has been said or not, I believe you're going to do well at this school if you could only curb that investigation streak you have and change some of your manners in how you ask questions, well, I think you'd be a much nicer boy. Still, you have years to perfect that." Kevin smiled back to his mum, then replied, "for now, mum, I just want to be a typical twelve-year-old, don't wish my life away," "I wouldn't dream of it Kevin," mum answered back," just listen to your elders and give them a little respect throughout your years, a little respect can go a long, long way," "ok, I hear you, mum, well, got a small piece of homework I need to get done for Mr. Godwill, so I'll go up and do that then I think I'll turn in for the night." Kevin got up, moved over to his mum, gently kissed her on the cheek, and told her, "Goodnight, mum," "Goodnight, dear," she replied, and Kevin trotted off up the stairs.

Friday came and went, along with Saturday. Nothing much happened apart from Kevin again getting excited about the match on Sunday morning. Kevin had gone through both books again that he had, studying spells and looking for that special place of the artifact, but still, only Nottingham stood out.

Sunday morning came with Kevin up early, cleaning his boots and having breakfast before heading off to the park, ready to go to the match. Once there, he met Russ, Brian, and the other team members. They got into cars and off to the match. The match went very well, Kevin's team winning by four goals. Kevin played in goal and did not have that much to do. Not once did he have to call upon his magical gift. He just played a normal game. As they drove home, Russ was talking to Kevin, saying that he was going to keep him in goal for the next couple of games if he didn't get injured. He was quite impressed with how Kevin had controlled his defence and how team members had worked hard together. When they got back to the park, Kevin noticed again the white dove flying overhead but continued going home. Once home, Kevin ran himself a bath and relaxed in it for a while, then got out and spent the rest of the day watching TV and doing nothing, but as he sat, his mind wandered to the white dove; it always seemed to be near him, was it something he needed to look into?, perhaps it was just coincidence, either way, he would ask Godwill if he needed to be worried about it. Monday came, and Kevin went to school; Vinnie was there at the gates again hobbling, "what have you done this time, mate?, Kevin asked, "got crocked whilst playing footy," Vinnie replied, "what, down the park?", Kevin asked, "no, listen, I play for Holbek st Johns on Saturday, that's why I didn't do the training for the Sunday team" Vinnie told Kevin, "but we play Holbek st Johns in our league," Kevin said quickly, "yep," replied Vinnie, "we train on Saturday and play on Sunday, it's a bit hard, especially if you end up like me getting hurt," "I'd say," Kevin replied, "it doesn't give you much chance to get overtraining before the main game, a bit mad if you ask me," he continued. "It was a way of definitely getting in a team as long as I stayed fit, your team has a few talented players in the position I play, all fighting for the place, and they don't, so I thought it the best bet." Both boys continued talking and laughing as they entered the school.

The day went as any other. Kevin was keeping his head down and starting to like and learn some of the lessons he was taking. Eventually, the bell went, and Kevin met his brother at the bike sheds; together, they rode to the spinney, ready for their first lesson of spells off Godwill. As the boys waited, they fed and talked to fireball the phoenix. Fireball was cooing and moving up and down his perch, the boys thoroughly engrossed in the antics of the legendary bird. The door swung open, and Godwill stepped in, "Right, let's get straight down to it. Open your books and find the section on Levitation," he said. The boys found the spell and sat listening to Godwill, explaining its uses and its problems. "The levitation spell is a common spell, able to be cast by even the youngest of wizards or witches," Godwill said, "Pro's, it can help raise items, small or large, to help use them in any way you choose, whether it is used for dropping something heavy on an assailant to knock him out or raising something so you can reach it. Con's, although easy to cast, you need to stay totally focused on it. Just a mile-second lap in concentration, and it will fail. All spells need total concentration; some need more than others, and some, after casting, also need inner strength to control it. Right, let's start by seeing if we can get this right. I'll show you how first, then, you will each take it in turns and practice it". Godwill walked down to the bottom of the room, turned, then said, "Ok, let's start small. We will start with the pencil on the table." Godwill took out his wand; it was the first time Kevin had seen it. He could only describe it as the same length as the one Merlin had given to him, but where Merlin's handle of the wand was ivory from the unicorn's horn, Godwill's was green. The top length was darker in colour, a different kind of wood. Godwill pointed his wand at the pencil and called, "Incantartum leverat" the pencil slowly rose from the table into the air, "once you have trained your mind," Godwill said, "it will be possible to do at least two things at once," Godwill slowly moved his wand and brought the pencil over to his hand, then back out to the table and down. "Now, you try Paul." Paul rose to his feet and cast the spell, just as Godwill had. The pencil didn't move; Paul called out again, "Incantartum leverat" "concentrate on It, Paul, lock your mind onto that little item and nothing else," Godwill said, slowly the pencil twitched and then slowly started to rise up off the table, "good, good, concentrate," Godwill kept saying. The pencil rose high in the air, "now, keep concentrating, but move your wand towards your hand, slowly," he said. Paul slowly did as Godwill had asked. The pencil followed his wand's movements over to his hand, "right, and back to the table."

As the pencil got halfway back toward the table, fireball let out a slight coo noise. Paul looked away for a slit second over towards the fireball, and the pencil fell to the ground. "You must not get distracted, not by anything, you see. Just the slightest bit of concentration lost will break the spell," Godwill explained as he walked over, picked up the pencil, and put it back on the table. "Try again," he said to Paul. This time Paul completed the task without any problems, "ok Kevin, you're up next," goodwill said. Kevin rose to his feet, focused his mind, and cast the spell. The pencil rose immediately, flew over to his hand, then back on the table with no problems, "good, very good, no problems there with your concentration. Pity it wasn't as good when you're in class", he smiled. "Ok, enough of that one. You can practice that in your own time, but make sure you are not seen doing it, go into some woods and practice different sticks, logs, or fallen tree trunks to gage the limits of weight you can control with comfort." Godwill now moved the table and chairs back from the end of the safe place, so only the wall was present in that open space, "now, the next two spells I will teach you really go hand in hand, you will understand when you see them, but, are just as tricky, if not more dangerous, it is the spell for casting fire and water."

Although Paul had already learned the spells he had just done and the ones he was about to do, he was still excited. Kevin could make out a few charred marks on the wall, ones when Paul had been taught in the safe place all those years before. Godwill placed a small piece of wood against the wall, "first," he said, "fire, Firentium Sparksum," he called. Sparks shot from his wand, moving at a great pace toward the piece of wood. The wood burst into flames, "now, water, to put it out, Disquelch Firentium," this time, a large water spray came from his wand covering the wood, the fire dyed out, and the wood returned to its normal state. Both Kevin and Paul looked at each other with smiles on their faces, "what you must remember here, boys, when using the fire spell particularly, is that it can cause considerable damage, not just to a person, but to people's belongings, it is not to be used for a whim, it is for a defence spell, and only that, do I make myself clear?". Both boys nodded their heads in agreement, "the water spell," continued Godwill, "is not quite so destructive, although you could still damage people's property if used incorrectly, so I ask you to use with caution, now, Paul, up you get, let us see what you've got." Paul stood where Godwill stood and cast the fire spell. Everything went as shown, then the water spell, again, as per Godwill's show. "Good, seems you have better concentration on destructive things than movement. I remember it was the same over three years ago. Still, Kevin, you are next."

Kevin got up, a little nervous but still very composed. He cast the fire spell, and instead of sparks coming from his wand, this time, a powerful length of fire shot along the line, completely engulfing the wood in its heat and dancing flames. Godwill moves alongside and casts the water-quelching spell. Kevin stepped back and then spoke, "what happened? I did as you asked, and Paul did. Why was it different?" Godwill put his hand on Kevin's shoulder, "don't worry, Kevin, it seems you are more powerful than both you nor I knew. You see, the power of the spell comes from inside you, and, as you are a very confident and strong-willed young man, then the power is that little bit more powerful than others, in time you will be able to control this, but this is what I was talking about in the class, many things will happen to you and with you", "I don't understand," Kevin said, "well," Godwill continued, "let me try and explain in simple terms, for over twelve years of your life, something has been telling you not to believe in anything that you can't see, touch, smell, hear, or that science has proved it to be, well, that has stored energy like a battery in your mind and soul, now when you let it out, it comes out like a bullet from a gun, and with as much force I see."

Kevin understood what Godwill was trying to say, "so young Kevin, I think the next thing I need to teach you is how to control what you have hidden inside" "is that hard to do?" Kevin asked, "that depends on you. How you want to do this is your choice, there are two ways. One is a very firm but easily learned way, although it will take many lessons to accomplish this, or," Godwill paused, "or what sir?" asked Kevin, "or, a more radical way that is proven, fewer lessons but will grow you up very quickly, I must warn you the second way will cause harm to you but will help control all that power inside you to use in its different stages as needed. Oh, by the way, I know I said it would cause you harm, but not for long as we can use

Pauls Heeling stone to, let us say, repair you". Kevin didn't like the sound of that but asked, "repair me, in what way? I won't get killed, will I?", Godwill replied, No, not killed, but yes, you could get hurt badly, but the healing stone will mend any breaks of bones, cuts, and bruises without any scares. I must say." Kevin looked over to his brother, who whispered, "are you mad? You're not actually considering the second option, are you? What are you, a masochist or something? I would take the first option." Kevin looked over at Godwill, "and how long will this second option go on if I choose it?", Godwill answered quickly, "I could complete the task in four lessons, I think," "you think" replied Kevin, "have you done this before?", "once, and to answer your next question, yes, it did work," Kevin walked over to fireball and stared the bird in its eyes, "what do you think I should do, little friend" he whispered. Fireball moved its head towards Kevin and rubbed its tiny head against his with a soft Coo as it did so.

Kevin moved away from fireball, looked at Godwill then said, "I need to think before I make my decision, when I have made up my mind then I will tell you, is that ok?", Godwill nodded then spoke, "but until you have made up your mind, and it needs to be quickly, we must suspend these lessons as other spells I am going to learn you with you in your frame of mind might not just be hazardous to others but me also, so choose quickly Kevin, there is still a lot to learn and time moves on, let me know of your decision". With that, goodwill turned and walked out the door and away. Kevin and Paul were left alone now to put the safe place back to how it was, as they moved things around, Paul spoke to Kevin, "look, so you know you have extraordinary power bottled up in you, we know there are two courses of action you can take, please, take the first option, I don't want to see you in pain, I know I wouldn't want to, fireball doesn't want it either, so do yourself a favour, go for option one". Kevin smiled at Paul and replied, "he wants me to take option two," "who does?" Paul asked, surprised, "Godwill," Kevin replied as he sat down, "Godwill, what makes you think that?". Kevin stared up at Paul and then replied, "did you hear him give a time for the control on option one because I didn't, that's why he did in option two, he wants me to take option two."

Paul snapped back, "Only because you never asked him about time in option one, you only asked how long in option two, don't do it, bro" Kevin got up from his seat, turned, then said, "Merlin chose me to complete a task for him, he knew what I was capable of, and he trusts Godwill, Merlin's time is getting less and less day by day, I have to act fast, of course, I don't look forward to getting hurt, no one in their right mind would, but bro, I have been given this gift to help someone in need, someone that believes in me, I can't stand back and betray their trust, let me think about it and I will contact Merlin this evening to try and find out more of what is needed of me to complete this. You are more than welcome to be with me when I ask, but please, it is my decision, not yours. Now come on, let us get home." The boys packed everything up and headed home.

That night before it was time to go to bed, both boys met in Kevin's bedroom, "so, have you been thinking anymore regarding the options?" Paul asked, "no, not as such," Kevin replied, "besides, until I know what each option entails, I won't really know, will I?". Paul and Kevin sat on the bed after Kevin had got the book out. He turned to the blank page and then asked, "Merlin, I need to speak with you," writing appeared, 'what is it you need to know, Kevin.' "The two options for curbing the power inside me," he said, "Godwill has stated that because I have significant power within me, it needs to be harnessed and controlled, one option will take a while to do, the other is radical, dangerous but he had stated he had done it before once and had worked. This option takes little time but can be very hazardous to me. Could you enlighten me, please"? The book revealed more writing, 'if what you say is true, then he is correct. If you deeply hold

91

immense power within you, it could cause others around you to harm, as well as yourself. Wands are a controlling part of the magic we use; we channel our energy through them to connect to a specific point of interest, but without them, the power is possible to be produced, but over a wider space. Controlling the power is what we learn to do to ensure loved ones or friends are not hurt when you either practice with them or fight with them to overwhelm a foe. You speak of two options that Godwill mentioned; the first will take a long while. It includes meditation to control your mind, and great self-motivation, the second a number of duels with an experienced master. Godwill speaks of this, you say, with this option, you must be prepared for training so hard, pain so great, and be able to learn so quickly that it is a very hard choice for one so young. Godwill is correct that it has worked before, but the wizard was a good six years older than you. I have given you the information you asked for. Now the choice is yours to make, young Kevin, but do not make it lightly.'

Paul stood up quickly after reading what the page had revealed and said to his brother, "well, it's clear, you got to take option one, Kevin. I know it will take time, but you can control that mind of yours quickly. I believe you can do this more than anyone. Look, you can't do option two, do the first one, will you?". Kevin put the book on the bed, "if you believe I can control my mind for the first option, then why do you think I can't do it for the second?", Kevin asked, "Pain, harm," Paul began, "do you really think you can put up with that?, because I'm three years older than you, and I'll tell you, bro, it scares the hell out of me just knowing what could happen. What are you going to do when the reality of this sets in, and you really feel the pain? I know I would not want to do that"? Kevin looked at his brother and then replied, "but Paul, you're not me, are you? We both know that there is a possibility that somewhere along the line, we are both going to experience pain, so why not taste it now? at least it will be less intent when it does happen." "You're mad," his brother replied, "just a masochist. I don't intend to get hurt if I can help it. If you want pain, then you go it alone. I guess you have already made your mind up, so I will save my breath, don't come crying to me when you are in that much pain you can hardly stand because that's what will happen, you mark my words", with that Paul turned and left Kevin's room.

Kevin went back to the book, took it on his lap, then asked, "tell me, Merlin, you once stated you look over my every move. How is that? I have a feeling you are there, but" Kevin paused, writing appeared on the page, 'but what?' Right from the start of this journey, as you put it, I have noticed on many occasions a single white dove flies in my direction when I'm away from the house and sits on the lamppost when I am home. It was present at the river where it all started. Tell me. You are the white dove that looks over me, aren't you?". The page filled with writing, 'finally you have worked it out, as you said, you are never alone for more than an hour, that is why you also encounter Jarez, it is at school he looks out for you even though you have Godwill, your brother and more there also, giving me time to rest or search for information that can help you on your journey,' "so I guess that Postromus taught you the animal changing spell for you to be able to do this?", Kevin asked.

"You are correct" the book revealed, 'but it gets harder each day as time goes on, because of the inner concentration strength needed to keep the spell in its form', "teach me Merlin, teach me the spell", Kevin said with conviction, the page went blank for a second, 'you wish to learn something so complex as this even though your journey has just began, you have stated that you have the need to harness the power within you on Godwills advise, what makes you think you have the concentration it takes to firstly complete this magic, and that you can sustain the concentration required to hold it in place?', came the reply, Kevin got up off the bed and walked around thinking before answering, "when we met on the Astral Plain Merlin, you said to me that you chose me because of that inner strength I have, the power inside me, to fulfil the task you need completing, if you doubt me know, then how do I know that what you said was true then, I have done what you have asked so far, without questioning you too much, my logic tells me, that if you are unwilling to share spells, secrets and Truth with me, then you have chosen for the sake of it, rather than the person that can actually complete the task". The page remained blank, "so," Kevin continued, "I guess then our journey is at an end, you should look for another protégée whom you believe in fully, to complete the tasks, Pity, I was just getting into this, and I believed I could do well at it".

Kevin closed the book and walked out of his bedroom and down the stairs. As he got to the bottom, he realised that there was no sound coming from the sitting room. He slowly rounded the corner to see his mother sitting watching television in her usual chair, but Merlin was also sitting on the settee, "come in, young man, I think we need to talk," he said. Paul had also heard Kevin go downstairs and open his door. Kevin walked into the sitting room and promptly said, "what's to talk about? You don't trust me, Merlin, so, as I said, it's over" with hearing Merlin's name Paul ran downstairs and into the room, "forgive me, Merlin," he called, "but my brother is very stubborn and very stupid sometimes," he continued, "he is very self-centered, strong-willed, and very immature a lot of the time, he doesn't really know what he is saying most of the time." Merlin laughed then replied, "it's exactly why I chose him," Paul looked amazed that firstly he was in the greatest wizard's presence, and secondly, why his brother was chosen over him. Kevin stared over at his brother, "self-centered, immature, and stupid," he said crossly, "where do you get off, bro" Merlin held his hand up then spoke, "enough, both of you, bickering is not why I am here, Kevin, you have worked out that I use the animal change to keep an eye on you, and, you wish to learn it. I have no worries about teaching you this spell. Also, I have no doubts that you can perform it. My problem is that you do not possess the knowledge to use it; remember the vision I gave you regarding Postromus. He died because of it" Kevin looked at Merlin and thought before saying, "Postromus died at the hand of Jarone and his men, in the form of a dragon," "correct," Merlin said, "but why?" asked Kevin, "as he was a wizard, why did he not turn himself back into a wizard and cast a different spell? I remember you telling me that you cannot spell cast in the animal form", Merlin rose to his feet, "rather than telling you, I will show you."

Merlin's spell cast, " Gradiation Columbine Morphious," both boys watched as Merlin slowly turned from man to dove, but it was not instantaneous. In real-life time, it actually took more than four seconds to transform, then another five seconds to change back. As Merlin returned to human form, he sank into the settee as if he was tired, "you see"; he said, "Postromus died because of the time factor it takes to turn from animal back to human. Not only that, if he had managed it in time, he would have been drained of his energy, stopping him from casting powerful spells, and apart from the killing spell, it is the most draining spell to cast and keep the form. Does this answer the question as to why I never said that I would or wouldn't teach it to you?, you have a great deal to go through harnessing that power of yours, I promise, once you have learned to do that, then, I will teach you this spell", Merlin held out his hand for Kevin to shake, Kevin looked at Merlin and his held out hand, "I never once regretted waiting for someone like you Kevin," Merlin said, "I never just chose you on a whim, I chose you for all the right reasons, reasons that you need to be aware of, but take slowly, I need you to be at your best all the time, or you might not last the journey, for me to teach, you must have the want to learn and not keep doubting me, yourself, your brother or anyone that deals in magic, if you still doubt in any one of the things I have just said then you are correct, your journey and mine is over, now what's it to be?".

Kevin looked at his brother this time, who just smiled back, then back to Merlin, took his hand, and shook it, "ok, I guess I'm just a little impatient. I know all this will take time, but I just get fidgety wanting to know it all, alright, no more doubting, no more immaturity", he said looking over towards his brother, "and, I will be taking the first option that Godwill mentioned, I know what you said Paul, but I think it is the right one for me. Besides, it might just be the thing I need to make me work harder". Merlin nodded then said, "well, as long as we have an understanding I guess it's time for me to leave, oh, one last thing Paul, it will be your journey to help your brother on the tasks, you need to believe in him and not doubt him, both of you need to learn how to become close and look out for each other, remember there is a certain advantage in numbers and a certain advantage in the power together, I will maintain my vigilance over you and your household, I am but a word away", with that Merlin cast the cancelling spell and time returned to normal, Merlin had gone. The boys mum turned to the boys and asked, "is there something wrong boys, I didn't hear you come down the stairs," "nothing's wrong mum, we just needed a drink, night mum," Paul said, "night, behave up there", she replied, the boys returned upstairs into Pauls room. Paul was like a new child in a sweet shop, smiling, and acting stupid, "whatever is the matter with you?", Kevin asked, Paul swung round, "I actually met Merlin, Merlin the greatest Magician the world ever knew", "so", Kevin said, "so, it's a big thing meeting him, you should show him more respect Kevin, you really should, listen, ok, I'll back you in this mental thing you're going to go through, I hear sometimes you may be very fatigued after it, so we need to work out a good story between us, and keep to it to tell mum and dad, we will work on that tomorrow, now, I need my sleep, so go get in your own room and have a good sleep bro, see you in the morning", Kevin returned to his room and went to bed.

The next morning everything started just as normal as any other day. Kevin had breakfast, then off to school, where he met up with his friends, completed his lessons, then, at the end of school, went to see Godwill. Kevin opened the door without knocking and walked straight in, he saw his friend Vinnie there talking to Godwill, but as he entered, they went quiet. "Sorry," Kevin said as both Godwill and Vinnie looked at him, "that's alright," Godwill answered, "we had finished anyway, ok, check out section two of the book, and if you have any problems let me know," he said to Vinnie, "ok sir, see you Kev," he said as he left the class. Kevin looked at Godwill and then back towards the disappearing figure of Vinnie. "I didn't know Vinnie was taking RE," he said to Godwill, "everyone takes it in the first three years, my boy, whether they like it or not, simply different classes regarding gradings," Godwill answered with a smile, "so what can I do for you?", he asked. Kevin sat down with Godwill and asked him to explain exactly what would happen if he took the first option they had discussed in the safe place. Godwill told him everything, the getting hurt part, getting healthy afterward, the main control of his power, how he would be able to use different strengths of it at different times when needed, the lot. Kevin listened without once taking his eyes off Godwill or missing a single thing he had said. In the end, Kevin got up from his seat and paced over to the window. "So, this will only take what, four, five lessons?" he asked, "depends on you," Godwill answered, "if you were strong enough and focused enough, then yes, but if you are not, then it will be a painful experience, even though an important one."

Kevin turned towards Godwill, "this other person you worked with on this, how many times did it take him or her?, you never mentioned their name, would I know them?", Godwill looked away from Kevin, "it took six lessons, and it was a boy, but as to you knowing them, it's possible, but I am not at liberty to tell you their name, they would not want that or want you pestering them for information, this is your decision, you must make the choice on your own, I can and will help you should you chose to go through it, now, are you up for it young Wilks?, or do we go down the long, slow path?". Kevin once again stared out of the window, "ok," he said, "but I must warn you sir, if I get hurt, I will be like a wounded lion, if I get hurt, you had better be prepared to be hurt also." Godwill laughed, "what's so funny, I mean it", Kevin blurted out, Godwill continued laughing but answered, "this is like going back in time, I remember John saying that as well", Kevin looked at Godwill, "John, is that the name of the wizard you taught?", Godwill stopped laughing then answered, "yes", he said quickly and then changed the subject, "now we will start your lessons after school, one a week, this will let you gain your strength back before the next lesson, oh, you might want to miss some football training, I don't think you will be in a to good mood to do both", Kevin stared now at Godwill, "miss footy training, not likely, you let me worry about my strengths and moods", again Godwill laughed, "well, spirited little man I must say, let's hope for your sake you have all that power to succeed in both. Now, off you go. We will meet on Monday after school for however long it takes to get you to the person you need to be. Tell your brother that lessons in the safe place are suspended until we have completed this task," Kevin nodded and then left the class.

On his way home, he once again saw the white dove flying nearby, "it's ok," he shouted out to it, "I have decided. I will tell you later." All of a sudden, Vinnie appeared cycling beside him, "what's ok, tell who later?", he asked, Kevin looked over in astonishment before answering, "oh, I thought I heard my brother calling me that's all", he said thinking quickly, "but your brothers nowhere to be seen Kevin, are you alright, you never took a blow to the old head at the weekend did you?, I must say, you have been a bit quiet lately, not your usual argumentative self, is there anything I can do to help mate?", Vinnie asked, "no, really mate, I'm fine, just a little tired with footy training, now the school footy trials, I guess I need to grow up quickly and find some more energy to do all this". Both boys laughed, "well, don't grow up to quickly Kevin or I won't have anyone to play with, after all, we are just kids," he said before racing off home. Kevin continued his journey home thinking about what Vinnie had said about being kids, "little does he know," thought Kevin, "if being a kid was his hardest thing to worry about, then he has no problems," again Kevin thought, finally he was home.

That night Kevin did his homework, had his tea, watched tv, then went to bed. Another day had passed, and now it was time to rest. That night as he slept, Kevin saw a vision with Godwill in it, there was a great wooded area with a clearing in the center, and Godwill was standing facing another boy. The face of the boy was not in focus, so he could not make out who it was. Kevin watched as Godwill and the other person cast spells at each other. Each time Godwill's spell connected with the boy, he could see that he was knocked down or thrown from where he was standing. "Get up, get up, and try again," he heard Godwill shout on several occasions. The boy got up very wearily and did as Godwill commanded him. Each time a new spell was cast from goodwill, the boy could not defend himself. Time after time, this went on, Godwill kept shouting for him to focus, but each time the spell struck home. After a time, Kevin saw Godwill walk over to the boy who lay on the ground and stands over him, "you're weak," he heard him say, "this lesson is over," with that Godwill cast a spell over the boy but Kevin saw Godwill holding a small but carved stone in his hand, Kevin stared hard at the stone, it looked almost like the one Paul had. The vision ended with Godwill helping the boy to his feet and both walking away.

Throughout the night, Kevin saw more visions with both Godwill and this boy in them. The next two were the first vision, then the next vision. It seemed to Kevin that the boy was finally getting to grips with the way to repel the spells and use them to fight back. The final vision he saw that night was a long and great fight between the two, this time the boy was definitely getting the best of Godwill, Kevin could still not make out the boy's face, but he was casting spells back at Godwill now, knocking him off his feet as well. Towards the end of the vision, Godwill knocked the boy off his feet and was just about to cast another spell when the boy turned over and cast a lightning spell from his hands, not using the wand as this had been knocked out of his hands, the spell hit Godwill full in the middle of the chest and knocked him down. There was no movement from Godwill. The boy raced over to him, got hold of the stone, and cast a spell that Kevin could not hear. Godwill flinched, then sat up. The boy helped Godwill to his feet, and the fight was over. He heard Godwill say to the boy, "you now hold in your hands the power to give or take life. Our lessons are at an end. Use the power wisely" with that, the two walked back through the woods and into the safe place, there, the visions faded, Kevin had seen an insight into what he must endure fulfilling this task. Kevin lay there now at ease; he drifted off into a deep sleep.

Controlling the power

The very next morning, Kevin did as he usually would do. He got up, had breakfast, and went to school. He met Vinnie there at the front gate and walked down the chase with him to the bike sheds, "so, did you speak to your brother when you got home?" Vinnie asked, "what" Kevin replied, "oh, yes, I told him that there was no need to come to the school trials on Friday; I don't need him to hold my hand. After all, I know we are still kids, but, really, he doesn't have to live in my pocket," Kevin laughed. Both boys put their bikes in the racks and went to school. At break time, Kevin hurried around the school until he found his brother. He told him of the visions he had that night with Godwill, the boy, and what looked like the stone Paul had. "Well," Paul started, "what you saw could be the first time Godwill practiced controlling, and yes, the stone you saw must have been the pendant given to me because Godwill asked if he could borrow it for a while. This boy, you said you couldn't make out his face, but his first name was John, it could be anyone, at least you saw what is going to happen, you sure you want to go through that, you can still change your mind you know, no one will think any worse of it". Kevin stared at his brother then replied, "I know I'm scared now, but, it will be for the best, I feel it in me, I can't put it into words, but it's the right thing to do," "ok " Paul replied, "rather you than me" and he walked off singing to himself. School went just as any other day. The final bell went, and the end of the school day came. Kevin went home to get ready for football training that evening.

The training went well again that evening, although tonight, Kevin spent more time working on his goalkeeping training than his outfield. At the end of it, Russ gave the team for this weekend's game at home against an extraordinarily strong Boslegg team. Kevin was in goal again with the team as it was from the last game. The next few days flew by, with no problems at school and no more visions, Sunday came, and Kevin went to the game. Although the opposing team was a little bigger than Kevin's team, they still managed to run out the winners with a four-goal to two-win. Kevin had not used any magic for the games since the very first one; he was quite pleased that the team had worked hard together, so magic was not needed to help. The rest of the day he spent just relaxing, when night came after a while of watching the television, he decided to go upstairs to his bedroom, whilst there he got out Merlin's book and looked through it. There were a number of spells he had not really looked at before, but now, as he had seen the vision of Godwill and the boy, he decided that he was going to be as ready as he could to stop as much pain coming his way. After a while of studying the words and remembering them, he turned to the blank page. "Merlin," he called, 'the page revealed some writing which Kevin read, 'What is it, young wizard?' "thank you for showing me the vision of Godwill teaching the boy how to control his power," he said, writing appearing once more, 'that was not me,' Kevin read, 'I knew of it, but it definitely was not me providing you with this knowledge,' "then it must have been goodwill," Kevin said. 'I think not,' replied the writing once more, "then who can it be?" Kevin asked. The page went bare then reappeared, 'perhaps the boy who went through this, perhaps he was showing you of what is to come, to prepare yourself as you are.' Kevin replied immediately as soon as he read this, "but how? the boy would be a man now, although Godwill did not seem any younger in the vision. How is this possible?" Kevin waited for the response, 'Looks can be deceiving. After all, just look at me. Although I look the late fifties to you, I am, in fact, hundreds of years old, the boy in the vision. He may be closer to you than you realize. I can say no more. The writing disappeared, "what, you mean Paul, my brother?" asked Kevin. With one last reveal from the page, the answer read,' not your brother,' that was it. Kevin asked more questions, but no answers came.

Kevin went into Paul's bedroom to see him, he told Paul about what he had seen the night before again and the conversation with Merlin, Paul sat deep in thought, "Well, it definitely was not me, I wouldn't go through that for love or money, someone close to you that you don't think of them as so", he clicked his fingers then said, "what about Vinnie, your mate", Kevin looked at his brother with a distant look, "Vinnie, Vinnie", he replied twice, " Godwill said his first name was John, how did you get from John to Vinnie, besides, Vinnie is no magic person, is he?", Paul looked away quickly answering nervously, "no, no, of course not, what was I thinking", ending with a nervous laugh, "you know something, I know when you get flustered, Vinnie is a wizard also, isn't he?", Paul looked back at Kevin, "I wish I could keep my bigmouth shut", he said as he sat on the bed, "Yes, Vinnie is a wizard also", Kevin stared at Paul, then spoke, "so why didn't you tell me before?, is there anyone else I should know about?", he asked. Paul stood up and then answered, "keep the noise down. Look, it was bad enough getting you to believe that you have the gift. What do you think you would have done if I said that some of you and my friends also possess the same gift? I don't think you would have handled things so well if you asked me" Kevin walked over to Paul then replied, "at least you could have given me a chance to" Kevin spun away from Paul, "it makes sense now," he said, "what does?", Paul asked, "Godwill said there were others around me, friends that can help and be relied upon." Kevin spun back towards Paul, then asked, "ok, if Vinnie is a magical person, who else? Where there's one, there's usually more, am I correct? So come on, you started to spill the beans, so let's have them all."

Paul stared Kevin into his eyes, then spoke, "what good will it do you? If you know, there are others looking after your interests. Then you are not going to try as hard as you should. Besides, the people who do look after you are of different stages in their development, one alone cannot help you, for all have different powers, but as a collection, we are quite powerful. I will not tell you who else yet. Perhaps after the ordeal with Godwill, you will get to meet them. Do not go pestering Vinnie, either. For the next four or five weeks, you had better concentrate on the work with Godwill, don't you?". Kevin looked at his brother and then replied, "I guess you're right. To tell you the truth, I'm not looking forward to tomorrow, but I think I may just give old Godwill a run for his money. See you in the morning" Kevin left and went back into his bedroom, thinking about Vinnie being a wizard. As he lay on his bed, a thought shot into his head, "if Vinnie was a wizard, then why did he not heal himself with the healing spell, unless he doesn't yet know it," Kevin toyed with who else could possibly be a wizard or witch that he was friends with, but everyone he thought of, he would dismiss, due to their characteristics of that person. He eventually fell asleep, and not a thought passed through his mind that night.

He woke the next morning with a heavy feeling in his heart, he really did not want to go through with the lessons after school with Godwill, but he had agreed, and he was not going to pull out now. When Kevin got to school, Vinnie was waiting for him at the gate as usual, "morning Kev," he said. Kevin just looked at Vinnie and kept riding down the chase. "Wait up," Vinnie cried as he ran after him. When he caught him up, Vinnie asked, "what's got your goat? Did you get out of bed on the wrong side this morning or what?" Kevin stared at Vinnie and answered, "or what" then he turned and put his bike in the rack, "you know what?" Kevin asked as he faced Vinnie again, "no," replied Vinnie, "I thought we were close friends, one's that don't keep secrets from each other" Vinnie looked at Kevin and asked, "but we are. What secrets? Who's been telling you stuff that isn't true, come on", "try my brother," Kevin replied snappily, "your brother, what's he been saying, I hardly know him only through you," Vinnie replied with a surprised look on his face, "really," Kevin went back, "well it must be truly a magical thing that has been going on, don't you think?", Vinnie still staring at Kevin replied, "what, what are you talking about, you're not making sense." Paul had just cycled around the corner and saw Kevin questioning Vinnie, "Kevin, what did I say", Vinnie looked at Paul as he put his bike in the rack, "this is neither the time or place to discuss things, I guess we all need to meet up and then we will talk, look Vinnie, he knows about you, but you know about him so your both even, now keep quiet and we will talk together later, now get going". Both Kevin and Vinnie went off to registration without another word. Later that day at lunch Kevin ran into Vinnie, "look Kevin, we need to sort this out, come on, let's go to the drama block, no one will be there, so we can talk," both boys headed to the drama block. When they arrived they checked to see that no one was in the block first before Vinnie spoke, "ok, so you know who and what I am, so what's the problem?", Kevin walked over to the window before speaking, "I just thought we were friends Vinnie", "but we are, just because I didn't tell you I can do magic doesn't change things, does it?, besides, when were you going to tell me about it?". Kevin looked as if he was going to speak, then fell silent, "you see," Vinnie said, some secrets must be kept from some people they care about. Not to hide things for the sake of it but to hide them so they do not get hurt. Listen, I know about the power control thing with Godwill, that day in the class when you walked in. Godwill was asking me to try and help prepare you for it, although I don't really know what I'm supposed to do to help you".

Kevin stared at Vinnie and then asked, "do you know the healing spell, Vinnie?", "of course, why don't you?" he replied, "I do, but never performed it," Kevin replied, "it's quite easy, really," Vinnie said, "not much to it, and not much concentration needed to cast it," "so when you had hurt your foot, why did you not heal yourself, I don't understand," Kevin replied. "It's simple," Vinnie replied, "it happened just as I said, training for holbek st Johns, where a few friends and, unfortunately, the family saw me get injured, well I could hardly whip out my wand and fix it in public could I, so I had to do it in stages, so I looked as though I was heeling at the normal rate, therefore not causing any suspicions from anyone. You know we must keep our magical world and normal worlds apart, don't you?" "of course," replied Kevin, "well, that's what I was doing," replied Vinnie. "I am so glad we do not have to pretend anymore to each other. It was hard, I can tell you. I wanted to tell you, but he Godwill make me promise until the time is right, well maybe a little sooner than he wanted, but now you know. Are we still friends?" Vinnie asked, holding out his hand for Kevin to shake. Kevin took hold and shook Vinnie's hand, "always," he said with a smile, "good, now we had better move it before someone comes in here," Vinnie said as he led the way out. Kevin was a bit more settled now he had heard Vinnie admit his magical ability and turned his thoughts to his pending lesson after school with Godwill.

The rest of the day went swiftly, with the final bell ringing for the school day to end. Kevin got on his bike and peddled to the spinney in wait for Godwill. It was not long before he arrived, "right then, come with me, and let's get this started," Godwill said to Kevin. As he followed Godwill into the spinney woods, he recognized the woods and the clearing where they stopped; it was the one in the vision. "right Kevin, I am going to teach you dueling first," Godwill said, "the art of casting and protecting yourself from spells, I am not going to lie to you, it will be a painful exercise but one that has to be learned to progress," Kevin nodded, "right, stand over there and raise your wand in front of you" Godwill commanded, "before we start, I had better slow time, so we are not interrupted, Timearium Discosure Afentium," time slowed rapidly, birds in flight seemed to be suspended in a motionless mode, trees that were swaying were now still. "Right. I hope you have been reading your books. I will go gently at; first. I don't want to harm you too much," Godwill said with a laugh. Both Godwill and Kevin raised their wands toward each other. As Godwill began casting a spell, Kevin quickly cast, "Transisomb."

A bolt of light shot from Kevin's wand and connected with Godwill's, sending it spinning out of his hand. Godwill stood looking at Kevin with a maddening expression on his face, "very good"; he said, although Kevin did not feel he meant it, "so, you know how to use the disarming spell? That's good, right we will try again, this time, no disarming, ok Wilks?", Kevin smiled and nodded in agreement. Both stood facing each other once more, again Godwill started to cast a spell a little quicker, but again Kevin was quicker still, "Sherek," in a flash, Kevin disappeared from in front of Godwill and reappeared behind him just as Godwill cast the lightning spell at him. Godwill turned to see Kevin standing there smiling back at him; Godwill now, even more cross, spoke severely to Kevin, "look, although it proves you have read the books and mastered the language of the spells, you need to stop yourself using them until you have successfully been taught them by an experienced wizard like myself, if cast wrongly, spells can do you more damage than your opposition, are we clear," Kevin paced back towards the starting position once again then spoke, "I've seen what you did to John in a set of visions, and I vowed I would not get hurt like him, so, I have put together a few simple get out of jail free spells to assist me, do you not think that was logical of me, or have you forgotten that I run on logic?". Godwill starting to go red in his face now cast "Windinium Ferosciate," a high wind started to whip up coming towards Kevin, "Crevatious Septimium" Kevin cast back, the wind changed direction knocking Godwill off his feet. As he rose, he cast "Firentay, Consunium, Derivarm," Kevin quickly cast back the electrical bolt now starting to appear from Godwills wand casting "Crevatious Septimium," the electric bolt turned in mid-air and slammed into Godwill, sending him spinning through the air. Godwill lay on the floor for a second before getting up, "you are unruly boy, just like in school, I said not to use those spells that you have not been taught," Kevin standing facing Godwill replied, "unruly sir, no, just a belief in myself and a greater concentration to help me from getting hurt."

Godwill now decided that enough was enough and cast three spells, "Disquelch Firentium, Firentium Sparksum, Windinium Ferosciate, in quick succession towards Kevin. Kevin stood still and thought, "shield," as he did so, an invisible shield folded around him, water bounced away, so did the fire, and the wind passed right over him without him being harmed. Godwill stood looking dumbstruck at how Kevin had produced a shield so strong to repel the spells. Godwill walked towards Kevin and stopped in front of him, "I have never known in my time, someone as young as you, to be so powerful as you are; in mind and soul, it seems that you do have a greater concentration within you than I first thought, duelling is not going to teach you anything, so we will try something else, put down your wand Kevin, now I want you to concentrate on the fire spell but let it flow through your arm, into your hand and out into the point beyond."

Kevin did as Godwill asked; as he cast "Firentium Sparksum," a broad ray of light started to appear from the end of his hand, changing into a torrent of fire aimed towards a tree. With a crackling sound, the tree was engulfed in fire, "now concentrate and try and narrow the broad width of the fire stream into a single fire stream," Godwill shouted. Kevin focused his mind, and sure enough, the broadness of the fire narrowed slowly into a single fire stream, "keep concentrating," repeated Godwill, "now, cast the water blast spell" Kevin did as he was asked, and the fire stream changed to a water blasting stream, putting out the fire. As the last remnants fizzled out, Kevin stopped the spell and fell to his knees in exhaustion. Godwill moved closer to Kevin, "not as easy as you thought it would be, is it, young wilks?" Kevin nodded in agreement, "you see," said Godwill. Although magic can do good or bad things, it also takes a great amount of concentration and strength to do it; this leaves you feeling weak, vulnerable, and easy to finish. I am here to help you enhance your power, to strengthen you, so it does not take so much of that needed energy away. If you were in a serious fight for your life now, you would be finished within a few minutes, right? Rest time is over, get up, this time let us try the lightning and wind spells". Kevin got to his feet and did as Godwill had asked, learning firstly with the wand, then without, at the end of it again sinking to his knees. "Get up, come on, again, water and hailstorms come on," Kevin looked at Godwill still on his knees, "I can't, I'm too tired, sir," he replied in a quiet voice, "come on, Wilks, push yourself, dig deep into that strength of yours, I know it's there and so do you, you just have to find it. The difference between living and dying is finding that little bit of strength you didn't know you had. Now come on", Kevin looked at Godwill still on his knees, "I can't, sir, I really can't," just as he said his last word Godwill cast a lightning spell towards Kevin, and it hit him full in the chest and knocked him on conscious, the last thing he could remember was a searing pain in his chest before he blacked out.

Kevin awoke to see Godwill holding the healing stone above him and chanting over and over again, "Compare-Relapsum" Kevin could feel his body healing itself, bit by bit, so he just lay there and rested. Eventually, Godwill stopped chanting; Kevin opened his eyes and sat up. He felt his chest, which still felt quite tender, "why on earth did you do that to me" he shouted at Godwill, "I was trying to get you to find that last bit of energy to protect yourself. Only you didn't. Therefore I must come to the conclusion that either you didn't have any left or you just took your mind off the game," Godwill replied. "Took my mind off the game. I told you I had no more. What didn't you understand about that?" Kevin got up a little groggy holding his chest. Godwill apologised and explained that this was the reason he needed to know how to control his energies, not to go full on and use all of it up in a quick session, "the last piece of energy that you can muster could be the thing that lets you escape from someone or something, or to bring them down, over the next few lessons we will work hard on that." Kevin still rubbing his chest, stared at Godwill then said, next few lessons, right, but I'll tell you this, sir," he said sarcastically, "I owe you one, and boy, am I going to deliver it to you," Godwill smiled but underneath he knew that although he was inflicting pain on Kevin, he knew that one day he was going to feel the pain of this pupil. Both Kevin and Godwill decided that enough was enough for this lesson. Godwill restarted time again, and the two left the spinney and headed to their homes.

When Kevin arrived home, his mother was in the kitchen and saw him walk through the door, "are you alright, Kevin? You don't look too good", she said. Kevin just looked at his mum and replied, I'm ok, just a little bunged up and feel a bit heavy, probably getting a cold, that's all. There are a lot of people in my class sneezing and going in a good one", "well I hope you're not coming down with it and pass it on to us, you'd better get in a hot bath, and I'll get you some medicine to try and catch it before it takes hold," Kevin just nodded and went upstairs to run his bath. Paul heard him coming upstairs and opened his door, "you alright bro?" he asked, "bit soar that's all, I'll get a bath then I'll fill you in, ok?", his brother nodded, Kevin, set about getting his bath ready. As he relaxed in the warm water, he remembered about the lesson Godwill had given him, occasionally smiling to himself as he remembered out witting his teacher.

As he came out of the bathroom, his brother was there waiting. Paul grabbed his arm and ushered Kevin into his room. "Easy," Kevin cried out as he rubbed down one side of his chest. "Sorry," Paul replied, "so, how did it go?" he asked. Kevin sat on the bed and told Paul all about the lesson. At the end of the conversation, Kevin asked his brother, "although I commanded the spells and protected myself, the power that drained out of me was to such an extent that I could do no more; why is this? does this happen to you?" Paul rose from the bed and walked towards the window, "Yes, but not so much now," he replied, "when I first started out, I was just like you. Lesson after lesson left me feeling so tired, a feeling as though my body wanted to give up. Every step sent a pain through my body that hurt like a knife being thrust into me. There were times like you I wanted to not believe in the wonders that I could do, pack it all in, and lead a normal separate life." "So, how did you get over these feelings?" Kevin asked. "It's not easy," Paul replied, "The feeling of being able to achieve something so special fought with the part of me that wanted to quit. Day after day, I fought with my conscience until, eventually, I realised that I had been chosen for the gift that was handed to me, to do something good with it. After that, even though many a day I came home after lessons feeling tired and drained, I knew I had to fulfill a destiny that would arise someday. So, I just stuck in there, listened to my teacher, and did what he asked of me, and slowly but surely, the tiredness slowly departed, the strength improved, and the concentration became more intense. This is the same path I feel you must tread. Also, there is no quick fix, but at the end of it, you will achieve more than most normal people could only imagine. Although you are young in years, you have an inner strength of a person that, if taught correctly, would equal that of any adult of which I can think. Pain will be your motivation for learning. The more you learn, the less the pain, until one day, there will be no pain."

Kevin looked at his brother with a look of disbelief on his face before replying, "so when did you become so deep and philosophical? All I wanted to know is how do I stop myself from being so tired?" Paul smiled at his brother and then said, "just eat sweet things; whenever you feel tired, have a bar of chocolate or a sweet fizzy drink, it worked for me." Both boys just stared at each other, then just burst out laughing together. "You could have just said that in the first place," Kevin said between laughs to his brother, "I know," Paul replied through his laughs. Not another word was said as the two brothers continued to laugh. Finally, Kevin got up and left Paul's bedroom, and went into his own. Still a little soar, he opened his wardrobe and took out Merlin's book. Kevin studied some more of the spells and their uses before going to sleep. After a while, Kevin started to see a vision appear; as it cleared, he could see himself walking down a path in some woods and then out into a clearing. In front of him was a small mountain range, one that he had seen before. It was the mountains where he saw Merlin and Postromus before the fateful day of his death. In his vision, Kevin could not see Merlin, only Postromus, beckoning him to go with him. Kevin moved forward and followed the wizard without speaking. Eventually, they walked into a forest where Kevin called out to Postromus, "where are we? What do you want with me? I saw you die. Are you a ghost?" Postromus just raised his finger to his lips as if to say be quiet. Then he pointed forward towards a waterfall.

Kevin saw himself move forward towards it. Through the waterfall, he could just make out a small cave. Kevin stopped before it and turned and asked, "what lies the other side of the water in the cave? Please, tell me, you bought me here for a reason. Can you not tell me why?" As Kevin asked his question, he saw the figure slowly disappear. As he faded away, Kevin heard the words, "It's your destiny to right a wrong. Ask Merlin." Kevin spun around and around, shouting, "what is my destiny? what's wrong?" time and time again, but there were no further answers; slowly, the mist appeared, and Kevin could see the vision no more.

Kevin woke with a start. He jumped out of bed and tip-toed to his brother's room, "Paul," he called softly, "you awake still?". A grunt came from his brothers' room, "what is it? what do you want now?" his brother asked sleepily. Kevin undid the door and went in, "I have had another vision," Kevin told his brother, "So what" his brother said with a snap in his voice, "do you know what time it is? I have to be up soon, it's alright for you, you can sleep in". Kevin sat on the bed and then said, "it was Postromus," Paul now seemed to take a little interest, "so, what happened?" He asked. Kevin told Paul all about the vision, "Wright a wrong, ask Merlin" Paul said," what is that all about? and what is the significance of the forest and waterfall?" Kevin just shrugged his shoulders and said, "I don't know, that is why I asked you." Paul sat up in bed thinking hard, "well" he started to say, "it's evident that all those years ago, something happened that should not have, something that may have involved Merlin, but what is the forest and waterfall got to do with it? Did you recognise any part of the forest? Was there a sign, a board with a name on it, anything that you can remember".

Kevin just shook his head, "nothing. The only thing I remember is that the trees were very, very tall, not a thick forest. In fact, in some places, I remember seeing what looked like small black marks on the ground like a small fire had been burned there." Paul looked at Kevin and then said, "Think, Kevin, think hard. Was there anything else you saw that you didn't take notice of at first." Kevin closed his eyes and thought hard, "at the waterfall, there was no river, just a shallow stream, but how can so much water crashing down only produce a stream" he said. Paul now sitting up straight in bed then said, "ok, so now concentrate on the waterfall, think hard Kevin, describes how the rocks are, how tall, is there anything you can see that stands out." Kevin again closed his eyes, "the waterfall is not high, quite narrow, a few rocks near the top with moss on them", Kevin said, "think Kevin" his brother snapped, "concentrate, there must be something about this waterfall that Postromus took you to in the vision, there must be something he knew you would remember about it, look deeper". Kevin tried hard to remember, but nothing was there, nothing that stood out to make him remember, "I can't, there is nothing else I can see, honestly", Kevin fell forward face down on Paul's bed, "ok" his brother said, "go back to bed and sleep, who knows, you may get a second chance, if you do, don't forget to look around in the vision, now I need some sleep, you can tell me what happens in the morning. Kevin returned to his bed and fell asleep. Nothing stirred until the light shone through the curtains waking him.

Chapter 8

Lesson After Lesson

As the bright sunlight shone through the curtains, Kevin yawned and got out of bed. He pulled his curtains open and grimaced with the pain that he still had in his chest from the lesson with Godwill. His mother had just come out of the bathroom and heard him cry. "Kevin," she called, "are you alright?" Kevin quickly replied, "I'm fine, mum, just stubbed my toe on the bed" his mum accepted that and replied, "well, stop messing about in there and get a wash and get dressed. Time is moving on, you know. You do not want to be late for school, do you." "No, mum," Kevin replied sarcastically as he looked out of the window.

As he did so, his eyes suddenly were transfixed on a cat riding on a dog's back. He chuckled to himself and then turned away. As he turned back to look again, there was no longer the cat and dog but a woman and a man staring up at his window. Kevin quickly shut his curtains and slowly peeped through a crack in the side of them. The people were still there, just staring up at his window. Kevin was now starting to feel a bit uneasy, he looked one more time, and they were still there. Kevin stared hard at both to see if he knew them or recognised anything about them, but nothing came to mind. He quickly dressed and ran downstairs and into the front room. He peered through the front window at the spot where the two strangers stood, but now they had gone. Kevin ran out of the front door and into the street, looking both ways, but no sign of either of them was apparent. As Kevin turned back to go down his path to the open front door, he noticed a piece of paper nestled in the rose bush at the edge of the path. Kevin picked it out and opened it up. As he straightened it, he could see that there was some sort of writing on the paper, but he could not make it out. Perhaps it was French or German, but nothing he understood. As he started to scrunch the paper back into a ball and throw it away, his mother appeared at the door. "What are you doing, Kevin? You're letting all the heat out of the house, that's what you're doing, my lad, and I hope you were not going to throw that paper in the street and be a litterbug," his mother called a little crossly. "Put that in your pocket and bring it into the bin. Come on. You need to get a move on. School waits for no one, you know," she said as she ushered Kevin into the house. Kevin had put the rolled-up paper in his pocket but forgot to put it in the bin before leaving for school. In fact, he totally forgot about it until he was back in the spinney that evening with Godwill.

"How's the chest, young wilks," Godwill asked unsympathetically. Kevin had not felt that much pain during the day but thought if he put it on a bit old, Godwill would take it easy on him this evening. "Not so good, sir, still hurts quite a bit," Godwill laughed out loud, then replied, "good, I see you have a sense of humour and a grotesque thing for lying also," he now said with a rather cross expression. Kevin knew Godwill was now even more upset with him as Godwill does not like liars. Kevin tried to lighten the mood by saying, "oh come on, you know I was just kidding, hoping you would take it a bit easier on me this time," he said with a smile. "Easy boy," Godwill grunted, "easy, will a powerful wizard standing in front of you want to kill you? Take it easy, no, he will whip out his wand and kill you stone dead before you can utter a single word. But, if you make jokes at him and try and make him laugh and forget that he wants to kill you, then go ahead, but do not do it on my time". As he finished his last word, he quickly chanted, "Weathio Corpus Evrader," "what are you doing you mad old fool" Kevin asked, "you have not even stopped time yet, people will see the weather coming," Kevin quickly thought of the shield and put it in place before the hail, blistering wind and lightning echoed through the sky. Quickly Kevin began chanting, "Eversage Momentum." The wind slowed down to a slight wind, hail now turned to rain, and the lightning slowly fizzled out. Kevin chanted again, "Timearium Discosure Afentium," time now slowed, and the spell Godwill had put in place also slowed its functioning down. Kevin, now very mad, shouted at Godwill with great rage. "What do you think you are doing? You're the one that stated we have to keep our lives separate, yet you blatantly went ahead and cast a spell without slowing time. You're a mad fool who has lost the plot, some teacher you are. I am out of here". Kevin turned and started to walk away, "don't walk away from me, boy. No one turns his back on me and gets away with it. Do you hear me, boy" Kevin stopped and turned back to face Godwill. Only Kevin now was thinking that something must be wrong with Godwill as he kept calling him boy, and Godwill mostly calls him Wilks or young Wilks.

"So what's your problem then, sir? Been drinking, have we?" Kevin mocked. Godwill was now getting very pumped up and angry, "Well," called Kevin, "Cat got your tongue, or are you just too drunk to answer me," Godwill now was fuming and cast "Firentay, Consunium, Derivarm" towards Kevin. Thinking quickly at the same time, Kevin cast "Sherek," a bolt of lightning shot through the air toward Kevin, but he disappeared before it hit. Kevin reappeared behind goodwill and cast "Disquelch Firentium," drenching him in water. Godwill turned quickly and cast at Kevin, "Firentium Sparksum," a fire bolt shot towards Kevin, who just closed his eyes and conjured up the shield. The fire blasted hard at the shield that Kevin had produced, and Kevin could feel himself getting weaker. As the fire blast slowed from Godwill, Kevin changed tactics, and again "Sherek," Kevin disappeared again behind Godwill, and as he reappeared, he cast "Elivio Consensious." The tree Godwill was standing under now came to life and thrashed its branches at Godwill, hitting him in the face and arms. Godwill dropped his wand and shielded his face as the tree continued to attack him. "Had enough yet, Godwill," called Kevin, laughing to himself. A voice came from behind him, "had enough, young Wilks. We have not even started." Kevin swung around in disbelief. "But if you are behind me, then who is that being attacked by the tree?" Godwill just replied, "no idea, but I think we should know who you have been fighting with, Godwill cast, "Evreko," the tree was still, and the body of Godwill lay cowering on his knees. Godwill pointed his wand at the form on the floor and chanted, "Optimus Reveal."

The second Godwill changed shape into Vinnie, "Kevin shouted, "what the hell do you think you were doing, Vinnie? You could have got hurt, really badly" Vinnie stood up slowly and then spoke; Mr. Godwell asked me to help you. Remember, I told you in the school, so I thought I would give it a go tonight. I knew Godwill was going to be late, and he asked me to tell you, but I thought it might be of some help if I didn't tell you and pretended to be him and challenge you." Godwill was not happy, "you chose my form to fight your friend," Godwell said crossly to Vinnie, then turning to Kevin "and you did not know that this imposter was not me?" "Well, actually, sir, I did know it wasn't you," both Godwill and Vinnie looked puzzled and then asked together, "How." Kevin then explained that Godwill always calls him young Wilks, whereas Vinnie in Godwells form called him boy every time. Also, the strength of the spells that were being cast was not as potent as the real Godwills spells, so "I thought I would go along with it and have some fun at last," he said with a smug look on his face. "Well, well, well, quite the little detective, young wilks," Kevin smiled and pointed to Godwell, making sure Vinnie knew." "What" Godwill bellowed. Kevin just laughed and shook his head. Godwill just realised what he had said and cracked a small smile himself before saying to Kevin, "well, you have had your fun, so now, can we continue the lesson." Kevins smile suddenly broke, "you mean now," he said to Godwill. "Of course, now, if I said tomorrow, then tomorrow it would be, but as I am here now, we will continue the lessons, right." Kevin, now extremely nervous, tried to speak, "what is it, wilks, stop mumbling and say what you have to say." "But sir, I feel weak after the fighting with you. I mean, Vinnie, can we not postpone this lesson until tomorrow until I have regained my strength, sir," Godwill smiled then spoke, "certainly not; here, eat this and be ready to go in five minutes." Godwill threw Kevin a bar of chocolate and turned and walked a little way on. Kevin remembered what his brother had said and ripped open the chocolate bar, and stuffed it into his mouth. "Easy, Kevin, you will choke on that if you are not careful. I must say, you are more advanced than I thought you would be. It took me a good while before I could control most of the spells you used against me. You are doing very well," Vinnie said. Kevin just smiled at him and then continued to tuck into the chocolate bar.

"Right," said Godwill, "it is time, come on, get to your feet, and Vinnie, if you're staying, you keep out of the way and do nothing at all during this lesson. Do I make myself clear?". Vinnie nodded and moved back, and sat on the other side of the tree, well out of harm's way. Kevin got to his feet and stood ready. "Ok, Wilks, ready?" asked Godwill. Kevin nodded and held out his wand. "Well at least look as if you mean it Wilks, for pities sake. Just as Godwill was finishing his sentence Kevin chanted "Elivio Consensious" pointing at the ground near Godwills feet. Tree routes started to creep towards Godwills feet entangling them around his legs and body, without a flinch Godwill bellowed "Gradiation Columbine Morphious" Godwill turned himself into a snake and the roots fell away from him. Kevin now chanted "Incantartum leverat," the snake or Godwill in its form rose into the sky, as it did the snake turned into an eagle and swooped at Kevin. Again, a chant came from Kevin just as the eagle was bowing down on him "Sherek," Kevin disappeared just as the eagle had its claws ready to tear into him. As Kevin reappeared next to the tree Kevin cast another spell at the eagle, "Firentay, Consunium, Derivarm," the lightning bolt hit the eagle in the middle of its back, and it fell to the ground. As it hit the ground the eagle turned back into Godwill who turned quickly and cast "Transisomb" at Kevin.

His wand shot out of his hand and away from him. Godwill stood pointing his wand at Kevin, "well, what are you waiting for, wilks? This is not a picnic, you know." Kevin stood with his arms open wide and his head bowed, "If I were an attacking wizard, I would have killed you by now, you remember nothing I have taught you so far, and I believe you will learn nothing more because of your stubborn streak that runs through your whole family. You are a lost cause. Why Merlin chose you, I do not know. It is over, Wilks, it is over". As he said his last words, he turned to move away when Kevin raised his head and looked at the back of Godwill moving off before saying," Over Godwill, it is just beginning." With that, Kevin held his arm, pointing directly at Godwill, and chanted, "Firentay, Consunium, Derivarm," the electric bolt shot from Kevin's hand and hit goodwill squarely in the back, knocking him down to the floor. As this immense electric bolt hit Godwill, Kevin then chanted another spell, "Gradiation Columbine Morphious," suddenly, Kevin had transformed into a large grizzly bear that had raced over to Godwill and now had him by the throat. As he stood there, he even managed to still be able to talk in the bear form. "No one says it is over until I say so. Do you yield Godwill, or do I have to do you serious harm as you do to me"?

Godwill closed his eyes and admitted defeat. Kevin let go and cast "Evreko," in a flash, the bear had gone, and there stood Kevin for a few seconds before falling to the floor with his eyes shut. The next thing Kevin knew was that he was in the lair of the spinney, slowly waking up with the phoenix crying tears down Kevin's face. As he eased himself up, he looked at the phoenix and smiled, "I never did give you a name, did I" Kevin said as he stroked the phoenix's head. "I know. I will call you Fergull; what do you think of that? Does that suit you?" The phoenix made a cooing noise and hopped up and down along its perch. "I think it likes it," Godwill said with a smile. Kevin turned to Godwill and said, "but I don't understand; phoenixes are supposed to heal cuts, wounds, and poisonings, so how did its tears help bring me back from unconsciousness." Godwill smiled, "there are many things we still do not know about the happenings of this world or any other. The tears of a phoenix are there for the person who takes care of it. It knows precisely what is needed for that special person, do not ask me how, but they know," he said as he also stroked its head. "Anyway, it is a good thing you have that bird to help bring you back. What were you doing changing the form like that? As I told you before, young Wilk's magic can be just as dangerous as rewarding if you are not trained in its use. This is just one of the cases in which you could have died. How would I explain that to your mother and father, ay."

Godwill got off the stool he was sitting on and walked towards the door. As he touched the handle, he turned to Kevin and said, "Perhaps I judged you too quickly. There is something inside you that can be harnessed for good; it took a lot of self-control to change form like you did today. I know wizards more advanced still cannot do this, but a mere boy can achieve this in some sort of way. We just must work on this self-control and willpower. Who knows, you just might become a great wizard yourself, but that is a long way off, yet, Wilks. Now, feed your bird and get off home. You too, Vinnie, ok." Godwill opened the door and started to walk through it and stopped halfway. He stuck his head back around the corner and said, "Oh, and don't forget to restart time, will you? There's a good lad," With that, Godwill closed the door and left.

The two boys sat a while talking about everything and were incredibly happy that no one got hurt through the evening's escapades. "How on earth do you know the Morpheus spell? Only major powerful wizards know that stuff"? Asked Vinnie. Kevin just looked his friend in the eye and replied, "I don't know; I asked Merlin to teach it to me, but he refused to until I had mastered the inner self-control of my power. I didn't even know it existed, but something in the back of my mind told me to use these words and", Kevin stopped speaking. "And what"? Vinnie asked. "I don't know. It was just the spur-of-the-moment thing that came out. I cannot explain it. All I know is it sure gave old Godwill a freight. Did you see the look on his face when I grabbed him by the throat?" Both boys fell silent for a brief time; then, both started laughing very loudly. Finally, Kevin restarted time, fed Fergull, and closed the hidden spot door. Both Kevin and Vinnie cycled home for a relaxing night, or what Kevin was hoping for, but things never go that way just lately for him.

As he rode along the road coming into his road, he noticed the man and woman he saw earlier that morning in exactly the same space they were in before. They were just looking straight ahead, looking toward Kevin's window. Kevin knowing no better, raced up to them and stopped right in front of the man. "Can I help you," Kevin said with a sarcastic voice. The man looked down at Kevin and then just returned to looking at the window. "Excuse me, but why are you looking at my bedroom window for? I saw you this morning doing the same thing, is something wrong with the brickwork or window? If there is, I had better tell dad." This time the lady looked at Kevin and spoke in a soft voice. "You live their little boy"? Kevin, not happy being called little, responded. "Of course, didn't I just say that a minute ago? So, what's the story? Why are you looking at my bedroom window with so much fascination, ay?" The woman looked at the man and smiled, "oh, nothing in particular; we just thought we saw an owl perched on the windowsill.

It's not there now. Is it your little boy?" Kevin was now getting angry being called a little boy and snapped back at the man and woman. "No, it's not mine, and I am not a little boy. My name is Kevin, so now you know my name, you can stop calling me little boy, OK." The woman gave a laugh as she turned to the man and then back. "A little touchy, are we, son? We mean you no harm. As I said, it is rare to see an owl around here, so we thought we would look for it. As you said, it was not yours. Perhaps you would also be on the lookout for it and let us know when you see it. Will you do that for me, dear?". Kevin was just about to answer when his brother came cycling up behind him, "you ok, bro? What's going on here? Come on, Kevin, race you to the front door". Both boys sped towards the front door, where Paul declared himself the winner. Kevin looked back to see the man and woman had gone. Paul moved so he could see what Kevin was looking at. "What were you talking about to the bloke and woman"? He asked. "Oh, nothing in particular. They just said they had seen an owl on the windowsill of my bedroom, that's all." Paul just grunted some sort of approval and then asked Kevin about the lesson he had this evening. Kevin told his brother he would tell him after tea, but something about the man and woman were troubling Kevin diverting his focus on what his brother was saying to him. Kevin just agreed with everything Paul said but heard nothing at all. Really, still, he could not put his finger on it, so he decided to go into the house and have tea and a nice warm bath afterward.

After tea, Kevin ran his bath and eased himself into it. As he was getting in, he noticed that the bruising on his chest was coming out, along with some other bruises on his arms and legs. He thought to himself that he had better not show any of these to his mum or dad, or they would be up the school stating that he was being bullied. Kevin sank back into the bath relaxing when a knock on the bathroom door came, "I'm in the bath; who is it?" No answer came, "Is that you, Paul, playing silly games? Well, I am not biting, you will just have to wait, and that's that." Kevin then began singing to himself in the bath when he noticed the door handle being tried to be opened. Fortunately, Kevin had put the bar lock on to stop anyone from coming into the bathroom while he was in there. "Alright, that's it. I am going to get really angry if you don't stop mucking about Paul. Pack it in. You can have the bathroom when I am finished in the bath ok, now go away." The door handle released itself, and nothing else was heard or seen, so Kevin again sank back down into his bath. After his bath, Kevin barged into Pauls's room and shouted, "it's all yours now. At least you could have had the decency to wait till I was finished before doing your childish games." Paul looked at his brother with a blank expression on his face, then said, "what are you going on about? Silly games, what silly games?" Kevin smiled, then replied, "Oh, playing the innocent guy, ay, so you didn't try the door handle to the bathroom a few minutes ago, I suppose?" "Actually, no, bro, I was downstairs and had only just come up. Ask mum; she will tell you." Kevin looked at his brother and then said, "really," "yes, really. Mum," called Paul. His mum came to the bottom of the stairs. "Are you annoying your brother again, Kevin? If you are, you had better stop it, or I will tell your dad?" Paul interrupted, "no, he's ok, but just tell him what I have been doing, will you? He seems to think I was trying to get into the bathroom whilst he was in the bath." A loud tut came from their mum, "and how is he supposed to do that, Kevin, when he has been down here watching TV with me all the time you were in the bath? He has only just gone upstairs. I do not know, Boys." Paul just raised his arms towards Kevin as if to say see. "Thanks, mum," he called, and his mum returned to the living room to watch more TV.

"I don't get it. Someone definitely tried the door handle to get in. I saw it move." Paul just looked at his brother and said, "Perhaps it is all the stress you are under making you see things that aren't real. I know I did when I first got involved with this thing." "Perhaps," Kevin replied, "So how did today go then? Learn anything new?" asked his brother. Kevin told Paul everything, including the part about fighting with Vinnie as Godwill. Both boys were laughing about it, but Kevin still had a lot of bruises that hurt his body, especially when he laughed.

After a long chat and a lot of laughing, Kevin decided it was time for him to get some sleep. He had another lesson tomorrow evening with Godwill, and he needed every bit of concentration and strength he could muster such a good night's sleep would do him a world of good.

As he drifted off to sleep, he found himself thinking about the evening's lesson. Slowly the memories faded away as he fell into a deep sleep. After about an hour, he suddenly was aware of himself being in a place he had been before. It was the Astral Plain that could only mean one thing, Merlin wanted a meeting.

Kevin now walked through the fields and followed the path the last time he had been in this place. Eventually, he turned up at the pond once again. He looked to where he last saw Merlin, sitting beside an old log by the willow trees, but there was no sign of him. Kevin called out, "Merlin, I'm here. What are you want?" The air was still. No sounds could be heard even from the pond's waters as it lapped against the banks. Again, Kevin called, "Merlin, are you here?" Finally, the shape of an elderly man appeared from behind the trees, "I am here, Kevin. What is it that you want of me?" Kevin looked puzzled at Merlin, then spoke, "what do you mean what do I want from you? You arranged this meeting, didn't you?" Merlin shook his head to say no, then stroked his long white beard, looking deep in thought. Finally, he answered, "is there something bothering you, Kevin? For us to be here, meeting like this suggests that you are troubled. I did not make this meeting, so the only other thing is that you yourself wished it to happen. The astral plain, as you well know, is a safe place for wizards and witches to meet and help each other in discussion, but those that have the power to conjure up the Astral Plain have been dealing in magic for some considerable time. I find it curious that you, so young and inexperienced, have this sort of power in you to do this." Kevin just stared at Merlin, "but I don't understand," he said eventually. I thought you had called this meeting. Merlin smiled, "no Kevin, it was you, you have done this through your subconscious without you even knowing it. It still confuses me that you have the power to do this, but now you here what is it that I can help you with?."

Kevin turned away from Merlin, slowly moving to the edge of the pond before turning and saying. "I am not sure, but I came across a middle-aged man and woman staring at my window. When I questioned them, they gave some story about an owl that had perched itself on my windowsill. That was not you, by any chance?" Kevin asked. "Merlin smiled, "no, it was not me, young wizard," he replied, "so could it be just an ordinary owl do you think?" Kevin asked, "perhaps," Merlin replied. "What did these two people look like, and did they describe anything else about the owl to you?" Kevin walked back towards Merlin, saying, "well, I am not too sure, you see the first thing I saw was a cat riding on the back of a dog, but when I looked back, the cat and dog had gone, and there in the animal's place was this man and woman. They asked if the owl was mine that they had seen on the windowsill as they are rare in the parts where I live. I know I was getting annoyed with them as they kept calling me little boy." Merlin laughed, "what's so funny" Kevin said crossly. "you are Kevin," Merlin said, "listen, if these people were a wizard and witch, then they could be hundreds, maybe thousands of years old like me, to them you are just an ordinary human boy that will live to maybe ninety if you're lucky, but to them that is merely just a blink of the eye in time to them." "Have you ever heard the phrase, don't judge a book by its cover? You have already judged these people. Now, what were they wearing? What else did they say to you?" Kevin described the clothes they were wearing as just normal clothes that any normal person would wear, and the only thing he could remember was them asking about the owl. Merlin sat down on the log near him, stroking his beard. "So, all they really wanted to know was if you owned the owl they had seen. Have you seen this owl, Kevin?"

"No, well, not really, not on my windowsill, but I have seen it perched on the telegraph pole near my window a couple of times. I thought it was you watching me." Merlin rose to his feet, "No, Kevin, it is not I keeping watch on you, but we must assume that there are others now that may have entered watching you. For what reason? I cannot tell you yet, but be careful, Kevin. We know of certain wizards from the past that has moved from time to time in search of certain artifacts that can make them more powerful." Kevin broke Merlin's speech, "to do what?" he asked. Merlin shook his head and then answered, "I don't really know at this present time, perhaps they come to stop me from gaining peace and freedom from my task, or it could be that they have another thing they wish to do that could jeopardise all those that may stand in their way to gain this power for their use. You must quickly learn, Kevin, what Godwill is teaching you. Always be on your guard. Sometimes those who are friendly towards you are not all they seem." Merlin walked over to Kevin and took him by the arm before saying, "I have been doing some more studying on the Power stone and may just have found out in what location this lies. But to get to it, the wizard that goes on this quest must be powerful, experienced, and level-headed to gain this artifact. Time is not our friend. Every day I grow weaker. I depend on you, Kevin, to help me. Once I have verified the place it is, I will tell you. Now go, watch your back and those close to you. We will talk again, on which you can depend." With that, Merlin waved his hand, and Kevin saw himself drifting back along the path until the path was clouded over, and he could see it no more. The vision faded, and Kevin drifted off back into a deep sleep.

The next morning Kevin got up, washed, had breakfast, and went off to school just like any other day. Kevin was now starting to think about schoolwork as dull and boring stuff and wanted only to concentrate on the magic. Although the school was not so appealing, he did manage to retain his enthusiasm for football and was still playing for his local boys' side at the weekends. That day after school, he was feeling ready for anything that Godwill was going to throw at him. Instead, when Godwill turned up at the spinney, it was quite different. "Ok, young Wilks, today we are going to see how well-developed that brain of yours really is. No dueling today." Kevin stood looking at his teacher with his mouth open staring in amazement, saying nothing. Godwill continued, "today we will try and concentrate on the art of form changing, not just animals but other objects also, chairs, tables, and so on, you get what I am saying, Wilks." Kevin just nodded in reply. "For this, I do not see why we have to slow time down as we will be doing everything in here, so let's get started, shall we." Kevin again nodded in agreement. "Right, the first thing we need to do is get our mind focused. To do that, we must decide which is the best way that we can obtain the perfect shape of what we wish to become. How do we do that, Wilks?"

Kevin stared at Godwill before speaking, then said, "I guess you clear your mind, think of the animal or object, and just do it." Godwill frowned, then blurted out, "you guess, what is to guess about? If you do not have the required conscience and thought to turn yourself into the object, then it can go horribly wrong, and you may get stuck forever more in that shape. This is what I said to you about how magic could harm you more than be useful. Now I suggest that you do not guess or have any doubts about this and let us see what you have got." Godwill stepped a little distance back and then continued. "Right, yesterday you turned yourself into a bear, no mean act I can say, but you could only hold that shape for a brief time, and when you changed back, it left you weak, did it not?" Kevin agreed, "Well then, let us start with something less strenuous first. I want you to focus on being a chair, just like this one," as he pulled the chair towards him. Look at the shape, the structure, concentrate on that, not the colour or height of it, just the basic shape. When you think you have it in your mind, say the chant, "Gradiation Columbine Morphious." Kevin chanted the spell and immediately changed in a flash to an exact copy of the chair. Godwill moved over to it and sat on it. Within three- or four seconds, Kevin changed back to himself and collapsed on the floor with Godwill on top of him. "Get off," Kevin shouted at Godwill, "what do you think you are doing?" Godwill got to his feet whilst Kevin lay there on the floor, tired. "What on earth was that all about, young Wilks? Is that the best you can do?"

Kevin slowly got up and then said, "well, I hardly thought that you would want to sit on me," he said. "But that is the idea. If anything was trying to harm you and you changed into a piece of furniture, then you must be able to maintain the shape and strength of it to not expose yourself, do you understand?" Kevin nodded, then said, "I think so, sir." Godwill stood with his hand on his forehead, "you think so" he bellowed, "if I was a bad wizard and this just happened, I would think nothing of killing you as you changed shape, believe me, it happened many years ago, and I do not want it to happen again." Kevin now standing straight quickly asked, "when, who was killed and who made the killing?" Godwill turned away and moved to the other side of the room, "who sir, tell me." Godwill looked sad and had a blank expression on his face, "no one you knew or will ever know," he said with a lowering of his voice and his eyes turned down to the floor. Kevin could see that Godwill was not happy to talk about it, so he left the inquiry for another time. "So, what now?" Kevin asked. "Now, now," Godwill boomed again, "we do not move onto something else until you master this first, so let us try again, and this time when I sit on you, do not relax and collapse. Stay in your form until I give you the command to change back, OK." Kevin once again concentrated and changed himself into the chair. Godwill sat on the chair and read some of the assignments that he needed to check from students. Eventually, after a time, he stood up and commanded Kevin to turn back to himself. With a small flash, Kevin had turned himself back, kneeling on the floor before collapsing altogether. Godwill helped him to his feet and into another chair. "Not so easy is it," Godwill said. "This is where we need to strengthen your mind and body, so it does not take it out of you when you do this. Here, eat this." Godwill handed Kevin what looked like a black root. "Go on. It will put back your energy quickly." Kevin took a bite of the root, it tasted like liquorice, but as he ate it, he could feel himself getting stronger.

After a while, Godwill got Kevin to turn himself into a bird, table, cat, dog, book, and, last of all, the bear he chose the day before. Each time Kevin changed back, he felt exhausted, but Godwill explained the more he practiced, the easier it would become and the longer he would be able to last in that shape without becoming exhausted. Godwill told Kevin to try these changes for small periods of time on a regular basis to get to know how to control them. The next lesson would be in one week's time, and by then, Godwill wanted to see a vast improvement in the making. At the end of the lesson, Godwill turned to Kevin and said, "study well, Wilks, I know you have the potential to do wonderful things, just like one of your family members did, but unfortunately, he did not want to follow the ways of our lifestyle. Do not question me for who it was because I will not tell you, but I know you will be even better than him. I feel it in my bones. Now, let us stop for the day, shall we? We have done enough." With that, the two walked out of the door and set off home, with Kevin wondering who Godwill could have been talking about.

When Kevin got home, Paul was there asking how and what had gone on in his lesson today. Kevin explained everything to Paul and even about what Godwill had said to him regarding a family member. "Do you know who he is talking about, Paul? Is it you?" Kevin asked. Paul shook his head, "no, not me, bro; it was me that noticed your potential and got you started on this path, no, not me, even though I did repent against it for a while. He is talking about someone else we do not even know about, but who could he mean? Is he still alive, or has he passed away? He could have been an uncle or cousin, but that does not tell us if he is still alive. I know of no one else apart from you and me in our family who has this gift. Certainly, there have been no suggestions for it. Are you sure that is what Godwill said"? Kevin snapped back at his brother, "of course I'm sure. What do you think that I imagined it?" Paul just ushered Kevin to keep his voice down by shushing him, then said, "well, you did say you saw the bathroom handle being turned when you were in the bath and thought it was me when I was downstairs, remember?" Kevin snapped back, "that's different, and for your information, I did see it turn so there, I am not seeing or hearing things, ok!" Paul just agreed, "ok, then we need to see if we can do some digging about and try and find out who this person is or was, but I have not got a clue where to start." The boys talked about uncles, granddads, and cousins for the next hour, trying to remember if they had noticed anything out of the ordinary or what their parents had told them regarding the ones that had passed away. Nothing came easy or was seen to be out of the ordinary from what they could think of. Eventually, it was teatime then bedtime, and the boys went off to the bedrooms and fell asleep., there must be something he knew you would remember about it. Look deeper". Kevin tried hard to remember, but nothing was there, nothing that stood out to make him remember, "I can't. There is nothing else I can see, honestly" Kevin fell forward face down on Paul's bed, "ok," his brother said, "go back to bed and sleep; who knows, you may get a second chance if you do, don't forget to look around in the vision, now I need some sleep, you can tell me what happens in the morning. Kevin returned to his bed and fell asleep

Chapter 9

Matrees and the Vision of Veraticous

Kevin lay cuddled up and warm in his bed as he heard his brother moving around, getting ready to do his morning paper round. A small knock on his bedroom door, then the door opened with his brother standing in the doorway, "morning, bro, any thoughts on what we discussed last night?" Kevin yawned and shook his head, "no, not one. Perhaps if we asked mum about our family tree, she might be able to put us on the right track," Kevin said. "Are you nuts?" Paul snapped back, "what do you think we are going to say to her? Oh, by the way, mum, do you happen to know if any of our family were witches or wizards throughout the ages, and are some still alive?" Kevin just smiled, "no, all we need to say is that we are doing a project at school about our family trees and see what materialises. You know she likes to help us in our schooling." Paul thought for a brief time, then answered, "maybe, but we will need both mums and dads' sides to see who we have that we can investigate." Kevin agreed as Paul left the bedroom, stating that he had to go to do his paper round and they would discuss it further later.

Kevin got up, dressed, and went downstairs and started to talk to his mum. "Mum, we are doing a project at school regarding family trees. Do you know anything about your side of the family?" His mum looked at him, thought, and replied.

"Well, I can tell you about your nans and grandad, Cussons, a few half Cussons that I know about, but if you need to know further back, then you will have to go to the church and look through the church records, although that will take some time. When has this project got to be done?" Kevin looked at his mum and then said, "by the end of the year." Kevin's mum stared at him, then said, "Well, the best person to speak to is granddad Wilks, he is a volunteer at the church, and he may be able to help with finding records depending on how far you need to go back, I would see him. I am guessing you need to know of your dads' side too, am I right?" Kevin nodded his head in agreement, "well then, you need to get started, as the end of the school year is only a month away and there will be a lot of work to get through. Who has asked you to do this?" Kevin, thinking, quickly replied, "Mr. Godwill, he thought it would be good to know who our ancestors were and if any of them worked for any charities or religious churches or maybe a missionary." Mum smiled, "that sounds like old Godwill, trying to get people interested in religion, ok, go see granddad and see if he can help you." Kevin smiled and grabbed a piece of toast from the table, and off he went to his granddad.

Kevin peddled to his granddad and found him in the garden watering his plants. "What are you doing, granddad? It is nearly winter; nothing is going to grow now," Kevin said. "Hello Kevin, you never know what will grow. It is not as though we have snow or frost at the moment, and well, I just thought I would try and get these flowers to bloom before the severe weather comes in", his granddad replied. "So, what brings you to see us on this lovely day?". Kevin parked his bike next to the shed and started asking his granddad about the records for the family tree. "Well, I can make a few enquiries, but there will be many records that need to be gone through, and the church will not let just anyone touch the records. Let me have a word with the vicar and see if he will let me have a look; who knows, he might just let us see. After all, he is a very dear friend of mine". Kevin hugged his granddad and then followed him into his house to see his nan. Kevin spent time talking to both grandparents for a while before cycling home again. Once home, Kevin met up with his brother a told him what had gone on. Paul now decided that they should go to the park in the afternoon and try and chill out and just see what would turn up. Kevin agreed, so the two boys had lunch and then went to the park. As they walked, they talked about what Kevin had learned so far regarding magic and shape-changing. They laughed and joked as they ran and walked through the park and back to the bikes. "I need to go and feed Fergull. You coming to Paul?" Kevin asked, "No, you go feed your bird, then go home. I have to go and see my mate Roger; I need to get some info from him regarding the chemistry assignment. See you at home, bro." Both boys peddled off in different directions until Kevin came to the spinney. He opened the door, and Fergull was there to greet him. Kevin walked over, stroked him, and then fed him. Kevin grabbed a couple of books that were on a dusty shelf and went and sat down to read them. Fergull flapped its wings and flew to where Kevin was sitting, perching itself on the back of the chair.

Kevin looked through the book until he came to a section in it regarding an extract on the Power stone. The section read, 'the alchemist Marcus Dwight originally made the Power stone, in the early 13th century with magical powers so great that the wearing of the stone would keep the occupier alive forever. Immortality was there, whoever owned the stone. As Kevin read on, it stated that the stone was the attraction of every wizard in the land, and many tried to steal it from Dwight throughout the ages but failed, and many died through trying. The stone has an ultimate power that can only be used for the good of the person who owns it. Many dark wizards had gained the stone and tried to do dark evil things with it, only for it to backfire on the wizard and kill him. Throughout time, spells have been formed to change the way it acts, so the stone became the most sought-after prize any wizard could collect. For this reason, after the last incident in the 15th century, Marcus Dwight decided that the stone could no longer be safe and tried to destroy it. The stone could not be destroyed, so he tried to hide it. Unfortunately, a gang of black wizards overpowered Dwight and took the stone from him. Without the stone, Dwight became vulnerable and was killed. Since then, many fought over the stone until it happened on by chance a wizard known as Cederic. Eventually, even Cederic, being plagued by wizards, decided to hide the stone in a location only known to him before dying. The stone was never found again. That was the last entry in the section. Kevin continued to flick through the book to try and find something else regarding the power stone, but he could find anything else. He then turned to the second book, which was handwritten and mentioned in a passage about historic locations throughout the ages regarding magical moonlight, mystic creatures being seen on different dates of the year, and mountain ranges around the world. There was no name in the book who wrote it but a single letter J on the inside of the cover.

Kevin flicked through both books again before placing them back on the dusty shelf and walking away. As he turned at the door to check on Fergull, he noticed that the books were no longer on the shelf; in fact, the books were not anywhere in the room. Kevin closed the door and went back to the shelf the books were on before. No imprints or even his fingerprints on the shelf were evident. Only a large build-up of dust that had not been cleaned for a long time. Kevin stood pondering and looking around the room; neither book could be seen. Kevin was confused but ended up leaving the spinney and cycling home, thinking of what he had read.

Once home, he put his bike in the shed, went into the house, and got himself a drink. His mother met him in the kitchen and asked, "did you see granddad? Will he help look for the records"? Kevin answered with a babbling, "what? Oh yes, he said he would have a word with the vicar about looking for the pieces." Kevin's mum looked at him then said, "pieces, what pieces?" Kevin snapped out of his thought then answered quickly, "people, I mean people." His mum looked at him in deep thought then asked, "are you alright, Kevin? You seem distracted. Why did you say pieces and people rather than ancestors, is something wrong? Are you sure you are ok"? Kevin took a sip of his water and then answered, "of course, mum, I was just thinking about something else Vinny said to me yesterday, that's all." His mum just gave a little sigh, then hugged him and said, "have you two fallen out again? You two are just like brothers, always fighting then making up, giving things time. Everything will be ok, you'll see." His mum gave Kevin a quick kiss on his forehead and then walked away into the living room.

Paul burst in and grabbed a drink of water, shouting, "what's up, bro? You look bothered. Anything I can do?" Kevin grabbed Paul and dragged him upstairs into his room, and closed the door. "Listen," he said as he told his brother all about the spinney and the books he had found in there. Paul listened with intent, then, in the end, said, "are you kidding me? You say you saw these books, then they just disappeared. Sure you did not just imagine it?" Paul laughed, then continued, "just like the bathroom door and the owl on the lamp post." Kevin snapped back, "no, I did not imagine it, and for your information, just remember that we live in a time of magic still, or are they just tricks we do? You never listen to me, you try to make me believe you are interested, but you are not. Why? Because I have been chosen for this, not you. You are bitter about that and don't forget who introduced me to all this, you, that's right, what? You could not handle it, so you thought you would pass it on, so if it fails, you are not the one who gets blamed by everyone, is that it?". Paul just waited until Kevin had finished his ranting, then said, "finished, are we? You know, when I first knew what I could do, I was truly angry also. I got to the stage where I started hatting everyone I knew. I felt like they were of no consequence to me at all, but I needed a reality check to bring me back to who I really was, and no, I did not pass this on to you to do so I do not get blamed for your exploits. Lastly, it was you who started all this. Remember the first football match of the season where you made the boy miss the ball, miss the penalty, do you? I just helped you along. I have not seen the astral plain, so tell me, am I jealous? Boy, you bet I am, but I am here to help you, not hinder you, and yes, although sometimes I think you may be imagining things, sometimes you say things that also make sense. Take, for instance, the Power Stone. The piece I had, which now Godwill has, is known as the Time stone, according to him. It can help slow time, repair injuries, and strengthen spells. This stone came from another. I remember him telling me so could be part of the Power stone, as you said you read about. You also said Merlin is searching for something, and it could be that he is trying to find the other pieces."

Kevin broke into the conversation with, "which means that Crandloss is also looking for the stone." Paul swung round and replied, "but Crandloss is no more. He has split into Matrees and Jerez; you know that." Kevin got off the bed and walked to the window, "I remember Merlin saying to me on the astral plain, be careful as people are not who they seem to be. What if instead of Jarez being the good side of Crandloss, he is just an imposter pretending to be good? What if both Matrees and Jerez are both bad and searching separately for the stone to try and cut time in finding them?" Paul sat staring at his brother, then said, "Crikey, I forgot you have a mega logic brain and deep thoughts. I suppose it is possible after you explained it that way that it could be possible, but what if they found it? What would they do with it?" Kevin shook his head, "I do not know, but we need to try and get this stone before they do. We need to talk to Godwill and find out the whole truth behind all this." Paul nodded his head in agreement, then said, "hang on, Godwill is off next week, holiday, which is why he told you to practice all this week whilst he was away."

Kevin replied, "but he never said he was going to be away, just to practice as the next lesson was going to be," Paul joined in also saying "in a week's time." Kevin sat back down on the bed, "what do we do know?" he said. Both boys went quiet for a while before Paul spoke, "well, you mentioned the books had the letter J at the back of them, perhaps, that is a clue that we need to try and find out first. Then, we need to concentrate on the places that you mentioned in the second book. This is where we need to start." "Kevin, when you go to sleep tonight, try to think of what you saw in the room at the spinney and try and see if you can remember all that you saw again. There is something you glanced at that you may be missing. We will talk in the morning, so for the rest of the day, try relaxing and see if anything comes to you."

For the rest of the day, Kevin relaxed, but however much he thought, he could not remember anything else before bedtime. At bedtime, Kevin took out his spell book and read it to the point that he fell asleep. As he slept, he started to dream. After a while, he felt himself moving to a place he had not been to before. The place was a heavily wooded grove, and two figures stood next to a large oak tree. As Kevin got closer, he managed to make out the people who stood there. It was Crandloss, but the second person he saw he would later know as Veraticous. As Kevin got closer, he could hear Veraticous talking to Crandloss about how the fool Dwight had tried to break the power stone into pieces but failed. Many wizards had tried to get the stone but failed until it was lost forever after being hidden by the last owner named, Cederic. However, a small piece of what was believed to be from the stone was now in circulation and in the control of Merlin. Kevin heard Crandloss say that he would get it from Merlin or he would suffer the same fate as his friend Postromus. Kevin was shocked to hear this then he heard veraticous tell Crandloss of a spell to split himself in two to help speed things up with finding the pieces of stone. It was a spell called Caristo Seperandum. It splits the soul into two parts, two people, but also has the effect of diminishing the power of spell casting. This can be done many times but only for short periods of time, no longer than three days maximum before the two must be reunited. Kevin heard Crandloss ask, "what happens if the two are not reunited within the time frame," Veraticous replied, "then the two will be separated forevermore and will eventually end up fighting for the power of the other. The strongest one will become the victor and eventually will become the whole person once again called Crandloss. You, my nephew, are bound for remarkable things. Already you have killed one of the greatest wizards ever known. To become the greatest, you still have one in your way, Merlin. You must find the stone to gain the power to defeat this wizard. Only then can you rule over the magical people of this world and the non-magic minions. No one will ever question your desires and will tremble when your name is spoken. Therefore, I will train you to be the greatest wizard of all time so that everyone will remember you throughout the thousands of years you rule. Remember, for this; you need to have the power stone, so you need to find it before that imbecilic Merlin. As Veraticous spoke these last words, Kevin felt himself drifting away from the site and back to his bed. He drifted off into a deep sleep and did not know anything else until the sun shone through the window for the beginning of another morning.

Kevin jumped out of bed and raced into Paul's bedroom, but he was not there. He had already left to go on his paper round, so he had to curb his enthusiasm until his brother got home.

Kevin dressed and raced downstairs, ready for breakfast. As he turned the corner from the stairs, he saw his mother standing looking out of the kitchen window. He walked up to her and noticed she was just standing, staring, with no eye movement, no body movement. Kevin looked in the direction of the garden his mum was transfixed in and noticed that the birds were not moving either, some captured in flight with still wings. Kevin turned quickly towards the room and noticed Matrees sitting in the corner of the kitchen, smiling at him. Kevin pulled out his wand and pointed it at Matrees. "Wait," cried Matrees, "I mean you no harm, wizard." Kevin stepped back, still pointing his wand at Matrees, "I don't believe you," replied Kevin, "I know who you are and what you are." "Oh, so you do you, then you will know what I am searching for then, boy." Matrees now got up from the chair and moved slowly towards Kevin. Kevin moved back further until he could go no further. "Stay where you are, Matrees. I know how to use this wand. I'm not scared either." Matrees stopped and bowed before Kevin, "as you wish, young wizard, but ask yourself the question, do you have the belief in yourself to control the magic within to stop me? Could I whip out my wand and kill you as easy as blinking an eye before you could gain the courage to cast a spell at me, could I?" Matrees laughed as he finished speaking. "I could have killed you and your pathetic family many times over. Oh, I know your brother has gained strength since the last meeting I had with him, and even old Godwill has much to offer, but why do they prepare you? I still need to know the answer to this. Does the fool Merlin think a boy like you could ever gain enough knowledge or strength to defeat me and stop me from becoming the greatest wizard of all time? People, yes, all people will live in fear of my name when I rule this entire world and have millions of worshipers and wizards and pathetic people doing my every bidding, and you, you are the one that is supposed to stop me".

Again, Matrees laughed aloud. Kevin, still with his wand held to Matrees then, answered quite calmly, "but you are forgetting one thing, Matrees," Matrees stopped laughing and paid attention to what Kevin was saying. "You are just one part of a vile man who killed to split himself in two, one good, one evil. To gain single occupancy and what you desire, you need two things." Matrees asked, "And what two things are they, boy?" Kevin smiled at Matrees, then answered, "you need to kill the good half that is just as powerful as you. Both share the brain that has been taught the spells and the confidence to use them. This will be hard for you because if you are successful, you will never again become the man you were before the split, never again be known as Crandloss." Matrees sniggered, then sneered before saying, "So what, I am Crandloss, here inside, to get rid of that goody two shoes will be a blessing. He is a conscience I never desired, a blot on my mind that has no meaning for life or ambition. Just a waste of space within me, I will think nothing of disposing of him. As for not being known as Crandloss, well, it is not such a terrible thing. The name of Matrees will still be as fearful. Mark my words, boy". Kevin shook his head in disbelief. "And what's the second thing you have to tell me, boy," Matrees enquired, "maybe I also have to get rid of that fool Merlin. Well, if I can defeat his friend Postromus when he was in his prime, then he should be no trouble". Matrees started to laugh again. Kevin broke Matrees laughter with a simple "No, what you need to destroy Merlin and the same to destroy you is the power stone. Without this, neither of you has the power to destroy the other. You gained power from killing Postromus but still do not have enough to finish Merlin off. So, you see, Matrees, I know of your quest for the stone, and I will do everything in my power to stop you." Matrees laughed once again, then said, "is that so, well" Matrees went to whip out his wand, and before he could do Kevin cast "Sherek," in a flash Kevin disappeared as Matrees cast "Transisomb," the disarming spell, but Kevin had already disappeared.

Kevin re-materialized behind Matrees and quickly snatched the wand out of his hand. Matrees then held his right arm out towards Kevin chanting, Elivio Consensious. Cups, knives and forks, chairs, and the table now powered their way toward Kevin. In a flash, Kevin chanted Crevatious Septimium, the return spell, which everything turned in a blink of an eye and hurtled back at Matrees, knocking him to the ground. Kevin now stood over him with both wands now pointing toward Matrees. "You see, Matrees, not so puny as you thought, I am a match for you, and I will get stronger, so do not come here again, or it will be your last." With that, Kevin snapped Matrees's wand. As the wand broke, Matrees let out an almighty blood-curdling cry of "NOOOOOO," a flash of light and a power so great it threw Kevin through the kitchen window into the backyard. He lay there dazed and unable to move as he watched the now fuming Matrees approach him. Matrees knelt in front of Kevin and whispered, "you are a fool to think that you will beat me. A wand is not the only power I possess. You and your family will pay dear for you breaking my mother's wand, and you will be killed. Matrees pointed his hand at Kevin as he lay bleeding on the ground and began to chant Excelious Painclos, the torture spell. Kevin was covered in immense pain from head to foot writhing around on the floor as Matrees's power got stronger and stronger. Kevin could hardly think of anything but the intense pain going through his body, but then let a chant "Crevatious Septimium," the return spell, as he freely raised his wand in Matrees's direction. With a crackling sound and another flash of light, the power from Kevin's wand found its way through the hand of Matrees and sent him shooting backward with a loud cry of pain. Just at that moment, Kevin's brother and a couple of his mates, who were also wizards, came around the corner and saw the flashes of light coming from his backyard. Paul and his friends had noticed that the time elements had slowed and now hurried back to his house to see his brother.

When Paul and his friends got to the rear of the house, he saw Kevin laying on the ground bleeding, with Matrees getting to his feet and moving back towards Kevin. Matrees stopped as he saw Kevin's brother and friends raise their wands in his direction. With a chant of "Gradiation Columbine Morphious," the changing spell, Matrees turned into what looked like a dust storm and hurtled towards Kevin; as he lay unconscious on the ground, he heard Matreeses voice. "This is not over, boy, you will lose, and you will die. It is invertible. There will be no saviours at our next meeting, so until then." The dust storm turned and hurtled between Paul and his friends, brushing them apart and knocking some to the ground, then silence. Paul raced over to his brother and cradled his head in his arms, and slowly uttered the chant, "Compare-Relapsum." Kevin's cuts slowly started to heal themselves as his brother continued to chant the charm. Finally, Kevin's cuts and grazes were gone, but Kevin still lay on the ground, not moving. Paul ushered his friends to help carry Kevin to his room which they did, then set about repairing the damage that Matrees had caused. Once everything was back to how it should be, Paul, still sitting by Kevin's bed, noticed something that his brother had in his hand that was now glowing.

Paul called to the others, who ran upstairs into Kevin's room and stared at what Paul was pointing at. The thing Kevin had in his hand was still part of Matrees's wand, and the power was now working its way into Kevin. A blue light was moving from the wand up Kevin's arm towards his head. Suddenly the light disappeared, and Kevin woke with a gasp and a painful cry. Then silence. He sat up, looked at his brother and his friends, and asked them, "what are you doing in my bedroom? What's going on, Paul, and what's this thing digging into my hand?" Paul looked at his brother and quietly asked, "do you not remember Kevin? You had a fight with Matrees; he nearly killed you." Kevin stood up quite woozy, holding his head, then replied, "Matrees nearly killed me. What are you going on about? I got kicked in the head during the football match we just played, that is why my head hurts and my arms, legs, hands, feet, in fact, my whole body hurts. Must have been one hard knock I took in the head." Kevin sat back down on the bed, holding his head still.

His brother, now trying to explain to him what had gone on, and about the blue light that was coming from what now looked like an ordinary twig still in Kevin's hand, which had covered him in light.

Unfortunately, Kevin did not remember anything about it. Roger, one of Paul's friends, now let out, "well, blow me down. He really does not remember anything of fighting Matrees and nearly dying for it. That must have been one powerful spell Matrees laid on him to blow his mind like that. What are we going to do, Paul? If he does not remember anything about the fight, does he remember he is a wizard"? Paul looked at Kevin and then asked, "well, do you remember that you aren't a wizard, bro"? Kevin stood again, this time in less pain, then answered his brother. "A what, a wizard, me? Do you mean someone that does magic tricks? You are having a laugh, aren't you?" Paul held his head in his hands and then said, "it's all gone. Nothing is in his head. I'm surprised he even remembers me." Paul gripped Kevin by the shoulders and shook him hard. "Now listen, you pipsqueak, you are a wizard, someone that can do extraordinary things through words and movements. Now remember, damn you." Paul was shouting as he ended his sentence, with his brother now being shaken around like a rag doll. Suddenly Kevin had had enough and, from nowhere, lifted his hand that propelled Paul to the ceiling holding him there. "Do not lay your hands on me again, or it just might be the last thing you do; do you hear me." Roger tried to go towards Kevin, but again Kevin pointed at Roger and the other two friends, and they were also pinned against the ceiling, unable to move.

Kevin stood with both arms held aloft, holding his brother and his friends fixed to the ceiling, when suddenly Paul shouted to his Brother, "Kevin, it's your brother Paul. Why are you doing this? We mean you no harm, we are here to help you and look over you to make sure nothing happens to you, please, stop it, you're hurting us". Kevin, now with his eyes transfixed on his brother, suddenly lowered his arms, and his brother and friends were slowly lowered to the floor. "What comes over you, bro? we are trying to help you; there is no need to try and harm us when we helped get rid of Matrees." Kevin just looked at his brother, then lowered his head and said, "sorry." Kevin just sat back on his bed and put his head in his hands and started crying. "What went on, it is real, so real, I could have been killed. It is what he said he wanted to do and what he was going to do. What am I going to do, Paul? I am nowhere as strong or knowledgeable in magic as him. Am I going to die"?.

Paul just sat beside his now very scared brother, hugging him hard, "No bro, your time is not now to die, and I certainly am not ready to die either. I will not let this happen to you, bro, I promise. You have friends you know about here and more that you do not know yet but will meet on your journey. I need to see Godwill and let him know what went on. Come on boys, let's go find him now." Kevin hung onto Paul's arm as if to say do not leave me. Paul just looked at his scared brother and said, "it's ok, Matrees will not be back today. You will be safe, I promise." Kevin looked hard at his brother and finally let go of his arm and nodded. "ok," he said in a quiet voice, "but please do not be too long." Paul just nodded and replied, "I will be back before you know it" then Paul and his friends raced away on their bikes to find Godwill.

Caulpolsier and Postromus

As the boys sped along on their bikes, talking about what had just happened, Paul skidded his bike to a stop. The others noticing Paul had stopped, turned back to meet him. "what's going on, Paul? Come on. We have to see Godwill, remember." Paul lowered his head then spoke, "that's just it. Godwill is on holiday, isn't he!" Roger looked up, then sighed, "of course, now what do we do? "Paul just sighed deeply, then said we must go to the spinney and look through the books to see if there is anything we can find out that will strengthen my brother and us. I don't know how Matrees found out about our address. Even when I had my incident with him, he never knew or visited our home. How has this happened"? The boys quickly cycled to the spinney in aid to find something that could lead them to some answers.

Whilst his brother and friends were trying to work things out, Kevin was lying on his bed and now starting to get bad headaches. The pain in his head was so immense that he called out in pain. Kevin's mother now came running upstairs as Roger had restarted the time before leaving with Paul and the other friends to see what the cries were all about. As she opened Kevin's bedroom door, she saw what looked to be an old man lying on Kevin's bed. Just for a split second, then it was Kevin. Kevin's mum shook her head and continued towards Kevin. She knelt by his bedside and placed a hand on his forehead, it was cold and sweaty, and Kevin's skin seemed to be a little off colour. In fact, she thought it looked like it had a light blue tint to it but thought that Kevin was coming down with something, so she ran downstairs and phoned the doctor. Kevin's pain continued for a while and then disappeared just before the doctor arrived. His mum showed the doctor up to Kevin's room and opened the door. There sat Kevin on the edge of the bed, reading a newspaper. "Now then, my boy, what's the problem? your mum said something about bad head pain and your skin being a little blue tinge to it, so let's have a look at you." Kevin stood up, "really, mum, I just got kicked in the head when a few friends and I were playing football. I must say it did give me a bad headache, but then wouldn't you have if you just got someone's boot in your face? As for the blue tinge to the skin, well, I cannot see anything, can you doctor"? The doctor just said, "well, whilst I'm here, we might as well look at you. It could be that you have a concussion or something, and we don't want anything bad happening to you, do we?"

The doctor shook his head, then examined Kevin and concluded that he needed a bit of rest to help stop the head from hurting. "I suggest, young man, you keep on your feet when playing football so you do not get kicked in the head again. Now take some aspirin and try to get some rest." The doctor then turned to Kevin's mum and said, "if he starts being sick or complaining of severe headaches, call for an ambulance and get him to hospital, you can't be too careful with head injuries, you know." Kevin's mum agreed and showed the doctor out. She immediately ran back upstairs to Kevin's room with two aspirin and a glass of water. "Here, take these and try and get some rest. I was very worried about you calling out in all that pain. I need to keep my eyes on you tonight, my boy. If it hurts that bad, then it is off to the hospital for you, just like the doctor said". Kevin took the aspirins and drank, then lay down on his bed. Soon he was off into a deep sleep.

After a while, Kevin woke suddenly and was aware that he was not in his bed but lying on the floor next to an old oak tree. He stood up and looked around the place where he was. He looked around and then thought it could only be the Astral plain, but why was he there? A faint sound of laughter was coming from a little way away, so he followed it to find out the source. As he turned a corner in the road, he saw two young children playing in the distance. He called out to them, but the children did not reply. They just kept on playing. Kevin moved nearer to speak to them, but it was as if they were not aware of his presence. Kevin noticed the children as a young boy and young girl, about 11 years old, playing merrily together, then a voice called to them." Postromus, Caulpolsier, it is time to come home now. Come on, you both have chores to do and practice to complete. Kevin looked on; a thin, tall man now stood in the middle of the field next to the two young children. Kevin thought for a moment. Caulpolsier, that's Crandloss's mother, and Postromus, "what's going on"? The children both answered at the same time, "coming, Mr. Lightfoot." Both children held hands, and off they went with the teacher. There was a mist that appeared that completely covered everything Kevin was looking at, then it started to disappear. When it was clear, Kevin noticed that the scenery had changed. No longer was there a field with great oak trees there but a small building that had several windows in it. Kevin peered through one of the windows only to see the tall thin man called Mr. Lightfoot teaching. This time the children were older than Postromus and Caulpolsier, whom he had seen only a short time ago, but Kevin noticed that 2 of the children seemed to look exactly like them.

A bell sounded, and the children rushed out into the street, all but Postromus and Caulposier. These two held hands and stole a kiss between them as no one was watching. Finally, the two emerged from the classroom and walked around the school and out into the open field that was behind it. Kevin followed them down to a brook where the two young people had laid down on the bank and were holding each other. Kevin made his way to a tree that was right by them and listened as both talked. "I am so happy," Kevin heard Postromus say to Caulpolsier, "I can't think what I would do without you. I am so in love with you that my heart yearns for you all the time." Caulpolsier laughed and hugged him. "If it hurts that much for me," she said, "then why not give your heart or a little piece of it to me to hold in my hands forever." Postromus laughed then said, "if only I could, my darling, I would gratefully give it to you if I knew that we will never be parted," again Caulposier laughed and pushed Postromus to the side, "of course, we will never be parted, I love you, and you love me, why should we ever want to be apart." Caulpolsier kissed him on the lips and then stood up. "If you really do love me, then there may be a way of holding part of your heart in my hands always." Postromus stood up and looked puzzled, then said, "I thought you were joking," he said with a look of dismay on his face. "Well, if you really love me as much as you say you do, then it will be a small thing to do so I can never be away from you, but if you do not love me as you say you do, then I guess we may never be completely together." Caulpolsier turned and started to walk away. "Wait," he shouted, "I do love you, and I wish I could prove it to you, but I know of nothing I can do to place a piece of my heart in your hands without me killing myself, if that is what you ask of me then I shall do it." Caulpolsier turned to him and flung her arms around his shoulders. "I do not want you to die, I love you, but it would prove to me that your love is true if I had just a small part of your heart that I could place in the main stem of my wand, knowing you will be there to always protect me from harm." Postromus held Caulpolsier tight and then said, "if there was only a way then I would gladly do this to keep you from harm." A large smile came over the lips of Caulpolsier then she said. "Master Lightfoot knows of such magic that can take but a small string of the heart tissue without the heart being injured. Could you do this for me?" Postromus turned away from Caulpolsier, then turned and faced her. "I would gladly do this for you, but what will you do for me"? Caulpolsier smiled at him then whispered, I will bare you many children to keep your name going through all ages." Postromus held Caulpolsier tight and kissed the side of her face. "Then I will do this for you. Besides, I must keep you safe if you are going to bare me many children." Both laughed and headed back to the school.

The mist came down once more, and as it cleared, Kevin found himself inside a small bedchamber with Postromus lying on the bed with Mr. Lightfoot standing over him, chanting something Kevin had not heard before. Then he took Caulpolsiers wand and waved it around the heart area of the young wizard. With a piercing cry from Postromus, a small blue thread came from out of the heart direction and wrapped itself around Caulpolsiers wand. It shone bright blue then it eased itself into the breach of the wand, where the light faded. Postromus stopped screaming and sank into the bed and unconscious. Caulpolsier and Mr. Lightfoot left the room. Again, the mist appeared, and this time, when it lifted, only Postromus in his bedroom was visible, holding a letter. Tears falling from his face, Kevin noticed as the letter fell from his hands onto the floor. Kevin knelt to read the letter. It was from Caulpolsier saying that her father forbids them to be together ever again, so he is taking her away and not to come looking for her, or her father will kill him. Postromus was distraught and did nothing but lay on his bed crying. The mist fell one last time, and when it had cleared showed that Postromus's mother and father were pleading with him to stay in the village and work his broken heart out with those who love him. The wizard turned to his family and said, "I do not deserve love, I do not show love, I have no love in me for anyone. Therefore so that I do not create hate instead of love, I must leave this place and live the life of a hermit, never to love again. Farewell, mother and father, do not look for me as I will never be in the same place for a long time. Farewell." With that, he turned and walked away. The mist rose again but did not clear this time. Kevin slipped into a deep heavy sleep.

The next thing he knew was the thumping of someone running up the stairs and into his brothers' room. Kevin got up and went to his brother's room and tried to open the door, but it was locked. "Paul, you in there" he called. A faint reply came from inside, go away, do not come in. I do not want to hurt you; please, leave me alone". Kevin, now completely confused, asked, what is going on, Paul? Are you ok?". Kevin could hear a rustling going on in the bedroom and then heard his brother ask, "I'm ok, but are you"? Kevin replied, "yes, mum got the doctor here, and I had to take a couple of aspirin, but no immediate danger, anyway. Whilst I was resting, I had another vision." Paul opened his door and ushered his brother in before shutting the door tight again.

Kevin explained what he had seen in the latest visions regarding Caulpolsier and Postromus. Paul, now more relaxed, replied, "well, it makes more sense now." "What does" Kevin replied. Paul came and sat down by his brother and began to talk. "After the showing of the blue light, Roger, Trish, Scotty, and I were going to go find Godwill but then realised he was on holiday, so we went to the spinney and looked through a few books. Whilst there, we came a crossed a letter in a book. It was incredibly old but just barely readable. The only thing was it was not in English, so we had to get Scottie's computer to try and find out what language it was in. It took ages, but we eventually found something like it and translated what we could read from it. It was the letter from Caulpolsier to Postromus." Kevin stood up and clasped his hands, "so the vision was true."

. Paul raised his hands, "Nearly," Kevin looked at his brother with some confusion, then asked, "what do you mean nearly?". Paul continued, "Well, we could not translate the letter, but it mentioned that Caulpolsier did not really love Postromus but was only using him to gain some power for herself with the base of his heartstring." Kevin was even now more confused, "What?" Paul continued, "don't you see" Kevin shook his head, "with the heart string of Postromus inside the wand it will always be part of the person who holds it." Kevin still did not understand, "Postromus could not kill the person who used the wand against him as it would end up killing him." Kevin sat on Paul's bed to think. "Come on, bro, "piece it together." Kevin thought about it but still could not conclude an answer. Paul stood up then said, "in your visions, who killed Postromus?" Kevin replied Crandloss," "correct," answered Paul. "Who was Crandloss's mother?" Kevin answered, "Caulpolsier." Whose wand did Crandloss kill Postromus with?" Kevin stood up, "Caulpolsiers," "Correct again," said his brother. "In the books, we found it stated that a blue light shone from the wand of Caulpolsier before it killed him, that was his heart string trying to fight back but could not as the power from the holder overcomes it and intensifies the spell." "When you broke Matrees wand or Crandlosses wand, it was his mothers, and now you have released the soul of Postromus. It attached itself to the nearest living thing, You." Kevin looked at his brother with a look of disbelief and then sarcasm, then said, "really, you expect me to believe that you are joking, aren't you" he said now looking at his brother and the expression on his face. Nothing, but silence could be heard for the next few seconds then Kevin spoke again. "Come on Paul, it is not true, magic is magic but someone being able to preserve life itself to be able to still be part of this world hundreds and thousands of years after death. Now that is stretching things too far," and he gave a little laugh when he finished. Paul just looked at Kevin still with a look of worry on his face, then said.

"If you do not believe in this, then how do you account for Merlin or Cranloss? I mean, Matrees and Jerez? There are not just 50 years old, Kevin. Add a few hundred years onto them for all, and there you have it,". Kevin answered very quickly, ah, "but I have only ever met Merlin in the Astral plain, a mystic place where magic is useless, so he could just be a figment of our imaginations" Kevin said with a big smirk on his face. Paul just got off his bed and walked towards his brother, then spoke, " So what about in our front room, Crandloss, Matrees, Jarez? They are all flesh and blood. You have seen them, touched them, felt them, are they imaginary images, or do your chest and arms hurt because you have done something else to them apart from getting hit by a magical spell in them". Paul just smirked back at his brother and walked towards the window. Kevin, now in deep thought, could say nothing. The two brothers turned towards each other before Kevin spoke. "So, what am I to do if the soul or heart of Postromus is inside me? How will I know when it is coming forth and not me?" Paul shook his head, "I do not know, bro, but you are going to need all that logical mind to be working all the time to keep him silent until we can work out what to do or how to control it. I do not mind telling you. It was pretty scary for me and the others to see the power emanating from your two arms without a wand. It had to be an increase in power from him through the heartstring you have now inside you. If that is just the tip of the iceberg, I don't want to feel the force of all his power, I can tell you".

"Look, all I can say is you need to be able to take yourself away from anything that makes you angry or upset until we have spoken to Godwill or you have been in touch with Merlin. The only problem is that will Postromus be friendly to Merlin in the Astral plain if you take him there." Kevin, again looking confused, asked, "why shouldn't he be? Both Merlin and he were old friends." Paul just said, "I am not sure he will be open arms for Merlin, so I think you had better try and control that brain of yours, bro, or there might just be another problem. I will try and find Godwill first thing tomorrow morning and get a meeting set up, until then unfortunately, you have had to grow up rapidly over these past few months, and I have got to say I am mighty proud of you as I do not think I would have been able to handle this at your age". The two brothers cuddled for a split second then parted. "Well, it's been a sort of interesting day, and there is more to come, I feel, so I suggest we get some sleep and rest. Just remember to try hard not to think of anything magic before you go to sleep or just stay awake if you can and control your mind, now off to your bedroom with you, I have an early start, night bro.". Kevin got up and went back into his bedroom and lay on his bed.

As he lay there, he became restless and started to get up from his bed when he felt a severe pain shoot through his head again. Holding his head in his hands and clenching his teeth together, he tried to muffle the sound of pain that he was feeling. After a short while, the pain subsided, and he fell back onto the pillows with his eyes closed in a cold sweat. How could he keep this from happening? he had no idea, but until something could be done, he knew that he was not alone. Kevin lay still on the bed with his eyes closed but could hear a distant voice talking to him in a language that Kevin could not understand. He tried to block the voice but found it difficult. He kept withering around on the bed until all was silent, and Kevin managed to fall into a deep sleep. Eventually, he woke feeling very tired, still as though he had not been to sleep but had just done a 10-mile cross-country run. His legs felt heavy, and his chest felt tight, but he struggled to his feet and leaned against the partially opened window staring out. There he saw again the grey owl sitting on the lamppost, just staring his way. Kevin closed his curtains, now blocking out the light, before sitting on the edge of his bed, feeling uneasy. As he rubbed his chest, he got up and moved toward the bathroom. His legs ached as though they were about to give way under his weight when he heard his mother starting to come up the stairs. He quickly stood straight and, with a smile on his face, greeted his mother as she got to the top of the stairs.

"Morning, mum," he called. His mother just looked at him and then asked if he was feeling better. With a nod of his head that really hurt him, and smile replied that he felt a lot better. "Good," she said, "gave me a fright when I heard you calling out in pain." She grabbed the sides of his face and looked deeply into his eyes, then said, "still look tired. You sure you are ok?" Kevin just smiled back and replied, "mum, I got a kick in the head from football, ok it hurt, it gave me a big headache, but it's gone now." His mother was still looking deep into his eyes with a look of doubt on her face, "honest mum, I'm ok," Kevin replied again. His mum let go of him and just said, "well, you need to take it easy for a couple of days, but it still means you will still have to go to school, I can't afford any time off, and your father is doing nightly shifts so will be in no state to look after you. I will explain to your form tutor about it and get the teachers to keep an eye on you and let me know immediately if something is wrong, ok!" Kevin just shook his head in disbelief which hurt him again, but he had to put a brave face on it before answering, "mum, stop fussing, I'm fine ok, now let me get on." His mother once again grabbed Kevin's head and kissed him on the forehead. "Ok, get ready and be downstairs in 10 minutes. Ok, it's nearly time for you to go to school". Kevin went into the bathroom and sat on the toilet, fully dressed, with his head in his hands, aching all over. He now had to summon up the strength and find a way to show his mum, teachers, and friends that he was ok and not in pain. This was going to be a gruelling day, he thought, then got up and washed before going downstairs for a quick breakfast.

Chapter 10

Jarez and the Power Stone

As Kevin left the house and got his cycle out of the shed, he turned to cycle down the path. As he did, he still noticed the grey owl sitting on the lamppost. He cycled over towards it, but just as he got to the lamppost, the owl flapped its wings and flew off. Kevin just shook his head and started the ride to school. As he passed the parking area, he looked all around to make sure there was no sign of Matrees. He quickened his cycling along this area but saw nothing of him. As he turned to enter the school chase, he had to pull up quickly as Godwill stood in the middle of the chase watching the buses and children arriving. "Watch it, Wilks," he called as Kevin came to a stop with Godwills hands on the cycle crossbars. "In a hurry or something," Kevin was pleased to see him and just smiled before answering. "Sorry sir, didn't see you," Godwill looked hard at Kevin and then stroked his beard before answering. "Well, mind your speed. You could have knocked someone down and hurt them. It's time we had a system where you youngsters get off your bikes before entering the school chase. I think I will talk to the headmaster about it; that will soon stop all the speeding." Just as he said that Kevin's friend Vinnie came around the other corner and had to swerve hard to miss both Godwill and Kevin. "Godwill bellowed at Vinnie about slowing down, but Vinnie just kept peddling on towards the bike sheds. Kevin, now looking at Godwill nervously, asked if he could continue. Godwill gestured with his hand towards the bike shed, so Kevin started to move forward. As he did, he heard Godwill call to him," And Wilks, I need to see you today. I have been told what went on these past two days. I have not been here, so I want to know everything. Meet me in the sixth form block at lunchtime." Kevin just turned his head and nodded back to Godwill, who then just gestured Kevin should go now, so he peddled off to the bike sheds.

As he put his bike in the slot, he turned to see his friend Vinnie still in the sheds talking to a young girl before coming over to Kevin to ask how he was. Kevin just looked at him with a blank expression, then said, "news travels fast, doesn't it?" Vinnie just laughed before whispering, "the magic network is fast and large; nothing gets missed by anyone within its circle." Vinnie just laughed and patted Kevin on the back, for which Kevin gave a quick, painful whimper. "Sorry mate, does it hurt that bad?" Kevin just stared at Vinnie and then said, "remember when you wanted to play Godwill and try and help train me, and I knocked you off your feet, and backward" Vinnie just smirked and then answered, "of course, it hurt like hell for a while," Kevin now staring Vinnie in the eyes spoke again, "well, take that and times it by at least ten, and that's how I feel. I feel that my body does not want to move, it aches all the time, I am getting bad headaches and", Vinnie stopped Kevin there, "ok, I get the picture, I don't need the ins and outs of every pain you have, I was only asking," Kevin staring at Vinnie just answered back, "well if you are not interested, why to ask?". Both boys stood toe to toe, staring at each other in silence before both boys started laughing aloud together. "Come on," Vinnie said, "or old Godwill will have our guts for garters and give us more detentions." The two boys went off happily toward the tutorial rooms for registration.

The morning lessons started well, especially for Kevin, as he had sport in his first two periods of the day, which he enjoyed very much, but after that, things didn't seem to go to plan.

As he walked along the corridor to his next lesson, History, he noticed someone trying to hide at the far pillar of the corridor. Kevin was with his mates Vinnie and Ivan all together walking to the lesson chatting to each other about the usual things, hate of teachers, lessons, and what they were doing over the weekend, when Kevin saw the figure gesture to him to follow him. Kevin turned to Vinnie and mentioned that he had forgotten something and would catch them up. Vinnie and Ivan went on towards class as Kevin veered off after the pillar to see who this person was that was beckoning him. As Kevin turned the corner, the person was no longer there, but he noticed that they had moved further along the corridor and were now trying to conceal themselves in a doorway of the chemistry lab. Kevin called out to ask what they wanted, but no answer came back, so Kevin just continued until he got to the door, where it was partially open. Kevin pushed open the door to look in, but no one was there. Kevin was about to close the door when he was tapped on the shoulder. As he turned around, he saw the young girl Vinnie was talking to in the bike sheds. "Hello, my name is Philipa, Philipa Cormack," she said as she took Kevin's hand and shook it. Kevin just looked at the girl with a pleasing look on his face before answering. "Hello, my name is," but was halted by the girl saying, "Kevin, Kevin Wilks." Kevin, now a little confused, asked her how she knew his name. Ruth just smiled and replied. "I was the girl your friend was talking to in the bike sheds. Not very observant, are you?" Kevin just smiled and lowered his head, "Sorry, got a lot on my mind at the moment; what can I do for you, Philipa?" Philipa just smiled back then said, "nothing really, I have just moved here and liked the look of you, so I asked your friend your name, just had the urge to meet you. I do not know why because usually I am quite shy, but something in me said you must meet this boy, don't ask me what, just did." Kevin, now feeling a little embarrassed, just smiled back at the girl and politely said, "well, it's been great meeting you Philipa, but got to get to lessons or the teachers will give me another detention." Philipa smiled then with a quick jibe answered, "oh, bad boy, I like that in guys, I guess we are bound to bump into each other again, so, I look forward to that time." With that, she turned and walked away singing. Kevin watched her walk away until she met some friends, and they continued towards the door, talking and laughing together, and Ruth occasionally looked back towards where Kevin stood. Suddenly, Kevin heard the next bell ring for the start of the next lesson, and with a quick "Damn," he ran off to the history lesson.

As he opened the door and looked around at his fellow people sitting in the lesson and then at the teacher, Mrs. Beaumont, who did not look best pleased, he thought he was going to be in trouble. The teacher moved towards the door and gestured for him to take his seat, then returned to teaching. Kevin sat down and felt relieved. All through the lesson, Kevin noticed the teacher kept looking at him in a funny kind of way but then turning away. As the bell went for the end of lessons, Kevin stood up, ready to go, when Mrs. Beaumont asked him to stay behind. Kevin thought he had got away with his lateness but now was not so sure.

As he stood waiting for the rest of the pupils to go, Mrs. Beaumont came over to him and asked him to sit down again. As Kevin sat, she asked how he was; Kevin just shrugged his shoulders in her direction. "Still feeling poorly. I heard from your mother about the accident on the football pitch, and she asked me to keep an eye on you, so, you ok?" Kevin nodded as if to say yes, but Mrs. Beaumont just blurted out, "come, come now, Kevin, did the accident take your speech? I expect more than this from you unless you are feeling bad". Kevin answered Mrs. Beaumont back, "Sorry, miss, I still have a bit of a headache, but I guess I'm ok." Kevin thought if he played on the illness, he would be dealt with more leniently. "You are sure you don't look that great. Perhaps you had better go see the school nurse and get checked out. We do not want something happening to our pupils, you know, so off you go, tell her I sent you". Kevin slowly got up to go and moved towards the door. As he did, Mrs. Beaumont spoke. "And Kevin, be careful, remember the boy that cried Wolfe, I expect you to be on time for my next lesson or the consequences will be severe, do I make myself understood?" Kevin just muttered quietly back, "yes miss," then shut the door and made his way down to the school nurses' room.

As he stood outside the nurse's room waiting to see the nurse, Jarez came out of the room. Kevin moved backward and looked around. No telephone noises, no noises anywhere of children. Kevin drew his wand and pointed it at Jarez. "Whoa, young wizard, it's me, Jarez. I mean you no harm." Kevin, now a little scared, just shouted out, "stay where you are. How do I know it's you and not Matrees? You two do look similar?" Jarez stood still with his arms open, showing no wand in place. "If I was my evil twin, do you think I would come unarmed to see you?" Kevin backed one more pace, then answered, "if it is you, Jarez, then what do you want with me?" Jarez moved forward, but Kevin kept his wand trained on him, which made him stop in his tracks. "Lower your wand, Kevin. I wish only to talk. Honestly, I mean you no harm." Kevin, still unsure, did not lower his wand but now held it tighter than before in case there was some trickery that went on. "Ok, talk." Jarez shook his head before answering, "No, not like this, not here. I will not talk whilst you hold my life to ransom in your hands. If you wish to talk, then you must trust me, lower your wand and follow me into this room." Kevin just bellowed back, "why into that room? Time is stopped. Why do you need me to follow you there? It's a trick. I know it is." Jarez again shook his head and answered, "young wizard, it is no more a trick than you are kicked in the head at football which you are trying to make everyone believe when we both know what really happened. You fought Matrees and, from what I hear, did well, but it is the consequences of that fight that I wish to talk to you about, but if you do not want to know, then I will take my leave." As Jarez turned to go, Kevin, shouted, "wait, ok, tell me, and no tricks or you shall feel my power." "As you wish," Jarez replied and pointed to the door. Kevin lowered his wand but kept a tight hold on it as he followed Jarez through the door. Inside the room, it looked just like a nurse's room, but then Jarez opened an adjacent door, and when he looked through, Kevin could see a meadow with flowers in it. Jarez moved through the door first, followed by an extremely nervous Kevin. As the door closed, Jarez looked back at Kevin and then spoke. "We are safe here; no harm can befall us." Kevin now ready to raise his wand, immediately asked, "what do you mean safe? Where are we?" Jarez moved over to a huge fallen tree trunk and sat down on it. "Come, I will tell you everything." Kevin moved over to the tree trunk and sat beside Jarez.

As they sat, Jarez told Kevin about the fight that had taken place between Matrees and him and then went on to describe what happened after. "When you broke the wand of my twin, a blue light came from it, did it not?" Kevin nodded, "This blue light, do you know what it was?" Again, Kevin just nodded. "Not very talkative, are you? Anyway, if you do know, then you know it is the heartstring of an enormously powerful wizard from many ages ago called Postromus. Until the unfortunate way his life ended, part of him was transferred to the wand my twin had. It was part of his own heart in the form of the base string. With this, no other witch or wizard could be as strong as the person holding the wand. It was Caulposier who controlled the wand, and she had been humiliated by Postromus in front of his friends." Kevin butted in, "I know all this. I have seen visions and the letter from her to Postromus stating that her father would not let them be together, which broke his heart." "Arr, but you do not know the whole story, I guess?" Jarez replied. Kevin just asked, "so tell me, what do I not know." "Patience, young wizard, the story continued. "After Caulposier had been humiliated, all she could concentrate on was how she would make him pay for his insolence towards her. Therefore she set about having a son with a non-magic person that could be taught the old ways and powers to control magic." Kevin again butted in, "yes, yes, I know all this. Tell me something that I do not know."

Jarez then stood up and turned away from Kevin, then back. "How insolent you are. You are still young, and you do not understand the great burden you will carry throughout your life." Kevin now hearing the word Burden, suddenly calmed down and asked. "Burden, what burden?" Jarez looked straight into Kevin's eyes and began to explain." Merlin has chosen you to collect some items, am I right?" Kevin just nodded. "Then this is your burden. Do you know what and why you must find these items?" Kevin answered, "of course, Merlin told me of a powerful magic stone that was made back in the olden days that provided the power for everlasting life. If this stone had fallen into the hands of a dark wizard, it would cause chaos and evil in the world as we know it." Correct young wizard," Jarez replied, "but the stone was sought after by many a wizard, good and evil. Many tried to gain it, many failed and died, and only one managed it. Caulpolsier found the identity of the wizard that had this stone and wanted it for herself. It was, of all people, Postromus. He alone had come a crossed it in a mountain range where it was hidden for many, many years by another wizard called cederic. Cederic had gained it by killing the wizard who had made this stone. Cederic was, on all occasions, a good wizard but had a lust for knowledge and power. Power, he wanted to use to improve the communities of people and magicians to live together in harmony, not by the ruling. Unfortunately, the stone has a power within itself that can turn even a great good wizard to the black side. This is what happened to Cederic as he defended the stone's presence. But, with the killing comes the blackness. A blackness that takes over the heart and souls of the person that owns such an item." Kevin again butted in, "so, how did Postromus get the stone"?.

After many years of fighting off wizards who would take such an item and kill them, the blackness was looming over Cederic. Although he wanted the power, he still had enough goodness in his heart to know that it must be destroyed. He tried many magic spells and many physical things to destroy the stone, but none could manage it. Finally, he decided that he would hide it until the day he could find something that could do this. However, many wizards kept trying to capture the stone they thought he still had in his possession until one day, Cederic met his match and was killed. No stone was found on him by a group of powerful wizards that killed him, and the search eventually ceased as all thought the stone had been lost. However, Cederic had hidden the stone in a cave in the mountains and closed the cave up so no one could open it until Postromus came along. Depressed for losing the love of his life moved from town to town and eventually wanted no more company, but his own made his way into the mountains.

Two hundred years had gone by since Cedric had hidden the stone in this cave in the mountains, and he had long died, so the magic that engulfed the cave entrance began failing. Postromus noticed a small opening in the side of the mountain pass and blasted open the cave. This is where he would make his home. Throughout the years, he dedicated himself to the magical ways, becoming increasingly powerful, but did not know the real reason why." Kevin interrupted once again. "You mean the stone, but how?" Jarez continued. "The stone omits a powerful invisible power to the person holding or near it. It provides nutrients for learning and contains the power of the maker and the spells conjured by him. Adding to an already powerful wizard, this thing is like, in your world, a power surge of information and power injection. Postromus eventually found the stone one evening when re-organising the cave for a better living. He knew nothing of it but a glowing rock that somehow helped him understand the old ways of magic. He did many things over the years with the stone in his presence, all good, I have to say, He healed a fallen horse, a man that was crippled, and many other things, but these things do not go unnoticed, and soon there were many questioning why the hermit that lived in the mountains was so comfortable." Again, Kevin had to question Jarez. He stood up and walked around the tree trunk. "But I do not understand if Postromus wanted to be cut off from civilisation, why did he do these things? He must have known that this would raise questions from normal people. For years he was a hermit, happy with his own company, so why the change?" Jarez just shrugged his shoulders and replied, "perhaps after many years of a recluse, he was ready to accept people back into his life. I have no answers for that young wizard, but, as I said, many had questions, and he was visited by many. Unfortunately, his method for helping people came from the power of the stone, which he waved over the person or animal that helped them get better. Soon word spread around the land, and many tried to steal the stone from him. He each time repelled the people but did not kill them until one day, powerful wizards visited him on the pretence of illness, wishing to be helped, which postromus started the ritual when the wizards turned on him. He had no choice but to defend himself and, unfortunately, killed one of the wizards whilst the other two fled. But the damage had been done; blackness soon started to take over him. He quickly realised that it was the power of the stone making this happen. So, he set about trying to do what no other wizard had been able to do before him. He tried to destroy the stone."

Kevin was listening intently now and asked, "well, did he do it?" "Oh yes, young wizard, Postromus was indeed a very powerful wizard, and eventually, after many spells cast at it, he finally found the spell to break the stone." Kevin, now extremely excited, stood up and said, "well, what was it?" Jarez just shrugged his shoulders once more, then spoke. "no one knows, only him." So, what happened next?" Kevin asked. "Well, he was still not a happy person, you see, even though he broke the stone into pieces, no one is sure how many pieces, but it has been rumoured that it was six pieces, they still omitted a power, only this time Postromus found out that each piece had a different power for doing things. As time went on, many other wizards and people tried still to take the stone or now stones he still had. He had to keep repelling them. Finally, he had made friends with some dwarfs, who had magical powers, and bid them to take a piece of the stone each and hide it in various locations for which he did not want to know the locations. However, he kept just one piece. This he called the Time stone, and I believe it is part of the original time stone that is around your neck." Kevin felt for the necklace and pulled it out. "What do you mean part of the Time stone? I was made to believe it was the whole original time stone." Jarez held his hand out as if to want to take a closer look at it. Kevin wrapped his hand around the necklace and said, "how do I not know this is still not a trick to get this stone?" Jarez looked Kevin in the eyes then said, "you don't, but why would I tell you all this if I do not wish to help you?."

Kevin then asked before handing it over. "So, how do you know of this? How do I not know it is just a story you have made up"? Jarez again spoke, "you do not, but I can assure you it is all true. This story has been passed down from father to son throughout the ages through many different families. Whether it is true or not, no one can tell you, but with what has happened so far, I would say there are some things that are as they have been told. All I can say is that if that stone on the necklace is part of the original stone pieces, it is why you are still here today after fighting Matrees. It must have some power to be able to repel the spell Matrees cast at you, and likewise, you did back at him to be still here, and why would he want it so bad, answer me that one young wizard." "But how does he know, or you know that I had the stone"? Jarez, still looking Kevin directly in the eyes, replied. "As I said, the stones omit a power; wizards pick up on the energy that it omits."

Kevin, now a little confused, replied, "so why can I not feel any power? After all, I was supposed to be a wizard, but I feel nothing." Jarez began laughing. "what's so funny? I don't think it's funny; if I do not feel the power as you say, then I can only confirm as I did to my brother that I am not a wizard." Jarez now laughed even louder, which made Kevin angry. "Stop it" he yelled. Jarez slowly finished laughing before answering. "You feel the power, but you are unaware of its presence, young wizard. You are just starting out in the life of magic and mysteries. It takes time to understand the presence of such power and how to use it. It is not a thing you can touch or feel physically. You will feel the power only when you are trained to understand the feelings, the awareness, and the mindset you need to be able to use this power. As I said, it is there. It is within you that you do not understand, or you would already be dead at the hands of Matrees. It provided power for shielding you from his attacks. In time with the right teacher, it will become apparent to you. You have a destiny, a destiny to be great one day, but it will be a dangerous and time-consuming journey. Do not doubt yourself, be confident, and all will come naturally." Kevin now started to understand what he was being told. After all, he was still here after Matrees' attack. Slowly he took off the necklace and put it into the out-stretch hand of Jarez.

Jarez studied the small stone in the necklace and then spoke. "See, see here, you can see where the split is. It is, as I suggested, just part of the time stone." Kevin looked at the stone as Jarez handed him back the necklace. "But could that be where the original stone was broken? How do you know it is just part of it, and how big was this stone"? Jarez sighed, then replied, "so many questions, young wizard, some for which I have no answers to give you. No –one knows apart from Cederic and Postromus the size of the stone, so no, I cannot be sure the mark is not from the original break, only that the power it omits I would have thought it to be stronger if whole than it is omitting." Kevin now replaced the necklace around his neck before Jarez stood up. "Now," he said, "it is time to resume your everyday existence, so we will return to the school." As they moved to a now visible doorway that led back to the school, Jarez stopped. Kevin looked round at him before he spoke. "Two things, young wizard, that may help or hinder you in your search. It was said many times that the dwarfs took the pieces and hid them in historic places down throughout the ages." Kevin asked, "Historical places like what, a castle, a different country, a church, how is that going to help me"? Jarez just looked at Kevin then said, "I do not know, young wizard, many have tried to find them, but none have, only that," Jarez stopped speaking. Kevin then asked, "only that what"? Jarez continued, "only that it was said by few throughout the ages that some are within this country, others in far off lands, and the power from each stone is picked up from one to another, the stone will glow when it is within the vicinity of another of the pieces." Kevin looked blank at Jarez then asked, "and who were the few that have said this?, it could just be another fairy tale story, now if there was some physical or verification on this was actually said by one of those that hid the stones then that would be interesting, but as this happened many hundreds of years ago I am guessing they are all dead, am I correct"?.

Kevin turned to walk to the door when Jarez replied, "you are correct." Kevin turned and then asked, "what, correct, they are dead or still alive"? Jarez turned away and then spoke, "one still alive." Kevin moved towards Jarez and then said, "are you joking with me? This happened hundreds of years ago. How can he still be alive unless he has some sort of magic," Kevin stopped speaking and looked at Jarez, then said, "power." Jarez nodded. Kevin then took hold of Jarez by the arms, so where is he, where"? Jarez stepped back to release himself from Kevin's grasp, "I do not know for sure, but it was last reported he keeps himself hidden and away from all in a big forest so no one can find him." Kevin was now quite excited again asked, "this is real, it is not another story, please tell me it is real." Jarez nodded, "so what forest, is it a far-off country or this?" Jarez spoke softly, "it is in this country young wizard." Kevin now even more excited than he had been before snapped at Jarez, "where, there are many in this country, give me some help, please." Jarez thought for a moment then said, "sorry, I do not know the name of the forest only that he dwells in a historical one." Kevin could not think of any at that moment as his mind was all over the place, so he turned and walked to the door. As he turned the handle, Jarez called to him again, which made him stop in the doorway, but he was still thinking of possible forests in England.

"Young wizard, the second thing I must tell you." Kevin stood in the doorway thinking hard and could not hear Jarez fully, but Jarez continued to talk. "As you know, there is also someone else who knows, that is Matrees as he is part of the same person that learned this information, but only half is with each of us, so he knows other details to what I know and has told you. Beware, young wizard. We shall meet again as this story has not been fully told yet." Kevin just waved as he passed through the door back into the waiting area for the nurse. He could hear the telephones ringing and children talking and see them running around the area, so he knew that everything was back to normal, or was it?

Kevin, now bursting at the seams to tell his brother and Godwill what Jarez had told him, did not even see the nurse come out of the office. "Are you ok young man?" she asked. Kevin spun around to see the nurse standing in front of him and quickly replied. "Oh, yes, I'm fine, just had a bit of a headache, but it has gone now. Sorry to waste your time, bye." With that, Kevin left the office area and headed toward Godwill's classroom.

Godwill and the Lessons

As Kevin hurried down the corridor knocking into a lot of other pupils, he came across a larger boy who swung round and caught him by the collar. "And where do you think you are going titch in such a hurry and in a clumsy way," the boy asked. Kevin now stopped in his tracks and struggled to get free before replying, "what's it to you?" The boy, now looking quite angry, grabbed Kevin's arm and led him into the toilet area. "Well, now, quite the little tough guy for a first year, you need to have some manners knocked into your little pipsqueak." Just as the larger boy was about to hit Kevin, he cast "Sherek." Kevin disappeared from the grasp of the big boy and reappeared behind him. With this, the boy had already swung at Kevin, who was now not there, and missed. Kevin now kicked the boy in the lower part of the legs that buckled the legs making the boy fall to the floor. Kevin now stood in front of the boy with his right hand outstretched, ready to cast another spell. Luckily for him, Godwill, at that moment, had entered the toilet areas and shouted, "Wilks, what's going on here." Kevin now lowered his hand, and the larger boy got to his feet. "So," Mr. Godwill continued, someone going to tell me, or do I put both of you on detention?" Kevin just lowered his head and said in a quiet voice, "just a misunderstanding, sir, that's all." The large boy looked at Kevin, then at Godwill, and repeated what Kevin had said. "If I find out that you two were fighting, you will be in detention for a month, do I make myself clear?" Both boys mumbled quietly "yes sir," "now get, and don't let me catch you two in here again," bellowed Mr. Godwill. The big boy straightened his shirt and walked out of the door. Just as Kevin got to the door, Godwill grabbed Kevin by the collar saying, "you, wilks, with me, now," and dragged Kevin out of the toilets and into his classroom, slamming the door as both got through it.

"Timearium Discosure Afentium," time slowed, and Godwill turned towards Kevin with a very angry face on him. "What do you think you were doing, Wilks? You cannot go around casting spells at everyone you take dislike, especially not normal people. Do you want them to know you are a freak? Well, do you?" Kevin, now also angry, replied, "is that what I am? a freak. I never asked to be one, and for your information, sir," Kevin said with a sarcastic expression on his face, "he grabbed me and hauled me into the toilets, not the other way round as you think." Godwill, now fuming, replied again, "that does not go giving you the right, just because you can beat any of these larger boys, by the use of your gift that takes a dislike to you to submit them to harm. Wake up, boy, I thought Merlin told you about keeping magic and normal worlds apart or did you not listen?" Kevin now still angry, made his way towards the door but said first, "yes, I did listen, but I am sure as hell not going to let some thugs give me a good hiding without doing something back to them." Kevin opened the door and started to go through it then stopped, turned towards Godwill, and said, "that goes for you also, so hope you are prepared for our next session." Kevin grabbed the door and slammed it shut as he walked off. Godwill opened the door calling out to Kevin as he continued down the corridor, "there will be no more lessons until you apologise and learn to curb that anger of yours, do you hear me Wilks, Wilks." Kevin just continued his journey to his next lesson. Godwill, still fuming, restarted time and slammed his door shut.

Kevin continued down the corridor until he met up with his two friends, Vinnie and Ivan, waiting outside the maths room. Vinnie took hold of Kevin's arm and led him to a quiet corner out of the hearsay way. "Did you notice that time stopped for a short while? Was it you?" Kevin explained to Vinnie what had gone on with the bigger boy than Godwill. "Are you mad? You know you should not use your magic in normal times. I bet Godwill was fuming. I heard that an occurrence happened here, a few years before from a previous boy, and Godwill made his life hell, so much that the boy had problems at home because of it." Kevin just dismissed what Vinnie was saying with, "he called me a freak, is that what we all are, and coming from him of all people." Vinnie now being quite firm with Kevin replied, "yes, we are to all these other kids that can't do the things we can do, and if anything got out then guess who they will cart off to the funny farm?, it won't be the big boy you were going at, no, it will be you, so I suggest you just keep that temper in place no matter what happens. Remember, you have immense power hidden inside you, more than you know, and you can certainly do considerable damage to some of these other kids. Is that what you want? You are a wizard, you have magic to use for good, not bad, or do you wish to end up like Matrees and go about killing people? Well, do you?" Kevin looked at Vinnie and knew he was right but was still incredibly angry with Godwill. "Ok, ok," Kevin replied, so I need to be able to control myself, it's just so frustrating, that's all." Vinnie, now had a smile on his face, replied, "likewise, but we have to be careful, ok mate?" Kevin nodded in agreement, then said. "I guess I will have to go crawling to Godwill and apologise." Vinnie, with an even bigger smile, then said, "yup, and I know how that is going to hurt you." The two friends just looked at each other in silence before bursting out in tears of laughter and then going into the math room.

As soon as the maths class had finished, Kevin came out of the door ready to head towards Godwills classroom. "Good luck," Vinnie wished his friend as he set off back down the corridor. As Kevin got to the classroom, Kevin could see his brother having an intense argument with Godwill through the glass in the door. Kevin knocked and opened the door, then entered. Immediately the argument between the two stopped. Godwill looked sternly towards Kevin, then spoke, "what is it, Wilks, upset someone else has set the school on fire?" Kevin did not like the tone of his voice but took a deep breath before answering. "No sir, I have had time to think about things and," Kevin paused for a time. "Well," bellowed Godwill; Kevin continued. "I have come to apologise." Kevin now lowered his head and looked at the ground. Godwill now moved over towards where Kevin stood before continuing to shout. "An apology is a thing you have to mean, Wilks, not just a small gesture said through words. I ask myself, do I believe you? I very much doubt it, but at least you have the courage to admit that you were wrong and man enough to admit it", Kevin, now feeling quite angry again, butted into Godwills speech. "Admit I was wrong, no, admit I should have thought about possibly using magic in normal time at school, yes. For your information, if my brother has not already told you, I had a near-death experience whilst you were away with a fight with Matrees, and now it seems to all purposes that I have the soul of Postromus lodged in my brain from Matrees's wand I broke during the fight. Also, a bigger boy than me takes a dislike of me and tries to thump me. Do you not think I am a bit scared or confused that I cannot do anything to help protect myself from this?". Godwill, now seeing the pain on Kevin's face as he spoke of these things, calmed down and perched himself on the edge of one of the desks near Kevin.

"Look," he said, "I know it is hard, but before your brother came in and told me of the events, I didn't know. I thought you were just an arrogant 13-and-a-half school kid, but I do have to apologise for my misgivings. You are special, more special than you could imagine, and yes, I bet you were scared to hell during the fight with Matrees, but you came through it; why? Because you are a better person than he is, and I guess you must have learned something from me, or you would not be here. I think that considering the events, we should start afresh; do you think we can do that, Wilks?" Godwill forgets that Kevin's brother is also in the room and hears both say yes together. Godwill turned around to see Paul now moving over towards his brother and gently giving him a quick hug. Godwill lowered his head to the ground before raising it again and saying, "so, anything else to tell me"? Kevin was now a little happier but still angry at remembering that Godwill called him a freak and decided to tell him what he had learned from Jarez at the last meeting. Godwill listened intently and, after hearing what Kevin had told him, spoke. "So, do you think he was telling you the truth?" Kevin shrugged his shoulders and then replied, "can't see why he would lie. After all, he is the good of Crandloss, and Merlin did give him the book to give to me. Why should he lie"? Godwill stood up and stroked his beard. As he was about to speak, the school bell went for the next lesson, "ok, let me see if I can look into it before we make any decisions. I will see you after school at the Spinney to continue the lessons, ok Wilks"? Again, both Paul and Kevin replied together. "Now off you go, and young Wilks, keep out of trouble and control that temper of yours, please." Kevin nodded and opened the door, and walked through it.

The rest of the day Kevin spent with his friends around him, keeping well clear of all trouble, but as the day ended and the two brothers set off towards the spinney on their bikes, Kevin had to pull to the side of the road and stop. He held his head as a searing pain shot through it. Kevin called out in a loud painful cry that made his brother stop and turns back towards his brother. As Paul pulled up next to his brother, he could see that he was in immense pain and was now off his bike and crouching down on the grass beside the road shouting with pain. Paul immediately got off his bike, knelt next to his brother, and held him tight, saying, "what's the matter, bro?" Kevin was trying to explain to his brother about the pain but the words coming from his mouth his brother could not understand. "Ismithian aggression tomarkis atholorian candrosin laticitate morthium," Kevin was saying, but his brother Paul could not understand and pulled back now from holding his brother. Paul also noted there was now a difference in the skin colour of his brother now starting to happen. "Kevin," his brother called to him, "I do not know what is happening, but whatever it is, fight it, control yourself, think of something nice, not magical, come on, do it, bro. You need to shut your mind down, do it, bro, or we are in big trouble out here in the open." With luck, Godwill was just passing by in his car and saw the two Wilks boys at the side of the grassy verge next to the road and knew something was not right, so he pulled up just in front of them and quickly got out of his car to see what was going on. "what's the problem wilks" he asked? Kevin now raised his head, and Godwill could see that Kevin had a look of anger and dislike aiming towards him.

Godwill quickly cast the time-stopping spell, and all time slowed to a stop. Kevin now pushed his brother with great force from beside him and stood tall and straight, staring at Godwill. A slight bluish tinge was now showing on his skin, and a fiery stare was coming from his eyes. Godwill, now standing just four feet from Kevin, spoke. "Wilks, fight this inside you. You cannot let this wizard's anger overwhelm you. You have to be strong until we can work out what we can do with it." Kevin spoke, but not in his voice but in that of the olden wizard Postromus. "Who are you, puny one? How dare you stand in front of me and try to keep me down. Do you not know who I am?" Godwill lowered his head before speaking, "of course I know great one who you are and what you are capable of, but the boy you have taken over is merely a poor substitute for a wizard as great as you. His body has not yet matured enough to be able to protect you from harm. Forgive me for saying these words to you, but you are still in possible danger from foes that have tried to enhance their powers through your own to become the supreme wizard that is indestructible. Therefore, I suggest you try to curb your power until we can get the boy's body you reside in up to strength to protect you, my lord."

Postromus was incredibly angry at being spoken to by what he considered to be a less important person than himself and started to get Kevin to raise his wand in the direction of Godwill. Just as a spell was about to be cast at Godwill, Kevin started to regain control of his mind and body. Godwill had already cast the spell "Crevatis Shouderit." A magical shield surrounded Godwill just as the words "Firentay, Consunium, Derivarm" came from Kevin's mouth, quickly followed by another spell, but this time in Kevin's voice, "Evreko." Just as the spell shot from his wand, it quickly disappeared, and then Kevin stood with his eyes shut but still talking. "you will not take over me, Postromus. You are or were a great wizard, but you have chosen the wrong person to mess with. I will fight you with all my strength to contain you until I can finally be rid of you. You are my pain in the backside that I did not ask for or need. Do you hear me ?" Suddenly, Kevin held his head and groaned again, with Postromus's voice now coming through once more. "How dare you talk to me like that, me, the supreme wizard, me the only being to be able to control this sorry place, me," he started to say again before Kevin again gained control, saying, "you, the once great wizard but lost it all through love and deceit, yet your class everyone a foe to you when there are people who would want to help but your to blind through anger and sadness that you cannot see that, and for that, you make more enemies rather than friends. Is that the thing you used to do when you were mortal and young? Because it certainly does not seem like it today. I saw visions of you with your true love and how she deceived you, and therefore you are like you are today. I suggest you stop all this anger and try and listen to the voice of reason if you can still listen. Until then, you will not be able to overpower me or speak to me until you can promise this. Now go, and think about what I have said to you."

With that, a crying, painful scream came from Kevin's mouth, and he and Godwill sank to the floor on their knees. Paul could not believe his eyes or ears of what he just saw and heard and was nervous about moving forward to help his brother or Godwill to their feet. As he was thinking about it, Godwill slowly groaned and got to his feet very unsteadily, shaking his head and stretching to straighten himself, then Kevin did the same. "Kevin," his brother asked nervously, then turned his attention to Godwill, "sir, are you alright?" Godwill moved towards Kevin and stood looking at him with a look of great admiration on his face. "Well, young Wilks, you ok?" Kevin looked at Godwill, no look of anguish or pain on his face but now only tiredness, "I'm ok, I think," he replied, then gave a small smile. Paul now throwing his arms around his brother and holding him tightly, said, "god, I thought that he would be a lot stronger than you, bro, but I knew when I saw the orbs beside you that someone was looking after you." Kevin pulled away from his brother and said with a look of puzzlement on his face, "orbs, what orbs? I couldn't see any orbs." Godwill smiled then laughed, there are many things you will see and not see, but your brother is right. There was clearly something radiantly coming from you while you were fighting mind to mind with Postromus that helped control him and speak to him." Kevin, still puzzled, looked at Godwill and asked, "so who is or was helping me?"

Kevin pointed towards Godwill, then Paul. "Don't look at me, bro, I don't have that much power or magical know-how, but there was a kind of an orange and red glowing orb attached to you, helping you somehow." Kevin quickly turned to Godwill, who was nodding his head, and then put his finger to his lips to say hush. Godwill looked at Kevin and then said, "it is called a mind projector. Someone other than me is looking out for you. We already know this with the things you mentioned before regarding the owl on the windowsill of your home and other bits you mentioned. I guess you could say you are an incredibly lucky boy to have so many people looking out for you". Kevin, still looking at Godwill, then said, "but if you were projecting to help me, who was the other person?" Kevin looked at Paul quickly then asked, "did you see a shape of anyone or just the orb as you said." Paul just smiled and said, "only the orb, but as Godwill said, someone else is looking out for you bro so you should take some sort of comfort in that, together Godwill, you and the other person have given you the inner strength to control Postromus at the moment, and you need to be able to strengthen that consciousness to be able to continue to do so. I do not mind admitting, bro. I nearly crapped myself when it was happening. Not a good feeling, I can tell you". All three looked at each other before bursting out laughing. "Ok, let's move to the spinney and see what we can work on to help you, young Wilks," said Godwill. With that, all three of them went to the spinney hideout and continued to work on spells, mind controls, and knowledge of orbs.

At the end of the lesson, Kevin could still not imagine who or what was looking after him. Godwill explains mind projection and the power it produces to help or even talk to someone. Paul had mentioned at the spinney to Godwill about the funny language that had come from Kevin's mouth during the Postromus thing, and he had written it down to try and discover the origin so he could find out what the words were. As the three of them left the spinney, Godwill restarted time, and the boys and teacher went their separate ways home. On the way home, Kevin was chatting to his brother about spells and what had happened regarding Postromus when he noticed a brown owl perched on the fencing of the park. As he got closer to it, the bird flapped its large wings and flew off over the park. Kevin remembered what Godwill had said about someone or something in the shape of the owl looking out for him and just came to a stop on his bike, staring at the bird as it flew off. His brother stopped beside him and looked where he was looking. "You ok, bro? What are you looking at?" Kevin just looked at his brother and smiled, then said, "oh, nothing, just a bird. Just looking at it and how peaceful it flies with no sound and how intelligent they are." His brother now started to laugh before saying, "birds intelligent, yer, right," then continued his way, still laughing to himself.

As they reached the estate, Kevin raced ahead of his brother and quickly rode his bike around the back of the house to put it in the shed. He parked his bike and ran into the house to find his mother getting tea ready. "Watch it, Kevin," she said, "you are not at school now, my boy. Get washed up before tea. Where is your brother?". Kevin just shrugged his shoulders as if to say do not know before saying, "I left him at the estate opening, so he should be here in a few minutes. Eventually, Paul turned up a good five minutes after Kevin and was looking a little worried. "You ok Paul, looks like you've seen a ghost or something" their mother said. "I'm ok mum, just had a bit of trouble with my chain on the bike, it slipped off but got it going again." Kevin, now looking at his brother, knew he was lying but did not say anything in front of his mother. The boys washed up and sat down to eat tea with their mum.

Chapter 11

Knowledge, Tempers, and Girls

That night just before the boys were due to go to bed, Paul called Kevin into his room. "what's up, Paul? Got a problem," Kevin asked. Paul looked at his brother and nodded. Kevin closed the door and sat on his brothers' bed. "So, what's the info?" Paul just looked at Kevin blankly before speaking. "When you sped off from me on entering the estate, I thought I caught a glimpse of a shadowy person near the turning, you sped off, not noticing it, but it noticed you. For a few seconds, it followed you, then stopped and came back to me. As it stopped in front of me, it materialised into an old man, someone I had never seen before, but he told me to tell you to go to the Sherwood Forest and seek out Sambia. He then just pointed towards the estate and disappeared." Kevin looked at his brother and then smiled before he spoke, "Sherwood Forest, Sambia, what's there, and who was this guy?" Paul did not know either but then continued, "He also mentioned that there is danger in the forest and to get what you will take the both of us." Kevin now looked a bit puzzled and replied, "to get what you want, what's there that we want? And needs both of us to do what? And what's this Sambia? Is it a man, animal, or something else"?

Paul looked at his brother and then said in a disconcerting voice, "well, how do I know? I'm only telling you what I was told by this old man. I'm not a book of knowledge. I guess I am just the postman or something like that." Kevin pondered for a minute before saying, "ok, so, first, you see a shadow figure that turned into an old man. What was he wearing"? His brother turned away in an angry way before turning back quickly to respond to his brother. "What am I now, a fashion guru or something? he had on a long smock or something, but it could have been a coat, I think." "What colour"? Asked Kevin, "why, you think you know someone that goes around like that in a red or black coat, get real brother, I cannot remember, anyway, what's the colour got to do with it? I was too scared to notice what he was wearing. It's not every day you see a shadowy figure materialise in front of you and then speak".

Kevin stood up and walked to the window with his hands on his head, thinking. "Ok, so it sounds like we have to go to Sherwood Forest to try and find something along with something or someone called Sambia. So, how are we going to get there? I know I can slow time, but traveling that distance how"? His brother shook his head as if to say he had no idea. They both decided to talk to Godwill the next day to see if there was anything he could help them with. With that, Kevin left his brother's bedroom and returned to his. With one last look out of the curtains, nothing unusual was noted. He cuddled down under his quilt and dropped off to sleep.

The next morning the two boys could not wait to get to school to talk to Godwill about the meeting Paul had with the strange man. As they ran down the corridor towards the classroom, they saw Godwill coming out. Kevin noticed that something was not right. Godwill seemed smaller and not so fat as usual. Kevin quickly grabbed his brother's arm and pulled him to a stop. "What are you doing, he is going to go away, and then we will have to talk to him another time. Kevin just whispered to his brother, "look, do you see anything different about Godwill today"? Paul looked at Godwill but turned to his brother and replied. "What, what do you see different that I can't? It's him. I think you are becoming paranoid, Kevin, come on, or he will go into the staff room, and then we will have to wait." Paul tugged at Kevin's arm, but Kevin was not having any of it. Kevin called out to Godwill about glowing Orbs where Godwill just raised his hand and replied, "very good boys." Paul stopped in his tracks; he knew if that were the real Godwill, he would have torn Kevin off a good strip." As Paul was closest to the Godwill-shaped person, he just stood still, watching as Godwill turned and walked towards the staff room. Kevin ushered Paul to follow him up until the reception area, where he saw Godwill go not into the staff room but into the nurse's office. Paul beckoned Kevin towards him, and when the two boys were together, they went towards the nurse's office. Just as Kevin put his hand onto the handle, Godwill came out of the staff room opposite the nurse's room.

"What do you want here? Not poorly, are you"? Kevin asked if they could go to his classroom to discuss a few things, which included himself. Godwill looked hard at the two boys, then nodded and went with them to his classroom. Once there, the boys started telling Godwill about the meeting of the old man and Paul, about Sherwood Forrest and Sambia. Godwill listened intently and then, when the boys had finished, spoke. "So, Sherwood Forest, there is something that is there that you want, so tell me, Wilks, what do you most want"? Kevin thought for a moment before speaking. "I guess I just want to be normal. I know I have been given this gift of magic, but I have to say that it has not been fun so far, so I guess I just want to be normal, as I said." Godwill, now a little angry, and also Kevin's brother, now looking puzzled at him, decided to speak together, saying, "what," Godwill continued, "you just want to be normal, well you can forget that, my lad, this gift is non-returnable, it's part of you, it's within you, part of your heritage from ancestors throughout time, so concentrate, what is it that you are seeking"?. Kevin looked at Godwill then said, "the Time stone." "Exactly," replied Godwill, "but how do we know that it's there, and why would someone or something tell you? Is it a trap? Or is it the truth, and what or who is Sambia? I need to do some research. Leave me now and come and see me at the end of school time". Both boys were about to leave the classroom when Kevin stopped, turned around, then spoke. "Oh, I'm not sure if it was Jaarez or someone else, but we saw you coming out of this class before and went into the nurse's room before you came out of the staff room. I would be aware there is someone else that is copying you, only" Kevin stopped there, "Well, go on, only what "? Kevin quickly replied. He is a little bit smaller and not so fat, sir." Kevin quickly closed the door and ran off with his brother down the corridor and out into the playground.

The day went quite quickly, and the final bell had rung for the end of school, so now Kevin met up with his brother and went to the classroom of Godwill. Just before going in, Kevin looked through the transparent glass and saw Godwill sitting at his desk. Paul pushed open the door, and both boys entered. Kevin stared hard at Godwill to try and determine if it was him or not. Eventually, Godwill had had enough of being starred at and not a word mentioned. He stood up and walked towards the boys, "well, Wilks, do I pass, or am I an imposter"? Kevin smiled when he saw that it was the actual Godwill and started to relax. "ok," said Godwill, now that we have verified that I am me, "I have been checking several books on this word Sambia, and come across nothing that is material but, I did come across something interesting. Apparently, it was the name of one of the magic dwarfs who was supposed to hide the pieces of the Power stone after it had been destroyed into smaller pieces. Look, here are the names of the others that were asked to do the hiding." Kevin and Paul looked at the list and noted that there were only five names on it." but sir," Kevin said, "when I visited the Astral plain and spoke to Merlin, he mentioned that there were six pieces described through tales of the olden time. If each dwarf was given a piece to hide, what happened to the sixth piece"? Godwill looked at Kevin and then stroked his beard before saying. "Hmm, you really are a bright lad, Wilks, but to answer your question, I cannot. No one knows where the pieces are or, in fact, that there were five or six pieces. These are tales told down through time to only the powerful wizards. In time, these stories may have gained momentum and additional pieces of information that is not true. Therefore this has been the problem in finding what is believed to be the power stone."

Kevin looked at Godwill with a confused look on his face. "So, tell me, sir, how much is true, how much is fairy-tale, and how did I get mixed up in this thing? I mean, I have been told and shown stories of a wicked wizard that tore his soul in two, a wicked mother who jilted a powerful wizard and transferred some of his power through a heartstring to an inanimate object, namely a wand, an old wizard legend called Merlin living in a special place but not human form, and you, so convince me that there is some truth in all of this or I walk and never come back". Godwill stopped time then pointed towards the desks and cast "Eloso Retriam." The desks parted to the sides of the classroom, Kevin just clapped his hands, "so this is your proof, I am not asking if magic exists, only what is true and what is not." Godwill shook his head and stared at Kevin before speaking. "Looks young Wilks, I have tried to find pieces of this stone for a long, long time but have had no luck in finding any. I have been to places mentioned by passers-by, other wizards, and witches but nothing. I cannot tell you that there is going to be a piece there or who told you it is right; the only thing is to investigate it and see if there is any truth in what was said. I have to say I have checked the forest myself but found nothing, but the forest is large. I will understand if you wish not to go there and see for yourselves." Kevin then butted into Godwills speech with, "ok, so how are we going to get there? As mentioned to my brother, I may be able to stop time but travelling, well, that's not happened as of yet." Godwill laughed loudly and then said, "travelling, that's kids' stuff. You should have covered that when you knew you had the gift. You mean you do not know how to travel using any piece of wood like brooms or even thought of travelling." Kevin and Paul looked at each other and then back to Godwill before answering together, "no." Godwill laughed even louder then tried to gain a straight face before saying, "well, we had better go back to basics and teach you this, I suggest we meet up at the spinney tomorrow after school, oh, and if you can bring a broom each or anything you can get your hands around and sit on that would be good." Godwill started laughing again, so the boys decided to leave and go home.

Once home, the boys met up in Paul's room to discuss travelling, where neither of them had learned how to fly or travel in other ways. Eventually, the boys got tired, so they decided to get some sleep.

The next morning Paul was out on his paper round again, and Kevin was getting ready for school when he heard his dad come home from work. "Hi, dad, good night at work?" he asked, "not bad, son, just the usual things. Not much going on there now, and I must say I'm pleased with that." His dad gave him a big grin after saying it. "So, what's the news on your front? I don't get to see too much of you these days, what with football training and school "? Kevin smiled back and then answered, "oh, just as busy as normal, learning and putting into practice what we learn, that's all." "So why the discontent in your voice than me, lad," his father asked. Kevin looking at his father, was a little apprehensive about asking his next question and decided to just not do it. Kevin just shrugged his shoulders and started to turn away when his dad replied, "come on, out with it. I know when something is bothering you. Not been in trouble again, have you?"

Kevin turned back to his dad and went and sat down at the breakfast table. "No, dad, honestly, but," Kevin paused on the but, "but what, come on, son, you can ask me or tell me anything. Not a new girlfriend, is it?" his father asked with a wink of his eye." "No, dad, not yet," Kevin replied with a smile, "pity" his dad replied, "so, what is the trouble?" he asked. Kevin thought for a moment, then replied, "how do you know if something you are told and shown, is true, I mean, we are taught about things that have supposed to have happened hundreds of years ago even thousands of years ago. Why do we need to learn about this stuff? Will it become useful for when we are grown up and need to find a job, and what significance does it have on today's life ?".

Kevin's dad looked at him before answering, "whoa, my lad. I can see your brain is in overdrive mode. What has history got to do with now day living? Well, if history was not recorded, don't you think that we would go around making the same mistakes again and again and not learn from the mistakes? That's why history is there, to stop those mistakes". Kevin looked at his dad and then replied, "I can see that, but what about myths and the bible? How can you say that these things are history, and we need to learn about them, take for instance, oh, I don't know, let's say, King Arthur and Merlin the Magician." Dad looked at Kevin and then replied, "First, you mention the Bible, then King Arthur and Merlin. Where is this all come from? I know they teach religious studies at school, but I didn't know there was anything about Arthur and Merlin, is it new?" Kevin smiled, "No, it is not new. It is just something I have been thinking about since Vinny lent me the old book a while ago. I was just wondering, could they have been real or just stories told by people as an attraction to others to get tangled up into"? "Well," dad answered, "The Bible is a very old book that was supposed to have been written by priests and disciples if I remember, but is it a true account? No one can prove or disprove some of the stories in it, but it gives people something to believe in. I'm sure Mr. Godwill has explained that to you in class, or maybe not. Still, as for Arthur and Merlin, well, let's just say that if Merlin was the magical person he was made out to be and there were others, where are they now? Did they have sons and daughters to pass the gift onto, and if they did, why do we not hear about it in the newspapers". His dad paused for breath.

"I see many people in my work Kevin, which have said they have seen God, Sorcerers, and all questionable things in my line of work, but I am afraid that these people are unfortunately just sick. Their minds are playing tricks on them and making them believe what they see and hear. I should not be saying this, but your mother and I were afraid a few years ago about your brother when we were having all that trouble with him, but luckily, we got help, and he is ok now. What people believe in or do not believe in is in the person. No one or thing will persuade the person otherwise, so if you want to believe in the bible, Arthur, and Merlin, you go ahead, but mind you keep it to yourself, or you just might find yourself going to a doctor to sort out your head. I hope this has answered your question. Now, it's time for you to go to school and for me to get some sleep before my next shift. Have a good day, Kevin, and stay out of trouble, ok?" Kevin nodded, hugged his dad, and then was off to school.

Kevin met up with Vinny, his best friend when he arrived at the school gates. "Morning Kev, everything ok?" he asked. Kevin smiled at his mate and replied, "never better. You got a game this weekend, Vinny?" he asked; Vinny shook his head, "No, been called off, was supposed to be playing Bostock rovers, but their manager was taken to hospital with appendicitis or something, so they cancelled, what about you?". Kevin smiled, "oh yes, we're playing the spaldwick rangers at home. It should be a good game; why not come and watch good footballers play," he said with a laugh. Vinny bumped his bike tire into Kevin's and then laughed as the boys took their bikes to the racks.

The school day started with the assembly, and then it was Maths class for the two friends. As they lined up, a couple of new girls walked past the class line and glanced and smiled at Kevin as they went by. Vinny saw it and gave a big "oooough, looks like someone likes you mate," Kevin blushed but just ignored his friend's suggestion and gave him a little thump on the arm as if to say, shut up. Vinny laughed, then the class door opened, and they went inside for their lesson. Eventually, the bell went for the end of the lesson, and the class left the classroom as they did Godwill was standing outside. "Young Wilks, a word, please," he said as he beckoned Kevin towards him. Kevin left his friend and walked away with Godwill. Godwill took Kevin to his class, shut the door, and stopped time.

"Right, young Wilks, I have been looking into things, and this is what is going to happen. Firstly, there is a school trip for second years going to the Sherwood Forest for a science class, checking on flowers and insects in the forest. I have put you and your brother down to go also. You need to look interested on the bus in science, but when you get there, you can stop time and have a good look around. Secondly, Sambia was indeed one of the magical dwarfs used to hide one of the pieces of the power stone; where or how he is still alive is unknown, but if you are to find anything, you will need to get more information on this character if he is still alive or where he was buried or anything that can help us, alright". Kevin nodded his head and was about to turn away and leave the class when Godwill bellowed again, "wait, Wilks, did I say I was finished with you, I don't think so," Kevin turned again and stood listening. "Thirdly, we need to meet up at the spinney tonight and teach you the travelling spell, now this is not going to be easy, and it may cause a little bit of sickness on your part, but I am sure you can take it," again Kevin nodded and then asked, "is that it sir, or do you have another thousand things for me to do because my calendar is still not full yet," he said sarcastically. Godwill was quite angry at the sarcasm but let it go as he knew all this had been thrown onto Kevin in a short time and had already seen how he reacted. "No, one last thing, yesterday you mentioned that you saw another me coming out of my class and into the nurse's room. Then I came out of the staff room. You mentioned it could have been Jaarez, but I have not known him to take the form of anyone yet, so why should he take my form? How did you know it was not me?" Kevin laughed before replying.

"As I said yesterday, sir, he was not as tall as you and not quite so big around the waist area, and if it was you, how did you go into the nurse's room and then come out just after from the staff room, I know it was Jaarez, just don't know what he is up to, best keep your guard up sir," he said before leaving the class again. Time started back up, and Kevin's mate came running down the corridor to him, shouting, "Kev, wait up." Kevin waited for his friend to catch up with him. Vinny, now a little out of breath, tried to compose himself before speaking, "well, what did old grumpy want?" he asked still catching his breath. Kevin just smiled at his friend then replied, "oh not much just wanted me to take on the universe, and kill a few demons," he replied laughing. Vinny not amused stood staring at his friend quietly as if to say really! Kevin smiled again then said, "he is going to teach me the travelling spell tonight after school, that's all." Vinny now aglow with excitement blurted out, "that's all, that's all, I've heard that only a very powerful wizard can do this, many have tried but some, well, let's just say that some were never heard of again and some never tried it again due to misfortunes."

Kevin looked at his friend and then said questionably, "misfortunes, what misfortunes?" Vinny started to walk away from his friend when Kevin caught hold of his friend's blazer arm, holding him back." What misfortunes, Vinney?" he asked. Vinney shook himself free before answering. "it's only what I have heard, nothing proven." "What did you hear, Vinney? Tell me," Kevin said with urgency. "Well, one boy I heard landed on some mountainside and was lost for a long while. He was eventually found dehydrated and talking about monsters and magical beasts, so they took him to a nutty hospital, another materialised in front of a car, and he was seriously injured and in hospital for months. I also heard about a girl that tried it and has never been found to this day, and," Kevin stopped his friend as he was about to say something else and asked. "Who told you this nonsense? Godwill will not put me in trouble without care. Besides, he did say it was part of the starting magic to be able to use the travelling spell, did he not? So, do you know how to use it? Vinney lowered his head before speaking in a quiet voice, "know of it, but too scared to use it, and for your information, the stories come from older wizards and witches, so it must be true." Kevin laughed at his friend then turned to walk away from the classroom door to his next class, with his friend following him.

The next lesson was PE, Kevin's favourite lesson. He would give up all his other lessons just to do PE all day, every day. As the boys changed, Vinney spoke to Kevin again. "Oh, I almost forgot, that girl that was interested in you, she's new, just come here from up North, her name is Rueth Davis, she is a little younger than us but quite a looker, ay mate?" Kevin looked at Vinney, smiled, and nodded. "Apparently, she likes Classical music. Well, that's a put-off straight away." Vinney laughed, but Kevin did not laugh, "what is wrong with classical music?" he asked his friend, "well, it's kind of geeky don't you think, and if you take that, you will have to be in old Bonzers and Loves lessons, and they are mad." Again, Vinney laughed, and this time Kevin also did, but still had the last word. "Rueth, you say her name is, she is quite a looker, and if she is into music must have some brains, I might just keep my eyes on her." Just then, Mr. Perry blew the whistle for all the boys to make their way onto the football pitch, so off they all went.

The lesson went too quickly for Kevin as he loved playing football. Soon it was break time, and the friends made their way out into the playground where Kevin's brother and some of his friends were waiting for him." Over here, bro," he called to Kevin. Kevin and Vinney moved towards his brother, but as he did so, he caught sight of the new girl Rueth, being taunted by some other boys pulling her bag from her and calling her names. Kevin made a beeline away from his brother towards the girl. He raced over to the pack and stood in front of one of the boys asking, "what are you doing? Leave her alone. What's she done wrong to you?" Paul looked on in dismay and just knew there was going to be trouble, so he made a dash toward his brother. Unfortunately, it was a little late. One of the boys had called Rueth a name, and Kevin hit out at him and knocked the boy off his feet. The boy's friends started to all have a go at Kevin as he threw punch after punch connecting with several of the boys' faces and heads before his brother pulled him off one of the boys. Paul's friends had also come with him, so now the boys had decided that enough was enough and got up and started running off just before Godwill, the duty playground teacher for that day, turned up. Paul struggling to hold his brother back, now whispered, "now you are for it, you fool." The last boy on the ground had now got up, holding a bloody nose, and started to cry. Godwill was there as if by magic; he had seen the scuffle and had covered a great deal of space in a brief time. He brushed Paul to one side, caught hold of Kevin and the boy called Richard Pickering by the ear, and was now marched both of them off to the office shouting, "No fighting allowed, you know the penalty," and disappeared into the car park area and back into school.

Vinney looked at his brother and then at Rueth. She lowered her head, picked up her bag then started to move away. "Hold on, young lady, what the hell just went on?" Rueth looked at Paul before speaking, "it's not my fault. I didn't ask him to do that. He just went off the handle." Paul walked towards Rueth and put his arm around her before saying, "it's ok, he's my brother, and I know he is a little hot-headed, but what did the boy do to make him start hitting out like that?" Rueth just looked down to the ground and started to cry, "I don't want to talk about it. Just leave me alone, please." Paul could see the girl was upset and let her go. Vinney now a little shocked, asked Paul, so what was all that about? It's unusual for Kevin to go bananas like that over some soppy girl". Paul agreed but was more concerned with what the repercussions were going to be for Godwill and his mother when she found out. The gang broke up as the school bell went, and then all went their separate ways to the next class.

Meanwhile, Kevin and the boy stood outside the headmaster's office, waiting for Godwill to come out and issue them their punishment. The boy had a large handkerchief holding it to his nose, stopping it from bleeding, while Kevin just stood there humming to himself. Suddenly the door opened, and the outcome was Godwill. He did not look best pleased. "Pilkington, Wilks, you will be on detention for two weeks. Every break time, you two will report to my class for detention. Now go to your next lessons and keep away from each other. If I see you two fighting again, it will not be detention but expulsion. Do I make myself clear?" The two boys mumbled together their reply and went separate ways to their next class. "Wilks, Come here." Kevin stopped in his tracks and turned slowly to face Godwill. "My class, now," he said as he sternly walked past Kevin knocking into him, nearly knocking him off his feet. Kevin regained himself and followed Godwill.

Once in the classroom, Godwill slammed the door shut. "What on earth made you do this, are you stupid or something" he shouted at Kevin. "Well, do you not have anything to say, Wilks?" Kevin now looked Godwill directly in the face with a look of anger, "Yes, sir, I have something to say about it. The boy called her a freak, for what reason I do not know, but on hearing this, it brought back the time at which, if you so rightly remember, you calling all us freaks, sir, remember, and I was not happy with being called it by you or anyone. Again, I ask you, is that what we all are? The more people call me or any of my friends freaks, then the more trouble I will get in because I will not be called that by you or anyone, sir." Godwill stood open-mouthed. Not a word was said by him at that present time, just silence. Godwill sat down and looked at Kevin, "this fight was just over a name-calling, and when you were hitting out at these boys did you think it was me you were hitting?" Kevin looked away from Godwill and said nothing. "It was, wasn't it, Wilks? Well, bless my soul, just because I called you once a freak. A laps time and word that was not supposed to be said, and this is what you hold against me and the world because you are not like others but special." "Special," replied Kevin, "not a freak then, sir." Godwill now took a softer tone to his voice, "No, Kevin, not a freak, but very special. I must say that if your anger is truly that forceful, then I can only say that the boy was lucky that you only used your fists instead of any magic." Kevin butted into Godwills speech, "well you and Merlin did say that we were to keep our two different lifestyles apart and I don't know how but I did." Godwill now had a small smile on his face staring toward Kevin. "So, this young lady, a friend of yours, is she?" Godwill asked. "Not really, only see her today. Apparently, she's new here, moved from up north according to my mate Vinney." Godwill stroked his beard then said, "well, it's obvious that there is some sort of attraction to you from her, but I tell you, having a girlfriend is not good for a young wizard, there is much to learn, and a girlfriend will distract you from your learning so I must advise that you make no romantic signs or suggestions towards her, do I make myself clear Wilks ?". Kevin now a little angry spoke severely, "so now you're telling me who I can and cannot associate with, that's just too much, I'm out of here, good luck with your quest." With that Kevin got up and left the classroom slamming the door behind him as Godwill was still shouting at him, "this is not the end of this Wilks, just the beginning, do you hear me, Wilks." Kevin just carried along the corridor to his next lesson.

The rest of the day went slowly, with every break being taken in Godwills class for detention and every finish of detention. Godwill tries to make Kevin see sense but to no avail.

Finally, the last school bell rang, and Kevin could not wait to get out of the school quickly enough. As he grabbed his bike and sped off down the school's chase to the gates, he saw the girl Rueth walking. He wanted to stop and talk to her but thought it could be awkward, so he continued to peddle on. Just as he was going by her, she called to him. He slammed on his brakes and skidded to a stop, where she ran up to him. "Look," she said, "I'm sorry you got into trouble with old fuzzy face, but I did not ask you to help but thank you." Kevin smiled at Rueth and just said, "you're welcome." There was a small silence between speaking, then Kevin said, "never liked that boy anyway." Now Kevin and Rueth were looking at each other, and a small smile came from her lips. "Anyway, thanks again." "Kevin," he answered, "Kevin Wilks," "Rueth Davis," the girl replied and held out her hand, which Kevin took and shook gently. Again, silence before Rueth spoke, "so, live near here?" "Not far," replied Kevin, "just the other side of town down Willders Garth" "you?" he inquired, "not far from there actually, just a bit further near the hospital." Kevin, now thinking he should ask to walk with her or not, was rudely interrupted by his brother now going by. "Where are you going, bro? Vinney told me you got a lesson to go to, or have you forgotten?" Kevin turned to his brother then said, "No, not forgotten, just not going. I have had enough of Godwill today, I'm not doing this anymore, it's over." Paul now looking terribly angry called out, "what do you mean it's over, you keep saying that, but you know nothing is over, get real, put the girl down and get your backside to the lesson or you know what old Godwill will be like tomorrow." Kevin looked at Rueth and just said, "so let him be angry. I don't care anymore." Rueth looked a little worried and said, "you should go, Kevin. You are already in hot water over me. I don't think I want to be the cause of you getting into deeper hot water with the old fuzzy face." Kevin looked at Rueth and then sighed and said, "ok, I guess I had better get this over with, come on bro, race you" Kevin turned his bike around and was just about to set off when Rueth said, "thank you once again, Kevin, I guess we will see each other around." Kevin smiled towards Rueth and replied, "I guess so. I will look forward to seeing you again," and rode off towards his brother, thinking of Rueth.

"Get your head out of the clouds, Kevin. You are going to need all the concentration you can muster for this lesson." His brother called to him, "ok, I hear you, but I don't know if old Godwill will turn up anyway after the things that I did and said today" he called back to his brother, "oh, he will still be there, trust me, remember, two lives kept separate, that's the way." Both boys sped on towards the spinney as fast as they could.

Chapter 12

Orbs and Matreese

When the three of them arrived at the spinney, Godwill announced that instead of learning the travelling spell today, they needed to try and understand more about the Orbs and mind projection and how it works. Paul asked, "but sir, I thought the travelling spell would be the most useful thing as it would allow them to be able to travel to far distant places in a very short time undetected." Godwill replied, "of course, it will, but after what just happened a little while ago, do you not think that we need to understand how your brother can control the force within him first and what, in fact, the Orbs' powers are of those that project them?" Paul gave a sigh as he really wanted to learn this spell then answered, I guess so sir," so all three set about looking through the number of books on the shelves for more information. After an age of looking through books, eventually, Godwill decided that enough bookwork was enough and decided to call it a night. Kevin was still a bit mystified about the number of books that had appeared suddenly in the spinney hideout that he had not noticed before, but he just went with the flow. In the time that they were there, they had searched the books on Orbs with mind projection and tried to find more information about this magical dwarf called Sambia but came to a dead end. In most books they read and talked about, it mentioned that all the magic dwarfs that hid the pieces of the power stone had died. However, one book alone mentioned that, in fact, the bodies or verification of two of the dwarfs' deaths were not actually confirmed but only presumed dead. Godwill stretched as he rose from the seat. "Well, I don't think that we are going to find out anymore in these books, so I guess the rest is up to intuition." Kevin looked at Godwill and then asked, "Intuition, what's that, sir?" Godwill smiled, then laughed, "Come young wilks, you don't know what intuition means?" Kevin looked at Godwill with a blank expression on his face and just shook his head. Godwill stopped laughing and then explained to Kevin that intuition meant that it was something that you must find out on your own through experience or just a feeling you have. Kevin understood then and gave a small smile.

"Well, come on, you two, let's get out of here, and then you two need to get some rest. You have a big trip coming up and things to do, so I do not want you, young Kevin thinking about that girl you met, ok?". Paul laughed, and Kevin turned to his brother with a look of anger on his face. "Easy now, it is you and not Postromus looking at me. Please say it's you?" Kevin had thought quickly shot into his mind thinking that he now had a way to be able how he could control his brother at certain times. "No, it's me, but I can't say that it will always be me. Just keep your comments to yourself when I am around, or you never know who or what is listening. Do I make myself clear?" Paul, now, took a couple of steps back towards the door, muttering, "ok, ok." Godwill was not so impressed. "Better you be the one that is in control all the time, young Wilks. Remember, Postromus is enormously powerful. You are not, not yet. Anyway, he can, and I guess eventually will, overwhelm you and take control if we cannot work out how to remove his presence from you. As for this girl, well, there will be plenty of time for those things later in life, provided we sort this whole thing out sooner rather than later." Kevin moved towards Furgill, the phoenix brushing the head of his bird and wanting to ask one last question. "Sir, how are we going to remove Postromus from me?" he asked nervously. Godwill stroked his beard and then spoke quietly, "I do not know at present Young wilks, but there are a lot of people working on it as we speak. They are exceptionally talented wizards, witches, and magical beings. I am sure one of them will produce a way, but until then, your mind needs to be strong and keep on with the situation that you are in. Who knows, you just might need his power to add to your own one day for something, so it could be a blessing. Now do not worry about it now. The time you went off home." With that, all three of them left the spinney after Godwill had restarted time again.

The boys cycled home in complete silence; not a word was said. When they arrived home, the boys put their bikes in the shed and went inside. Their mother was there getting tea ready, singing happily to herself. "Good day at schoolboys," she asked. Both brothers looked at each other before answering. "fine," Paul said as he went on through and up to his bedroom. "And what about you, Kevin? Everything ok?" she asked. Kevin gave a smile and replied, "not bad, just the usual things, although I did meet a new girl that has come to our school, she seems nice, apart from that, just the same boring things." Kevin's mum looked at him and said, "now, young man, boring things, you mean lessons? Well, let me tell you, when you get older, you will look back on your school days and just remember how good they really were. Oh, I know you do not think that way now, but mark my words, you will. So, who is this girl you like then?" Kevin blushed, "I didn't say I liked her mum, just that I met her today, that's all." Kevin's mum Wiped her hands clean on the tea towel by the oven before replying. "Well, you haven't mentioned a meeting with a girl before, so she must be cutey for you to notice and mention," and gave Kevin a smile. "Mum, leave off," Kevin replied before running up the stairs to his room.

That night, Kevin got out his books to look for more spells that he could learn when he felt a throbbing in his head. Kevin held his head tightly, muttering, "no, no, no." His brother heard him from his bedroom and went racing into his bedroom to find out what the trouble was. As he opened the door and saw his brother there in pain, he quickly shut the door and got out his wand. Kevin now struggling to control things, suddenly stood up and opened his eyes. Paul stepped back a pace then just said quietly, "Kevin, you ok?" Kevin stood still, not murmuring a word. He then shut his eyes again and stood perfectly still, not a movement of any part of his body, only his eyes moving inside his closed eyelids. Paul still scared, asked again, "Bro, you, ok? speak to me." Still, Kevin did not move or open his eyes. He just stood there motionless. Eventually, he did open his eyes and sank back onto his bed. He turned his head towards his brother and muttered. "Get me a pen and paper, now." Paul scrambled back to his bedroom and quickly returned with both, which he gave to his brother. Kevin, without looking at the paper, started to scribble a picture down on the paper and a few words, some in English, some in a language Paul could not recognise. Eventually, Kevin stopped drawing and writing and then closed his eyes again. The paper and pen fell from his fingers, and Kevin now lay on his bed, fast asleep. Paul, not wanting to wake him picked up the paper and pen and took it back to his bedroom. He looked hard at the pictures Kevin had drawn. One was of what he thought looked like a small waterfall, another a small cave, and the final drawing looked like a pool inside a cave with arrows pointing both up and down at the entrance. Paul then looked at the writing that his brother had done. The writing he could make out said, "to open this mouth, you need the food to feed it," also, "one will die alone trying to succeed in this quest," And the last thing he looked at said, "if this person still lives, they will be needed for help and strength." Paul also noted on the scribbled papers some words, 'Alicatan Vasiley Drawench,' Sareptamus Comonulitous Gertainhes Powerglukit Cerentium' and Thesep tomackar witchestum seperatum momentum. Paul decided to go back one last time to his brother's bedroom to check on him and noticed he was no longer in there. Paul ran out of his brother's bedroom and knocked on the bathroom door. No answer came back, so Paul raced downstairs to where his mother was sitting watching television in the living room. She turned to Paul and asked, "you ok, Paul? You look worried," Paul just shrugged his shoulders and replied, "no, I'm ok. I just wanted a drink, that's all." His mother just turned back to watching the television as Paul went through to the kitchen to get a drink.

As Paul got himself a drink of water, he noticed out of the kitchen window Kevin, just standing at the bottom of the garden staring at a tree. Paul went out towards his brother and saw him with his hands in front of him, holding a glowing orange orb in them. Paul quietly spoke. "Kevin, what are you doing? What's that? Stop it. People will see." Kevin smiled and answered his brother. "isn't it beautiful? It just appeared and drew me out here." Paul, now a little concerned, replied, "so, what is it, and why out here to this spot?" Again, Kevin smiled and then replied, "it's," Kevin went silent before carrying on," you would not understand", Paul just uttered, "try me. Nothing surprises me anymore". Kevin just closed his eyes and muttered, "Loseterum," the orb slowly started to dim before it disappeared. Kevin gave a shudder, then turned to his brother, "The orb is that of Bartholamew, Merlin's friend. It was he who was helping control Postromus." Paul looked in disbelief, then said, "but Kevin, Bartholamew died. You saw it yourself in the visions that Merlin showed you, how can this be?" Kevin looked at his brother then replied, "I don't know, but there are a lot of things we don't know, remember that is what Godwill also said, all I know is that there are magical things around me that I have not noticed before or known about that are out there for good and not just bad or evil. It is time we grew up and started to recognise these things." Kevin then walked back into the house and back upstairs to his room. Paul ran in also after Kevin had left him and ran to his brother's bedroom, where he found him sound asleep. Paul returned to his bedroom, still not sure of what had gone on this evening but decided enough was enough and decided to get some sleep.

The next morning the two brothers made their way to school. Once there, Paul left his brother in the cycle sheds with his mate Vinney saying, "I just got to have a word with someone. Catch you later, Kev." Kevin just raised his hand up to acknowledge his brother. As the two boys walked into the main school, chatting about football and the new girls that had arrived at the school, Godwill met them as soon as they entered through the door. "Morning Wilks, Rose, so pray. What is on your agenda for today?" Vinnie looked at Kevin with a look of disbelief on his face as he had never heard Godwill talk this way before. "Excuse me, sir, what did you just say," asked Vinnie. Godwill, now a little sterner, replied, "don't be flippant, Rose. I just wanted to know what lessons you and Wilks had today, that's all" Vinnie sighed with a look of relief on his face as now he understood what Godwill was talking about. However, Kevin was a little more concerned and replied, " why do you wish to know that, sir? After all, with what's going on, I thought you would be tracking my every move and lesson I attend, am I not right ?" Godwill looked down and muttered, "of course, wilks, I know all the lessons you are taking, but we have to be careful that no one else knows this. Am I right?" With that, Kevin took out his wand, cast Timearium Discosure Afentium ", then quickly cast another spell at Godwill, "Revalto" Vinnie jumped back in alarm at what Kevin was doing only to see the shape of Godwill change from that of a teacher to the shape of his brothers best friend, Roger Cranbridge. Vinnie now looking at Kevin stuttered to ask the question of how he knew. "Roger just laughed when he saw Vinnie's expression on his face, then spoke. "So how did you know I was not Godwill, Kevin? I guess if I were, then you would be in deep trouble for casting that spell at him." Roger laughed as Kevin slowly started to explain. "Well, first, Roger, the fool you are, you just do not listen when goodwill talks to me. He is not polite but bullish; he never just calls me Wilks, as Vinnie also found out when he tried to become Godwill and challenged me that time at the spinney. He only calls me young wilks, and the last thing he would never ask is what lessons I have in the day, as he knows. The reason that he knows is that he needs me to complete something for him and a higher power, so he needs to know exactly what I am doing and where I am. Also, I am a little confused about your account. As you know, I have with me always at present an immensely powerful and angry wizard that could show himself at any time, and even though I hate to say it could do you some serious harm. Why would you even want to try this? do you wish to be harmed?" Roger now a little afraid, stuttered himself, trying to explain that it was his brother's idea and that they thought it would be funny. "Funny, really, well I hope that I can contain Postromus long enough for you to get away as I feel that he is not happy and wants to show his anger, so if I was you, I would run, and run fast and tell my brother I will have a chat with him at home and that he might get also to talk to Postromus, that should keep him amused". With that, Roger ran as fast as he could down the corridor but kept looking back to see if there was any sign of Postromus anger coming towards him. Kevin let out a laugh, but Vinnie was looking at him with disbelief. "What, "Kevin asked. Vinnie just shook his head and said quietly," Postromus, who is he when things are said and done," Kevin just looked at Vinnie and said, "never mind, Vinnie, I will tell you about it someday, but until then, I had better restart the time, and we need to get to the class." "Hold on," Vinnie then said, "so how did you know it was not Godwill?" Kevin just looked at his friend and said, "Vinnie, do you ever listen to a whole conversation? I just told you and Roger how I knew it was not the real Godwill, can't you remember that?" Vinnie looked down at the ground with a quiet mutter replied, "oh yes" then Kevin restarted time, and the boys continued to the class.

The day went quickly, and no incidents were noted on that day, but at home time, there was something that was going to happen that would really stay with Kevin for the rest of his life.

Godwill met Kevin as he was ready to get his bike from the bike shed. "Young Wilks, where is your brother? We need to meet at a safe place now." Kevin thought that his brother had got out a bit earlier than him, and he was now on his way home. Kevin looked across from where he stored his bike only to see his brothers still in the bike shed where he stored his. "I do not know, sir; his bike is still here, so that must mean he is still here. Maybe he is in the common room doing some extra studying or something." With that, Godwill grunted towards Kevin with a forceful "come, we must find him." Both Godwill and Kevin set off towards the common room to see if his brother was there. When they got to the common room, the lights were off, but it looked as if Sharpe bolts of lightning were thrashing around inside. As they moved closer, they could hear cries of pain coming from inside. Godwill tells Kevin to stay behind and follow quietly. The two crept inside the building and along the corridor. Each footstep closer, the cries got louder until they reached the door, and Godwill pushed it open quickly. As he gazed inside, he could see Kevin's brother lying on the floor with Matreese standing over him. Godwill wiped out his wand and cast "Transisomb," the spell shot Matreeses' wand from his hand, and the wizard moved back away from Paul. With his wand still pointing at Matreese, Godwill shouted, "what do you want here with that boy? he is no use to you."

Matreese smirked and answered, "You are a right old man, but there is someone here that I do need, and I shall have him and all that goes with him." Godwill, now angrier shouted back, that is not going to happen as long as I draw breath", Matreese stared at Godwill then replied, "well, that can be arranged, old man. You are nothing, an old man with a little power, not like me, a powerful being that could wipe you and the rest of your kind right off this world. However, it seems that you have the upper hand at present, so I will go but be aware, no ware is safe, and no one will stop me from gaining further power when I Matreese, find the stone parts and become invincible. That day, you will wish that this had never taken place. Kevin wilks, we will meet again, and next time there will be no saviour like the times before, until then" Matreese waved his hands quickly, and a flash of light and a gust of wind-powered its way through the common room and out through the open window at the end. Kevin now rushed towards his brother with Godwill, asking for the stone around Kevin's neck. Kevin quickly gave Godwill the stone, and he waved it over his brother chanting "Compare-Relapsum" many times. Paul's open cuts and bloody body now started to heal, and life started to appear back on his brother's face. With a gasp of breath and a last cry of pain, Paul lay still for what seemed to Kevin to be an age. Then opened his eyes looking straight up at Godwill and then to the side to see his brother kneeling beside him.

With a small smile and a whispering word said, "I could do nothing, nothing, he is too strong for me and you, Kevin, Godwill, we need help, please help us." Godwill cradle Paul's head in his hands, quietly hushing Paul to save his strength and to calm him down. Goodwill turned to Kevin and said, stop the time. Your brother needs rest, and he cannot go home whilst he is like this. We need to work out a plan to be alert and in pairs, at least until we can eliminate Matreese from here." Kevin was a little taken aback by what Godwill had said but understood also. "So, I think I need to up my lessons, sir, to be ready and stronger. This will not happen again. I promise you that." Godwill quickly lowered Paul's head onto the ground and, in the same movement, jumped to his feet and grabbed Kevin's shirt front at the tie area. "You promise this will not happen again. How can you say this, a mere boy of what twelve and a half thinks he can defeat a wizard of age experience, wisdom, and black arts, well I bow to you, but excuse me for saying, your brother, who is three years older, more knowledge than you, more understanding of the magical ways could do nothing so what makes you sure you can? Are you a chosen one or a special one, boy?"

"Kevin, now beginning to get annoyed at how close and bullish the way Godwill was acting towards him, raised his hand to the tie position that Godwill was holding onto him tightly and wrapped his hand around Godwills. As Kevin stared into Godwills eyes without blinking, he slowly started to speak but not in Kevin's voice but in that of Postromus. "You dare to lay your hands on me, Postromus, the great and powerful wizard; I will teach you to respect me." Godwill sank to his knees with a cry of pain coming from his lips. Kevin stepped back, held his arms aloft, and then pointed them toward Godwill. A shot of lightning flew from Kevin's arms towards Godwill, but at the same time, an orange orb covered Godwill, and the lightning seemed to rebound back towards Kevin, knocking him off his feet and where he lay still. The orb disappeared, and Godwill got to his feet, gradually looking at both Paul and Kevin lying there on the floor. Godwill moved closer toward Kevin and stood over him, wondering what had happened. Kevin's eyes opened, and he stared at Godwill. Godwill took a step backward as he could see there was still a slight tinge to the colouring on Kevin's face, and he knew that Postromus was still there. Kevin now quickly shot up off the floor and stood looking at Godwill, staring hard at him, saying nothing. "Forgive me, great one," Godwill murmured. I mean you no harm. I wish only to help these two young wizards to become great like you and to be able to protect themselves against evil and corruptness. No harm was intended towards you, but as you look upon these two youngsters, I wish only that you help and look over them in these dark times." Godwill now lowered his head as Kevin still stared at Godwill then spoke. "Tell me, wizard, why should I help you when my best friend Merlin never helped me when I called for him? Why should I help anyone in this world when all they can do is cause misery and suffering? Is it not better to kill and eliminate the soft and meek to provide a strong community where all are equal, so no fighting takes place? Tell me that I am wrong, convince me, and I will help you. If you do not convince me, then I will kill you, these two, and many more until I make this puny world bearable to live in once again".

Godwill held his head up high and looked Wilks/Postromus in the eye before speaking.

"Merlin did not forsake you at the time you needed him. He was misled by a maiden to a place by the men that killed your body as the dragon. They knew of you teaching a young wizard in your ways, so they entrapped him just like you were entrapped with Caulpolsier. She knew of your strength and dedication to magic. She knew if she could harness this within her wand that her dear beloved son Crandlos would be near invincible. She used you to get that strength. It was she also that arranged the entrapment of Merlin so he could not come to aid you and thus become the drive behind your move towards the darkness and revenge. We had seen letters from old describing what went on when she stated that her father was sending her away from you when this was a lie, and the only purpose was to hurt you and make you vulnerable." Kevin's head started to twitch, the colour of his skin started to turn a darker shade of blue as Godwill spoke of this. Suddenly a cry from Kevin's mouth came that uttered, "you lie, wizard, she would never do this to me, she loved me, we were both deeply in love, and Merlin let me down and allowed them to kill me, this is the truth, not the rubbish you are saying."

Godwill slowly moved closer to where Kevin was standing and spoke again. "The wizard that did this to the boy and the subject you are lodged in is no other than Caulpolsier's son, a dark magician called Crandloss. He killed other good magicians, sorcerers, and mythical animals to gain their power. Finally, he killed the unicorn and drank the blood of the pure animal, then ripped his soul into two and became both light and dark. He now seeks the pieces of the Time stone that you had and broke into pieces to gain further power to defeat you and any other magical person or creature that stands in his way of becoming the almighty ruler of this world. Is this what you want, is this what you, the great wizard of olden times, are going to allow him to do?." goodwill then became silent and bowed his head once again but kept his eyes open and fixed on the face of Kevin. With a moan and a groan, Kevin's face contorted, and then the answer came from his lips.

"I, Postromus, do not know if you tell the truth or lie, somethings you say are true, and that did happen. Some things I find hard to believe, then I think them to be a lie. All I will say, wizard, for now, is that you may keep your life until I have thought about this longer. Until then, do not attempt to harm this body I am in, or the consequences will be fateful for you. I will deliver my verdict to you or this organic body I am in when I am ready. For now, the area is safe, so I suggest that you be careful in what you say and do." With that, Kevin's skin returned to the flesh colour it was originally, and he fell to the floor in a heap of exhaustion. Godwill knelt beside Kevin and slowly helped him to his feet. "Come, young Wilks, we need to deal with your brother, everything is safe at the moment, but we need to prepare for any further encounters with Matreese or others that may come." They returned to where Paul was lying and dealt with him. His wounds were healed, but he was still quite weak from the encounter and was quite sore all over his body. He explained that he felt like he had been hit by a car. Kevin cracked a smile and just said to his brother, "well, I can't say I can agree with you as I have never been hit by one, so I don't know how you're feeling, but believe me, I guess it has made a small improvement in your looks at the least."

Both Kevin and Godwill laughed, with Paul also cracking a smile but also feeling still the pain from around his body. Both boys were escorted home by Godwill, and he restarted the time shift as they entered the pathway to the house. Just before leaving them, Godwill spoke to Kevin. "I am sorry for what both you and your brother have gone through so far. I guess that I have not been of any real help to you, but, with the outcome of today, I promise to both of you, I will do all in my power to bring you up to speed on all magical spells, potions, and all other magical things I have in my power to help. You are quite lucky, you know,

Wilks, someone or something is looking over you to protect you from dreadful things. I do not know who they are or what they are, but they are there for a reason, and that reason is to keep you safe and from harm and turn towards blackness. Remember these young Wilks, as there is a long journey ahead for all of us if we wish to be able to complete these tasks. Now get you inside and get a decent night's sleep, and hopefully, things will look different in the morning." With that, Godwill ushered the boys towards the door, and as they turned back to look again at Godwill, they saw him turn into a hawk and fly off over the estate. Paul looked at Kevin and just said "you have to admire the old guy, he sure has style," both boys just laughed and went inside the house where they were greeted by their mum.

Chapter 13

Sherwood Forest

The boys slept well that night, with only a slight stirring from Kevin happening. During this stirring, Kevin had a vision about the Time stone. Again, he saw the forest he was to go to, a waterfall and tree surrounding and a cloaked person near the fountain. Kevin could not make out the face of this person, but he was quite small and moved with a shuffle in his step. Although Kevin's mind was trying hard to try and get closer to this figure, he could not. At the waterfall, Kevin noticed there was a small opening that looked dark inside, but he did not get to enter it. Then the vision moved quickly to an opening in the forest that showed a little hut with smoke rising from the chimney. Outside the hut was a wooden frame from which dead rats and small deer hung. It appears someone was living there, but again, Kevin got no closer in the vision to be able to check this for sure. The vision then disappeared, and Kevin returned to the slumber of sleep.

The next morning Kevin met his brother at the breakfast table and was starting to discuss what he had seen that night when his mother interrupted the conversation. "Sherwood Forest, waterfall, hut, what is that all about, Kevin? You have had some funny dreams lately. I have heard you moaning in your sleep some nights. Are you ok, dear?" Kevin looked at his mother then replied. "Yes, mum, sorry about the moaning. It's just things staying on my mind that we have learned from school, that's all." Kevin's mum looked at him with a thoughtful gaze and then replied, "Well, I do not know what they teach you nowadays, but some of the things I heard coming from your room did not make any sense. It was as though you were speaking a foreign language but had never heard of any of them. It was not French or German. Are you taking any other language classes about which I do not know?" Kevin smiled and replied, no, mum, it was probably some words of Latin we must learn in some subjects as that is what they are mostly known through." "Latin, you say," replied mum, "guess it could be. I was never any good with any Latin names, had to try and learn a few when I was at school, but never remembered any of them," she smiled back at him. Kevin just turned away, smiling and uttering the word "mum" in a comical fashion. Paul gave his brother a quick tap on foot under the table and a quick wink of the eye as if to say, nice one, which Kevin saw, but mum did not.

After breakfast had finished, the two boys got on the bikes and left to go to school. During the journey, they both discussed what Kevin had seen during this vision and tried to decide when they got to Sherwood Forest that day on the school trip.

They boarded the bus with the other children, Mr. Tingle, the biology teacher, and Mrs. Woodstock, the rural science teacher. Both teachers greeted both Paul and Kevin when they were seated. "Nice to see you both here on this trip. Mr. Godwill says you have a passion for rural science and biology. I did not know that Paul, you were miles away when you attended my classes on this subject, but I guess people can change. I will be counting on your support, being older than most of these children, for help in controlling them, alright, deary." Paul just muttered and stammered as he replied, "oh yes, Mrs. Woodstock, you can rely on me." As she turned to walk back to her seat, Paul just laughed then said quietly, yer right, if that is going to happen," Kevin just gave a dig in the ribs to his brother as he smiled and sat back in his seat, ready for the journey. During this journey, all the children had separate ways of keeping themselves amused, some listening to music on their phones, some singing together some just sleeping. As the journey went on, Paul asked Kevin quietly, "you know, I just thought of something; I wonder when we stop or slow time if that happens only where we are or all over the world?" Kevin, who had not even given this thought a consideration looked at his brother with a strange look on his face as if to say well, how do I know that? Then replied. "Well, it only happens in the area we are, or if you think about it, there must be others like us all over the world, and if any of those did this, then the world's time zones would be a complete mess. Time must continue, or I guess the world would stop spinning, and then we would be in an awfully bad way, but I have to say that is a question that to me seems very intellectual for you, Paul. Where did that come from?" Paul just shrugged his shoulders and replied, "Don't know, really, it has only just popped into my mind, and you being so logical, thought that you may just be the person to give me some ideas about it. That's all." Kevin just smiled and closed his eyes.

Eventually, the bus arrived at a parkway at the edge of Sherwood Forrest, and the children got off. All huddled together, they listened to some information on the history of the forest, about the age of trees, animals that dwell in the Forrest, and a little about the famous person called Robin Hood. Both Paul and Kevin were deeply concentrated, looking around the area to see if there were any signs of smoke, waterfalls, or any clues as to where they needed to go. Then their concentration was broken when Mr. Tingle mentioned the size of the Forrest and how this area is under conservation to be maintained in the condition for visitors to walk through. Kevin looked at Paul and then whispered, "how are we going to be able to cover all this forest to find what we need? This will take weeks, not just a day." Kevin shrugged his shoulders as if to say he had no idea. During this small conversation, Mr. Tingle had noticed Paul talking to his brother and cried out, "something you wish to share with the whole class Wilks?" Paul looked at Mr. Tingle and replied, "no sir, sorry, I was just saying how good the trees looked and if the same tree was present throughout the Forrest to my brother." Mr. Tingle looked quite happy with this reply and answered, "well, for your and others' information, most trees in this forest are oak. They live for hundreds of years, and I dare say that if they could talk, then they would have some great secrets of things that have happened here." Paul just nodded toward Mr. Tingle as if to say thank you. The teachers then started to break the children into groups that would go off in separate ways to look at key elements of the Forrest. With a last mention from the teachers about keeping to the paths only and not straying, it was time to go.

Paul and Kevin had been put in separate groups heading in different directions, which was not Paul's choice. He wanted to stay with his brother, but unfortunately, Mr. Tingle had a different idea. As the groups started to leave and entered the Forrest, Kevin cast the time spell. All time slowed down then stopped. Paul now raced over to where his brother was puffing and panting. "Glad you did that. I didn't fancy going through there with Mrs. Woodstock." Kevin laughed and then got down to the matter of why they were there. "Ok, this is going to be a nightmare. Do we split up or stay together? That is the first question; the second is how we are going to remember where we have been. We need to devise a plan of remembering or drawing a plan where we have been so as not to get lost and be able to return to this spot and to know where we have covered." Paul looked at his brother then said, "right, so the plan is?" Kevin stood looking at his brother with a confused look on his face before answering, " I don't know, you are the older brother and supposed to be more brainy in these situations," Paul held his hand in front of his brother before replying, "hold on there little brother, older I may be, brainier, definitely not, anyway, there's two of you in there and only one of me, so the majority gets to decide." Kevin now a little frustrated, decided that it was no good standing there discussing this when their time could be spent better trying to find the items he saw. "Ok, he said, we will stay together but need to draw a map and make some sort of trail items that we can follow on our return." "Great," Paul answered, so what and how are we going to do this"? Kevin just raised his head towards the sky with a muffled "god, give me strength." He just grabbed his brother's arm and forced him in front to get moving.

Kevin took out his pen and some paper and started to draw some things on it as he walked. After going through brambles and passing many trees that all looked the same, Paul stopped and turned to his brother. "This is hopeless. We don't know if we are going in the right direction, we don't know if we are lost and how we are going to get back to the meeting spot, and I'm hungry." Kevin barged passed his brother, not even replying to him.

Deeper, they ventured into the forest, coming across many animals they would not usually see, especially in mid-flow of running or movement. Paul came across a small deer that had stopped in its tracks of movement when the time had stopped. He petted the small dear on the head as he followed his brother marking off things on his paper and just following him in a silent mode. Suddenly Kevin stopped and looked forward, then back, then up to the sky. Paul moved beside his brother, looking in the same direction his brother was looking, then said. "What, what are you looking for, are we completely lost?" Kevin said nothing but continued to look around, then said, "do you smell that?" Paul looked at his brother, then replied, smell what? All I can smell is trees and moss. Is that what you are asking?" Kevin shook his head and then replied, "Smoke," Paul looked confused but sniffed the air. "Nope, only trees and moss." Kevin started to walk further on, and his brother followed, sniffing the air but shaking his head as if to say he could not smell anything like his brother had said. Further, they ventured through trees and brambles, scratching themselves as they continued until they came to a clearing. As the boys entered further into the clearing, Kevin swore. He saw movement on the far side and moved towards this area.

As they crossed the clearing, the ground seemed to become wetter and boggier, slowing the walking down with Paul now getting concerned that his feet were getting wet and his shoes and trousers dirty. Eventually, they made it to the next part of the forest, where Kevin stopped and gazed around. Paul was about to speak when Kevin held his finger to his lips at his brother, and Paul immediately stopped speaking. Kevin slowly moved forward, looking through the forestry brambles and moving them aside to progress. Suddenly a small shape made a sudden movement moving away from them in a quick fashion. Both Paul and Kevin moved forward quicker, now trying to follow this shape. Whilst running, Paul shouted out to his brother, "what is it? Who is it," Kevin did not answer. He just kept running forward. Suddenly he stopped. His brother caught up to him, puffing and panting, and both stood looking in front of them with surprise. Where they stood, they could see a kind of recess area, clear of anything apart from two broomsticks standing straight up from the ground. "Now that's something you don't see every day," Paul said jokingly. Kevin turned to his brother with a look of discussed on his face. Both boys moved forward towards the brooms looking around the open area as they ventured forward. When they reached the brooms, Kevin noted that something was attached to one of the brooms. It was a note saying, "to use me, you must command me; to command me, you must utter the words 'Ebrackium Fortunas.' As Kevin read out the controls to his brother with a look of confusion on his face, the broom that had the note attached suddenly moved quickly in between his legs, where it was as if Kevin was now sitting on it.

Kevin gave a gaze towards his brother then the broom started to jerk forward, with movements of upper and downward motions. Kevin gripped the broom pole hard then shouted the words once again. The broom stopped jerking under his control. He then spoke. Up." As soon as he said this, the broom shot straight upwards with Kevin holding on for dear life. He shouted out, "level" the broom stopped moving upwards and levelled out to a smooth movement flying forward. Kevin adjusted his body movements, and the broom travelled in the direction of the body movements. Kevin flew around the clearing for a brief time, then ordered the broom "down" the broom suddenly moved in a vertical motion, hurtling towards the ground when Kevin was now screaming, "level, stop, land" all together. The broom jerked in the movements as he called and finally came towards the ground, where it completely stopped about six feet from the ground then just fell. Kevin fell with it crashing to the ground and landing heavily. His brother just stood there laughing as Kevin got to his feet, holding his leg. "What's so funny is you try and do better. I bet you can't?" Paul, still laughing, just answered, "no fear, I don't want to be hurt, thank you." Kevin now getting more annoyed with his brother moved towards him and shouted, take it, these must be here for a purpose, and it will get us around quicker if we can master them, don't you think? Also, it will be easier to get back to the meeting spot unless, of course, you want to continue to walk all the way?."

Paul not looking at all impressed, decided that it may be a good idea. However, he was not too sure that this was going to be easy. "I wish Godwill had taught us the travelling spell before we came here," "well, he didn't, but here is a chance to learn something for ourselves, isn't it, and show old goodwill that we can do things on our own." Paul not at all convinced, grabbed the second broom and gave the command.

As the broom sat under him, he spoke, "levitate" the broom did not twitch but just raised a couple of feet off the ground and stayed there. Paul now looking smug towards his brother, let go of the broom's neck and laughed, then said, "easy when you know how, not like you saying up" with that, the broom shot in an upward motion tipping Paul off the broom back to the ground with a thud. The broom returned down beside him, standing in a vertical way. Kevin laughed, then said, "easy hey" and laughed some more as he helped his brother to his feet. "Right, let's try this again together." Paul was not happy with this but did as his brother told him to do. Both boys uttered the command and sat on the brooms. Firstly, Kevin said, "Levitate" the broom followed his command. Paul now did the same, holding more tightly to the broom pole. Kevin now gave the second command, "Slowly up" Kevin's broom now started to ascend in a more controlled fashion until he shouted again, "levitate" the broom came to a holt just hanging there, Kevin still holding tight, called to his brother, "now you," Paul nervously gave the same commands as his brother and found that it worked and flew beside his brother and came to a holt. "Wow, quite high up, aren't we?" Kevin nodded and then commanded, "slowly forward," the broom did as it was told, and Kevin moved off, holding tight. Paul, now left behind, copied his brothers' commands and followed him, shouting, "wait up." Eventually, the two boys flew around areas of the Forrest dodging large trees and static birds held in mid-flight until Kevin noted that there was a screen of smoke rising from below in another clearing. He shifted his movement and gave lower commands to the broom, which did as it was asked until they entered the clearing, and there in front of them was the hut that Kevin had seen in the vision the night before. He thought to himself, "could this be the hut and then lowered himself to the ground in-front of the structure that had rats and small deer hanging from it. Paul followed but landed quite hard as he had not remembered to command the broom correctly and ended up in a heap on the floor again. Kevin turned to his brother and laughed, then again held his finger to his mouth as if to say quiet.

Kevin now moved further towards the door of the hut very nervously when it sprung open, and there standing in front of him was a small man holding his wand in-front of him. Suddenly he cast a spell at Kevin

"Firentay, Consunium, Derivarm." Kevin knocked backward away from the hut door and landed in a heap with a large thud. The small man now ran towards Paul again, starting to cast a spell at him when Kevin called out, "wait, Sambia." The little man turned quickly and ran over towards Kevin, again pointing his wand at him. "How do you know my name? Who are you, speak up, or I will send you to a place you only hear nightmares of?" Kevin, now shielding his face towards Sambia, nervously spoke. "You are Sambia, one of the good dwarfs chosen by Promostrus to hide a piece of the time stone. I mean you no harm. I come in search of help from both Promostrus and Merlin to find this article." You lie, boy. Both Merlin and Promostrus died centuries ago, you are here through Crandloos to gain the item for evil, and now I will dispatch you to your grave to join my master and friend." Just as Sambia started to raise his wand, Kevin felt strange, and suddenly Promostrus came through shouting some strange word towards Sambia. "Alicatan Vasiley Drawench,' Sareptamus Comonulitous Gertainhes Powerglukit Cerentium, Thesep tomackar witchestum seperatum momentum" Sambia backed away from Kevin on hearing these words and bowed in-front. Kevin now got to his feet and stood over the dwarf, staring down at him. "Why do you wish to do me harm," asked Postromus. "Forgive me, my lord, as I could not see you, only this boy asking about the stone you gave me." Kevin, now trying to take control back over Postromus, fought hard within himself, and slowly the blue tinge on his skin faded back to the flesh colour of himself. Kevin then spoke to the dwarf. "Why would you want to hurt me for just asking about the stone, Sambia?" Sambia, on seeing the change in Kevin's features, leaped to his feet and stepped back from him. "How is this possible, human? How do you have the master's voice and words? Is this trick? Because if it is, then I will surely deal with you the same way I have dealt with others."

Kevin stared the dwarf in the eyes and replied. "I assure you, wise dwarf, I am not here to steal or use the stone's mystical powers for evil, I am on a quest for Merlin, and this is my brother, a wizard, to help me in this quest. I will reach down and bring my wand out so that you will recognise that I am telling the truth." Kevin slowly grabbed his leg where the wand was and slowly drew it from its place. Sambia kept his eyes on Kevin, staring intently and still ready to raise his wand and cast a spell. Kevin now turned the wand around, so the main end pointed at himself, and the ivory handle was now being offered to Sambia. The dwarf stepped forward and gently took the wand from Kevin's hand to inspect. "This wand is indeed Merlin's. I recognise the carvings on the handle. Where did you get it from, wizard as legend says that this wand had been destroyed when Merlin met his death. How do you come to have his wand, and how do you seem to have our master within you?." Kevin now knelt before the dwarf then spoke. Good Sambia, I have many tails to tell you if you allow me, and hopefully, you will see I am no threat to you, Postromus, Merlin, or anyone else. Please, take the time to hear me out." Sambia thought for a second, then slowly lowered his wand. "You seem young, and the intent seems true. I will let you talk, but head my warning wizard, if you try to trick me like all others before you, to will end up on my trophy stake you see before you." Paul took a large intake of air and then squeakily spoke. "You mean these are other people, not forest animals?" Sambia laughed, then replied. My, you are a vain and irresponsible young wizard. Of course, these are witches and wizards that tried to harm me for the knowledge of the stone." Sambias face then went from happy to mad before he continued. "And this will be your fate if you are not who you say you are and are trying to hurt or trick me, understand." Paul, now on his feet, nodded his head with an expression on it that Kevin could only decipher as help. Let us get out of here. Kevin spoke to Sambia, who reassured the dwarf of the boy's intentions. Sambia grunted, then slowly led them into his hut.

On entering the hut, both Paul and Kevin were shocked as the hut outside looked exceedingly small and would be cramped once inside. However, the room space was enormous with lofty ceilings, plenty of space to move around in, and very pleasant. Sambia, still holding Merlin's wand, beckoned the boys to seats. "Now, young wizard, firstly, who do I have the pleasure or misfortune to be speaking to?" Kevin replied, "my name is Kevin Wilks, and this is my brother Paul." Sambia, now stroking a small light beard on the chin of his face, grunted back, "is that so?" Both Kevin and Paul nodded. "And you say you are on this quest, so who gave you the quest, laddie?" Kevin now started to explain what had happened to his visions and how now Crandloos was two persons. Sambia quickly got to his feet with a shouting cry and called out to Kevin, "You lie, boy. Merlin, Bartholmew, and Postromus are all dead. How can they still be with us in body or soul when their bodies were discovered and properly buried in the traditional way"? Kevin now stood also, and the dwarf turned Merlin's wand towards him as if he were going to use it. "Go on then, Sambia, use it, make me another of the trophies you claim, do it, go on, or are you just scarred?" Sambia cast the lightning spell towards Kevin when suddenly he was engulfed in an orange globe light. The lightning rebounded off the light and back at the dwarf, which knocked him clear off his feet and along the floor. Sambia came to a halt leaning up against the wall and looking at Kevin, who still stood.

Sambia got to his feet and, this time, pointed his wand toward Kevin. Kevin raised his hands, pointing at the dwarf, and cast the water spell. Water torrents shot from his hands and forced the dwarf up against the wall. The water continued to hold the dwarf in place, rendering him moveless. Kevin now walked towards the dwarf and slowly collected Merlin's wand and the dwarf's wand before stopping the spell. Sambia again fell to the floor. Kevin bent down and offered his hand to help the dwarf up to his feet. Sambia sat looking into Kevin's eyes before accepting his help. Once on his feet, Kevin offered the dwarf his wand back. Paul just started to scream at Kevin. "What did you do that for? He will make us one of his trophies. You mark my words." Kevin just smiled at his brother then said, "If it is to be, then that is what we must accept." Paul now looked frightened at his brother and dropped his wand, then knelt. Sambia stood looking at Kevin with a puzzled face, thinking about what had just happened, then lowered his wand and then knelt before Kevin. Sambia spoke, "I am truly sorry, master Kevin. I now see that you are a good wizard, and for that, I will help in your quest any way I can." Kevin stepped back before speaking to Sambia, saying, "firstly, dwarf, I am no one's master. Secondly, I have no intent of hurting anyone, and thirdly, I just love magic." Sambia raised his head and then gave a small laugh that turned into a full-scale one that echoed through the forest. "You truly are a mystical person, young Kevin, and I can see a lot of things you have that I have seen before in all good wizards." Paul broke into the conversation, "and what is that?" Sambia turned towards Paul now, who stepped back quickly before Sambia answered calmly. "A good heart." Both boys looked at each other and then smiled before Sambia asked for help in putting his home straight again. All three wizards cast spells to mend broken items, levitate items back into their rightful place, and just do a general clean up. Once this was done, they began talking again, only this time as equals and friends. After a while, Kevin got up and then went to the window, looking out into the clearing, and further crossed to the forest edge.

He turned to Sambia and asked, "So, was it you that put the broomsticks in the clearing Sambia?" Sambia shook his head, "no, not me, young wizard" Paul then butted into the conversation. "So, if it wasn't you, then who did it, Kevin?" Kevin turned to his brother and calmly replied, "I don't know, Paul, but if you remember what Godwill said, there are people or magical creatures looking after me, so I have not got a clue, but I got to say I am very thankful for the help." Paul nodded in agreement and then heard Sambia call out, "Godwill, is that old goat still alive and kicking? I knew him as a young wizard two centuries ago". Kevin and Paul looked at each other with a look of surprise on their faces. "You mean Godwill is over two hundred years old? no, it must have been another Godwill, surely." Sambia described the features of Godwill to the boys and his stern way of talking. "Yep, that's got to be old Godwill, alright? Well, I never," Paul said as he shook his head in disbelief.

After a further chat with Sambia and a few laughs, Kevin returned to the window and gazed out once again. Staring through the open space as if in a trance, Kevin suddenly felt a cold breeze travel down his neck, which made him shudder. Then he noticed a small dark figure standing in the forest gathering, standing still, but he could not make out any of the figure's face as it was too far for him to see. "Sambia," he called, "come here." Sambia got to his feet and moved beside Kevin. "I just saw someone or something out there over towards those trees. Do you have regular visitors here?" Sambia shook his head as he stared toward where Kevin had mentioned. "No, young wizard, sometimes I get a little bit like you and think I see things and go and have a look, but usually, there is nothing there that I find." Paul butted into the conversation, "What do you mean usually?" Sambia moved away from the window, but Kevin stood staring now at the same place he looked at before with nothing in view. As Sambia returned to his seat, he started talking about years ago. He had seen something and chased into the forest after it and found a Gruffalo. Paul and Kevin both asked at the same time, "A Gruffalo, what's that?" Sambia laughed before answering the two wizards. "What, you never heard of a Gruffalo?" Sambia laughed again before carrying on. "A Gruffalo is a magical creature, probably about the size of one of those small ponies you have wandering about in the forest." Kevin answered, "do you mean a Shetland pony?" "Yes, that is it. I cannot remember all these spare spangled animals you have now in this place, but yes. However, unlike the pony you mention, it also has small wings so it can fly and is also able to cloak itself so it cannot be seen, I did not think there were any of those left after all this time, but there it was plain as the eye could see."

Paul now looked hard at Sambia and asked, "are they friendly?" Sambia replied, "oh yes, they are timid and can become very friendly. They can give you a nip sometimes when they get frisky, but they are good." Paul felt relieved as he thought he did not want to particularly come across one of these animals if it was not nice. "So, what else have you seen here, Sambia?" Kevin asked. "Well, a long time back, I swear I saw a unicorn but did not see it again after that day, then there was the pestrolon. Kevin butted into the conversation this time "a what?" he asked. "A pestrolon, it is like a small dragon. They can give you a nasty fright. I can tell you when you come across them. They do not like being disturbed. Get all nasty and anxious if you disturb them. They do, and they breath small fields of fire at you. Nothing more than a quick blast but can still cause fires and a small burn on you, so you better be careful out there as they roam, and you never know when you might bump into one of those annoying things." Again, Paul was not happy hearing this and sank further into his chair with a look of despair on his face.

Kevin just laughed then asked, "surely you are just playing with us, Sambia. Nothing lives in this forest like that. It just scares stories!" Sambia looked over to Kevin with a stern look on his face before answering. "Why would I want to do that, young wizard, especially with my master inside you? He would be able to verify what I say is true, but if you do not believe me, then you're a fool and do not deserve to be in the presence of my master, so this conversation is finished, and I wish you to go now please". Kevin replied, "forgive me Sambia, I did not want to upset you, but you must look at things from my point of view. Until some months ago, I was a normal boy, playing football, kissing girls, and doing normal things. Then suddenly, I am thrust into a world that I only read stories about and become a player in this world. I have magic, see things people have only read about in books, meet historical fictional characters, be bequeathed a quest from the most famous magician ever known called Merlin to find the time stone that I knew nothing about, see visions of other witches and wizards and going on, and now be told that there are mythical creatures still alive in our world today. What do you think I would say regarding all this?" Kevin then sank into a seat with a look of despair on his face and his head held low. Sambia stood up and walked over to Kevin. With one hand resting on Kevin's head, then began to mutter a few words that neither Kevin nor Paul could make out. Kevin began to start glowing a blueish colour as Sambia continued to talk. "What are you doing to my brother?" Paul asked as he got up from his chair quickly and started to move towards Kevin and Sambia. "Sambia held his other arm in front of Paul, who came to a stop and could not move. Paul cried out to Kevin to move away from Sambia, but Kevin could not; he just sat there.

Finally, Sambia stopped and removed his hand away from Kevin's head but kept Paul at a distance with the magic from the other arm. Kevin slowly raised his head and smiled at Sambia, and said, "thank you, I needed that." Sambia slowly lowered his arm, keeping Paul at bay, and he rushed over towards Kevin as Sambia stepped back.

"What did he do to you?" Paul now turned quickly with his wand in his hand, shouting at Sambia, "Tell me, what have you done to my brother, speak now, or I will." Sambia just laughed then replied, "You will do what, young wizard? I could eliminate you in the flick of my hand with what power you have over me." Paul began to raise his wand, and Sambia's face turned into a look of nastiness. Kevin then stood up," wait, Paul, just drop it. He did me no harm. In fact, he showed me many things from the past that even Godwill would be amazed at. Sambia meant no harm but to give me knowledge of past times and a clue." Paul lowered his wand and looked at Kevin, then at Sambia, who also was looking at Kevin. "A clue, what sort of a clue?" Paul then looked at Sambia, who just shrugged his shoulders and answered, "don't look at me. I have no idea what he is on about." Kevin then spoke, "in the visions you gave me, there was a waterfall, a clearing near it, and a large dead oak tree. For a split second, as I was looking around this vision, I saw a small opening at the bottom of the tree, not noticeably big but big enough for a small person to get into. What was significant about this area? In the other visions, I saw wonderful mythical creatures roaming around the forest, people of olden times working on the land areas, and children singing."

Kevin's face then turned sad before continuing. "I also saw wizards fighting, killing each other to gain a stone. The same stone for which we searched, I remember it was yellow in colour, small, crystal-shaped with rugged areas around it, but in some wizards, hands glowed but not in other wizards' hands that had killed previously for it." Kevin looked at Sambia and asked, "Why was that Sambia?" Sambia walked towards the window silently and stood gazing across the open patch before answering. "The stone is magical, all right, and as you know, is a small part of a bigger stone that will give the person or wizard that has its immense power to do whatever they like with it. But, when the stone was shattered into pieces, some pieces were enchanted with a magical cover by my master to be good and evil. The stone, as you would understand, can sense the character of the wizard that has it and would either help protect the good but turn the nasty ones towards the black side and kill for no reason. This was done so that, in the end, only the good could hold that amount of power in their hands and use it for good throughout. Thus, our master gave the seven of us trusted dwarfs a piece each to go and place them in places that were safe, away from harm doing, and to never be found until the day a powerful good magician can seek these pieces and only use them for good. Each of the seven of us went our own ways to far-off distant lands, to places that were not known before but, due to time, have been found in this time and age. Many of my brother's dwarfs were found and tortured by evil magicians more powerful than themselves and, alas, killed but taking the secret of the place of the stone they had to the grave with them. None of us have been in contact since that day when my master Postromos gave this mission to us. I do not know if any others survived like myself, but they still came and found me here. I have moved around this forest so many times after confrontations with other wizards that seek the stone I had. Luckily, I have overcome all that has come, but there will be a time when even I will not be strong enough to defeat my foes." Sambia lowered his head and fell silent.

"Listen, we have taken up enough of your time today, but may I ask can we come back and discuss further with you things that we need to know?" Sambia raised his head, "of course, young wizard, now we are acquainted, and I know who you are and what your purpose is. I will be only too pleased to help, but let me tell you, after all these years and continual movement around the forest, if you think I remember where the stone is, I have to say sorry. Over the years, my mind has lapsed, and fights have taken a lot away from me, sometimes I wake in the morning and do not even know where I am or why I am here, so please, do not pin all your hopes on me to be able to help find the stone for master Merlin, but will help of course in any way I can".

With that, the two boys headed outside and towards the brooms they came on. Sambia spoke to Kevin, "if you head straight towards the big outflowing branches of that oak and then turn right, you should be able to pick up the trail back." Both Kevin and Paul thanked Sambia for his advice and rose on the broomsticks, and headed toward the old oak. As they flew onto the path they needed to take, Kevin suddenly had a thought come into his mind and halted in mid-air as his brother shot past. Paul quickly, but still clumsily, turned and headed back towards his brother. With slight adjustments, Paul held flight alongside his brother, asking what the problem was. Kevin looked at his brother then back from where they came from and replied. "If Sambia knows the way back to our meeting point, then he must have seen us when we were trying to find him. How is that possible?" Paul shrugged his shoulders and then replied, "I don't know, but there are still a lot of things I am learning in this business, so all I can say is he must have eyes everywhere. After all, he did say he has had confrontations throughout the years with others and moved on, so how did he see those people?" Paul smiled and then continued, "Listen, we have seen and heard a lot today; I suggest we now get back, finish the day, and report to Godwill. I am sure he will know what to do next." Kevin agreed, and the two boys flew back to the opening near the rest of the students, still stuck in a time delay. The boys landed and hid the brooms inside the bus, then joined the others, and Kevin restarted time.

The rest of the day, they travelled around in their separate groups looking at trees and plants and taking cuttings back to be able to study further at the school. When they got back to the school, it was late in the evening, so the two boys got their bikes from the bike sheds and rode home. Once they reached home, their mother was there to ask them how everything had gone during the day. Both boys looked at each other, smiled, and told their mum how boring it had been but had opened their eyes to some things in the great Sherwood Forest. After that, it was bath time, then bed.

Chapter 14

Restless Night

As Kevin lay in his bed that night after the visit to Sherwood Forest, several questions popped into his head regarding what he had seen and heard during the visit. As he lay there with each question, his facial expressions changed, some with a smile on his face and some with a stern look and expression of disbelief. But he could not stop the questions from coming, so much so that he got out of bed and headed downstairs to get a drink. As he stood there in the moonlight shining through the kitchen window, he had a sense that he was not alone. He turned to see the figure of Merlin standing there in the doorway, smiling at him. Kevin spoke softly, "what are you doing here? Someone will notice you." Merlin spoke, "there is no need to speak so softly, Kevin. I am slightly hard of hearing but sensed an uneasiness from you, so I thought I needed to come to you." Kevin shook his head as he looked straight at Merlin. He could see straight through his form and knew it was just an apparition. "You cannot sleep; what is troubling you, young wizard?" asked Merlin. Kevin started to explain what had gone on in the forest and the questions he had regarding things.

"Merlin smiled before speaking, "so, you met Sambia. I knew him for a short while during my mentoring with Postromus, he and his brothers were quite good at magic, really, and I must say one brother called Tugay taught me as much as Postromus did. Truly knowledgeable dwarf and good with spells. However, had a weakness for the ladies, but, still exceptionally good. Then if I remember, there was another brother called Isaac, a quiet sort of dwarf who kept himself to himself, did not shine in anything but again was skilled in the art of magic. Of course, there were other brothers, but I have to say cannot remember their names at present. Anyway, you seem to have questions regarding Sambia. Can I help?" Kevin asked Merlin "how can a dwarf so old give me visions of past and present things that had gone on but then say that his memory is lacking? Surely, these visions come from the memory, so therefore, must have been trying to throw us off the track regarding finding the stone?" Merlin smiled at Kevin before answering. "You know, Kevin, throughout the ages, I have met many sorts of people. Some are noticeably confident. Some have amazing memory capabilities, and some, like yourself, have an intense sense of logicality, but how do people remember things? In age, memory fails. Small pieces are lost over time, put to the back of your mind to either try and forget or just get lost as they have not been thought of for such a long time. However, even those memories can be retrieved by the slightest thing, a smell of something smelt from the past ago, a sight of something, or even words that can trigger the memory. I guess with what has happened throughout time, Sambia has locked memories away and is trying not to regain those as they are painful memories. No one really wants to have those sorts of memories that causes anyone sadness, would you not agree?"

Kevin nodded in agreement but then entered another question. "When we arrived, Sambia was hostile towards us, and if it were not for Postromus making me speak words to Sambia that I could not speak now, he would have hurt us. Two young boys strayed from a path, and he was ready to hurt or kill us. Why would he do this?" Again, merlin looked at Kevin and then replied, "for someone so logical as yourself, you are not thinking straight, are you? as you stated, Sambia has had many confrontations with witches and wizards in the past. Do you think that they will always appear as grown-ups? No, some had heard of the dwarf, and what he could do so they tried to trick him into being kind to them in the forms of children? I do not know if you know, but dwarfs were accustomed to having large families and thrived on the number of children they could produce, so happy when children were around and very protective towards them. Then after being taken in by the witches and wizards, they would turn into their normal shape and try and gain information about where the stone is through punishment and even on pain of death. So, you see, my boy, Sambia, was unnerved to see two young boys turn up at his lodgings especially flying in on broomsticks." Kevin looked suppressed at Merlin on this comment, then spoke. "I didn't mention anything about us finding the broomsticks and flying into Sambias glade. I just mentioned things that we talked about when we were there, so it was you that did this. I knew there had to be somebody behind it, but how did you know? How did you know we were going to be in Sherwood forest?." Merlin's form turned and walked into the lounge area and took a seat in the chair his mum usually sits in. Kevin followed. "I know and hear a lot of things, do not forget, you have Godwill as your mentor. Do you not think that he keeps me up to date on what is going on? And then there are others keeping an eye on you and your brother that you do not know about, and best you do not until the time that you need them. As I said to you before, Kevin, there are many people and creatures looking over you to help in this quest, all of them good and loyal to me. There will be many things that happen in the coming times that sometimes will be at hand, but sometimes not, so you need to be ready for those things."

Kevin looked hard at Merlin again before posing yet another question. "So, who or what helped with the brooms? When we got to an area of clearing, I saw a figure that raced along quickly through the forestry bushes, no offence Merlin but that could not have been you, so who was it"? "No offence taken, Kevin," merlin answered, "you are right, it was not me, but again I will not tell you who it was as in time you may need to know, but for now, it was just a friend that's all you need to know." Kevin then replied, "so this friend also hung around near Sambias hut during our stay with him as I saw him through the window at the far end of the open ground to the forest but could not make him out." That is correct," merlin answered. "Now, any other things troubling you, young wizard, or have we set your mind at ease?" Kevin nodded, then replied, "no, I guess now I can put my questions to bed, but not happy not knowing how these things came about. It would be better for me to understand more and be, as you said, ready for things. Do you not agree?" Merlin shook his head and then replied. "Do not be impatient, Kevin. Magic is a gift and a gift to be taught in stages; each stage has a significant path in which way you will tread. Time is the factor. Some parts of the magical tuition need longer than others to learn and understand; if taught too quickly and used incorrectly, then the consequences could be fatal. I know I have impressed upon you that we need to find these pieces of the stone as quickly as we can, but I would never intentionally put anyone in harm's way to complete this. For now, you have some useful information for which I am sure your mentor Godwill will be able to help. Now, it is sleep time for both of us, me especially. You do not know how much energy this takes out of this old body to be able to metamorphosis, so I will say good night to you now, and if you do need me, you know I am always available in the astral plain". With that, Merlin's figure slowly disappeared, leaving Kevin sitting in the dark of the lounge.

Suddenly the stairway light came on, and Kevin's mum came trundling down the stairs. She went straight into the living room and turned the light on, only to be shocked to see Kevin sitting on the sofa drinking. "Oh, my word Kevin, you scarred me. What in the dickens are you doing down here?" Kevin just looked at his mum before answering, "couldn't sleep, so thought I would get a drink to see if that would help." Kevin's mum then replied, "I'm sure I heard voices down here. Who were you talking to?" Kevin quickly replied, "no-one mum, must have been me humming and singing to myself that you heard."

"Singing," his mother replied, "do you know what time it is, and you are creating that racket at this time of night? You have no regard for others, young man. Think if it had woken your brother, who is up early to do his paper round, you need to stop this and get back to bed, and I warn you, if any more of this happens, then I will tell your dad and he will not be pleased about this young man I can tell you, now, off to bed with you".

Kevin went back upstairs to his bedroom and shut the door. He heard his mother follow him and return to her bed before she fell asleep. Kevin lay there still awake, still not totally convinced of what Merlin had told him, but slowly drifted off to sleep during his thoughts.

As he lay there sleeping, images of what Sambia had shown him that day started to reappear in his mind. He could see them more clearly now, and it was as if he were now in the images. He could see large families of dwarfs and elves all living together in this village, and things were as he could make out normal. People worked the land, growing crops, and children went to school and sang as they played, but then the vision turned. From the happy village to a burning village, men, women, and children were crying, bodies of others lay on the ground with others crying over them. Figures in dark cloaks with fire and lightning coming from wands aiming at people and houses all were turned into fireballs, or the people just fell to the ground. Kevin tried hard to see if he could make out the figures doing this destruction, but the faces of the one's doing this were blurred. Although how hard he tried, he could not get closer enough but did hear names mentioned. He saw where the cloaked figures had a couple of elves tied together and wands pointing at them, asking questions regarding the whereabouts of the wizard Postromus, but the elves did not answer, so they were put to death. On killing the elves, Kevin heard the two magicians talking to each other, calling themselves by the names of Veraticus and Zephron. These two wizards were on the dark side. Nothing good about them. They used their power to maim and kill others to impact the fear of others. Kevin looked further, suddenly, he saw three dwarfs come to the aid of others. One he could make out looked like Sambia, and the other two he could see their shape, and they were of the dwarf clan, but I did not know who they were until after a battle that ended with Veraticus and Zephron being run out of town, both hurt but still alive and a lot of damage to more housing and people. Kevin heard the three dwarfs talking afterward as they dowsed fires and dealt with the wounded. The names of the dwarfs were Sambia, Tugay, and Frelic. These were three of the brothers that took on the wizards and beat them, but not without the deaths of their parents in the attack. The next vision saw the seven brothers standing over the graves of their parents with another figure beside them. It was Postromus. He had befriended the dwarfs during his stay in their village but had gone off to look for the unicorn of Evendure, A forest some miles away, and noted the attack from afar and tried to return but did not manage it in time.

Kevin heard Postromus promise to the dwarf brothers that he would look after them now and would seek out the killers of their parents and avenge them. He then heard Sambia reply back to postromus that killing another person would not make up for what had happened. Even though the brothers' hearts were heavy with grief, they did not want a friend to be turned over to the dark side because of this.

The vision then changed, and this time it was of another village again where Kevin could clearly see postromus and the Severn brothers working together, being happy together, and postromus teaching the dwarfs all new manners of magic from turning metal into gold and animals into other things but of course, always returning the item back to its original shape and characteristic. Then the vision showed a traveller entering the village. Kevin had seen this person in a vision before. It was that of alchemist Nicolas Flammel.

163

Kevin's intent bordered around this person. In time, it showed how Nicolas became exceptionally good friends with postromus, and they set about life in a happy way. Then it showed Nicolas in his workshop producing a stone the size of a cricket ball that glowed when it was touched. Nicolas was overly excited. Kevin could see in the vision as Nicolas ran with the stone to the postromus and the seven dwarf brothers to tell them what he had made.

Kevin could not hear everything the people were talking about but caught a few words. The words Power stone, immortality, and darkness. There their vision faded for a while, then reappeared.

Next, Kevin saw Nicolas, postromus, and the seven dwarf brothers holding the stone in turn and chanting spells. Each time the power of the spell was enhanced, and things appeared and disappeared that would not normally. All the friends were laughing and enjoying life, hailing the alchemist as a founder. Then, it looked as if years had passed, and Nicolas had left the village and travelled far afield with his stone. Other wizards had got to hear of the bragging stories told by Nicolas that wanted the stone. Many tried to seize it by power but failed, but Nicolas was always in peril whilst he had the stone, so he decided to journey back towards his good friend postromus for sanctuary. During the journey, Kevin repeatedly saw the torment of having to fight for his life as he would not give up the stone. As he neared the village, he came across a figure that was immensely powerful, a wizard by the name of Veraticus who took Nicolas to the limit of nearly dying but managed to escape with the stone intact back to his friend postromus. In his poor state of health, Nicolas finally managed to get to the postromus, where his friend tried to heal his wounds, but that meant taking the stone away from Nicolas whilst doing this. As the stone created immortality, it did not stop severe damage from being undertaken to the body but would sustain the life force so the body could heal itself. When postromus removed the stone from Nicolas's hand, the alchemist gave a last gasp, closed his eyes, and died. Postromus was in a fearful rage and tried to break the stone up, but each spell he tried did nothing. He was enraged that an object like this would cause so much pain and misery rather than do good. It had caused the death of one of his particularly good friends, and he knew that there would be others looking for the stone to take it for themselves, and he could not allow anyone else dear to him to die. Kevin saw in the vision that throughout time, many heard of the stone's whereabouts and tried to get it for themselves, but each time, postromus and the seven brothers repelled the attacks, but finally, after seeing the pain and misery, it was causing, decided that he would not put his friends in any more danger and decided to leave the village and become a loner and travel to a new place that no one would find him and try to work out how to destroy the stone so it could cause no further misery to anyone.

As time went by in the vision, Kevin saw a postromus in a cave in some mountain ranges. It was the cave where merlin would stay with postromus and learn his trade. Month after month, year after year, Kevin saw postromus trying to destroy the stone, learning new spells, trying them against the stone but all in vain, until one day, a visitor passed by the cave-dwelling of postromus. This old man was on a journey to find the enlightenment of life when he came across a postromus sitting outside his cave, holding the stone in his hand, deep in thought. The man approached the prostromus and spoke. "Such a deep thought must mean there is a problem, young man. May I be of assistance?" Postromus gave a sigh and then replied, be gone, old man. I know it is the stone you come in search of, and I will not allow you to take it. My goal is to destroy such a thing that can only cause misery to whoever holds it." The old man bowed to the postromus and then replied. "If that stone is the cause of your woe, then why not throw it away or break it into pieces that will cause you less grief."

Postromus was now a little angry and replied sternly. "Throw it away, so you can pick it up and do with it what you will." The old man again bowed before postromus and again replied. "I mean no solace towards you, sir, but it is merely a rock; why does it mean so much misery to you? Have you been segregated from others for a long time and now going mad relying on rocks for the company?" Postromus, now even angrier, shouted at the old man, "you think I am a mad old man? No, not mad in the head but mad in the heart, and to answer your question further, no, I do not talk to rocks or rely on them for company. This rock has caused so much pain and anguish throughout the years, I do not know how to destroy it, and I would not throw it away as I said to someone that may use it for bad things". The old man then sighed, "oh, so this must be the rock so many have talked about from that person Nicolas somebody." Postromus withdrew his wand and pointed it at the old man. The old man coward in front of postromus shouting, "forgive me sire as I knew you not to be a magician, please spare me, I mean no harm. I am but a lowly hermit travelling on my own quest for enlightenment, I assure you." Postromus lowered his wand and turned away from the old man before the old man spoke again. "I have heard of words, or in your terms, for breaking things that cannot be broken but not destroyed. Postromus turned quickly again towards the old man, "and what are these words, and where did you hear them, old man? Only a wizard would be able to conjure up a spell to do this, so if you know of a spell, then you must be a wizard, and you are here to steal the stone for which you will die in trying." Again, the man coward before postromus saying, "I am no wizard, I have no magical strings attached to me, but there was this magician in the town of Licidium far to the north of here where I was travelling amusing people with his tricks. One of them was a simple word chant that produced light from his wand that entered a rock. A dust cloud engulfed the rock, and when it disappeared, the rock had diminished into small rocks. I do not know if this were true or not, as the dust cloud was there for a while, whereupon he could have removed the one rock and replaced it with many. I am only telling you what I saw." Postromus again lowered his wand and asked a little more patiently, this time but still in a firm manner. "And what prey were these words, old man?" The old man thought for a time and tried to remember the words. "Come on, old man, or are you just an old man trying to confuse me with these things? be going on your way before I do something I may regret." The old man then stood tall, wagging his finger towards Postromus, and said quietly, "CIGRO, FREDSOM, BOMBARDO SEPRUM." Postromus looked at the old man then said, "This will never work. It must have been a trick, like you said, old man. I have wasted enough time talking to you, so be on your way and tell no one of our meeting or conversation, or I will hunt you down, and you will wish you had never come across me". With that, the old man bowed to Postromus and took his leave.

Postromus continued to cast spells he had already cast at the rock in the coming days to no avail. Then he remembered what the old man had said and decided to give that spell a go. He cast it, and as the old man said, a dust cloud engulfed the stone, but on its disappearance, the stone lay intact. He repeatedly tried to no avail, so he decided to give up for the time being and just keep it hidden. Postromus spent years alone working on new spells gaining knowledge and expertise in the powers from them but did not try to destroy the stone again. Then after he had even forgotten about the stone came upon it when he was having a clear out of the cave. He picked it up and took it out into the moonlight. He placed it on a high rock and started to cast spells at it. Nothing happened, then in one final gesture cast the spell he had been told about years before by the old man. A big boom went into the night sky, a thick cloud of dust rose from the area covering everything in its way, and then the dust settled to the amazement of postromus. The rock was now split into seven pieces. Each piece glows a distinct colour caught in moonlight rays. He picked up the pieces and started to jump up and down with happiness.

The next day he decided to make a journey back to his long friend, the dwarf's village. As he got closer, Kevin could see in the vision that all was not well. Charred buildings and burnt land lay before the out rim of the village. As postromus ran to the house that was now in a poor state of repair, he came across a solitary grave that the headstone read. Steric is a beloved brother to many. Postromus continued to the door of the dwarfs, where he was greeted by Sambia. A large embrace went on between the two for a time, and then they went indoors. Now only six of the brothers remained after an attack two years previously by wizards in search of the stone. Sambia explained that no one knew where Postromus had gone, so could not fetch him to help.

Kevin could see that again. Postromus was hurt deep in the heart and set about getting the dwarf's help in hiding the pieces of stone. He stated that each dwarf must not tell anyone or any other brother where they had hidden their piece of the stone. If they did this, then the misery would end, and they would all get back together and be united and safe together. The dwarfs agreed, and each of the six brothers took a piece of the stone. Postromus stated wherever the stone lies then, there must be a covering spell to protect it from any evil. The time will come again when the purity of a magician will find the stone bits and piece them together again for good only. The last thing Kevin saw in the vision was all the dwarfs leaving to go hide the pieces of stone. There the vision ended, and Kevin then fell into a deep sleep until the sunshine of the next day shone through the curtains to wake him.

Kevin opened his eyes to the bright sunlight shielding them with his hand as his mother entered his room. "Come on, Kevin, time to get up and go to school. Your brother has been long up and already gone." She looked at Kevin with a sort of concern on her face before speaking again. "Did you get to sleep last night? you did give me a scare sitting in the dark all alone down there." Kevin just grunted. "Anyway, come on, get you up and get off to school. I have some toast ready, so you can chew on that on your way." Kevin got up, dressed, grabbed a piece of toast, and then cycled to school, where on arrival met up with Vinny, his friend in the bike shelter. "God, you look rough, Kevin. Hard night? or you are coming down with something?" Kevin, again not fully awake, just gave Vinny a sarcastic grin and then went towards the school door.

They were greeted by Mr. Godwill as they walked through the doorway. "You ok young Wilks," he asked, "you look a bit under the weather." Kevin raised his head and replied, "oh, I'm ok, but I could do with a chat, sir, when you have time." Godwill looked at his watch and then replied, "well, there is no time now, but come and see me at lunchtime, ok?" Kevin nodded, and the two boys went off to the classroom for registration.

"What's that all about?" Vinny asked Kevin, "oh, nothing, just need to see when the next visit to Sherwood Forest is," Kevin replied. "You got to be kidding me; you want to go again? is there a girl on the trip I should know about?" Vinny asked as he nudged Kevin in the side and gave a wink. "Cause if there is, I think I might put down to go." Kevin just smiled back and replied, "no Vinny, no girl, just actually, it was a peaceful day roaming through trees, not thinking about anything. It was good to get away and relax, that is all." Vinny just gave a look of discussion, then replied, "really, you're not normal to think that way." Kevin again grinned sarcastically at his friend, then uttered, "but Vinny, we are not normal, remember." There the two left the conversation.

The morning in school went without any hitches. Only a couple of times did the teachers call out to Kevin for yawning, saying, "Sorry, Wilks, we keeping you awake with this?" Kevin just took the sarcastic comment and tried to look interested in the subject. Finally, the lunch bell rang, and Kevin made his way to Godwills classroom on his own. As he opened the door, he saw Godwill, Vinny, and his brother already in conversation.

Chapter 15

Girls and Godwill's Talk

As Kevin entered the room and shut the door, his friend Vinny ran over to him, "blimey Kevin, just heard what went on in Sherwood Forest from your brother. Next time, count me in on these trips, sounds a lot of fun, more fun than here that is for sure". Kevin stared at his brother as if to say, "what have you been talking about?" Godwill gestured Kevin towards him, which Kevin obliged. "So," Godwill said, "seems you had different things happen on this trip, young Wilks, any good come of these things?" Paul, now starting to get excited, jumped in." Any use of these things, I just told you of what happened." Godwill raised his finger to his lips looking at Paul where he shut up then turned back to Kevin and said, "Well?" Kevin stood looking at Godwill before speaking.

"Good sir, I do not know what you are asking. New figures in the Forrest, broom sticks in a clearing, flying on them, meeting one of the dwarf brothers, being set upon by that dwarf, information on past times that have caused me a headache. What is good in those things?" Godwill turned away from Kevin and stared out of the window before turning back to Kevin and then asking again. "But did you make any sense or head way where the piece of the stone is hidden?" Kevin just answered with one question, "at the moment, no, but talking to Sambia bought a question to me, which is, who actually are you and how old are you as Sambia said he knew you from long ago when I say long ago, I mean long ago like a couple of hundred years or so ago. So again, I ask, who are you"? Paul looked at Kevin in disbelief and said, "who is he? Godwill is our teacher and mentor in this quest. What are you going on about?" Kevin looked sternly at his brother before turning back to Godwill and asking again, "well, are you going to tell me"? Godwill looked at Kevin and then turned away before answering.

"Perhaps you have the right to know, perhaps not. However, this is neither the time nor place to discuss this here." Kevin then turned towards the door and spoke as he walked towards it, saying, "then our conversation is ended until I get some information." Paul shocked at his brother's attitude, jumped in front of him and stopped Kevin in his tracks. "What are you doing, Kevin? You know who Godwill is, Merlin, Postromus, you know that insane magician you have attached to you. The things that have gone on and what needs to be done, how dare you to question the one person who can help us." Kevin looked at his brother then replied. "Help us, if you remember, dear brother, I wanted nothing to do with any of this right from the start." Paul jumped in and interrupted Kevin speaking. "But since you knew you are special, you have to admit you were very happy with what you can do, am I not right?" Kevin again spoke, "Listen, Paul, since knowing what you have said, I have endured pain, headaches, a wizard trying to kill me at our home, another wanting to kill me that has somehow attached itself in my body for existence and a man or creature that is hundreds of years old teaching me things that you would only read in books as fairy tales, what or who do you think you would trust if these things happened to you. For God's sake, Paul, I am thirteen and a half going on fourteen, and I want to see a life further on, but at this moment, I think if anyone found out about this, they would drag me off to a nutty farm. Also, what do you know about Godwill Paul, so he can do magic, but do you truly know the person or whatever he is? Until he tells us who or what he is, and the reason he is here, this thing is finished with any of my concerns." Kevin pushed his brother aside and took hold of the doorknob, and started to turn it to go out. Godwill spoke, "Very well, young Wilks, you shall have all you asked for, but not here. Meet me at the safe place after school, and we will discuss things, but be aware young wizard, and that is what you are. You will not be able to comprehend all that I tell and show you, but perhaps it will settle that inquisitive mind of yours, so you understand the magnitude of what is going on". Kevin turned back and glanced at Godwill before opening the door and going out into the corridor, where he shut the door and went off to the canteen to get lunch.

Whilst sitting in the canteen, Kevin was joined by both Vinny and his brother, still going on about what had gone on in Godwills classroom before. Kevin was now getting very mad with both, and he just stood up and shouted, "enough, you two, leave it alone." The canteen that is used to noise going on in it suddenly became silent as he shouted this. Everyone just stared at Kevin as he took the rest of his meal, went to the tray area, slammed down the tray, and left the canteen. Paul just stood up and gestured towards his brother, just saying "brothers," and went out after him. As they got to the entrance, Paul and Kevin's mum stopped them, who had heard the commotion and questioned Paul about what had just gone on.

Paul just smiled at his mother, saying that there had been a bit of a misunderstanding and Kevin had got the hump over it. As his mother questioned further, Paul just said, "look, mum, it's nothing. We will find him and straighten this out." Paul's mum looked at him with a concerned look and then said, "you had better. I do not take kindly of my boys arguing in public. When you find him, tell him we will be talking about this when we get home, now go sort it". Paul and Vinny ran out of the canteen to find Kevin, but they did not see which way Kevin had gone, so they decided to split up and go separate ways to try and find him and talk to him.

Kevin knew they would try to find him, so he made his way to the music room, where he thought they would not look. When entering the music classroom, Kevin saw the girl he had helped before called Rueth. "Oh high, your, Kevin, aren't you?" Kevin just nodded and could not answer. "Thank you for helping me out with those others. It's nice to see chivalry is not dead in today's age." Kevin just smiled without replying but just stared at Rueth. "So, you here to learn how to play something? or just interested in music." Kevin just nodded again with a stupid smile on his face and again said nothing. Rueth just smiled back, then finally asked, "cat got your tongue, Kevin?" Kevin looked at Rueth, then finally spoke, "sorry, I have a lot on my mind and just hiding from my brother and friend, so am I interested in learning about music or instruments? Not really, but I could be persuaded, I guess." Rueth looked at Kevin and smiled, then spoke again. "Music is good to listen to. It can help you forget the worries of life and help you relax. Also, playing an instrument gives you the satisfaction of being able to do this. You should try it; you might like it." Kevin again, staring at Rueth, just nodded again, then stumbled out, "well, I might think about it. Do you come here most lunchtimes?" Rueth nodded and replied, "yes, it's a good getaway from the playground and confrontations, so this is like my safe haven," Kevin just smiled. Rueth then went on, "would you like to share my safe haven with me, Kevin?" Kevin did not really hear what Rueth had said but just smiled and nodded. He was just so taken by the beauty he could see in Rueth. She was his age, red-haired, and incredibly beautiful. It was like a rabbit being caught by the light in the eyes where it stands still.

Suddenly the end of lunch bell rang, and Rueth just smiled at Kevin and then said, "Oh, better get going now to my next class. Perhaps we will meet here again tomorrow and continue our love for music or let me try to incise you into its relaxing element". With that, Rueth walked past Kevin and out into the main corridor and away. Kevin, just standing still reflecting on Rueth, was rudely brought back down to earth by

Vinny knocking on the door and seeing Kevin there. "Been looking for you everywhere, Kevin. Need to talk but got to go to the next class now, so catch up later, ok?" Both boys now wandered off to the next class. The rest of Kevin's day went by in a haze as he remembered everything about Rueth, and the day was a blur. Finally, the home time came, and Kevin was making his way home when his brother and Vinny stopped him and asked where he was going. "Home," Kevin said, "Why?" Paul just shouted at him, "home, what about Godwill? we need to go to the Spinney, remember, or are you just not interested anymore as you said in the classroom?" Kevin just looked at his brother and Vinny then agreed to go and see what he had to say.

When the boys arrived at the safe location, they entered the secret room to find Godwill already there. Paul and Vinny sat down whilst Kevin just stood waiting for Godwill to speak. Finally, Godwill did speak, "Paul, Vinny, away you go. This is just between your brother and me." Paul and Vinny stayed seated and said they both wanted to hear what was being said. Again, Godwill spoke, this time more harshly, "I said away with you, now." Both Paul and Vinny left their seats quickly and went outside, closing the door as they left. Godwill now beckoned Kevin to sit near him. Kevin, a little apprehensive, slowly moved towards Godwill, beckoned, and sat down.

"Now, young Wilks, you really want to know about me because this is not a thing I can show and tell you in five minutes. My life has been long, filled with happiness and a lot of sadness. It has had highs and lows; I have seen beautiful things and fearful and nasty things. Is this what you really want to know about?" Kevin nodded and said politely, "yes, please. I need to understand more what is happening and what all this really has to do with me." "Alright, but I need to slow time first. As I said, this is not something I can tell you in five minutes." Gowill cast the time spell, then got up and walked over towards Fergull, sitting on his perch, cooing lightly. "Magnificent creatures, the phoenix is, live their lives to help others. They have immense strength, rebirth themselves every twenty years, have tears of healing, and are very loyal to their owners." Godwill stroked the head of Fergul, which made it coo even more. Kevin turned to look at Godwill as he was speaking. Godwill then asked, "so, ask your questions young Wilks and I will do the best to answer." Kevin started off by asking exactly what age Godwill was. "Well, I guess I am around nine hundred years old, I don't really remember my birthday, but you can say it's about my age, not bad for an old man," Godwill winked at Kevin as he said it. Kevin just shook his head and said, "Really, you want me to believe that you are that old, and how is that possible? Even science of today cannot keep people alive over a hundred years old, so you are telling me you are an alien or something?" Godwill laughed, alien, me, no, but I am around nine hundred years old, I can assure you of that. I have lived through old times of knights, bandits, holly wars, world wars, and the beginning of the space age, which I have to say still baffles me how far humans have progressed through my time." Again, Kevin shook his head before asking, "Prove it!" "And how do you want me to prove it?" answered Godwill, "tell you of my exploits during the times?" Kevin again shook his head before answering, "No, anyone can read books, and the things you tell me could just be from books you read." "Then how young Wilks, you tell me." Kevin stood up and asked, do you or did you have any brothers or sisters?" Godwill stroked his beard then replied, "No, no other family."

"So tell me, give me some names of people you have met during these times and not from story books." Godwill again stroked his beard before answering. He looked Kevin directly in his eyes and then said, why?, whoever I say, you will not believe me. If I said I was part of the King Arthur age, you would not believe me. If I said I lived as a hermit for a hundred years or more and saw no one, you would not believe me, so why bother? You have made up your mind that I must be lying to you. I can see it in your face". Kevin again questioned Godwill, hang on, so have you always been called Godwill or by other names?" Godwill smiled, "I think you may be onto something here, young Wilks, but not going to help you only with the answer of no. I have not just been Godwill throughout the ages. I was known by another name or names to other people."

"Anyone can say this rubbish. Where is the proof I asked for? When did you start to know you had magic you could use? If these other people like Postromus, Crandloss, and others I have seen in visions, where are their deeds recorded? what happened to Nicholas Flamel, really?" Godwill held his hand up and shook it side to side as if to say stop, one question at a time. Kevin went quiet, and Godwill shook his head, then answered, "My, so many questions all at once, that mind is doing overtime. How do you live with so much going on in there? Firstly, you have seen visions of past times, people, lands, and other things. I have taught you how to use magic, and you have seen it in front of your very own eyes, things changing shape, fire, water, and lightning. This is magic. Believe me; it is happening. As for me, I am your mentor. A mentor picked you because I recognised the potential you have but do not know it yet, but you will. You doubt not magic but yourself. This is normal for someone so young, but in time, you will come to deal with this and become as great a wizard as," Godwill paused before carrying on and saying, "Merlin."

"You keep saying your age, so tell me, how is this possible?" Godwill looked hard at Kevin before answering. "Please, sit and let me explain." Kevin sat beside Godwill as he started to speak. "Do you still have the time stone with you?" Kevin pulled the stone out of his pocket and held it in the palm of his hand. "This stone is not actually the time stone; it is another stone Nicholas Flamel made that has the power to be able to slow time. It was one of three that he completed. Remember who can alter time during your move into magic?" Kevin thought hard, then replied, "Well, there is you, me, and Merlin, so each of us has the three stones for stopping time." Godwill shook his head, "so what about Jarez? You mentioned that time was at a standstill on his meetings?" Kevin nodded, "Yes, that's true, so does that mean that he has one of these stones as well, but you said there were only three, Were there more that were made that you did not know about?" Godwill shook his head, "No, listen, concentrate, Young Wilks, come on, you're supposed to be a bright, logical-minded boy, now use that grey matter you have in your head, or do I need to really spell it out to you?"

Kevin sat there thinking then, "three stones, one I have, one you have, one Merlin has, but Jarez can also stop time. I can't think. It's so confusing." Goodwill, now a little frustrated, got up and swung around the other side of the seats stating, "three stones, you, me, which I got from Merlin and the other one Crandloss had. The stones do not stop time. It produces a time pocket, a moment within a space of time, it enables us to move around not slower but at a great speed, the speed that other people cannot see, only magic folk can as they are unaffected by the timelines, each minute of a normal person life is like ten hours of our lives". Kevin now even more confused state, "Hang on, so every time the time is slowed then we age depending on the amount of time that has been stopped for by around a hundred times difference?" Godwill shook his head again, "No, remember, the time has no relevance here. It is just a tool to ensure that normal people do not see what is going on in the world. There are wizards and witches all over this world, in every country, city, town, and village, but they have to keep their lives separate from the normal folk or just imagine what would happen, these people would be taken away to lunatic institutions you call them in this time, but before many years ago they would be burnt at stake or killed in other ways, but innocent people still got hurt or murdered during these times. This is what could happen right here if we do not find these pieces of stone and sort the power they have into one for good only to try to banish the olden-time death threats."

Again Kevin looked confused but asked again, "So what has this all to do with me? I am no saviour, major wizard. How is it that I am involved in all this?" Godwill sank to the floor, holding his knees and head in his lap. "Because young Wilks, during your life, you have had magic all around you without you even knowing. The magic gene is passed down throughout your family. Although your brother has the gene, also, it is evident that you have the positive gene, whereas your brother has the negative gene. This means that his magic can never be as strong as the magic you can produce. At times this may cause confrontations between you two, but you must play things down. There will be days when his magic will be required to help you in your quest and life. You must not hold grudges against each other, or this could cause the blackness to overcome you and turn you to the other side of magic. Tragic, hate-filled magic that is only succumbed by causing pain and death instead of things of beauty and for good. Promise me this, Young Wilks, promise me." Kevin Promised, as he was a little scared at what Godwill had told him.

Godwill looked at Kevin and then said in a soft voice. "What has happened in the past is irrelevant but has a significant impact on others. It is how now you shape your own and others' futures. People have abilities that they do not know about to do whatever they please, but only if they believe in what they want. It is important that we do things because we want to and not because it is expected of us." Kevin broke into the conversation, saying, "Well, how does that work? I knew or did not want to have anything to do with this, but you and Paul are commanding me to follow this path". Godwill smiled before answering. "But you are following the path, are you not? A bit confused, but you are on the journey. You have learned things you can do that no one else can. You have used magic for your own use but need to be careful not to overdo things in the public's eyes. You are not sure or confident yet that you did not choose magic, but magic chose you because of who you are. Magic is not just using tricks to amuse people but a reality of things you can do for good. Throughout time, wizards and witches have bent the meaning of magic, some for good, some for bad, but each wizard or witch has changed the olden day spells giving it their twist to make the spells stronger for their own security." Kevin looked at Godwill with a puzzled look on his face, then answered. "Change the spells, how?" Godwill looked at Kevin then replied, "oh yes, the spells you have in the books, and what I taught you are, as you will probably understand basic spells, certain words, actions as casting the spells can transform the spell into something else and making it more potent. Also, new spells have been made by others that I guess still are not known. This is why you need to know as much as possible to be able to repel or stop what may be cast at you during your journey."

Kevin stood up with a look of frustration on his face saying, "so, any magician I meet may still be a lot better than me no matter what I learn from you and Merlin. After all, if what you say is true and you have lived for all these years, so have others that may have perfected spells further than you. That does not sound good, especially for me." Kevin again stated, "This is why I do not think that I will ever become as good as you or Merlin, and it puts not only me in jeopardy but my family. Why have you done this to me? Why do I have to be one? Why?" Kevin sank back onto the seat with a heavy heart before Godwill again spoke. "Remember what I said about putting a twist into the magic? Well, I believe that you can do this. This is your time. You need to trust yourself and be confident. I have seen other wizards that have projected shields and plasma bolts both from their wands and hands. How do you think they did this? they perfected these spells by working on them. You now have the power inside of you, but you need to believe in young Wilks, believe in yourself, believe in magic, and you can do anything you want to. This is your time, and only you can decide if this is what you want. I had this conversation with someone else many years ago, but unfortunately, I guess they were not ready and did not believe in themselves, but this is different. I feel it in my bones. You can be an amazing wizard Young Wilks. Trust me, trust yourself, and above all, trust and believe that magic is part of your soul, part of your reason for living, and above all for the people that trust in you."

Kevin said nothing but looked hard at Godwill without speaking. He then got up, went across to Fergul, and stroked him before struggling to say," hm, ok, I do not fully understand everything you said but will give it a go and see what plays out, but I warn you. I will not be bullied into anything. Do you hear me, sir?" Godwill laughed before speaking, "I would expect nothing else from you, young Wilks. It is that strong mentality and resolvents that gives you the person you are; however, respect costs nothing but should be given to those with more knowledge than you, so I must ask, you will respect me and not challenge me on anything, especially in front of your brother or friends again, do you understand me?" Kevin nodded, then spoke again.

"So," Kevin went on, "did we really accomplish anything about me knowing anything about you or why this is to do with me?" Godwill looked at Kevin, then answered, "I don't know, young Wilks, did we?" Kevin thought for a moment, then said: "ok, let's recap as I find this a good thing to do. You are around nine hundred years old, although there is nothing to prove this or how it has been achieved, no brothers or sisters, got into magic at a very early age, I guess never been married, and knew some people of greatness throughout ages, but these can be seen in books, oh, so how have you been able to be a teacher for so long as my mother new you being at the school for a long time now ?" Godwill smiled, then replied, "Well, let's see, firstly, I know your mother. She is a good woman, and your dad a great man, more than you know. Next, as I tried to explain regarding the stones we have, they slowly time but also have healing power and age-stopping power to them. This is how I have been able to live for so long, along with Merlin and Crandloss". Kevin then realised that the stones were the key, "ok, then how do you account for Sambia? As he knew you, he reckoned about two centuries ago?", again Godwill smiled then answered, well, I will give you a couple of books to read over the next few weeks which describe the life existence of dwarfs and elves. It explains their body makeup and life capabilities. This should help answer this question."

Kevin took the books from Godwill and started to flick through them when Godwill slapped his hands and said, "well, I think you have had enough time now to ask your questions, so I think this is at an end, agree, young Wilks?" Kevin looked up from the books and just said, "for now." "Good, so let's get things back to normal and be off out of here, shall we?" Kevin nodded in agreement and rose from his seat, and walked towards the door. Before opening it, Godwill re-started time to the usual setting, and Kevin opened the door, His brother and Vinny were waiting outside for him, but before he stepped out, he turned back to Godwill and said, "you know with more information comes more questions, I will be asking you so this session is not ended just postponed until then." Godwill laughed, "of course, young Wilks, I expected nothing less. However, diplomacy is needed. Remember, I am incredibly old and do not take kindly to being summoned by a young upstart like you, but at this time, I thought that you needed questions answered just like," Godwill stop himself from saying anything else. "Just like who?" Kevin asked? Godwill turned away from Kevin, saying, "oh nothing, it is not important, now off you go, or your mum will be questioning you why you were not home." Kevin shrugged his shoulders and went out the door, and joined his brother and friend, ready to start the journey home. Question after question came from these two to Kevin during the bike ride home, but Kevin just gave quick, snappy answers that really were not relevant and changed the conversation. At the crossroads, Vinny left to go on his way home. Paul continued to question Kevin, but he gave nothing away about what was said between him and Godwill during the time together.

Eventually, they arrived home, where their mum was waiting with quite a frown on her face. As the boys got off their bikes and put them in the shed, she launched questions at them regarding the shouting at lunchtime in the canteen. Eventually, after a lot of talking and yelling from their mum, Kevin just said, "Look, mum, leave it, please. It was just over a girl I met in the music room called Rueth. Paul thinks that I should concentrate on my studies and sport rather than girls at this stage. What right does he have to say this?" Kevin's mum went quiet, then answered cautiously, "A girl, hey Kevin, is she nice?" Kevin just blushed and then said she is beautiful, mum. Now let us leave it there, can we?" Kevin was then pushed passed by his brother and went up to his bedroom. "Well, Kevin's smitten by this girl, is he? I think I need to see for myself what this is all about. It's not a girl war, is it Paul? You like her too, is that it?"

Paul just looked at his mum and then answered quite sternly. "Mum, she is Kevin's age, not mine. Why would I like someone that age? I like girls more my age and a little older; who do you think I am, I ask you." Paul was quite angry at what his mother had just asked him and continued with, "he is not doing too well in his studies, but he is an incredibly good footballer. He can go far, mum; in this, why would he want to jeopardize this for a girl? He has a gift, and if this girl gets involved, then he will lose interest in the game. Dad will understand, he was once very good in his time and had trials for top teams, and I would like to think he would want him to do better than him". Mum just turned away, saying, "football, that's all you boys think about, and what if he does not make it in the so-called good teams, what will he do then, I will tell you, nothing," Paul butted in with "exactly, this is why he needs to study also so he needs to start putting girls out of his mind and start studying. This is what the argument in the canteen was all about." Mum looked at Paul and then replied, "So you were only trying to give your brother some helpful advice?" "Yes, said Paul but you know how hot-headed Kevin is, and he got the hump." Mum just looked at Paul before saying, "Well, I am sorry dear. I guess I jumped to the wrong conclusion about you two fighting over something trivial. Still, you need to use more tact when talking to your brother; you know that. Do not argue with him but keep me updated with him and this girl, and I will talk to him next time, ok dear?" Paul agreed and then went upstairs to his room.

Knowledge is not always a good thing.

That night whilst in his room, Kevin took out the books Godwill had given him and started to read them. In the books, Kevin read of past spells for different things, but these books were not just of spells, but scribblings of things that had happened throughout time recorded in these books. They mentioned things regarding mythical creatures like dragons, unicorns, griffins, and others. Kevin had never heard of, like the Montrose bull, flying mandrel, and one that had a small drawing of one called the firedrate. This creature took Kevin's attention as it had the head of a snake, the body of a large rhino, and six legs. Under the picture, it reads, breathes fire and ice, and moves quicker than an eagle both on the floor and in the air. The blood of this creature, if drinking, can help prevent death from occurring for a period but not for ever. Time spans depend upon the person's build, mind, and strength. Kevin starred at the book with this creature on its pages, thinking how it would be to meet such a creature and be able to see if it really existed or was just a drawing from someone that wanted to make a storybook. He decided to carry on looking through the first book, where several spells were written down, but he could not make out all the words, so he decided to try one that he could.

It was for lighting up a space of darkness, so he whispered the words. "Iluminum Cantarta." A blast of dazzling light came from the wand he had by his side that shone through the doorway of his room. It was like a thousand-watt light bulb had been turned on. The light fed through his curtains and out of the window, shinning bright with a long ray flowing from it. Kevin, now panicking, quickly said, "Evreko," the light faded quickly. Kevin heard his mum now coming up the stairs to find out what had happened. Kevin hid the books under his quilt and quickly got out the book of Rome they were studying for history. His mum opened the door quickly, asking, "what is going on? Did you see that beam of light shining out? Where did it come from? Was it from here? What are you doing?" Kevin looked at his mum before answering, "Mum, what? What light? I did not see any light, just me and my bedroom light on while reading this book on Rome for the history class got tomorrow." Kevin's mum pulled back the curtains and looked out. A couple of people were standing on the corner of the street, pointing up towards the window where mum closed the curtains. "I know something just went on in here, my boy. There are people standing looking at your window now. Why would they be doing that?" Kevin thought quickly, then said, "I have no idea. I know there were a couple of people out there when I put my light on to read before closing my curtains, but I have no idea, mum." Kevin's mum looked at him with a kind of a cross look on her face before sighing and then leaving Kevin's bedroom, saying, "there had better not be any monkey business going on here, or your dad will get to know my lad." With that, she shut the door and went downstairs.

Kevin gave a big sigh of relief and sank back into the pillows on his bed. As he lay there, he thought to himself how hard it was to be able to keep secrets from his parents and if it was all necessary. As the thoughts started to gain momentum, he slowly closed his eyes for a brief time, only to be wakened by a feeling of a presence in his bedroom with him.

Slowly he opened one eye and was surprised to see the figure of Merlin standing at the bottom of his bed. Kevin sat up quickly, asking him, "what are you doing here?" Merlin put his finger to his lips as if to say quiet, then silently moved around the bed and sat on the side near Kevin. "I sensed a great power through your thoughts and decided to see what it is that was causing you so many troubles." Kevin pulled the book out from under the bed covers and turned to the page of the Firedrate. Merlin gave a little "now I see. The interesting creature, the firedrate, caused problems back in the old days." Kevin looked at Merlin and answered, "old days, what old days?" Merlin smiled before answering. He rose from the bed and walked over to the bookcase before he spoke. "The old days I refer to is I would think the fourteen hundred's, yes definitely the fourteen hundred's." Kevin smiled and shook his head, "And how do you know about this, next you will be telling me that you were around then also!" Merlin stared at Kevin and then asked, "And what makes you think I wasn't?"

Kevin then replied, "Because when we met on the astral plain, you said, if I remember correctly, you were only around two hundred years old, which I find very doubtful. Now you are saying you're older? So which is it, and what do I believe ?"

Merlin again smiled, then spoke, "firstly, young man, part of life is actually seeing what is in front of you. Secondly, it is opening your mind to what can happen, and lastly, has it happened? As I stand in front of you, I have to say I am all three. Part of me is still here; part of me has long gone; however, what you see of me is the future of where I have come from." Kevin looked puzzled and then asked again. "Just tell me, were you there in these times or not?" Merlin just once again smiled, then said, "All I will say is that I know of and have seen a firedrate." Kevin looked, then replied, "Do they still exist?"

Merlin chirped quickly, "oh yes, they do. However, not many are alive, but a few survived the time and are in a place where no one will disturb them." Kevin got quite excited after hearing this. "Can we go and visit them?" Merlin shook his head as if to say no. "That would not be a good thing to do. The Firedrate is a creature that does not take kindly to having its territory invaded. Its gift is powerful. People have tried to befriend one of these creatures and died for it." Kevin sank back into his pillows and slammed the book shut. "Then why are they mentioned? How did they know that the blood of this creature could fend off death for a time? Why have these creatures never been written about?" Merlin gave a smile, then once again put his fingers to his lips to say quietly. Kevin stopped the questioning but was quite frustrated as he did not know the answers. Merlin spoke, "still you ask questions, however, to gain the knowledge you must ask one question at a time and wait for the answer. Although you crave to understand everything, you are still young, inexperienced, and sometimes extremely hot-headed." Kevin burst in with, "I am not." Merlin again smiled then answered, "see Kevin, very defensive before all the answers are spoken. What I was going to continue to say was that passion for something is not always right or wrong. Sometimes it can lead you down a dangerous path, one that is fraught with things you know nothing about, so you are not scared of it until it happens. The other path is a good path; plenty of wonderful things are happening, and if they do not threaten you, it is something you do not read into or try to understand it. Either way will have light and dark patches believe me, I have been along many of both paths and managed to try and understand both ways, but even in the many years I have lived, I can say to you that there is more that happens that goes un-noticed than noticed." Kevin, now getting very confused, did not really understand anything Merlin had just said but nodded as though he did.

Kevin then asked, "so you say the firedrate exists? What about the other animals mentioned in the book? Are any of them still around?" Merlin took the book and slowly flicked through the pages saying softly, "Yes, yes, no, no, and no, not that I know of." Kevin took the book from Merlin and flicked through it again with Merlin saying, "Yes to the dragons" Merlin nodded, "Yes to the Unicorns," again Merlin nodded, "No to the griffins" Merlin stroked his beard, then replied, "not sure on that one as not heard of any sightings for a couple of hundred years, but that does not mean some do not still exist," "no to the Montrose bull and flying mandrel." Merlin got up off the side of the bed, then turned to Kevin and asked, "what is your fascination with these creatures anyway?" Kevin just shrugged his shoulders and replied, "Do not know. I saw a picture someone had drawn and thought, did they really exist? It is a bit like you, Merlin. Many stories of a great wizard called Merlin have been written, and even films made of the things you did but were they real, yet here you stand in front of me or someone claiming to be Merlin, who is hundreds of years old. Do I think this is real? Well, you're in front of me. We have been to the astral plain, a place I never knew existed before. I have your wand that can do a lot of stuff, and someone who also has lived for a long time tried to kill me, so do I now think that this is real?" Kevin smiled at Merlin before continuing. "I guess so." Merlin now had a cross look on his face. "you guess so? What does that mean? You've felt pain through spells, you've seen things only a select few can, you have the power to slow time, make things appear and disappear, and you guess so," Merlin said in a stern voice.

"I think that our conversation is over here for tonight and would say to you, young wizard, to learn more respect for the older generation. Without that, the only path you will take is the dark one, and believe me. It can be a lonely and dangerous path on your own. Think about what we have talked about and try to sort out that inquisitive streak before you upset people. Now, I must go. I know you mean no harm to me or the others, but things said in jest, or a certain way can rub people up the wrong way. I will still monitor your thoughts and be of as much help in your quest as I can, but for now, sleep, for tomorrow is another day of unpredictable circumstances that can happen, and you will need all that brain matter working in harmony as best you can." With that, Merlin called out softly, "Conceptium troversum." It seemed to Kevin that Merlin's form was now starting to waver in the light and was finally gone. Kevin rubbed his eyes, put his books away, then sank back into his pillows, slowly shutting his eyes. His mind was too tired to think about any other questions, so he just drifted off to sleep. Kevin slept well for the first time in ages. When he awoke the next morning, he felt brighter, fitter, and more alert. He ran downstairs and sat at the breakfast table, ready for his breakfast. "Morning dear, you seem to be in a better frame of mind and health today. I must say that sleep did you well." Kevin hummed to himself and was incredibly happy with himself until his brother appeared and mentioned the frame of mind he was in. "Is it because you are going to see that girl again today?" Paul asked. Kevin's frame of mind changed in an instant. "What's it to you? If it is, keep your snout out and just do what you should do and don't interfere, ok"?

Their mum immediately spoke, "Paul leave your brother alone. What did I tell you when we had this conversation last time? It has nothing to do with you. Let the boy be". Paul just grunted a noise that really had no meaning whatsoever but did not feel happy being told off by his mum, so he just grabbed a piece of toast and went out, ready to do his paper round.

Kevin quickly followed him to the shed where his bike was. "For your information, I had a visit from Merlin last night and worked on a plan for finding this stone. Anyway, what's it to do with you if I am seeing Rueth again today?" Paul just grunted again and said in a low voice, "well, I hope she does not distract you from what we need to be doing" with that, he cycled off to do his paper round.

That morning, Kevin cycled to school on his own as Paul was a little late back from his round, where Kevin met up with Vinny along the way. Vinny was always asking questions regarding what was going on and do they need his help in anything. Eventually, they arrived at school, where Vinny was still going on until Kevin saw Rueth getting off the bus at the school gates. From that moment, all Kevin could hear was white noise, nothing going in and being thought of, just Rueth. Eventually, Vinny noticed Kevin's stares towards her and just left him standing there alone looking. Rueth made her way down the school chase to where Kevin still stood. "Morning Kevin, everything all right? Is there a seam down on my skirt, as you are keeping a keen eye open on me?" Kevin just shook his head and then answered, "what? Sorry, I was miles away. Must have been a bad night's sleep I had last night." Rueth's face dropped when she heard this and marched off. Paul had just come into the bike rack area and heard what he said. "Well, if that was a chat-up line, bro, then you got no hope with that one," and he laughed as he parked his bike in the rack.

Kevin turned to his brother with a scowl on his face, then bellowed, "Listen, just shut your mouth on this, or I will" Kevin stopped speaking. "You'll what?" Paul finished. "Remember what Godwill and Merling said about keeping the magical and normal life separate? Just hear those words, or you might just find that you are being carted off to the funny farm."

Kevin was about to storm off when suddenly he snapped to his brother, "we need to talk to Godwill now. Help me find him." Paul, now noticing the shift in Kevin's voice, followed straight away as he was a little concerned.

Godwill was in the teacher's staff room preparing for the day's lessons he had. When the two boys got to the reception part, they asked for him to see them, and they were told that he was busy and could not be disturbed. Kevin now quite angry, demanded to see him, and if he did not come to them, then they would go to him. They started to bypass the receptionist when Godwill appeared at the door. "What's all this commotion, Wilks? What do you want? The school has not started yet. Can't it wait?" Kevin explained that it could not, and they needed to see him on a personal level rather than school. Godwill agreed and told them to meet in his classroom in 5 minutes. The boys made their way towards the classroom when suddenly Kevin noted that there seemed to be something not right. As he looked out of the glass windows along the corridor, he saw birds in flight but stationary. Kevin turned to Paul, who looked at him to say, "What"? It was then that Paul also noted what Kevin had seen.

They turned around to go back down the corridor when suddenly a shape appeared in front of them. It was Jarez. "Well, well, well," Jarez said, "Long time no see, young wizard or wizards. Things have been spoken about you visiting Sambia. For what reason, prey tell me?" Kevin walked towards Jarez whilst speaking. "You know what for, so why did you ask?" Jarez smiled, "Sambia is a great magician. I guess he did not take it too well with you turning up unannounced like that. I guess he was angry and wanted to do you harm." Kevin smiled before speaking, "Not at all, he was only too pleased to be of any help he could, but unfortunately, he had a memory lapse over his lifetime and could not help"> Jarez laughed out loud, "Is that what he told you and you believed it well, I guess you're not all the wizard they say you are. All magical folk have extremely long memories and can recall all that has happened to them in their lifetime, so he was playing you. He did not believe your quest and thought you were imposters. Still, to get that close to him is another thing. So, you seemed troubled and stuck in your mindset, wizard. Is there anything you wish to ask of me that could possibly help"?

Kevin pondered for a moment, then just stated, "No, not yet. When I need help, that will cost me as it usually does speaking to you, then I will ask". Jarez was not happy with this comment. Kevin said and snapped back, "Beware, wizard, I may be the good side of Crandloss, but even the good can go bad, and with comments like that, it would not be too long before that happens." As if in a flash, Godwill appeared, "Now then Jarez, the boy did not mean any harm and nor should you take any, he is confused with what is happening here and therefore speaks out of turn quite often. I guess this little misunderstanding needs to be put behind us, and we all keep working on the same side for the good of all man." Jarez agreed and then disappeared. "You two, classroom now, move" Godwill bellowed. "What the dickens do you think you were doing demanding to see me like that and talking to Jarez in that tone of voice Wilks"? Kevin said sorry but needed to see him regarding the next step for finding the stone. "I do not care at present, I have senior teachers now demanding I punish both of you for what you did, no-one demands to see a teacher, especially before the school day begins." "But sir" Kevin spluttered, "Don't but sir me Wilks, you belittled me in front of the other teachers this is not acceptable, you both will serve a three-day detention after school starting tomorrow evening, and you best let your mum know or I will today at lunch time, do I make myself clear"? Both boys, now realizing that this was not the best way to have gone about things, agreed. Godwill fumed off after the timeline had been re-set as Jarez did not do it before leaving. Paul turned towards Kevin with a hateful look on his face. "You just had to do it and drag me into it also. Why, why can't you think before you speak, you little idiot" and then stormed off. Kevin slowly made his way to the kitchen where his mother worked to tell her what had just happened. She was not happy. " I knew it. You just had to upset the most respected teacher at the school and demand to see him, and what for? You won't even explain that to me. Well, not only will you do the detentions, you will be banned from playing for your football team for two weeks, do you hear me? So best you explain that to them also, my boy. You will learn to respect grown-ups. You will." His mother now turned away and went back to work in the kitchen.

Kevin was having a really dreadful day, and it started so promising and just went downhill from the moment he set foot outside the house. Kevin made his way toward the music room, hoping to see Rueth try to cheer himself up. As he got there, Rueth was coming out and totally walked by him without saying a word or looking at him. Now he was sinking into depression. Kevin felt angry with Godwill, his mother, his brother, and his mum. He just wanted to let off steam and was about to cast a spell when Paul's mates walked by and grabbed him, stopping him from doing this. Kevin struggled, and slowly a blue tinge started to appear in his skin colour. "Whoa, little man, control yourself; this is not the place or time for this, so calm down, please." Kevin continued to struggle, and the frustration got worse. Kevin now threw the three boys off him and stood there staring at them with a hateful stare. Godwill had seen what was going on and cast the time-slowing spell, then came out. "Wilks, stop this. You need to calm yourself down now. These people are trying to help you, not hurt you."

Kevin turned to face Godwill now, "You do not control me. You think you are all powerful, but you have not felt the power of me, Postromus, not this child's feeble body I am within. How dare you talk to me in this way." "Kevin, if you are in there, try to control him, don't let him take you over because if he does, then you will be no more. I can assure you of that," Godwill shouted. A piercing laughter came from Kevin's mouth with the further comment, "you think this child is stronger than me, old man, I am the powerful Postromus, and I control him, can't you see?" Kevin held out his arm, and Godwill was propelled backward, knocking him off his feet. Kevin started to sink to his knees, struggling to take back control of his body. Kevin's body shacked and curved, and the blue tinge went more vivid for a while, then reduced and finally disappeared. Kevin rose to his knees, and Paul's three friends went to help him up. "Get off, get off. You are no friend of mine. Just leave me alone, all of you, can't you see? I never wanted to get involved in this, never, go away or I will." Godwill, having gotten to his feet after the incident, moved towards Kevin, but he was having none of it. He just got to his feet and raced off down the school, chasing out of the gate and away.

"Shall we go after him, sir"? Asked Roger. Godwill shook his head to say no. "Let him be for now. If Pstromus raises his head again, it could be fateful for you. I have a hunch about where he might be going. I will go there and see him, now, leave the time as it is for now until I get this sorted, find the older Wilks boy and explain to him what has gone on but to do nothing until you hear from me, ok"? The boys and Godwill moved away in different directions to do what needed to be done.

Godwill arrived at the spinney looking for Kevin, but no sign of him. Godwill pondered, "where are you, young Wilks, you don't know what dangers are waiting out there for you." Godwill returned to the school and spoke to Paul. Wilks, where would your brother go in his state of mind"? Paul stuttered by saying, "I don't know, sir, is he not at the spinney"? "No," came the reply from Godwill, "think boy, where else would he go"? Paul thought again, then remembered the comment his friend Roger had said to him.

Paul shouted out, "oh no, he must have gone back to the place where it all began, Baxter's barn on the river Holland, he is going to try to throw the books and all back in where it started. He does not know he can do this, he tried when the book and wand were first caught on his fishing line, but I guess he is not thinking straight". "OK, Wilks, you come with me, and you boys keep look out at the spinney just in case he is not at the river and returns to there."

Paul looked bemused by Godwills comment, then asked, "how are we going to go there in your car, sir"? Godwill shook his head, then said, "Car, no Wilks, we will use the travel spell, take my arm and hold on tight. I don't want you falling off somewhere during the travel." Paul looked a little worried on hearing this and clung to Godwill's arm tightly. "Conceptium Troversum," Godwill spoke. In a flash, the two had disappeared and reformed on the bank of the river next to Baxter's barn. "Wow, that is so brilliant, I must learn that," laughed Paul, "so now we wait for my brother to get here, that could be ages, sir", Godwill just laughed then said, "why? he is already here", Paul looked confused, then asked, "how, Kevin can't do this spell, and his bike does not go that fast." "Really, Wilks, so how do you explain that young man sitting on the riverbank over there dressed as your brother then"? Paul looked in disbelief, "How the hell did he do that? Oh, sorry, sir, I did not mean to voice my opinion, but I got to ask how?" Again, Godwill laughed and just gestured for Paul to follow him.

On moving towards Kevin, Godwill saw the books, wand, and time slowing stone on the bank next to him. "It won't do you no good young Wilks or postromus, which either one you are, the task has been given and cannot be undone by anyone apart from the taskmaster himself." Kevin just stared at the water and replied quietly. "I know, I keep trying, but they just come back. I did not want this. I cannot do this. How can I live with this thing inside of me that controls me now and again? What if I do something to serious harm or even kill someone when he is me, I can't do this, I really can't". Kevin now looked at Godwill and Paul with tears in his eyes and asked, "help me, what can I do, I am turning into a monster that cannot be controlled. I never wanted to hurt anyone, but now I get so angry that it brings him out, and terrible things happen. I am afraid. Please, please help me before I go mad" Kevin's head lowered, and more tears flooded from his eyes. Godwill walked and sat down beside Kevin before placing a hand on his head, softly cradling it, then said in a soft and calm voice. "I know, lad. I remember the first time that I had these thoughts and feelings years ago. Does it stop you from being human? Of course not. We are all human with feelings and thoughts. At your young age, this still does not seem real, but unfortunately, it is, it is here, now, and it will not go away until the end". Kevin raised his head and asked with a quiet question, "the end sir," "yes, the end young wilks, when the world is safe from harm from bad wizards, witches, warlocks, and other things that we do not even know about yet. It is a long journey, and even I cannot live forever even though I have done so yet, but there will come a day when I will be ready for it. So much has happened in my one long lifetime, changes in the world, some good, some bad, but I have had a good relationship with it all and learned to adapt. This is now what you must do, young Wilks, adapt. You need to become stronger in mind and body to control the inside you and use him for your benefit only when needed in a dire situation. This will be hard and time-consuming, but you can do it. I feel greatness in you already. That is a rare trait to find in someone so young, I can tell you." Godwill smiled at Kevin, which calmed him down, and agreed once more to toe the line and learn and move forward.

"So, shall we go now, young Wilks, and work on this together"? Asked Godwill. Paul chirped in, "I guess so. What do you say, Kevin"? Kevin nodded and got to his feet. "Hang on though," Paul said, "I don't think I am still happy being given the detention for something Kevin did. I was only with him. Can I get my detention remised, sir"? Godwill looked at Paul and then said sternly, "No." "That is so unfair, sir. I think I shall just stay here and sulk as my little brother did," Paul said and sat down. "Please yourself, Wilks, but how are you going to get back to school from here? You don't have a car, bike, or broomstick, and it is a long walk, so I guess you might get the detention increased for slopping off school also." Paul thought about this and then said, "OK, sir, I get it, but still not happy with the detention thing." Godwill turned to Kevin, "ready young Wilks"? "Ready for what, sir"? Kevin answered. "To go back to the school, of course," Godwill replied with a smile, "but how sir, will you use the travel spell I wanted to ask you to teach me"? Godwill smiled then replied, "but you already know it, Wilks, how did you get here if you did not use that then"? Kevin pondered, "but, I just wished I was back at the river, the next thing I was sitting here, did I really do that or the other person inside me"? Well, the only person that can decide if you young wilks, does he control what you do, or is it you? Only you can tell me that." Paul looked at his brother with a gaping mouth expression, then blurted, "you can do that. Wow, neat, bro." "So, give it a go then, young Wilks? I would head towards my classroom; do you wish to lead, or should we go first?"

Kevin closed his eyes and thought of the classroom, and when he opened them there, he was standing facing the blackboard in front of him. Soon after, Godwill and his brother clinging on for dear life appeared also. "That was fun," Godwill said, "now, young wilks, you know you have greater powers within you to do wonderful things, but you just need to take a step back and be calm before using some of them." Kevin looked a bit confused and then asked, "some of them, sir?" Godwill sat at his desk and then said, "oh yes, you need immense concentration to use. Some will come naturally. I knew you could do this spell. Remember the fight with your friend Vinny where you disappeared from in front of him and appeared behind him, then struck the vital blow using the trees to do your work? Ingenious move, but with that one split second, I knew you were stronger than you thought of yourself, so this was no surprise that you could accomplish this spell." "But could I travel with others rather than just myself?" Again, Godwill looked at Kevin and then said, "well, if your concentration is good, you should be able to. What I suggest is you use your brother as a guinea pig," Paul looked at goodwill with a disarming stare on this. "Start with just small travels, something like a couple of feet, then a mile, then further if it works, but make sure you think of the solid piece of ground, or you could end up in a river or sea or something like that. You must clearly propel the image to where you want to go to, just like the riverbank you chose and went to". Kevin nodded in agreement, but Paul was still a little worried regarding these comments and asked, "could you just not teach me the travelling spell, so I don't have to do this please sir"? Godwill smiled then replied, "in time Wilks but at this moment your brother is the stronger of you two so you should go with this I think." Paul just muttered sarcastically "great."

"Now, time has been slowed long enough now I think, it is time you and your brother return to the normal world and see me after school to discuss the thing you demanded to see me about. By the way Wilks" he said turning to Paul, "let the others know everything is ok again now and to return to school." Paul nodded then started to leave the classroom but before going out the door mumbled, "wow, I have all the hard jobs to do, I will have to bike there I guess as I don't know the travel spell," Kevin smiled then said, "why not take the broom stick then Paul"? "Ah, the broomstick, why did I not think of that." Paul tapped himself on the head and left the classroom. Kevin and Godwill laughed together then kevin left the class also to continue the day ahead.

Chapter 16

Tugay, Sambia and the Forrest

The rest of that day went without any other hitches as far as Kevin was concerned. Paul and his friends met up with Kevin during the lunchbreak to talk about the early mornings happenings with the boys all impressed that Kevin knew how to use the travel spell. At the end of the day Paul and Kevin made their way to Godwills class for the talk they agreed on.

Godwill was as good as his word and was waiting there for them. As Both boys walked through the door Godwill spoke, "so, this important thing you wish to speak about, does it have anything to re-visit Sambia and the forest"? Paul looked at Kevin and whispered "he must be a mind reader or something" "on the contrary Wilks" replied Godwill. "Only something this big would raise the passion and mindset of young Wilks there to do this, but again, I must ask you to curb your enthusiasm Kevin, you need to maintain the magical and human lifetime lines apart and not raise any eyebrows is it you say"? Kevin laughed to himself then closed the door and sat in front of Godwill. "It is hard sir being the person I am to do that, but I will try." "That is all I can ask of you young wilks, now, what is so important for you to confide in me" replied Godwill. Kevin explained the visions and what Jarez had said in the meeting when Godwill broke it up. "I know this already" Godwill said, so what do you want me to do about it"? Paul blurted in, "Well you could always quash our detention so we can find a way of doing this." Godwill laughed, "you really have not thought about this, have you, Wilks," he said, speaking to Paul, "I gave you both three days detention after school. The three evenings slowing time should give you enough time to find and visit Sambia again to gain further information in your quest."

Paul looked at Kevin then had a smile where it appeared the penny had dropped and now Paul got it. Then a cross expression came across his face, with a comment of "hang on, mum got to hear of this and now we both have to miss the next three weekend football games due to this incident; I hardly think that is fair, I just got in the team and the manager is going to drop me because of this". Godwill stroked his beard thinking then said, "ok, I will have a word with your mum and see what I can do with getting that removed, but I can't say she will do it, I have known your mum for a while and she can be quite stubborn, a trait young Wilks has gained from her." Paul nodded in agreement then sat back on the seat. Kevin listened to the conversation but still had quite questions running through his head that he wanted answering. Finally, he blurted out. "Sir, so I can do the travel spell, but can I take anyone with me when I do this, I have only travelled on my own?, When in the forest, will Sambia still be in the same place we found him or is he likely to have moved?, Is there a time line slow that will revert back to normal time?, Will there be anyone there who we can relies on if it comes to a nasty situation"?.

Godwill raised his hand and then said, "Whoa young wilks, you are giving me a headache just listening to you, one question at a time, so, Sambia moves around the forest often, so he is hard to find so I suggest you take the brooms with you and jet around until you find him again. The time slow envelope is creditable for about ten hours, that is ten hours normal time not magic time so this should give you well enough time to do what you need to, but keep in mind, this will not all be done in one visit that is why I decided that the 3 days detention should be incorporated, also we have to think of your mum waiting to get home, detention starts at three thirty after school, and you need to be back by five normal time, this will give you sufficient time each day. Someone or something will always be present near you even though you will never see them unless in dire need of their assistance but be warned both of you, there are things in the forest that are not there for your assistance, dark evil things that may be there from other wizards that have tried to find Sambia but have been left after they have gone so keep your wits about you and never separate, that is important, the two of you are strong, apart you have vulnerabilities so stay together". Both boys looked at each other and agreed.

The conversation went on with the description of the vision again and what needed to be looked for. After a lengthy conversation Godwill stated enough is enough for today and the boys should get a good night's sleep before the beginning of this part of the quest. The boys agreed and started to leave the class, Paul looked back and then said, "you will have a word with mum please sir"? "Yes, yes, yes, now go" replied Godwill. Paul closed the door, and the two boys made their way home.

When the two boys arrived home, there was mum standing at the front of the house with an angry expression on her face. "Christ, we are for it now" Paul said to his brother, "So much for Godwill having a word with her." As the boys got off their bicycles their mum started. " How dare you upset and demand to see Mr Godwill, what on earth think you two young scallions have the right to do this, it is unacceptable for anyone to demand anything of anyone, he was very angry and upset with the both of you and I have told him to give you the whole week of detentions for this, I am embarrassed to be your mum at this moment. Another thing, the 3 weeks football detention, well my boys, make that a month also, now what do you say to that? Your dad is not happy with you either when I told him, I think he will also have something to say regarding this." Paul tried to say "Mum, that is so unfair, we have spoken to Mr Godwill this evening and apologised for our behaviour and even though the detention is still going ahead and on reflection I guess it is fair but to stop us playing football in a team we have had a struggle to get in I think this is unfair and Godwill was going to have a word with you regarding this". "It is Mr Godwill to you Paul, where is your respect for your elders and it doesn't matter what he says you two need to learn respect so this is what will happen and there is no compromise do you hear young man, now get inside, eat your tea, do your homework then it is bed for both of you and I don't want to hear another word from either of you". Kevin just looked at his mum and mumbled "but I didn't say anything", "that's enough of that back chat from you Kevin, I bet you are the ring leader in this whole thing, trouble seems to follow you around no matter where you are and you bring everyone else into it also". With that mum started to have tears appear in her eyes due to the anger and disappointment she was feeling towards her two boys at that present moment.

"Now get in and no more back chat, go on go," mum said as she turned and opened the door for them all to go inside.

After a rathe silent tea the boys went to their separate bedrooms with Paul being very despondent to his brother. "See you later" Kevin just said to his brother at his bedroom door, Paul just looked and said, "Piss off, you are the cause of all this, now I will not get chance to play for the team again I bet because of this, I hope your happy." Paul opened his door and slammed it shut. Kevin now feeling sad and a little depressed opened his door only to see his bedroom a mess. Clothes, books all over the place, his bed turned on its side. Kevin closed his door then his curtains. He took out his wand and cast the repair spell to put everything back in place. As he did this, he heard his mother coming up stairs calling "what is all that noise, you two stop that, if you are fighting, I will clip your ears for you both." Kevins door burst open just as he sat on the bed after putting everything right, with his mum starring at him. "What are you doing Kevin, why the noise, just because you're not happy ,does that give you the right to make that thunderous noise up here, you haven't even considered the neighbours, just think what they will say hearing all this, now, no more noise or you will be for it I tell you young man, now get your homework done and open those curtains to let light in and switch the light off, we are not made of money for you to burn". With that mum slammed the door shut and went downstairs. Kevin sighed heavily and started to get his books out of his satchel then remembered the state of the room. He opened his wardrobe and checked for his magic book. After moving a load of clothes, he saw it, but it was upside down and not how he had left it. Kevin grabbed the book and rested it on his legs as he lay on his bed before opening it. As he did, he noticed that a couple of pages had been added that were not fixed to the binder. He looked hard at them starring at the blank pages where nothing appeared. Kevin scratched his head and started thinking, why the room so messed up, where did these pages come from and what is there significance if there is nothing on them?

Kevin moved the book from his legs and stood up, staring out of his window. To his surprise, he saw something he could only describe as a small man shuffling away down the street, but he had a thought that he recognised this little man. Kevin suddenly had the urge to find out about this man and slowed time there and then. As he came out of his bedroom, Paul appeared. "What the hell are you doing now? You're going to get us in more trouble; pack it in and restart the timeline now." "Sorry, Paul, but I just saw something out of my window I need to investigate." With that, Kevin ran down the stairs and out the front door with Paul calling, "well, go on then, and don't call me if you get into trouble because I won't be there".

As Kevin ran up the street following the path the small man was on, Paul just looked out of the window, saw Kevin running down the street, thought, "Sod it," and ran after him. Slowly the distance got shorter, and Kevin caught up with the old man. "Excuse me, but who are you"? The man now slowly turned. As the man's face appeared, Kevin did not recognise him.

"My name is Tugay, brother of Sambia, who you met in the Sherwood Forrest, and what is it to you, young wizard"? Paul came running up beside Kevin with his wand in his hand. Tugay immediately raised his wand to cast a spell. Kevin grabbed his brother and thought shield. The spell rebounded off the shield and back onto Tugay knocking him off his feet to the floor. "Wait," cried Kevin before Tugay could cast another spell, "We mean you no harm, honestly." Tugay, still posing his wand in front of him, replied, "and why should I believe you? I am not my brother. You cannot fool me; you are the younglings of a dark wizard trying to gain the stone for yourself." "You're wrong" Paul shouted. Have you not seen your brother and talked with him? We do the quest for Merlin and Posromus, not Crandloss".

"Only dark wizards would say this and utter the dark wizard's name in jest. You will not capture me and torture me like my brother Sambia. Where have you taken him, tell me, or as sure as I stand here, I will kill you no matter how young you are". Kevin, now standing straight, looked at the dwarf and spoke. "Then you too would move over to the dark side and never repent your sins you have committed. I met your brother in good faith for the quest we have spoken of. I need to find Sambia again to help in this quest. If you wish to call me dark, then I guess it would be right for you to try to kill me. However, be warned, I am not alone, and you may wish to reconsider this statement before you do anything further that may cause you harm." The dwarf looked confused and frustrated before pointing his wand at Kevin and casting a spell, but Kevin was quicker. Kevin's wand was in his hand and cast "Crevatious Septimium." As the spell Tugay cast hit back at the dwarf knocking him again off his feet, Kevin cast another spell, "Transisomb," the

185

dwarf's wand flew out of his hand, and now Kevin stood over the dwarf staring at him. As he stood staring down at the dwarf, his skin started to turn blue with the captured Postromus now speaking the words the dwarf understood. Tugay scrambled to his feet and made for his wand. Kevin is now cast "Haliofit."

Tugay stopped in motion, not being able to move but could speak. "Who are you, wizard? I will tell you nothing of the stones' whereabouts, so you might as well finish me off." Postromus came through and spoke in English this time. "Tugay, my friend, do you not recognise me? It is me, Postromus. Look at me. I am your friend, I vowed to find your mother's and father's killer, and that is what I am trying to do. I am set in this small, frail body of a boy, but I need his shape to survive. Without it, I am lost." Tugay looked hard at Kevin as he knelt beside the dwarf, unable to move. "If you really are who you say you are, why did you leave us when the deed was done? You returned after this was done and vowed, then disappeared again. Why should I believe either of you? My brothers have been hunted over the course of time to find this stone that flammel made, and I wish it never happened, or we never met you and befriended you, as this was our misfortune. Now, if you truly are who you say you are, then let me go. If not, kill me and be done with it." Kevin raised his wand again, pointing at the dwarf. Tugay closed his eyes, awaiting the killing spell, but it did not come. Kevin cast "Evreko." The dwarf now slowly opened his eyes, looked at Kevin, and grabbed for his wand. "Go ahead then," Called Kevin. If you are sure we are not who we say we are, then perhaps it will be a blessing that you put us out of our misery." Postromus was not happy with these comments and now started to come through stronger. Kevin fought this and slowly managed to get him under control with words said in English and more in another language that No-one knew apart from magical people that had lived with the dwarfs and magical creatures. Tugay stood still, pointing his wand at Kevin, listening to the argument that was taking place inside of him. Suddenly the dwarf dropped his wand and bowed his head toward Kevin.

"Forgive me, Postromus, it is truly you in there, but how? it was said that you were killed centuries ago, and no one knew if it was true or false as nobody was found to bury," Postromus continued talking through Kevin. It is partly true, Tugay, my friend. I will explain." Postromus talked with Tugay regarding the love of his life and the heartstring he took and gave to her, which was inserted into a wand. Tugay listened in disbelief but accepted this conversation as true. After the conversation, Postromus slowly started to fade with the comment that Tugay was to help this boy on the quest so that one day he could take the proper form he once was; Tugay agreed. All three now sat on the curb, talking regarding the whereabouts of Sambia and of the first stone. Tugat was a little coy with the information but promised to help as much as he could, especially to try to find his brother whom he had been searching for hundreds of years.

The three discussed meeting at the school the next evening when the two boys were supposed to be doing the detention. Tugay apologised for the state of Kevin's room was left in, but he was trying to find some sort of information as to where his brother was. Kevin smiled and then just said, "no harm done, but I was a little taken back that it had been searched through. Did you find what you were looking for"? Tugay said, "Naa, just the books I saw with magic in them, so I knew you must have been a wizard or something so high towered out of there." "The two sheets you left there, what are those? I tried to get them to appear, but nothing would work," Kevin replied, "So that is where I left them, bring them with you for our meeting tomorrow, and I will show them and explain them to you." Kevin agreed, and the three new friends shook hands, saying, "until tomorrow, then." Tugay scampered off whilst the boys returned to their house.

As the two boys ran up to their bedrooms, Paul talked all the time regarding the fights, the trust between them and Tugay, and what would happen next. Kevin stopped him at the top of the stairs. "Look, this is new development has happened. Godwill said this would not be easy; harsh times will come and go, things we need to be ready for Paul. I need to know that my brother, all older, is there for me to help get this done. The sooner we get it sorted, then maybe, just maybe, we can get our normal lives back on track and put this magic nonsense behind us, until then we deal with it, yes"? Paul just stared at Kevin after he said this wondering if he should be talked to like that by his younger brother, but he agreed. Both the boys went into their bedrooms, where Kevin restarted the timeline. Nothing was out of the usual for the rest of the night apart from mum still not happy with the two boys' attitude. They could hear her talking to herself about them downstairs, but eventually, both boys fell asleep that night.

The next morning they went down to breakfast to see their mum still angry with them both, and she continued to lay down the laws and what would happen if they didn't start to toe the line. After this much demoralizing telling off, the boys went off to school. The day passed, and then they met outside the classroom of Godwill, ready for the meeting.

Kevin walked through the door first and was amazed that Godwill, Tugay, and Jarez were all present. Paul followed Kevin in and was a little bit shocked to see Jarez. The door closed, and Godwill slowed the timeline down. "Right, you two, over here, you need to listen to what we have been talking about." Kevin being his usual inquisitive self, asked how and what Jarez was doing there when the timeline had not changed. Jarez smiled and then answered. "I may be a magician, but not always do the timelines have to change for me to be able to appear. Who do you think you saw at Sambias hut"? Kevin stared, "so I did see someone, and it was you. Did you also put the brooms in place"? "of course, young wizards, perhaps you will stop giving me such a tough time and accept I am good and here to help you." Kevin still had concerns in his mind but nodded in acceptance. Paul sat astride a chair near the collect people saying, "So, what's new and what's going on"? Godwill stared at Paul at what he asked and the way he was sitting. Paul got up and sat on the chair the correct way. Godwill just looked away as he did this.

Godwill explained what they were all doing there, and each had information regarding clues to the origin of the stone's whereabouts. Turgay explained, "firstly, the stones were hidden by each one of my brothers as requested by our friend Postromus." Tugay looked hard at Kevin when speaking of this, to which Kevin replied, "I know this. I saw it in the visions and talked with Merlin on this, so"? Tugay continued. The twist to this was that when the brother placed the stone part into hiding, he was then to proceed to the next brother's area to protect it. This meant that this brother never actually knew where the stone piece was hidden, just the area. In doing this, the brothers would set up magical barriers in the areas, but they were not sure if it were the resting place for the stone or not. With doing this, many magicians seeking the stones would be misled in their search for them, not knowing that it was or was not the place" Paul now very confused, blurted out, "Well, that is just not helpful. How do we know where to look, what is or isn't the correct area, and what lies in store for us? I just can't get my mind around this." Kevin looked at his brother and put his finger to his mouth to quieten down. "Go on," continued Kevin. Tugay continued, "The only other piece of information I can give you is that they are all on this island in special places. Places throughout history are recognised in your books and records. Remember, many places have changed throughout the ages, with buildings built and demolished. Areas changed, so this is not going to be easy to retrieve these stones." Kevin sat back and thought for a minute with all the others looking on, then said, "So you, yourself, hid a piece of the stone in a location. Where was that?" Tugay looked at Kevin then replied.

"I do not know for sure when this was assigned to us. The places we were to hide them were of our own choosing, but" Tugay stopped there. "But," replied Kevin. "But the other part of the condition of change around was to put in place a memory charm by the other brother so that when entering this area, the memory charm would wipe all the memories of the locations from each other and only ensure that magical barriers were to be put in place in that area." Jarez gave a laugh then said, "do you really expect us to believe this nonsense you are spouting, A memory wipe charm, what next a three-eyed ogre hiding by the stone, really, you all really going to believe in all this rubbish"? Tugay was not impressed by Jarezs outburst and stood up, staring at him. "That is the truth. If you do not believe me, ask him." Tugay pointed to Kevin. "The boy, how is he going to know." Tuguy interrupted Jarez, saying, "Not the boy, but postromus." Jarez laughed even louder, pointing at Kevin, saying, "Postromus, you boy, you got to be kidding me." Godwill immediately rose in a nervous state on hearing this, "Jarez, I suggest you be quiet, or you could be in considerable danger," Jarez kept laughing then replied, "from who, the boy, he is still learning what will he do?" All the others were staring at Kevin and taking a step backward slowly. Godwill again tells Jarez to stop the laughter and be quiet for a while. Jarez continued even though he had been told not to. Suddenly a bellowing voice came from behind Jarez, which startled the wizard. He took out his wand but was disarmed and pushed up against the wall by a now very blue-skinned Kevin. Only it was not Kevin but Postromus coming through. "So, you mock the boy and me, little man do you, I know not of your name, nor do I care, but what I do care about is my friends, the dwarfs. To insult them is to insult me, and I would advise that this will not end well for you." Kevin's hands raised and slowly pointed towards Jarez. Godwill looked at Tugay, saying, "say something, Tugay, we need Jarez."

"My friend, stop. He means me no harm. He does not understand what went on and what was asked of us. Please, confirm what I have said. We also need him to help us." The boy's mind is telling me you are part of that dark wizard Crandloss. How do I know if you are good or bad? How did he manage to split himself? Answer me, or I will take your life now." Jarez, now realizing that this was indeed Postromus cowered before answering. "I am sorry great Postromus. I am good, not evil. The other part of us is indeed Crandloss, who searches for the stones to gain the power never to be challenged again in this world. I, being the good side of Crandloss, he dismissed from the body to try to prevent this from occurring. This is my quest to complete. On completion, then I too will live my life out without prejudice or worry that someone will try to kill me." Postromus growled, then lowered Jarez to the floor but still fixed him in place so he could not move.

Kevin/Postromus now walked around to face him straight in the eye and then said. "My friend speaks the truth; a memory charm was put in place by each dwarf that hides the stone part. This was my idea, along with the magical barriers to be done. However, I know no whereabouts of the stones' locations or what barriers are in place, and neither do the dwarfs due to the memory wipe. All I can say to you, little wizards' is do not ever try to diss me again, or it will be the last time you will ever do anything. Do I make myself clear"? Jarez nodded. Then Kevin/postromus turned towards Godwill, Paul, and Tugay, "I have no advice I can give, no memory recovery charm to help, but you will succeed, or I will be lost forever. This mortal child will become part of me forever, and you will lose him. In this form, I am still great but need a better substance for which to grow and gain the power to become mortal again" slowly, the blue tinge to Kevin's skin started to discolour back to the normal colour of his skin with postromus now seemingly crying out in pain until Kevin dropped to his knees and quiet bestowed the classroom. Godwill ordered the others to help Kevin into a chair. "You ok, Young Wilks?" asked Godwill. Kevin now raised his head and answered. "Yes, but feel quite weak. I found it easier to control him the longer it went on. During the power surge when he controlled Jarez, I felt him weakening from then. Is this going to happen continuously when getting mad?" Asked Kevin. Godwill shook his head, "I do not know, young Wilks, but we need to do something to try and control it. Tugay knows a way to strengthen the mind block to do this. Dwarfs have amazing powers."

"That's right," Paul added, remember when Sambia laid his hand on your head, and I thought he was hurting you, but he was actually showing you visions." Tugay stood back quickly and asked, "He did what"? Paul started to explain again when Tugay stopped him in his tracks. "What visions did he show you, boy"? Kevin explained about the waterfall and opening at the bottom of an old oak tree. Tugay stroked his beard then muttered, "but how, how has he done this." Godwill asked, "Done what"? Tugay explained that what Sambia showed him was the area where the stone had been hidden. "He must have come across it when looking for something else, but although the location is shown, he did not show you anything else, boy"? "No, that was it, just a waterfall and opening at the tree, as I said" Tugay turned and looked out the window in thought, then turned quickly and said, "ok, so we need to find Sambia and see if there is anything else we need to know."

Paul butted in once again. "That's great, but do you have the power to put these so-called barriers in Kevin's mind to stop, you know, who keep rising and causing trouble." Tugay looked at Paul before speaking. "Yes, young wizard, but at his time, I suggest that he waits for another day because we may need the power and aid of Postromus in this search due to not knowing what we will meet in the forest. Do you not agree"? Paul looked at Kevin, then Godwill and Jaez, who all nodded in agreement. "Then it is settled. We need to make our way to the Forrest and find Sambia. I suggest you two brothers head for the east side of the Forrest, and we will take the west side. Make your way towards the centre where we will meet. Before you go, take this." Tugay handed a special small horn to Paul. "That is a magical horn from a unicorn. When blown, all magical creatures will come to the blower's aid. Dwarfs can also hear it from a long distance and will be alerted to come to the blower's aid." Kevin then said, "so why not when we get to the forest just blow the horn, and this will alert Sambia to come to us,"? Tugay shook his head. "It does not just work on the good magical creatures. It also alerts the bad ones also present there, so only blow it in dire circumstances. Do you hear me? it is not a musical instrument." Both Kevin and Paul nodded in agreement.

"So, shall we go then"? Tugay asked. All stood ready. Godwill spoke, "I know you have not tried this before taking your brother on the travelling spell. Are you ok? Feel confident and strong young Wilks"? Kevin nodded, "well, see you in the forest," with the three wizards clasped each other's hands and, with a flash, were gone. Paul, a little nervous, asked the same question again as Godwill had asked but continued, "you sure you can do this, bro? I don't want to be landing in a bog, river, or somewhere nasty". Kevin laughed, and then flash, they were gone. In a second, they were transported to the east side of the forest, where they were meant to be. Paul opened his eyes to find out that they had landed on a quite nice, firm accessible area and was well impressed by his brother and smiled at him. "So which way do we go then now," asked Paul. Kevin looked towards the sky; Paul looked up, wondering what his brother was looking at. "So, what have you seen, Kevin? What is up there." Kevin just answered. He was looking at where the sun was and decided on the way to go. The two boys ventured forward into the forest through trees and bracken, some parts hard to get through, some easy to get through. Eventually, they came to another clearing, an accessible area that was clear of all obstacles in their way.

The two boys started moving a crossed it happily until halfway across when vines started to come out of the ground in different areas moving slowly towards the boys who were unaware of them. The further they moved forward, the more the vines grew and followed. Paul heard a noise behind them and stopped to look. Just at that moment, the vines wrapped around his legs and started to drag him backward. Paul gave a loud scream pleading with his brother to do something. Kevin took out his wand casting "Ferentium Sparksum," a firebolt shot from his wand into the vines, frying them and releasing his brother. Kevin ran to him, picked him up, and shouted, "quick, this way," both boys were now running fast toward the trees out of the clearing, but the vines gathered momentum and caught hold of Kevin's legs, now pulling him to the floor. Being dragged backward towards a hole that had now formed, he cried out to his brother, who repeated the spell cast Kevin had done. Again, the fire hit the vines that released him, and Kevin scrambled away and looked up towards his brother, only to see a large patch of vines starting to wrap itself around his brother.

Kevin knew if he hit these vines wrapped around his brother, it could also seriously damage him, so he opted for a different spell. "CIGRO, FREDSOM, BOMBARDO SEPRUM." A flash from his wand sent a blinding pulse towards the roots of the vines, which, when it hit, dissolved into tiny pieces and lay dormant. Kevin unwrapped his brother from the rest of the vines and dragged him to the edge of the clearing. "Bloody hell, what the hell was that all about," asked Paul, shaking. Kevin just answered, "Come on, keep moving. Not sure what else will happen, but keep your wits about you" Paul followed Kevin with wand ready just in case anything else was encountered. They continued through more bracken, stopping to listen and view what was in front of them. As they slowed the movement, Kevin was aware that something was making him feel uneasy, but he was not sure what. Then, he found out. Suddenly, they were charged by an animal that was two animals in one. The body of a bull with the head of a big lizard. "Run like crazy, Paul," Kevin shouted. Paul looked up and saw the animal racing towards them and decided that it was the best option. As they ran into the forest, they knew the animal was catching up with them fast. Kevin screamed, "split up, it will confuse it" Kevin ran to the left whilst Paul ran to the right. The animal stopped where they had split up, smelling the ground, then went right the same way as Paul had gone. Kevin stopped and doubled back, and ran after the animal. Eventually, he came upon where his brother had been caught by some bracken struggling to get free whilst the animal stood gazing at him hissing. Kevin picked up a rock and threw it at the animal, which turned to see him throwing more stones at it. Then it charged towards him. Kevin waited and waited until the animal was right upon him and cast the travel spell. Kevin disappeared, and the animal ran headlong into the big thick oak tree that was behind him. Kevin reappeared a few paces behind the animal as it smashed into the tree knocking it senseless for a while. Again, Kevin helped his brother out of the bracken, and they ran onwards.

Eventually, Paul had to stop to catch his breath. "Come on, Paul, we can't stop now, that thing might be coming back after us, and we need to move now. Come on." Paul gathered himself together and followed his brother. After what seemed a long time, the brothers came to another clearing. Paul was on his way ahead when Kevin said, "Paul, come back. Remember the last opening"? Paul stopped dead in his tracks as he looked back at his brother. Then pointing towards him, shouting, "Kevin, run." Kevin looked around only to see the animal that had previously been chasing them had caught up with them again and was now standing a little way back from Kevin.

The animal charged again towards Kevin where he cast "Incartartum leverat," pointing his wand at the animal, where it lifted off the ground and raced by, where Kevin lowered it away from Paul into the clearing. As it landed, the vines that were travelling towards Paul changed direction towards this animal and caught hold of it, dragging it back towards another hole that had appeared. "Run forward, Paul, quickly," shouted Kevin and chased off towards his brother and passed him. Paul did not need a second warning, and both made it to the other side of the clearing, resting to see the animal disappearing into the hole in the ground, making a terrible hissing noise. Both boys, shocked and tired, moved on. Finally, they came to an area where Kevin stopped. "What now," Paul asked nervously, looking around. "Smell that," Kevin asked. Paul stood tall and sniffed the air. "Is that a smoky smell?" he asked. Kevin nodded and moved forward. After a few minutes of nervous twitching from sounds that they heard, they came to another clearing where they saw the same hut that Sambia had where they had met earlier in the journey. Kevin walked towards the hut looking all around the area, with his brother following, doing the same. Finally, they came to the door. Kevin heard voices coming from inside, which seemed familiar. The door opened, and there stood Sambia. Behind him, sitting on the chairs, were Godwill, Jarez, and Tugay. "So, you finally found it then," Godwill said with a laugh. Both boys walked into the hut, very dirty and exhausted. Tugay laughed when he saw the condition of the two boy's clothes. "What have you been doing," he asked. Paul started to explain about the vines and the animal. Sambia broke in, "so you met the Montrose bull then did yer, quite the fellow. Normally he runs around scaring folk, but he really would not hurt a fly. He has been around here for a few hundred years. Looks scary though if you have never seen one before". Kevin and Paul looked at each other, then lowered their heads and said nothing else.

Godwill laughed again when looking at the boys and shook his head. "Good job, your mother does not see you in this condition, or she will be asking me what I do on these detentions," all the others laughed when he said this. "So, how did you get here so fast Paul asked"? Godwill looked at the boys and just said, "brooms, my dear boy, remember, I did say this to you before Wilks. It just goes to show that you do not pay attention enough when I speak, doesn't it?" Paul looked at Kevin with an angry expression on his face which Kevin just turned away and walked over to the settee and sat by Godwill.

"So, what have you been talking about whilst waiting for us," Kevin asked. Godwill looked at Kevin, then rose from the settee and walked over to the window, staring out into the forest. "Sambia has developed a weakness in the mind block that Postromus had implanted on them and now can recall certain things from long ago. When he gave you those visions when you were last here, that is all he could remember. However, in talking to him further." Sambia quickly cut in with, "but I have remembered something else since our last meeting, young wizard. I showed you the waterfall and the old oak tree where an opening is present somewhere in the forest. Now I also remember something about there being a dark force also present in this area." "A dark force, what dark force," Paul asked nervously? "That is the thing. I cannot remember what it is, just a dark force," Sambia said. "Well, that is just not helpful at all," Paul said in an angry manner. Sambia turned on Paul with a truly angry expression on his face before saying, "what do you expect of me, wizard? I try to help, and you, just like others, ridicule me because I am a dwarf. If you think you are more knowledgeable than me, then go look for it yourself." Kevin rose and looked at Paul before saying, "forgive my brother, please, Sambia. Although he is three years older, he sometimes lets his inner child come out too often before thinking about what to speak". Sambia looked at Kevin and then just walked away from Paul. Paul looked hard at Kevin, then said, "Yes, yes, sorry, I just get nervous when someone says there is a dark force around. I have no idea how to handle or what to do about it."

Kevin moved towards Sambia, "Can you give me the visions again, please, Sambia?" "Why, young wizard, I have shown you them once. Why do you need to see them again? They should be imprinted on your mind." Kevin looked at Sambia and spoke again. "You showed me those visions last time, but now you remember that a dark force lay in the area. Is it not possible that during the visions, you show me this time that something may show me what that force is"? Godwill looked at Kevin and then spoke. "It could do, Sambia. Will you do this?" Sambia stroked his beard whilst thinking about it. Finally, he spoke, "it is possible, I guess, that this could unlock the memories, but it could also be dangerous. Too much information could overload that tint brain you have in their young wizard. Will you be prepared for this and what it could do to you? I say this because not only do I have these memories, but a lot more that may flood through and hit you with many visions and visions from the deep past and the present. Will you be able to pick through them and find what you need, and will you still be yourself, or will it change you? I have to ask this as I do not want to be the cause of your untimely harm or even death". Godwill moved towards Kevin and placed his hands on his shoulders, looking at him in the eyes, then spoke softly. "I know you have great inner strength and a real manner problem, but I believe that you can do this. I believe that this will show you more of the puzzle, and you be able to guide us to where we need to go." Paul then butted in, "now hang on the one-minute, mental strain, possible death, Kevin, do not do it, how would I explain this to mum if that happened? If this is significant, then why do you not do it, Godwill? You are the oldest here, the more experienced. Why should it only be Kevin that can do this?" Kevin looked at his brother then replied, "good question, bro, so why me, why not you?" Godwill turned away from Kevin then said quietly, "because it is you chosen by Merlin to conduct this quest, not me. It is you he chose as he saw an intelligent child with a big heart and manner. It is you that Postromus chose to abide with. Do these things not tell you that what is happening to you young wilks that you are destined for greatness? Therefore it must be you". He then looked at Paul and said, "and it is your job, just like mine, to help in any way to complete this quest as it is ours. I feel terrible things are awaiting in the future for all of us, but your brother will be the key to be able to stop these nasty things from occurring. So, you see Wilks. It must be him. We all will be looking after him and each other. It is like what you would call a brotherhood, one that, when others are needed, will step in no matter the cost." Jarez started to slowly hand clap and just said, "Bravo, old man, now, can we get on with this now, please?"

Tugay, now a little angry, stood up and moved over towards Jarez, but Kevin just stopped him and turned to Sambia and said, "OK, let us do this. Show me the whole thing."

Sambia looked at his brother with a worried look on his face. Tugat just nodded, and a small smile came onto his face. "If you have this power, the brother, then it is up to you if you wish to do this, but the boy is strong, and Postromus lies within. He was and still is our friend. We need to be able to do this to stop others that seek the stone for themselves from doing wrong and terrible things. These are honourable wizards that can stop this from coming about. Help them." Sambia smiled back and showed Kevin to a seat by the table. "Well, young wizard, if you wish this and my brother has this belief in you, then who am I to distrust you." Kevin sat on the chair and looked at Sambia and just said, "Sambia, my name is Kevin, a friend, not an enemy. Please, call me, Kevin." Sambia looked at Kevin as he sat there and smiled. With that, he said to

Kevin, "close your eyes, Kevin, clear your mind, and I will do my best to enlighten you into our past and present. The visions you will see are mixed, some good, some bad, let us hope you can see the truth and gain the information you desire to be able to help in this quest."

Sambia placed both hands on the top of Kevin's head and then just said, "let us begin." A white light shot through Kevin's mind, with visions all colliding through. He saw the dwarfs playing happily together with others and the parents happy with their children, then bright lights flashing that obscured the visions. When they became clear, a desolate area where war had taken place with buildings and dwarfs lying dead on the ground, other visions seen were of wizards fighting, killing others and themselves in search of the stone. Finally, piece, a forest, and a cave. The visions continued while walking through this cave. A shadow appeared, that of an animal not known to Kevin. It was not big but very quick; it was a small-looking lizard but then grew to the size of a house. Fire, sharp claws, and a piercing cry. Kevin saw bodies of others that had tried to move through the cave littered on the ground, wands also on the floor. In looking hard, he could see men dressed in medieval chain mail with swords and shields. Finally, at the end of the cave came where looking out, there was the waterfall and an old large oak tree with an opening at the base. This is where the vision cut out. Sambia fell to his knees with a cry of despair. Kevin's eyes opened as Godwill, Tugay, and Paul all went toward Sambia. Jarez just sat still.

"Brother, you ok?" asked Tugay. Sambia was helped to his feet and moved over to the settee. Kevin still sat still in the chair with his eyes wide open, not moving a muscle. Godwill now turned his attention to Kevin. "Young Wilks, you ok?" Kevin lowered his head and shut his eyes which had tears slowly falling. Godwill put his hands on Kevin's shoulders and then gently removed a couple of tears from his right eye. Kevin was still whilst still seated and seemed to be asleep. Sambia sitting with his brother, just said, "it is not my fault. I did not want to do this, but you had to keep pushing." Paul now very distraught about what condition his brother was in, turned and pulled out his wand, pointing it at Sambia. "What have you done to my brother? Speak, or I will surely take my anger out on you." With that, Kevin opened his eyes, and the wand flew out of his brother's hand, "wait," Kevin spoke. All now looked at Kevin as he sat staring at them all.

He stood up and walked over to the window, staring out. Suddenly, he turned and said, "we have to go. Go now; we are not alone." Tugay moved to the window and saw shadows on the edge of the clearing, "he is right. Time to go." Tugay grabbed his brother, who also held the hand of Kevin. The next thing he knew was he had been transported away back to the school where they came from. Godwill, Jarez, and Paul followed quickly. Once all there, Kevin spoke, "Who or what were those shadows we saw." Sambia turned away and said, "Dark wizards seeking what you want to find. It has been a long and perilous journey we have had since this all came about. I must move locations regularly as they find me wherever I go to. I am running out of places to find, but I must stay in this area to keep the stone from falling into the wrong hands. I hope you got what you wanted to know, Kevin. If you find this, it will make the area a more peaceful place where to live as they will no longer seek the piece there. However, if or when you do find it, then there will be more on yourself as it will spread quickly that you were the finder, so they will search for you. As Godwill stated at the hut, there will be further dark times ahead of you, and you will need all the friends you have by your side to help out until this is over."

Paul, now chirping in, asked, "by the way, where will you stay now? The shadows would certainly have destroyed the hut you live in?". Sambia looked at Paul and then smiled before answering. "Oh, I don't think that is a problem, young wizard. After all, are we not wizards?" He pulled out of his pocket something and opened his hand. Inside the palm was a small miniature version of the hut. Paul just looked and smiled, "Oh, so you shrink it then enlarge it. How do you do that?" Kevin butted in, "look, we need to focus on our next move. We know that there are more forces involved looking into the whereabouts of the stone and we need to concentrate on that." "You are correct young Wilks; we need to unravel the vision and work on where it will take us next. I suggest that we meet at the Spinney tomorrow after school and discuss this intently. Young Wilks, tonight we need you to map out what the vision gave you with information so we can produce a plan." All agreed. Sambia and Tugay disappeared whilst Jarez just stayed looking at Kevin. "How do we know that this young wizard does not lead us into a wrong direction, how do we know he does not want the stone for himself to become more powerful?" Kevin just stared at Jarez on hearing this comment and replied. "How do we know that you really are the good half spilled of Crandloss?" Jarez bowed his head and just said "touché" then disappeared. Kevin and Paul looked at each other and how dirty their clothes were and their condition of them. Godwill took out his wand and just gently waved it over them. The dirt disappeared, and the clothes looked as if they had just been ironed. "Thank you, Godwill," Kevin said before leaving the class.

The timeline had been restored, and the two boys made their way home talking about the adventures they had had during the detention. Finally, arriving at home and put the bicycles in the shed. Tea was waiting on the table as the boys entered the house. Their mother was busy around the kitchen cooking different things, with the smells filling the whole room. The boys loved these smells and happily sat at the table and started to dig into the food in front of them. "I hope you learned something on this detention spell," their mother said, looking at the boys. They both nodded as they could not speak due to having their mouths full. Mother just gave a glancing look at them when they did not answer and went back to cooking the delicious things she was doing. Not another word was said, and the boys thanked their mother for the tea and then went upstairs to their rooms. Paul ushered Kevin into his bedroom and closed the door. That night the two brothers concentrated on the vision Sambia had given to Kevin, with Paul not being of use. They decided to go to bed and get a good night's sleep.

Chapter 17

The Vision and the Trail

That night Kevin lay on his bed thinking of the vision he saw through Sambia. Many things ran through his head regarding the vision. The dwarfs as youngsters, the turmoil of the dark wizard's entrance, and Postromus. Suddenly he felt that Postromus was trying to push through his mental block, which Kevin eventually let through. Now it was a dual conversation, with both trying to speak at the same time. "So, you have seen the things that once were and the things that are as now. What do you intend to do, young wizard?" Kevin thought for a moment before answering but was suddenly interrupted by Postromus again. "When do you plan to do this then, boy"? Kevin began to say quietly, "why do you read my thoughts? If you know what I am thinking, perhaps you can help me understand this better, so maybe, just maybe, we can work as a team and try to get this done so you can be rid of me once and forever. Remember, I did not ask you to be inside or attached to me; you just did it." Postromus laughed before replying. "It was you that let me through when you broke the wizard's wand; remember that young wizard? If you had not done this, then I would still be in my dormant state, but now I am here, and although you are a miserable excuse for a sole attachment, I guess I must say also thank you." Kevin had a question shoot through his head when suddenly Postromus answered. "Do not be such a smug boy. With what I said, it is just at least I get to see through your eyes and thoughts what is going on now."

Kevin lay back on his pillow, continuing the conversation with Postromus. "So, we know the piece of the stone is in the forest where a cave is that has something in it that will kill and devour any living thing that enters it, and you cannot see it. After that, there is a path that leads to the waterfall where a large oak tree is, and at the base, an opening. I wonder what else lies there also?" Postromus then came through with, "Why should there be anything else there, boy? As you see, the shadow beast has stopped people and wizards through the ages from getting any closer to gaining the stone." Kevin sat up and then said, "But what if something or someone had worked out a way to get through that area? Would you not want another block in place also to prevent this from happening?" Postromus replied, "Mmm, I know why goodwill says you think too much, boy. If there was something else, then Sambia would have shown it to you and me through you. There is nothing else." Kevin was not sure, and Postromus could sense this, "believe me, boy, there is nothing else. Now, what are you going to do to get through this path?" Kevin tried to think of different things and spells, but each time Postromus just kept coming through, saying that it would not work. Eventually, Kevin decided to think harder to block out Postromus, and slowly, he disappeared from his mind. Kevin, now very tired, lay back and closed his eyes and went to sleep.

That night for a long time, Kevin had a good night's sleep and woke refreshed and alert. He got up, washed, dressed, and ran downstairs. As he got to the kitchen, he could see his father talking to his mother with a worried look on his face. "Morning, dad. Is everything ok?" he asked. Kevin's dad looked at him and answered in an unhappy manner, "it's your grandad. He was taken to hospital last night feeling very poorly." Kevin lowered his head and said quietly, "but he will be ok, won't he? Dad, grandad is strong." Kevin's mum and dad both answered at the same time, saying, "of course, but for now, the hospital wants to keep him in to do some tests just to make sure he has not got anything serious, so we will be going to the hospital tonight to see him, but unfortunately, they do not allow children to go at the night visits so you and your brother will have to stay here and Barbara next door will keep you company until we return. We should only be gone a couple of hours, so it should be no problem." Kevin looked at his parents' faces and saw that their expressions did not match what they were saying but just answered, "ok, but make sure you give him my regards and tell him to get better soon." Kevin's dad just ruffled Kevin's hair then said, "will do." With that dad kissed mum on the forehead and said, "will see you later love," then walked out the door and away back to his work.

Kevin's mum continued getting ready for work before she, too, had to leave the house. "Now, Barbara knows you two are at the detention again tonight, but mind you pop round when you get home and let her know you are here. Tea will be sandwiches and crisps, which will be in the fridge when you get home. Make sure you do your homework, and please, do not get into any more mischief for the rest of the week. I have enough to think about with your grandad, so please, be good if you can, Kevin." Kevin looked at his mum, then gave a little smile and said, "I will, mum. Honestly, I am worried about grandad also, so I do not want to be the one that causes you more grief." Kevin's mum looked hard at him, then just smiled and left for work. Just then, Paul turned up from his paper round and grabbed a bit of breakfast before the two boys headed towards school. On the way to the school, they discussed their grandad, remembering the fishing trip they took with him that started all that had come about. Kevin was getting increasingly upset with Paul going off on the magic thing rather than remembering other things about their grandad and finally shouting out at him. "Is that all you can think of? Our grandad is ill in hospital, and all you can come up with is this pathetic magic world I have been thrust into. Can't you see that mum and dad are very worried about him?" Kevin just raced off in front of Paul with an incredibly angry expression on his face. "Wait up, bro, I am worried too, I really am," and he tried to catch Kevin. As they got to the school gate, they walked down the driveway to the bike shed with Paul still chatting on about grandad and the vision. Kevin rammed his bike into the bike support and turned, and walked away.

Suddenly Kevin stopped and was just staring in front of him when Paul caught him up. He looked where Kevin was looking and saw that his sight was fixed on the girl Rueth in-front of him, staring back at him. Paul just gave a sigh and then said, "Girls, they will be the downfall of you, Kevin and then just brushed passed him. Rueth walked forward towards Kevin and just said, "morning Kevin, you ok? you look as if you have the weight of the world on your shoulders." Kevin just sighed and then replied, "oh, sorry, my grandad has been taken to hospital as he is not well, so I got a lot on my mind." Rueth just looked at him, then gently grabbed his hand and gave a little squeeze. "I am sure he will be ok; the hospitals do wonderous things for people nowadays." Kevin looked down at the two hands held together, then back up at Rueth. "I guess so," he answered, removing his hand from Rueths, then politely excused himself to go to registration.

As he walked towards his registration along the corridor, he saw Godwill standing in front of his classroom. "Morning, young Wilks, you look worried. Is there something you wish to discuss?" Kevin just shook his head and walked past without saying a word. Godwill turned and said again, "my door is always open, Wilks. If you need to talk, then just let me know, and don't forget about the detention tonight." Kevin just walked on to the registration class. It was a typical day at school for the day, classes Kevin did not like but had to go to prevent any further grief from his mother for not going, so he just put his head down and got on with them. During the break times, Kevin tried to avoid Rueth, that now had a special fascination with him, but eventually, she caught up with him at lunchtime. "Are you trying to avoid me, Kevin? I thought we were friends?" Kevin answered her back, saying that they were, but he was still very worried about his grandad, and this was his main concern. Rueth just smiled and then said, "look, he will be alright, but if you are that worried, why not go and see him for yourself?" Kevin explained that visiting times at night do not allow children as his mother had said to visit at that time. Rueth smiled and said, "so what about during school time?" Kevin Shook his head, saying he could not do that as he was already in detention for the week for doing things he should not have done. Rueth smiled again before answering.

"A rebel; I like those sorts of people. It must be that is why I like you, Kevin." It was clear that Kevin was blushing with a now reddening face. Rueth smiled again and leaned forward, and kissed Kevin on the cheek. Just at that moment, his brother Paul and his friends were walking nearby and saw what had just happened. "Oh yes," Paul said with his friends laughing aloud as they continued past. Kevin just turned and said in an angry manner, "What?" Paul and his friends continued walking, now showing arms around each other, pretending to kiss. Kevin looked up at Rueth and stormed off, leaving her routed to the spot.

Kevin, now truly angry, walked down the corridor towards the end when suddenly he noted that the time envelope was now happening. Kevin stopped and looked back down the corridor, where he saw Jarez come out from Godwill's class, beckoning him towards it. Kevin, still angry, eventually went towards the class. As he walked through the door, Godwill, Jarez, Sambia, and Tugay were all present. Kevin strode through the door with a very arrogant "What now?" Godwill looked hard at Kevin before signalling for him to sit down and be quiet. Sambia and Tugay turned to look at Kevin. Kevin saw that both looked as if they had been through hell and back with marks across their faces. "What happened to you two?" Kevin asked.

Sambia stared at Kevin and then spoke. "We found the cave, but so did someone else." Kevin looked at Sambia as he stopped speaking. "Who?" asked Kevin. "Matrees was there also with a couple of his followers." Kevin looked at Godwill with a worried expression on his face, then replied. "Matrees, how has he found out where the cave was?" Tugay answered, "We went to the site of the vision Sambia gave you, but when we were near the area, we jumped and had to fight our way out of the area. During the fight, we were caught and tortured by Matrees to find out the location through Matrees's memory charm. If it were not for the firedrate, we would be dead now." Kevin, now puzzled, spoke, "Firedrate, I thought they had died out years ago, or that was what I was led to believe. Do these creatures still live?" Kevin asked. Sambia nodded, "oh yes, wizard, some still exist, not many, but some are still in existence over the world. It just so happens there are a pair of them in the forest. I had never seen them before, but they came to our rescue. They keep their eyes on those who are good and come to the aid of them should any peril be noted by them." Kevin shook his head. "This is getting beyond belief. Is there anything else that lives in that Forrest, good or bad?" he asked? Tugay just shook his shoulders and answered, "We do not know. Some creatures are extremely hard to see or find; some are there all the time, but you do not detect them."

Kevin stood up and walked over to the window, and looked out. "And are there any others out of the forest also, like, could be over there in the park, for instance?" Godwill moved over to the window. "Why, do you see something?" Kevin just shook his head and answered, "No, but how do I? I mean, we know what is out there awaiting us?" Godwill just shook his head and answered, "We don't, young Wilks. Let us hope that there are no other suppresses awaiting you on this quest." Kevin reared up at Godwill, "awaiting me, why me? Are we not a team? Is it all to do with me?" Godwill looked at Kevin and then answered, "Merlin chose you for this task. Many tasks have been given to many wizards and witches to prove themselves; each had a team, as you put it, to be able to help in the quests, but it is the chosen one's task to complete the quest." Kevin now very unhappy again shouted at all of them, "so, my team including Paul, does this also include Vinny? are there any others in this so-called team that I should know about?" This time it was Jarez that spoke. "There will always be help for the one that asks for it or deserves it. There are good wizards and witches that you will meet over the course of the quest, but also others that are not good. These could be associates of Matrees." Kevin looked at Jarez and asked another question. So how will I know or be able to tell who it is?" Sambia answered this question. "Only you will be able to fathom out the devoted friend or the true enemy; it is in your nature, mind, and inquisitive nature. All you need to know is that you will never be far from help." Kevin was not happy with these comments, but they went onto the dwarf's encounter with Matrees and the firedrate.

The brothers explained they had managed to find a trail leading towards a cave, but that was as far as they got when Matrees found them. After fighting and being captured, the Firedrate appeared. The animal was large, with a glowing orange body spouting fire and rays of light from the horn on its head that scattered Matrees and the followers in separate ways. As the firedrate flew after Matrees, the two dwarfs managed to get free and travel out of the area and away, but not before Matrees had used the memory unblock charm that had given him the vision also of the whereabouts of the stone.

Godwill spoke, "we have to go tonight to get the stone. If Matrees gets it first, it will add power to him, and that means he will be stronger and harder to defeat. I know we ask a lot of you, young Wilks, but do you feel as though you are ready for this?" Kevin just looked hard and sternly back at Godwill and asked, "do you think I am ready?" Godwill first looked back at Kevin and then turned away without answering. "I thought so," said Kevin. "So, you do not think I am ready for this encounter, but you still want me to undertake it. I need to speak to Merlin, as both you and I know I am not ready. I need to get him to remove this quest from me and give it to someone else that is ready like, well, how about you, Godwill?" The dwarfs and Jarez looked firstly at Kevin, then Godwill. Goodwill turned quickly and said in a loud voice, "because it is you that has been set this quest, you young Wilks, not me, your brother or anybody else. You, the quest, cannot be passed onto anyone else. It is yours to complete." Kevin now angry himself now, shouted back. "Well, you can forget it; I will not do it, and I never wanted any of this, as I said from the start. Get some other puppet to do your task because I am out of here and all this magic rubbish." Kevin moved towards the door to open it, but goodwill chanted a spell that locked the door. Kevin tried to open it but could not. "Godwill spoke, "however much you kick and complain young Wilks, you are in this world, and nothing is going to change it, nothing you hear." Kevin looked back at Godwill, took out his wand, and cast "CIGRO, FREDSOM, BOMBARDO SEPRUM." A large blast and boom echoed through the room, and the door blew off the supports. Godwill and the others shielded their faces and ears as this happened. Kevin looked back towards them and then left through the now gaping hole where the door used to be. Kevin just walked on towards the playground, where his brother and friends came running along the corridor with their wands in their hands. They stopped and looked at Kevin as he passed by and then continued onto the classroom for Godwill. As they looked in, they saw the others looking at each other in silence. Paul just looked at the hole now and just said quietly, "sweet," then turned away to go after his brother. Goodwill eventually waved his wand, and the doorway moved back together piece by piece so no one knew it had ever happened.

As Kevin got to the playground, Paul caught up with him, asking what went on in there. Kevin now pacing backward and forwards with a truly angry look on his face, raised his wand towards his brother, who stood in front with a very suppressed look of shock on his face. "Leave me alone, Paul. Just walk away, or I may do something I regret later; just go." Paul now backed away slowly, saying, "ok, Kev, just lower your wand, just calm down, or you know who will come." "Back off, Paul. I won't tell you again." Paul's friends now also caught up with them, and Kevin's attention now went towards them. "Wait," called Paul to his friends, "walk away, now, go" the friends with wands now raised towards Kevin slowly lowered them and slowly backed off. Kevin lowered his wand and then used the travel spell to leave the area. "What the hell is going on," asked Roger to Paul. "I don't know, but we need to ask Godwill to find out. Come on, let's find him and find out." With that, Paul and his friends headed toward Godwill's class. When Kevin had travelled out from the playground, he ended up at the safe house, where he entered and went to Fergus. There he stood, stroking him as Godwill entered the room. Kevin turned quickly, holding his wand ready and pointing at Godwill. "Wait, young Wilks, it is only me this time" Kevin still had his wand pointing at Godwill starring at him. Fergus squawked towards Kevin, who looked at the bird. A couple of tears were seen coming down from the bird's eyes, and Kevin knew that he was sad. Kevin lowered his wand and sank to the floor. "What is happening to me? I never asked for any of this. Why do you persist in pushing me to do this? Do you not understand that this is confusing me to the point that it brings out my anger, and that can be so harmful? I worry about what I can do, especially with this thing inside me that is getting harder and harder to control. What if I kill someone when I am angry? What will happen to me?" Goodwill slowly moved towards Kevin, speaking quietly.

"You are no different to all witches and wizards when this comes of light. We all went through the same feelings, the same questions you ask, and the mood swings, but we worked hard in being able to understand the consequences that this also could have, so we worked on how to control the terribly angry feelings inside so we could remain within the community of others and be there should others need help. I am not talking about magic folk but un-given". Kevin raised his head and then said, "Un-given, who are those?" The Un-given, normal people are not of the magic type. People that have not been given the gift of magic. People that think magic is just someone doing cheap tricks with mirrors and quickness of the hand." Godwill now moved over to Fergus and stroked his head. "People that will never know such animals and creatures exist like Fergus here or the Firedrate or dragons. They only see them in books and in films that people have made using technology to produce a vision of such animals, but they do exist, but they cannot see them. Only the magic folk can do that. That is the way it is and has always been. Therefore, it is so hard to keep the normal existence and magic world apart, as I told you at the very beginning." Kevin rose to his feet and stroked Fergus, who now was chirping happily. Kevin sat at one of the chairs and asked. "Tell me goodwill, honestly now, no lies. Why was I picked by Merlin for this task? Why not you or Paul or even Vinny?" Godwill stroked his beard before answering. "Well, young Wilks, I have my own thoughts on this, but Merlin must have seen something in you, some strength, greatness, or maybe something else. I don't know for sure, but it was you he entrusted his wand to, and this wand has great power within it, but the wizard that yields it will have even more power. The wand also will only give the power to the wizard that holds it if it trusts them." Kevin, now looking puzzled on hearing this, asked, "what did you say? The wand has feelings and knows who it is to work for?" Godwill nodded, "that's right young Wilks. Many say that a wand picks the witch or wizard to be with. Personally, this is still an old wife's tale. I think you call it, but there is some evidence that different wands react to different people that use them. Also, in each wand, there is an added item."

Kevin now blurted in, "You mean like a heartstring like Postromus?" Godwill nodded and stoked his beard again. "That is right, but I have to say. Usually, it is a unicorn's hair or dragon heartstring or even a fired rates brain string, but I have to say that I have never before heard of someone being able to split their heart into pieces and install it within a wand." Kevin again blurted out, "Well, what about Crandloss? He split himself in two, didn't he? causing Matrees and Jarez?" Godwill nodded again, then replied. "Magic is like the earth. Things change and evolve, sometimes for the better but also sometimes for the worst. The stone Flammel made was the beginning of evolved magic that happened and had been going on for hundreds of years. Dark magic is growing stronger each millennium. We have seen it and what it is causing. It is essential we find the pieces and properly destroy the stone forever so it can be stopped." Kevin asked one further question. "So, let us say we do find all the pieces, what then, how will they be destroyed beyond all recognition? Who will or has the power to do this? I know it is not me. I am the puppet seeker that you are using for this, but who is the puppet master, the one that can end this for good so our lives can be normal or as normal as possible?" Godwill looked at Kevin and finally answered, "I cannot tell you that at this present time, but a way will be found to do this, I assure you." Kevin just dismissed this reply with the content it had in. "so we possibly know where one piece is but who knows where any of the other pieces are?" "We have Sambia and Tuguy. It was Sambia that was able to unblock his memory for the area of this piece, he can then unblock Tuguy's memory also, so we may be able to find a second piece, but we need to work on the first piece at present. Young Wilks, I do honestly believe in you even though you are very infuriating most of the time spent with you, but that is probably why I believe in you. You're not a yes child or one that will back away from things, so you asked me in the classroom whether I think you are ready. The answer is yes, it has always been yes, but I have to be sure that you think the same. Sometimes, you need a test thrown at you to see if you believe in what you have become. I got to say the door exit spell is quite brilliant. I believe your brother still has not mastered that spell yet." Godwill gave a little laugh and then winked at Kevin. "Now, I guess we had better go back, don't you, and one thing, young Wilks, please, remember, magic is only to be used when Un-givens are not present, or there could be dire consequences, Ok?" Kevin nodded, and they both travelled back to the school, where the envelope was once more removed, and time went on as if nothing had occurred.

Before leaving each other Godwill said to Kevin, "I hear your grandpa is not very well, I suggest you go see him, he is a good man and could do with some cheering up, take your brother with you also young wilks". "But sir, they won't allow us to visit him at nights and we are at school during the day so there is no chance of that happening" Kevin said. "I promised mum that I would not cause any more trouble so I cannot just leave the school as she will know it." Goodwill winked again at Kevin then said, "where there is a will there is a way, Oh, I think that your next periods for you and your brother has just been cancelled due to illness of the teachers." Goodwill turned with his back to the school and quickly waved his wand. Mr Sidel and Mrs Wallace who were eating in the dining room suddenly became very sick with wanting to vomit and ran out of the dining room where a lot of people were eating. "There, free period, make it count young wilks, I will ensure your mum does not find out, now, get your brother and go see him, but be back before registration, ok?" Kevin nodded and just answered, "Thank you, we will." Off kevin ran to find his brother who was still upset at his brother for pointing his wand at him before but after Kevin explained agreed to go with him. As they were near to the entrance of the gate Godwill passed them by just saying "remember the time boys, don't let me down or there could be further consequences." With that Kevin slowed time again and travelled his brother and himself outside the hospital. Once there Kevin re-started the timeline and the two walked into the hospital to find out where their grandad was.

Grandad, Rueth, Davey, and Mr. Perry

After a lot of speaking to nurses at the main reception, they found out which ward their grandpa was in and made their way to it. As they walked into the ward, they saw their grandad sitting up in bed. "Hello, you two. What are you doing here at this time? Should you not be at school?" Kevin answered, "Mr. Godwill, let us have the afternoon off to come to see you as the teachers are sick for the afternoon." Kevin's grandad looked hard at Kevin and asked, "is that right? I hope you're not lying to me, Kevin. It is not nice to lie, you know," replied his grandad. Kevin convinced him, with Paul's help, that what Kevin had said was true, which grandad accepted. Paul asked, "So, grandad, what are you doing in here? You seem ok." Grandad just smiled before replying, "oh, it must just be a bug or something. It started about a couple of months ago, and well, I am no young man now, so they brought me in here to keep an eye on me, but every now and again, I get a bit tired and breathless, but it soon goes away." Kevin looked at his grandad with an inquisitive look and then asked, "So I bet you're missing your fishing then." His grandad nodded. "It must have been a couple of months since we all went fishing at Baxter's. Do you think you got stung or something happened whilst we were there?" His grandad looked hard at Kevin, then just shrugged his shoulders and said, "maybe, but I cannot remember anything that happened there but come to mention it, it does look like a coincidence. Maybe I should get them to investigate a connection with bugs or water rat issues. That could be a good catch, Kevin; I never thought about it but your right. It did start when we had been there."

They continued talking throughout the next hour talking about school, Nan, and other things. "By the way, how did you get on regarding your school assignment regarding the family tree and the records you looked at the church archive when I took you there?" Kevin replied quite quickly, and they were extremely impressed. "I think it was just trying to get the students to trace their past and not let it all pass by without knowing the true family and what our previous ancestors had been doing." Grandad laughed, "I see school never changes its ways. I remember when your Uncles John, Malcolm, and Aunty Christine all had the same assignment. You would think that as the world evolves, then schooling needs to evolve and not stand still." Both Paul and Kevin laughed and agreed. Paull spoke, saying, "well, they can only teach us with what has actually happened and not what is going to happen as they don't know until it has occurred." Both grandad and Kevin looked at Paul and said together, "yes, right" then laughed again. "Talking of historical things, I found a couple of old books in my loft that I do not need anymore that may be of some further use for you two if you have any more ancestors' assignments. I found a few names in these that were not in the archives and did not give it a second thought until I saw them the day before I came in here. Mind you, the writing is in lain, I think, and I do not read Latin; perhaps you do at the school?" Paul just said, "No, just French, German, and Spanish." "Oh well, they're at home. If you want them, just ask Nan to get them. They're by the sideboard." Both boys thanked him. "Well, you get better, grandad, so we can do some more fishing." Grandad nodded, and the boys kissed him on the cheek before starting to set off. Kevin turned around and then said, "One thing, grandad, don't say anything to mum or dad that we have been here, please. There already upset that you're not well." Grandad just wagged his finger at him and then said, "I knew it, my lad. Ok, I won't say anything to them, but don't do this again unless you're with your mum and dad, or it could drop me in it too, ok?" Kevin nodded, then waved goodbye, and the boys left.

Kevin slowed time and the two boys used the travel spell back to the school where he re-started it again. Whilst walking back to the registration class the boys talked. "Do you not find it funny that grandad went down with this illness the day I got the wand" kevin asked his brother, "and that it got worse when I broke Matrees's wand and had Postromus attach himself into me?" Paul just looked at him puzzled and said, "just a coincidence I guess," Kevin stopped his brother from walking on." ok, so answer me this, Uncle John, Malcolm, and auntie Christine all looking into the family archives like us for some made up ancestor family tree assignment, what is that all about?" "Again, a coincidence" answered Paul. "Really, when we looked at their side of the tree there was little to go on and markings that we could not decipher" Paul just shrugged his shoulders and answered again, "what, you say that there is something not right with them, I can't see it, you are thinking into things too much again Kevin". "I want those books that grandad was talking about, perhaps they can fill in a couple of answers I have spinning around my mind." Paul just started walking on saying, "don't know when you will get them bro as we haven't seen Nan either since our last fishing trip, it was the only time we get to see both of them, and mum will not want us bothering her over a couple of old books whilst grandad is ill in the hospital". Kevin agreed and walked on but still had questions going on in his head that he could not answer.

After the afternoons registration the boys made their way to Godwills class for the detention only to find it locked. Whilst waiting outside Mr Perry was passing by stating that Mr Godwill had to leave early today so the detention had been cancelled but will continue tomorrow when he returns. The boys looked at each other, then just walked off back to the bike shed to get their bikes. As they rode home kevin continued to talk to Paul regarding the uncles, aunts, and the books so much that Paul just shouted, "look Kevin, the things your stating are purely a coincidence nothing more so let it drop."

Finally, they arrived home with their mum surprised to see them. "What are you doing home, should you not be in detention, have you missed it?" she asked with a maddening look on her face. "No mum" Paul answered, "Mr Godwill was called away earlier today so they cancelled it, but it will be going on tomorrow when he is back, honest, you can check with Mr Perry who told us." Mum frowned then said, "I will be doing that my lad and if you have lied to me then you'll miss even more of your precious football matches I can tell you." "By the way, tomorrow Barbara next door is out so I will be taking you two to your Nans tomorrow to look after you whilst we see your grandad and she feels a little tired so we told her to take a break and we will go. I expect you to be on your best behaviour there, she is getting on and cannot be up and down to watch you two, OK?" Kevin looked at his brother and they smiled and agreed. Kevin thought that things maybe a coincidence but were all fitting together quicker than he expected. After tea, the boys completed their homework before going to bed. That night as Kevin lay asleep the thoughts were still running through his head making him toss and turn. So much that eventually it woke him up. Sitting up in bed he saw a faint light appear towards the bottom of his bed and then finally Merlin appeared. "What troubles you, young wizard?" he asked as he sat on the side of the bed by Kevin. Kevin whispered "quite a lot. Why did you choose me for this so-called quest, it is so confusing and making me very angry at most times causing me and the other people grief"? Merlin smiled, "it is because of your strong-minded manner and the sometimes recklessness of your nature. You seem to forget; we all grow up in time and our manners change. You remind me of myself. Oh yes, I was once exactly like you, but I grew up in a quite different era, one that magic was everywhere then and trying just to be normal was harder than showing you are of the magic blood. So, you see, it is the opposite of what I was like. I had been watching from afar for a long time all the way through from your birth right up to now. You have a kind of ore around you that you do not know about that can attract the attention of people and magic folk. Throughout your life, this ora around you, has grown stronger with the thought and mannerisms you have growth through, now, it is at a state of let us say, near perfection. You have much inside you that you can accomplish but do not know it yet, but you will. I have to say reports from Godwill have been very encouraging although he states you still have an incredibly angry temper on you and that is when you are at your most powerful state. I think he is beginning to like you, young wizard".

Merlin rose from the side of the bed and walked around. Kevin then asked, "so what am I to do with this vision Sambia gave me? it looks as though Matrees has already found the area where the stone was, and the two dwarf brothers only just escaped with their lives with help from the Firedrate." "I know," Merlin said, "A Firedrate, I thought them to be extinct for over a couple of hundred years, but they still exist, marvellous creatures, so I am told. I never got to see one, but from what I hear, they are good magical creatures and will be a force to align with on your quest." "But, if Matrees is already there, how do we know that he does not already have the stone?" Merlin turned towards Kevin," Many questions asked, many not answered, we do not know, but we have to think that he has not got it yet or he would have already left the area, and my sources still say he is still there searching, so I guess through that deduction that he has not found it yet." Kevin again looked at Merlin and then spoke. "So, if I go to this location, who will be with me? As the dwarf brothers said, Matrees had a couple of followers with him. I cannot do this myself, Merlin." Merlin sat on the bed again." You will never be alone; you have friends and guardians you know nothing of yet that will be with you. Your strength and manner will be the main tool you use against the said foe. All you need to do is believe in yourself and what you can achieve. If you have this, there is not a man, wizard, or creature that will defeat you. Mind you, use the gift you have for the wrong purpose, then it will start you down the dark path, and there is nothing that can return you from this way. All I will say before going is to believe, be strong, and above all, follow your heart rather than your mind, and in certain circumstances, you may have to use both at the same time, but you will know when that must happen. Anyway, I have kept you awake for long enough but remember, I can sense and feel your thoughts and frustrations, and I am only a thought away. Now, rest, for tomorrow will be a big day for you, I feel." As Merlin started to disappear, Kevin shouted, "wait, what do you mean big day tomorrow?" Merlin smiling at Kevin, slowly disappeared without a word. Kevin, now even more confused, cuddled down, closed his eyes, and eventually fell into a deep satisfying sleep.

Kevin's mum heard him call out and thought that he and his brother were arguing and came rushing upstairs and burst into his room. Kevin woke with a start and see his mum standing at the door. "What on earth is going on?" Kevin bleary eyed answered her. "Nothing mum, I must have been having a nightmare I think" Mum stared at him then spoke. "And what was the nightmare about?" Kevin shrugged his shoulders and answered. "I do not know, cannot remember." Mum again stared hard at him and then said quietly but sternly. "Well cuddle down now, try to be quiet as you know your brother is up early to do his paper round in the morning. He needs that job to earn his money so he can buy the stuff with which we cannot help. If he does not keep that job, then it will be down to you keeping him awake at nights so just think about that my lad." Kevin sighed then slowly said, "sorry mum, I will go back to sleep. Sorry." Mum turned and closed the door and then checked on Paul who was fast asleep. She quietly closed his door then went back downstairs.

The next morning Kevin met his brother in the kitchen, and they had breakfast before going to school. On the journey Kevin told Paul about the visit. Paul was listening but also concentrating on something more that he had noticed in-front of them. "Stop Kevin" Kevin applied the brakes to his bike and pulled up." What?" he asked. Paul pointed to a small opening at the side of the park where he thought he saw something moving around. The boys got off their bikes and slowly approached the area. As they peered around the side way, they saw something that neither had seen before in their lives. It was Rueth walking around chanting spells and a wand was seen in her hand. Kevin wanted to rush out, but his brother grabbed him back and hushed him. "Why" kevin whispered, Paul replied quietly "she is not in our order therefore she could be a follower of you know who?" Kevin just shrugged his hand away holding him back and moved forward. Rueth immediately turned around pointing the wand at Kevin. He stopped and laughed. "What are you doing Rueth, practicing being a witch or something with that twig?" Rueth not happy that Kevin had seen her cast a spell of "Iluminum Cantarta" Slowly kevin felt himself starting to float and then cast "Evreko". Kevin landed back on the floor. "What are you trying to do Rueth, you know if you're of magic that you do not do this in front of un-givens" he shouted to her. Rueth just smiled and put away her wand. "I wanted to show you that I am not just a normal girl, I like you Kevin, but you really do not seem to want to know me. I thought it was because you thought I was just a normal silly little girl and not a witch." Kevin walked towards her saying, "But how did you know what I am, I have tried to keep it separate so give no signs?" Rueth laughed. "You really do not know do you? The order here has a lot of witches and wizard meetings, and you are the discussion point". Kevin looked back at his brother who was now standing by the bikes beckoning him to come back. "Leave mine there Paul, I will walk in with Rueth as I have questions for her I need to be answered." Paul shook his head then laid Kevins bike on the ground and rode his to school. On the small walk to the school both Kevin and Rueth talked about the order and un-given magic folk. "So, what order are you with as my brother said you are not in our order?" Rueth just smiled before answering. "There are many orders around here kevin. I guess you would call them house orders." "House orders?" kevin replied. "What the heck are those?"

Rueth explained that the magic order has houses that were given names through the wizard or witch that had followers. "Our order is that of the witch Driomatus. I believe that she was a powerfully good witch back in the olden times. So, what order are you in?" Kevin shrugged his shoulders and answered. "Do not know. This is the first time that someone has told me this. I thought that all witches, wizards, and others were just the same but some good, some bad. So how many orders are there?" Rueth did not know for sure but just said. "Many I guess, but no-one knows for sure. There are no scriptures that I have checked that state the number of orders, just that there are many around the world. Anyway, we need to get to school or the teachers there will do their nut at us and be on our backs so come on".

When at the school gate, Rueth turned to Kevin and gave him a quick kiss on the cheek before running off to go find her friends. Kevin walked his bike down the chase to the shed to store it where his brother was waiting. Paul immediately started with, "Why did you do it? How do you know she is one of us and not of Matrees's followers? Really, bro, you must be more careful. Do not let your heart rule your head." Just as he was having a go at his brother, Kevin's friend Vinny turned up. "Hi, Kevin, Paul," he said as he looked hard at Kevin's brother, "What gives?" Paul just went quiet when he saw Vinny and turned to walk away by just saying, "Be careful, bro, you really don't know who to trust here," and walked off. "What's he say? he doesn't trust me?" Kevin shook his head and led Vinny away from the bike shed towards the registration building, talking about Rueth and what had happened. Vinny was listening carefully and giving out a few smiles and laughs as the two boys discussed things. "So, where have you been, Vinny? Haven't seen you for a while now. I thought you were sick or something." Vinny just laughed and then replied, "No, my parents decided to take a short holiday. They got cheap, and I had to go with them as they could find no one to look after me whilst they were going away. It has been the most boring week of my life, I can tell you. "And then laughed. "It seems as though plenty has been going on here, though, and Rueth, wow, she is quite a looker. You could do worse than her, mate. She got any nice friends she could introduce me to?" The two boys laughed together and finally went into the registration class.

After registration had been completed, the two boys went off to their first lesson of the day and it was for religious education, a class Godwill was the teacher for. "I need to speak to him with what is going on and ask him why the cancellation of the detention occurred," said Kevin. As they opened the door to their surprise goodwill was not present but their stood Mr Perry instead. "Hello sir, didn't know you did religious education, where is Mr goodwill?" Mr Perry just smiled and pointed to a seat for the boys to go to. "Mr Godwill is not feeling well today so I have been given the task of taking his class so sit down get your books out and turn to page 34 and read the section on the Garden of Eden". The two boys sat, removed their books, and opened them at the page given. As others turned up for the class the two boys looked at each other and began to talk quietly about where Godwill was and that he never misses a class. Mr Perry saw the two boys talking and bellowed "Is there something you wish to share with the class Mr Wilks?" Kevin just said, "No sir" and then went back to reading the book in a quiet fashion. For the rest of that period the work was as normal as it should be. Mr Perry taking the class through certain elements of the book. At the end of the class the bell rang for break time. All left the class with Kevin and Vinny now going through the door when Mr Perry stopped them. "Mr Godwill has said that your detention continuous tonight so do not be late. I guess I should add you to the fold and Rose also for talking in the class." Vinny was not happy, "But why sir, it was just the once and I apologised." "Still rose, we cannot keep you two young friends apart, so we had better keep you together. Mr Godwill will not be here so it will be myself taking the detention." Kevin looked at Vinny and gave a sigh of disbelief then answered, "Yes sir, we will be here" and the two boys left.

Outside Kevin was not happy, "A detention with Perry, this is really going to be boring. I wonder why Godwill is not here, what's going on?" he asked his friend. "Beats me but now I have to explain to mum and dad that I got a detention, the first day back and already in trouble, they are not going to be happy." The two boys went off to the playground where they come upon Paul and his friends. Kevin asked him "Where is Godwill, just had Perry for class instead of Godwill and he is also taking the detention. How are we going to get this thing done with Godwill not controlling it?" Paul looked at Kevin and answered. "I don't know bro but there has to be something significant that is happening as Godwill is never ill or misses class, well not since I have been here, although." Paul stopped speaking for a moment with Kevin and Vinny looking on." There was that time when things were not good during my time as a trainee wizard. That was also to do with Crandloss back then I remember, I guess whatever it is he has a good reason but your right, the detention will be boring and the usual rubbish of reading books in quiet." Kevin walked away with Vinny chasing after him. Next, they came upon Rueth and a couple of her friends together talking. As the boys walked past the girls laughed aloud where Kevin and Vinny just walked faster past.

The next lesson went off as usual, and now lunch was here. The bell rang, and the boys made their way to the dining room where Kevin's mother was serving. As he got to the serving hatch, his mother said, "I talked to Mr. Perry, and he told me what you said last night, but he would also be taking the detention tonight, so make sure you are there. Do not forget, when you come home, put your bikes away and then walk down to Nans as you and your brother are to go there and do not play her up, you hear? We will pick you up from there when we get back from the hospital" Kevin nodded. "Hello, Vinny; not seen you for a while, been ill dear?" Vinny quickly explained what had gone on, and the two boys now moved to a table to eat their lunch. Whilst there, Paul and his friends also joined them at the table to eat, and they discussed further the plight of the forthcoming boredom of the detention with Mr. Perry. After they had eaten, the boys got up and left the dining hall. As they walked down the corridor towards the playground, they noticed that all did not seem right. Time had slowed. From Godwill's class, Sambia exited, beckoning the boys towards it. The boys all followed to the class and entered it. Instead of the class, there now was a mountain range with bright sun shining overhead. The boys all looked at each other, then in front of them. There stood Sambia, Tugay, Jarez, and another dwarf they did not know. "This is Davey, another of my brothers. We travelled long distances to find him and convince him to help, but he has some reservations about who you really are and what you intend to do with the stone once all the pieces are gathered".

"So young wizard, what makes you the special one?, and what do you intend to do with the pieces once gained should you manage to be able to get them?, each stone part is power and glory in the magical world, for what do you want with them? To gain power yourself to do good or bad, tell me wizard why I should fall in beside you like my witless brothers. You cannot fool me like you fooled them with a body show of Postromus. Speak or I leave." Kevin slowly walked forward towards Davey. "I have been thrown into this world of magic, I did not ask for it, I have been assigned this quest through Merlin, one that I have many disagreements about, but it has still been put on my shoulders. The light body show you so aptly describe is not a show but real. Postromus attached himself to me when I broke Matrees's wand, I mean crandloss's wand. All here are magic folk for doing good, not bad. As for what will happen when or if the pieces are gained as you spoke, I have no idea for I have not been told of this but purely to gain them for Merlin. It is him you should be asking, not me."

Davey laughed then replied. "A satisfactory answer wizard, but still I am not convinced. Merlin has been dead for hundreds of years and Postromus, a good tale but extraordinarily talented said. Do not waste my time or my brothers in this story of a quest, I will take no part and I suggest brothers you do the same. If Postromus was still alive and present it would be what he prevailed upon us." Davey started to turn and walk away when Kevin held out an arm towards Davey which made him stop in his tracks. "What is this magic, I cannot move, release me boy and I will show you what you are dealing with." Kevin now showing a tint of blueness to his skin slowly turned his hand around where Davey now was being elevated slowly in the air and turned to face him. As Davey turned, he saw the blueness of Kevins skin and see what he was doing. Slowly Kevin spoke. "You wish to challenge me, that is good, but do you also wish to challenge Postromus." There the English stopped but Kevin kept speaking in dwarfish. Davey tried to struggle but could not move. Slowly Kevins arm moved backwards, and Davey slowly moved towards him. The other two brothers spoke, "Please. Sire, he does not know or believe that it is you, please, he is our brother, your friend from long ago, do not hurt him." Davey now still elevated was listening to the language being spoken. A tear rolled down one of his cheeks as the talk continued. Tuguy now raised his wand towards Kevin where Vinny also raised his towards the dwarf. "Stop, you fool" bellowed the voice from Kevin. "Put away your wands, we are one, one of magic for good not evil, this is what Crandloss wants, to tear us apart from inside where he can become stronger than any one of us. I have explained to Davey what is going on and now it is up to him to decide to follow and help or leave, the choice is his." Kevin lowered his arm and Davey was set back on the ground. Davey stood looking at Kevin for a long time before speaking. "I do not know what to say, how do you speak dwarfish, the power I felt in your presence, it felt like that Postromus had but yet." The dwarf fell silent then continued. "I still am not sure about you; therefore, I will have no further dealings with you until I have worked this all out. For now, brothers I will leave you, but should you need me you now know where to find me unless I must move due to being hunted like you all my brothers, but someday we will all meet again when we will not be hunted". With that Davey turned and walked down the mountain path and disappeared.

Tugay looked at first his brother then Kevin. "He will be there when it is needed, I am sure of that." Sambia grunted, "Really, you really believe that from Davey. He has always been a bit head strong and does only what he wants even if it is the wrong thing to do. He has no shame." Vinny butted in "Sounds like someone we all know" as he stared at Kevin. Kevin now had returned to himself just gave Vinny a friendly push. With that Sambia waved his wand and the mountain pass disappeared and they were now all back in Godwills classroom. With a nod and a smile, the dwarf brothers disappeared just leaving Jarez. "I to must go wizard but listen first. To accomplish the deed that must be done, you must find a way to bring together all involved, or you will fail." With that Jarez clicked his fingers and was gone. Now only the boys stood in the classroom wondering what had just past and what the meaning of Jarez comment meant. The bell went and they decided to speak together about it later so went off to the next lesson.

That afternoon Kevin's thoughts were not really on the lessons he was learning, with more questions popping through his head than answers. Many a time, the teachers called out to him to concentrate on what they were teaching rather than daydreaming. Finally, the lessons ended for the day, with Kevin and Vinny meeting up in the registration room. "You ok, Kev? It seems you have been a little distracted this afternoon?" Kevin looked at Vinny, then answered, "And you're not?" Vinny just shrugged his shoulders and sat down for registration. After this had been completed, the boys made their way to Godwills class and became part of the detention being run now by Mr. Perry. As they entered the class, they saw Paul, his friend roger, Rueth, and Susan Rich. "Hello Kevin, long time no see. Although I do see you around quite a lot, you seem to be in another world." Kevin smiled when he saw rueth, then asked, "So what are all of you doing here? Old Perry, did you also lot for something or nothing?"

Just as he said this, Mr Perry was walking into the classroom and heard. "So, still mouthing your thoughts then Mr Wilks, old I may be but useless behaviour for detaining pupils definitely not. Now sit." Mr Perry now handed out a book to all. The book read 'spell casting and ways to repel.' All looked around at each other with puzzled faces on all. Just then Mr Perry took out a wand, waved it, and chanted the time envelope spell. All the pupils stood up and clapped and shouted in joy. "Well, you really didn't think I was just a boring old sports and religious education teacher, did you?" With that time slowed and a whirl of wind came into the classroom where Godwill appeared. "Sorry I'm late Markus." "That's ok Godwill, I think this has given a bit of a surprise to our students here" replied Mr Perry. "I bet, especially young Wilks." Both teachers laughed then went to the side of the main teacher's desk.

Godwill spoke first, "I guess you are all wondering why I was not at school yesterday and took the detention, well, I have been busy following leads to other possible locations of pieces of the stones." Kevin butted in "But sir, surely, we need to concentrate on the first part rather than the others or does this mean the first has been found by Matrees?" A murmur from the others started to happen around the class.

Goodwill held his hand up and spoke, "Quiet, no, it does not mean that this first piece has been found, but we need to be on the ball and first to any other pieces we may find. Of course, you are right as usual young Wilks, but we do need to keep our options open. Now, we have new members to our fold I see. Ms Davis, Ms Rich, nice to see you. I hope both your parents are well and fine. Give my regards to them, I remember teaching them years ago." Both Susan and Rueth looked at each other and asked between them quietly "how old is he." Paul heard their question and answered, "no-one knows for sure, but you could say he is ancient" The girls laughed. "Got something to say Wilks asked Mr Perry. "No sir" replied Paul.

"Now, as you can see, Mr Perry here is also a warlock, a magician with an enormous knowledge for spells. He will take you through different spells, correct casting, and the most significant thing how to repel them. Of course, all spells can be repelled apart from one." Vinny piped up with "The killing spell." "That is correct Mr Rose. The killing spell is what it says, if cast at you, you will die, there is no chant or potion that will stop this from occurring. It is time for all of you to know this. Some of you have been in confrontations where different spells have been cast at you. Some mild some harsh that will leave you in riving pain like the torture spell. Mr Perry's job is to teach you how to repel most of these spells or cut the power of them, so they do the least damage to you during any confrontations."

Paul's friend Roger now spoke. "Well, you certainly know how to scare people. Just look at the younger ones here. They must be scared on hearing this". "Quite right, Mr. Cranbridge, but do you not think they have the right to hear this being so young and being able to train earlier in the likelihood this may occur?" Roger went quiet, but Kevin then spoke. "So let me get this right, Mr. Perry is going to teach us things we already know but may teach us new things? And whilst we are learning, Matrees is getting closer to getting the stone. How does this help?" Mr. Perry now came in with, "So you think you are ready to take on Matrees and his followers, all wizards and witches with more experience and knowledge than yourself, do you, Wilks? Even with that thing or so-called Postromus inside you, you are no match for him yet. You need experience, mind enhancement, and above all, knowledge. So, to tell me you need not learn from what I am to teach you is just a boy's thoughts, a mere boy's thoughts, not a wizard's thoughts. A wizard will gain as much knowledge and experience to gain the slightest advantage over your opponent as possible. That way, you may just make it out of the incident alive." Kevin looked at Mr. Perry and, in a way, knew he was right but really did not want to hear what he had just been told, but apologised for his outburst.

"So, now, if there are no more interruptions, shall we begin?" asked Mr Perry.

Chapter 18

Spell Casting and the Books

In the classroom, Mr. Perry waved his wand, and the chairs and desks slowly moved to the side of the room. "Now, I want you to break into pairs. It would be good if we had an older one with a younger one. Saying that this does not mean your elders take for granted that you are teaching and learning and not hurting the youngsters. If I see this, then I will intervene and bestow on you the same grief. Do I make myself clear to everyone? All nodded, then paired up with disagreements going on before all was settled, with who would be with who. Once suited, Mr. Perry began the lesson.

"First spell I will teach or go over to those that know it is the spell to produce fire from your wand called Firentium Sparksum. As he said the words, a small stream of fire appeared at the end of his wand. Kevin sighed and looked away. Mr. Perry, now looking at Kevin, spoke. "So, I guess you know this spell, young Wilks? "Know it, used It, and a counterspell to quenched it." Mr. Perry just waved his wand and pointed it at Kevin. Fire shot towards Kevin at a quick rate, but not before Kevin had cast back Disquelch Wateriade. A blast of water shot from Kevin's wand, engulfing the fire and forcing it back to Mr. Perry's wand, which eventually drenched him. The students all laughed aloud as Mr. Perry stood dripping wet, staring at Kevin with a mad look on his face. Mr. Perry then cast Windinium Ferosciate at Kevin, again Kevin recast back to Mr. Perry Crevatious Septimium. As the storm wind came from Mr. Perry's wand and the cast back Kevin did, turned this towards Mr. Perry, knocking him off his feet and blowing him across the floor. All the others stood holding their coats down and holding onto something so they did not get caught up in the flow of the storm wind. As it faded, Mr. Perry rose to his feet and was about to cast yet another spell when Kevin chanted Transisomb. Mr. Perry's wand flew out of his hands and over to Kevin, who caught it. Mr. Perry now truly angry, stood looking at Kevin and was about to shout at him when Godwill stepped in and shouted, "Enough," he walked over to Kevin and snatched the wand back, and gave it back to Mr. Perry. "This is not an ego trip for you two, and this is a teaching exercise for all. Mr. Perry, and Mr. Wilks, I would ask you to calm yourselves and take the time to learn and better yourselves in the spells and their powers they carry. Each spell will have different amounts of power cast by the wizard doing the spell based on experience and mind control. From what I just saw, both of you are equal in power, with your young Wilks a little stronger in the mind controls, but that does not allow you to think that you are both good enough and experienced enough to repel any spell cast at you. Now, all the others may be included within these teachings, as this is what they are here for. Do you not agree, Mr. Perry" Mr. Perry nodded and apologised for his outburst. "Young Wilks." Kevin nodded and agreed also. "Good, now, into your pairs and work on the spells, Mr. Perry, and I will give them to you to practice." All got back into the pairs and went through the spells given to them to react to and repel against.

After a long while, Godwill ended the class with several spells retaught and new ones added. Each student had notebooks to write down the spells to remember them and read up on in the spell books for the differences the spells could be used for. Kevin, a little disheartened as he knew a lot of these spells before and had tried them out on his own in different areas where no one knew he had gone to do this, did the lesson. In the end, all were leaving when Godwill stopped Kevin. "Can we have a word, young Wilks"

Kevin nodded to Vinny to go and joined both the teachers. When the class was empty and the door shut, Godwill spoke. "I am not sure what that was all about with you two, but it was certainly not called for. Markus, what were you thinking? Mr. Perry replied, "I am not sure. When we started, it was just a teaching thing I was doing, but then, something changed within me, something that made me feel uneasy, a feeling of ore, a power trying to hurt me, so it was just an instinct to protect myself that took over." "And what of you, young Wilks? What were your feelings inside? Kevin spoke, I guess the same, but with a difference, I suppose. The difference was that I had the belief that I could repel anything and turn it around. An overwhelming calmness and feeling of power within me to do this." Godwill stroked his beard, then spoke. "Although young yourself, with Postromus inside you, you are incredibly powerful. I am guessing that this is what Markus felt and changed his mind and actions towards you with what went on. If this is so, then it may be a terrible thing, as others will also get this feeling and try to search you out. Therefore, it is imperative you learn quickly and gain the experience and knowledge to be able to protect yourself. Markus, I need you to do the training, will you be ok to do this, or do you think there could be a problem? Mr. Perry looked at Kevin, then answered. "I can do this, Godwill; I can harness this energy from myself and transport his energy so it will become even stronger. You will have to read and train a lot of information from now on, Wilks. Are you prepared to do this? There will be tears and pain involved in the training, but it is only to make you stronger. Can you cope with this? I do not want to waste my time if you are not going to complete this requirement. Kevin listening to the comments by Mr. Perry, thought for a second before answering. "Tears, pain, who would want to sign up for anything like that? You both think I must be stupid and agree with that. No, forget it. What I think you both still do not realise is I am just a 13-year-old boy, not an adult, not a warlock or wizard, just someone who has been into this world and has a gift. A gift that is supposed to be for good but could be for evil, also. I just wanted to be a normal boy, that is all" Godwill looked at Kevin and again replied.

"Normal, what is normal? People kill each other with knives and guns, is that normal? You have a gift that may help prevent actions or death on the streets if you see it just by uttering certain words and causing things to happen" But sir, when this started you said that we have to keep thew magic out of the normal life to ensure people do not get frightened of us"? Godwill then spoke quickly, "so, you do believe in the magic, then there is no turning back, magic is and always has been part of your life. For this, others will look towards you for help and knowledge on things to come to prevent any re-occurrences, you, not Markus, not me. Therefore, Merlin chose you, a mere boy but a talented and powerful youngster who will eliminate the land of evil for good. A guardian you call them." Mr Perry now also spoke. "I felt the power within you young Wilks, you have a power that is even stronger than mine which I have to say is a bit alarming, but what Godwill has said is the truth. Give me the chance to enhance and capture the power you must improve the mind set of yourself so you can become the great wizard you should be." Kevin looking at both wanted to speak but just could not find the words to say. Eventually he spoke, "ok, ok, I will go along with you lot for now. What do I need to do to become this so-called great wizard? I have to say not into this bit about the pain though, just understand I will be like a wounded animal if you inflict pain onto me and the boy, will I give pain back. Are you also prepared for this Mr Perry? Remember also, you are not just taking on me but my co-host, not sure what he will think about this" Godwill replied, "That is the thing Young Wilks, Markus and I need to train your mind in how to control him and when to let him loose. This could be painful for all of us if this does not work but we must try." Kevin agreed. "Now, you need to get home, the time started a while ago and if you are late then your mum will be worried what is going on. Go home, read the books, understand the spells, when you get chance continue to try them out, but make sure you put things back to normal after you have done this, please. Leaving things after you have been there is a tale tell sign to other wizards in the area that another wizard is present so may go looking for them" Kevin agreed. There the conversations finished, and Kevin went to the bike shed where Vinny was still waiting for him.

"So, what went on there then"? Kevin shrugged his shoulders and answered, "just some clap trap about I am powerful, and I don't know it yet that's all." Kevin got his bike and both the boys set off home. When Kevin arrived, his mum was in the kitchen. "Oh, so you made it home then. Get washed and then tea will be on the table. I hope you manged to behave with Mr Perry during your detention, I will know as I will ask him tomorrow" Kevin sighed, yes mum, I was good, Godwill was there also, so had both present at the detention." "Godwill, it is Mr Godwill to you, young man, show respect to people Kevin. I do not know where you get this disrespect from, certainly not my side of the family, best you mind your words young man or this will get you into a lot more trouble in future times let me tell you" "Yes mum, sorry, Mr Godwill was also present and I will try to think before I speak in future" "mind you do my lad, now, get washed and then it will be tea" mum replied. Kevin went upstairs, washed then came down for tea. Paul arrived home and they all sat at the table having tea as the phone rang. "Hello" mum answered, it was nana on the phone, she was just phoning to ask that when the boys come down that they bring a drink with them as she did not have any at hers for them. When mum put the phone down, she told Paul to take the bottle of squash with them to drink at nans. Soon after tea the boys left to go to their Nans. On the way they were discussing things regarding spells and things that have happened in a short space of time since the whole thing of magic was known by both. When they got there, they went inside to greet Nan. Nan was sitting in a chair looking out the window so see them coming.

As both boys entered the bungalow, they greeted their nan. They went to the front room sat down and started to talk. "So how is grandad nan, is he getting better?" Nan nodded and then answered. "Well, he looks ok, think it was just a touch of the flue that knocked him off his feet. But you know your grandad, stubborn as usual. He did not want to admit that he was ill and just kept going until it got too much for him. That is when I stepped in and called the doctor who admitted him to the hospital. Have to say boys, it was a worry to start off but now." She gave a grin then continued. "It has been a bit of a rest for me since he has been in there. Always pottering about and doing things even though he did not need to." Both boys laughed when they saw nana grin. "Bet he is missing his fishing though whilst he is in there?" Paul said. Nana smiled. "Of course, he loves getting out on that bike and going down riverbanks. Me, personally, I just do not see the fascination in what you lot do. I mean, you sit there waiting for ages, for poor fish to eat something as it is hungry, and only to be hauled out of the water, and put in a net. Poor things, I wonder what goes through its mind when that happens?" The boys laughed at what he said. "Nan, fish do not have a mind of thoughts that go through their heads" kevin said. "And how do you know that my lad? How do you know they do not feel pain or hunger? Are they not animals or fish that need to eat to survive, how can you say they do not feel pain until you have been one? Have you ever been a fish kevin, no, of course not because you are a human not a fish"? Kevin looked at his brother with a confused look on his face and then shrugged his shoulders. "I just thought that what I said was what all anglers say that is all nan. I did not mean to get you upset." Nan smiled, upset, me, no, sometimes you young ones, talk of things you know nothing about but give your own opinion on them without doing any research into things before talking about them. I guess, that is what school should be there to teach people the knowledge, and stuff to understand different things." Both boys looked at nan and agreed with her.

211

After further chatting about things at school and friends, kevin asked nan about any books that grandad of nan had that could be of any use for the family tree assignment to help them further understand their tree lines. "Funny you should Say that, but grandad got a couple of books out and left on the side of his bookcase in the bedroom. I had a quick look but not sure that they will be of any use as they are not in English. Looks to be a funny sort of language or gobble gook to me." Paul went to get the books. When he walked through, he was looking at the top one. "Looks like Latin to me bro." Paul handed the other book to kevin to look at. As they flicked through pages, they noticed that pencil marks had been added on certain pages but could not really understand them. "As I said, gobble gook" nan said. Paul answered. "We have teachers at the school who read Latin so they could help translating them so could still be of use to them." "Well, take them and see what you can learn." Both the boys thanked their nan for the books. The rest of the evening they talked amongst each other about things including memories of both nan and grandad what they used to get up to when they were young. Soon, mum and dad turned up after they had been to see grandad. They came in and spent time with all together explaining that grandad was on the mend and would soon be home. Nan looked at the boys and gave a wink to them. "Oh well, there goes the peace and quiet again" they all laughed. As dad stood, he said. "Right boys, time for home and let nan get some rest, she must be tired after looking after you too" Nan immediately replied. "No Derek, the boys have been fine. We had a laugh, a catch up, I have to say they have been nothing than the perfect little gentlemen listening to an old lady talking. You should be proud of them."

Both Paul and kevin felt a warm glow through their bodies when nan said this as it is not usual for either to get compliments from the older generation. Both Paul and kevin said "thank you nan" at the same time and started to walk out the house. "What is that you both have there?" dad asked. Paul showed dad the book he had. "Nan and grandad have leant us these books to try help with our family tree assignment given to us by Godwill" Mum gave a cough then spoke to Paul, "You mean Mr Godwill." Paul lowered his head and then replied. "Sorry, Mr Godwill gave us." Dad looked at the books. "Hmm, seems like Latin to me." Paul asked, "you read Latin dad?" "No, just seen somethings in Latin that your grandad showed me when I was younger so just took an educated guess that is all" replied dad. Dad looked at mum and then they all took their leave from Nan's house to go home. Not a word was said in the car, but both boys see that dad looked at mum a few times on the journey but not a word said. When they got home it was time to wash and bed. The boys did as they usually do and went into their bedrooms.

A little while later, dad went to Kevin's room and sat on the end of his bed. "So, old Godwill is getting you to do the old family tree thing. Nothing changes at schools. I had to do this with my old teacher called Mr Biggerdyke." Kevin asked, "so, is there any use in doing it dad? I mean, should we not concentrate on where we are going and not where we have come from"? Dad smiled, "There is a lot of stuff you can learn from where your roots come from. Some of it can be good but some not so good. I remember one thing from all those years ago I looked through. One of our ancestors was a slave trader and animal exporter to make their money. Today this is not allowed, and is out lawed but sometimes, people had to do things then at that time to survive, just like we must work to earn money to feed and clothe us all. Decisions made then, could impact on the futures of all further on. What I would say my lad is, whatever you find out about our tree, do not take things too much to heart of what they did. Think of what we do now, that is all that matters." Kevin now with a puzzled look on his face spoke. "But dad, did you not say that what they had to do then could impact on later stuff?" Dad looked at kevin, smiled and then spoke. "Do you know Kevin, your mum thinks that you only cause trouble to get attention, me, personally, I think for your age, you are more advanced than some sixteen-year-olds. You think about what is said but blurt out anything that is a question without thinking about it, just like what you asked me there" Kevin lowered his head and then said. "Sorry dad, I cannot hold myself back when I have a question, is it wrong to do this when I look for information or to gain more knowledge?" Dad smiled back at kevin, "Not in the least, but be carefully how you word the question and the attitude you use in asking it. Sometimes an innocent question asked in a different manner could cause trouble. Just think on that my lad. Now, time for you to cuddle down. Sleep well kevin." Dad got up and walked out the door. Kevin heard his dad enter Paul's bedroom for a while and again left and went downstairs. Kevin then drifted off to sleep.

The next morning as Kevin got up, he noted that it was raining hard. Kevin came to sit at the table to have his breakfast when his brother walked in after his paper round. Paul was soaked through with water dripping from his coat and trousers all over the kitchen floor. "Get those wet clothes off now, Paul, or you will go down with a cold," mum bellowed at him. "And when you have done that, you can dry the floor where you were standing." Paul took off his coat and shoes and ran upstairs. Kevin gave a little smirk which mum noted. "And what is so funny, my lad?" Kevin looked away, saying, "nothing, mum." "There had better not be, and you have all this to come to, my lad. Should we laugh at you like you do your brother when you get wet? It is not nice to do so." Again, Kevin said sorry and continued to eat his breakfast. Soon it was time for the boys to leave to go to school. As they rode along the road, Kevin asked his brother why he did not slow time which would halt the rain, which meant he would not have got wet during his paper round. Paul immediately stopped his bike in front of Kevin's.

"Look, you cannot just stop and start time when you think you want to, remember, we try to keep magic away from normal life. Suppose I did what you said there, and I walk in dry as a bone, but the weather is chucking it down all morning. What do you think mum would say and start asking me how when it is pouring, and I am perfectly dry? She would think and give me a tough time asking if I was doing the paper round and where was I getting the money from. That is just a stupid suggestion you asked kevin. You need to really think about things before you speak or you could land both of us in serious trouble. Do you hear me little bro?" "Alright, God, I just asked a question. Why should we not use these things we can do that we have been given? They are useless unless we can use them to help us" kevin asked with a bad attitude. "There you go again" Paul answered, "did you not here what I just said, evidently not. Just shut that mouth of yours and do not speak until you can ask things for the right reasons in the right way. You will drop yourself in it trust me, I was once in your shoes and it was not good so take a little experience of someone who is older and now wiser, be quiet." Kevin let out a loud laugh. "You, wiser, more experienced, leave it out bro." Paul now incredibly angry with his brother cycled off fast leaving kevin by the side of the road.

Eventually, Kevin reached the school chase, rode down it, and parked his bike in the bike shed. His mate Vinny was there. "Wow, what is up with your brother, mate? He has a face like thunder and just ignored me when I said morning?" Kevin smiled, "he has just a bee in his bonnet with me, mate. Do not worry. He will lose that by the time we see him again." Vinny laughed. The two friends then went off to the registration. As the day went along, nothing of any importance seemed to be happening. Just another boring day at school. Then at lunchtime, as the bell went, as the two friends walked towards the lunch hall, Paul and his friends stood halfway down the corridor, blocking their path. As they got nearer, Paul stepped forward and grabbed Kevin by the arm, and pushed him toward the wall. "What the heck do you want, bro?" Paul standing looking at him with a bad expression on his face, pushed his face towards his brother.

"Look, you little squirt, I am angry with your whole attitude and think you are the king or something. You are not, ok? You're just a silly little boy who, at the moment, if you got in trouble, I would not bat my eyelid to help you. Your mouth spurts out rubbish, and you have a bad attitude to everything that is happening, and it needs to stop. Do you hear me, little bro? You need to show respect not just to the teachers but to me also. Next time you give me attitude, whether or not you have that other person in you, I will knock your block off. Is that clear?"

Kevin struggled free. "what the hell has gotten into you bro, and you can try to as you say knock my block off, but just remember, postromus or not, before this all happed I beat you in scraps before and I can do it again so do not go threatening me or it could get messy for you, now back off and take your mates with them before something happens to them also". Paul stared deeply into Kevin's eyes. Pauls mate roger pushed forward but Paul held his arm out and stopped him. "Leave him for now, let us hope that he gets a visit from the nasties and wants our help. Then, we just turn and walk away" Paul's mates all smiled and nodded. They all just turned and walked away. As they walked away, kevin shouted out to them. "Yer, keep walking, that is all your good for, come a fight that is what you would do also." Vinny tried to pull kevin away from what he was doing and asked." Are you mad kevin, you know what we are up against, and you have just alienated your brother and friends. What happens if we do need them at a troubled time to help, what we going to do then"? Vinny looked at kevin and just lowered his head before saying, perhaps your brother is right kevin, you changed since all this began, I really do not know also where I stand with you". Vinny walked on as kevin stood looking at his oldest mate walking away from him. He wanted to shout at Vinny also, but something made him stop before he did it. As he looked round, he saw rueth looking at him from the classroom entrance just a few metres in front of him.

Rueth slowly walked towards kevin and stood looking at him. "I heard the whole thing kevin, what was said to all in the conversations. Is Vinny right what he said, has all this that has been thrust at you changed you that much? I cannot say as I have only known you for a brief time and when you are with me your different, happy, is it a man thing that is going on?" Kevin looked at Rueth, "I do not know Rueth, I get so mad, so confused that it drives my temper to the limit, but with you, I do not feel that I feel calm, happy, perhaps it is a man thing with all the other guys, I just get so angry and it is impossible to stop being angry". Rueth looked at kevin again gazing into his eyes, "look, it is the same with all us girls, we go through the same things as you boys do, but very rarely will it get to fighting stages, we just avoid each other for a while and things blow over, I suggest that is what you do if you do not mind me saying?" Kevin lowered his head. "I guess I can do this although it will be hard. Can I spend time together with you for a while to help me get over this?" Rueth laughed. "You want to hang out with me, a girl, others will think we are boyfriend/girlfriend." Kevin looked at Rueth, "What is so bad with that? Do you have a boyfriend already?" Rueth now looked at kevin and then whispered in his ear "No, I do not have a boyfriend but could be looking for one." She then kissed him softly on the cheek and ran off towards the lunch hall with a big smile on her face.

Kevin slowly walked to the lunch hall, where the room was quite busy with people all eating. Kevin stood in line, waiting to get to the hatch where the food was. As he slowly moved along in the Que, he looked around for a place to sit. Paul and his friends were all at a table, just staring at him, so Kevin looked somewhere else. Vinny was with his friends again, looking straight at him. Kevin felt a little nervous about what had gone on before and looked away from all the areas. As he got to the serving hatch, there was his mum. "What is up Kevin, you been in trouble again? You have that sheepish look on your face. You had better tell me, my boy, as you know I will find out." Just then, mums' friend Lilly came to the hatch. "June, leave the boy alone. Can you not see there is something troubling him." Kevin's mum turned to Lilly and then said, "that is what bothers me, always in trouble. It seems the same as when Paul was his age, always trouble wherever he went, and now the same with this one." Lilly just beckoned Kevin on as she gave a smile. "Boys will be boys, June. It is in their hormones, I have the same with Gordon, but you must deal with it. There are only thirteen or fourteen, and they need some understanding. My Gordon has got better since his dad, and I sit down with him each night before tea and just talk. Talk about what has gone on that day, good and bad, and then offer advice on things but not throw things down their throats, like telling him he must be better. I guess you could call it psychotherapy." June just looked at Lilly and then spoke. "You are turning into a psychic mum now, Lilly? Seems that it is a bit of a soft way to deal with things if you ask me." Lilly spoke back, "but I am not asking you to do this. It is just a better way for the family can share without any bad feelings around. You might want to try it; it might work for you." June just put the food on Kevin's plate and ushered him away. Kevin moved to a space on a table and sat there alone, eating his lunch. Soon, Vinny and Rueth moved and sat down beside him. Quiet was in the air until Vinny spoke.

"Look, mate, there is a whole load of things going on. Sorry, I did not mean to sound you out like that. I was simply confused as to who or what you are becoming. I want my old mate Kevin back, the one where we have fun together. I know it is hard what has been put upon you, but I am sure we can all get through this by sticking together." Kevin looked at Vinny and eventually smiled. "I want that too Vinny. You're one of my best friends, and I do not want to lose you or fight against you." Vinny smiled. "You betcha, anyway. You would not want to be knocked off your feet again like the last time, would you?" Both boys started to laugh, and eventually, Rueth laughed too with a quiet comment of "Boys."

After lunch, the three got up to walk out of the room. However, Paul and his friends were still staring hard at Kevin. He started to feel angry and was going to walk over to his brother and question him on what he was looking at. Vinny grabbed his arm to stop him." leave it, Kev, it is not worth it. Just ignore them." Kevin looked at Vinny and just smiled and nodded, then walked out of the lunchroom and on their way outside, which was a nice sunny day.

Brotherly love and the forrest.

Outside all was good, the sound of birds, the sun shining, and happy children running around kicking a ball or playing other games. This seemed to calm Kevin down, and he started to relax. As the two boys and Rueth walked around, Rueth just excused herself from seeing her friends. As she left, Vinny spoke to Kevin. "Wow, mate, she is a looker. You're in there mate." Kevin gave Vinny a push as if to say do not be silly. Vinny, laughing, just said, "Well, if you're not bothered with her, perhaps I should ask her out. What do you think"? Kevin laughed, "If you want to, mate, but I guess we do have a certain connection." Both boys laughed and then started to join the other boys kicking a ball about. The bell went for the end of lunch, and all went inside to the next lessons. The afternoon was just like any other afternoon; quite boring, Kevin thought, but soon it was over. After registration, Kevin and Vinny made their way back to Godwill's class for detention. As Vinny opened the door, Godwill and Mr. Perry were in what the two friends could see was quite a heated discussion which stopped as they walked in. "Do not stop on our account," Vinny said. Godwill waved his wand and slowed time. "What is all this about you two? Your brother has deep concerns over your young wilks with your attitude towards your brother and friends. He states that your attitude, in his words, stinks. Tell me, why is this so?" Kevin just looked at Godwill and replied. "Don't know, sir, it is not as if his attitude towards me is any better. Maybe he is jealous of me, and what is going on is that he is not the top dog, I guess," Vinny smirked at Kevin's reply. Mr. Perry then butted in. "Think that is funny, Rose? I can tell you it is not. A house divided is a weak house. We cannot allow this as there is too much that can happen. Others sense it and will thrive on the weakness shown. We must be together and strong and not argue amongst ourselves. Now, we need to get this power struggle sorted. Both you, Winks, sit down, let us get things aired, and maybe we can move on to what is important. Do you not agree?" Godwill looked and Mr. Perry, "Well said, Markus." Both Paul and Kevin were staring at each other when Mr perry waved his wand. The two boys were transported into chairs near each other. Kevin now reached for his wand. Godwill looked at Kevin and shouted, "now, now, young Wilks, none of that." Kevin moved his hand away from his wand and sat there, waiting for something to be said.

"Well," Mr. Perry spoke, "who wants to go first?" Absolute silence. Neither wanted to speak, but eventually, Kevin did speak. "Better ask him, as he is the one with a bee in his bonnet." "There he goes again," Paul replied, "everything is about everyone else and never you. Is it Kevin? No thought or respect is given to anyone. It is all you, you, you." Kevin looked at his brother, "What does dad say? Respect has to be earned, not just given." "And what does that mean? Hey, respect has to be earned. Do you even know what that means and how to earn people's respect? I doubt if you even know what respect means, do you, little brother." Kevin, now starting to get a little angry with his brother, rose to move out of his chair before goodwill spoke. "Now Wilks, I seem to remember a few years ago we were having this same conversation, maybe not on respect but attitude, do you not remember?" Paul also rose, "I do, sir, but I have to say his attitude is double what I had." "Really," replied Godwill. "I think not, Wilks. It is all about growing up. I guess Mr. Perry and myself also went through such things during our early years. Things are done and said that at the time appear harmful, but on reflection, they are but just motions in time. We eventually grow up, and we look back and laugh at some we remain angry at. But you cannot stay angry all your life. That is a certain path you would take down the dark road. Brothers argue, fight, and even despise each other at early ages, but in time, that can and will pass. Brothers eventually re-bond, making them strong. We need this to happen sooner rather than later. Do you hear you two?"

The two boys listened to Godwill but still looked at each other with anger in their eyes. After a short while, Kevin spoke. "Look, if what you say is true, then maybe you had better speak to Davey, one of the dwarf brothers because as I see it, he still does not trust or get on with his brothers after all this time." "What did you say, young Wilks?" Godwill asked. Kevin told them of the meeting he had with the dwarf brothers, and it seemed to Kevin that Davey had a big chip on his shoulder. Paul laughed, "Seems like someone I know," looking at Kevin as he said it. Kevin again stared at his brother, but Godwill continued, "So, Sambia has found his brothers. We must meet with them as soon as possible. Did he say how to contact him, young wilks?" Kevin shrugged his shoulders and replied, "No sir" Mr. Perry then spoke, "Terrance, if Sambia did find the dwarf brothers, there is a good possibility that Matrees could also find them." Mr perry turned to Kevin, who was smirking at the name Terrance. Mr. Perry just called Godwill. Both Godwill and Mr. Perry stood looking at Kevin before going on. "Think Young wilks. Did he give any clues to the whereabouts of him or the brothers during the meeting? Think hard." Kevin thought for a moment but came up with nothing. Paul then spoke, "What about the cabin in the forest we visited?" Godwill stroked his beard, "I doubt it as Matrees, and maybe some of his followers would also be in that area, so he may have moved somewhere else." Kevin then spoke, "But, is it not Sambias duty given by Prostromus to guard the area where the stone is so? If that is so, I doubt if he would be far away from the cabin, would you not think?" Godwill smiled, "There is the logical thought process that we hate in you, Young Wilks, but it may just give us a starting place to look. Mr. Perry looked at Godwill. "So, we go to the cabin and search from there?" "exactly," replied Godwill. Kevin looked at his brother and spoke. "Look, Paul, I know I am just another annoying kid to you, and your just another annoying brother to me, but" Kevin paused, "sometimes, I cannot hold my temper or my thoughts. I am sorry this time for upsetting you, but." Godwill broke into Kevin's talk, "No buts, young wilks, I am sure your brother will accept your apology, won't you, Winks?" Paul looked at his brother and just said, "yes, for now." Godwill quickly interrupted the speech again, "Good, now, there is no time like the present, Markus, you take Winks and his friends with you, and I will take young Wilks and Rose with me. We enter the cabin if it is safe to do so, then if Sambia is not there, we split up into our teams. Markus, you go right away from the cabin, and we will go left. Be careful. We do not know what we may meet but try to be always on your guard and rely on each other." All agreed. With that, Godwill asked each to pair off to travel through the travelling spell to meet at the cabin. Kevin and Vinny linked arms, and then Kevin chanted Conceptium Troversum.

In a flash, Kevin and Vinny found themselves outside the cabin. Godwill appeared next, then Mr. Perry and Paul with his friends. Vinny started to cough and thought he would throw up. "Never easy that spell when you first do it," laughed Godwill. "I felt the same young Rose." Godwill entered the cabin and then returned very quickly. "No sign of Sambia, just as I thought." Kevin now looked at Godwill and asked. "What do you mean as you thought"? Mr. Perry then spoke, "You do not think Matrees has been here, Terrance, do you?" "Well, there seems to have been no struggle inside the cabin, so if there was anything, it would have to have happened out here, but everything thing looks the same as when I was last here, so probably not. Guess he may be out looking after the creatures in the forest." "Do we wait for Terrance or go look for him"? Asked Mr. Perry. "Well, we could wait, but it could be some time before he returns. Then again, we could go look for him and never find him in this forest. Also, there could be Matrees and his followers we could run into in the forest, another thing to consider." Kevin looked at Godwill and smiled, then turned away. "What, young Wilks?" Godwill asked. Kevin just stared at him and then spoke. "So, there is some logic in grown-ups then. For a minute, that is what I was going to say, but you beat me to it, sir." Everyone laughed for a brief time then Godwill spoke. "Enough now, so, what do you think we should do," he asked all. Paul and Roger started to wait for a while whilst Kevin, Vinny, and Mr. Perry all wanted to find Sambia. "Ok, the majority has spoken, and we will go look for Sambia," Godwill explained.

Although Paul and Roger were not too happy with this, they fell in to do what Godwill asked them to. "Right, Markus, you take Wilks and Cranbridge with you, and I will look after these two." Mr. Perry agreed. "Take your boys around to the right of the forest and look for him. Keep your eyes open, Markus. We do not know what else apart from Sambia lurks in the forest." Mr. Perry nodded in agreement. Slowly they walked towards the forest part. "Hang on," Kevin said, "for how long are we going to look for Sambia? This forest is huge. He could be anywhere, and how are we going to keep to a time limit as time is slowed"? Godwill stroked his beard. "Good question, young Wilks," he replied. "Markus, when the sun is at two o clocks in the sky, return your party to the cabin, and we will do the same." All agreed that this was a good plan, and both parties went their separate ways into the forest. Godwill moved quite quickly for an older man, and Kevin and Vinny were struggling to keep up with him at times. Sometimes Godwill had to turn and see the boys a distance behind him, so he waited until they caught up. "Keep up, you two, we need to move quickly through the forest, or time will run out before we have to go back." Kevin and Vinny agreed and set off once again. Kevin looked around and saw what he thought were birds sitting on tree branches in this area when Godwill stopped moving and turned to the young boys with his finger to his mouth as if to say quietly. Both boys see Godwill draw his wand, and they also do. All crouched down and stayed very still for a while.

Eventually, Godwill waved his wand forward to indicate for them to move on but quietly. Kevin and Vinny looked at each other and slowly moved. Suddenly, Godwill shouted, "Run." All three ran forward into the thicker part of the forest. They ran towards large Oak trees in front of them, and Godwill started to climb very quickly. Kevin and Vinny did the same, but Vinny dropped his wand whilst climbing. "Wait," he called. I dropped my wand. I need to get it." Vinny started to head back down the tree just as a creature ran to the tree. This creature was exceptionally large, with the body of a wolfe but with a long flowing main extending from both sides of the head. Also, a third eye was noted in the centre of the wolfe's head. Vinny climbed back up quickly. "What is it," Vinny shouted to Godwill. "A Scaret Wolfe, I think," Godwill replied nervously. "Another creature that is supposed to be extinct for many hundreds of years." Kevin looked down at the creature as it peered back at him. "Look away, young Wilks. From what I can remember of this creature, it uses the third eye to send the foe to sleep. When asleep, the wolfe kills the foe and carries it off to eat. Shut your eyes, now."

Kevin closed his eyes and heard the wolfe let out a loud howl. It paced around the trees the three were in for a long while and kept looking up at them. Eventually, with another loud howl, the Secrat left. Vinny was now eager to get to his wand starting to climb down the tree. "Wait, Rose. It is still not safe to go down yet. Those animals travel long distances very quickly, and even though I cannot see or hear them anymore, it does not mean has left the area." Vinny stayed where he was. Kevin then looked at Vinny then waved his wand, chanting Incantartum leverat down towards Vinny's wand, which slowly started to rise towards them. Suddenly the Scaret Wolfe sprang back towards the tree. Kevin raised Vinny's wand quickly and hovered it over to his friend. Godwill cast a spell out in the forest, which caused a large crashing noise. The Scaret Wolfe turned and ran off in the direction of the noise. "Right, down you go and keep moving forward, quickly do you hear?" All got down from the tree and moved off. They moved very quickly through bracken and trees.

Chapter 19

Matrees and the Cave Entrance

Further on into the forest, the party came to a clearing. Godwill stopped. "What is it the two boys asked nervously again and drew their wands quickly. Godwill motioned to lower their wands. "Nothing," he said as he sat on an old tree stump. "Just needed to take a quick breather, that's all." Kevin and Vinny still stood with their wands ready. "How did you know that thing was there?" Vinny asked Godwill. "Did you not smell anything different in the area we were travelling through?" He asked Vinny. "No, it all smells like trees and ferns to me," replied Vinny. Kevin agreed with Vinny also. "This is where you need to gain the knowledge and understanding. To consider the smallest changes in the physical or odour senses. Things in the magical world can look just the same in the non-magic world but can be extremely dangerous for either of the people in both worlds. The Scaret woolfe is more like part of the cat family I remember. It sprays the area with its odour to state that that area is his and if anything should move into that area to go or it will face a battle to the death." Kevin then said, "so it was marking its territory then." Godwill nodded. "Right, come on, time to move on, time waits for no man." Vinny laughed then said quietly "unless you can slow it or stop it like us wizards." Godwill, turned round quickly and stared at Vinny. "No Mr rose, time waits for no man or wizard, it keeps rolling on no matter what you can do with it, no move on." All walked further on until they came to a Brooke. They followed the Brooke as it wound its way through the forest until it brought them to a dead end where massive boulders stacked like a wall lay before them. Godwill walked towards the boulder wall and lay his hands on the front rock. He wiped dirt and debris off the rocky surface and see what he thought were indents into the rock. It appeared to be what he thought was a sign. Two lines close standing vertically, a small star in the middle of the two lines and arrows which had points at both ends pointing towards the centre lines. Godwill beckoned the boys towards him and pushed them behind him raising his wand very quickly and pointing it in front of him. "What is it, sir, not the woolfe again?" Asked kevin quietly, "shush" Godwill said quickly.

"Show yourself, I know you are there" Kevin and Vinny now raised their wands also. Kevin quietly chanted Ilustria Evapsum. Suddenly Matrees appeared with five of his followers behind him. Also, Sambia bound and tied at the rear of Matrees's party. "So, you found the hiding place of the stone also old man. Looks as if it could be a bit of a stand-off. I suggest you leave now or there could be dire consequences happen to you and the young boys" Matrees said with a big smile on his face. "Vinny shouted out, "You mean it will be bad for us but there again, it will be also very bad for you, and your gang of thugs, I promise you." "Quiet Rose" shouted Godwill, "There does not need to be anyone hurt here Matrees, I have others coming to this area and will be here anytime now so just leave us the dwarf and move off before this gets ugly." Matrees laughed, those three imbecilic idiots, I sent them on a wild journey. They are most probably lost in the forest, so, that leaves you three against us six, double your number of people, mine with more experience. Therefore, it is you that needs to move away, or things will get very messy." Just after Matrees finished speaking Vinny cast Transisomb at one of the five followers. The boy's wand flew out of his hand and away on the floor. Matrees now angry pointed his wand at viny and cast Excelious Painclos towards Vinny. Godwill stepped in front of Vinny and cast back Crevatious Septimium. This returned to Matrees knocking him off his feet. "Quickly, into the trees now move" Godwill shouted at the two young boys and ran into cover by trees. As Matrees got to his feet he cast towards the running trio Firentay, Consunium, Derivarm. Godwill waved his wand at the spell calling Evreko. This cancelled out the spell as they got to the trees. The five followers now moved towards Godwills party casting different spells at them but missing every spell they cast. Godwill crouching down looked at Vinny with a mad look on his face. "You just had to Rose didn't you, now we are in a major pickle, one that could be hard to get out of. You are a young fool boy." With that a blast of fire shot through the trees where they were. Kevin cast Disquelch Wateriade. The water dosed the fire and it disappeared quickly.

Godwill saw that three of the followers had got together in one area and were now shooting off spells towards them at the same time. He could not see where the other two had gone. As he cast back spells at the three which were behind boulders, he saw out of the corner of his eye one of the two missing from the five. Kevin saw him glance and cast in that direction Elivio Consensious. Suddenly, the trees the spell hit, wound around the follower's feet, dragging him up in the air and waving him around causing him to drop his wand to the floor. Kevin then cast Crevatis Shouderit. A magic shield surrounded the party now deflecting any spell cast at them. "That is great young Wilks but both of you still stay low as there is one spell that shield cannot stop, and you both know that." Godwill caught sight of the second follower moving back towards the other three. Godwill cast CIGRO, FREDSOM, BOMBARDO SEPRUM. A loud explosion noise was heard, where the boulders they were hiding behind now exploded throwing the three followers back and unconscious. Matrees shouted "Stop, or I will kill the dwarf and any of you to get what is needed" Godwill now could see Matrees was incredibly angry and holding his wand against Sambias head. Sambia shouted "I die for you Prostromus, I told him nothing where the stone is or how to get it."

Matrees stared at Sambia with hate in his eyes. "Why do you call Prostromus, that fool died hundreds of years ago, he is not here to save you dwarf. But, as you stated you die for him, then I will grant your wish for a dead old useless wizard who really did not grace the magical world of us true magical folk." As Matrees was saying this kevin felt a stir in his body and slowly the blue tinge appeared in his skin. Kevin/Prostromus stood up calling to Matrees. Godwill tried to push kevin back down but kevin/postromus was far too strong, and Godwill was thrown to the other side of the tree. "How dare you call me old and not of true magical folk, you, who are just a bad half of a once great powerful wizard, you, just a half of true magical folk. Why do you not dare to fight me then you little creature because that is all you are, nothing but a creature. No man, no wizard, just a piece of dirt that needs sweeping away." Matrees looked puzzled, all these words coming from a small 13-year-old boy that appeared that he had a blue tinge to the skin. Matrees now starting to smile answered. "Very good little boy, you sound quite grown up, so let us see what you do without your wand. Matrees disarmed kevin sending his wand away to the floor behind him. Kevin/Postromus now standing in the clearing with no wand did not move. Matrees then cast Excelious Painclos. AS the spell got to kevin, he waived his hand at the spell casting Crevatious Septimium. The spell shot back to Matrees and hurled him to the floor in pain and agony. Kevin now walked closer to Matrees with his hand held out in his direction. Every slight twist of the hand made the spell become stronger. Matrees was in pain calling out "this cannot be so." Kevin stood smiling as he got directly over Matrees. "You dirty little creature, as I said, I am Postromus, come back to get the stones so I can be whole again. If you or any others get in my way again, I will not be so nice next time. Do you hear me"? Matrees uttered "yes." "No, go, leave this place and if you ever hurt any of my friends, I will hunt you down and kill you. This is no threat but a promise. I should be disposing of you now, but you do not deserve to die here, just go." Kevin lowered his hand. Matrees grabbed his wand and chanted the travelling spell. He and the followers vanished.

Kevin now turned his attention to Godwill. Kevin had his wand pointing at Godwill. "If you ever, interrupt again, I will have no problem disposing off you either, do you understand me wizard"? Godwill stared at kevin. Let the boy speak Prostromus, it is he who will decide who lives or dies, not you." Kevin/Postromus now angry started to speak. How dare you speak to me in that manner. The boys are but a carrier for me until I can become whole again. I will use this body how I feel like it and nothing you can do will change that." Sambia spoke, "Mighty Postromus, these are good people, killing them will send you down the dark path where there is no return from. I am sure that this is not your true goal as it was all those hundreds of years ago. If you kill them, then you might as kill me also as I will no longer follow or help you, nor will my brothers. This quest needs to be completed by many, as different challenges lay ahead. Please sire, be the Postromus we once knew and loved and would die for yet again." Kevin/Postromus looked at Sambia, slowly lowered his wand and slowly started to let kevin back in. The blue tinge slowly disappeared from his skin. As it did, kevin now fell to the floor feeling exhausted. Vinny ran to kevin and slowly helped him up. As the party got together, Mr Perry, Paul and Roger turned up running through the trees with wands pointing forward. As they got to the clearing, they stopped. Terrance, are you ok"? Godwill nodded, "we are now Markus, but it was touch and go for a while I must say. The boys done good, better than I expected, and we had a visit from our local wizard Postromus also, so, I think in the end we outnumbered them I would say would you not also Winks, Rose"? Godwill winked at the two boys. Mr Perry explained that Matrees had tricked them into moving further away than closer to Godwill and his party and apologised for it. Godwill shook his hand as if to say it was all right but thank you anyway. The sun was now at the peak where Godwill had said to return to the cabin. Mr Perry walked over to the boulders in front and see the marks Godwill had found. "Is this the place where the stone is? Surely, we are so close, we cannot go now until we get it." Sambia spoke, "No, this is not the place, the marks are a map to the actual place the stone rests. I do not know what they mean only that a faint memory of placing those at an area to fool anyone that could be looking."

"So now what Terrance"? Godwill shouted, Get behind me, now." The party all assembled behind Godwill with wands pointing ahead in Sambia's direction. Godwill shouted to Sambia also to get behind him. Sambia stood looking at Godwill and asked, "Why"? Godwill pointed past Sambia and then said, "because of that." Sambia turned to see the Sacret Wolfe standing there looking at him. Sambia laughed, then turned to the wolfe and said, "hello Dion, I was looking for you" Kevin looked at Vinny then said "Dion." Sambiah was now stroking the scaret woolfe. "Yes. This is an old friend of mine that I bought here when I moved into the forest, just like Frank." Again, Kevin and Vinny looked at each other and gave a little smile. "But that thing chased us and wanted to kill us," said Godwill. "Kill you, what nonsense, maybe scare you or, at the worst, hurt you, so you left the area, but he would never kill anyone unless I commanded him to." Kevin stepped away from Godwill and slowly walked towards the woolfe. The woolfe moved forward very hesitantly and met Kevin, who stood still. "What are you doing, Kevin? That thing is going to do some serious harm to you. Get away from it."

Kevin knelt in front of the woolfe who stood looking at his every move. When kevin was on his knees, Dion lay down beside kevin. Kevin tentatively held out his hand and slowly stroked the woolfe on the head. Dion allowed the petting to continue until eventually kevin rose to his feet. Dion now looked at Sambia then kevin and slowly brushed up against both before turning a running off into the forest. "Looks like you made a friend there young wizard" Sambia said. "Once a scaret woolfes friend always a friend. If you get into any trouble it will appear to help its friend." Vinny a little confused by this comment asked Sambia, "So, you are friends with Dion, how come he did not help you then"? Sambiah lowered his head and answered. Dion was helping me when Matrees came a crossed us until he used the disappearance spell. Dion can only help what he sees, although he has an exceptional nose and can smell different smells it is hard to track, therefore he could not help to his fullest power and believe me, even Matrees feared him". Vinny then thought and said, "So Mr Godwill, are you a scaret woolfe in disguise"? then laughed. Godwill smiled back and answered, perhaps Rose, which is why you should do what I tell you to, or you might just feel the force of the woolfe too" and laughed also.

We need to head back to the cabin now and back to school also. Let us get Sambia back first then us back home also. We will come back to this spot and see where it leads from here possibly tomorrow." Vinny chimed in "I do not think so sir, tomorrow is Saturday, no school and as it is there is football training taking place in the morning so will have to be another week day" Godwill looked sternly at Vinny, "I guess so young Rose, but also we cannot let Matrees get back here and find the location of the stone can we, so I will re-visit over the weekend whilst he is still licking his wounds". With that, the party travelled back to the cabin and left Sambia at the cabin door. Then returned to the school classroom where they left earlier. Godwill re-started time to the usual running speed. With one last look at both kevin and Vinny just said. "You both did well today but Rose, I thought it was young wilks was the hot headed one not you, but this time it worked out. Just be more controlled, any time certain things can change rapidly, and dire consequences can happen. Do not do this again." Vinny said sorry and lowered his head. "As for you young Wilks, your spell casting and the spells cast were excellent, however, we still have work to do with that certain thing or person inside you. Until we can control him better this is going to be a challenging thing to do. At any time, he could choose to change paths like thought he was going to today. Good job Sambia was there, or it could have ended very much differently. Also, to stop and cast spells from the hand like you did, that is un-heard of from a young wizard your age, where did you learn how to do that"? Kevin just looked at Godwill and answered. "It was not me sir, it was prostromus, I cannot do anything like that, but when he takes control, it is like the power is immense, he has overcome me, and I become him using all the power he emits. I can see it happening but cannot do anything to take back control." Godwill put his hand on Kevin's shoulder and just said, "For now young winks but we will work on that." Godwill then opened the door, and all walked out, kevin, Vinny, Paul, and Roger. All walked to the bike shed without a word said. Vinny turned to kevin and just said, "see you later mate" kevin smiled and nodded. The boys biked home again with nothing said.

Merlin and the astral plain.

That evening was noticeably quiet with hardly any conversations held between the boys or their mother. Each only spoke when they thought there was a need to. Soon it was time for bed. The two boys kissed their mum on the cheek and went upstairs to their own rooms. Kevin went to close his curtains but stopped when he saw the owl on the windowsill. With a hard stare at the owl, kevin swiped the curtains a crossed to close out the outside world. He lay on his bed thinking about the events that took place this day. Suddenly, the apparition of Merlin appeared. Kevin ignored it. Merlin then spoke, "I feel anger, confusion and also frustration all in one young wizard, tell me, what are the basis of these troubles"? Kevin sat up quickly," leave me alone will you, you keep getting into my head and then causing me more confusion. All I want is to be left alone for once. I am tired and I have football training tomorrow morning so need to be at my best if I am to make the team this weekend." Merlin smiled "Oh, I see, Football and erm" Merlin stuttered "Girls, is it? That is more important than what is happening here at the present? Kevin snapped back, "you bet. That is the fact so get off my case and leave me alone." Merlin looked at kevin, "ok young wizard, but I will be waiting for you in the astral plain, and you will come later, and we can have a good chat then." "Not going to happen so just go." Merlin smiled once more and waved his hand as if to say goodbye as his apparition disappeared.

Kevin lay back down terribly angry with what just occurred but closed his eyes. Soon, he was in a deep sleep. Kevin suddenly awoke to find himself on the astral plain and Merlin was sitting on a tree trunk by a Brooke. Kevin just stood looking at Merlin with an angry look on his face. Merlin stood, "Well young wizard, I see you came just as I said you would" Merlin beckoned kevin to the other tree stump where he was. "Why did you bring me here when I said that I did not want to come"? Merlin laughed. "I did not bring you here, you come on your own thoughts. I just knew for sure with what I could feel inside your mind that you needed to talk, so, talk young wizard." Kevin moved to the other stump but before sitting down angrily said to Merlin. "My name is Kevin, not young wizard, stop calling me that will you"? Merlin just gazed at kevin and nodded. "So young" Merlin stopped there then continued, "kevin, tell me what all these thoughts are which is clouding your judgment". "Clouding my judgment" kevin asked, "my judgment is not cloudy as what you say" Merlin then replied. "So, what is causing you concern then? Is that better for you"? "That sounds better" kevin replied. "Well, I am not sure if Godwill has filled you in with what went on in Sherwood Forest this afternoon"? Merlin just said, "yes but go on." Kevin continued, "for some time now, it has been bothering me when my brov keeps reminding me that something happened when he was my age that really upset mum and dad, something to do with magic, can you tell me what that was"? Merlin rose from the tree stump and took a couple of paces away from it. "I cannot tell you Kevin, you must get that from your brother, only he can explain what happened then. All I can say is that it became quite messy and your brov as you call him nearly had what you would understand was a breakdown. It is he; you need to get that information about." Kevin stood also and moved towards Merlin. "Why can't you tell me? Was it really that bad"? he asked. Merlin just stood looking at kevin. "You must ask your brother kevin, I will not say anything else on this matter." "What else kevin troubles you"? Merlin asked. Kevin was feeling more frustrated in not getting an answer from Merlin just turned and said, "if that is how you are going to be then there is no further point discussing anything with you." Merlin stared at kevin, "there it is, just as Godwill said" Kevin snapped back "And what did old Godwill say then"?

Merlin snapped back at kevin, "Have some respect for your elders, what he says is that you have none, there is part of your problem young wizard" Kevin was ready to snap back when Merlin raised his finger as if to say stop. "What he also told me was that you are both good but dangerous." Kevin replied, "Dangerous, how, I have been doing what I have been asked to do, how is that dangerous"? Merlin again starred at Kevin before speaking.

"The spells you are using, the way that you bring them to the immediate actions for what they are needed, the power they are cast with, these are the things, wizards your age should not be able to do this, granted a very select few have mastered them and used them but I cannot work out how you can do this". Kevin laughed, "you what? Use the spells, cast the spells, is that not what teaches us in the books and in the special classroom sessions held"? Merlin was about to answer when kevin spoke again. "Also, what is this about a select few? How do you know then I am not one of this so called select few, are you for real"? Merlin now with a cross look on his face answered again. The select few are wizards, witches and w2orlocks who have a specific talent and powerful brain to be able to cast these spells, and at the recognised power to do harm or good. You keep saying you are only a boy of thirteen years of age, well, when I was your age, I was like you but if not a little better. Each year I got older, I learnt more powerful spells and the right power to cast them. Tell me, you used the shield around you all during the fight with Matrees and his followers did you not? How did you know the right power that would work for the shield to prevent any spell getting through, tell me that young wizard"? Kevin just stood looking at Merlin with a blank look on his face and eventually answered. "Blind look I guess, I did not even think about power needed, just conjured up the shield without thinking about it." "There, Dangerous as I said, that could have ended in a major catastrophe with you all being killed." Kevin snapped back, "how, only the killing spell can do that is that not right"? Merlin turned away. "All wizards, mythical creatures can die and not just through the killing spell, what if you get seriously hurt and bleeding, and there is no-one there to heal the wounds for you if you are unconscious. The killing spell kills there and then, but do not think because of the magic you possess, you cannot die through other spells." Kevin was now starting to get nervous and afraid with what he had just heard. "This is why wizards never usually travel on their own just in-case something like this happens. You must obey this principle to young wizard. One day, it could help save your life or someone else." Kevin stood quiet. "Trust me, you are not immortal."

Merlin returned to the tree stump and sat down. Kevin did the same still noticeably quiet. "What else do you want to ask"? Merlin said. Kevin now started to think. "I have been told that the wand I use is your wand." "Correct" answered Merlin. Why give it to me? I know in the past you have said because you see something in me but why not my brother, why not Godwill or Mr Perry? Are they not, better people to hand this to"? Asked Kevin. Merlin answered. "I am aware of your brother as he is of magic folk and used for a previous task before. I came to him one night to speak to him, but before I left, I heard a smaller boy crying in his bedroom. When I walked in there, you must have been about eight. I guess. I asked you what was wrong? You told me that you had broken one of your favourite toys and your mum would be angry with you. I asked to see the toy. You showed two halves of an old toy I believe it was one of your grandads toys years ago, and you should not have been playing with it. I waved my wand, fixed the toy. Got you top put it back where it came from. You stopped crying and you said thank you to me. I have to say, that was the last time I have heard you say those words since then. As you grew, you became more outspoken, used your mind to question specific things that were hard to show evidence to convince you. Using your mind helped your strength in your inner self, now, you have strength, mor than you know. This drew me to you to give you the wand and book and see if anything could materialise from it, and of course, it has. Now, magic is not a given thing, it is either in you or not, also magic folk do not have to come from pure bloods or magical folk. Every now and then, a magical person can come from a non-magic family. It is a bit like the odd one out born. Distinct colour, but still the same animal. Magic people are just the same. As with non-magic could have a magic baby, pure bloods could have children that are not magic folk. You do not hear of these babies surviving as the parents used to and to what I hear still kill them."

Kevin spoke, "That is horrid, why kill a baby, it is not their fault they were born that way," Merlin agreed. "I still feel there is something else that troubles you"? "Well, When I had the first encounter with Matrees, I broke his wand and the heart string of Postromus entered through my skin and into me" Merlin said, "Go on," "Well, firstly, why does he not appear when I get angry here on the astral plain? And, when I lost my wand, I was able to cast a spell without it, how"? Merlin stroked his beard before answering. "Well now, let us see. Firstly, when you sleep, I guess Postromus sleeps, but your conscience can wander but he is unaware of it that is why he has not appeared but does not mean to say that it may never happen. I know of Postromus and his anger, he can do powerful things, become havoc, I think you young people say. Secondly, it was not you, casting the spell by hand without your wand but Postromus. He was angry and showed his power in what he can do. When he is present, you are not I guess, am I right young wizard"? Kevin nodded, "I can see and hear everything, but he is too powerful to let me come back through until he decides it is right to do so." "Then we must work overtime to strengthen your mind so you can control him and not the other way round. When you can do this, you will be a formidable opponent to anyone including myself."

Kevin liked this comment and nodded again. "Now, you have your football tomorrow and Sunday, Godwill is going back to the forest to see if he can find out anything else from Sambiah and the rock with the markings on he found. By the way, the Scaret Woolfe, what made you go up to it? You did not know it was Sambiah's friend"? Kevin just shrugged his shoulders and said, "I love all animals, both non-magic and magic, I wish to know as many as I can, is that wrong"? Merlin smiled, "No" he said, "but, not all are good, and you just might meet the wrong one's as well as the good ones, you must be careful." Kevin then asked one last question. "So, in Matrees wand it had the heart string of Postromus," Merlin broke in, "his mother's wand, not his" Kevin nodded, "So, is there different wands out there? Are they made by the magic folk or are they made by specific wand makers? What does your wand have inside? Merlin turned away from kevin, "So many questions in one young wizard. Let me explain things to help you understand things better."

Merlin again stroked his beard then answered Kevin's question. "Well, where to start. So, wands are made from certain wood, could be oak, walnut, you are correct that there are special people that make wands, trained in the art of wand making. Apiece of wood on its own does nothing, however, a wand that has a certain central pin let us call it, can help channel the power from the wizard, warlock, and witch, to enhance that power coming from it. Many wands I have known of other magical folk, have centre pins, such as unicorn main strands, dragon heart strings, Sacrat Woolfe main and other things. These as I said help to channel the power of the one using it" Kevin looked at Merlin with great interest discussing this item. Merlin continued, "it is said by some wand makers that a wand chooses the master when purchased from these wand makers shops." Kevin then asked quite surprised, "the wand chooses the wizard, how does that work"? Merlin smiled, "if a wizard chose the wrong wand, then it would never truly trust that person and therefore not work for that wizard. I have known and seen for myself where the wrong wands have channelled less power coming from it and then left the wizard in peril during fights. Some so much so, that the wizard's wand even backfired, and the spell cast instead of going to the one in front and sent the wizards off his feet and hurt them. When growing up, there are certain things that the parents can see where the strength is in that young one, so, they ask the wand makers to either tailor the wand to those strengths or make one to that youngster. I seem to remember that your brother's wand has a griffin heart string in, Godwills has a dragon heart string, Markus has the brain string of the flying Mantrel but do not know where that come from as they have been extinct for hundreds of years unless it was passed down from one family member to another. But there is no certainty that that wand would work for that person like the previous owner. Magic as I said is not a given thing." Kevin then butted in. "So, you gave me your wand to use but had no idea it would work for or against me, I call that being either optimistic or stupid on your part. What if it backfired like you said and hurt me, what if it still might later? I have to say that I am less likely to use your wand now after you are telling me this."

Merlin again spoke. "You are correct young wizard, but it did work for you did it not? When I entrusted you with my wand, I had already looked deep in your mind and heart before even deciding to do this. As I said, you reminded me in part of myself when I was growing up." "In part" kevin replied, "yes, in part. No person is the same, some are born to do nasty things some to do good, however, there is what I call a light switch in us all. It only takes one or two trivial things to grow big that the switch can be turned by that person from good to bad. Sometimes it can be such things as for money, power, glory, or something else that the person so wants that bad." Kevin then asked part of his question again to Merlin, "So, as I asked before, when you were growing up what did your family have put in your wand"? Merlin got up from the tree trunk and paced towards the Brooke. "Nothing that you need to know right now but maybe later in your quest we will discuss this, but it is time for you to head back now. You have a busy weekend with that football of yours" Kevin still wanted to ask questions from Merlin, but Merlin turned to him and just waved his wand saying sleep. The next thing kevin knew he was now waking up on the Saturday morning at home in his bed.

Chapter 20

Football and Discussions

Kevin got up, washed, and ran downstairs to the waiting breakfast on the table. His brother had just returned from doing his paper round and joined the table. Paul was still not talking to kevin and had still quite an angry look on his face. Mum noticed this and asked, "you ok Paul, was there a problem on the paper round this morning? You do not look happy." Paul just answered, "little tired, that's all, been a heavy week at school this week but I am ok." "Good" mum said, "now, both at football practice soon, when your finished get back home as we are going to the hospital to fetch grandad home, is that not good news"? Both boys answered together, "great, I bet he will be glad to be home. I know how he hates hospitals," replied Paul, mum just laughed and nodded. "Well, if you are both good and grandad not too tired maybe we can take you round and see him tomorrow for a short time after your matches if you are both good" Both Paul and kevin looked at each other and nodded.

Time moved on fast, and the two boys were now leaving the house to go to the park for training. As they turned the first corner, Kevin moved his bike in front of his brothers and stopped making Paul brake hard and stop too. "Watch it squirt," Paul said angrily. Kevin now shouted, "Look, what is with you, bro? I want to try and apologise, but you are having none of it. You said I had a chip on my shoulder. It seems to me if I did, it has now gone over to yours. Why won't you listen?" Paul tried to move his bike away, but Kevin stopped him from doing this. "We need to talk, Paul. I need your help with all of this that is happening. Speak to me, please." Paul looked at Kevin, "you want my help; right from the first time I showed you what I could do, you ridiculed me. You have Merlin's wand and Merlin's book, and you think you are better than anyone else. Your attitude stinks, and that is not just from me but your mate Vinny, Roger, and Godwill. How do you expect me to be with you, you are concerned about yourself, and just you, now, get out of my way so at least I am not late for training."

Paul pushed passed kevin and his bike and rode off towards the park. Kevin tried to catch him up, but Paul was more physically fit than kevin and had no chance of catching him. Kevin turned into the park entrance and rode to the bike shed. He got his bag and ran off to the others in the area for his training. Russ Hoyt was waiting, looking at his watch, tapping it as kevin ran up. "Sorry Russ, I had a bit of bike problem on the way here" kevin said. After accepting his apology Russ broke the boys into teams to do specific training. Kevin went with Brian who was Russ's assistant. Today's training was about command of the goal area. Most of the time of the training the young keepers, were made to come out of the goal catch the ball after it was crossed and look for out balls to unmarked players. Kevin did this very well. It appeared to Brian that Kevin's mind was sharp, good at anticipating where the ball was going to be and to the look both ways to feed out the out feed to players. After an hour of this, Russ blew the whistle and brought all back into the huddle. He then set out two teams to play against each other for the remainder of the training. At the end, he picked the team to play at home against their archrivals spaldwick on Sunday morning. Kevin was in the team. He felt good to know that. Paul had also made his team to also play in the spaldwick in the afternoon. As they left the field Brian and Russ came over to kevin and asked him to also try out for the under thirteens, not as goalkeeper but as a defender. They both said that he had a cracking powerful right foot and can leap high to head the ball, a certain quality that the under fourteens lacked so far. Kevin smiled and just said "sure, why not, thanks." They all walked off the field and kevin went to his bike. When he got there, he noticed that Paul had already gone, and his bike now had both his tyres flat. Kevin started to get angry at the thought his brother had done this to him.

As Kevin reached the park gate, he noticed Rueth standing there. "Hi Rueth, fancy seeing you here." Rueth smiled, "Was just having a walk out to Susan's, she only lives around the corner from the park." Kevin just nodded. "So, what is wrong with your bike?" She asked. "Oh, Paul must have thought it funny to let my tyres down and take my pump off with him." Rueth just sighed, "Boys, so why not inflate them magically, or do not tell me you do not know that spell?" Kevin just said, "No, he wants to play games then I will let mum deal with him. When she is angry boy, she can rally give you an ear bashing." Both Rueth and kevin laughed. "Seems that brother of yours is a pain, never understands you, never sticks up for you, if you ask me, he is jealous of you. But it is not just your brother, Godwill and Perry are the same you know, there jealous also. Jealousy is not a pleasant thing; it can lead to things happening that could be of a dark nature. Once someone starts down that path, then there is no turning back. Are you sure your brother has not started on this path yet kevin"? She asked. "Well, now you mention it, with the pushing about in the corridor yesterday and before that he has been quite horrible on several occasions, I am not sure now you mention it." Rueth just looked at kevin. "Why do you say that about Godwill and Pery though? Are they not there to help me"?

Rueth smiled, "There only goal is to get someone to collect the stones for them to pass onto Merlin is it not? They do not care who or how they get them just that they succeed in getting them. Keep your eyes open and your mind sharp kevin, personally, I would not trust him or the others. Brotherly rivalry is one thing but this, it is certainly not brotherly rivalry." Kevin nodded. "Well, enjoy your walk home but I would still do what I said but guess you have your own way in dealing with this which is commendable" Rueth then just said bye and walked off. Kevin walked home with thoughts in his head what Rueth had said. When he turned into the back yard his father was there. "What two punctures kevin, you really need to be more careful where you ride my boy." Kevin just shook his head, "No dad, I think Paul let them down and he took my pump so I could not blow them up." "Why would he do that"? Asked dad, "You two been fighting again? I hope not, you know you will both be for it if she finds out. Anyway, does your friends at football not have a pump you could have borrowed and blown the tyres up"? Kevin shook his head, "No dad, I was a little later leaving as Russ and Brian were asking me to try out for the under fourteens in defence, they think I could do a good job there." "Well," dad said, "under fourteens, those boys will be harder than the ones you play against, well indeed, make sure you give it your all son. Only good things can come from that." Kevin nodded, "oh I will, playing for two teams, that will certainly get up Paul's nose" Dad looked at kevin, "now, stop that gloating, just say nothing is the best policy, one that I know is hard for you son, but you need to hold tight on that enthusiasm, or some would say conflict remarks. Now, let us get a pump and see if those tyres are good or need repairing." Dad got the pump and blew the tyres up. "No punctures, which is good. Say nothing to your brother kevin, I will have a little word with him when we are alone ok"? Kevin nodded to say ok. Kevin put his bike away and went inside.

The rest of the day and evening kevin was outside with his other friends. Paul came out to call him in for tea. Kevin went in and walked by his brother just making a grunting noise. That night when the two boys had gone to bed, Paul decided to creep into Kevin's room. Kevin heard the door open and see his brother standing there. "What do you want, get out" Paul just hushed him and started to talk quietly to him. "So, you told dad that I let your tyres down and stole your pump." "Well, you did, didn't you"? Paul said "No, why would I do that"? Kevin answered, "because your jealous of me, and hate me because I was the chosen one for this quest, not you. What happened when you were chosen for something earlier? Merlin told me that you were given something to do. As you are not willing to talk about it, then you must have failed." Paul slowed time then sat on Kevin's bed. "Yes, little brother, I was given a quest as you call it, but it did go horribly wrong, so much that two people died, and me also. Suppose it were not for Roger finding me, then I, too would not be here. He has been my best friend and savour throughout this whole thing." Kevin sat up in bed. "Hold on, Roger finding you, what sort of quest were you on and how did he find you where you were at the time"? Paul stood, "That is the problem, I cannot remember what I was doing or for who, it is though my memory was wiped, not completely, but most of it. I still remember things that come back in flashes but not enough to piece together. All I remember is Roger leaning over me when I was in big trouble, casting the healing spell and travelling me from somewhere to the safe house in the spinney. That's it. I do not know how I got to where I was, what happened to put me in that big trouble either. It is all blank." Kevin looked at his brother who had tears rolling down his cheeks. "Are you telling me a lie brother, I do not know if you are being truthful or just trying to pull a fast one. I met Rueth at the park gate, and she warned me against you, saying of your jealousy and arguments you pick on me, it is not right. She also asked if it looked as though you were starting down the dark path or not. Well, are you Paul"? kevin asked. Paul now wiping his tears away just started time again and said, "think what you want, all I want is that the same does not happen to you. Even though I wish bad things on you, that is only brotherly rivalry, but I do not mean them. Believe it or not, when this whole thing started, I just wanted you to throw everything back in the river, but, I just did not have the guts to say so. Anyway, think what you will of me, things will change between us during growing up, I just hope it is for the good and not bad." With that Paul walked out Kevin's bedroom and back to his. Kevin now very tired just closed his eyes and dropped off to sleep.

Sunday came, and the morning match with Spaldwick. Although the two teams had played a few weeks before, it was a different game. Kevin decided no magic this time, just his goalkeeping expertise would be on show this week. As the two teams lined up, Kevin looked to see if Paul had come to see his team play. His brother was nowhere to be seen. The game started, and heavy pressure was on his team from the opposition right from the start. Kevin had a great game by stopping several shots from the opposing side and setting up a quick break which led to his side scoring in the first half. Both Dedger and Nutty also scored in the second half, so the end score was 3-0 for Kevin's side. All shook hands as they left the pitch. Kevin got changed and rode home. When he got there, he saw his brother Paul sitting outside in the backyard. "We won, bro, 3-0, good game, pity you missed it, and it was only me, if you know what I mean, no funny stuff". Paul looked at his brother and just smiled. "So, soon it be time for your game. You want me to come and watch"? Paul shook his head, "No thanks. Been thinking most of the morning about what you said last night, and well, I think we need to follow our own paths from now on. Just do what you need to, and I will do the same. That way, we should be able to live quietly in the same house and stop arguments or anger. I am so sick of all the things happening, so just let us see where we can go to get things back to normal, shall we, little bro."

Paul got up and walked inside. Kevin really did not know what had just been said and how to take it but put his bike up and went inside. A little while later Paul set off to the park for his game, not a word said again between the two brothers as he left. Kevin sat down and watched some television until tea when Paul arrived home. "So, how did it go bro. Paul just said 1-0 to the opposition. Two of his team got sent off for bad tackles but he did not say who. The night fell and bedtime approached. Paul had been in a very quiet mood that night and mum noticed it too. "You pk Paul, you do not seem to be your usual self? It is not because your team lost was it"? Paul just said quietly, "could be, but I do not feel well, feel run down." Mum went over to him and felt his brow, "Hmm, little warm my boy, maybe coming down with a cold, right, take some tablets with lemon and honey drink and up to bed you go my lad. A good night sleep will sort that out." Paul agreed. He did as his mum said and then went to bed. Soon, it was also time for kevin to head upstairs also. He went into his bedroom and then to bed.

Morning came for the start of another week. The sun was shining as Kevin went downstairs for breakfast. His brother was already there after doing his paper round. The boys ate and then got ready and biked off to school. Paul was still a little quiet but did talk to Kevin regarding the football at the weekend. As they got to the school, Kevin saw Rueth just getting off the bus. He biked up beside her. "Hi Rueth, did you go to Susan's after all?" Rueth looked at him, "When, Kevin?" Kevin looked at Rueth, "Saturday. Remember I met you after training at the park?" Rueth looked at Kevin and then replied, "Saturday, no, I was not at the park. I was with mum and dad. We went to see grandma. Was there most of the day, in fact," Kevin just looked at Rueth with a questionable expression on his face. "But you were there, remember, I had both my bike tires flat that my brother let down. You said not to trust my brother, Godwill or Perry also" Rueth looked at Kevin now with also a questionable expression, then spoke. "It was not me, honest Kevin, and I would never say anything like that about Mr. Godwill or Mr. Perry. Not too sure about your brother, but I would not say anything about him either, as I do not really know him to get that judgment. Are you ok? You did not get a bump on the head at the weekend, did you, as you are acting a little strange?" Kevin did not know what to say. He thought Rueth was playing with him, but the expression on her face told him she was not. Kevin just said, "never mind, forget it, hope you have a good day, probably run into you later."

Kevin then cycled down the chase to the bike shed. Once there, he saw his friend Vinny waiting. After putting his bike into the shed, they left to go to Registration. Kevin told Vinny what had gone on at the weekend and the conversation he had just had with Rueth. Vinny stopped. "But if she said it was not her, who was it? Does she have a twin sister"? Vinny asked. "Not that I know of," Kevin replied. "But if it was really not her, then" Vinny stopped talking. "Then what mate? don't start a conversation and then just stop in the middle." Vinny carried on, "Do you think it could be Matrees"? Kevin looked hard at Vinny, "Matrees, really, he is a guy, not a girl." Vinny looked at Kevin, then shook his head. "Either Rueth is lying to you, or it was Matrees. Remember the spell for changing yourself" Kevin nodded and then replied. "Yes, but that is to change into an animal or something else, not a person, is it?" Vinny laughed, "Really, remember at the spinney when I changed into Godwill that time, and you knocked me off my feet? That really hurt." Kevin laughed, "oh yes, but you changed from boy to man. Can you change from man to girl or woman with that spell"? Vinny shrugged his shoulders, "Why not? I guess you just focus on what you want to change to, so if Rueth definitely was not there on Saturday, it only leaves me the option of it being him. You need to tell Godwill about this." Kevin agreed. The boys went to registration.

During the first school break, Kevin went off to Godwills class to talk to him. When he opened the door, no one was in there. He closed the door and started to run to the reception area and the staff office. "Walk,

Young Wilks," was heard behind him. Kevin stopped, turned around, and there stood Mr. Perry. "Sorry sir, but I need to speak to Godwill as soon as possible," Mr. Perry just replied, "Who, I think it should be Mr. Godwill. Show some respect, boy." Kevin said sorry and asked about where Mr. Godwill was. Mr. Perry said that Godwill had been away all weekend looking for the cave, and he was due back to school tomorrow. Mr. Perry ushered Kevin into a class near them when he saw some students walking down the corridor.

"So, what is so important, Wilks, that you need to talk to Mr. Godwill? Kevin began to tell Mr. Perry about what had happened on Saturday, then stopped talking. Mr. Perry stood listening, but when Kevin stopped, he asked, "Well, carry on" Kevin just replied, don't worry, sire, I will speak to Mr. Godwill tomorrow morning about it, but, whilst you are here, there is something I need to understand if you have time" Mr. Perry stared at Kevin, "Look, I am a busy man, I do not have time to play your games, Wilks, spit it out son". Kevin asked Mr. Perry about the magic order houses, what they were and who is in them, how were they put in them. Mr. Perry looked at Kevin and replied, "What, you don't know of these. I thought Godwill had discussed this earlier on" Kevin shook his head, "Also, sir, I am studying the family tree, my grandad gave me a book that could help with it, but he says it is in Latin. Do you know of anyone here that can understand it?" Mr. Perry looked at the book. "As it so happens, Wilks, I studied Latin at my university, so yes, I can understand it, but I neither have the time nor want to do this at present with what is going on." Kevin lowered his head, "Oh, ok, sir, it would be nice to know what is in there. I guess I will look for someone else to help with it." Mr. Perry held onto the book as Kevin went to take it from him. "Leave it with me, Wilks, I will look, but it will take time to go through it, do not keep pestering me for information on it, or I will give it back, and you can then try to find someone else. Good look in that matter, as there are not too many people who can read Latin anymore. Such an old language that slowly disappeared. Leave it with me." Kevin said thank you to Mr. Perry, "Look, have you got a few minutes after school?" Kevin nodded. "Meet me at the safe house, and I will discuss the houses, ok?" Again, Kevin nodded and agreed.

They left the classroom and walked their separate ways down the corridor. The day went through, as usual, class after class. Kevin went to the music room at lunchtime, hoping to see Rueth in there, but she was not. He waited for a short while and then left the music class. As he came out, he saw Roger. "Hi, roger," Kevin said, "Oh, it's you. What do you want"? "Look, I have spoken to Paul and think all is ok again for now," Roger looked at him. "I need to ask you something about my brother, please. Nothing nasty, I just want to know what happened when he was on his quest at my age." Roger turned away, "Ask your brother," he said sharply. "I did, but for some reason, he tells me that he cannot remember all that went on, only that you were there to help him out when things went very wrong. Please, I am not snooting into his past, but I just need to know why he is like he is towards me" Roger turned back towards Kevin with a saddened face. "So, it worked for him. Let sleeping dogs lie, Kevin. It is not a good story to tell you. In fact, it is very hard for anyone who was there to talk about it. Such a painful memory." Kevin looked at Roger and saw he was upset. "If it is that bad, do you not think I should know? Please, Roger, I need to know if something like that awaits me, please," Kevin asked again. Roger put his hand on Kevin's shoulder, "perhaps another time when you are older and can learn and understand it. Then I will probably discuss it with you". Kevin looked at him and again spoke, "later, when I am older, what if I do not get older? What if something this bad happens to me and this time, no one is there to help me like you were for my brother" Roger just stared back at Kevin. "Look, I am at basketball training tonight after school, but if you really want to know, meet me at the spinney tomorrow after school, and we will talk. But, if I do tell you, you are to say nothing to your brother or anyone else do you hear me"? Kevin agreed. Roger nodded, and off they went to the next class.

The school continued until the final bell. Registration was completed, and Kevin went to get his bike. "Hold up," Vinny shouted, "Where are you going in such a hurry"? Kevin explained that he was meeting Perry at the spinney to discuss the magic houses. "Cool, can I come too, please? It would be good to understand all this again." Kevin looked at Vinny, "Again, you know about it? Why did you not tell me about the houses"? Vinny just replied, "Thought you knew, always wondered what house you are in." Kevin just agreed for him to come with him. When they got to the spinney, Kevin cast the magic words that showed the entrance to the safe house. Kevin walked in, and the first thing he saw was Fergull. Fergull squawked at Kevin and slowly lowered his head. Kevin went over and slowly stroked the phoenix. Mr. Perry entered the room.

"Well now, young Rose also, what has Mr. Godwill be doing? I thought all knew the houses and who is in which," Vinny answered, "Yes sir, I do, but I did not really know how or why I was put into Wilfred's house, so it would be good for me to understand it better. Hope you do not mind, sir?" Mr. Perry smiled, "Ok, Rose, we will go through it all again to help you understand." Kevin looked at Vinny, "Wilfred house, and when were you going to tell me this"? Vinny smiled, "As I said, I was not sure what house you were in, and like the schoolhouses, there is a certain rivalry between the houses, is that not so, Mr. Perry?" Mr. Perry laughed, "Some rivalry Rose, but nothing nasty, I can assure you." Mr. Perry went over to the desk in the room and sat down with both Kevin and Vinny. He took out four books from his case and put them on the table. Each book had names on them. The house of Dromitus, the house of Wilfred, the house of Flammel, and the house of Petromore. Kevin looked at the books and the covers with intent. Mr. Perry then explained that each house has a set of expectations for witches and wizards to meet. Each person would be asked several questions to be asked and several things to do to show which house they would be suited for. Kevin asked, "These questions and things to do, who set them"? "Good question, young Wilks," replied Mr. Perry. "Each housemaster set the questions and tasks to judge the person on what their strengths and weakness were. Taking these all into consideration, a house would be assigned to that person taking the tasks to help and make them stronger in that field".

Kevin looked at the books and then spoke, "I know of Flammel. That would be Nicholas Flammel, the alchemist." "Correct young wilks." Kevin then asked, "What is an alchemist"? Vinny then interrupted. "An Alchemist is a person that can make things from nothing, really. They can turn rock into gold, glass into diamonds, and other stuff, too, am I right, sir?" Mr. Perry smiled, "nearly Rose, they did so much more. Also, they created spells for power, items that could be held to enhance power, but they were the people who worked out that if certain things are incorporated into wands, they also could enhance the power coming from the person down and through the wand which clearly gives an edge to whatever spell be cast. In the olden days, there were very few of these gifted people that walked this earth. They were sorted by many, both good and bad. Nicholas Flammel was probably one of a kind. He worked out the process of immortality. Through magic and all chemistry, he was able to transmit himself to be immortal by the ingestion of a fluid that had magical powers that enabled him to live forever. At the present time, his location is not known. He moves around a lot, avoiding being seen or known about." Kevin asked, "Why?" Mr. Perry then continued there are a lot of wizards that have been able through time to split their souls so they can survive through time. However, once all the splits are destroyed, then they are destroyed. Nichols flamel does not have this split, so many wizards have been seeking him, trying to get him to give them the formulae to be immortal without the soul split." Kevin then spoke again, so for this house, you must be able to use the right power and potions. Is that right to make something else more powerful to be used?" Mr. Perry nodded.

Kevin then laid his hand on the house of Wilfred. "So, this house is what?" Mr. Perry spoke. "The house of Wilfred. This was one of the most powerful Warlocks ever known. He was Merlin's friend back in the yonder years. This man was always good at heart and helped anyone in distress. He created many spells that worked in different ways with wizards and witches depending on the controls and power they could emit.

He was not only a great warlock but a very good teacher. He taught magic and non-magic folk in the same classes. He would have many tenders travelling around different lands collecting information on all sorts of things. They would give him the information so he could teach it. Payment for these things was money for non-magic tenders and spells for magic people. Everyone always looked forward to meeting such a great wise person. So, really, he was there to help the little and needy people. He worked his magic on trying to help make the world happier and a less painful place to be in." Kevin looked at Mr. Perry. "Seems like a nice guy then" "Indeed, young winks, many still have the followings of this great Worlock and will always uphold his requirements."

Kevin then moved to the next one. The house of Domotrus. Mr. Perry looked at Kevin with his hand over the book. "Hmm, the house of Dromotrus, well, Dromotrus was Merlin's mother. She was an incredible potions master and a somewhat good witch. She was taught by her mother and grandmother the are to potions. Her grandfather was a well-known wizard but not that powerful. Dromotrus grew up learning both powerful potions and even became a more powerful Witch at casting spells than her father. Potions she made through hard work and a lot of trials, and I must say knockbacks occurred before she got things right occurred. She developed hallucination potions, love potions, death potions, and happiness potions. In all, she was always good at heart but knew that there would be days when drastic measures may be needed, so that is why she also bought the death potion using Hemlock as the main ingredient. She lived until old age and eventually died through her old age, which I have to say was recorded as 237 years old". Kevin sat back in the chair, "Really, you really believe that I can accept that? People live until eighty to ninety. How did she live until that age? If you look at the Tudor times, you were classed as old when you got to forty and were most likely to die by the age of fifty. You are now telling me that first Nicholas Flammel is what over four hundred years old, was he not around in the thirteen hundred, then you say this woman lived two hundred and thirty-seven years. Come on, sir. You really believe this?" Mr. Perry looked sternly at Kevin. "Firstly, Young Wilks, Nicholas Flammel was born in 1355, it is documented, and he is still alive today. I met him when I was about your age. He was what you would say was a very old man, shuffling around to get to places, but, when called upon, had immense magic power he could draw upon to use. So yes, I do believe it, and so should you, as it is the truth whether you like it or not." "So, you never mentioned at what age did Wilfred die"? Mr. Perry replied, "Mr. Wilfred died young. He was a mere one hundred and eighty-seven years old. He was taken from this world by," Kevin butted in. "Crandloss" Mr. Perry looked surprised at Kevin. "Yes, but how did you know"? Kevin replied, "I saw it in a vision when this all started. It was clear as day," Mr. Perry stood up. "My my, so you have vision power along with spell casting. Well then, this would lead to the final house, which I would say you should be in. The house of Petromore. This witch was the witch of all time. She was powerful. She received insights into things before they happened or when they happened. Immensely powerful at casting spells. It was said she drew her power through the very earth she stood on. She defeated many dark wizards in duels and helped many mythical creatures when they were in peril."

Vinny butted in, "just like you, Kevin, animals do seem to like you, and have to say that Scarett Wolfe seemed to understand and like you when it knew you were not a threat." "Precisely, Rose," said Mr. Perry, but that now brings in a little problem." Kevin and Vinny looked at each other, and both said together. "What problem, sir?" Mr... Perry replied. "Well, you see, young Wilks, you have every trait of the house of Petromore, but your brother is in the house of Wilfred. Usually, there is a wizard ruling that the brother of or sister of a previous house member will enter that house also." Kevin looked at Mr. Perry, "But that is stupid. It is clear we all do not have the same things we can all do. As you mentioned, with all these houses, does that mean I will be going into House Wilfred instead of House Petromore?" Mr. Perry replied, "Well, you seem a good fit for house Petromore, but I do not have the right by myself to assign you to that house. It will have to be with the other three when we all decide which house to put you in." Kevin spoke, "the other three, who are they"? Mr. Perry then replied, Mr. Godwill, Mr. Peterson, Miss Barnard, and me." Kevin and Vinny looked at Mr. Perry, "Miss Barnard, who is she?" Mr. Perry replied, "Miss Barnard is from the UK Circle of magic. She is there not just to choose with the others which house you go in but to record what things you can do and work on a teaching strategy to enhance these skills." Vinny then spoke, "oh, that was the funny lady at my enrolment then I guess, wondered who she was as I do not remember her being a teacher at this school." "Correct, Mr. Rose, but do not let her hear you call her a funny lady. She is far from funny, let me tell you." Time had not been stopped and was moving on quickly. "So, there is the information regarding the houses, Mr. Rose. You already have the house assigned to you, young Wilks. I guess this will be completed in the near future, which means by next week in your language, ok? You will be notified. House selection will be held at the school after school finishes in Mr. Godwills class. Any other questions before we leave"? Kevin then piped up. "So, our headmaster Mr. Peterson is also what, a wizard, Worlock, What?" Mr. Perry just answered. He is a magical person. That is all you need to know at present, Wilks. Now off with you, home or your mum will give me another ear bashing young Wilks tomorrow why you were late home." Both Kevin and Vinny laughed. Kevin fed and petted Fergull before leaving. Mr. Perry cast the spell to hide the safe house, and all went their separate ways home.

Godwill and Rogers meetings

The next day when Kevin got to school, he made his way toward Godwills classroom. As he opened the door, he saw Godwill sitting at his desk talking to Mr. Perry. Kevin walked into the classroom. "Ever heard of knocking young Wilks?" Asked Godwill. "Sorry, sir, but I do need to talk to you. It is urgent, I think." Godwill looked at Mr. Perry, "You think, if you are not sure, then it cannot be urgent, so I suggest you leave and come back later, perhaps at lunchtime." Kevin turned around but was muttering. "Well, if you do not want to know about Matrees, then perhaps I will not come back at lunchtime." Kevin opened the door and started to walk through. "Wait," Shouted Godwill, "What is it then you wish to talk to me about regarding Matrees?" Kevin stood still, turned then walked back into the class. Kevin sat down near Godwill's table and told him what had occurred at the park, what Rueth had said when he asked her about the meeting. Mr. Perry laughed, "You call this urgent; the girl was probably lying to you. Tell me, when you asked her, did she have friends with her?" Kevin explained she had just got off the bus when he asked her, so she did not see any of her friends either near or with her." Why do you ask, sir?" Mr. Perry explained that perhaps this girl had arranged to meet a friend and went to someone else, so he did not want to upset any other person plans had been made with. Godwill just looked at Mr. Perry and signalled with his finger to be quiet. Kevin went on to explain his conversation with his friend Vinny regarding changing shape. He asked Godwill if this could be done from man to girl or woman. Godwill spoke, "I have not heard of this, but I guess if you can change into an animal or piece of furniture, then it may be possible to change into another person. Mr. Rose showed that did he not when he changed himself into me during your sparing session." Kevin nodded, "Yes, but I knew it was not you due to the height of the person he changed into and the way he spoke to me. Rueth or Matrees gave me nothing to say; it was not her. Same height, same way of speaking as she does to me." Godwill stared out of the window. "It seems that Matrees has perfected transformation. If this is so, then who could he change into, Markus, me, Mr. Peterson? It could be anyone. You said this happened on Saturday lunchtime. What time exactly do you know?" Kevin thought, well, training finished at eleven thirty. I got to my bike around twelve and saw that both my tires were flat. I started walking down the park pass and came upon Rueth around twelve-fifteen then, I guess." Godwill looked at Mr. Perry, "At the same time, I saw him disappear from the forest where I was looking for clues to where the stone lay." This girlfriend of yours, young Wilks, she absolutely denied it was not her?" Kevin nodded. "Hmm, Markus, you need to feed this out to your house and let the other masters of the houses know also. There needs to be some sort of checking when the magic folk meets to question who they are." Markus agreed. "Better tell the circle and the head, just so they are in the loop, I will do that," Godwill said.

"Wilks, this girl Rueth, what house is she in?" "Driomatus, she said, but I had no idea we had magic houses. I met with Mr. Perry last night at the safe house, and he explained all about the houses and when I will be getting placed in a house." Godwill laughed, "Placing in a house always makes me laugh, but it really is no laughing matter. I was the same back when this was happening to me. Anyway, thank you for bringing this to our attention. It was good that you did." Kevin got off his seat and started to walk to the door. "Did you find anything in the forest, sir, this weekend?" Godwill replied as if I would not find something. Matrees and some of his followers were in the areas I was which left me to believe they knew of the area where the stone lays but not the actual place. I had to hide several times to avoid being seen or heard, but I think I found the place where the stone was but could not get closer enough to verify it due to his followers near the area I wanted to check. I plan to go back there tonight and try to look some more. Hopefully, I will be able to confirm if it is the resting place of the stone. I will call Sambia to assist and see if he can remember anything about the area. Will let you all know tomorrow at a meeting after school in the Safehouse, so make sure you are there, young Wilks. Kevin nodded and then walked out of the classroom.

As he started to walk, he saw Vinny in front of him. "What was such an important, mate, that you could not wait for me in the bike shed as we always do"? Kevin started to explain he had to talk to Godwill about what took place at the weekend. "Oh, that, what? You had to tell him your team beat Spaldwick?" Kevin now took a step back and drew his wand. Vinny backed off. "What are you doing? Someone will see you." Kevin then asked abruptly, "What is the name of the Pheonix I have in the den"? Vinny looked at Kevin and replied, "What, the phoenix's name? I can't remember that. I remember you calling it something like furgus or something." Kevin now pointed his wand harder at Vinny. "That is not his name, Kevin cast optimus revealed. Nothing happened, just Vinny still in front of him. "What the heck are you doing?" Kevin lowered his wand slightly, "ok, so either you are my friend Vinny, or you have perfected a way to prevent your true identity Matrees." "Matrees, you think I am a no-good old wizard that is bad? Well, thanks for that, mate, I don't think." Prove to me you are Vinny. "Vinny, now a little angry, snapped back. "You really are blinded by all this. You question everyone and anything you see. No wonder your brother is angry with you too. You really know how to upset people. Tell me, Kevin, is it a gift, or does it come naturally?" Kevin snapped back, "Answer my question. "Vinny looked at Kevin, "What do you want me to say? We have been friends for years. We went to junior school together. Your dad and mine are great friends. You have a great right foot for football. The first bike you got was a red racer which you repeatedly beat me in races; your cat's name is Tommy. What else do you want me to say?" Kevin lowered his wand and apologised to his friend. He explained what Godwill had said and what was going to be put forward to the circle and the houses. Vinny sighed, "So you thought that I could have been Matrees in disguise, in this school where he knows there are many witches and wizards present? If you were him, would you come into what they say is the lion's den"? Kevin smiled and replied, who knows what he is capable of, but we have to be more on our toes, that is for sure". Vinny replied. "Are you sure Rueth told you the truth and was lying when she said it was not her"? Kevin looked at his friend and answered. "Why would she? She is one of us, is she not. She is in the Driomatus house, so I have no reason to believe she would be anyone different than who she is." Vinny held his head, "Stop, you're giving me a headache just listening and thinking about what you are saying." Kevin smiled again, "Come on mate, better get off to the classes, or we will be in trouble again." Just then the bell rang for registration.

The day went as usual as any other day with Kevin's classes which were English literature, geography, and Mathematics. Lunch, Chemistry followed by French lessons and finally for the day Biology. Nothing out of the ordinary happened apart from the earlier meeting with Godwill. The end-of-school bell rang, and registration was completed. Kevin and Vinny headed to the bike shed. When the two boys got to the shed, Roger was waiting. "So, you still want to do this, Kevin?" Vinny looked, "Do what?" he asked. Roger looked at Vinny and spoke, "nothing to do with you, Rose, so be on your bike off home" Vinny just stood and answered, "Hang on a minute, Cranbridge, if you are going to have an issue with Kevin, then it is with me too" "Commendable Rose, but no, it is nothing like this, just some information Kevin has asked for regarding his family tree, that's all." Kevin looked at Vinny, "It is alright. It's as he said. He is helping me with trying to find things out of my family tree." Vinny looked hard at Cranbridge, "Well, that is ok then." Kevin thanked his friend for his backup. Vinny took his bike and cycled off, shouting back. "See you tomorrow, Kev" Kevin waved towards him to say bye. Roger then said, "ok, meet me at the safe house in five minutes" Kevin nodded. Both set off towards the spinney. Once there, Roger waved his wand, and the safe house appeared. They entered the room. Fergus sat on his perch and cooed. Kevin walked over to him, saying, "Well, my friend, twice in two days we have been together" Kevin stroked Fergus on the head. Roger beckoned Kevin to the table as the two boys sat down. Roger began to talk." Firstly, Kevin, I need your vow that what we talk about stays here and is told to no one else and especially not your brother, is that clear." Kevin nodded and wanted to say something, but Roger shushed him. "No interruptions during what I tell you. If you have anything to say, then you can ask after I have told you the whole thing. Is that also clear?" Kevin sat back and nodded.

"When we came to this school, both your brother and I were well, like you and Rose. True friends grew up together and did mainly the same sort of things together. We entered the magic realm at around the same age as you are. Paul was a good student, learned spells and potions very quickly, a lot quicker than me, I might add. After a while, Mr. Peterson called us into his classroom and assigned Paul a quest. He asked me to assist as I was his closest friend, so I agreed. Looking back now, I wish we had not" Kevin sat forward and tried to speak. Roger put his finger to his lips. Kevin sank back in the chair. Roger continued. "The quest was to find and get back the Pharynx. A powerful book with spells written in the hidden text but also a two-way script to learn from. We were told that two young dark wizards had stolen the book from one of our masters and needed to get it back. During our training, Paul took everything hard as he wanted to be the best wizard in time, but his attention span was very low. If he could not do the spells by the third attempt, he got very mad. We duelled a lot, and most of the time, I beat him, which made him even angry. His anger grew over time, so much so that it changed his whole outlook on life. His attitude towards all, your mum, dad, you, me, teachers, and others, was so bad that it was causing a lot of concern for us all. The amount of power he used when the spells were cast, they were very potent, let us say. Stronger than Peterson could cast. Some of us had the feeling that this was the start of something very bad as if he was starting to thread down the dark path. Time went on, and things did not change but seemed to get even worse. Eventually, Peterson thought we were ready. We set off on the quest. However, he had voiced his opinion to the circle that he was not sure your brother was in the right mind for this quest. We tracked the two wizards with the book, trying to sell it in a non-magic town called Wibeck. After trying to get the book back through conversation, the two started to fight, casting spells at us. Peterson shrouded us in shields to protect us as we cast spells back to try and disarm them. This all took place in a non-magic area where non-magic folk was also. They clearly see the fighting using thunder, fire, water, and other spells. It was a right mess. If Mr. Robertson was with us, the shield held strong. However, he saw one of the two wizards runaway who had the book on him. Robertson ran off after the boy, and I followed. The shield broke, leaving Paul fighting this other wizard boy. Spell after spell was cast from Paul's wand toward the other wizard, eventually overwhelming the wizard. As Paul walked toward the wizard as he was kneeling on the ground, the wizard still had his wand and cast the Excelious Painclos spell. Paul sank to the ground in extreme pain, another cast from the dark wizard boy shot from his wand, wounding your brother, causing a wound that bled now. The dark wizard boy was now laughing at Paul. With one last cast, your brother cast Lithio killentious. The killing spell. The dark wizard tumbled to the ground, his wand flew out of his hands, and he lay there dead, eyes open. Paul was in a bad way when Peterson and I returned. Many non-magic people had seen it all. Some of the crowd now moved towards Paul, lying bleeding on the floor, and the dead boy. We arrived just in time and travelled both Paul and the dead wizard away from the area. We travelled to a deserted roadside away from the town. There I healed your brother's wounds whilst Peterson dug a grave and put the dead wizard in. Then Peterson used a memory charm to remove most of the memories of what had happened. Paul, never fully recovered from this quest, has very little memory of it, that is what he told you, and that is the truth. Peterson made me vow not to say a word of this to anyone, and I have kept this until now. The reason I have agreed to tell you the truth about this matter is that you are now on the same path as your brother was those years ago. Bad attitude, little respect for anyone, argumentative. These are all the things that your brother had. Now you are on a bigger quest than what he was. None of us want to kill, but in some circumstances, it may be necessary for you to survive. It is how you deal with that. Peterson could not take the chance that your brother would start to enjoy this feeling and enter down the dark path. Your brother was then suspended from the circle and house of Wilfred, his mind wiped of magic, and he became what you call a normal boy until that fateful day when Merlin chose you for the quest. Somehow, it opened all his memories of magic, and he started to read and do magic again. He was eventually accepted back into the circle and house of Wilfred only after your acceptance had been taken up of the quest. He still has a very stubborn streak in him, and some of the heads are still not sure of the right mindset he has. That is why

I have been assigned to, well, let us call it, babysit your brother and inform the heads of any changes I think are significant. So, in the end, you can see with what he has in his memory he does not want anything serious happening to you. His attitude towards you is quite hostile to warn you away from things that could happen. It is not because he hates you or even despises you, but it is his way of dealing with things now. You must never tell him of any of this. If he learns any of this, it may be the start of you sending him down the dark path, and we do not want that do we, Kevin?" Kevin just looked at Roger and said nothing, just a look of amazement on his face. Eventually, Kevin did speak.

"So, let me get this right, Mr. Peterson is the headmaster of our school and part of the circle of magic"? Roger nodded, then spoke. "Correct. At this time, he was head of chemistry and physics, not the headmaster then." Kevin continued. "Paul's attitude changed because he what? Had thoughts that he was better than anyone else? Even the teachers"? Again, Roger replied, "Correct." Kevin now stood up and started to walk around the room. "And you and Peterson left my brother with an older, more experienced dark wizard to fight him so you could get the Pharynx back. A boy of my age, limited magic experience, alone." Roger looked at Kevin. "Then, when he used the killing spell as a last resort, as you said we may need to, is dealt with being kicked out of the magic circle and memory wiped, well, most of it. Tell me, why only some of it and not all? Why leave just small parts of memory, and when he was allowed back, why has he not been coached in what happened?" Roger started to talk. "The reason for leaving some part of the memory is to embed itself in someone to know that something dreadful happened and could happen again. To what that was is the part to remove. The feeling is still there deep in the mind of that person and hopes that they will be wary of the use of the killing spell as a normal spell." Kevin then continued, "I know you said that if he kept the thoughts, it could turn him towards the dark side. What is the dark side? Do we all not have good and bad in us? It only takes that one thing to flip the switch. How do you stop that? My answer is you cannot. Perhaps Peterson was right to have concerns over my brother, and in saying that, I guess they may also have concerns over me as things are panning out just the same way as you said, Roger. Do you have concerns about me"?

Roger looked away and said, "Truthfully, Kevin, yes, not because you are Paul's brother, but in the attitude you have. Change that, and the concerns would go away. Not just from me but Godwill, Perry, and others". Kevin heard what Roger had to say and just stood there, taking in all that was said. He then thanked Roger for telling him what had happened to his brother. As they left the room, Kevin stroked Fergulls head again. The phoenix looked hard at Kevin in his eyes for a short time, then rubbed his head against Kevin's. Roger sees this and then feels a little better about having told Kevin of Paul's quest. He also, when seeing Fergus rubbing heads, knew that Kevin had a lot of good inside of him, or the phoenix would see this and would not have made this gesture. Both left the safe house and went home.

Chapter 21

House Assignment

Whilst at home, Kevin pondered what Roger had told him regarding his brother. A lot of thoughts were going through his head all that night. So much his mum noticed that Kevin was not very talkative, which he usually was. "You ok, Kevin? You are not your chatty self this evening." Kevin looked at his mum. "I'm ok, just a bit tired. Been a busy day in all." "Well, as long as you are not going down with anything, you just have to deal with the other stuff," replied his mum. Kevin nodded. Dad then walked in. "glad that shift is over, been manic. A few of the residents were going nuts today. Had to restrain a couple and tranquilise them." Mum just looked at Kevin and then back to dad. "Just been saying to Kevin, you just got to handle things day by day. It is not that those things happen every day." Now, dad and Kevin looked at each other, and both just said, "right." Dad winked at Kevin and then went to get washed up before tea.

After tea, Kevin went to his room to do some homework. As he completed it, he lay back on his bed, thinking of different things. Some that he smiled at when he thought of them, some that were lingering in his mind that he could not find answers to. Paul ran upstairs to his room and then came out and opened Kevin's door. Kevin sat up. "Paul closed the door and spoke to Kevin. "Mum said you were not your usual self tonight and asked if we had a falling out. I told her no. So, do you need to talk to someone? I know we have not been that close over the last few weeks. Both of us have had reasons for this, though, but I am not going to go into that now. Talk to me, tell me what is causing you problems. Who knows, I may be able to help." Kevin looked at his brother. He wanted to talk about what Roger had told him but knew that it would cause more problems than not talking to him about it. "I'm ok, honestly. Just a few things that I am trying to work out, that is all." "Like what, bro?" Kevin thought quickly, then replied. "When we were in the forest, the Matrees meeting, he was going to kill Sambiah. I had no panic, and no worries, when I stood up and walked toward him. When he disarmed me, I was still able to cast spells by hand and not with the use of the wand. How is that possible, Paul? Can you do that?" Paul looked at his brother. "No, I cannot do that, nor can I project a strong shield as you did. I guess, really, you cannot either, but with Postromus inside you, it gives you more strength and power than your project. He was a very experienced wizard, and he also did not need a wand to cast spells. I did a bit of research into him after this thing happened to you when you broke Matrees wand. I went through a lot of books searching for items on him. Not that many were available, but what I did find was that when he finally died, his powers started to go. He eventually died when the dark wizards attacked him, and he was in the form of a dragon. Although powerful, he did not have the strength nor power to turn himself back quickly enough and escape. There is no record of birth, only the death date. However, in one journal I read, it said he was two hundred and thirty-seven years old."

Kevin butted in sarcastically. "Really, two hundred and thirty-seven, are these people aliens? As last time I heard, the average human will live between fifty and one hundred if they are lucky. Back in the olden times also, men were lucky to live longer than forty. It shows that in history books." Paul shook his head. "I know none of this makes sense, but I believe it to be true. Things were very much different back in those days. Magic, although thought to be bad, was all over the country, no, the world. I have seen many wizards, warlocks, and witches that are in many different countries. And the mythical creatures, well, some of them make the ones we have seen like pussy cats." Kevin stared at his brother, "Where did you find these journals"? Kevin asked. Paul smiled, "They are right in front of you, at the safe house. Did you not pick any of those books out and sit and read through any one of them"? Kevin shook his head, "not sure we are allowed to, so leave them alone," he replied. "I would suggest then that you go there and check a few things out in those books. Most are in English, but there are some in French, Spanish, German, and some other languages that I cannot read, but it is not Latin; I know that for sure. Some of the books you cannot take from the shelves. For some reason, they are held in place by a spell, I guess, so only the person or people that put them there can go to them." "Why would they do that?" Kevin replied, "Do not know. There must be a reason for it, but you never asked or bothered any of the house masters to why, and you should not either. Just go read some of the other books. You might also find some useful spells, and potions magic in some of them also may be good for you." Kevin thought hard and agreed. Paul was about to get up and leave when Kevin asked. "So, what happens at these house assignments then"?

Paul looked at his brother, "Arr, I knew there was something else on your mind. Do not worry, little bro. There is nothing dangerous that happens. A bunch of the masters and someone from the Circle decides which house you would be suited to. They ask you questions, get you to do a few things, and then decide on the house. That's it. Anyway, you have no problems as you will be enrolled in the Wifred house, the one I am in. All brothers and sisters tend to go in the same house as the brother or sister." Kevin nodded and then spoke. "I know that, but when speaking to Mr. Perry, he explained what each house stood for and the skills needed to enter the house. He also said what did you do, then, because it is not just me, is it?" Kevin pointed to his heart, "Mr. Perry thought that I might be put into the house of Petromore. Because of the visions, the strength of spell casting, he thought that this would be a good fit." Paul looked at his brother, "maybe, but not a usual thing to happen. Anyway, go with the flow, and we will see what house they put you in. Whichever house they choose for you, go to the safe house. There are a few books with descriptions of the four main houses and how they come about. This may also help you, bro." Kevin nodded. "Thanks, Bro, this talk has helped a lot. Pity we cannot be like this all the time." Paul stood up and laughed. "What, and break the brotherly rivalry, it is never going to happen, but just on occasions, some sort of rivalry can become brotherly love too. But do not tell anyone I said that, or you're for it." Paul laughed as he said the last words. Kevin laughed also and promised. Paul went back to his room, and Kevin cuddled down and fell asleep.

Kevin had slept well, the first time in a while. He raced downstairs after getting washed and sat eating his breakfast as his brother walked in. Kevin looked at Paul and smiled. "What is with the smile? Something funny happened"? Paul asked. Kevin just shook his head, "No, bro, just feel that today is going to be a good day." Mum chimed in. "Well, that will be a change. So, no mischief planned for today or disrespecting your teachers for no reason" she asked. Kevin laughed. "Of course not, mum. Really, I do not plan to upset anyone honestly, I guess things change, and that can cause me to get upset. Unfortunately, I say it as it is. I do not do these things on purpose. They just seem to happen." "Right, not on purpose," replied his mum. "You just have the knack for saying something or being in the wrong place at the wrong time every time Kevin. Your great great grandad was exactly like you. I remember nan telling us about all the little things he used to do to try to play one teacher off another. Always get someone else in trouble rather than admitting he was the cause of that trouble. I do not want you to be like he was!" Kevin rose from the table. "Do not worry. I won't. I am sure it will grow out of me sooner rather than later." Mum starred at Kevin. "Sooner would be better than later, my lad." Paul laughed. "And you are not Mr perfect either, Paul, but you have grown up better since Kevin's age. Those years were a nightmare, and I am not going through them again. Do you both hear me"? Both boys looked at each other, then nodded. Both boys then went on their way to school. As they rode to school, both brothers talked about different things that made them laugh. Kevin really enjoyed the ride with his brother on this day. Usually, they were never together, they usually rode one in front of the other with hardly anything said, but today, all was different.

Kevin rode down to the bike shed where his friend Vinny was waiting. "Morning, Vinny," Kevin said. Vinny nodded. They left the bike shed and went off to registration. After registration, the bell went for the first lesson. Both boys headed towards the physics class, where Mr. Peterson was standing at the door where Mr. Geldof usually stood. "Morning, sir," the boys said. Mr. Peterson smiled and let them through. The class went as any other physics class. No unusual things happened until they left the class. Mr. Robertson called Kevin back in. Vinny walked away. "So, today is the housing assignment, young Wilks. I guess there are many questions you have and had in the time you have been given the gift. I understand from Mr. Godwill that he has been mentoring you in your studies. I also guess that you were a little confused to hear of me in the Circle. I am sure through time all will be explained and come clearer for you. Now, you have heard about the four houses Mr. Perry, what the usual process is, but, I have to say, you are no usual case, are you, young Wilks?" Kevin looked at Mr. Peterson. "Unusual case, sir, in what way?" Mr Peterson replied, "Come come now, young Wilks, with all that has happened, and with him also present inside you, giving you different things and powers of a boy your age, well, that is unusual." Kevin just nodded. "We will be meeting at the safe house after school with also Miss Barnard from the Circle also present to talk to you, get you to do a few things outside before we assign which house and master to assign you to help continue your growth and learning. Do not be late, as Miss Barnard is a very busy woman and hates being kept waiting, you hear?" Kevin nodded. "Well, off you go, have a nice day, and try to keep out of trouble, young Wilks," Kevin promised he would do his best. Kevin ran out of the classroom to try to find his friend Vinny. "Walk, Wilks," bellowed Mr. Peterson. Kevin slowed to a walk and headed towards his friend, waiting.

The school day passed quickly, and now it was the end of the day. Registration was taken, and Kevin and Vinny walked to the bike shed. Paul and Roger stood waiting. "Well, today is the day," his brother said. "You finally get your house you will be in and working for. As I said, it should be Wilfred house as I am already there, so do not be disappointed little bro if that is what they tell you. We have a great bunch of people in the house. All of that can help you in different ways. I had and still have my friends who are still teaching me new things all the time. The thing is, you must impress the team masters and the circle that you are responsible, want to learn, and are dependable in hard times. So, please, do not go letting that mouth loose saying stupid things. Listen to their questions and think before you answer. Do not just blurt out the first thing in that head of yours, and you will walk through this easily." Roger then spoke. "There is a lot going on and around now, do not let that cloud your answers or judgment, Kevin. I knew when I spoke to you that you appear older and wiser than your age states. Ok, you have an elder in you also, but when we spoke, it was you doing the talking, not Postromus. This must also be when you are being assigned. Keep him out of this or." Roger stopped talking. "Or what?" Kevin asked. Paul replied, "well, it is not a given that everyone is accepted. Some have been turned away and turned down to the dark side. We certainly do not want that to happen. Those wizards and witches are a nuisance. They have no masters to learn from, so their magic is weak. However, there are the occasional ones who hook up with other dark wizards and learn together and can become quite strong." Kevin glanced toward Roger, who just nodded. Kevin knew it was

241

a signal to stay quiet. "Anyway, good luck, bro, and I hope to see you in Wilfred's house tonight when you get home. I will tell mum you got footy practice at school in the gym tonight. You did have gym today, did you not, and have your kit?" Kevin nodded. "Good, at least mum cannot find us out for telling a lie if she asks me." Paul was looking at Kevin and waiting for him to bite and start arguing back, but nothing. Paul was quite surprised by this and smiled. With that, Vinny wished Kevin good luck and left to go home. Kevin cycled to the Spinney and the safe house.

Once at the safe house, Kevin entered the room. Mr. Peterson, Godwill, and Mr. Perry were there, along with a tall skinny woman who was Miss Barnard. "Good, right on time young Wilks Godwill said. Well, let us take a seat and start the assignment, shall we?" After sitting, the teachers and miss Barnard took out folders and opened them. Mr. Peterson led the questions. He asked questions about family, school, and what his thoughts were when the gift of magic came to him. Kevin answered them honestly and to the best of his thought process. Mr. Pery then continued the questioning on things of the magic learning he had received or researched on. Again, Kevin did well when answering Mr. Perry's thoughts. Next, it was Godwill. He asked just one question. "So young Wilks, since the gift was given, you have constantly moaned to me that you never wanted it, that you are but a boy of a young age. Since then, you have learned spells from us and books, and even, I must say, perfected them further than anyone your age should be able to do. What are your thoughts now, at this very time?" Kevin went quiet for a while, thinking how to answer this, and eventually spoke. "Sir, when this all came about, I was just a normal boy with a normal life. Getting into trouble is just one of those things that boys my age does. It is all about growing up and learning from mistakes and hardships to prevent them from occurring during the latter part of our lives. Things that occur, good or bad, usually just, well, happen. It is what we do, then, to try to oust them right when a wrong has occurred. As I said, I am but twelve coming twelve soon so still growing in body and mind. We all must learn to get better always, not just once. So, to answer your question, I am both happy and incredibly nervous for this gift. Happy that I can do things my other friends cannot, but nervous about making a mistake that can cause terrible things to happen. As a teacher and head of one of the houses, I guess, as you are here, do you not still have those feelings too?" Godwill looked at Kevin, smiled, and then replied. "Good answer young Wilks, and to answer your question, yes, even though I am a very experienced wizard, sometimes, nerves do rise, especially like the last meeting we had with Matrees. When you stood up and walked out, I wanted to try and stop you but froze solid at that point. It can happen to anyone even you young Wilks, so, train that mind of yours and become strong inside as well as outside." Then it was miss Barnards turn. All teachers and she had been making notes on the pads in front of them.

"Tell me, young man, for what I have heard, you have a certain wizard attached inside of you," Kevin answered, "Yes, mam, Postromus." She held her hand up and in front to stop Kevin from talking. "He has, or had, so I have been told, the immense power that he can use you to emit from. He is as I hear quite strong and can come through ahead of your thoughts and controls when angry. What are you doing to try to control this addition to you, and how far are you in that"? Godwill looked sternly at Ms. Barnard. "Let me assure you, Ms. Barnard, we are all working on helping young Wilks to be able to do this step by step. It is not something he will be able to turn on and turn off at a flick of a switch, you know." Ms. Barnard answered. "Mr. Godwill, we at the circle need to know that whatever has happened will not cause the magic world to become exposed to the non-magic folk. Imagine if that happened, there would be mass hysteria from the non-magic folk, and then they would start to try to hunt us down and try to irradicate us just like they did in the olden times. Do you want that to happen just because of one boy doing something wrong? It was not so many years ago when we faced a grave issue when it was his brother that caused us a big problem at the circle." Kevin stood up quickly. "If, mam, you are talking about my brother who fought a dark wizard and used the killing spell to prevent him from being killed, and then I have to say that he did it to be able to live, not to become a problem." Kevin looked at Godwill. "Yes, I know of this and what happened to remove certain parts of his memory so he cannot recall it. If you are asking if I would use this spell, then the answer is yes. If it were the last thing I could do before I was killed, would you not do if you were in a really bad situation either, Ms. Barnard?" Mr. Peterson stood up and told Kevin to be quiet. "I do not see what this all is to assign a house to the young wizard Ms. Barnard. That was not just a question but a hard statement to try and make young Wilks angry, so you could bring out Prostromus. Then, what would you do if he were angry and started casting spells at us, harming us, and if things got a bad ending in someone's death? What are you doing? What are you searching for?"

Ms. Barnard then stood up. "I see from the circle heads that you all protect this boy. All of you are making him soft, not hard. He needs to learn and learn quickly. Two meetings with Matrees, the first saved by his brother and friend, the second, he made Postromus come through and cast spells from his hand, not his wand. Even very experienced wizards, witches, and warlocks cannot do that. Dark wizards can get through learnings from the olden wizard Crandloss. We at the circle need to be sure he is not a descendant from Crandloss and, therefore, a sheep in wolf's clothing. I think you would call it Petterson. I have to say I am not impressed by this gathering and the questions and answer time. We will now go outside and see what you have then boy, shall we?" Kevin stepped back from his chair, "Yer, let's do it," Kevin replied sarcastically.

Outside there were things lying around on the ground and two men standing on either side of where the items were. "Wait a minute," Godwill shouted. "What is all this? It is supposed to be a fact-finding exercise to see which house the boy goes into, not a trial." Kevin looked at Godwill, "Trial, for what?" He asked. Ms. Barnard then stepped forward. "It is not a trial, just a walkthrough of what you can do with each item you see and how you would use them to your best advantage under pressure from other wizards." Mr. Perry then spoke harshly. "It is not a done thing in the circle for this to happen until the young wizard moves forward after their whole teachings and can be responsible for others, namely perfect. Davey, you must stop this now." Mr. Peterson now walked towards Miss Barnard. "I will not allow this as a master of the circle and want to know who at the circle has allowed you to do this"? Miss Barnard pulled a piece of paper out of her folder and handed it to Mr. Peterson. It was authorized by the minister of the circle that she could conduct this testing of one Kevin Wilks printed on the paper. Mr. Peterson handed Godwill the order to read.

"I really would like to know what the fascination in this boy is to the circle. Is it one of them he could become something very special or perhaps a threat" he asked Miss Barnard. Miss Barnard just smiled and answered, "At this minute Mr. Godwill, the minister is unsure, and I have been given the task to collect this information and report back to him. It is he who will make that decision, not me. I am but the factfinder, so shall we start, gentlemen." Godwill was not happy and unsure of what could unfold. He took Kevin to one side. "This is none of our doings, young Wilks, but once the minister has decreed this order, it has to be completed. In front of you are different things. Each item has different uses. Some you will be aware of, some not. How you use these items will show the power you have using them. The two men on either side are there to ensure if you use an item wrong, they will battle you to prevent you from using them to hurt anyone hear." Kevin looked at Godwill and replied, "hurting anyone here? Why would I do that." Godwill replied quietly, "I have reason to believe that Miss Barnard has put a spell on certain items which will cause you anxiety, frustration, and even possibly memory block to force through Postromus from you. She believes he is uncontrollable and would cause you, in his anger, to do something very bad. If it does, then the two men will try to either control or hurt you. I have to say this is one of the hardest trials I have seen or known about. Whatever happens, you must keep calm and open-minded and control the beast inside of you to prevent him from coming through. I am sure that if things start to go bad that all of us will cut this trial against the minister's wish and stop it before it gets out of hand."

Kevin looked at Godwill and whispered to him. "This is why I did not want this gift; I do not want to harm anyone, but if I should need to do so, then that is what will be." Godwill stepped back and looked at Kevin with a worried look on his face. Kevin was then beckoned to the start of the trial on the field. In front of him was a red orb, then further down the field was a rusty sword, a little further was a closed box on a stool, then what appeared to be a stool with a purple potion in a flask seated on the stool. Finally, at the end of the field was a griffon chained up and appeared to be very angry. Kevin looked nervously at Godwill, asking him what the creature was at the far end. Godwill answered. "It is a Griffon, the body of a lion, head, and wings of an eagle. Griffons are magical creatures and very powerful in the body. They do not like to be cornered, chained, or restricted from roaming. Be careful young Wilks. This one seems to be very angry and could be the greatest threat. Your task is to calm the beast and then release it. If you succeed, the Griffon will just fly off, but if you do not do this, then it will attack and try and will probably do you great harm. Should we as masters feel things are going wrong, we will step in to help but then will anger miss Barnard and could become very ugly. I have seen what you can do. Believe in yourself, young wizard. Think hard about all the tests before actually taking them on".

Kevin looked at Godwill and smiled. "Since when have I thought about things, sir? I do what comes to me at that time." "This is different Young Wilks; these tests are there to see what your strengths and weaknesses are. Doing something half-handed shows weakness. Just think before you do," replied Godwill. At the start of the trial, the two men moved to the side of the field areas where Kevin was due to set off. Kevin now slowly walked towards the red orb. As he got closer, the orb shone brighter, so bright that it was becoming painful for Kevin to look at it. He kept moving forward, now totally blinded by the light coming from it. He reached for the orb, picked it up, and then reached for his wand. As he did, the two men had their wands pointing at Kevin in anticipation that something could happen. Kevin felt around the orb and found a top screw unit. Before unscrewing the top of the orb, he stopped, then, with his wand, he cast Optimus Reveal. The bright light started to dim until he noticed inside the orb was a creature that appeared to be very sad. The light had all but gone, and Kevin looked at the sad creature inside. He was not sure if this was a good or bad creature but took a gamble and opened the top. The creature eased itself out of the orb and onto the ground. Once on the ground, the creature began to grow. Kevin took a step back. The creature was a Doriatriel. Kevin had neither heard of nor seen any photos or sketches of this creature. Kevin looked at the creature and then spoke to it. "Why so sad? You look just like my cat when it is waiting for food." As soon as he said that, Doriatriel turned into a black cat sitting there cleaning its paws. Kevin lowered his wand and slowly bent down to pet the cat. The Doriatriel looked up at him as his had closed towards the head of the creature. Kevin stopped moving, stared at the creature then slowly continued to move his hand forward. The creature raised its head towards his hand, and again Kevin stopped moving it. The Doriatriel slowly sniffed at Kevin's hand, stared at Kevin, then bowed its head. Kevin then slowly placed his hand on the creature's head, saying quietly, "Do not be afraid. I mean you no harm," Kevin heard a small voice inside his head replying. "I know, young wizard, thank you." Kevin then stood up and looked at Godwill. Godwill smiled and nodded toward Kevin. On seeing this, the three teachers sighed a sigh of relief and started to discuss the Doriatriel and what it could do. Miss Barnard was not so impressed as the teachers.

Kevin now walked towards the sword. As he started to get close, he began to feel an uneasiness within himself. As he stood over the sword, he noticed that there was still red staining on the blade of the sword. Kevin looked over towards the two men, now casting a shield spell around them. Kevin knew that this was not good. As he knelt to pick the sword up, he felt the presence of Postromus trying to get through. Kevin spoke. "What is it? Why are you angry? Please, calm yourself." Postromus burst through and stood Kevin up straight with the sword in his hand. "Where are you who tried to kill me? I will deal with you this time so that you never bother me again Kevin shouted. On hearing this, the teachers and Miss Barnard took cover behind some large rocks that were to the side of them. The two men were now pointing their wands directly at Kevin.

Kevin held the sword high and began to cast Firentay, Consunium, then stopped before he cast the last word of the spell. Kevin fought back and shouted, "No, you will not harm anyone here. These people are mainly good. They just want to see with you inside me how far you will push me before you take full control of me. That is never going to happen, Postromus, never you hear." Then the voice of Postromus came through again. "You dare to challenge and control me, me, a true blood wizard of the ages. You, as I said before, are nothing to me, no use or good to anyone, let alone me." Kevin again fought back. "We have discussed this before. Without me, you are gone, so really, no use to you is not the right thing to say, is it? You, the almighty Postromus, are all but gone apart from one small thread of you. I, on the other hand, am whole. I can walk in the sunshine, eat, drink, laugh, and cry. What can you do? Nothing unless it is through me. Therefore, you need me more than I need you, as we talked about before. You promised that you would be good and controlled until we can find a way to get you out of me and into a body after retrieving the stone. Now, I can live with you inside me, but can you live with being inside me"? Postromus was still angry and still holding the sword high in the air. Kevin continued, "So what is with the sword, sire?" Postromus answered. "This young wizard is the sword that slew me used by that dark wizard Crandloss and his army of dark creatures and wizards. Why would you have this sword? Have you killed Crandloss? Is this to show me you used the same sword to slay him that he slayed me with"? Kevin again answered. No, Sire, I have been given a magic trial to complete, and this sword was one of the items that were put here to get you out and angry and see how I can control you to prevent you from doing any harm. I have to say this is not going well. The two men on either side point their wands at me, ready to cast spells at me. You hold the sword aloft and are ready to cast spells at them. My teachers and the lady from the magic circle are all over behind the rocks in case you should try to harm them. I have to say, Sire, this has not gone well, but you could help by calming yourself and letting me deal with the trial by myself unless I need your help. Then I can call for you." Postromus listened but was not happy with what Kevin had discussed. He only agreed to it if they could talk after the trial had finished, and then he would calm down and leave Kevin to it. Kevin agreed. Postromus lowered the sword and plunged it into the floor. Then, calmed himself and let Kevin take back control. Kevin sank to his knees. Godwill slowly moved out from behind the rocks. "I hope you are pleased with this; you were sure he would take over the boy and cause harm or death. You put all in peril except yourself. Have you no pity for anyone else"? Miss Barnard looked at Godwill and smiled, then spoke. "Pity is for fools and the weak, I am neither, so no Godwill, I have no pity in me." She then turned and shouted to Kevin, "Get up, boy, continue."

Kevin looked round towards Miss Bernard. Kevin got to his feet and walked onto the closed box. There were two catches on the right-hand side of the box. He unclipped one; then the box started to make a movement. Kevin put his hand on the top of the box and closed his eyes. As he did, he could feel and saw a quick glimpse of a snake inside the box. Kevin drew his wand and undone the last latch when the top burst open, and out sprang a coiled snake. The snake glared at Kevin as it was about to strike. Kevin cast Firentium Sparksum. A fire bolt shot from his wand and engulfed the snake burning it to the ground and dead. Kevin turned towards the group. "Is this what you want from me, is it? Am I being bad enough for the circle because this really sucks? I have had it. No more trial, I am done" Kevin started to walk back towards the start when the two men then cast Transisomb. Kevin's wand shot out of his hand. Kevin stood still and looked at Godwill. "What are you doing, Miss Barnard? Tell your men to back off, or they could be in big trouble." Miss Barnard stared at Godwill. "Do not tell me, housemaster, what I can or cannot do. No one, and I repeat, no one, will cancel the trial, only I can do that, and it is not happening. Now, boy, back to the trial now," she bellowed at Kevin. Kevin waved his hand, and the wand returned to him. The two men on either side looked at each other in disbelief, as this had never been done before. Next, Kevin waved first his wand, then his left hand. The two men's wands and Ms. Barnard's wand came out of her bag and pointed in mid-air directly at them. They moved back the wand moved with them. "How dare you take another wizard and witch's wand; this is intolerable. What are you doing, boy? How are you doing, this boy" Ms. Barnard asked. As Kevin walked towards her, he just replied, Magic, mam, magic. The trial is over. Now it is time for you to leave, please, but before you do go, the purple liquid, what was it." Before Miss Barnard could answer, Peterson spoke, "Antidote, I am guessing, as she planned for the snake to bite you and see what you would do to get to it" "And the Griffon, what has that done so bad it has to be chained up"? This time Miss Barnard answered. "A chained Griffon is an angry Griffon, another possibility to prove you have Postromus under control, but I guess we will never know as you refuse to finish the trial." Kevin stood looking at her whilst smiling. "Oh, by the way, did I pass, mam? Because I think I did. I controlled both Postromus and myself, you made me kill an animal, and your two henchmen were ready to do me harm but prevented that from occurring. So, in my book, it sounds like a pass to me. Do you not agree, Mr. Godwill, Peterson, and Perry?" All three agreed.

Mr. Peterson "Well then, after all that excitement, we should go and recess inside. As they turned to walk away, Kevin stood staring at the unhappy Griffon. "What about the Griffon, sir? We cannot just leave it there like that," Peterson agreed, "I will set it free. You lot go inside. I will join you later." Kevin looked at Me, Peterson, and politely said, "can I do it, sir, please?" Godwill looked at Petterson and smiled. Godwill spoke, "It is said that Griffons are loyal mythical creatures. A good deed deserves another in their eyes. Perhaps we should let young Wilks do this, master." Petterson thought for a moment, then replied. "OK, but A griffon maybe not be that loyal. We do not know what the circle did to catch it or from where. Be very careful, boy, do not get too close. Just shoot the chain holdings to free it and allow it to fly off. Do nothing else, ok?" Kevin agreed and walked back to the Griffon. As Kevin approached the Griffon, it started snarling and squawking at him and moving about. Kevin held his hand in front of him and closed his eyes. The chains fell from the Griffon. The Griffon now prowled around Kevin. Peterson, Godwill, and Perry started to run over toward him with wands at the ready. Kevin projected a shield in front of them which stopped them in their tracks. The Griffon sees this happening whilst also snarling toward the oncoming wizards. Kevin then spoke to the Griffon. "Do not worry about them. They just want to make sure you do me no harm. They cannot get any further. Now, you are free, go and live free, and run/fly wherever you want. Be careful of anyone that comes near you. Keep safe, now, go."

The Griffon moved closer toward Kevin and smelt the hand he had in front of him. The Griffon then lowered his head, and Kevin slowly put his hand on the Griffon's head. The Griffon stopped snarling and gave a little moan. It then raised its head, stared at Kevin in his eyes which were now open, then flew off. Kevin lowered the shield. When Godwill got closer, he started to shout at Kevin, asking what he thought he was doing, as those animals were very aggressive and could have turned on him. Kevin looked at Godwill, then answered. "Let us just say we came to a joint decision that neither would be forceful with the other and left it at that." Petterson then asked, "So what was the thing with the hand in front of you towards the beast? Why did you do that"? Kevin smiled. "I see Sambiah do it with Dion, so guessed it would work with the Griffon." "Guessed," shouted Mr. Perry, "You guessed it would work with the Griffon. How? Sambiah and Dion have been together since he was a puppy. They know each other instinctively. How on earth did you think that you would be able to get away with that? It is not sound judgment if you ask me for someone who is very logical." Kevin smiled again, "Let us just call it Magic, shall we." Mr. Perry looked hard at Kevin, then turned towards Godwill and Peterson. All of them gave a laugh and went inside the safe house.

As the masters all sat, they decided that with what had gone on, then, there was no better house for Kevin to join the Petromore house. The master was Mr. Petterson. "Congratulations, young Wilks. I am sure you will make a great student and a great wizard in years to come. There will be a lot of hard work, magic meetings with House members, and other get-togethers. You can meet your fellow house members starting tomorrow in the six-year block after school. But for now, I think we have had enough excitement for one evening. Time to go home." Mr. Petterson thanked Godwill and Perry for their support during the assignment. As they did this, Kevin walked over to Furgus, who cooed at him in a happy manner. Kevin stroked his head, gave him some seed, then went outside the safe house. He moved towards the trial field, which now looked like a normal field with long grass growing. Godwill comes to him. "This was truly one of the hardest assignments to any house I have seen or known young wizard. The circle must have either great things planned for you or worries about you. They will be keeping a sharp eye on you, so stay alert. Whatever you do from now on, they will be there watching you even though you do not see them. Mr. Petterson is your housemaster, but should you need to, Mr. Perry and I are always available to help out whenever we can". Godwill smiled at Kevin, which was quite uncommon. "No, go home, young Wilks, rest and continue your learning," Godwill told Kevin. Kevin smiled back, then left and went home.

Chapter 22

The Talk with Postromus

That night when Kevin went to bed, he felt Postromus within him trying to push through. Kevin spoke quietly. "Wait, this is neither the time nor the place to talk." He heard the voice answer, "When then, young wizard, I will not wait until I am summoned like a dog?" Kevin again quietly answered. "Tomorrow, after school, I will go to the safe house where we can talk safely and honestly." Kevin heard a laugh in a sarcastic manner. "Honestly, what is this? You know nothing of honesty. How could you, young one? All young people lie and cheat at your age, I did it myself, and you are no better than me when I was your age." Kevin again answered. "When we talk, I will not lie, but I also need your honesty in questions I have for you. Do you promise to be honest with me also, Postromus?" Kevin heard a growl, then a very angry reply. "How dare you speak to me in this manner. I am a very powerful wizard who could kill you in a blink of an eye. I will not be spoken to by a mere boy like you." Kevin answered, "we have discussed this many a time during the sharing of the two of us. Without me, you will not be, I do not wish to upset you, but I would like to understand many things, many things of which I think you could teach me like you did, Merlin. Please, wait until tomorrow, and then we can talk all you want, I promise you." For a little time, there was no answer; finally, "very well, young wizard, but head my warning, should this not occur, I will not kill you but, I will hurt you from the inside so much that you will regret that you did not complete the task you have given to complete, do I make myself clear"? Kevin answered with a worried "yes, I understand" "Very well young wizard, until tomorrow." Kevin felt the presence slowly disappear, and he now lay down and drifted off to sleep.

The sun shone through the curtains on the arrival of the morning. Kevin woke, got up, washed, and went downstairs. Breakfast was on the table, waiting for him, along with his brother sitting eating. "So, you decided to get up then, bro. Had a good sleep?" his brother asked. Kevin looked at the time, it had just gone past 8 am, and it would be soon time to leave to go to school. Kevin finished breakfast quickly, ran upstairs, and got his books for what he needed that day. The boys left the house and cycled to school. On the way, they talked about a few things to break any silence. Paul eventually asked Kevin if he had any after-school activities planned today that he should know about. Kevin looked a bit puzzled at his brother. "Why do you ask Paul?" Kevin asked. Paul smiled, "nothing really, just thought we could go to the spinney and do some training if you get what I mean?" Kevin smiled, "oh, some training. Sorry, not today, bro. I have something else I need to do after school today. Something I have been pushed into from deep inside of me, if you get my drift." Paul looked hard at his brother with a face of emptiness. "Has Godwill got you doing something that I do not know about?" he asked. Kevin shook his head, "No bro, a certain person inside of me wants a chat with me, and I arranged to do it today at the safe house where we will not be interrupted, so I do not look like I am a right weirdo if someone sees me talking to myself and have a bit of a blue tinge to me". Paul looked at his brother, "Oh, a talk with him, I see, that should be fascinating, two strong minds standing each other off. Would like to be a fly on the wall when that happens." Kevin laughed, "I would not say that a fly on the wall would make it out of the safe house. I am sure Postromus would sense something and do something about it, so just stay away, bro, please, for your safety." "For my safety, what about your safety"? Kevin laughed then replied, "Did not know you cared that much for me, bro, which is really touching" Paul turned away then answered, "care no, wonder what I would have to tell mum and dad, yes, so do not let him overpower you and do something stupid if you can tell, bro. That is all I am saying." The boys had finally reached the school gate and went to put their bikes away in the bike shed.

The school day went through quickly with lesson after lesson, some break times where Kevin and his friends met up to just chill in the bright sunshine and just talked about normal things such as football and girls. As they were talking and sat on the green beside the gym Rueth and her friends walked by. Kevin glanced at Rueth, and their gazes met. Kevin smiled, and so did Rueth. Her friends just laughed and ushered her away from the area of the boys. The bell went, and school continued. The rest of the day went in a blur until the bell went to end school. After registration, Kevin and Vinny went off to the bike sheds to get their bikes. Paul and his friends were already there. As they got their bikes, all said goodbye and cycled off down the long school chase. Kevin turned towards the spinney rather than towards home. Vinny called Kevin, "Where are you going? That is the wrong way, mate?" Kevin shouted back. "Got to feed Fergus before I go home. See you tomorrow, mate." Vinny just waved bye, and off he went. Kevin arrived in the spinney and cast the spell to show the door entrance to the safe house. Once inside, he stroked Fergus and stood thinking what would go on when Postromus came through. Unfortunately for him, it was not long before this happened. "So, young wizard, you kept your word, but that does not mean I trust you just based on this one thing" Kevin moved to the table and sat down before speaking. "So, what is it you wish to talk about, Postromus? I mean no disrespect, but there are so many questions I have and need answers to. Should I be able to gain this information, then it may help our co-existence better. Please, may I speak first?" Kevin felt himself begin to laugh. Postromus then spoke. "With all your chittering young wizard and your questions, you remind me of a wizard I used to know many years ago." Kevin then answered, "I know, it was Merlin." "That is right. How do you know of this wizard?" Kevin replied, "I have been chosen by Merlin to complete a quest, a quest which is hard and has danger in every corner I turn." "And what be the quest young wizard that Merlin has given you?" Kevin answered, "I have the quest to find the power stone" Kevin stood up, pushing the chair he was sitting on back and over. "Why would Merlin seek the power stone? For what use does he need it"? Kevin answered, "I do not know, just that this is what he has asked of me." A quietness was around the room for a few short seconds. "You have met Merlin, young wizard?" Kevin answered, "I have, sir," "You lie, young wizard, Merlin was a great wizard but not one that would live all this time. It is impossible, and you are a liar." Kevin then spoke, "But are you not hundreds of years in age, but clearly here you are attached inside of me. This was from a heart thread that was in the wand of Matrees, which I broke, and you attached yourself to me. In answer to your question, I have met Merlin on the astral plain." "So, the astral plain, it still exists then. This is good news for once," Postromus said. Kevin took out his wand and placed it on the table. "Do you remember this, sir?" Postromus recognised Merlin's wand. "How did you get that boy?" Kevin explained what happened with Postromus, asking a few questions as they talked. After a time, Postromus seemed calmer and finally asked.

"Very well, young wizard, you said you have questions for me. Ask, and I will see if you are worthy of an answer." Kevin was not too sure he liked this answer but asked the questions. "In the vision when Merlin travelled to you, you appeared first as a dragon, then a dove. You also could speak in these animal forms. Could you teach me the spell for doing these things, please?" Postromus made Kevin laugh, then answered. "You, you want to master the changing spell completely. You are not ready or strong enough for that powerful magic yet young wizard. It takes immense strength and mind control to do this. Perhaps in another fifty years or so, you may be nearly ready." Kevin continued to ask, "When we last met Matrees and fought him, he disarmed me, but I was still able to cast spells using only my hand. How is that possible?" Postromus answered. "Well, it was not you doing the casting. It was me that did this. A weak wizard like yourself would never be able to do this. I guess you also want me to help and teach you this spell also, young wizard?" Kevin just replied, "yes," Postromus went quiet. Kevin carried on." Once, a young wizard came to you for help, learning, and a way to move forward with the knowledge to do good and not bad. You helped him although you knew his father, Cormious, so he had an advantage, but you still helped and schooled him. Why not me?" Postromus spoke, "How do you know all these things and people you speak of"? Kevin replied. "It was in the visions Merlin gave me with what terrible things happened all those hundreds of years ago. Visions of Merlin and his family, Mr. Wilfred, Bartholomew, Crandloss." Postromus then flew into a bad temper on the name of Crandloss. "Do not ever mention that man's name again in front of me. He turned to pure evil and darkness. Killed many friends, good wizards, and witches in his quest for power overall."

Kevin tried to calm Posrtromus. "Crandloss is no more, sir. However, he found a way to spit his soul and body into a good and bad half of crandloss. The good half is called Jarez, and the bad half we met in the forest. It is Matrees. In the vision, he slayed a unicorn and drank the blood of the creature. Not just a small part of what Merlin did to sustain life but a lot. This split Crandloos into two. I have just started," Postromus spoke, "I see. I never thought it possible that this could be done, but he was always a student that took things further than they should. Mr. Wilfred, who you mentioned I knew of and spoke a few times as I passed through that way." Kevin answered, "Yes, like the time you initiated Merlin into the magic sect, which I also see in the visions Merlin gave me." "Very good young wizard. I see Merlin has been able to maintain the magic he possessed then and still now. Merlin was, and I guess still is, a great good wizard. He must have a great interest in you to choose you above all others for this quest, so I will make you a bargain, young wizard. When Merlin came to me, he was in his twenties. You, being younger, lack the age, experience, and maturity of what he was. However, Merlin was and still will be a dear friend of mine. Therefore, the bargain. I need you to find out why he needs the power stone and tell me. In doing so, I will help try teaching you certain spells that could help you along your path. In learning these spells, there will be pain and suffering on your part to be able to do them correctly. Are you willing to take this pain and suffering, young wizard"? Kevin thought for a moment and replied, "I am" Postromus made Kevin laugh again and spoke, "A boy's answer, not a man's. Do you really think you can take the pain? It is crippling in some parts of the body until you have mastered the spells. The transformation-changing spell especially, if the mind is not strong and you change, you may not be able to change back to the human form. Are you ready to live with that should it happen?"

Kevin, now very quiet, sat thinking. "I hear your thoughts, young wizard, and you are not sure. Due to this, I will not be teaching you this spell as it is too dangerous," Kevin then replied. "Until we can work out how to remove you from me into another body for your own, then you will be with me for a while, I guess. My strength and yours will not allow that to happen, so I would still like to try to learn it, please. When we met Matrees, you already said it was you casting the spells from your hands at Matrees, not me, so I really do not see where I/we will be stuck in an animal form, do you?" Postromus went quiet. Eventually, he replied, "You had some small bouts of wisdom in you, boy, the same as Merlin when he came to me. Alright, it seems we will be forever together, so I guess you need to know a lot of stuff to keep up with other wizards of old that may still be around from yester years. A bargain is a bargain, neither will break it, or consequences will be dealt to the one that does, do you hear me, young wizard?" Kevin agreed. "One last thing, young wizard," Kevin butted in. "My name is Kevin, not boy, not a young wizard. Your name is Postromus, not an old wizard or old man. Can we be civil and use the names, please" Postromus was not again happy with this but agreed. "As I was saying, Kevin, the power stone is but one part of the puzzle. The original stone made by Flammel and Marcus Dwight was eventually shattered into six pieces. The stone itself was a truly magic stone with the greatest power ever known to exist. It can enhance spell casting, take, and give life. It was sought after by many dark wizards, so eventually, the stone was passed to me. I spent years developing a spell to try to destroy it, but all I could do was shatter it into six pieces. Each piece was given to one of my friends, the dwarfs, to hide a piece in different areas and put magical barriers in place. On return to the house, I met them and wiped their minds of where they put those pieces of the stone. This would prevent any dark wizards and witches from capturing the dwarfs and finding the stones." Kevin spoke, "I know, we found Sambia, and I have met other dwarf brothers of his that were given the task of hiding them. We have found a place in Sherwood Forest where we think a stone piece could be. Sambiah was with us, but we could not remember the exact area. This is where Matrees was when we fought him. Godwill is searching for the right area to check out." "Godwill, who is this?" Kevin replied, "Godwill is master of the Wilfred house of the circle of magic. It is like a ministry that governs magic throughout the land" "Ministry sounds like the druid sect in my time," spoke Postromus. We must not let any of the stone pieces fall into Matrees or any dark wizards willing to join him, or it could be very bad." Kevin agreed.

"Go to the book stands in the corner, Kevin" Kevin got up and went to the bookcase. Postromus uttered some words at a book in the case. It was a book that Kevin previously tried to get but could not as it appeared to have a magical barrier around it. The book now became free, and Kevin pulled it from the shelf. "Magical spells are in many languages, but with the words, I have just spoken, the language changes to the wizard reading and casting the spell. It sounds to the caster in their language, but what is being said is the language the spell is written in. You must take your time, go through the book, look at the spells in there, and practice. Some need a lot of minds to control, some not. This is the first step, Kevin. I give you this within the bargain, do not break it." With that, Postromus drifted quiet, and it was just Kevin and Fergus in the room. Kevin looked at the time and then thought he had better get home before his mum started questioning him. Kevin put the book into his bag, then left the safe house and rode home.

Spell learning. Memory cast spell

When Kevin arrived home, his brother was outside cleaning his bike. "So, where you been then, Kev? Mum has been asking me all sorts of questions about where you were." Kevin smiled and said, "Been for a chat with our friend that is close inside me if you get what I am saying. Cleared the air and got to understand more about him. What sets his anger off, and what happened in the olden days? He even removed the spell holding his spell book, which he has allowed me to look through and learn from." Paul looked at his brother, "Does Godwill know you have the book? He will go crazy when he sees it missing. You must tell him, or there will be trouble, bro, not just for you but for all of us." Kevin saw that there was a look of worry on his brother's face. "Ok, I will talk to him in the morning and explain that I have the book and how I got it, but I do not expect him to understand, but we will see." Just then, Kevin's mum came out and saw him. "And where do you think you have been until this time, my boy?" Kevin thought quickly. "Sorry mum, I have been in the park with" Kevin stopped and looked at his brother as if asking for help. "I know why you went to the park; it's Rueth, isn't it" Paul quickly replied. "Kevin has got himself a girlfriend, then laughed." Kevin pushed his brother in fun. "A girlfriend then, Kevin? Do I know her?" asked his mother. Kevin shrugged his shoulders, "Guess so. She eats in the canteen like all of us, so you must have seen her." Paul butted in again. "It's the pretty redhead mum, usually with around four to five of her friends all moving in a pack." Kevin again pushed his brother. His mum looked and then smiled. "Well, do not go doing something you should not, do you hear, my young lad? We do not want her mother or father coming after us because you two got too friendly if you get my meaning." Kevin looked at his mum, "no, mum, I promise." His mum was about to go back inside, then stopped. "Next time, at least let me know if you are meeting with her after school, so I know you are not in trouble with the teachers like you usually are. For once, Kevin, I feel quite happy and proud of you, but you need to tell me not me get it from your brother, ok"? Kevin nodded and replied, "Sorry, mum, I will." His mum then went inside, humming a happy song to herself. Kevin looked hard at his brother. "No mickey taking, bro. Glad you stepped in to help but do not go telling all your friends at school, so it gets around, or it might put Rueth off me." Paul looked at him and saw that Kevin was not angry but had a weird look on his face, one of happiness. "You do like her, don't you, bro?" Kevin started to turn away from his brother and replied, "So, do not tell me you do not like Denise, I see you looking at her when she walks past you, and I know you two have had meetings together." Paul looked at Kevin. "It was for helping each other with homework, that is all." Kevin smiled, "If you say so, bro," and smiled as he said it. Paul just snarled at his brother and then put his bike up. As he came out of the shed, Kevin was still there. "You had better start to look at that book then, Kevin, and get some understanding of the things inside." Kevin pulled the book out of the bag. It was heavy and very thick. "Where do I start? There must be hundreds of spells and things inside," Paul laughed, "Better start from the beginning then and worked your way through it bit by bit. If you need help, I guess I can help you out, but we must be careful not to be late home or have a good excuse to give to mum." Kevin looked at his brother. "Excuse to tell mum, why"? Paul looked hard at his brother. "Well, you can hardly test spells out at home, can you? It needs to be done at the safe house, so no one can see or know about them." Kevin smiled, "I guess so, bro. I did not think of that." Paul now moved towards the house door but stopped. "Do not forget to talk to Godwill about this tomorrow either." Kevin nodded and went inside.

That night when Kevin went to bed, he took the book out and slowly flicked through it, stopping at a few pages to read. There were many things in the book, not just spells and potions but also pages of the writings of Postromus on certain days about his life and things that had happened. All became a little muddled, and he slowly felt tired, so he put the book away and went to sleep. The new morning broke, and Kevin awoke. He felt full of energy and was feeling happy. He washed, dressed, and ran downstairs. "Morning mum, Paul, nice morning, isn't it?" His mum looked at him and then replied, "Well, seems you got out the right side of the bed which is unusual for you, me lad. Bit of a spring in your step. It must be this girl you were speaking of." Kevin blushed, "Oh, don't worry, it is nice to see a change in you, a change I hope for the better." Kevin sat down and started to eat his breakfast. "Are you seeing Rueth after school today?" Asked his mum. Kevin looked at Paul, smiled, then replied, "Guess so, had not planned it, but I do not know what goes on in their minds, so could be is all I can say." Kevin's mum looked at him, smiled, and then answered. "You boys, just be nice and do not push her, or she will drop you quickly. Take your time and just get to know each other. No girl likes to be pressured into anything, even if it is just getting to know someone. If she asks, just agree. If she does not, then say nothing and do nothing. You will find out that things can move along quicker that way." Kevin looked at his mum. "Mum, leave it out. I do not plan on doing anything silly; she is a nice girl, and she likes music and sport, so I guess we have this in common. That is all at the moment." "Music, you say what? She sings, plays an instrument, or just like studying music?" Kevin looked at his mum. "Now, who is pressing someone with all these questions?" Both Paul and Kevin laughed at the same time. Mum just looked at the boys and then laughed herself. "That was quite a good answer, Kevin, and I have to say said in happiness and not anger. This girl could be good for you. I hope all goes well with the both of you." She then turned and washed the breakfast pots up as the boys set off towards school.

On the ride to school, both boys were talking. "Got away with that then, bro, and it could work for you to be having time at the safe house for the learning you need to do," said Paul. Kevin agreed. "But you got to keep this girl thing going and hope mum does not see Rueth and talk to her about you. That could scuttle things for you if she gets to know it is a lie." Kevin replied, "Why is it a lie, I like her, and I think she likes me, so it is not a lie, well, not in my case anyway." Paul laughed, "ooo, Kevin has a real girlfriend, kissy kissy." Kevin now turning angry, replied, just like Paul and Denise, oooooo, Kissy, kissy Paul." Paul just shouted, "Shut up. I said it was homework, that is all." "Oh, so homework is on kissing; which class is that you take because I must enroll in it," Kevin answered sarcastically. "I see you and Denise a couple of times in the park holding hands and kissing, do not deny it, bro." Paul went very quiet and just rode quicker. Soon they were at the school gates, and Rueth was getting off the bus. Kevin stopped and walked down the chase with her to the bike shed. Rueth walked on to see her friends whilst Kevin met up with his friend Vinny. As the two friends walked to registration, Kevin told Vinny about the trial test and the housing assignment he had gone through, and the Postromus talk. Vinny was all ears and listened to Kevin without butting in. When Kevin had finished, he spoke. "So, you got to go to Godwill and explain about the book and how you got it. Have you looked at it yet? I bet there are loads of new spells we have not been given yet to try"? Kevin looked at his friend. "I guess. I had a quick look, but it is not just magic stuff. There are pages in there also with what I believe to be Postromus' daily life things he did." Vinny looked at his friend. "Postromus' daily life things he did, what is that all about? Do you mean like a diary?" Kevin nodded. Vinny looked puzzled. "Why would he write a magic spell book with diary entries in it? I just do not get it," Vinny said. "I don't know, but as I read it, maybe that will become why he did this. Anyway, let's get to registration, then I will go see Godwill after the first lesson." Both boys went off to the registration room and then onto the first lesson of the day, which Kevin liked. It was chemistry.

As the bell went, Kevin headed towards Godwills classroom. As he entered the class, Godwill sat at his desk with a look on his face as if he were thinking hard about something. Godwill saw Kevin enter and spoke abruptly. "How many times, boy, do I have to remind you that it is courtesy to knock before entering? Kevin stood still, looking hard at Godwill. He was about to speak when goodwill rose from his seat and continued to speak loudly toward him. Kevin now had a few thoughts running through his head. He slowly moved towards Godwill but clasped his wand by the side of his leg. Just then, Godwill burst through the classroom door. The images of Godwill now stood in front and behind Kevin. Kevin wiped out his wand, but the Godwill in front clapped his hands above his head, muttered a spell, and disappeared. Godwill burst past Kevin towards the smoke as it started to clear. Only the one Godwill now stand there. "Young Wilks, you ok"? he asked. "Yes sir, who was that in your place?" Godwill shook his head, "Not sure, but I guess I could have been one of the followers of Matrees. What did you say to him?" Kevin shook his head, "Nothing, sir, but I knew it was not you as he called me boy. You never called me that, and he was quite aggressive when asking me, although sometimes you do that. I just knew it was not you." "Anyway, why are you here, young Wilks?" Kevin quickly explained what had happened after the trial and the talk with Postromus and the book. Godwill stroked his beard, "hmm, so Postromus has taken it upon himself to become another of your teachers on your journey for information as to why Merlin would want the stones.

Young Wilks, in that book you have, there lies a great deal of knowledge, some good, some bad, very bad. The reason it was held under the spell was that in the great wizard's existence, he had to do things that were not of good nature. However, it did not mean he had turned to the dark side; he merely had to be better and more prepared for stronger and more knowledgeable wizards, warlocks, and witches than himself. He laid bare his soul and recorded all that occurred. Only the masters have the reading of this book, but it can be of great help should anything become truly bad. He has struck a bargain with you for which it is said as an unbreakable vow. Any wizard, warlock, or witch that breaks the unbreakable vow will suffer bad fortune and fate. In doing this, you have opened yourself to that possibility. Merlin will never tell anyone why the stones are of importance." Kevin sat down beside the desk, thinking. "But sir, why would he get me to enter this unbreakable vow when if I do not give him what he wants, it will cause me harm? Without me, he cannot exist. We discussed this during our talk and came to an agreement. It does not make any sense what you are saying. When I met Merlin on the astral plain, he mentioned that the stones, when all were got, would be right a terrible wrong. What wrong was so terrible that it needs to be righted"? Godwill shook his head. "I do not know, young Wilks, but there are others after the stones that Postromus told you about. I fear it is for no good and would probably become the worst catastrophe ever known in the time of the magic realms throughout time. Whatever happens, you must guard the book now yourself. Once the spell is broken by the person, the book will only answer to you until it has been got by another using the same spell." "Answers to me, what do you mean? I have had a quick look through it, but it is merely a book. What answers can it give and in what way?" Godwill explained that along with just being a book, it has memories implanted within pages. You can ask it questions on those pages to which it will answer, but only the wizard or person can hear it once they have mastered the memory spell. I suggest you look and concentrate on that one first. Once mastered, you will not only hear the answers from the book but will be able to talk and understand the mythical creatures' voices." Kevin nodded as if he understood. "Sir, when I released the Doriatriel, I spoke to it but heard it saying thank you when I explained I meant it no harm. Is the Doriatriel not a mythical creature"?

Godwill looked hard into Kevin's eyes before answering. "Yes, but what I think occurred was that you did not actually hear it talking to you but what you wanted it to answer to you. The spell I am talking about is the most complex and extremely hard to master. It will be even harder for you being so young. Your mind is not of the capacity for the learning of this possible, and the strength it takes to be able to cast and maintain that strength needed to continue the talk and listening is immense. As I said, this spell not only allows you to talk but to call upon any mythical creature you have encountered through time to aid you in any way it can. You need to try to find the spell in the book, ask questions of the book many times, and gain the knowledge and information that your mind can take. Then, expand your mind further to gain further control so this can be done. It is of most importance as I fear that this could be immensely helpful in the quest Merlin has set you." Kevin, now looking quite nervous after hearing what Godwill had said, stood up and walked out of the door and slowly to the next class.

The day passed in a haze for Kevin as his thoughts were being repeated of the words Godwill had told him that morning and the other Godwill that was already in the class. The bell eventually went to the end of school for that day. Vinny noted that Kevin had not been himself that day and asked what was up in the bike shed. Kevin just answered, "a lot on my mind, mate, I met Godwill, but someone else was there that was in Godwill's place before Godwill came in. The other Godwill disappear. We talked about the book and some things that I need to do with it and for myself, so, just a lot happening, mate." Vinny looked at

254

his friend, "anything I can help with, Kev? You know you only have to ask, don't you?" Kevin looked at his friend. "Thanks, mate, and I am sure there will be times I will need you, but for now, I just got to fathom a few things out for myself. But thanks, you're a really good friend." Vinny smiled, "Just let me know, and I will be there by your side, mate, anytime, anywhere." Kevin smiled again. He took his bike out and went off to the safe house. When he entered the safe house, he made his way to Fergus, stroked his head, fed him some seeds, and then sat with the book. Kevin opened it and slowly turned page after page through the book until he came a crossed the memory spell. Kevin sat reading the spell repeatedly. He read it so many times that it became a blur. The more he read it, the less he remembered the spell. Kevin became annoyed that he could not remember parts of the spell without going back to the book to read again. Eventually, he slammed the book closed. He got up and walked over to Fergus and tried the spell on the phoenix, but nothing happened. Fergus just cooed all the way through as Kevin tried to cast the spell. Suddenly in an outburst, Kevin shouted. "Why can I not do this? It is a simple spell. Why?" Kevin felt a sense of Postromus filtering through his mind. "Why so angry, wizard? Why do you call me from the depths to come forward? Kevin spoke, "how am I to do this spell? I have read it many a time, I have cast it, but nothing happens; why?" Postromus laughed. "You try to learn a spell that requires great strength of mind to be able to do this. Why do you waste time on this spell when there are many that you need to learn that would best suit you."

Kevin sat down. "But I have been told by Godwill that I may need this spell on my quest for the stones. If I cannot do this, then the quest may be over for me, and someone bad will gain the stones. I need help, please, Sire, help me in this spell, I beg of you." Again, Postromus laughed, "You beg me. Begging is a sign of weakness. If you are weak, then how do you expect me to help you? You must find your strength first. Master some of the other spells in my book first, then and only then I will think of possibly helping you if I can," Kevin now replied, "I am not weak, young I may be, but weak never. I have a mind that takes in a lot of knowledge and the ability to think and mostly contradicts the things I have been taught as there is no evidence to sustain the teachings. Is it that you are not so great and incapable of help in completing the task I have asked help for?" Postromus, now angry, replied, "You dare me, boy, a dare I would tell you to apologise for, especially for the dribble you have just had come from that mouth of yours. I can teach any spell to anyone if they have the right mind and strength. At present, you have neither, so I will not help until you can prove to me that you have changed and have the right qualities for you to learn." Kevin spoke, "If you do not help, then it is you that will break the unbreakable vow, not me. Therefore, it will be you that suffers the consequences of the curse it brings." Postromus spoke harshly, "How is that possible? Have you found out what Merlin wants and needs the stones for? No, so it is not me but you that is breaking this vow." Kevin again replied, "Your wrong. When I said I would find out why he needed the stones, I set no timelines to gain the information. It could have been one day, one month, a year, or longer. I just said I would find out. On the other hand, you promised to help me become better, stronger, and more knowledgeable to gain both the information and the stones. You released the book to learn from, so your part has already started and should continue. Therefore, I say it is you breaking the vow." Postromus was quiet. "Very well then, if you do not help me, then the book can be restored to the shelf, and I will learn from other better wizards than what you think you are," Kevin said. He stood up and was about to start to walk over to the bookshelf when he felt himself being sat back down. The book slid out of his hands onto the table and opened at the memory spell.

"Very well, young wizard, what do you need of me?" Kevin answered, "I have cast the spell and tried it on my phoenix, who is a mythical creature, but I hear nothing but the cuoos from the bird; why?"

Postromus laughed. "The spell you are trying to master is indeed a powerful one for talking to mythical creatures. However, it does not work on all mythical creatures. On casting the spell, the mythical creature can understand you but may not be able to talk or memory-cast talking to you. They are not like cats, dogs, pigs, chickens, or any other animal that does not have the ability to talk," Kevin thought, "So if I cast the memory spell and asked Fergus to fly over to here, he will he could not answer me?" Correct young wizard, try it. Kevin looked at Fergus and cast the memory spell, then asked him to come to him. Fergus looked at Kevin and then flapped his wings and flew onto the table where Kevin was sitting. Fergus sat looking at Kevin's eye to eye. Kevin thought, "Thank you, Fergus," Ferguss cuooed happily to Kevin, then flew back to the porch. "Very good young wizard, so you have mastered the first step in being able to talk to the mythical creature but not hearing the voice. This is your next step. This step will be either easy or painful." Kevin asked, "painful, in what way," "If you mind cast and talk through your mind to a mythical creature and it does not reply, then it may try to harm you. You will need to be on your toes all the time in the presence of the creatures you meet, not knowing whether you can talk with them or not. Some also may be of the old religion and believe you wish harm upon them. It is then you must convince them this is not the case. Some can feel your fear or strength that will decide what that creature does. Although you have managed step one of the memory spell, I feel within you that for step two, you still do not have that strength inside you to accomplish this." Kevin replied, "So how do I get this strength you keep talking about?" "It is not a given thing; it is a thing that you must do. To strengthen your mind, you must do things, things you would fear doing and conquer them, and be able to face any fears that hold you back. The more you do and conquer, the stronger and belief in yourself you will gain. The stronger you get, the more spells you will be able to learn and use effectively. This is my help to you, young wizard. Now, strengthen that mind and find me the information I have asked of you." Kevin sat. Still, he felt Postromus fade and sat thinking. He suddenly had an idea, Frank and Dion in Sherwood Forest, he could go to them and see. Kevin put the book in his bag and went home.

The next day Kevin had a plan in place to go to the forest and find Sambiah first, then look for Frank and Dion. The school day soon ended, and Kevin said goodbye to his friend Vinny. He then headed to the safe house. Once there, he cast the travelling spell and found himself in the forest by Sambiah's cabin. As he looked towards the cabin, he could see that there was stillness around the area and the cabin. Kevin knocked on the door, but no answer came. He tried the door, which opened easily. Kevin stepped in but with an uneasy feeling inside of him. Tables were tipped over, shelves on the floor, and generally was a mess. Kevin then remembered the meeting and fought in the forest where Matrees had Sambiah and was going to kill him. Kevin stepped outside and stared into the forest. Suddenly he saw bushes moving and heard a thundering sound on the ground as if a pack of large animals was running toward him. Kevin pulled out his wand, ready to repel and protect himself. Into the open came Frank charging towards him. Kevin raised his hand and cast the memory spell. "Wait, Frank, I am here not to harm you or Sambiah, but I just need to talk to him." Frank continued to charge toward him. Kevin now raised his wand and pointed it towards Frank as he thundered towards him. Kevin was about to cast a spell when Frank stopped right in front of him. "So, you can talk to me and understand me then, young wizard. I remember what you did to me when I first saw you. Why are you here if not to harm me or sambiah?" Kevin sat on the steps of the cabin and explained to him what had occurred with the meeting and fight with Matrees, the talk to Postromus, and the challenging task of trying to master the memory spell. He heard Frank laugh. Frank lay down at the bottom of the steps looking at Kevin. So, you are a friend of Sambiah. I heard what occurred, as you said, with the fight of Matrees and how you saved my friend. But tell me, young wizard, how, when

256

Matrees disarmed you, did you continue to cast spells using just your hand? That is not something a normal wizard can do, especially one so young." Kevin explained that it was not his casting but Postromus inside of him. "It was like Postromus was protecting me and Sambiah, his long-lost friend. My magic is nowhere near as powerful as his and probably will never be, as he was a true master." Frank looked at Kevin and then spoke through the memory spell.

"I see you doubt yourself, your abilities, and the world of magic. However, your ore around you is very strong, glowing, in fact." Kevin laughed, "That Ore is probably from Postromus, not me, but thank you for saying a nice thing like that". Frank continued, "No, young wizard, it is your ore I see. Am I speaking with you or the mighty Postromus"? Kevin answered, "Well, it is me, of course, Frank." "Then it is your ore. Many mythical creatures can see ores, the colours, and the depths of the ore. Good ores are different from bad dark ores. This we are given the knowledge to see them passed down from our parents. When I first saw you and the other wizard, your ore stood out as a light blue colour pulsating from you. The other wizard you were with was of orange colour. Therefore I ran towards you to try and help" Kevin looked at Frank and asked, "To try and help who? Both of us?" Frank replied, "to help you, not the other wizard with you." "But I do not understand, he is my brother, why would he or be a different colour, and why do you say you were to help me"? Frank raised onto his feet. "The colour ores around wizard's are different in many ways, each colour tells us who is good and who is from the dark side. Blue, green, violet, and yellow are good, and orange, red, and deep purple are from bad wizards, witches, and warlocks. All mythical creatures have this gift to see the ores of magic folk. As is said, this gift is passed down through the family to try to help us from befriending the wrong magic folk. However, there are still some creatures out there that have been brutely harmed to bend to the dark side by powerful magic folk. An ore also changes around magic folk when a bad deed has been committed. Tell me, young wizard, your brother, who does he follow." Kevin looked at Frank and asked, "Follow? I do not understand. He was given a quest by Merlin, but that went wrong." "Wrong, in what way" asked Frank. Kevin explained what he had been told by one of his brothers' friends and that Paul had the memory of the kill removed but was left with some part of the memory to make him more thoughtful but scared of using it again. Frank stared at Kevin, "So, he used the kill spell, a dark spell that should never be used but is throughout the whole of time. As he has killed, this will change the colour of the ore that surrounds him or anyone that uses it. The more they kill, the more the colour change, but the more they kill, the more the dark side calls. Eventually, the killer is so dark that they will never again return to the good side. It seems your brother has started on that journey, be careful young wizard. With what you have told me, I have to say he may be untrustworthy and could compromise you."

Kevin stood up. "No, you're wrong, Frank. He is my brother. He will only help me, not do anything to cause me harm. He saved me with the first meeting of Matrees." Frank replied, "was it done for your safety or to get you to think that all is good and he is good? I do not wish him to be bad, but the ore around him does not lie. Be aware and keep a good eye on him. I hope I am wrong, but I have never been wrong ever throughout my life." Kevin just nodded. "You must not doubt your power, young wizard. I have a sense that greatness uses you. It is a feeling of good, and yet somehow, you feel a burden. Magic is a gift, a gift to do good. The ore around you tells me to do good, keep my heart true, be good in your journey that has been patched by Merlin, and remember, your gift is like a switch, although the light shines bright when the switch is in the up position, it may not take something too bad to switch it down and then the dark appears. Follow the path of light always. It will lead to many rewards. Think before you do, way up the good and bad that can happen when you cast spells at people or even animals you encounter." Kevin thought, "you sound like old goodwill telling me to do this do that." Frank snorted at Kevin. "Just because you think that answer, do you not think I cannot hear you, young wizard? You do not have to speak for me to understand you. We, the mythical creatures, can hear your thoughts and hear what you can speak. Who is this Godwill anyway"? Kevin said sorry and explained who goodwill was. Frank accepted Kevin's apology but again warned him of the gift he has and what can and cannot be done. Frank then spoke. "So, young wizard, you look for sambiah. He moved after what Matrees did to him when he found him. Travel through the forest to the west side. You will come to a brook. Beyond the brook, there is a small cave entrance, and there you will find my friend Sambiah. But beware, young wizard, many mythical creatures live in the forest, so you can see. Some you can only hear but never see. Not all mythical creatures can speak through the memory cast. I will accompany you to the brook, but from there, it is you on your own. Kevin looked at the time and noted that it had raced on. "Frank, thank you for your words of wisdom and help. I must return to my home for now but will return tomorrow. Could you meet me here, and we will go tomorrow to see Sambiah." Frank stared at Kevin. "As you wish, young wizard, I will be here waiting for you until tomorrow then." Kevin thanked Frank and then used the travelling spell. He found himself back at the safe house, where he petted Fergus and then went home.

That night as Kevin lay in his bed reading the book of Postromus, he felt the great wizard coming through in his mind. "So, young wizard, I feel from you that you achieved a great thing today. Your mind cast the memory cast and spoke with the Montrose bull," Kevin replied, "His name is Frank, and he is a friend of Sambiah. He explained a lot to me about the ore we have around us, the feelings that can change us from light to dark, and a lot more," Postromus laughed, "So, young wizard, you are learning, and I must say strengthening that mind of yours quicker than I expected. This is good. Maybe you will become a great wizard who I can trust and help along your journey. I also feel there is some doubt in your mind, but it is not clear to me. Tell me, what is this doubt about." Kevin answered, "Oh, nothing, just something Frank said to me that I feel is not true, but I will always be thankful to him for raising a small concern in me."

Postromus was quiet, then spoke, "hmm, your brother, I feel. What did he say about your wizard brother?" Kevin just said, "I cannot say here, perhaps we will speak about it in the future at the safe house, but for now, I need sleep. This magic thing is tiring, and I need to travel back to the forest tomorrow to see Sambiah." Postromus replied. "Why do you seek my friend?" Kevin just smiled to himself, "I need his help in understanding the memory cast. Further, I have spoken to Frank but would also like to speak to Dion, the Sackrat Woolfe, if I can." "Beware, young wizard, the sackrat Wolfe is powerful, stubborn, and has a doubting mentality. It will rather try to hurt you than befriend you. I would not recommend you follow this course." Kevin just answered, "But you are not me, well, not all of me anyway, just a little bit of me. I wish to do this, so I will." Postromus answered, "Very well, young wizard, but heed my warning. I feel a powerful strength comes through you. Do not think this strength is always going to be present. Sometimes freight is as good as strength. It was freight that allowed you to talk to Frank on this occasion. You removed your wand, ready to harm the beast rather than the confidence needed to be used instead. Your main gift is the ore around you. This, too, will help mythical creatures see this and know the difference between who you are but remember, a young wizard, not all mythical creatures can talk, and some may be already on the dark path. Be very careful on your journey." Postromus then disappeared out of Kevin's thoughts. He closed the book and went to sleep.

Chapter 23

Questions for Merlin

As Kevin slept, he drifted into a deep sleep but found himself on the Astral plain. He found himself on a path where a tree was. In the tree, a dove sat. Kevin looked at the dove and spoke." Why am I here? I never asked to come here." The dove did not speak. It just flew down the right path, which Kevin then followed. As he walked, he saw many areas where many figures of mythical creatures were in. Some just ignored him as he passed, and some looked at him with expressions of anger, sorrow, and nervousness as he passed. Kevin carried on down the path and eventually came to the brook he remembered when he had previously met Merlin. Merlin was there, sitting on an old tree trunk where they had been before. Kevin approached Merlin. "I feel there are many things going on with you, young wizard, that you are looking for answers to but cannot find them. How can I help" Merlin asked. Kevin sat down beside Merlin. "You are correct, Merlin. The stone you have asked me to find and get, what is the use of this stone, what wrong do you need it to the right, what mythical creatures still exist in my time, and how do I know who is good and who is bad?" Merlin laughed. So many questions in one go. Perhaps if we start from the first one and work our way through, perhaps, we can answer as many as I can that is possible. So, the first one, the power stone I asked you to help find and get. This is but one part of a big stone that has immense power. The power omitted from it can do great things." Kevin butted in. "I know this. I was told by Postromus of the main stone that Flamel and Dwight had made through alchemy. The stone was eventually broken into six pieces. Each piece on its own has a different power that omits from it and can be used. So, what does the power stone omit from it." Merlin smiled, "You are a very inquisitive young wizard. What my dear friend Postromus has told you is correct. The power stone is but one of six; on its own, it omits the power for mind spell casting and further strength to enforce the magic shield. The power helps the mind strengthen so memory casting can be sent further and reach people of creatures at a far-off distance. The power also omits the way shields can be conjured up. Some shields are small or like a small wall. With this, the shield will surround the person or people next to that person for the protection of spells cast against them." Kevin butted in again, "But not the killing spell?" Merlin looked at Kevin, "No, unfortunately not. There is nothing in the magic world that can prevent that."

Merlin stood and beckoned Kevin to walk with him. Kevin now walked beside Merlin back to the field where the mythical creatures were. "You asked what mythical creatures still exist in your world. Well, I see you have seen a few, both in books and real, the ones which are present in this field. The Montrose bull is a fascinating creature; it has the strength to move heavy rocks but also can help tear down magical barriers. The sacerat Wolfe, hmm, this animal is of the old religion. They prey on the unwilling souls of the magic world. This creature has a double quality, part good, part dark. Again, it has the ability to tear down magical barriers but can turn against the master if not treated with respect; not a creature to mess with, really. Many non-magic and magic folk have fallen fowl to this creature. You must be on your guard should you come a crossed this again. The Doriatriel is a creature that is not of any real worry but can change into anything the magic folk is thinking of to try to scare other folks. It usually does this as a protection for itself. The Griffion is a dark creature that has mystical powers along with strength. This is definitely a creature to steer clear of at all costs, as it could end in a fatality. There is talk that still further creatures still exist even after all this time from the olden days that you have not met but have the possibility to meet should they still be around a specific area. "Kevin looked at Merlin and asked. "Like what, Merlin?" Merlin waved his hand, and the images of the mythical creatures changed.

In their place stood a firedrate; the creature had the look of a part bear with the head of an eagle that spits fire. "The firedrate was used in the old religion for the maters of good magic. This creature was born of magic and helped when marauders came after their masters, but they still had an aggressive attitude even with their masters challenged them. It was said that they eventually were killed off as too many were caught by dark wizards to do their deeds or be punished to the extent that they were nearly killed. Many bad things happened during a hundred years whilst they were present. Many bad things." Merlin lowered his head and went quiet. Kevin asked, "Can the Firedrate and flying mantral be talked to through the mind-cast memory spell" Merlin looked at Kevin and asked, "Why do you need to know this? What purpose would this serve you, young wizard?"

Kevin shrugged his shoulders, "Do not know, but if they can be contacted and become a use for good, then perhaps, they may be of use for the quest." Merlin stroked his beard, "I really think you need to dismiss this of these creatures' young wizards. They are more of the dark side than the light. I really do not think they could be of any use but for harm, your harm at that. Do not try this, or you could be in considerable danger," Merlin then went onto the biggest thing he made appear. "The welsh dragon, magnificent creature, born of magic, has the ability to fly many leagues in a blink of an eye, has an outer skin of armour. It was said that they were of the dark side, but I have known wizards and warlocks that had dragons for friends and protection, so not all dragons were bad, but they are like any other mythical creatures, given the right circumstances or pain they can turn to the dark side like anything or anyone." Kevin looked at the images with fascination. Merlin could sense that there was a feeling inside Kevin that longed to meet these creatures. "As I said, young wizard, be aware of what I have said. I feel you want to meet or see these creatures close up. It could be the worst thing you could do." Kevin just looked at Merlin and then lowered his head. They made their way back to the tree stumps and sat. "I sense there is another trouble on your mind, young wizard, one connected to your brother, you spoke to the motrose bull called Frank, and he warned you of your brother" Merlin raised his hand towards Kevin's head, "Hmm, so he used the killing spell and had to have this memory removed, the ore around him has changed colour, you are fighting with thoughts based on this conversation about your brother." Kevin looked at Merlin with a sad look on his face. Merlin stood up and paced backward and forwards. "Killing anyone or anything is not an easy thing to do. It is either in the mind of the magical person or not. In the memory, I just see your brother did it as a last resort to enable him to live. Does that mean he has gone over to the dark side? I cannot say the ore around him has changed colour to signify that he has used this spell. All mythical creatures will see this and will attack to preserve themselves against this person from doing them harm. I also saw that he prevented Matrees from seriously hurting you and chased him off during the meeting. To me, this shows courage and needs to be taken into consideration. All I would say is that there are many paths that all can take, some the right path, some the wrong path. It is unclear which path your brother is treading at the present time, so be aware of this young wizard, but for now, the doubt you have is unfounded that he has chosen the dark path. Wizards, throughout time, have changed paths in both directions, good to bad, bad to good. It is down to him which path he continues. No matter what you think, what you do will change the mind set of your brother. Only he can decide the path. The worse things happen, then the dark path call is strong. The better things then the good path calls for him to come back and follow" Kevin looked at Merlin and nodded as if he understood. "Now, it is time you went back to your world and rest, there is still much to do in the coming months, and you need to be strong and sure of yourself both in magic abilities and the right frame of mind." Kevin agreed and started back down the path from where he came from.

As he started to walk, he stopped, turned to Merlin then said, "You did not answer one of the questions I asked. Why?" Merlin looked at Kevin then replied, "To right a wrong that occurred, I cannot give you an answer to this young wizard, not yet. When we have the stones, then I may answer this question. Until then, be patient. All will be revealed, I promise you." Kevin stared at Merlin, another question; then I promise it would be the last one this visit. Merlin looked hard at Kevin, "Very well, young wizard, but it will be the last I will answer tonight." Kevin walked back towards Merlin. "When I come here, it is only me, no Postromus, yet he is firmly inside of me. How does he not come through and wish to speak, and how is it that both you and he can read my thoughts and feelings? Is this another spell that I ned to learn so I can also do this"? Merlin laughed loudly before speaking, "I said one question. You have given two. Therefore, I will answer but one. Which one will you choose, young wizard?" Kevin thought, "OK, why does Postromus not come through? Why we are here." Merlin replied, "This is a magical place where the soul can escape to another place, leaving the body for a short time. Postromus is firmly attached to your body, not your soul. Therefore, he cannot enter this realm, which is the reason why it would be a great wish of mine to see again my dear friend and teacher Postromus, something I have wished for throughout time. There, I have answered your question. Now it is time for you to go." Kevin looked at Merlin and then spoke. "With every question and answer I get, I get further questions that I have that need to be answered. They leave me confused when I cannot answer them. Why does this happen?" Merlin replied, "You do ask a lot of searching questions, young wizard, but they cannot all be answered where and when you want, there are times and places for answers to appear, and for tonight, I feel tired also, so leave now and we will speak at a later date." Kevin agreed and walked off down the path. The next thing he knew was the sun shining through the curtains in his bedroom. A new day had begun.

End of the school term.

The coming days came and passed with just the usual school things happening. Although Kevin kept himself from getting into trouble with the teachers, he still went daily down to the safe house after school to continue learning more spells from the book of Postromus. On occasions, he met with Godwill asking him questions about what was happening and has he had found the place where the stone was. Unfortunately, Godwill's answer was the same. "Not yet, young wilks, I keep going back to the forest searching different areas, but still, I cannot find any sign or notice where the location could be." Kevin knew that the end of term was closing fast and was feeling quite frustrated. His parents had planned a holiday during the school holidays, and Kevin wanted to know what would happen should Godwill find a clue as to where the place was. "Do not worry, young wilks, as long as we can keep an eye on Matrees also to ensure he does not find it either, then it will wait, or we can get the stone without you. I know Merlin gave you this quest, but should things move in a dramatic fashion, then we need to have a plan B, and we have looked at this and have some ideas about how and who will go to get the stone." Kevin was not impressed by this answer. "So, all this time that you and the rest of the wizard masters have been training me for, you would give the task to someone else? Why was I chosen for this quest when you could have given it to someone else in the first place"? Godwill looked angrily at Kevin, then replied. "So, you think that just because you were chosen, this makes it that only you are to get this stone? Do you really think you are that important? I must let you know, young Wilks, the main thing is to gain the stone. Even though Merlin asked you, if you cannot be there, then the stone is the most important thing, not you, not me. We work together as a family, a collect, to get the task done. We will not or cannot expose the non-magic world and people to us. What do you think would happen if your mother and father knew you and your brother were wizards? She would think you are ill and need to be sent to a place for treatment for a mental issue. This nearly happened to your brother. Should it happen again, and you were the same, I have no doubts she would set those things into motion. It is imperative that we all look after each other and keep our gifts secret. So, if anything happens whilst you are away on the family holiday, we will attend to what needs to be done. You just enjoy yourself as you said you always wanted, being a normal boy of your age, Do not worry, young wizard, there will be lots to do once you are back. The quest does not finish until we have all the stones that Merlin requires." Kevin looked at Godwill and accepted what he had said even though he was still upset. He left the classroom, as usual, to go to the next class.

The days passed by so quickly that Kevin and Vinny kept talking about the task at hand and the new spells Kevin had learned from the new book he had gained through Postromus. Occasionally Kevin kept trying the memory cast a spell on cats and dogs as he met them, but nothing happened. This made Kevin a little down, but he kept trying no matter what. Each night after school, he went to the spinney safe house and tried new spells he had learned in the open field shielded by the magic cast so no normal people could see what was going on. He set up different things so spells could be used against them to ensure they would work or not. Some did some did not. Although frustrated, Kevin kept reading and retrying to cast the spells until he accomplished them. Time after time, he tried, which made him feel quite tired at the end of it. Each night before he left, he spoke to Fergus about all his thoughts and worries whilst stroking the phoenix, even though he knew Fergus would not answer before feeding him and going home. Night after night, Kevin tried questioning his brother if anything had been said to him, but he had not talked to Kevin about it. Paul was getting annoyed with this as he gave the same answer every time to his brother, which was No. He would let him know if anything had been done, although some things could be of a sensitive nature that it would be on a need-to-know basis only. This made Kevin angry, thinking that something was going on, but he was not part of it. During his sleep, there had been no contact with Merlin on the astral plain or Postromus pushing through like he had done before whilst Kevin had all these thoughts. Kevin's attitude had also changed so much that his mum had noted it also. The final day comes during the school year. As Kevin went downstairs to get breakfast, his mum beckoned him to sit at the table for breakfast.

"Everything alright, Kevin?" asked his mum. Kevin looked at his mum and replied. "Yes, mum, why do you ask?" "Call it a mother's intuition, but just lately. You seem to be slipping back into your normal self, questioning everyone, more anger coming out, and disrespecting the older generation. I guess you and this young girl have split up. Pity, you were becoming quite a nice boy. Look, you are young. You will have many young loves before you find the right person to be with. Both your dad and I went through the same thing when we were young. I know that it hurts when things go wrong between young people, but you just must keep moving forward. Do not slip back into the old Kevin. No one wants to see that, least of all me, your mum. If there is any help or you just want to talk about it, you know you can." Kevin looked surprised at his mum and answered her. "No, mum, Rueth and I are still boyfriend and girlfriend. It has been doing these tests at school, which was the problem, that is all." Kevin's mum looked at him, "So, you think you have not done well in them? I have to say, at the beginning of the year, you did not really take to the work, but I have to say, in the last month since you have been with Rueth, was it? You seem to have calmed down and got on with the work, and from what I have heard from some teachers at school, you are doing well now. Let's just wait and see what the results are. I guess you will know later today, as it is the usual thing for them to publish results on the main classroom notice boards. Let me know when you get home how it all went, and if there is a problem with a subject, then we can always get someone to help you with that. A kind of extra home tuition if it is needed". Kevin looked at his mum. "I really do not think that will be necessary," Kevin replied. "Well, let's just wait and see," his mum replied. Just then, Paul walked into the kitchen for breakfast after he had completed his paper round, so mum got up from the table and got Paul's breakfast.

As the last school morning of the term began, Kevin kept thinking about what mum had said regarding some teachers who had told her he was doing well and was trying to think which one it would have been. As he thought about this, he walked into Rueth. "Morning Rueth," he said, sorry I bumped into you" and laughed. Rueth smiled, "you do not need to do this to get my attention, Kevin. I look for you each and every day." She smiled and gently kissed his cheek, which made him blush. The reason for this was his mate Vinny had just come round the corner and seen it. Rueth sees Vinny, too, with a big smile on his face Rueth also blushes and then runs off to find her friends. "Wow, mate, she kissed you. She must be really into you to do that. The last time I tried anything like that, I just got a smack around my face from the girl I tried it on. Perhaps, if you really like her, Kevin, you might want to take control and kiss her first, not wait for her to do that." Kevin looked at his mate. "Why," he said. "Mate, don't you know anything about girls? Most of them want a strong, confident bloke who can show he really likes her. I think Rueth is one of those girls." Kevin smiled and looked at Vinny. "So, when did you become the love guru, mate?" "Love, who said anything about love? Are you telling me you have fallen in love with her? Are you sure she has not cast a spell over you to get you like this and do stupid things?" "Stupid things, what stupid things?" Vinny looked at Kevin, "Well, one thing is that you are not as angry as you have been in the past since you two became an item" Kevin stared at his friend again. "An item. What are you talking about, Vinny? We are just, I guess, boyfriend/girlfriend. Two people that are getting to know each other but just friends, that's it." Vinny smiled, "For now, mate, but love could easily blossom. I have seen it in both yours and Rueth's eyes when you look at each other." Kevin laughed and gave Vinny a friendly soft punch on his shoulder before they went off to the class.

In each class they went in, they looked at the test results. Kevin and his mate were surprised as Kevin's name was near the top of every test. Vinny checked for his name and saw that some he had done well, some not so well. At lunch, Vinny spoke to Kevin. "See, since you have got with Rueth, your mind has expanded, and you have done well in all the tests. I remember the time when you said to me you cannot be bothered with tests and learning apart from the lessons you like. But it has proven that this girl has really helped you unlock your mind and take things in to do the tests" Kevin looked hard at Vinny. "The only thing that could have done what you say is learning all the stuff in Postromus' book. It has been so hard to learn and do the things in that book. I guess as I have been learning those things, it has also helped me take in things from the school classes, not Rueth." Vinny smiled at Kevin, "Whatever, if that is what you think, then you just keep on thinking that, mate." Both boys stood in the dinner queue to get lunch. As they got to the serving hatch, Kevin saw his mum and Lily serving. "Hi, Kevin. I just had your young lady through here a little earlier with her friends. She really is a sweet girl, quite a catch for you, my young lad," Lilly butted in, "June, stop it, you're embarrassing the lad and not in front of his friends also. You are awful, June." Kevin smiled at Lilly then just pointed to what he wanted for lunch. Both his mum and Lilly smiled then off the boys went to the table. "Not a word, mate, do you hear?" Vinny did a sign as if he were zipping his lips at Kevin, then laughed. After lunch, the two friends were on the way outside into the playground when Mr. Perry stopped them. "Mr. Godwill has been looking for you. He wants you to go to his classroom as soon as possible, so off you go." Both boys headed down to Godwills classroom, knocked, opened the door, and walked in.

Godwill was sitting at his desk and beckoned them over. The two boys sat down. Godwill looked at them and gave a sigh, "It is the last day of school, and we still have not found where the stone may be. I have been backward and forward to the forest but have found nothing. I am not sure if this really is the place where it is," he said. Kevin looked at him and replied, "Do you want us to go and look then?" Godwill looked hard at Kevin, then replied, "I just said I have been over the whole forest, and I could not find anything. What makes you think you can do any better young Wilks." Kevin shrugged his shoulders and then replied, "I meant no disrespect, sir, but a different set of eyes, a different way of looking, might reveal something". Godwill gave a little laugh, "No disrespect," he said after a sarcastic smile. "Well, that would be a first for you, young Wilks." Vinny smiled and gave a little laugh. Kevin kept his eyes on Godwill as he was speaking, then without memory, mind casting thought, "What are you not telling us, sir? I see some sadness and pain in you. What is it?" Godwill stood up and stared hard at Kevin. He then thought back to Kevin, you can mind casting young Wilks, but how, you are so young, and it takes immense power to be able to do this." Vinny stared at Godwill as if he were expecting Godwill to speak. "You were saying, sir, before Kevin said that two eyes are better than one." Godwill looked at Vinny and then at Kevin. "Rose does not have this power, does he, young Wilks? Kevin replied through the mind cast, "No sir, I guess not." Godwill smiled, then spoke to Vinny. "I am not saying that you could not find anything but Rose, there is a presence of Matrees in the forest, and it could be dangerous, and I do not want to put any of you in any possible harm." As he spoke, Mr. Perry came running into Godwills class. "Markus, I guess you are here with what is going on. Kevin heard Mr. Perry ask, "Is it true, master?" as he looked at Kevin. Kevin replied through his thoughts. "Yes, sir, I have learned and mastered the thought-casting spell I learned from the book of Postromus. Vinny was looking firstly at Mr. Perry and then at Godwill. To him, there was a deadly silence, and he was wondering who or what would be said next. Mr. Perry noticed Vinnie's expression and then spoke. "Are you asking the boys to go to the forest Godwill? Because, if you are, then I will go with them to help them just in case there is anything that could be troublesome" Vinny smiled and then said, "Well, thank you, sir, I did not know you cared." Mr. Perry looked sternly at Vinny, then replied, was that supposed to be funny, Rose, as I did not think so." Vinny stopped smiling. "Now, Markus, thank you for this. Perhaps young Wilks could be right. My eyesight is not what it was many years ago. I may have missed something small that could be a clue. I suggest that you go after school today. Slow time as you cannot be away too long, or the boy's parents may start phoning the school to see where their children are." Mr. Perry nodded in agreement. "Right, off you two go, be careful tonight, boys, Markus. Make sure you look after these two to the best of your ability." All agreed. The boys stood and walked towards the door. "Young wilks, can I just have a word with you regarding your last test score, please." Vinny looked at Kevin and then walked out of the class.

Kevin walked back in and closed the door. "So, Young Wilks, you can mind cast without even casting a spell to do this. It is tremendous and also a little concerning," Godwill said. Kevin looked at Godwill. Concerning sir, in what way?" Mr. Perry then spoke, "I heard you down at the school entry point speaking in my mind, which is why I came running in case it was an imposter in your form that could be trying to attack Godwill." Kevin looked at Mr. Perry first, then Godwill. "But I was only speaking to Mr. Godwill. I thought, how did you hear what I was saying." Godwill stood up, then walked behind Kevin and placed his hands on Kevin's shoulders. "Usually, mind speaking, as we call it, is just the two parties. Let me ask you, young Wilks, have you heard any other voices in any way since you mastered this gift?" Kevin shook his head. "Why, sir" Godwill stroked his beard and thought. "Although you spoke to me, Markus also heard it. Therefore, I think that any magical person at a certain distance from you can also hear it. Markus said he could hear you from the school entrance, which must be a good eight hundred meters away. I just wonder how far your thought cast will project. In your lesson in the book, was there anything regarding hearing other thoughts or just how to cast?" Kevin thought and just remembered the mind cast and was going to speak, but both Godwill and Mr. Perry nodded as if they heard his thoughts when he was thinking them. Kevin looked at both. "You heard my thoughts when I was going through thinking what was in the book" Godwill and Mr. Perry both nodded. "This is now my concern, many others that have mastered this gift may also be able to hear you. Therefore, what you think, what you cast is the concern." Kevin understood what they were saying. "Do you think Matrees has this ability? I know my brother does not, and my friends do either, but he is part of a once very experienced wizard. I guess he would be able to pick up on this?" just as Kevin finished speaking, there was a bright light shining in the front of the class, and as it disappeared, there stood Jarez.

Kevin grabbed his wand and pointed it at Jarez. Godwill shouted, "wait, Young Wilks." Jarez smiled at Godwill and then spoke. "Thank you, master Godwill, it is I, Jarez, that stands before you. I, too, heard your mind cast many leagues away from here, so I travelled here to see you. It is indeed a great thing that you can do this and set your mind to rest. Yes, only I heard the mind cast. My previous form of Crandloss could do this and hear many thoughts of wizards and witches that also could do this, but when we were separated, it came with me, not Matrees. The reason being, he learned this when he was young, older than you young wizard when he was still a good person. Therefore, as the good of Cranloss, it was separated from me when it happened. However, Matrees has followers from other dark wizards, which I cannot say do not also have the gift could inform him what your thoughts are. The mind cast usually can only be done by two or three people whilst they are in sight of each other, but then it grew stronger that others could also feel and hear the thoughts that were being cast. You must now learn to control the spell even further young wizard, to keep you safe and any location you may be in. Otherwise, it could be your undoing." Mr. Perry butted in, "And how does he do this? How do any of us do this if what you say is true?" Jarez turned towards Mr. Perry. You have the book of Postromus, I feel. You have learned this spell from that book, but I feel you have access to the great wizard also. Although I do not know how this is possible, you must ask for his help as I have never come to a cross anything in any book to be able to do this." Jarez stared at Kevin and then spoke, "You are a remarkable wizard with great power. As you grow older, the power will also grow, almost to the strength of the great wizard Postromus and maybe even the great Merlin. I say to you, young wizard, learn the controls; master them. This will keep you and all in your sight safe. As to the whereabouts of the power stone you seek, be true to yourself, be true to your power, and above all, be true to the mythical creatures you have and will come crossed in this search." Godwill spoke, "And to what do you mention this power stone Jarez"? Jarez smiled, "Do not take me as a fool, Godwill. There are many that know you seek this stone and the others, for exactly what reason is not clear yet, but, as I said, it is not just Matrees that also seeks the stone," he replied. "Tell me then, Jarez, do you also seek the stones?" Jarez smiled again, "I will neither say yes nor no to answer your question. Many say that when the stones are found and repositioned correctly, the main stone will again fix itself and give the holder the greatest power ever known to the magic world. This stone could be used for good or evil. It all depends on who finds and connects it and wields it will be the answer. Tell me, why does Merlin seek these stones." Kevin did not speak but did think in his mind without even thinking that he had done this "to right a wrong" Jarez looked at Kevin, "Hmm, to right a wrong, hey? I wonder what wrong needs to be righted." Godwill looked angrily at Kevin. "Young Wilks does not think or speak whilst this wizard is here." Kevin just looked at Godwill and stared at Jarez. "Do not worry, young wizard. I mean you no harm or ill fate. In fact, if you need my help with anything, you can call me. I am true to my word. My purpose in life is to help. This is my destiny now throughout the rest of my existence." Godwill looked into the eyes of Jarez before speaking." Although you say the words, I still do not trust you, Jarez." Jarez smiled, "That is your thought, but I assure you, when the time comes, you will see, I am a wizard of my word." With that, the bright light shone again, and Jarez disappeared.

As the three of them stood looking out at the beyond, Godwill turned to Kevin. "Do as Jarez said and get Postromus to help you master better the mind cast, or it could be a big problem for us. Markus, when you go to the forest later, do not be too far apart from the young wizards so you can speak clearly to hear each other. Do not mind cast whilst there. There could be, as Jarez said, others in the forest vicinity that could pick up on this and give your location away" Mr. Perry nodded in agreement. Kevin then left the classroom and went to find his friend Vinny.

Chapter 24

Return to the Forest

School finished, Kevin and Vinny headed to the sports hall to meet Mr. Perry. When they went in, Paul, Roger, and a couple of other people who Kevin did not recognise were already there waiting. Once all together, Mr. Perry gave them a talk on what they were going to be doing and grouping-wise. Kevin being inquisitive, asked Mr. Perry, "Where is Mr. Godwill, sir?" Mr. Perry answered, "he is already in the forest. He left as soon as the bell went. We are to meet up at the spot where the marks you saw on the rock on the last visit, and then we will move on from there. You all need to be very quiet, observant, and young wilks, with no mind casting. Remember what Jarez and Godwill said?" Kevin nodded in agreement. All uttered the travelling spell and disappeared from the sports hall. As they appeared one by one at the location, Kevin did not. When Kevin appeared, he stood looking at a high pile of boulders but not where he should have been. The others all started to look around for him where they were and knew he was not there. Mr. Perry looked very nervous and troubled. He turned to the others and spoke. "Young Wilks must have been transported somewhere else; I hope he is alright, but our task is to find the stone. Break up into your groups and search for clues to where we go next." Vinny looked at Mr. Perry, "try mind casting him, sir. He could be in trouble." Mr. Perry looked at Vinny, "I can't, young Rose. Remember, there may be Matrees and others in the location also, which may give our locations away and become trouble for us. I am sure he will turn up sooner or later; you just watch and see." Vinny was not as sure as Mr. Perry but got to his group, and off they went.

Kevin now stood staring at the boulders where he was and had a little feeling that he was not where he was supposed to be. The more he looked, the more his feeling grew. He walked up to one of the large boulders and gently put his hand on it. To his surprise, his hand disappeared through the rock. He pulled it back quickly, then did the same again. This time he pushed his arm through the rock and eventually walked through the boulders.

Once on the other side, he looked back and could see through the rocks to the side where he was before. Kevin stood looking in a concerned way, then turned to face even more rocks in front of him. He walked towards them and thought he could walk through them also but walked into what appeared to be true rocks this time, or so he thought. He tried to feel around the rocks, but to his surprise, his hand was nowhere near the rock face as it was stopped by an invisible physical barrier. Kevin felt along the barrier, but there was no way through it. He stood looking and was thinking how he could get through when he heard a voice in his head say to him.

"Call the mythical creatures around you, young wizard." Kevin spoke softly, "Is that you, Postromus?" There was no answer he heard. Kevin knew what goodwill had said regarding mind casting and wondered what he should do. As he stood wondering, he noticed a figure standing at the far end of the rocks looking at him. It was Frelic, one of Sambiahs dwarf brothers. Kevin moved closer toward the dwarf and started to speak when Frelic put his finger to his mouth as if to say be quiet. Kevin stopped speaking and just looked at Frelic. The dwarf moved quickly to Kevin's side and then spoke softly. "Sambiah asked me to keep a close eye on you, a young wizard, and help in any way I can. You know none of us to know where the stones are, but we have also been hunting the spots for hundreds of years for them also." Kevin asked, "Why are you looking for the stones?" Frelic looked at Kevin, then answered. "We have been hunted for hundreds of years by evil dark wizards to give them the locations where they are. We, as the elderly dwarfs, decided a long time ago to either help good wizards to find them or do it ourselves to get them to one place where no good or evil will be able to get to them again." Kevin looked at Frelic, "Where is that, I ask?" Frelic looked at Kevin then answered, "The dragon's belly." Kevin now even more confused, just repeated what Frelic had said and then continued, "is this a place somewhere as you cannot mean a real dragon's belly? There are no such things as dragons. They were just a myth, surely?" Frelic again smiled at Kevin, "If that is what you believe, then you still have a lot to learn, young wizard. Dragons were and are still real to this day. Not many have survived over the time span since their coming due to environments, and more powerful spells have been created to defeat them. However, there is one dragon who is immune to any magic that has come from the ages. The magic the dragon possesses is more advanced and extreme than not one wizard, warlock, or witch has ever matched it. Therefore, the stone parts need to be taken to the dragon, and he devour them. Inside a dragon, the stones, even though magical, will be dissolved through the dragon's stomach juices and therefore no longer be a problem." Kevin strangely understood this but was still quite nervous. At that point, Kevin grabbed his wand and pointed it at Frelic. "What are you doing, wizard? You have seen me with Sambiah and know me." Kevin replied, "How do I know you really are who you say you are? Tell me, how many brothers do you have, and where is Sambiah right now"? Frelic looked hard at Kevin, "You dare to challenge me, young wizard. Who do you think you are? Kevin then heard a voice within him, Kevin began to speak dwarfishly, and Frelic then knelt on the ground before Kevin. Kevin knew it was Postromus coming through. "You were right to challenge him, young wizard, although even though it be right, this can then cause my great friends to distrust you. My words to you are that if in doubt, try the reveal spell first. It is of great magic where no one can hide from it once cast." Kevin then felt the feeling from Postromus disappears. Kevin spoke, "I am truly sorry, Frelic, but Matrees has shape changed before to try to trick me, and I must be certain I am in the person's presence who they really are. Frelic got to his feet and stared hard at Kevin. "Do you wish my help, young wizard, or not? Now, we are in a very unsafe area. Although non-magic folk cannot see through the illusion, other wizards can. We must get through this barrier. My magic cannot do this, although you have master Postromus with you. Not even if we all come together can we do this. However, there are magical creatures around that, when they come together, can. You need to call upon them for their help." Kevin again looked at Frelic, "Why me? Could you not call them?" Frelic shook his head, "Only the right wizard who is given the task can call upon these creatures. I can call them, but they will only come to help me in dire circumstances." "Is this not a dire circumstance we are in?" asked Kevin.

Frelic now started to walk backward and forward in frustration. "Call them young wizards. Now, I feel there are others near, and we need to get through this barrier as quickly as we can." Kevin was feeling pressured and then asked, "others near, who? And to which creatures are you referring to that I call?" Frelic just shouted, "Call the creatures, young wizard. I feel darkness is coming. Call them now. When we get through this barrier, there may be other challenges in front of that. We need to move quickly to put space between us and the darkness, I feel. Call the Montrose bull and Sacret wolfe you met." Kevin stood looking at Frelic with a blank expression on his face, "Frank and Dion," Frelic spoke quickly, "If that is what they are called, now, call them to us." Kevin was very doubtful and not sure he should, but he could see Frelic was getting very nervous looking through the illusion barrier. Kevin's mind cast the spell and called to both the mythical creatures. "Frank, Dion, it is Kevin, the young wizard you met. I need your help, please. Come help me at the illusion barrier." As soon as he did this, Mr. Perry and Godwill also heard it. Godwill was indeed with Sambiah and questioned him where the barrier was. Sambiah answered, "I do not know Godwill; I have tried to remember, but there is nothing there." "Why would he call the mythical creatures to him?" Sambiah just shook his head, I really do not know, but we heard, and that means others will too. However, at least he has not given away the location just at the illusion barrier. If I try to contact Frank, maybe, he could take us to the place". Godwill stroked his beard then said, "call him, but not to come here to us but to meet at a special place only the two of you know so no others can hear and understand." Sambiah agreed and mind cast Frank to meet at their special place. Both Godwill and Sambiah used the travelling spell to go there.

The special place was by a running stream, the land around it was shrouded by trees, and the sun still shone through. Sambiah and Godwill sat on a rock near the stream, waiting. Frank came thundering through and stopped in front of Sambiah. "You heard the call for help, Frank. The young wizard mentioned the illusion barrier. Do you know this place. Frank looked at both Sambiah and Godwill and nodded. "Can you take us there, Frank?" asked Sambiah. Frank snorted and mind cast, "I can, but it will take time. Dion is already en route and should be there soon. Quick, we must go. Follow on your broomsticks and try to keep up. There is a lot of lands to cover, and some areas are very congested by trees and bushes. You will need to stay low as you will not see where I am going from the sky, as you will not be able to see me through the trees." Both agreed and called for the broomsticks. As they landed in front of them, goodwill and sambiah mounted the broomsticks. Frank nodded and set off at a blistering pace. Godwill and Sambiah followed. Darting in-between trees and over shrubs, they eventually came to the place where Dion was sitting waiting. Frank mind cast to Dion, "Did you see anything or anyone on your visit here, Dion?" Dion replied, "There are a couple of groups of wizards heading this way, although I feel they do not know what they are looking for. I had seen some of them before with the young wizard who called. There are also more groups of other witches and wizards further back, also heading this way. I feel these are not of the good magical folk." Frank snorted, "Ok, let us help out how we can, Dion" Dion nodded and pushed through the illusion barrier. Frank followed, and so did Godwill and Sambiah. Once through all, see Kevin and Frelic. "I should have known," said Sambiah. Kevin looked at Sambiah and asked, "What should you have known"? Sambiah answered, "My dear brother who just keeps getting into trouble, always has, always will" Frank now mind cast, "Very touching, but we need to get through this barrier, Dion. Do you remember what we were told and shown how to do this?" Dion's mind cast back, "Of course, although it has been a very long while, this will always stay with me until I am unable to draw breath" Dion moved towards the barrier. "When I get it to the brittle stage Frank, you know what you must do." Frank nodded. Dion stood staring at the barrier in front of him. Kevin watched as Dion closed both his eyes, but a light shot from his third eye. Godwill shouted, "Do not look into the light anyone, or you will be sent to sleep." All turned apart from Frank, who was immune to this magic. Dion was concentrating hard and starting to slowly yelp as if in pain. Frank called to Dion, "Now, my friend?" Dion's mind cast back, "Not yet, wait, wait, wait, now." Frank burst at the barrier with as much speed and weight as he could put behind him. The barrier shook and then cracked and fell as Frank made contact. As the barrier fell, Frank continued to carry on through it.

The others looked round to see Frank now lying on the ground, exhausted. Dion also lay on the floor. Kevin ran to Dion and stroked his head, mind casting, "You done it, both of you, you were brilliant" Dion raised his head and looked at Kevin and licked his face. Kevin then moved to Frank and again stroked his large head, mind casting, "Thank you, Frank. We would not have been able to get here without you and

Dion." Frank raised his head and cast. "It is not over yet, young wizard, the open ground you see before you have also been enchanted with things to prevent anyone from getting near the stone's location. Be aware, be on your guard, all of you." Sambiah looked at Frank and asked by speaking, "Can we use broomsticks to cross my friend"? Frank shook his head as if to say no. Dion's mind cast to them. "To get to the location, you must cross the open land on foot only. Should you use any other method, then the cave where the stone is will never be seen. There is a spell that covers the precise location, which will not be removed until you have crossed the land and found the five keys scattered around. Once you have the keys, then, at the other end, you will come a crossed another barrier. In this barrier, there will be a keyhole. Insert the right key into the keyhole, and it will open. You need to do this with the first three tries. If not, the barrier will not open, and you will have to leave or face certain peril. Once you start to cross the land, you have but 3 hours to find the keys, get to the barrier, and go through. If you fail, further magical things are lurking in the underground that will come free and attack you. The magic here is much stronger than anywhere else you have encountered on your journey and may not be as useful as you have gotten this far." Kevin then asked Dion, "So, we have three hours to find five keys, of which only one is correct, there are magical things out there to slow us down or harm us, and if we do not do this in three hours, we could perish. What am I doing here? We are never going to do this. No way, we should just go?" Frank looked at Kevin and mind cast. "Young wizard, you have been chosen for this task because of who you are. Someone that is strong-minded does not have much respect for traditions, does not follow what you are told but lives by his own instincts and gut feelings. It is not a bad thing sometimes when you use these together. However, although they may bring a bit of luck sometimes with them, they can also be your downfall. Today, I feel as if it could be the lucky side that will come through on this journey." Kevin looked at Frank and smiled, then stroked his head and said, "thank you, Frank." Kevin looked at both the mystical animals and spoke. "Well, you have rested enough. Time to kick on, I guess?"

Dion's mind cast to Kevin, "Sorry young wizard, but this is as far as we are permitted to go. Should we step out into the ground, we will die. This has been another of the magic enchantments laid down. No magic creature can cross the land." As he finished speaking, Frank turned towards where the barrier came down and was snorting in that direction. Godwill shouted, "Wands ready." They pointed them in the direction of the noise they heard coming towards them when Mr. Perry and the groups appeared. "Markus, you found us." Mr. Perry walked towards Godwill, "It was not easy. I can tell you, and the woods are crawling with others out there that we kept well away from as they could be with Matrees or even someone else. I have been listening on our way here. It seems to me that we keep the groups and cross with them. Each key found needs to be given to one of the group to get through to the other side and meet with the others that have the key." Dion mind cast. "Good plan, may I say, but the only person that can put the key into the lock is the one assigned the task. Should someone else try, they will be hit with the lightning spell from above. This, too, is also one of the enchantments." Kevin now looked hard at Dion. "So, let me go through this again. The stone has been here for hundreds of years. No one has been given the task of finding and getting them back to me. How does that work for me? It sounds like a load of nonsense. How does it know I am the one to complete the task and not hit me with lightning? Who said it would be me, and how on earth has this been thought of from hundreds of years ago?" Sambiah laughed and turned to Godwill. "He certainly asks a lot of questions, just as you said, Godwill. Young wizard, you have books available to you. In these books, it was proclaimed that a child from this year's time would come of magic and would become one of the greatest wizards ever known in the history of the magical world. This is you, have you not seen that? You can do things that even older wizards have tried to do but fail with spells, mind-casting, and understanding the way in front of you. That is why Merlin has chosen you. This is the reason why the ones around you have come together to help you. Do you think the incident with Matrees and you having the core of Postromus enter you was an accident? No, it had been mapped out in books throughout the years gone by. We all knew this was to happen. We did not know when, though."

Kevin, on hearing this, looked at his mate Vinny who just smiled at his friend. "So, I guess we move on," Kevin said. Godwill nodded. Sambiah spoke. Frelic, Frank, Dion, and I will try to give you time and hold anyone up that may get to this place. We will meet again once this is over. Good luck to you all."

As they split into groups, Godwill gave each group instructions on where they would go through the land. "Be very careful and observant. We do not know what lies in front or beneath the ground. Each group has a senior wizard with the group. It will be their task to help protect the others and get the key to the other side. Time waits for no man in this area, and time cannot be halted, so I suggest we move off. Good hunting and luck to you all, and I hope we all get to see each other on the other side."

The groups all looked at each other and set off a cross the land in front of them. Mr. Perry's group was following the right outer side of the land. Godwill stayed with Kevin's group whilst Paul and his friend Roger had a couple of others with them and went left. As they crossed over the land, it appeared calm and open, with very little of anything in the sight of any of them. Just then, Mr. Perry called out that there was a bucket they were coming across. Godwill mind cast, "be extremely careful, Markus. It may be nothing or something that will test you and the group's nerve." Markus relayed the message from Godwill to the group. Wands pointing out in front, they approached the bucket. Paul then also called out, "we have a broken tree trunk coming up. All, be ready just as Godwill has said." Kevin kept moving along with the group who were now out in front of the three groups but could see nothing in sight. Markus had now reached the bucket and was slowly walking around, looking at each angle with his group holding their wands and pointing at the bucket. Markus then stopped and looked harder; he could see a silver key just under the bucket base rim. "I can see a key, be ready when I grab it. We do not know what or if anything will happen" Markus slowly moved his hand towards the key, and gently he took hold of the key. As he did, smoke appeared from the bottom of the bucket, which rose into the sky. As the smoke disappeared, there in place was a flying Mantrel. Markus quickly cast a shield that covered the group and pointed to walk forward through where the Mantrel was. The group moved cautiously forward. The Mantrel spat out a ball of fire towards them, which hit the shield but bounced off. It then flew hard at the shield, trying to break through. Again it bounced off, but the shield was damaged. Markus told the group to all cast the spell Firentay, Consunium, and Derivarm, Markus dropped what has left of the shield, and the group all cast the spell at the same time. The electric charges from each of their wands formed one line and hit the Mantrel. With a piercing cry as the charge hit the Mantrel, he fell to the ground. It lay dormant as if it had been killed. Smoke surrounded the grounded Mantrel then both disappeared. A great cheer from the group was heard by the others.

"Key one got," Markus' mind cast to the others. Paul's group, now happy, walked further toward the tree trunk. Before they got within two feet, the ground started to rumble, and two snakes appeared in front of them. Roger fired off the Firentium Sparksum, which hit one of the snakes, which immediately disappeared, but the other wrapped itself around Roger, squeezing him so he could not breathe. Roger was in pain and starting to feel faint. Paul immediately cried out to Roger, "Roger change shape, come on, you can do this." Roger heard his friend and cast " Gradiation Columbine Morphious" Roger then changed shape to a mouse, fell through the coils of the snake, and ran back to the group. Paul shouted, all, Firentium

271

Sparksum" On hearing this, the group shot the spell at the snake, which engulfed it in the fire. Withering and falling to the floor, smoke again encircled the snake, which disappeared. Where it originally lay, there now was a silver key. Paul's wand in hand moved forward slowly and picked the key up. A big cheer went through the group, which the others heard. Paul now turned to the mouse and said, time to change back, my friend. In a flash, Roger now appeared very tired but un-hurt through his ordeal. Paul looked at his friend and said, "Good, but a little stupid thinking of the mouse Roger," roger stared at Paul and then replied, "stupid, why stupid"? Paul laughed. Snakes eat mice for food, which is why you are a little stupid. Brilliant for the shape and being able to escape, but perhaps if you use that again, you might want to think of something a lot larger than the foe that has you." The group laughed all together after patting their friend on the shoulder. The group then started to walk further on.

Kevin was now getting frustrated; both the other groups had found a key but nothing. Godwill sensed this and spoke to him. "Keep calm, things may be looking bleak here, but something will turn up, young Wilks. You mark my words." As sooner said that a chair appeared in front of them with what appeared to be a small elf sitting on it. The group stopped and looked at the elf. "Greetings, wizards. You are in search of the silver keys to open the far barrier. I do not plan to harm or slow your journey down unless you are not of knowledge and pure heart. To this, I have three questions that the group can answer. If you get all correct, I will give you the key. Should a question be answered wrongly, then one of your group will be hurt. Do you accept my challenge?" The group looked at each other, and all agreed, although they did not know how to hurt or even who could be hurt in case a question was answered wrong. Kevin stepped forward just as the elf was about to ask the first question. "Elf, the questions you ask need to be of a magic nature only based on the medieval times and not after." The Elf stared at Kevin with an angry face. "You dare to challenge me when I am the master of the questions." Kevin answered, "I do, and, within these questions, there cannot be a right or wrong answer, only the truth, no myths" The Elf was now very angry. The group was becoming uncomfortable in seeing the Elf getting so angry. Godwill looked and noticed something that the others did not and smiled at Kevin, nodding to him as to continue to ask more questions of the Elf.

The Elf, about to come out with the first question, was interrupted by Kevin again, "in challenging us. Therefore, you must also be challenged for knowledge and purity of heart. Do you accept my challenge?" the Elf now really very angry was jumping up and down on the stool with steam coming from his head. "Do you accept my challenge, Elf?" without thinking, the Elf shouted out, "This is not how this challenge works" again, Kevin shouted, "do you accept my challenge or not, which means you are not pure of heart." The Elf was now beside itself with anger and shouted back, "yes, I do, but it will do," Kevin then asked quickly, "who is Postromus?" The Elf stopped jumping up and down on the stool, then looked at Kevin and smiled with a big smile on its face. "You, boy, have just committed the ultimate sin and therefore will be hurt," Kevin shouted again, "answer my question, Elf." The group, now very nervous about what the Elf had said, stood with wands ready. Smiling still, the Elf answered the question. "You said truth and knowledge. Well, the truth is there is no person who lived with that name, so you forfeit the question. The Elf raised its hand to cast a spell at Kevin when suddenly Kevin felt Postromus coming through and cast the spell "Excelious Painclos" The spell hit the dwarf with immense power knocking it off the stool. The Elf lay dazed and hurt on the floor as Kevin approached it. Postromus now spoke elfish through Kevin to the Elf on the floor. After the Elf was now cowering on the floor, Kevin's voice now came back. "You tell lies and have no knowledge of the old times; therefore, you are no true of heart and therefore need to be banished from this area." Kevin held his wand over the Elf, who looked up at him. "I maybe not of the true heart or knowledgeable as you, young wizard, but a test is a test. I lost. Therefore I leave you with this thought. Many are travelling to this place to try to gain the stone. Only the pure heart and trusting wizard has any chance of gaining it. Stay true to your heart and trust all with you, or you will never retrieve the goal" A mist appeared over the Elf and disappeared. There on the ground lay a silver key. Kevin bent down and picked it up. The group all cheered and felt relieved as they moved forward. Godwill mind cast to the others, "that is three keys, there are still two more to get, and time is ticking on. We have but one hour left to find them and get through the barrier, so keep moving forward."

As the groups continued forward, it was Kevin's group that came across the next problem. The ground rumbled, and a gap in the ground appeared. From the open ground came two creatures believed to be Monocerus. Godwill calls the group to come to him where he casts the shield around them. Kevin asked, "what on earth are those creatures? I have not come across them in any book before?" Godwill answered they are Monocerus, dark creatures with immense strength and hard to kill or get rid of as they are stubborn as hell." The two creatures looked at each other and then lowered their heads as ready to charge. "Can the shield protect us from these creatures?" Kevin asked, "I do not know, I have never faced one before," Vinny looked at Godwill and shouted, let me out. Perhaps I can move them away from here whilst you lot carry on". Godwill spoke, "I commend your bravery or stupidity, but we need to stick together. There is more strength in the lot of us rather than the few." Kevin then asked, "you had better think quickly as they are about to charge." Vinny now cast "Weathio Corpus Evrader." High winds, hail, and electric charges directed at the two creatures. Both creatures were hit but just kept coming. Kevin now cast "Ilustria." Kevin cast an illusion of a dragon flying over the heads of the two creatures and flying towards the gap in the ground. The two creatures now changed their direction and headed back to the ground gap. Godwill now spoke, "keep that going, Kevin, whilst I work out what we can do next." "Got it," Godwill said after a few seconds, "ok, everyone, I need you to split into different parties. One goes left, one right. This will confuse the creatures. Use the Iluminum Cantarta spell first to try to blind the sight with light, then use Firentium Sparksum, follow it quickly but the next spell Firentay, Consunium, Derivarm. If we can hit both these creatures with all three in split seconds, we may have a chance to defeat them." Kevin asked, "to what percentage do you think this will work?" Godwill looked at Kevin then said, "fifty/fifty, not sure but we should give it a try at least do you not think?" Kevin looked at the others all terrified. "Ok, let's do this, we need to all be on the same song sheet, so timing is critical. Let's do this." Kevin cancelled the dragon illusion, and the group split into two and moved forward. The creatures saw what was going on, and each chose a group to concentrate on and began the charge. As described by Godwill, the groups waited until Godwill gave the order to cast the spells. Each cast at the very same time onto each of the creatures. The light blinded them, and they started to slow down on the charge. Then fireballs were sent at each creature which hurt them considerably, and finally, the powerful electric charges tore through the creatures causing them to explode. The two groups sank to their knees in tiredness but were, at present safe. The gap in the ground closed, and on top lay a silver key. This time Godwill picked it up and let the others know they were safe and had key four.

Now just one more key needed to be found. The groups carried on and did not come across any other areas where possible locations of another key were noted. Eventually, they crossed the land and reached the invisible barrier. "Now what do we do?" Markus asked. "We only have four of the keys, and it was stated we need five. What do we do, Godwill?" Godwill stroked his beard, looking at the barrier. "First, we need to see where the keyhole is," Vinny then asked, "what is the use of that? What if the fifth key is one that we

273

need to open, we are going to get killed if we stay here. At least if we run back now, we will get possibly halfway over the ground before what is to happen happens." The group was convinced by Vinny's statement. "Hold on, Rose, what if we already have the key here? Remember, we have three attempts to open the door before what happens. Should we not give it a go rather than hoping in vain?" The group now agreed with Godwill. "Ok, we had better find this door quickly, or we can say good night to all. We have just five minutes left, so all get looking," Markus said. All the group started to look around and feel the invisible barrier.

"it is no good. We are never going to find it," Vinny said as he leaned on the barrier where a door appeared with a key lock present. Kevin shouted, "well done, Vinny, you found it," Kevin now took out the four keys that had been given to him, ready to try in the lock. "So which ones do I use and in what order?" "We do not have time to discuss this, young Wilks. Use your gut judgment. We trust in you," replied Godwill. Kevin tried the first key, which did not unlock the door, and neither did the second key. "I guess it was just hope, I guess, but it seems that possibly Rose's comment on running from here was the right choice to do. I am sorry, a bad judgment call on my case," said Godwill. Just then, Kevin heard Postromus say to him, "put all four keys together and insert them into the lock," Kevin questioned but did as he had been told. The air over the area became heavy, dark, and electric charges were noted coming directly over the group. Kevin turned the key, and with a final turn, the door sprung open. "Everyone, through now, "Kevin shouted. All dived through the door and slammed it shut. As it shut, the barrier broke like glass and disappeared. The sky then became sunny and warm. The group got to their feet and congratulated Kevin on their success. Godwill put his hand on Kevin's shoulder, "I guess it was a gut feeling, young Winks?" "No sir, Postromus told me to do it, so we have someone on the inside also helping us, I guess" Both laughed along with the group.

Chapter 25

The Cave, the Brother Ship, and the Stone

As the group stood looking in the distance, they could see a winding path that lay before them. "I guess we follow the path and see where it takes us then," Godwill said. Mr. Perry just looked at Godwill. "Guess we do," Mr. Perry said, "but all be on your guard. What looks easy to do is very rarely that easy. There may be other things we come a crossed on this part of the journey" Godwill nodded. The group moved off down the path with caution.

As they moved along the path, the day was still bright, and the ground was firm and smooth. Halfway along it, they see in the distance a rock face with an opening in it. "Look, there, an opening. This must be the place we need to head to," Vinny cried. Godwill stopped and spoke. "It appears so, but why would it be this easy to get to? Something does not feel right." Kevin then asked, "what is it, sir? What makes you say this? The path leads directly to it. We clearly can see along the path that there are no strange things we can see, so we need to carry on and get to the opening." Godwill stared at Kevin, "have you just forgotten what we just came through, young Wilks, some of those things were not visible when we moved a crossed the land that suddenly appeared. This feels the same to me. We need to be careful. All, break into your groups again and follow the path but in a staggered movement as we did, moving a crossed the land and paying attention to the slightest thing that appears unusual" Mr. Perry nodded, this time in complete agreeance.

With the groups reformed, they moved off down the path slowly. Step by step, they could see the rock face getting closer and closer until they were now at the opening. "Well, that was easy. I told you it would be ok," Vinny said. Godwill turned to him with his finger to his mouth to quieten the boy. Vinny looked at Godwill in disbelief, and some confusion. Godwill pointed to the inside of the cavern and beckoned the group to move forward slowly. On entering the cavern, they could see a clear pathway that was lit by fire lamps. Each section they moved through burst into flame to light the next part of the route. The deeper they went, the group started to hear some noises coming from the distance. Godwill kept the group moving until the cavern now split into a two-way path. Mr. Perry now looked at Godwill, "so which one do we take, Godwill?" Godwill stood looking, "I do not know which path is the correct one, but I am sure that there will be possible things that will happen on both. One clear thing is that only young Wilks can gain the stone. Others that try may perish. It is, therefore, imperative that we break into two groups and follow both paths. Should the whereabouts of the stone's location be found by either group, we must mind cast to each other to state it has been found. I also have a feeling we are not alone in this cavern which may be a problem when alerting each other of the location." Kevin interrupted, "mind casting will not work, sir," Godwill looked at Kevin, "and how do you know this young Wilks?" Kevin smiled, "well you did not speak back to me just a minute ago when I asked you what could be ahead of us through mind casting." Godwill looked at Kevin. "You tried to ask me a question through mind casting, which was very stupid young Wilks. What if it did work, and you let other wizards or dark creatures know we are in here?" Kevin's face dropped, "I was only trying to help to test the methodology of your words, which proved to be wrong, sir." "So how do you think we can communicate with each other than young Wilks? Seems my idea is not working," said Godwill in a gruff voice. Kevin replied, "Maybe with Ilumino Trevelesto. Godwill thought for a moment, then nodded, "it may work, but again it may also notify anyone or thing in here to also follow it, but we need to be able to use something to converse. It seems that certain magic cannot be used in this cavern, which makes it more dangerous to all. Be aware of this and not really on it to help you." All agreed and broke into two groups, and each travelled a different path. Godwill decided that he would travel as the lead in Kevin's party whilst Mr. Perry took the other group.

Moving down the path, Kevin and his brother were whispering to each other about things that had happened. "Got something to say, Wilks?" Paul looked at Godwill and shook his head as if to say no. "Then I suggest you pay attention like all of us and not rely on us to find things," Godwill said again in a bad-tempered frame of voice. The group continued along the path until Godwill held his hand up to stop. The group all huddled together, looking forward. An opening was present ahead of them with what appeared to be a griffin standing at it. Kevin looked hard and saw it was the Griffin he had helped at the spinney to become free. Kevin whispered to Godwill, "it is the Griffin I released at the spinney during my test." Godwill whispered, "how can you be so sure young Wilks, all Griffins look alike." Kevin shook his head. This is the Griffin I released. See, it has a white spot towards the side of the back legs, which the Griffin had on the one I released. All Griffins are totally black all over. I know it is the same Griffin." Godwill looked and saw what Kevin had told him, then nodded, "but why would that Griffin be here but to protect the stone? They are violent beasts at the best of times," whispered Godwill. Kevin replied, "let me walk to it and talk to it, then we will see", Godwill grumpily whispered back, "and what if you are wrong? Also, how are you going to talk to it, as no mind casting can take place here? You proved that it could rip you apart in a second". Kevin then felt something inside of him that he knew was Postromus. "I have Postromus with me. He has just let me know that I need to do this." Again, Godwill stared hard at Kevin. "And how did he let you know? Can you both still talk to each other in here"? Kevin nodded and then started to walk out towards Griffin cautiously.

The Griffin saw Kevin approaching and moved towards the hem. Kevin stopped. He then spoke, "we cannot mind cast in here,   so I cannot feel what you wish to talk about." The Griffin growled at Kevin, which made him step back. As he did, he felt Postromus come through and growl in Griffin's back to the beast. The beast continued to growl many times toward Kevin with what appeared to be the others of the group. Kevin was growling back. Finally, after several minutes of the two growling at each other, Griffin bowed toward Kevin. Postromus then spoke to Kevin. "The Griffin is indeed the one you let loose, and he wants to repay you for doing this. He made his way to this place after reading your thoughts back on the test area. What he has said is that a cavern is at the end of this path for which only the chosen one can enter to gain the stone, but it is not without difficulty to get it. You must choose one other to assist you in the quest and one only. That second person cannot enter the cavern only to assist from outside. Choose wisely, young wizard, for if you do not; then you will be lost forever." There Postromus faded away from Kevin's thoughts as he moved back to the group to tell them what had just happened.

Godwill stroked his beard, then asked Vinny to send the light to Mr. Perry to get them to come to them. Vinny did this immediately. "So young Wilks, you need a champion with you to help. Who will you choose from us all? Remember, whoever you choose can only assist from outside the cavern as the Griffin said," Godwill asked. Kevin looked around at each of the group presents. A few questions come from some of the group in the manner of what will happen if that person enters the cavern to help, what the Griffin means by perish forever, and how we even know the stone is in the cavern. Kevin stood tall and spoke. "I can only tell you what Postromus told me. The Griffin knows that the stone is present in the cavern and came here to try and help because I showed it some leniency. Now mention how the person, me, can perish or what would happen if the second person enters the cavern. Let us take it that it will not end well for both, so we need to focus on what we need to do and get this stone so we can get out of here all alive ok?"

Just then, Mr. Perry and the other group turned up. Godwill explains the situation to him. Mr. Perry immediately spoke, "I will accompany young Wilks. He will need someone he can rely on with superior magic knowledge and experience." Kevin thanked Mr. Perry but shook his head, "No, thank you, Mr. Perry, but I think I will take my brother Paul with me." Paul looked shocked, along with the group. "Why him?" Godwill asks, "He is my brother, my blood, and I believe we have a connection that will be needed to do this." Kevin looked at his brother, "You up for this, Bro?" Paul looking scared at Kevin, replied, "are you sure you are probably a better wizard than me already? What do you think I can bring to help you?" Kevin smiled, "brotherly love at the end, Paul. We have had our differences growing up, but I feel it is the best thing for us to complete this mission. Remember back at the park when you showed me that you had magic? Then at the river, we were fishing for the dove, the book, and the wand. That would not have happened without reason; therefore, I choose you. So, I ask you again, are you up for this, bro, or not?" Paul looked at everyone in surprise, then answered, "let's do it, Kevin, just let me know what you need me to do." A lot of handshakes, pats on the backs of both two boys occurred. Godwill asked "are you sure that you want your brother to accompany you on this dangerous test, how will I explain to your mum if something goes extremely bad and neither comes back. She will have a major breakdown like she did when your brother had a problem growing up with magic." Kevin smiled, "this is my wish. You once said that I am headstrong, unruly, and skeptical, at least about magic. I have seen things now that convinced me it is not a dream but a reality. Blood is thicker than water, so again. Therefore, I chose my brother, and I know he will not let me down in a dire situation". Kevin looked at his brother. "Right, bro?" Paul smiled back to his brother, "Right, bro, let's do this." The boys then headed towards the cavern.

As they walked, the two boys talked about things that had occurred until they came to an opening. There they could see a pedestal above a small pond. The opening appeared to have an overhanging wall construction that looked like a door. The two boys looked at each other, and Kevin thought about what could happen. "Ok, Paul, what I see is that I walk through, but you cannot, as if you do, the door will fall down and shut us both in where we will not be able to get out." Paul laughed, "but Kevin, we have magic. We can bombard this brick wall to smithereens." Kevin shook his head, remember, bro, we cannot use all our magic, and the person who put this here would have done something to prevent that from happening." Paul stopped laughing. "So how do we know what magic we can or cannot use here?" "We don't, not until we try something, but by that time, it may already be too late to stop anything from happening." Paul now looked worried, "so what can I do to help when I do not know how I can help?" His brother asked. "You don't, but I am sure you will do the right thing, do not think. Just do is my thought," replied Kevin. Paul, now worried, "I don't think you thought this through. You would have been better off with old Godwill or Perry. I am not sure I can do this." "Too late, bro, we are here, and I have faith in you." Just at that moment, the Griffin appeared at the doorway. Kevin heard a mind cast from it. "To do this, young wizard, you must both be as one, with the right thought patterns and the right motivation. Your brother does not give out this feeling I am sensing. You sure you do not want to turn back now and live longer"? Kevin then mind cast, "so we can mind cast here now as I hear you. Does that mean my brother can mind cast also"? Paul then mind cast, "yep, I heard what this animal had to say. That was not a true beast, he is my brother, and I do not intend to let anything happen to him do you hear." The Griffin just growled back towards Paul. Kevin then heard the final mind cast of the Griffin, "if you do not work together then you will both be doomed. Should you work together, then you may get out of here alive. It is down to the both of you now."

The Griffin then just stood back but did not leave the doorway. Kevin took a further look into the cavern and discussed it with his brother. "So, I guess there is something on the pedestal that will cause something else to happen to get to the stone. No matter what happens there, you cannot come in to help. You can only help from outside. You understand, Paul?" Paul nodded. So if the door starts to close, what are you going to do if I am not out?" Kevin asked. Paul just smiled and replied, "I do not know, bro, but something heroic, I guess. Somehow the door is not going to close until you are out. I promise you this." Kevin smiled. That is what I want to hear, bro." Both boys hugged for a few seconds. "Ready Paul?" Kevin asked. "When you're ready, bro, be careful and get your backside out of there as soon as possible. I will be waiting for you." Kevin sighed, looked forward, and then slowly stepped inside the cavern.

Kevin walked towards the pedestal and looked around it. "There is a gap on the side of the pedestal where it looks as though there is a handle that needs to be pulled," he called out to his brother, "I can see a small shinny thing towards the bottom of a shallow pond beside it that could be stone but not sure." Kevin continued to look around the area. "The ceiling looks jagged with a few rocks that look loose over the pond. Let me think about this before doing anything." Kevin thought hard but was voicing his thoughts as he thought them, "so if I pull the handle will that drain the pond or release those rocks into the pond, which may crush me trying to get the stone? If the pond drains, will it take the stone as it drains, so I cannot get it? What happens, then? Will the door shut, and I will be blocked in here for eternity"? Paul now spoke, "I can hear you thinking or rather talking through your thoughts, and none of it is very positive, bro." "Sorry, just have to voice my thoughts so I can work through them easier," Kevin replied. Then his thought was interrupted by the Griffin mind casting. "One thing I forgot to tell you is that there is a time limit set as you cross the thresh hold and the clock is ticking, young wizard." Kevin's mind cast back, "now you're telling me this, so how long is the timer set for"? The griffin replied, "in your human time fifteen minutes, in magic time a heartbeat." Kevin was now getting a little stressed as he had already been in the cavern for five minutes. His brother could see this and tried to calm him down, but it did not seem to work. "Ok, gut feeling, what is my gut feeling," he asked himself. Suddenly, he just took the handle and pulled it.

The pond started to have a cover come over the top. Kevin tried the spell "Gradiation Columbine Morphious" Kevin changed form into an otter that quickly jumped into the pond, swam down, and grabbed the stone. He swam upwards and just managed to get out of the pond before the closure sealed the pond. The next minute, the jagged rocks started to fall, and the door started to close. Kevin still in the otter form, scampered towards the door. Paul was now calling out to his brother to change back, but Kevin was dodging the rocks falling. Paul also conjured up the same spell and changed into a large dragon. As the door came down, he moved its large body directly under the door, where it crashed down on his back. The pressure was so great that he started to buckle at the knee areas. Kevin, still not near the door, was trying to move quickly, but it seemed that the door would close before he would get to it. Just then, the Griffing moved beside his brother's form and stood to help hold the door also. Griffin and his brother were beginning to be crushed under the force. Kevin reached the door just as Griffin and his brother could take no more pain and moved away from it. With a large crashing noise, the door fell shut, the area cloaked in heavy dust where no view by anyone could be seen. Paul changed back to his normal self, lying coughing with the dust in his lungs. The Griffin was also coughing hard. When the dust slightly started to disappear, Paul called out at the door for his brother, but no reply. Paul sat there crying, not knowing what to do. Suddenly, he heard a mind cast from Kevin. "We definitely are not doing anything as stupid as this again, bro," Paul's mind cast back. Where are you, Kevin? You on the other side of this door?" Kevin answered, "no bro, can you take your foot off my tail, though? It is painful as hell."

Paul looked down to see the otter form at his feet with his foot on the otter's tail. "Sorry, bro. I thought I had lost you behind the door." Kevin now changed back to his normal form. Kevin was weak but still answered. "I thought I was a goner too, bro. If it was not for Griffin, that helped keep the door open for a few more seconds, then I would have been gone forever. Quick thinking on your part, a dragon, one with immense strength." Paul looked in happiness, "I just conjured the spell, not knowing if it would or not work. As you said, the magic here is disarmed, or most of it." Kevin laughed, "well, not sure that was all true. When the Griffin mind cast me, I thought that if it could do this, then there must be magic able to be used. Good job in a way, or I would never have got the stone without being an otter". Paul just hugged his brother, saying, "you and that logic mind have come through this time, but it is not always you know that Kevin?" Kevin smiled, "well for this thing it served me well that is all I can say." Kevin then felt Postromus coming through and spoke to him. "You did well, young wizards, so the first stone has been gained. Now it needs to be stored in a safe place as we collect the others to reform the whole stone. This has been the easiest one to get. The others get harder on each task I seem to think or remember. Others are going to be alerted of this and will also be looking for you to get the stone from you, so I would suggest giving it to someone that they will not suspect." Kevin agreed. Postromus slowly fading had a last comment. "Get out of here now, as others are coming. Get to the group. Go now." Kevin stood and hugged his brother and mind cast to Griffin. "Thank you, Griffin, for helping my brother keep the door open for me to escape." The griffin replied, "Well, young wizard, you helped me, so it was only the right thing to help back, but now we are even, do not expect my help in any further tasks you undertake. For now, farewell. I am sure our paths will cross each other over time." The Griffin flapped its wings and flew off. Kevin and Paul headed back to the group, where they were so relieved to see both safe and unharmed. The group left the cavern immediately after what Kevin told Godwill and Mr. Perry what the Griffin had told them.

Once out of the cavern, the group used the travelling spell, which worked to travel back to the school. Once there, the time was re-started. Godwill used a spell to clean both Paul's and Kevin's uniforms so they were in perfect condition. Godwill took the stone from Kevin, stating that it would be placed in a special place to be held until the others could be found and got. After a lot of happy people cheering each other and congratulating each other, the group dispersed and went home. Before Kevin and Paul left, Godwill wanted a word with each. "This is the first stone we have found and retrieved. You both have been put in immense danger to do this, for which I cannot express my gratitude to both of you. Kevin, your comment about blood being thicker than water did not really make sense to me, but it did to you. I now see why it did. You are a naughty school child with quick thoughts, but some, I have to say, quite ingenious sometimes. However, there is a place for gut feelings and the right way to use magic. You must still work on these olden-day theories to implement because somewhere along the line, gut feeling is going to let you down, and when it does, it could be catastrophic. On saying all of this, I understand why Merlin chose you for this task as you are not black and white, you have your own mindset, and you do not follow anyone in authority" Godwill paused at this comment. He then winked at Kevin and spoke, "A bit like someone else and I were too at your age." Godwill smiled, "now go home and relax but not too much. See you at school tomorrow." Both Paul and Kevin smiled back and left the school building to the bike shed. There Paul met Roger and Kevin met Vinny. The friends now all joined together in a small hug before going home. "Looks like things are going to change around here for sure now. What do you think, Kevin?" Kevin answered, "certainly looks like it, mate. Guess we are in it for the long ride, and thank you, Vinny." Vinny looked at Kevin in some confusion, "What for"? Kevin replied, "remember when you changed shape into Godwill at the spinney? Well, it was you who gave me the thought of form shifting, so I could get the stone." Both boys laughed. "Your welcome, mate. See you tomorrow." With that, the boys cycled off to their homes with the daylight still shinning bright in the sky.

That night as Kevin lay in his bed asleep, he sensed he was being called to the Astral plane by Merlin. The next thing he remembered was opening his eyes in the Astral plane and Merlin sitting on a log by a Brooke. Kevin approached Merlin and spoke, "we did it. We got the stone," Merlin turned towards Kevin and smiled, "I know, young wizard. I have been informed by Godwill of this. Come, sit with me." Kevin sat on the log beside Merlin. "It has been a test of your beliefs and arduous journey to gain this first stone, but there are more adventures and even greater dangers to come in finding and gaining the next than the next after that. You showed great loyalty towards your brother in choosing him to help, but something troubles me in your judgment." Kevin stared at Merlin before speaking. "What troubles are you talking about," Kevin asked. Merlin stood and looked at Kevin. "Tell me, Kevin, what made you choose your brother, especially after you knew what had gone on in the past with him?" Kevin just answered straight back, "Why not? He is my brother, ok, we have had our differences throughout our lives, but I had a gut feeling that he was the one that would really help me in a situation; blood is thicker than friendship. I knew that if there was anything that would happen, he would be there to try and help me through it" Kevin smiled, "just think what he would get in the neck from mum if something did happen to me." Merlin smiled first, then turned his face to a different look as if in anger. "You are smiling about this, but it is very real. People can die, then how do you think your mother and father would take it if they had to be told of this?" Kevin then thought for a second without speaking. He then stood and faced Merlin. "I really did not think of that," "No, that is evident in the attitude you are showing. Look, you are a great magician, but no one is immortal, not even me." Kevin smiled again, then spoke, "Well, you are doing great at present for someone so old to me." Merlin again growled at Kevin. "Again, your attitude shows me you are both great but dangerous in that thought mentality you show the young wizard. This seriously needs to change to ensure you understand what is going on here." Kevin stared at Merlin, "You chose me, not the other way round, remember? I did not believe in this magic stuff, remember, and now you say I am dangerous because of how I think and what I can do with this gift I have. Perhaps it is you, Godwill, and the others that need to change your thoughts on me. I have a remnant of a great wizard inside me from the past. Has this ever been done before? No, I do not think so. If, again, this is about just me deciding to choose my brother to help. Then it was a gut feeling also. Tell me, Merlin, when you roamed this earth many, many years ago, did you ever have a gut feeling you followed that worked out for you?" Merlin turned away from Kevin and then spoke softly, "Once, but unfortunately, it did not work out as well as yours has, but that is not to say that the feeling was of good thought to take." Merlin turned back towards Kevin.

What I am trying to say is that there are many wizards, witches, and other magical folks out there who once were on the path of light, and when the danger appeared, tried your gut feeling and either perished or turned them onto the dark path. This is what happened to Matrees and so many others. Why your brother also was close to treading down the dark path if his memories had not been blocked and removed from the fateful day that occurred? I do not want this to happen to you. You are special, not just to your parents but both to me and Godwill." Kevin looked at Merlin now with an expression of confusion. "I once was a boy like you, thrown into the magical world and did not understand it, just like you. But I had to quickly learn that the magical community around me was there to help and teach me to stay on the light path. It took many years for them to do this, and I guess this will be the same. In all, Kevin, we did not choose you as a champion, but a really gifted strong boy that we knew could get things done. It is our job to help and assist you, but again, only when you need to call upon us for that help. I hope in the future you will call on us to give that help to bring things to a close so you and everyone can live a safe and peaceful life," Kevin, again looking at Merlin, replied. "I will, Merlin, but one thing I guess I have to change is thinking I am a wizard rather than being a gifted individual with magic to use only for good. Sometimes people forget that I am just a boy, and boys' minds are not yet mature to the state of a full understanding of things. I will try and improve this with the help of others. I think that there will be rocky times ahead with things I do that may be questionable, but that is only the beast of nature with frustration, so the others need to understand that."

Merlin now laughed out loud. "I would not expect anything else from you, young wizard. Now, it is time for you to leave and get some rest. Godwill and the dwarfs are already looking for clues to the whereabouts of the second part of the stone. Perhaps my old friend Postromus could help also, so call upon him when you feel it is needed. One last thing before you go, thank you for being the person you are, and thank you for being so abrupt but logical in what you say. Sometimes it needs a jolt from someone like you to remind the older folk of the past, the present, and what lies ahead in the future for us all" Kevin then smiled and walked past Brooke. The next thing he remembered was waking up to a beautiful sunny morning.

Ingram Content Group UK Ltd.
Milton Keynes UK
UKHW050728260623
424053UK00012B/594